#1 *New York Times* bestselling author **Susan Mall**[…] millions of reade[…]escribed as 'imm[…]tional' (RT Book[…] (Publishers Week[…]eciates the accola[…], Mallery is even more honoured by the enthusiasm of her readers and the word of mouth that catapults her toward the top of the bestseller lists time and again.

Mallery lives in not-so-sunny Seattle with her husband and a toy poodle who makes her laugh every day and who's not even a little bit impressed by her growing fame. Visit Susan online at www.susanmallery.com.

Susan Mallery

Dreaming of Christmas

Published in Great Britain 2016
By Mills & Boon, an imprint of HarperCollins*Publishers*
1 London Bridge Street, London, SE1 9GF

ISBN: 978-0-263-92684-2

9-1016

Our policy is to use papers that are natural, renewable and recyclable products and made from wood grown in sustainable forests.
The logging and manufacturing processes conform to the legal environmental regulations of the country of origin.

Printed and bound in Spain
by CPI, Barcelona

A FOOL'S GOLD CHRISTMAS

To the 2011 Head Cheerleader Char,
who has such an amazing heart that she
wanted to share this dedication with the entire
Fool's Gold Varsity Cheerleading squad in
the spirit of Christmas. This one is for you.

One

THE SOUND OF eight tiny reindeer had nothing on a half-dozen eight-year-olds clog dancing, Dante Jefferson thought as he held the phone more closely to his ear.

"You'll have to repeat that," he yelled in to the receiver. "I'm having trouble hearing you."

The steady thudding above his head paused briefly, then started up again.

"What's going on there?" Franklin asked, his voice barely audible over the banging that nearly kept time with the damned piano music. "Construction?"

"I wish," Dante muttered. "Look, I'll call you back in a couple of hours." The stupid dance class would be over by then. At least he hoped so.

"Sure. I'll be here." Franklin hung up.

Dante glanced at the bottom right of his computer screen. The ever-present clock told him it was seven-fifteen. In the evening. Which meant it was eleven-fifteen in the morning in Shanghai. He'd stayed late specifically to speak to Franklin about an international business deal that had developed a few glitches. The clog dancers had made the conversation impossible.

He saved the spreadsheet and went to work on his email. He and his business partner had plenty of other projects that needed his attention.

Just before eight, he heard the clog dancers going down the stairs. They laughed and shrieked, obviously not worn out by an hour of misstepping practice. He, on the other hand, had a pounding pain right behind his eyes and the thought that he would cheerfully strangle Rafe first thing in the morning. His business partner had been the one to rent the temporary space. Either Rafe hadn't noticed or didn't care about the dance school parked directly above. The offices were in an older part of Fool's Gold and had been built long before the invention of soundproofing. Rafe didn't seem to mind the noise that started promptly at three every single afternoon and went well into the evening. Dante, on the other hand, was ready to beg the nearest judge for an injunction.

Now he got out of his chair and headed for the stairs. He made his way to the studio. He and whoever was in charge were going to have to come to terms. He had to spend the next couple of weeks working out the problems of the Shanghai deal.

Which meant needing access to his computer, contracts and blueprints. Some of which he couldn't take home. He needed to able to use his phone, in his *office,* while speaking in a normal voice.

He paused outside the door that led to the studio. It was as old-fashioned as the rest of the building, with frosted glass and the name of the business—Dominique's School of Dance—painted in fancy gold script. He pushed open the door and entered.

The reception area was utilitarian at best. There was a low desk, a computer that had been old a decade ago, backless benches by the wall and several coatracks. He could see through into the studio itself—a square room with mirrors, a barre that was attached to the wall and, of course, hardwood floors. There wasn't a piano, and he realized the endless, repetitive song that had driven him insane had come from a compact stereo.

He rubbed his temples and wished the pounding would stop, then walked purposefully into the studio. He was a coldhearted bastard lawyer, or so he'd been told endlessly by those he bested. He planned to reduce the dance instructor to a blob of fear, get her to agree to lay off with the dancing and then go back to his phone call. All in the next ten minutes.

"We have to talk," he announced as he came to a halt in the center of the room.

He realized there were mirrors on three walls, so he was seeing himself from unfamiliar angles. His shirt was wrinkled, his hair mussed, and he looked tired, he thought briefly, before turning his attention to—

Dante swore under his breath as he took in the tall, slender woman dressed in nothing more than a black leotard and tights. Despite the fact that she was covered from collarbone to toes, the clinging outfit left nothing to the imagination. He almost felt as if he'd walked in on a woman undressing. A sexy woman with big green eyes and honey-blond hair. A woman who was completely untouchable, for a host of reasons.

He ground his teeth together. Why hadn't Rafe mentioned that his sister was now working here? But even if his business partner didn't kill him for looking, Dante had a firm list of rules that were never broken. Not getting emotionally involved was number one. Anyone who taught little kids to dance had to be softhearted. Nothing got him running faster than a hint of emotion.

"What are you doing here?" Evangeline Stryker asked.

Yes, he thought as he stared at her. Rafe's baby sister. She was responsible for the nightmare that was his life. She and those unbelievably loud mini-dancers she taught. So much for reducing the dance instructor to anything.

"Dante?"

"Sorry," he said, doing his best to keep his voice from growling. "I didn't know you worked here."

Evie gave him a wide-eyed stare, then a strange half laugh. "Right. I work here. I teach dance. Lucky me."

Dante knew Evie had broken her leg a few months ago, but he didn't remember hearing anything about a head injury. "Are you all right?"

"No," she snapped and put her hands on her hips. "Do I look all right?"

He took a step back, not wanting to get in the middle of whatever she had going on. "I came upstairs because I can't work like this anymore. The pounding, the same piece of music playing over and over again. I have to talk to Shanghai tonight, and instead of peace and quiet, there were clog dancers. You've got to make it stop."

He held out both hands, palms up, speaking in what he knew to be his most reasonable tone.

"Make it stop? Make it *stop?*" Her voice rose with each word. "Are you kidding?"

EVIE KNEW SHE sounded shrill. She was sure she was wide-eyed, flushed and more than a little scary, but right now she didn't care. She was in full panic mode and now Dante was stuck listening to her rant.

"You want to talk to me about your troubles?"

she continued. "Fine. Here are mine. In approximately six weeks it's Christmas Eve. That night, the town of Fool's Gold expects yet another chance to see their annual favorite—*The Dance of the Winter King.* You've never heard of it, you say? I know. Me, either. But it's a huge deal here. Huge!"

She paused for breath, wondering if it was possible for her head to actually explode. She could feel a sort of panicked pressure building. It was as if she was in a nightmare where she was going to be naked in front of a room full of strangers. Not that being naked in front of a room full of people she knew was any better.

"I won't go into the details about the storyline," she continued, her chest getting tighter and tighter. "Let's just say it's a lot of students dancing. Oh, and the dances they're doing this year are different than the ones they did last year because, hey, they move up. Which wouldn't be a problem because there's always Miss Monica, who's been teaching here for the last five-hundred-and-fifty years."

She was getting shrill again, she realized, and consciously lowered her voice. "The only problem is Miss Monica has run off with her gentleman friend. The woman has to be pushing seventy, so I should probably be impressed or at least respectful that she has a love life, except she took off with no warning. She left me a note."

Evie pointed to the piece of paper still taped to the mirror.

"She's gone," she repeated. "Left town. Flying out of the country first thing in the morning. Which leaves me with close to sixty girls to teach dances I don't know for a production I've never heard of, let alone seen. There's no choreography to speak of, I'm not sure of the music and I heard the sets are old and need to be completely refurbished. In the next six weeks."

She paused for air. "It's up to me. Do you want to know how long I've been teaching dance? Two months. That's right. This is my first ever, on the planet, teaching job. I have sixty girls depending on me to make their dreams come true. Their dreams of being beautiful and graceful, because you know what? For some of them, this is all they have."

She knew she was skating uncomfortably close to talking about herself. About how, when she'd been younger, dance had been all *she'd* had. She might not have any teaching experience, but she knew what it was like to want to be special and, by God, she was going to make that happen for her students.

She stalked toward him and jabbed her finger into his chest. More specifically, she felt the cool silk of his fancy tie. It probably cost more than she spent on groceries in a month. She didn't know very much about Dante Jefferson beyond the fact that he was her brother's business partner and therefore disgustingly rich. Okay—he was reasonably good-looking, but that didn't help her right now, so she wasn't going to care.

"If you for one second think I'm going to stop having practice here," she told him, "you can forget it. I have a serious crisis. If you want to have a conversation with Shanghai, you can do it somewhere else. I'm hanging on by a thread and when it snaps, we're all going down."

Dante stared at her for a long moment, then nodded. "Fair enough."

With that, he turned and walked out of the studio.

She glared at his retreating back. Sure. *He* got to leave and go back to his fancy life. Not her. She had to figure out what to do next. While running in circles and screaming might feel good in the moment, it wasn't going to get the job done. Nor was railing at the unfairness, kicking something or eating chocolate. She might have failed in other areas of her life, but she wasn't going to fail her students.

"You have to rally," she told herself. "You're tough. You can do it."

And she would, she thought as she sank onto the floor and rested her head on her knees. She would figure out *The Dance of the Winter King* and teach her students and let them have one magical night.

First thing in the morning. But now, she was going to take a few minutes and feel massively sorry for herself. It was a small thing to ask, and she'd earned it.

THE NEXT MORNING, Evie started her day with a heart full of determination. She had survived worse than this before and probably would have to again. Mounting a production she'd never seen with no help might seem daunting, but so what? Her pep talk lasted through her first cup of coffee, then faded completely, leaving the sense of panic to return and knot her stomach. Obviously the first step was to stop trying to do this all alone. She needed help. The question was, where to get it.

She was new in town, which meant no support network. Well, that wasn't totally true. Her brothers had taken a surprising interest in her lately. Rafe had even prepaid for her townhouse, against her wishes. But they would be useless in this situation, her mother wasn't an option and going up to strangers to ask them what they knew about *The Dance of the Winter King* seemed questionable at best. Which left the women in her brothers' lives.

She had one sister-in-law and two sisters-in-law to-be. Of the three of them, Charlie seemed the easiest to approach. She was blunt but kind-hearted. So after a quick routine of stretching to overcome the stiffness of her still-healing leg, Evie got dressed and started out for the center of town.

Fool's Gold was a small town nestled in the foothills of the Sierra Nevada—on the California side. The residential areas boasted tidy lawns and well-kept houses while the downtown held nearly a half-dozen traffic lights, making it practically metropolitan. There were plenty of pumpkins by front doors and paper turkeys in windows. Orange, red and yellow leaves flew across the sidewalk. It had yet to snow at this elevation, but the temperatures were close to freezing at night, and the ski resorts higher up the mountain had opened the previous weekend.

The whole place was one happy small town postcard, Evie thought, shoving her hands into her coat pockets and longing to be somewhere else. Los Angeles would be nice. Warm and, hey, big enough that nobody knew her name—which was how she preferred things. She just wanted to live her life without getting involved with other people. Was that too much to ask?

A stupid question, she reminded herself. She was here now, and responsible for a holiday tradition. She would get it right because she knew what it was like to be disappointed, and there was no way she was doing that to her students.

She rounded a corner and walked up to the fire station in the center of town. The building was older, mostly brick, with giant garage doors that would open if there was an emergency.

Charlie was a firefighter. From what Evie had been able to piece together, Charlie drove one of the big trucks. She was competent, sarcastic and just a little intimidating. She was also a bit of a misfit, which made Evie more comfortable around her. In addition, Clay, Evie's youngest brother, was crazy about her. Over-the-moon, can't-stop-looking-at-her in love.

Clay had been married before, and Evie had adored his late wife. Now that she thought about it, Clay kind of had extraordinary taste when it came to women. After years of mourning his first wife, he'd stumbled into a relationship with Charlie, only to find himself giving his heart and everything else he had. It was kind of nice to see someone as perfect as Clay brought to his knees by an emotion.

Evie hesitated by the entrance leading into the fire station. She told herself to just open the door and walk in. Which she would. In a second. It was just…asking for help was not her favorite thing. She could easily list ninety-seven ways she would rather spend her time. Maybe more.

The door swung open unexpectedly, and Charlie Dixon stepped out. "Evie? Are you okay?"

Charlie was a little taller than Evie, and much bigger. The other woman was all broad shoulders and muscle. The latter no doubt necessary because of her job. Evie had spent her life in search of the perfect combination of being strong enough to dance and thin enough to look good in whatever costume her job required. Which meant being hungry every day of her life since her fourteenth birthday.

"Hey, Charlie," Evie said and forced a smile. "Do you have a second?"

"Sure. Come on in."

The fire station was warm and brightly lit. The big trucks gleamed, and holiday music played over a hidden sound system. Charlie led the way to a massive kitchen with seating for maybe fifteen or twenty, long counters and a six-burner, restaurant-style stove. A big pot of coffee sat by the window, and there was an open box of donuts on the table.

Charlie poured them each a mug of coffee and handed her one, then settled right next to the box of donuts and grabbed a maple bar. As Evie watched, she took a bite and chewed.

Just like that, Evie thought, both impressed and horrified. Depending on the size of the donut, the maple bar would be anywhere from two hundred and fifty calories to over five hundred. Evie had learned shortly after puberty, she was destined to be pear-shaped, with every extra ounce going to her hips, thighs and butt. While the medical community might want her to believe that pear-shaped was perfectly healthy, more than one costume director had pointed out no one wanted to watch a ballerina with a big ass and jiggly thighs.

Evie gripped her coffee mug with both hands, averted her gaze from the box of donuts, whose contents had started to quietly call her name, and stared at Charlie.

"I wondered if I could talk to you about *The Dance of the Winter King.* Do you know about the production?"

"Sure," Charlie said, dropping half the donut onto a napkin and reaching for her coffee. "It happens every year on Christmas Eve. It's kind of a big deal." She smiled, her blue eyes bright with humor. "That's right. You're working for Miss Monica now. Nervous about the big show?"

"You have no idea." Evie knew the situation was complicated even more by the fact that, while Miss Monica was in charge of the studio, the business had recently been purchased by Charlie's mother. Evie had left the new owner a message the previous night, bringing her up-to-date, but had yet to hear from her.

"Miss Monica ran off yesterday." Evie quickly explained about the older woman's flight with her gentleman friend. "I've never seen the dance, and there aren't very many notes on the production. Miss Monica mentioned many of the sets need to be refurbished, and I don't even know where they're kept. I have sixty students who expect to dance in front of their families in six weeks and no idea what I'm doing. Worse, there aren't any videos of the production in the studio. If Miss Monica had any, they're in her house, and she's on her way to Italy."

She stopped and forced herself to inhale. The panic had returned and with it the need for sugar. She started to reach for a small, plain cake donut, then gave in to the inevitable and picked up a chocolate glazed. As her teeth sank into the sweet, light center, the world slowly righted itself.

Charlie ran her hands through her short hair and groaned. "I'm trying desperately not to imagine Miss Monica and her gentleman friend."

Evie chewed and swallowed. "I know exactly what you mean. The terror helps me overcome that image."

"I'll bet." Charlie reached for her coffee. "Okay, let me think. I've seen the dance every year I've been in town, but I can't remember the details. So, start with your students. Their parents will have the production on video, right? You can watch them and figure out what's going on."

Evie sagged back in the chair and nodded.

"You're right. They'll all have it filmed. That's perfect. Thanks."

Charlie stood and moved back toward the kitchen. She pulled open a drawer. When she returned to the table, she had a pad of paper and a pen.

"The sets are going to be in one of the warehouses on the edge of town. There should be a receipt for the monthly rent in the studio's records. This is the guy who manages the warehouses." She wrote down a name. "Tell him who you are, and he'll let you in, even without a key. Then you can evaluate the sets. Let me know how much work there is and we'll organize a work party."

Evie blinked at her. "A what?"

"A work party. People come and help repair the sets. You'll have to provide the materials, but they'll give you all the labor you need."

"I don't understand. You mean there's a group I can hire to fix the sets?" She wasn't sure what the budget would be. Maybe her new boss would want to cancel the production completely.

Charlie sighed and patted her hand. "Not hire. People will help you with the sets for free. Because they want to."

"Why?"

"Because this is Fool's Gold and that's what we do. Just pick a day and I'll get the word out. Trust me, it will be fine."

"Sure," Evie murmured, even though she didn't believe it for a second. Why would people she didn't know show up to work on sets for her production? For free? "I don't suppose these miracle workers can also alter costumes and do hair for the show?"

"Probably not, but there are a couple of salons in town." Charlie wrote on the paper again. "Someone's been taking care of all that every year. Start here. Ask them who normally handles the hair and makeup for the show. I suspect it's either Bella or Julia. Maybe both." She picked up the second half of her maple bar. "They're feuding sisters who own competing salons. It makes for some pretty fun entertainment."

Evie's recently injured leg began to ache. "Let me see if I have this straight. I'm going to talk to parents of my students to get videos of a production I've never seen so I can teach it to their daughters. In the meantime, a man who doesn't know me from a rock is going to let me into a warehouse so I can evaluate the sets. You're going to arrange a work party of perfect strangers to repair those sets—all of which will happen for free. Then feuding sister stylists may or may not know who does the hair and makeup for my sixty dancers."

Charlie grinned. "That about sums it up. Now

tell me the truth. Do you feel better or worse than you did before you got here?"

Evie shook her head. "Honestly? I haven't a clue."

Two

EVIE WALKED HOME after her last class that evening. The night was cool and clear and smelled like fall. All leaves and earth and woodsmoke. She might be more a big-city girl, but there were things she liked about Fool's Gold. Not having to drive her car everywhere was nice, as was being able to see stars in the sky. Now if only she could find a good Chinese place that delivered.

She turned onto her street, aware that most of the townhouses had Thanksgiving decorations in the windows and on the porches. She'd only been in her place a few weeks—it was a rental and had come furnished. She wasn't interested in putting down roots, and buying furniture wasn't in her budget. But maybe she should stick a flameless candle in the window or something.

Somewhere a door slammed shut. She heard laughter and a dog barking. Homey sounds. For a second she allowed herself to admit she was, well, lonely. Except for her family, she barely knew anyone in town. The most contact she'd had with her neighbors had been to wave to the young couple who lived across the street. She'd never even seen the people next door.

She couldn't shake the feeling of being out of place. The sensation wasn't new. In Los Angeles, she'd had plenty of friends but no real direction for her life. She'd been waiting for something. A sign. She'd been going through the motions of living without a sense of belonging. She'd always figured "one day" she would have the answer. Now she was starting to think there wasn't going to be one day. There was now, and it was up to her to figure out what she wanted.

One of those would be a start, she thought with a quiet laugh as a fancy black sedan pulled into the driveway next to hers. Actually she would settle for having over a hundred dollars in her checking account at any given time.

Evie watched the driver's door open and prepared to at least pretend to be friendly. But her halfhearted wave had barely begun when she recognized Dante Jefferson.

"What are you doing here?" she asked. Was he checking on her? Typical. Her brothers couldn't even get the address right. Dante was in the wrong driveway.

"I live here."

"Where?"

He pointed to the townhouse next to hers.

She dropped her arm to her side. "Seriously? For how long?"

"I moved in the weekend after you."

"You knew you were moving in next to me?" she asked.

He shrugged. "There weren't a lot of choices. I don't know if I want to buy or not, so I took a short-term lease. Hungry?"

"What?" She was still dealing with the fact that her brother's business partner was her neighbor.

Dante pulled a large white bag out of the car. "I got Italian. There's plenty. Come on." He started toward his front door before she could decide if she was going to say yes or not.

He was her brother's business partner. That alone was reason enough to say no. He was connected with her family, and she wanted to avoid her family. Mostly because every time she was around them, she got hurt. It was a rule she'd learned early—people who were supposed to love you usually didn't. Staying far, far away meant keeping herself safe.

"And wine," he called over his shoulder.

She could have ignored the bag of food and the offer of wine except for two things. Her stomach growled, reminding her she was starving. And a very delicious smell drifted to her.

"Garlic bread?" she asked, inhaling the fragrance of garlic as visions of cheesy goodness made her mouth water.

Dante paused at the front door and laughed. "Sure. Thanks for making it clear your willingness to have dinner with me is about the menu and not my sparkling personality."

"I really shouldn't," she began, even as she took a step toward him.

He smiled and shook the bag again. "Come on. Just this once. You can do it."

Just this once, she agreed silently. That would be safe.

She walked up and joined him on the porch. He handed her the bag containing dinner, then opened the front door and flipped on the light.

His place was the mirror image of hers, with a living-dining area, a small gas fireplace and the kitchen beyond. She knew there was a half-bath tucked under the stairs. The second floor had a master and a second bedroom with an attached full bath.

Dante's furnishings were all black leather and glass. From his place in San Francisco, she would guess, setting the food on the table and shrugging out of her coat. Her brother had mentioned Dante had moved from the coastal city just a few months ago.

Dante dropped his suit jacket and tie onto the

sofa. He rolled up his sleeves to his elbows as he walked into the kitchen. He was tall, she thought, taking in the short blond hair and killer blue eyes. The man was easy on the eyes. Her gaze dropped as he moved to the cupboards. Nice butt. He moved well. Athletic. He'd been a jock once and kept in shape.

"I'm going to use the guest bath," she said, motioning to the short hallway on the right.

"Help yourself."

She ducked inside and quickly washed her hands. Her face was pale, her eyes too large. She looked tired. No doubt because she was still healing.

By the time she returned to the dining area, Dante had opened the wine and poured. There were plates and paper napkins. Several containers of food were open on the bar area.

"Help yourself," he told her.

"A take-out buffet. Very nice." She took lasagna and a bit of salad, along with two slices of garlic bread. Her brain quickly added up the calories, but she dismissed the number. Staying at her dancing weight wasn't an issue anymore. Besides, she was tired of being hungry.

They sat across from each other. She leaned back in her chair, picked up her glass of wine and smiled. "How are things in Shanghai?"

"Better. We're building a high-rise and the permits have come through." He paused. "I'm going to guess you don't want the actual details."

"You can tell me if it's important."

"You'll pretend interest?"

She laughed. "Yes. Even wide-eyed amazement if it's called for."

"I'll take a rain check." He studied her. "How about your crisis? Getting any better? You aren't as..." He hesitated.

"Shrill?" she asked.

"I would have picked a different word."

"A smart man who understands women." She picked up her fork. "I'm still dealing with everything that's happening, but I'll get through it."

"How's the leg?"

Evie winced. Not something she wanted to talk about.

For two years she'd been a cheerleader for the Los Angeles Stallions football team. Earlier this season, she'd been plowed down by one of the players. She'd fractured a bone, torn a few tendons and generally ended any chance she'd had at ever dancing again professionally.

In a belated attempt to take care of her, her family had converged on the hospital. When she'd been released, they'd taken advantage of her still-drugged state and brought her to Fool's Gold. When she'd finally surfaced, she'd discovered her belongings moved, her physical therapy set up and her brothers and mother hovering. She'd gotten a job at the dance studio and moved out as soon as she was able. But in a town this small, it was impossible to escape them completely.

The bright spot in her recent, uncomfortable past was she'd discovered she loved teaching dance. She'd always been the one to help classmates conquer difficult steps and passages. She might not have the necessary brilliance to be a star, but she understood how to break down a dance and teach it to others. Funny how she'd never thought to turn that into a career. But working with her students had her thinking she might finally have found the direction she'd been looking for.

"I'm healing," she said. "There are a few lingering aches and pains, but nothing I can't handle."

He took a bite of lasagna, swallowed and chewed. "Did the manager of the studio really take off and leave you with the Christmas program?"

"*The Dance of the Winter King,* open to all faiths," she corrected and nodded. "She sure did. You'd think life in a place like this would be easy, but it's not. There are expectations and complicated relationships."

"Like?"

She drew in a breath. "Okay, Miss Monica ran the studio and she's the one who hired me. But the owner is Dominique Guérin." She paused.

Dante waited expectantly.

"You've never heard of her?" she asked.

"No. Should I have?"

"She's a famous ballerina. Or she was. You're not into dance or the dance world, are you?"

"Do I look like I'm into dance?"

"Fair enough." Although he had nice bone structure, she thought. "Then let's try this another way. Dominique is Charlie's mother."

Dante stared at her. "Clay's Charlie?"

"Uh-huh."

"But Charlie's..." He took a big bite of lasagna and mumbled something unintelligible.

She grinned. "What was that?" she asked sweetly.

He motioned to his still-full mouth, as if indicating there was no way he could possibly speak.

"I understand the point you're avoiding," she said. "Charlie doesn't look like a dancer. From what I understand, she takes after her father. Anyway, I've left a message for Dominique to tell her what's going on with the dance studio, but I haven't heard back. In the meantime, I have to assume we're still planning on the Christmas Eve performance, which means getting organized in ways I'm not sure I can even comprehend. I've never been in charge like this before."

Her appetite faded, and she pushed away her plate. "Charlie suggested I ask some of the parents for copies of any recordings they have. So

I'll be able to see those. Then there are costumes and steps and music." She stopped. "We should change the subject or I'll get shrill again. Neither of us wants that."

He swallowed. "It's a lot."

She poked at her salad. "Like I said, we can talk about something else." She looked at him. "So, how did you meet my brother?"

"Rafe?"

"He's the one you do business with. I'm assuming you met Shane and Clay through him."

Dante leaned back in his chair. "You don't know?"

"We're not that close." She'd left for Juilliard when she was seventeen and hadn't had a whole lot of contact with her family ever since. She'd seen them more since her football accident than she had in the past eight years.

"Even to your mom?" he asked.

She sighed. "Let me guess. You and your mom are close and you call at least twice a week. For what it's worth, I really admire that." From an emotional distance, she thought. No way she could relate to it.

Dante picked up his wine. "My mother died a long time ago."

"Oh." Evie felt herself flush. "I'm sorry."

"Like I said, it was a long time ago." He leaned

toward her. "Rafe and I met while we were both in college. We were working construction."

She remembered that her brother had taken summer jobs to supplement his scholarships. After finding out about Dante's mother, she wasn't going to do any more assuming.

"You went into the family business?" she asked.

He chuckled. "No, I was paying the bills. I found out I was a lot more popular with girls in college when I could afford to take them on dates. I was a scholarship student, too."

"Intelligent and good-looking," she teased. "So why are you still single?"

"I like the chase, but I'm not so big on the catch."

"A man who avoids commitments." She knew the type. With those broad shoulders and blue eyes, he would have no trouble getting a woman to notice him. The money and success wouldn't hurt, either. "Do they line up at a set time, or is it more like concert lotteries? You pass out numbers and then call them randomly?"

"Impressive," he told her. "Mocking me and my dates at the same time."

"I was gently teasing. There's a difference."

"You're right." He studied her over his wineglass. "What about you? No fancy Mr. King of the Dance coming to rescue you from the backwater that is Fool's Gold?"

"I'm between kings right now. And, at the risk of sounding like Jane Austen, content to be so. Miss Monica is welcome to her gentleman friend. I'm more focused on the upcoming performance." Not to mention avoiding her family as much as possible.

"Did you see all the Thanksgiving decorations around town?" he asked.

"The turkey population is well represented."

"Christmas is going to be worse," he grumbled.

"Candy canes on every mailbox."

"Wreaths on every door." He looked at her. "It's going to be like living in a snow globe."

"Tell me about it." She sipped her wine. "Do you know this town doesn't have a grocery store that stays open twenty-four hours a day? What's up with that? What if someone needs something at two in the morning?"

"Like aspirin after listening to clog dancers for an hour?"

"You'll adore them when you see them perform."

"Maybe." He frowned. "Hey, why aren't you a big fan of Christmas? With your family, I would think loving the season would be a given. I'll bet your mom made Christmas special for you."

Evie put down her wine and pressed a hand to her stomach. Sudden churning made her uncomfortable.

No doubt Dante saw May as a warm, caring parent. The kind of woman who would bake cookies and sew Christmas stockings. Maybe she had once—Evie's brothers each had a carefully embroidered stocking. But Evie's was store-bought and not personalized. There hadn't been many traditions for her. She'd always found Christmas kind of lonely and wasn't looking forward to an entire town showing her all the ways she didn't fit in.

"I suppose I've gotten out of the habit of the holidays," she said, hedging. She barely knew Dante. There was no reason to go into the gory details of her past with the man.

"Then we'll have to stay strong together," he told her. "There's only the two of us against all of them."

She laughed. "Grinches together?"

"Absolutely." He pointed at her nearly untouched plate. "Okay, you're either going to have to eat more or explain to the chef why you didn't like his very excellent lasagna."

"I wouldn't want that."

An hour later, they'd finished most of the wine. Dante had explained more about the Shanghai project and she'd told funny stories about her days touring with a third-rate ballet company. He insisted on packing up the leftovers for her to take home and then escorted her across their shared driveway and to her front door. Once there, he waited until she'd put her key in the lock and pushed open the door.

"If you need anything, pound on the wall," he told her. "Ah, the one between us. If you pound on the other one, you'll confuse the neighbors and get a bad reputation in the development."

"I wouldn't want that." She held up the bag of food. "Thanks for this."

"You're skinny. Eat more." With that, he bent down and lightly kissed her cheek. "'Night, Evie."

"'Night."

She watched him walk back to his place and step inside. Then she stepped into her house and shut the door. She stood in the dark for a second, the feel of his kiss lingering on her cheek.

She'd had fun tonight. Talking, sharing a meal with a friend. Dante was easy to talk to. Charming. He was the kind of man who made a woman think about more than kissing. Even someone who knew how dangerous that could be.

"My brother's business partner and a player," she said as she turned on the light in the entryway. There were a thousand reasons not to play the what-if game with Dante Jefferson. She was smart enough to remember every one of them.

"YOU KNOW THIS isn't normal, right," Dante said as he stood on the porch of the house and stared out at the elephant. "Ranches are supposed to have things like horses and goats. What were you thinking?"

Rafe shook his head. "It wasn't me."

Dante continued to study the elephant. "What is she wearing?"

"A blanket. It gets cold here. She goes into a heated barn at night, but she likes to be out during the day. Mom had the blanket made for her."

Dante thought longingly of his life back in San Francisco. Season tickets to the Giants and the 49ers. Poker nights with his buddies. Dinners with beautiful women. Okay, sure, he'd had a beautiful woman at his place last night, but that was different. She was his partner's sister. The price of getting lucky could be the loss of a very treasured body part. Although he would have to admit watching Evie move was almost worth it. He supposed it was years of dance training, but she made even the act of picking up a fork look graceful.

"I know what you're thinking," Rafe said.

Dante doubted that.

"I changed my life for Heidi," Rafe continued. "It's worth it. And I want to be here on the ranch. I like Fool's Gold."

"I figured as much when you moved the business here."

"Come on." Rafe turned toward the house. "Let's go inside. We'll have brownies while you tell me about what's going on in Shanghai."

They settled at the kitchen table. The company's rented office space didn't have any private offices, which meant any sensitive business had to be discussed elsewhere.

Over the next couple of hours, they reviewed several ongoing projects, and Dante brought Rafe up-to-date on a few legal matters. When they were finished, Rafe poured them each more coffee.

"You staying in Fool's Gold for Thanksgiving?" he asked.

Dante shrugged. "Probably."

"Come to dinner, then. I wasn't going to get between you and your latest conquest, but if you're flying solo, we'd love to have you."

"Thanks. I'll bring wine."

"Not a salad or dessert?" Rafe joked.

"Maybe next year." He collected the folders he'd brought. "Evie's pretty panicked about the Christmas Eve dance show."

Rafe frowned. "What are you talking about?"

"The show. *The Dance of the Winter King.* The manager of the dance studio took off and left everything to her."

"I didn't know that."

The statement confirmed what Evie had hinted at the previous night. That she and her family didn't have much to do with each other.

"You and your brothers have always been close," Dante said. "But you barely mention Evie.

We'd been in business about three years before I even knew you had a sister. What's up with that?"

Rafe shrugged. "After my dad died, things were tough. My mom was devastated, money was tight. I tried to handle the family, but I was a kid."

Eight or nine, Dante thought, remembering what his friend had told him over the years. He knew what it was like to look out for a parent. He'd done the same with his mom. It had always been the two of them against the world. Until Dante had joined a gang. His actions had broken her heart and ultimately cost her everything.

What he would give to go back and change that, he thought grimly. To have his family back. But he'd learned about the perils of close ties.

"Mom was crying all the time," Rafe continued. "We knew she was sad. Shane met this cowboy in town for one of the festivals and brought him home for dinner. Nine months later, Evie showed up."

"You're kidding."

"No. She's technically our half sister. The four of us were a unit and Evie never seemed to find her place. I should have tried harder with her. I'm trying now. I don't know that it's enough." He stared at Dante. "You live close to her, don't you?"

"Next door." Dante braced himself for the next line. Where Rafe said to stay away from his sister.

"So do me a favor. Look out for her. Make sure she's okay."

That was it? No dire warning? Rafe knew Dante's reputation with women. It's not that Dante was a bad guy—he simply didn't believe in long-term commitments. Four months was a personal best in his world.

"Sure thing," he said easily. "I'm happy to help."

"Good. She'd tell me that it's too little, too late, but as far as I'm concerned, having Evie in town is a second chance for all of us."

Three

Evie stared at the battered ledger that served as a scheduling calendar. While Miss Monica had been a pleasant enough person and a good teacher, she hadn't believed in any invention that surfaced after 1960. The Smithsonian had been calling to ask if their old computer could be put on display in the history of technology section and the answering machine had to be from the 1980s. The worn tape had contained a single message that morning. Dominique Guérin, the new owner, had returned Evie's call. Her response to Evie's slightly panicked info dump about the loss of the head instructor and the upcoming ballet, about which Evie knew nothing, had been a cheerful "I have every confidence in you, my dear. I can't wait to see the production on Christmas Eve."

"Great," Evie said, clutching her mug of tea in her hands and willing her heart to stop beating at hummingbird speed. She felt as if she were trapped in some old black-and-white movie. "Come on, boys and girls. Let's put on a show!"

Only there was no production staff waiting in the shadows to work the cinematic magic. There was her, a battered ledger and sheer force of will. Oh, and sixty students she wasn't willing to disappoint.

She picked up her purse and crossed to the small mirror on the wall. After brushing her hair, she separated it into two sections and braided each one. She expertly wrapped the braids around her head and pinned them in place, then returned her purse to the desk drawer. Now she was ready to dance.

She heard footsteps on the stairs leading up to the studio. A few seconds later, a smiling woman with brown hair hurried into the reception area. Evie recognized her as one of the mothers but had no idea of her name.

"I'm running late," she proclaimed, handing Evie three CDs in cases. "Here's what you need. I hope. I mean I know it's what you wanted, I just hope they help."

The woman was in her late twenties, pretty, wearing a long-sleeved T-shirt with a large embroidered cartoon turkey on the front.

The woman laughed. "You look blank. I'm Patience McGraw. Lillie's mother."

"Oh. Lillie. Sure." Sweet girl with absolutely no talent, Evie thought. But she loved dancing and worked hard. Sometimes that was more important than ability.

"Charlie called me," Patience continued. "OMG, to quote my daughter. Miss Monica ran off with a man? I haven't been on a date in maybe three years, but my daughter's seventy-year-old dance teacher gets lucky? I can't decide if I should be depressed or inspired."

"I'm both," Evie admitted. "Slightly more depressed, though."

"Tell me about it." Patience gave a rueful laugh. "Anyway, Charlie explained that you're feeling completely abandoned and pressured. I can't help with the dance stuff. Lillie inherited her lack of coordination from me, I'm afraid. But I'm good at getting things done. So those are recordings of previous years' shows. One is mine. The other two come from other mothers. They're also for different years. I thought that might help."

Evie tightened her hold on the CDs. Right now, these were her best shot at figuring out what the program was supposed to look like.

"Thank you. You've saved me."

Patience laughed. "I'm barely getting started." She pulled a piece of paper out of her jeans's front pocket. "My phone number. I'll help get the work party together for the sets. Charlie mentioned those, too. So, a Saturday would work best. I suggest the first Saturday in December. All that's going on in town is the tree lighting and that's not until dusk. We'd have all day to spruce and paint and do whatever needs doing."

Evie took the paper with her free hand. In addition to Patience's phone number was a man's name.

"This guy is your contact at the hardware store in town. Tell him who you are and what you need the supplies for. He'll give you a great discount. Once you get that coordinated, get back to me and I'll spread the word about the work party. Oh, we'll also need to coordinate for the costumes."

Evie felt as if she were being pushed by an out-of-control tide. "You sew?"

"Enough to repair a costume. But I have the names of the talented ladies who do the real work. Plus, we need to schedule the fittings and then the run-through for hair and makeup." She drew in a breath and planted her hands on her hips. "Drat. There's one more thing that I can't… Brunch!" She grinned. "Thanksgiving morning we all meet at Jo's Bar. We have yummy brunch food, enough champagne so that we don't care about the turkey we're cooking and we watch the parade on TV. Girls only. You have to come. It's really fun. After we're stuffed and drunk, we head outside to watch the Fool's Gold parade through town."

"Okay," Evie said slowly, still overwhelmed by names, promises and information.

"Be there at nine." Patience pulled her phone

out of her pocket and glanced at the screen. "I'm running late. Nothing new, right? I have to get back to work. Call me with any questions." She started for the door. "And pick a date for the work party. We need to claim our labor."

Evie stood in the center of her studio. She was holding three CD cases and a small piece of paper, but she would swear she'd been buried under a giant mound of boxes or something. She tucked the CD cases into her purse. Tonight she would watch the recordings and start to make notes. As for the rest of it, she would have to sort through all she'd learned and make up some kind of schedule. She still wasn't convinced about the work party, but maybe a few parents would be willing to help.

She walked into the main studio and settled in front of the barre. A half hour or so of practice would settle her mind for the lessons to come. Slowly, carefully, conscious of her still-healing leg, she began to warm up. Two minutes later, her cell phone rang.

She straightened, slid her right foot back to the floor and walked over to where the phone sat on the reception desk.

The calling number was unfamiliar.

"Hello?"

"Evie? Hi, it's Heidi."

Heidi was Rafe's new wife. She lived on the

ranch and raised goats. A pretty blonde who had welcomed Evie with genuine warmth.

"Hi," Evie said, more cautious than excited about contact with her family.

"I wanted to make sure you knew we were having dinner at four on Thanksgiving. Rafe couldn't remember if you'd been told." Heidi sighed. "Men. Because social details aren't that interesting to them, right?"

Thanksgiving dinner? Evie held in a groan. She wasn't up to dinner with her relatives.

"Oh, and that morning we watch the parade at Jo's Bar. You know about that, right? It's a huge crowd. Girls only brunch. You'll love it. It's a great chance to meet everyone. Just be careful. The champagne goes down way too easy. Last year I had to call my grandfather to drive me home. I vowed I wasn't touching the stuff this year and I'm holding myself to that. Oh, it's on a local channel that starts the replay at nine our time. Just so you don't freak out and think you have to get up too early."

Evie heard a crash in the background.

Heidi gasped. "I think that was my new batch of cheese. I gotta run. Save the date."

The phone went silent.

Evie slowly pushed the end button, then replaced the phone in her bag and set the bag in the bottom drawer. As far as Heidi was concerned,

Evie had just accepted both invitations. Calling back to say no would mean answering questions and coming up with a reason why she wasn't joining the only people she knew in a town she'd just moved to. Talk about awkward.

In truth, she didn't mind spending time with her brothers. With new wives and fiancées hanging around, Evie should find it easy enough to avoid her mother.

She glanced at the clock on the wall, then walked to the stairs. Once she was on the main floor, she stepped into her brother's offices and moved toward Dante's desk. He was staring at his computer screen but glanced up as she approached.

"Hey," she said. "I wanted to warn you that tonight there's more clog dancing. No tap classes until tomorrow. Ballet the rest of the time. Ballet is quieter. Except for the music. But you seem to have this thing against the clog girls, so I'm letting you know in advance."

Dante sat at his desk, his blue eyes fixed on her, the oddest expression on his face.

"What?" she demanded, raising her hands to her head to make sure her braids were tightly in place.

He swore under his breath. "Is it legal?"

"Clog dancing? The last time I checked."

He opened his mouth, then closed it. "What you're wearing."

She glanced down at herself. She had on black

tights and a leotard. It was exactly what she wore nearly every day of her life. Scuffed ballet shoes covered her feet. Later, she would put on toe shoes to demonstrate some steps, but she wasn't going to walk around in them. She found that awkward and, okay, a little pretentious.

She pulled at the stretchy material. "It's worn, I'll admit, but I'm dressed."

Dante glanced around, as if checking to see who was watching them. As far as Evie could tell, everyone else was busy with work.

"You're practically naked."

She laughed. "I'm fully covered."

"Technically. But…" He waved his hand up and down in front of her body. "Shouldn't you put on a coat?"

She didn't understand. "Because why?"

"You're distracting."

"Really?"

"Look around. Do you see anyone else wearing an outfit like that?"

"It's not office wear."

He seemed a little glazed and frantic. For a second she allowed herself to believe he found her sexy. Wouldn't that be nice?

"You're killing me," he muttered.

She smiled. "That's so lovely. Thank you."

"You're welcome. Oh, the guy at the hardware store called me about the set."

"What? Why would he call you?"

"Because Charlie told him to. She has this idea that you don't know squat about construction."

"I don't, but it's my responsibility anyway." She was going to make sure her students weren't disappointed.

"Yeah, well, now I'm going to help, too. I thought we could go look at the sets together, and I'll put together a list of what needs doing."

She took a step back. "No, thanks. I appreciate the offer, but no."

"Why not?"

"Because, um, you're busy." Lame, but it was better than the truth. She wasn't willing to risk getting sucked in. Dante was pretty tempting. Handsome, funny, interesting. Sexy. Hard to resist.

"Why not?" he repeated.

She sighed. "You're my brother's business partner. I'm not looking to get more involved with my family. We have a long, complicated history. I won't bore you with it, but believe me when I say, stay far, far away."

He studied her. "Interesting. A mystery. I love a good mystery."

"Don't be intrigued. I'm a seriously boring person. You're sweet to offer, but no. I'll do it myself."

His phone rang. He swore quietly. "I have to take this call, but our conversation isn't over."

He couldn't be more wrong, she thought, giving

a cheerful wave and hurrying away. Dante was a complication she didn't need and couldn't afford. Him being nice would make staying away more difficult, but even more necessary.

THE OFFICE CLEARED OUT a little after five. Dante kept working. Right on time, the thudding of clog-clad feet pounded above his head. He turned off his computer and ducked out while he could. But an hour later he returned and made his way upstairs. Evie was turning out the lights in the studio, obviously done for the night.

She turned and looked at him, her expression slightly guarded. He took in her bulky sweatshirt and fitted jeans, and raised his eyebrows.

"You changed."

She pointed at him. "You did, too."

"I don't think my suit would get the same reaction as your work clothes."

"I don't know," she told him. "I do love a man in a tie."

"Now you're just messing with me."

"You make it easy."

Her eyes were big and green, with dark lashes. He would guess she wasn't wearing much in the way of makeup, which was fine by him. He liked women in all shapes and sizes. From high-maintenance divas to the most casual of tree-huggers.

"I'm going to help you with the sets," he said. "You can accept gracefully or you can fight me, but in the end, I'll win. I always win."

"Doing your civic duty?"

"Helping out a friend."

He liked her. She was Rafe's sister. As for the way she looked in dance clothes, that was his problem alone. He knew better than to go down dangerous paths.

He thought briefly of his mother, how she would have liked Evie and adored the little girls who danced. His mother had wanted so much more than the hardscrabble life she'd been forced to deal with. She'd wanted him to be a success. She would be happy about that, too.

Knowing her, she would accept the price she'd had to pay to get him on the right road. Something he could never accept or forgive in himself. He supposed that made her the better person. Hardly a surprise.

"It's Christmas," he said. "Think of this as me getting in the spirit."

"You don't like Christmas spirit."

"Maybe helping you will change my mind." He shrugged. "You know you can't do it alone. Accept the inevitable and say thank you."

She drew in a breath. "I know I can't do it alone, and for what it's worth, I trust you."

"I think there's a compliment buried in there."

"There is. Thank you."

He smiled. "Was that so hard?"

"You have no idea."

"Then while you're still wrestling with your personal growth, let me add, your brother invited me to Thanksgiving dinner." He braced himself for her rant.

"Good. I was hoping for a big crowd."

Unexpected, he thought. "Should I ask why?"

"No. You should assume I'm just one of those friendly types who loves humanity."

"Your recent resistance to me helping aside." He leaned against her desk.

"Yes."

"And your feelings on humanity?"

"Okay in small groups." She held up a piece of paper. "I was visited earlier by one of the moms. Patience. She swears there really can be a work party to restore my sets."

"Good. We'll make the list of what needs fixing and get it organized."

He studied her. From what he could tell, she wore her hair up for her lessons—two braids wrapped around her head. But now, with her work done for the day, she'd left it loose. Wavy strands of honey-blond hair fell past her shoulders and halfway down her back.

He would bet she had soft hair, he thought, imagining her bending over him. He could practically feel the cool silk in his fingers. She would be all muscle, he thought absently. Long legs. Incredibly flexible.

"Dante?"

He blinked himself back into the room. "Sorry."

She tilted her head, her mouth curving into a smile. "Want to tell me where you went?"

"Nope."

"Are you going to help me?" She paused. "Go with me to look at the sets?"

Was that what they'd been talking about? "Sure. When do you want to do that?"

"You weren't listening at all, were you?"

"Not even a little."

"At least you're honest about it." She folded her arms across her chest. "Now. I suggested we go now."

"Works for me." He studied her, wondering how much trouble he would get in for kissing her, and knowing it would be worth it. "Here's the thing."

She raised her eyebrows. "You're putting conditions on helping me? You're the one who insisted."

"No. I'm telling you that when I said I was a player, I wasn't kidding. I never get serious. I don't do relationships and I'm not the guy you take home to meet the parents."

"You're already having dinner with my mother on Thanksgiving."

"That's different. It's not a date."

She tilted her head. "You're warning me off."

"Yes."

"I haven't expressed any interest in you. Is this your ego talking? Are you assuming that a woman can't be in the same room with you without begging for your attention?"

"I wish, but, no."

Her gaze was steady. "You're going to make a move."

"Most likely."

One corner of her mouth turned up. "Announcing it up front isn't exactly smooth."

"You're difficult to resist."

She laughed. "Oh, please. I'm very resistible. Trust me."

He moved a little closer. He liked the sound of her laughter and how she wasn't aware of her appeal.

She put her hand on his chest. "Let me see if I have this straight. You're warning me that you're not someone I want to be involved with, and at the same time, you're convinced you have enough going for you that I'll give in anyway."

"Absolutely."

He put his hand on hers, liking the feel of her fingers against his chest. Skin on skin would be better, but a man had to take what he could get.

She pulled free and dropped her arm to her side,

then shook her head. “You’re a weird guy, you know that?”

“I’ve been called worse.”

“I’m sure you have. Let me get my coat, and while we head to the warehouse, you can share all the details. Knowing the depth of your awfulness will help me resist you.”

“Now you’re mocking me.”

“Hey, you think you can seduce me against my will. I think a little mocking is called for.”

Four

Evie wasn't sure about brunch at a bar, but she showed up right on time anyway. She was a little bleary-eyed from spending every free moment over the past few days watching the videos of *The Dance of the Winter King.* She'd broken down the choreography of over half of the production. With luck, by the end of the holiday weekend, she would have the whole dance down on paper and then be able to put it all together for the girls.

While each age group had already learned the basic steps they would need for their section of the production, there were no transitions, no flow and the order of the dances had yet to be determined. Traditionally, the younger, less experienced students would go first, but Evie was playing with the idea of having the older soloists do short routines in between each group. Although, with time ticking, that might not be a smart move.

She walked into Jo's Bar to find the main room

already filled with a couple of dozen women. Unlike regular bars she'd been to, this one had flattering lighting, the TVs already tuned to the parade and the smell of cinnamon and vanilla filling the air.

The bar itself was being used as a buffet. Large chafing dishes sat in a row, with a stack of plates at one end. Big trays of cut up fresh fruit offered healthy choices next to a display of pastries that made Evie's mouth water. Even the voice in her head—the one that warned about potential butt and thigh growth—was silent with carb anticipation.

A tall no-nonsense thirtysomething woman walked over carrying a tray of glasses of champagne. She stopped in front of Evie.

"I don't know you," she said, a friendly smile buffering her blunt statement. "Visiting relatives?"

"Evie Stryker."

The woman's eyes widened. "The mysterious dancing sister of the cowboy brothers. Everyone wants to meet you."

"I can't decide if that's a compliment or if it makes me sound like the villain in a horror movie."

The woman laughed. "Dancer killer. I like it. I'm Jo, by the way. This is my bar." She nodded toward a guy opening bottles of champagne behind the bar. "I promised everyone this would be girls only, but he's married to me, so technically he doesn't count. Besides, he's a good guy, so that's something. Your group is over at that table. Enjoy."

Evie walked in the direction Jo had indicated, not sure what she would find. Heidi, Annabelle and Charlie were already there, which allowed her to relax.

Annabelle, Shane's pregnant fiancée, jumped to her feet when she spotted Evie. "Thank goodness. Charlie is not willing to drink for two, which is very selfish of her, and Heidi's resisting drinking at all."

"I have to handle dinner later," Heidi protested. "I'm responsible for the turkey. Do you really want me wielding a sharp knife after a couple of glasses of champagne? I don't think so. If I hurt myself, one of you will have to milk the goats."

Annabelle sighed. "Fine. Be reasonable." She drew Evie to the table. "I'm dying for champagne. Can you drink a glass now so I can watch you and experience it vicariously? Please?"

"Ah, sure," Evie said, not clear on what Annabelle wanted. She didn't think watching someone else drink would be very satisfying, but she was willing to go along with it.

She sipped from the glass Annabelle handed her. "Delicious."

Annabelle sighed. "I knew it. I miss champagne."

"I'd miss coffee more," Charlie muttered. "The

whole pregnancy thing is a giant pain in the ass, if you ask me."

"It's not really your ass that hurts," Annabelle said in a mock whisper.

Charlie rolled her eyes. "Thanks for the update."

"I thought you were hearing the pitter-patter of little feet," Heidi said.

Charlie ran her hands through her cropped hair. "We're still negotiating." The strong, competent firefighter flushed. "Clay is worried that once I'm pregnant we're going to have to, um, spend less time…you know. He wants a few more months of us alone."

Evie stared at her, not sure what she was talking about. Wouldn't they still be alone during the pregnancy?

Annabelle leaned toward her. "Sex. She's talking about sex. Clay's worried that Charlie might have morning sickness or something and he won't be getting as much. They need the bloom to wear off the rose, so to speak."

Evie covered her ears. "Okay, I'm not having that conversation. Clay's my brother and that's just disgusting."

The other three laughed.

Conversation shifted to the plans for the day—what was happening when. The four of them walked over to get started on the buffet.

"Oh, Dante said he'd drive you, if you want,"

Heidi told Evie. "He said to knock on his door when you were ready."

"Thanks."

She hadn't seen Dante since their trip to the warehouse a couple of days before. Despite the flirtatious teasing at the dance studio, once they'd arrived to view the sets, he'd been all business. His claims to have worked in construction had turned out to be true. He'd studied the sets, had taken notes on what needed to be fixed and started a preliminary supply list.

All things that would help, Evie told herself. She had a big job ahead of her, and she didn't have the time to complicate her life with a guy. Still, there was something about Dante....

Something best left unexplored, she cautioned herself. A philosophy he obviously embraced. For all his flirty ways, after the set viewing, he'd simply dropped her off at her place with a quick goodbye and left. Apparently the only thing he'd exaggerated had been his attraction to her.

Evie collected a small piece of stuffed French toast and some bacon. Heidi chose a lot of protein, while Charlie filled her plate with food for twenty. Annabelle kept touching her stomach, as if trying to figure out what she and the baby were in the mood for.

Five women walked in together, and most of

those already in the bar called out greetings. Heidi moved close to Evie.

"The Hendrix family women," she murmured. "Denise is the mother. The three who look exactly alike are triplets. Dakota, Montana and Nevada. Nevada's the one who's pregnant. The one who doesn't look like the others is Liz Sutton, the writer. She's married to Denise's oldest son."

The women looked happy to be together, Evie thought, watching them. The sisters and sister-in-law seemed especially close and kept near their mom.

She knew her brothers had grown up tight and, even when Rafe was at his most imperious, had kept in touch with the other brothers. She'd always been the odd one out. Never fitting in. As a kid, she'd felt as if everyone was mad at her all the time, but she never knew why.

She started back to the table, only to come to a stop in front of her mother.

"Hello, Evie," May said with a tentative smile.

"Um, hi. I didn't know you were going to be here."

"I drove in after Heidi. I wanted to get a few things started for dinner tonight."

Evie nodded, wondering if her sister-in-law had known May was coming to the brunch all along, but had failed to mention it. Had Heidi made that clear, Evie would have found a reason not to attend.

Evie started to step around her. May put her hand on her arm.

"Wait," her mother said. "Evie, we should talk." May glanced around at the crowded bar. "Maybe not here. But soon."

Evie looked for a place to set down her plate. She'd suddenly lost her appetite. "There's not very much for us to talk about."

"Of course there is. It's been so long. I want..." May drew in a breath. "I'd like us to stop being angry with each other."

To anyone else, that was probably a very reasonable statement. Evie fought against the sudden rush of tears in her eyes. "Sure. But first answer me a question. What do you have to be mad about? Me being born? Because that's not anything I could control."

May stiffened. "That came out wrong. I'm sorry."

Evie shook her head. "I don't think it came out wrong at all. I think you've been angry with me for a long time. As for talking, as far as I'm concerned, until you can tell me what it is you think I did, we have nothing to say to each other."

With that she walked back to the table. She set down her plate, picked up her champagne glass and drained it. Then she went in search of a refill.

"ARE YOU DRUNK?" Dante asked.

Evie leaned back into the soft leather of his very expensive, very German car. She'd been driving the same dented, slightly rusty old Chevy for nearly five years. The seats were more spring than foam, the windows didn't close right and the mechanic actually sighed every time she took her car in for service.

"This is nice," she said, stroking the side of the heated seat. "I'll try not to throw up."

"Gee, thanks," Dante said, turning his attention back to the road. "You *are* drunk."

"I'm buzzed. There's a difference."

"It's one in the afternoon."

"I was at a brunch and there was champagne. Plus I had a fight with my mom and that took away my appetite." She frowned, or at least tried to. She couldn't exactly feel her forehead. "We didn't fight. Not really. She said we should stop being mad at each other. I'm the kid. What did I ever do? That's what I asked. Is she pissed I was born? But she didn't have an answer. There's never a good reason, you know?"

She turned to Dante and blinked. "What were we talking about?"

"You need to eat something."

"Turkey. I'll eat turkey."

"That'll help." He glanced at her. "She said she was angry?"

Evie tried to remember May's exact words. "She said she would like us to stop being angry at each other. Being annoyed at me is kind of implied."

"Poor kid." Dante briefly put his hand on top of hers.

For a second Evie enjoyed the warmth of the contact, then the meaning of his words sank into her slightly soggy brain. Poor kid? Poor *kid?* Is that how he saw her? As a child? What happened to her being a sexy vixen? Not that he'd ever used that phrase, but still. He'd implied she was. Or at least her dancer work clothes. She didn't want to be a kid. She wanted to be vixeny. Vixenish. Whatever.

She leaned her head back against the seat and sighed. Life was far from fair.

Two hours later she'd munched her way through a fair amount of the veggie platter Heidi had put out and finished off about a half gallon of water. The buzz was long gone, as was the faint headache that had followed. Through careful maneuvering, she'd managed to avoid spending any time alone with her mother. Oddly enough, Dante had helped more than a little. He'd stuck beside her from the second they walked in the door.

Painfully aware that his concern was more fraternal than she would like, she told herself not to read anything into his actions. Dante was practically family. There was no way to avoid him while she was in Fool's Gold, and as her plans had her staying well into the new year, logic needed to win over longing. Well, not longing. Acknowledging that Dante was smart and sexy was simply stating the obvious. It wasn't as if she had a thing for him or wanted anything other than casual friendship.

"Halftime," Heidi said, walking into the living room. "It's time, people."

"Time for what?" Dante asked.

"I have no idea," Evie admitted, but stood along with everyone else.

Shane sighed. "It's Thanksgiving."

Evie pointed to the kitchen. "You know, the big turkey in the oven was our first clue."

"Funny. It's Thanksgiving, and if we get a big feast, so do the animals," Shane said.

Dante groaned. "Including the elephant?"

"Especially the elephant. My racehorses have a very controlled diet, but everybody else gets a treat. Do you know what a watermelon costs this time of year?"

They all followed Shane and Heidi outside where a truck waited. The back of the pickup was filled with all kinds of holiday goodies. There was the massive watermelon for Priscilla, the elephant, carrots and apples for the goats, Reno, the pony, Wilbur, the pig, and the riding horses. Something from the local butcher for the feral cat who had taken up residence with Priscilla and Reno.

Evie and Dante were assigned the riding horses.

"You know what you're doing?" Shane asked.

Evie sniffed. "Yes. We'll be fine."

They walked toward the corral. Six horses trotted over to greet them. Dante hesitated.

"They have really big teeth," he said. "You're okay with that?"

She smiled. "Keep your fingers away from their teeth and you'll be fine."

She took the knife Heidi had provided and sliced the apple in quarters, then put a piece on her hand, straightened her fingers so her palm was flat and offered it to the first horse. He took it gently, his lips barely brushing her skin.

"Impressive," Dante said and did the same with another quarter of apple.

"Look out!" she yelled, just as the horse reached for him.

He jumped back, dropping the apple piece. "What?"

She grinned. "Nothing. Just messing with you."

"Charming." He took another piece of apple and held it out to the horse. "Sorry about that," he said. "You know women."

"Um, you're talking to a girl horse."

"She understands just fine."

They finished giving the horses their holiday treats, then headed back to the house. When they stepped onto the porch, Dante paused. "Did you grow up here?"

Evie looked out at the rolling hills of the ranch. The air was cool, but the sky blue. To the east, snow-capped mountains rose toward the sun.

"Technically I was born in Fool's Gold," she admitted. "But I don't remember much about it. We moved when I was pretty young."

Her earliest memories were of the tiny apartment they'd had in Los Angeles. The three boys had been crammed into the larger of the two bedrooms. May had taken the smaller bedroom for herself and Evie had slept on the sofa.

"Are you happy to be back?"

"I like teaching dance," she said, willing to admit that much of the truth. "I wasn't sure I would, but it's gratifying. The girls are enthusiastic and excited to learn." A few were talented, but she'd discovered she was less interested in skill than attitude when it came to her students.

"Let me guess," he said, glancing at her. "The clog dancing is your favorite."

She laughed. "It's a very important art form."

"It's loud and on top of my head."

For a second she allowed herself to get lost in his dark blue eyes. Then common sense took over, and she gave him her best sympathetic smile. "It's for the children, Dante. Not everything is about you."

"It should be," he grumbled. "Come on. The second half is starting."

"You know, I was run over by a football player only a few months ago. Does it occur to you that watching the game could be traumatic?"

"Is it?"

"No. I'm just saying it could be."

He wrapped his arm around her and drew her inside. "Stay close. I'll protect you."

For a second she allowed herself to believe he wasn't just being funny. That he was someone she could depend on. She knew better, of course. Her family had taught her that the people who were supposed to love you back usually didn't and that it was far safer to simply be alone. She was done with love.

DINNER WAS MORE ENJOYABLE than Evie had allowed herself to hope was possible. With ten people sitting around a large table, it was easy to avoid awkward silences and difficult questions. Even more fortunate, May had sat at the opposite end, on the same side, so Evie didn't have to try to avoid her at all.

Once everyone had eaten their fill of turkey, dressing, mashed potatoes, sweet potato casserole, vegetables, olives, rolls and a very confusing Jell-O mold, conversation turned to the holiday season in Fool's Gold.

"You pretty much need a schedule of events on the refrigerator," Charlie was saying. "The town starts decorating this weekend. Next Saturday night is the tree lighting."

Heidi leaned against Rafe. "We're doing hayrides."

Dante turned to her. "What?"

Shane groaned. "Hayrides. Horses pulling sleighs." He glanced out at the rapidly darkening night. "Or wagons if we don't get snow."

Evie knew he sounded exasperated but guessed it was all an act. Shane liked everything about the ranch, including the close proximity to town. More important to him was how Annabelle enjoyed the holidays.

She glanced around the table, startled to realize all her relatives were paired up. A year ago everyone had been single. Since the last holiday season, Rafe and May had both married and Shane and Clay had gotten engaged. Annabelle was pregnant. This time next year Shane and Annabelle would have their baby. Heidi and Charlie would probably *be* pregnant, and she would be gone.

"I ate too much," Glen, May's husband, said as he pushed back from the table. "Wonderful dinner. Thank you."

May smiled at him. "It wasn't just me. Everyone helped."

"Not me," Evie said, suddenly wanting a few minutes away from her family. "So I insist on cleaning up. Everyone carry your plates into the kitchen, then leave me to it."

"You can't do all the dishes yourself," Heidi said.

"There's a brand-new dishwasher that says otherwise," Evie told her.

"I'll help," Dante said. "I'm good at taking orders."

"We all know that's not true," Rafe said. "But, hey, if he wants to wash, I say let him."

It only took a few minutes to clear the table. Heidi took charge of the leftovers and put them neatly away in the refrigerator, then Evie shooed her out so she could start rinsing the dishes. As promised, Dante stayed behind and began stacking serving pieces.

May walked in. "I want to help."

Evie forced a smile. "You made most of the dinner. I can handle this."

Her mother stared at her. "You really hate me, don't you?"

Evie felt her shoulders slump. "Mom, it's Thanksgiving. Why do you have to make me helping with cleanup more than it is?"

"Because you've been avoiding me." She pressed her lips together. "I know you had a difficult childhood and it's my fault. It's just that you..." Tears filled her eyes, and she looked away.

Evie told herself to be sympathetic. That nothing would be gained by snapping or complaining. There was no new material here. Just the same half-truths and partial explanations.

May sniffed. “Can’t you forgive me?”

Evie folded her arms across her chest in what she knew was a protective and not very subtle gesture. “Sure. You’re forgiven.”

“You’re still angry.” May drew in a breath. “I know I wasn’t there for you, when you were little. There were so many responsibilities.”

“I’m sure it was difficult to raise four children on your own,” Evie told her. “But we both know that’s not the problem. The problem is you had a one-night stand a few months after your husband died, and I’m the result. The problem is, every time you look at me, you’re reminded of your moment of weakness. You never wanted me, and, growing up, you made sure I knew it. It’s not enough that I don’t even know who my father is. I ended up with a mother who didn’t give a damn.”

May clutched at her throat. “That’s not true.”

“Isn’t it? You blamed me for being born. That’s my big crime. When I was little, you wanted nothing to do with me. You were never there for me. You weren’t overtly mean, but you also weren’t interested. You and my brothers had special things you did together. Rituals and celebrations. Things I wasn’t a part of. It was the four of you as a family and then me on the outside looking in. My brothers did their best with me, but it wasn't their job to raise me. It was yours and you didn't bother."

Evie felt herself starting to shake. She tried to hold it all together but knew she was seconds from a complete meltdown.

"I left home as soon as I could because there was no reason to stay. I never wanted to come back and wouldn't be here now if you and my brothers hadn't literally brought me here while I was unconscious after the accident." She almost blurted out that she wasn't planning on staying, either, but May didn't deserve to know her plans. She wouldn't be a part of her future.

"I was seventeen when I took off, and it was over a year until I heard from you. You never checked on me or wondered where I was or what I was doing."

"You were at Juilliard," May whispered.

"Right. For the first six months. Then I left. Did you ever wonder how a seventeen-year-old girl makes it on her own in the world? Did you bother to ask?"

The room blurred, and it took her a minute to realize she was crying.

"So, sure, Mom," she said, her voice thickening. "I forgive you. You were everything I ever wanted in a parent."

Then she was running. She went out through the back porch and down the stairs. Somewhere along the path to the goat barn, she stumbled and nearly fell. The only thing that kept her from going down was a pair of strong arms.

Dante pulled her against him and held her tight. He didn't say anything. He just hung on and let her sob until she had nothing left.

Five

DANTE WAS SURPRISED to find Rafe in the office Friday morning. "Why aren't you home with Heidi?" he asked.

Rafe looked up from his computer. "She's making cheese and let me know I was getting in her way. Figured I'd get some work done. What about you?"

"Heidi pretty much only has eyes for you."

Rafe chuckled. "I'm lucky that way."

Dante walked to his desk and turned on his computer, then poured himself a cup of coffee. They were the only two working that morning. The staff had been given the long weekend off.

"How's your mom?" Dante asked.

"Fine. Why?"

Dante had wondered if May had told anyone what had happened. He'd let Evie cry herself out, then had driven her home. This morning he'd wanted to go check on her, but there'd been no sign she was awake when he'd left.

He'd been forced to walk away, still feeling protective but with nothing to do.

"She and Evie got into it last night," Dante said and recapped the conversation.

Rafe shifted uncomfortably in his chair. "I wish they wouldn't talk about the past. There's nothing that can be done to fix it."

"Was Evie telling the truth?" Dante asked. "Was she that isolated as a kid?"

"It was complicated," Rafe admitted. "She was a lot younger, and I think she was a reminder of that one night for my mom. The four of us were used to being together, then Evie came along…." His voice trailed off.

Dante had lost his mother when he'd been fifteen. While he hadn't been the one to pull the trigger, a case could be made that he was responsible. They'd always been there for each other, and to this day, he would give anything to have her back. He couldn't comprehend what it would be like to have family and not be close to them.

"She's your sister," he began.

"I know." He sighed. "I was too busy being the man of the family. I figured the rest of them would worry about Evie. But that never happened. She was always an afterthought." He shook his head. "There's no excuse."

Dante had known Rafe a lot of years and trusted him completely. From what he'd seen, May was a sweet, loving person. So how had everyone managed to ignore what was going on with Evie?

"She's here now," Rafe continued. "We want to make things up to her."

"Good luck with that."

"You think she'll resist?"

"If you were her, how forgiving would you be?"

Rafe sighed. "Yeah, I see your point. I appreciate you looking out for her." He stared at Dante. "That's all it is, right? You're not getting involved?"

Dante knew exactly what his friend was asking. Telling Rafe he thought Evie was sexy as hell, from the way she walked to her hard-won smile, wasn't a smart move. Instead he settled on the truth.

"You know how I feel about relationships." In his world, love had deadly consequences. He'd learned the lesson early and had never let it go.

THE FRIDAY AFTER Thanksgiving wasn't a school day, so Evie had scheduled her dance classes early. She was done by three and showered, dressed and settled in front of her television by four. She pushed the play button on her remote, cuing up the DVD of the performance, then settled back on her sofa to watch it for the fortieth time.

The story was simple. The Winter King had dozens of daughters. The girls wanted to go free in the world, but he loved them too much to let them go. So his daughters danced to convince him they were ready to leave. At the end, the girls were revealed as beautiful snowflakes and he released them into the world as Christmas snow.

The girls danced in groups. They were mostly divided by age, with the younger performers having more simple choreography. Every student had a few seconds of a solo with the more advanced students having longer in the spotlight. Several styles of dance were represented. Modern, tap, clog and, of course, ballet.

The sets were simple, the lighting basic. The music was a collection of classic holiday songs, leaning heavily on Tchaikovsky. What would the world have done without his beautiful *Nutcracker?* The biggest problem in her mind was the transitions. They were awkward in some places, nonexistent in others. Sometimes the girls simply walked off the stage, and the next group walked on. Every time she watched that part of the performance, she winced.

Evie made a few notes, then rewound to the clog dancers who opened the show. Some of their steps were similar to tap, she thought. The sounds could echo each other. Slower, then faster. She stood and moved along with the girls on the recording. But as they turned to leave, she kept dancing, going a little more quickly, finding the rhythm of the tap dancers as they moved onto the stage.

She paused the frame and wrote some more, then made a couple of quick drawings to capture the exact poses she imagined. She moved on to the next transition and made changes there. She was just starting the third when someone rang her doorbell.

Her first thought was that it might be her mother. Dread coiled in her stomach. She wasn't ready to face May, to deal with the family trauma again. Was hiding and ignoring the interruption too cowardly?

Whoever was at the door rang the bell again. Reluctantly, she walked over and opened it.

Relief was instant. Dante stood on her doorstep. He smiled at her.

"You're home. I didn't hear any pounding above my head, so I thought maybe you'd finished early. Get your coat."

He looked good, she thought, studying his amused expression. He wore a leather jacket over jeans and a scarf. He had on boots. She could feel the cold of the rapidly darkening late afternoon.

She put her hands on her hips. "Get my coat? Was that an order? Newsflash. I don't work for you."

"Good. Because I don't take anyone on my staff

out." He sighed. "Seriously, you're going to be difficult?"

"No. I'm going to ask where we're going."

"Didn't I say 'out'? I would swear I did."

She laughed. "Out where?"

"To the center of town. They're decorating. Neither of us particularly likes the holiday season, so we need to be with people who are less corrupt. It will be good for us."

"Will it?" She stepped back to allow him inside. "When did you make this discovery?"

"Earlier. So are you coming or what?"

"Give me a second."

She turned off her TV and the laptop she'd hooked up for the DVDs, then stepped into boots and pulled them on. After shoving her house keys and a few dollars into her jeans pockets, she shrugged on her coat.

"I'm ready."

Dante stared at her. "Impressive. Less than two minutes."

"You've never had to change costumes during a performance of *Swan Lake*."

"That's true. How perceptive of you."

They walked outside. She locked the door, then followed him to the sidewalk.

The couple across the street was putting up Christmas lights. Several other townhouses had wreathes on doors and lights twinkling from doors and rooftops.

"We're really going into town?" she asked.

"Yes. The whole place has transformed."

"I noticed a few Christmas decorations being put up this morning," she admitted, "but nothing that earth-shattering."

He took her hand in his. "You walked home the back way, didn't you? Through the residential part of town."

"Uh-huh."

His fingers were warm and strong next to hers. His skin smooth without being too soft. She couldn't remember the last time she'd held hands with a guy. This was nice, she told herself. She and Dante weren't dating—she wasn't that stupid. She knew better than to fall for her brother's business partner. But some gentle flirting, a little handsome male company, wasn't going to hurt anyone.

"You'd be amazed what this town can do in a day," he told her.

"You sound impressed."

"You will be, too. How's the dance prep coming? I heard the clog dancers earlier."

She laughed. "Sorry about that. I don't know how to make it quiet."

"I'm getting used to the noise and they're getting better."

"How can you tell?"

"They're more rhythmic."

"That's true. At least most of the students are studying ballet. It's quieter."

"Unless they fall."

She winced, remembering the mass tumble during her two o'clock class. "You heard that?"

"It registered as a minor earthquake. The local seismology office called to see if we were okay."

She shoved him in the arm. "It wasn't that bad."

"They didn't do it on your head."

"Smug lawyer type," she grumbled. "They're learning. It doesn't always go well."

"I didn't say it had to stop. I'm looking forward to seeing the performance."

"You'll be intimately familiar with the music." She glanced at him. "Will you really come see the show? Won't you be off visiting family?"

"There's just me."

"What about your dad?"

"I never knew him."

"I didn't know mine, either. But you probably guessed that from the slight altercation you witnessed yesterday."

He drew her close and kissed her cheek. "It sucks."

The blunt assessment was oddly comforting. "It does," she admitted. "Hey, I don't know anything about you."

"I like being mysterious. Sort of a James Bond of the lawyer set."

She laughed. "Hardly. So tell me something interesting."

"That's too much pressure. Ask me a question."

"Have you ever been arrested?"

"Yes."

She stopped on the sidewalk and stared at him. "Seriously?"

"More than once."

"You went to jail?"

"I served time."

"No way. You can't have a criminal record and be a lawyer."

"Pretty and smart," he told her. "That makes you irresistible. Okay, you're right. I was a juvenile. My records were expunged."

"What did you do?"

His normally open expression tightened. "Bad stuff. I was in a gang."

Evie tried to imagine the well-dressed, smooth man next to her as a kid in a gang. Her imagination wasn't that good. Before she could figure out what else to ask, he tugged her along and they turned a corner, entering one of the main streets of Fool's Gold.

Just yesterday the stores and windows had featured turkeys and pumpkins. Any lights had been orange, and garlands had been made of leaves. In the space of a few hours, the transformation to the Christmas holidays had begun.

Baskets of holiday greens with shiny silver and red decorations hung from the lampposts. The windows were now covered with painted holiday displays—pictures of wrapped packages or snowmen, a few nutcrackers. Morgan's Books had stacks of popular children's books on tables and a sign promising Santa would be coming to read *'Twas the Night Before Christmas* next Saturday, after the town Christmas tree lighting.

Up ahead, in the main square, a large crane was being attached to the biggest live Christmas tree Evie had ever seen in real life. It had to be twenty feet tall.

"But it was Thanksgiving yesterday," she said, feeling as if she was going to see snow and Dickens carolers any second.

"Tell me about it," Dante told her. "There's more."

He led her toward the center of town, past the tree on the flatbed. Booths had been set up selling everything from hot chocolate to pizza slices.

"Because nothing says the holidays like pepperoni?" she asked.

Dante grinned. "Come on. I'll buy you a slice."

They got pizza and soda and walked over to watch the tree being secured by thick chains before being raised into place. The scent of pine filled the air. The pizza was hot and gooey and more calories than Evie usually allowed herself in a day.

She wasn't a professional dancer anymore, she reminded herself. Or a cheerleader. She could afford to have a BMI over twenty.

Families crowded around them. She recognized one of the women from the brunch yesterday morning, but couldn't remember her name. She was a pretty blonde, with an adorable toddler in her arms. Her husband held a baby boy.

The little girl pointed to the tree slowly rising from the truck bed. "We have one like that?" she asked.

Her father chuckled. "Sorry, Hannah. Our ceiling isn't that high. But we'll pick out a good tree. You'll see."

The woman leaned into her husband. They shared a look—one that spoke of love and promise. Aware she'd caught a glimpse of something private, Evie turned away.

Back when she'd still been young enough to believe in miracles, she'd assumed she would find love and have a family. That one day a man would promise to be with her forever. She would belong, and that belonging would finally heal her.

Several bad boyfriends later, she was less sure love was something she could count on and more convinced people who were supposed to love you usually didn't. She wanted to tell herself it could still happen, but she had a feeling that was just the Christmas tree talking.

She glanced toward Dante. "Thanks for your help yesterday. For getting me home and everything."

"No problem. Families can be complicated."

"My mom's a nightmare."

"It's not just her."

"You mean my brothers?"

Dante looked into her eyes. "Sure, they hold part of the blame, but so do you."

If they hadn't been in the middle of a crowd, she would have taken a step back. But more people had stopped to watch the tree put in place, and there was nowhere to go.

"Me? I'm the kid here."

"You were," Dante told her gently, his voice low. "You're an adult now, and if you want things to work out with your family, you have to make a little effort. Does keeping your mom at bay really make you happy? Don't you want more? A connection?"

She wanted to say no but remembered that he didn't have anyone. No doubt he would tell her to be careful what she wished for. He was the kind of man who would take care of people, only there wasn't anyone to watch over in his life. Right now, she had the benefit of his instincts.

"I like the theory of family," she admitted, "if

not the practice. It was so bad for so long, I don't know how to let go of the hurt."

"You take baby steps."

"I'd rather leave."

"Is that the plan?"

She nodded. "I like teaching dance. I think I want to continue that. I'm going to stick around for a while and learn all I can, while saving money. Then go open a studio somewhere else."

She braced herself for Dante's judgment, but he only nodded slowly. "That's an option."

"My family doesn't know."

"I won't say anything. How long's 'a while'?"

"Maybe a year." She wrinkled her nose. "Okay, okay, I get your point. That's long enough to try to work things out with my family. I should give them a break, or at least credit for trying."

He leaned in and kissed her nose. "See, it's like I said. Smart *and* pretty."

She shoved at his chest. "It's not a compliment when you're being annoying."

He chuckled and put his arm around her. They both watched as the tree was pulled upright, then slowly lowered into place. Everyone cheered.

Evie leaned into him, enjoying being a part of the happy crowd more than she would have thought.

When the tree was secure, Dante led her back toward the booths. "We need hot chocolate."

She shivered slightly. "I could use something warm."

He bought them each a cup and they checked out the rest of the booths. One of them was selling ornaments in bright colors.

"They come with your name painted on them," the woman in the booth said with a smile. "How about a lovely star?"

She held up a red one.

"We'll take it," Dante told her, then spelled Evie's name.

"I don't have a tree," she said.

"We'll get one of those later. You need an ornament with your name on it."

"Only if you get one, too."

"You going to let me put it on your tree?"

She laughed and leaned close. "Yes, but why does that question sound dirty?"

"Because it was supposed to."

They both laughed.

He paid for both ornaments and tucked the small bag into his coat pocket. They continued to wander through the center of town, then turned back toward their neighborhood.

Somewhere in the distance, a church clock chimed the hour. She could hear Christmas music. There were a thousand stars in the sky, and her breath made puffy clouds in the cold air.

"I'll admit it," she told him. "There is something

just a little magical about this place. The tree, the hot cocoa, the window decorations."

He stopped and faced her. "It's going to get worse."

"What do you mean?"

"Your family at the holidays? There are going to be a lot of get-togethers."

She could only imagine. "I tend to stay on the fringes. It's easier that way."

"You're assuming they'll let you. I think the easiest solution is practice."

She had no idea what he was talking about, but it didn't matter. Staring into Dante's blue eyes was kind of a nice way to spend an evening. She didn't even care that she was freezing.

"For example," he continued, his gaze locked with hers. "What if there's mistletoe somewhere? We'll be expected to kiss."

She felt herself smile. "Oh, right. That could be awkward. We barely know each other. What if we bump noses?"

"Our timing could be off. People would talk. I know you wouldn't want that."

"I wouldn't." Anticipation tiptoed through her stomach, warming her from the inside out. She tilted her head. "So you think we should practice?"

He sighed heavily. "It's probably for the best."

"You're such a giver."

"I am."

With that, he lowered his head and pressed his mouth to hers.

His lips were warm and tasted faintly of chocolate. He kissed gently, lingering as if he'd been waiting for this his whole day and planned to enjoy every second of it. She put her hand on his chest while he held her lightly by the waist.

They were on the edge of the main square, neatly tucked in a doorway to a closed shop. Around them twinkle lights flashed on and off. It was like something out of a Christmas movie, she thought, letting her eyes flutter shut as she concentrated on the heat burning through her.

They stayed there for what felt like a long time. While part of her wanted to deepen the kiss, another part was content to leave things as they were. Uncomplicated, with just enough zing to make her thighs tighten. The perfect combination, she thought hazily.

Dante drew back and rested his forehead on hers.

"I'd give us a B."

She opened her eyes and glared at him. "Excuse me?"

He grinned. "Kidding. That was nice. But we probably need more practice."

"What did you have in mind?"

"We have a month until Christmas. That gives us time to work out the kinks."

She laughed and linked arms with him. "You're the strangest man I know."

"That's what all the girls say. Admit it. You like me."

She laughed again, and they started for home. In truth, she did like Dante. She wasn't an idiot—she knew he was a player and that expecting anything but a little fun was a mistake. But he was exactly what she needed right now. In the midst of preparation for the Christmas Eve performance and having to deal with her family, Dante was a distraction. One any girl could appreciate.

Six

DANTE WALKED INTO the Fool's Gold fire station with a list and an idea for a plan. He spotted Charlie by her rig and called out to her.

She turned to him and raised her eyebrows. "You're wearing a suit."

He glanced down at his clothes and then back at her. "Yes."

"Looks uncomfortable."

"I'm used to it."

Charlie was tall, over five-ten, he would guess, with broad shoulders and plenty of muscle. He didn't know much about what it took to be a firefighter, but he knew physical strength was a part of it. Still, at that moment, she had the happy, glowing smile of a woman in love.

"You didn't come here to model clothes," she said. "What's up?"

"I heard you spoke to Evie about a work party

for her sets. I wanted to talk to you about that. How do I get something like that organized?"

"You volunteering?"

"I am."

"Know which end of a hammer hits the nail?"

"I've done construction."

She looked him up and down. "I have my doubts."

"It's how I got through my fancy college."

"Was it fancy?"

"There were bows and lace."

She grinned. "Okay, I like a man who can take a little teasing. Now, about the work party. Do you know Patience McGraw?"

"No."

"She's a hair stylist, and her daughter is in Evie's class. Which means nothing to you. Okay, the point is she mentioned the work party, as well. So we've been coordinating. Let me get my notes."

She disappeared out a side door, then reappeared a minute later, carrying a piece of paper. There were a couple of dozen names and phone numbers on it.

"Evie has a supply list," Dante told her. "We put that together when we went to see the sets."

"Good. We're thinking next Saturday. It's early enough in the season that not everyone is busy." She waved the names and phone numbers. "How many people are you willing to call?"

"As many as you want."

"I like that. You have potential." She tore the paper in half and handed one of the pieces to him. "Oh, and make sure Rafe, Shane and Clay are there. I keep meaning to mention it, but I haven't yet and I'm working a double shift."

"I'll get them there."

Charlie glanced at the list, then back at him. "Why are you helping Evie?"

A seemingly simple question with a complicated answer. Because the more he learned about her past, the more he wanted to knock a few heads together. As he couldn't do that, making her current dance crisis better was the other option. Because she was dynamite in tights and he was a man who enjoyed a beautiful woman. But maybe, most honestly, because this time of year he always missed his mom and he knew that helping out Evie would make his mother proud.

"Christmas is my thing," he said instead.

"Why do I think there's more to that story?"

EVIE PUSHED THE play button on the CD player and waited for the familiar music to begin. She'd warmed up already, and her first class wasn't for an hour. While there was plenty of paperwork to do and she still had to decide on the last transition in the show, she was restless. Her muscles nearly twitched, and her brain was fuzzy. She knew the solution. The question was, would her body cooperate?

She banged the box of her toe shoes against the floor a couple of times to make sure she'd tied them on correctly. The music surrounded her as she raised her arm. She silently counted to eight in her head, then, as the familiar notes filled the studio, moved both her feet and arms.

She'd never performed the "Dance of the Sugar Plum Fairy," although she'd been an understudy twice. Now she kept time with the music, landing in *effacé en fondu.* Her body wobbled slightly, but she kept on. *Revelé* and *passé.* Up. With ballet, the dancer was always lifting. In modern dance, she would go down first, as if scooping from the earth before going up, but in ballet, the goal was the sky. A turn and—

Pain ripped through her leg and her hip. Ignoring the fiery sensation, she raised herself again, her pelvis tucked, her body a perfect line from her head to her toes. Arms extended, her fingers curved delicately. The music guided her, the count pulsing in rhythm with her heartbeat.

She risked a glance in the mirror and immediately saw everything that was wrong. The sloppy extension, the bend of her elbow, the slight tilt. Voices echoed in her head. Calls for more crisp footwork, faster beats. Precision, perfection. The room seemed to bend and fade as time shifted.

She was seventeen again and walking into class at Juilliard.

The dance continued, and when the last note was silent, she came down on her feet and walked to the remote to start it again.

By the third time through, her leotard was damp with sweat. By the fifth, every muscle trembled and the fire in her leg had become a volcano of pain. She was both here and in her past. Remembering how eager she'd been, how full of dreams. How six months into her first year at the prestigious dance school she'd been told she didn't have what it took. Yes, she worked hard, was disciplined and determined. But she lacked the raw talent. The best she could hope for was the corps, with a second-rate company. They offered her the chance to leave rather than to be thrown out. A testament to their affection for her.

Evie's right leg gave way. Still-recovering muscles had reached the point of exhaustion, and she went down hard on the wood floor. She lay there, panting, shivering. After a few minutes she sat up and untied her shoes, then tossed them across the room and rested her head against her knees.

There were no tears. Nothing to cry for. She couldn't complain about what had been lost. Not when she'd never had it in the first place. Slowly the pain became manageable. She forced herself to her feet and limped over to the CD player to silence it before heading to the small restroom in the back of the studio.

She washed her face and made sure the braids around her head were still secure. She could see the sadness in her eyes, the lingering shadows of the pain, but doubted anyone else would notice. Her girls were excited about the performance. They all wanted to do their best.

She remembered what it was like to feel that way—back before she'd known that those kinds of dreams were impossible to hold on to. But maybe one of her students would have what it took. Maybe one of them would make it onto the stage and dance with a major company. They were on a journey, and she wanted to offer whatever guidance she could.

"I DON'T WORK for you."

Shane made the statement from his place on the sofa in Rafe's ranch house living room.

Dante nodded. "I'm glad you recognize that."

"Technically I don't work *for* him," Rafe pointed out. "I work with him."

"I'm with Shane," Clay said. He was sprawled in the big recliner with the best view of the big screen. Not that the TV was on. "So I don't come to your meetings."

"All evidence to the contrary," Dante told him.

It was shortly after noon on Tuesday. Rafe had

been working from home. As Shane's horses were on his property next to his brother's, getting him over to Rafe's house had been easy enough. Clay had texted he was available, as well, so here they all were.

"This Saturday is a work party. Charlie and Patience are setting it up."

"Patience?" Rafe asked. "Do I know her?"

"She's a hair stylist," Clay said. "Friends with Charlie, Heidi and Annabelle. You've met her."

"I don't think so," Rafe said, then glanced back at Dante. "But, okay. What does Patience have to do with anything?"

Dante groaned. "The point is the work party."

"What's it for?" Shane asked.

"Your sister."

The three brothers stared at him blankly.

"I thought she was renting her townhouse," Clay said. "What does she need help with?"

"The sets," Dante told them.

"Sets of what?" Rafe asked.

Dante had unexpected empathy for the women in his life who, from time to time, had stared at him like he was the stupidest man on earth.

"The sets for the dance."

Shane frowned. "Evie's going to a school dance?"

"*The Dance of the Winter King,* you morons. Your sister teaches dance. There's a performance on Christmas Eve. The manager of the school took off, leaving Evie in charge of everything. This is a big deal to the town, and she has to make it happen. The sets for the production are in bad shape. There's going to be a work party to refurbish them, and you will all be there to help."

The brothers looked at each other and then back at Dante.

"Sure," Shane said. "Why didn't you just say so?"

Dante sank into the chair behind him and rested his head in his hands. "It's too early for a beer, right?"

Rafe chuckled. "Don't sweat it. Of course we'll be there. When is it?"

"Saturday." Dante told them where to be. "Bring tools and paintbrushes." He raised his head. "Let me be clear. There won't be any excuses and you will be on time. You'll work hard, be cooperative and not do anything to upset your sister. Oh, and while I have you here, this is where I tell you that you will also be attending the performance. Got it?"

"Of course we'll be there," Rafe said, shifting in his seat. "We, ah, were always going to come."

"Right." Dante scowled at him. "You're a crappy liar."

"I know, but that makes me a good business

partner." Rafe drew in a breath. "Thanks for looking out for her."

"You're welcome."

THE FIFTEEN OR SO GIRLS were crowded around Evie's laptop, watching the DVD of the performance from three years ago.

"This is the part I was talking about," Evie said. "Until that last four-count, the dance is beautiful. See how everyone moves together? Then it comes to an end and there are three beats of nothing, followed by everyone clomping off the stage."

Melissa Sutton turned to Evie. "Do you really think they clomped?"

"I'm sure not in their hearts, but that's what it looks like." She walked away from the group, exaggerating her steps so she sounded more like an elephant than a dancer.

The girls all laughed.

"So we need something different," Evie said. "Something more lyrical."

Fifteen pairs of eyes watched her anxiously, both excited and a little nervous.

Her other classes were divided by age, skill level and style of dance. She had the six-year-olds who were awkward but adorable. The beginning class in tap and ballet for seven- to eleven-year-olds was popular. She taught one clog dancing class, several in modern dance. There were classes for those near-teens, who had several years of experience, and finally a ballet class for one group of serious students. Then there was this group—fifteen girls of all ages and abilities who were new to dance.

Melissa Sutton was the oldest, at fifteen. Her younger sister, Abby, was also in the class. The rest were around twelve or thirteen. The girls were tall, short and everything in between. A few were here because they had weight problems, and their pediatrician had suggested dance as a way to get exercise. None of them had any experience, and most lacked a sense of rhythm. But they were fun and enthused and Evie enjoyed teaching them. They were already nervous about the performance, and she wasn't looking to increase their anxiety.

"I thought we would try something simple. Who here has seen *Swan Lake?*"

A few of the girls raised their hands.

Evie walked over to her computer and changed the DVDs. "There's something called 'Pas de Quartre of the Small Swans.' It's four dancers together. I thought we could do something like that, but in groups of five."

She found the right part of the ballet and pushed the play button. The girls gathered around her computer. As the dance began, their eyes widened, and they all turned to stare at her.

"We can't do that," Melissa said. "We don't

know ballet. This is modern dance. And to go up on our toes like that?"

One of the bigger girls bit her lower lip. "I'd look stupid trying."

"No," Evie said quickly. "I'm not asking you to dance *en pointe.* I'm showing you the style of what I'm thinking we'll do for our exit."

She moved to the center of the room. "At the end of your dance, you're all in a row. Bent over like this." She counted the beats, then straightened and moved her arms.

"Now pretend I'm at the end of the row. We'll do three groups of five dancers, so I would go forward three counts." She motioned for Melissa to join her. "Stand here, with your arms crossed."

Melissa took Evie's left hand with her right.

"Good. Now quick steps to the right, on the balls of your feet, and one and two and three and four, straight, lifting."

Melissa did as she said, and they moved across the floor. Evie released her. She bent forward, her arms still crossed in front of her, then straightened and moved four more steps.

"I haven't gone to the stage yet, to do the actual count. I'm thinking it will be three combinations. As the first row moves to the right, the second row will move forward and follow."

Melissa nodded slowly. "I get it. It's the spirit of that bit from *Swan Lake,* without the scary parts."

Evie laughed. "Exactly. Want to do it with me?"

"Sure."

Evie put the music in the CD player. "We'll start from the beginning."

"One and two and three and four."

Evie and Melissa moved together in the simple dance. Her leg was still sore from her workout the previous day, but she was used to working through the pain. As they finished the three-minute routine, she reached for Melissa's hand and stepped to the side. The girl kept up, only stumbling twice.

"And we're off the stage," she said. "Easy enough?"

Her class glanced at each other, then back at her. Abby, Melissa's sister, nodded.

"I can do that."

"Me, too," one of the other girls said.

"I knew you could," Evie told them. "Now everyone line up, and we'll take it from the top."

It took the rest of class, but by the end all the girls were comfortable with the transition. As her students walked out of the studio, Evie went to turn off the CD. Melissa followed her.

"You're really patient with us," the teen said.

"You're great to work with."

"I know we're not as good as some of the other classes. I've seen Grace dance. She's amazing."

Grace was fourteen and one of the school's most promising students. Starting in January, Evie would be working with her privately. While each of the performers would get a chance to shine at the show, Grace had one of the only two longer solos.

"She's been studying since she was four," Evie told Melissa. "That's a long time."

"I know. I really like coming here, though."

"I'm glad. I hope you continue to dance."

Melissa wrinkled her nose. "Could I ever dance on my toes?"

"Of course. It's not that hard."

"Does it hurt?"

"Yes," Evie said with a laugh. "But you get used to it."

Melissa grinned. "I can't wait." She hugged Evie, then ran out.

Evie followed her toward the reception area and was surprised to find Dante there. Several of the mothers were helping their daughters into winter coats and boots, although Evie noticed more than a few of the moms were glancing toward the handsome attorney.

She couldn't blame them. The man dazzled in a suit. She had a feeling he would look just as good without one.

She watched her students leave, then turned to him.

"There's no clog dancing tonight," she said. "You have no reason to complain."

His blue eyes were dark with an emotion she couldn't read. He looked at the door, then back at her.

"Last class of the night?" he asked.

She nodded. "Everything will be quiet. Do you have to phone Shanghai again?"

"Not exactly."

He took a step toward her, then put his hands on her waist and drew her against him. She went easily, wanting to feel his arms around her. She was overwhelmed by all she had to accomplish before the performance, a little freaked out by the holiday season and uncomfortable about having her family so close. The idea of forgetting all that in a passionate embrace suddenly seemed like a great idea.

He lowered his mouth to hers. She tilted her head, let her eyes close and her hands settle on his broad shoulders. Then she gave herself over to the soft, warm insistence of Dante's kiss.

Seven

DANTE TASTED OF mint and warmth. His mouth moved against hers, back and forth, exploring, teasing. She found herself wanting more from him, so she tightened her hold on his shoulders and leaned in slightly.

Her body came in contact with his. He was all hard muscles. She felt delicate next to him—feminine. His hands spanned her back, his fingers pressing lightly against her. The leotard didn't offer much in the way of a barrier, and he quickly heated her.

She kissed him back, moving her mouth as well, then parted her lips. He slipped inside, his tongue lightly stroking hers. She went up on tiptoe and wrapped her arms around his neck, even as they kissed more deeply.

Low in her belly, wanting blossomed. Her thighs ached for a reason that had nothing to do with exercise and everything to do with anticipation. Her blood moved more quickly, spreading desire to every part of her.

He drew back enough to stare into her eyes. "You're dangerous."

She smiled. "Hardly."

"Sexy, tempting and the whole dance thing. I'm getting all these images in my head."

"Imagining what I can do?" she asked.

"Oh, yeah."

Dante was one of those men who liked to be in control, she thought. It came with his profession and partially from his personality. She would guess he nearly always had the upper hand in his relationships.

Still on tiptoe, she leaned in to whisper in his ear. "Whatever you're thinking, I can do more."

She slowly lowered herself until she was standing flat-footed. Dante's eyes were glazed, his mouth slightly parted. The comment was mostly cheap talk. Sure, she was limber and strong and could probably get in positions that he'd only dreamed about, but so what? That didn't mean she was any more secure than other women. She still worried about how she looked naked and whether or not the relationship would have a happy ending.

He shook his head, as if clearing his mind, then swore under his breath. "It's the dancing," he muttered. "You're too sexy."

"Thank you, but the truth is, I'm not that good a dancer."

"You're the best I've ever seen."

She laughed. "Again, a lovely compliment, but you're hardly a discriminating audience." She thought about the feel of his mouth on hers. "Good kisses, though."

"You like them?"

"I do."

"Good. Then we should plan to kiss more."

A goal she could get behind. Dante might not be long-term material, but didn't she deserve a little fun? It was the holiday season. He could be her gift to herself. Being with him was easy and natural. She needed more of that in her life.

He cleared his throat and deliberately put space between them. "Okay, there's a reason I came to talk to you."

"Which is?"

"The work party is arranged. Charlie and Patience have taken care of most of the volunteers. I'm picking up the supplies tomorrow. We're starting at eight on Saturday morning."

"At the warehouse?"

He nodded. "We have a big workspace. If everyone who says he's coming does, we're going to need it." He paused. "Your brothers will be there."

She looked at him. "Your doing?"

"Maybe."

She wanted to say she didn't need them, that she would be fine on her own. But the truth was, she didn't know anything about refurbishing sets for a production. She needed help, and she would be grateful for anyone who showed up.

"Thank you," she told him.

"You mean that?"

"Nearly."

He laughed and kissed her lightly on the mouth. "Close enough. I gotta go. See you Saturday?"

"I'm looking forward to it."

"Me, too."

EVIE MANAGED TO hang on to the post-kiss tingles during her walk home. A trick, considering the temperature had to be close to freezing. There were plenty of stars in the sky, but the next storm would bring snow to Fool's Gold.

Still, despite the occasional shiver, she felt warm inside. Or maybe just quivery. There was something about a man who knew how to kiss. No doubt Dante had plenty of practice with the women in his life. Something she should remember to keep herself safe. In the meantime, she would enjoy the anticipation.

As she turned onto her street, she noticed there were more decorations on the various houses and townhomes. Lights on roof lines, and plastic snowmen and Santas on lawns. By contrast, Dante's place was completely dark and hers only had a few flameless candles in the front windows. Maybe she should find out about getting some lights for the front window and maybe a wreath for her door.

As she walked up to the porch, she glanced next door. Obviously Dante wasn't home yet. She wondered how late he was going to work and wished they had the kind of relationship where she could simply call and invite him over for dinner. Not that she had anything to eat. Still, they could get takeout. Maybe Chinese.

She went inside and flipped on lights. After hanging up her jacket, she hit the switch for the gas fireplace, then waited for the *whoosh* as it started up. She wandered into the kitchen, already knowing there was nothing to eat, and wondered why ordering takeout for one didn't sound as exciting as when it was for two.

Someone rang her doorbell.

Evie felt herself starting to smile as she hurried back to the living room. Dante was home, she thought happily. He'd decided to come over and—

She pulled open the door, then felt her whole body tense as she stared at her mother.

"Hello, Evie," May said.

"Mom." She automatically stepped back to allow the other woman in, then wished she hadn't.

"How are you?" May asked.

"Fine. I just got home from work."

"The girls are getting ready for their performance?"

Evie nodded, then watched as her mother slipped off her coat and hung it on the back of a chair.

The Stryker brothers all shared similar looks. Dark hair and eyes they'd inherited from both their parents. The brothers were tall, with broad shoulders and muscles. Evie assumed she took after her father—not only with her light coloring, but with her lean build. When the family was together, no one questioned who the brothers belonged to. Strangers had always assumed Evie was someone else's child. As she'd gotten older, she'd been presumed to be the girlfriend or a neighbor.

"I thought we could talk," May said, sitting on the sofa and patting the cushion next to her.

Evie tried to figure out a way to say she was too busy, but she couldn't come up with an excuse. And knowing May, her mother would want to know what was more important than them talking.

"All right."

Evie sat in a chair across from her mother, rather than next to her, and waited.

May looked around. "You don't have a lot of furniture."

"The place came furnished."

May nodded. "That's right. Your apartment in Los Angeles was furnished, too."

"I like to travel light."

"Eventually you'll want to settle down." Her mother looked at her. "I was hoping you'd stay at the ranch a little longer. It was nice having you there."

Evie drew in a breath. "With me working in town, this is more convenient." She hoped she would get points for being polite because what she really wanted to say was "Why on earth would I want to live anywhere near you?" But that sounded harsh, even in her own mind.

It wasn't fair—her mother had been horrible to her for years and years. But Evie was now expected to be reasonable. To understand, maybe even forgive. When was it her turn to be the mean one? Not that she wanted to be mean, but she wanted some kind of payback.

No, that wasn't right, she thought, shifting on the chair. She honestly wasn't sure what she wanted, but it wasn't them pretending all was well.

May drew in a breath. "Fool's Gold has many holiday traditions. Even more than I remember from when we lived here before. On the fifteenth is the annual Day of Giving. The town welcomes all kinds of charities to come in and talk about what they do. There are booths set up, and people can ask questions. The same day is the Take Home a Pet Adoption."

Evie wasn't sure where this was going. Money

was always tight in her world, and right now she was saving every extra penny she had. Not that there were very many of them.

"Carina McKenzie started the pet adoption last year, but she's pregnant now and can't be on her feet that much. Rina, as everyone calls her, is married to Cameron McKenzie."

May paused expectantly.

Evie shrugged. "Okay," she said cautiously. "Should I know who that is?"

May smiled. "Right. Sorry. You have no reason to. Cameron is our local vet."

Evie thought about all the animals on the ranch. There was everything from goats to horses and even Priscilla, an aging Indian elephant.

"You must want to keep him happy," she said.

May laughed. "Exactly. So when Rina started to freak out about the pet adoption, I told her I would help. I thought it was something we could do together."

At first Evie thought her mother meant "together," as in "with Rina." It took her a second to process the hopeful stare and realize May wanted her only daughter to help.

"I know, I know," her mother said quickly. "You're very busy with the dance. I understand that. Rina is going to arrange all the advertising and get the word out about the adoption. I'm handling the pet end. Going to see the animals at the shelter, arranging for grooming, setting up for the event and handling the actual adoptions. It's only one Saturday. We could have fun."

May paused, her expression hopeful.

Evie opened her mouth, then closed it. Everything about the situation was unfair, she thought with mild annoyance. If she said no, she was the bad guy. If she said yes, she would get stuck doing something she didn't want to do.

"It wouldn't be much time," her mother added.

Evie drew in a breath. "Sure," she said slowly, knowing if she didn't agree, the guilt would keep her awake that night.

May beamed at her. "Wonderful. I'll handle all the details, I promise. We only have a couple of weeks until the adoption and I want it to go well."

May bounced to her feet. Evie instinctively stood as well, then found herself pulled into her mother's embrace. They stood there for a second, hugging. Evie couldn't remember the last time that had happened, but she told herself to simply relax and accept the gesture in the spirit in which it was meant.

For a second, she allowed herself to feel the longing she'd lived with as a kid. Shut out of her family, always the outsider. Never fitting in or knowing how to belong. Back then, having her mom hug her would have meant the world. Now it was simply awkward.

She thought about what Dante had told her—that now some of the responsibility was hers. That if she wanted things to be better, she was going to have to be a part of the solution. But as she stood there, uncomfortable and unsure, she realized she didn't have a clue as to how to change anything. Nor did she know if she was really willing to risk her heart one more time.

Eight

EVIE WAS DRESSED and hovering by the front door fifteen minutes before Dante was due to arrive. It was barely seven and well below freezing. But the skies were clear, so there still wasn't any snow.

This morning was the work party for her sets and she was nervous about everything getting done. While the sets were simple and the dancers the focus of the performances, the backdrops provided context and mood. No one would expect perfection from an amateur show, but she was determined to get as close to professional as possible.

She opened the front door when she saw him walking up the front steps. He smiled when he saw her.

"You look nervous," he said.

"What if we don't get everything done? I'm trying not to freak out, and it's difficult."

He leaned in and kissed her cheek. "Have a little faith."

"I have great faith in you," she told him. "It's myself and everyone else who causes me doubt. I've barely held a paintbrush."

"Now you'll be able to practice."

She grabbed her jacket and followed him outside. Instead of his sleek German import, a large pickup truck was parked in his driveway.

"Compliments of your sister-in-law," he said.

She slid onto the seat and stared at him. "You borrowed Heidi's truck?"

He shrugged. "I knew if I asked one of your brothers to trade with me, he would probably drive my car. Heidi won't."

She grinned. "Are you sure about that? She has a bit of a wild streak. What if she takes one of her goats for a joyride?"

"Now you're just messing with me. Come on. We need to get our supplies and be at the warehouse before our workers show up."

Ten minutes later Dante was backing toward the loading dock of the Fool's Gold hardware store. Two teenagers were ready with stacks of paint, brushes, tarps, glue and bags filled with Evie wasn't sure what. Dante went over his master list, and Evie signed the purchase order. The store would bill Dominique, the dance studio's owner, directly.

By quarter to eight, they'd stopped for coffee and were on their way to the warehouse. Evie told herself that whatever work they got done would be enough and that she shouldn't be disappointed if no one showed up to help. People had busy lives, and it wasn't as if she had a bunch of friends in town. Sure, Charlie and Patience had offered to make a few calls, but would that make a difference? Patience would be there, Evie knew, but Charlie had to work at the fire station. Still, with one or two parents and her brothers, they could make some serious progress.

Dante pulled into the storage warehouse parking lot. She saw there were already about ten or fifteen cars and trucks there.

As she climbed out of the truck, Patience hurried toward her, her long brown hair pulled back in a ponytail.

"'Morning," she said cheerfully. "I'm just organizing the work parties now. The sets have already been pulled out and grouped together by scene. I was waiting to hear what you think about how we're going to do this."

Not sure she would have an opinion, Evie followed her inside the large building.

Instead of the sets being stacked together in the cramped storage locker, they were spread out in the long, open hallway of the warehouse. Sure enough, they had been clustered together by scene and in chronological order. She could look at them and see the flow of the show.

More surprising was the setup. Long tables stood at one end. Heaters were plugged in the whole length of the hall. Lights blazed overhead. But the most amazing part of all was the people waiting. There had to be at least twenty adults and several of her dance students. As Evie blinked in astonishment, two more families arrived, including Melissa and Abby Sutton. They were accompanied by a boy, who was probably their brother, and their parents. Rafe, Shane and Clay were also there, smiling at her with an annoying combination of pride and smugness.

"Surprised?" Clay asked.

"Yes," she admitted.

"Good. We decided you needed more surprises in your life."

"Lucky me."

"By eight-thirty we won't be able to move in here," Patience told her. "But, hey, the more hands, the better, right? This way, we'll get it all done by noon."

Evie opened her mouth, then closed it. Her throat was tight, and she had the horrifying thought that she might actually start to cry. She'd been hoping for a couple of parents to show up. Not a flood of assistance from people she didn't even know.

"I, um," she began, then waved her arms, not sure what to say.

Dante took one of her hands in his and squeezed her fingers. “I’m the professional here,” he told her. “Why don’t you let me organize everyone into groups? You can supervise.”

“Thank you,” she said, vowing to bake him a cake or something later. Okay, maybe baking wasn’t the best way to show her appreciation, but she would come up with a plan.

“Stryker brothers,” he called. “Come with me to unload the truck. Everyone else, pick a set and go stand by it. Make sure you divide yourselves evenly.”

Five other guys went with Dante and her brothers. By the time they’d returned, there were at least twenty more people there to help. The hallway was loud and crowded. While a few people had collected by sets, most were just laughing and talking. They’d moved from controlled chaos to a party.

“How do you want to handle this?” Dante asked. He had a paint can in each hand.

Patience stood with her clipboard but didn’t look as if she was going to take charge. Evie knew she was ultimately responsible for the project. What was that old saying? An embarrassment of riches. She needed to get over it, she told herself.

She walked over to a folding chair and climbed onto the seat. Her injured leg protested slightly, but she ignored the twinge and waited as people turned toward her and grew quiet.

Everyone was staring at her, she thought, feeling herself flush. She knew less than a third of the adults in the room. The only time she'd ever been anything close to a leader was while she was teaching. Still, the performance was her responsibility, and that made the sets her problem.

"I'd like to thank everyone for taking time out of your Saturday to come here and help. I know the holidays are especially busy, so your generosity is all the more appreciated. For those of you who arrived in the past fifteen minutes, we're asking everyone to gather around the set you want to work on."

She pointed to the chronological beginning of the story. "I'll walk down the line and tell you what I would like done. The supplies will be on those tables at the end. We may have to share cans of paint and brushes."

"I brought tools," a man called. "Three toolboxes, nails, screws, extra lumber."

"Thank you." Evie smiled at the crowd. "You're all fantastic for coming out here today. I hope you'll enjoy our performance."

"We always love the show," a woman said.

Everyone applauded and Evie stepped down.

She walked over to the first set. Patience walked with her.

"I'll take notes," the other woman said. "So we can keep track of what's going to be done."

"Thank you."

One of the men standing by the first set, a good-looking blond guy with an easy smile, pointed to the back of the tall trees.

"The supports are all busted," he said. "We should replace them while we're painting. It won't take long and Ethan is here to give us novices advice."

Evie cleared her throat. "Ethan?"

"The guy who said he had tools."

A pretty, obviously pregnant woman with brown hair joined the man. "Josh, start with the basics." She smiled at Evie. "I'm Charity Golden. This is my husband, Josh. Ethan Hendrix is a local contractor."

"Thanks for coming."

"Oh, we love helping out. This is a fun project. Our daughter is still too tiny to be involved in anything, so we're practicing for when she's older."

Josh leaned over and patted his wife's tummy. "And he."

Charity rolled her eyes. "Yes, this one is a boy and Josh is too proud for words." But there was love in her voice as she spoke, and the couple shared a look that spoke of devotion and caring.

Evie went over the rest of the repairs and agreed that, yes, this was a good time to deal with the trees.

She and Patience went down the line. Her brothers and Dante had claimed the throne where the Winter King sat. She looked at the four of them. "Tell me you know what you're doing."

Clay pressed a hand to his chest. "Mortal blow. Come on, sis, we're good. Dante and Rafe have both done construction, and Shane and I will follow their instructions."

She sighed. "Fine, but no fighting."

By eight-thirty, everyone was hard at work. She walked up and down the line, pleased with how quickly things were progressing. Close to nine, a tall, dark-haired man walked into the warehouse. He had as many muscles as Wolverine and looked nearly as dangerous. He glanced around at everyone working, caught sight of Evie and headed directly for her.

"I'm Gideon," he told her, his low voice rubbing against her skin like velvet. Or maybe chocolate.

"Okay," she said, wanting to get him to speak again. A voice like that was magic. "I'm Evie."

His dark eyes glinted with amusement but his mouth didn't smile. "I own both radio stations here in town."

"That's nice."

Patience cleared her throat and leaned close. "He's, ah, doing the narration for the performance."

Evie looked back at him. "Oh. Gideon. We've emailed." Had she known what his voice sounded like, she would have asked that they speak on the phone instead of meeting in person. "Nice to meet you."

They shook hands.

"I've watched the performances on DVD," he said. "And I went over the script. I thought about making a few changes." He handed her several sheets of paper. "To smooth things out and make the story flow better."

"Sure. I'm open to that." She took the papers he offered.

He was a good-looking guy with a seductive voice. She was currently unattached, although secretly attracted to her neighbor. Shouldn't Gideon be getting her tingles on? After all, she could simply close her eyes and listen to the magic of him speaking.

She glanced at the script, all the while trying to imagine sharing dinner with the smooth-talking stranger. But instead of enjoying the visual, her brain replaced Gideon with Dante and then got all quivery. So much for the magic voice working on her sexually. Apparently she simply enjoyed it the way she enjoyed good music or a latte. At least now she didn't have to find out if he was single.

She smiled at him. "There are too many distractions for me to read this now. Can I get back to you?"

"Sure." He glanced around. "You've got quite the party here."

"I know. Patience and Charlie put out word that I needed help and look what happened." She lowered her voice. "I'm not from here, so it's kind of a surprise."

"I know what you mean. I've only been in town for about two months and it's not like anywhere else I've lived."

"Big-city guy?" she asked.

He shrugged. "That works as well as any other description. I'm retired military, so I've been all over the world."

"How did you find Fool's Gold?"

"A buddy told me about it. I came for a weekend and ended up buying the radio stations."

Melissa hurried over. "We're putting on the glitter. Can you come tell us if it's okay?"

"Sure." Evie smiled at Gideon. "Nice to finally meet you."

"You, too."

She followed Melissa over to one of the sets. When she turned back, Gideon was gone.

Work continued. Just before ten, Morgan, the owner of Morgan's Books and the man who played the famous Winter King, showed up with coffee and cupcakes for everyone. Evie introduced herself to the older man.

"I like what you're doing," he told her, his

brown eyes kind as he spoke. "A few of the girls have stopped by to tell me about the changes you're making in the show. They're very excited."

"I hope everyone enjoys the performance."

"They will." He nodded toward the throne. "The fur is a nice touch."

"Fur?" She followed his gaze and saw her brothers had attached faux snow-leopard fur trim to the throne. "Excuse me," she said to Morgan, then hurried the length of the hall.

"Fur?" she demanded when she reached the throne. "Are you serious?"

"Annabelle thought it would look nice," Shane said, his tone warning. "She gave it to me and I put it on."

"Fine." Evie liked her sister-in-law to-be and wasn't about to take on Shane over fur. "Any other surprises?"

"If we told you, they wouldn't be surprises," Clay said.

"Great."

Patience appeared at her side, clipboard in hand. "We're making great progress. With everyone drinking coffee and eating cupcakes, we should get a nice rush in productivity and have all the work done in another hour or so."

This time yesterday Evie would have said there was no way the sets could be spruced up in less than four hours. But now, surrounded by thirty or forty people digging in and getting it done, she realized it was more than possible.

"Thank you," Evie told her. "This wouldn't have happened without you and Charlie helping me."

"You're wonderful with Lillie, so I figure we're even. Oh, I forgot to tell you, we're all confirmed for the costumes and the makeup and hair. You know that's all provided, right? We have a fitting and make sure the girls are set with the clothes, then talk about hair and makeup."

The throat tightness was back again as she remembered the feuding stylist sisters story. "Let me guess. A couple of the local salons team up to take care of hair and makeup?"

"Exactly."

"Is this place even real?"

"Of course it is. I know it seems like we're really nice, but the truth is we're pretty nosy, and getting involved means we get the good gossip first."

Evie laughed. "I think the motivations are more altruistic than that."

"Which means we have you fooled." Patience started to say something else, but despite her open mouth, she was silent.

"What?" Evie asked, turning to follow her gaze. All she saw was some older woman with white hair walking into the warehouse. "You know her?"

"That's Mayor Marsha," Patience said, her voice hushed.

"Okay. Is it bad she's here?"

"No. She always comes to things like this. It's just…" Patience pointed. "Look."

Evie did and saw nothing out of the ordinary. "You've got to give me a clue."

"Look at what she's wearing!"

"Jeans and a cardigan over a turtleneck?"

"She's in *pants.*"

"Uh-huh. You know women have been wearing pants out in public for maybe a hundred years."

"Not Mayor Marsha. She always wears a suit with a skirt. OMG."

Evie started to laugh. "You did not just say OMG."

"It's Mayor Marsha in jeans. It's an OMG moment. I have to go call my mom. She'll die when I tell her."

Patience pulled her cell phone out of her jacket pocket and pushed a button. Evie shook her head and walked back toward the people working.

Over the next hour, each of the sets was completed. Evie thanked the teams as they finished. She introduced herself to the mayor, who was a very pleasant woman. From what Evie could tell, no one else had shared Patience's reaction to the mayor wearing pants.

"Thank you," Evie told a blonde woman and her husband. "I'm sorry, I know you said your name, but I…" The woman was one of the triplets, but Evie had no idea which one.

"Don't worry. You've met way too many people today. You can't keep us all straight. I'm Nevada Janack and this is my husband, Tucker."

Evie shook hands with both of them, telling herself Nevada was pregnant. That information would help her keep the name with the face, at least until Nevada gave birth. "You were both wonderful. You didn't need to rebuild that whole section."

"It needed it," Tucker said. "Not to worry. Nevada and I are both in construction. So's Will." He pointed to the man who had been assisting them.

The three of them had taken apart the last set and basically created a new version from scratch. Now it was painted, and the pulley system for the falling snow gleamed with new hardware.

"Good luck with the show," Tucker said, then turned to his wife. "I'm going to help Will load the truck."

"Sure," Nevada said, then she looked at Evie. "My two sisters said to say they're sorry they couldn't make it. They both have kids on the tail end of colds."

"That's fine. We had plenty of people."

Nevada leaned toward her and lowered her voice. "Be grateful they didn't come. One of my brothers is in the military. He just told us he's not reenlisting, which means he's coming home next year."

Evie wasn't sure what that had to do with her sets. "Okay. You must all be happy."

"We are. We haven't spent any time with Ford in years. But the thing is, my sisters are determined to get him married off as quickly as possible. They're making a list of potential women and you're on it."

"Oh." Evie took a step back. "While I'm flattered, I, ah..."

"Can get your own guy? That's what I told them. Not that they'll listen. Ford's great. Don't get me wrong, but matchmaking is a slick road to disaster."

"I appreciate the warning."

"Anytime."

Technically, it wouldn't ever be an issue, Evie thought. She wasn't planning to be here a year from now. Although it made her kind of sad to think she wouldn't be working on the dance again.

Nevada, Tucker and Will gathered their tools and left. Evie's brothers had finished with the throne and were now checking to see which sets were dry and ready to be put away.

The nearly empty hallway smelled of paint and glue. The coffee and cupcakes had disappeared, and sometime when she hadn't been looking, someone had cleaned up the brushes and neatly stacked the cans of paint.

Shane and Rafe wheeled the throne back into the storage locker while Clay crossed to Evie.

"Five of the sets need to dry a little more before we store them," he told her. "I talked to the manager, and he said we can leave the sets out as long as they're not in the way. I'll swing by later and put them back into storage."

"I can do it," she said, surprised he would offer.

"Some of them are heavy. I'll take care of it." He draped his arm over her shoulder. "Then you'll owe me and I like the sound of that."

"Thanks," she told him.

"No problem."

Clay joined his brothers. A few minutes later, Dante and Evie were left alone in the warehouse. She pulled out her phone and glanced at the time.

"It's not even noon."

"Told you," Dante said. "You have to have a little faith in people."

"Oh, please. You're a lawyer. Faith is hardly your strong suit."

"I have my moments." He tucked a strand of hair behind her ear. "The tree lighting ceremony is tonight. Want to go with me?"

The sense of anticipation that had been so obviously quiet when she'd been speaking to Gideon fluttered to life in her tummy. She felt herself smiling up at Dante and hoped she didn't look as foolish as she felt.

"I'd like that."

"Pick you up at six. We'll eat on the way."

Nine

"YOU WERE RIGHT," Evie said, sipping the tea Charlie had made for them.

Charlie sat across from her in the kitchen at the fire station and smiled. "That never gets old. Maybe you could say it again."

Evie laughed. "I'm happy to. You were right. People showed up to help me with the sets. Lots of people. I didn't know most of them and yet there they were. Everything was done by noon. I never expected anything like that to happen. And yes, I know. I need to have faith in people. I've been told."

"Then my work here is done." Charlie leaned back in her chair.

"I met Gideon."

"What's he like? I've heard him on the radio. Sexy voice."

"Tell me about it. He's attractive, in a dangerous sort of way."

"That should make him irresistible." Charlie arched her eyebrows. "Any interest?" She held up a hand. "Never mind. I apologize for asking. I can't believe I'm turning into one of those women who falls in love and then wants to see everyone around her paired up, as well. It's horrible."

"I don't mind. And sorry, no. Gideon seemed very nice, but there was no chemistry." She wasn't about to mention her attraction to Dante. The fewer people who knew about that, the better.

"I'm glad the town came through for you," Charlie told her. "This place is always special, but even more so at the holidays." She hesitated. "Now I'm going to say something else I'll have to apologize for, but I can't help myself."

Evie held on to her mug and waited.

"It's your mom," Charlie began.

Evie stiffened. "What about her?"

"It's not my business," she began.

"You're right, it's not."

Charlie sighed. "And I always hated when people gave me advice about my mother. She and I didn't get along, either. But last summer she showed up here and wanted us to be close. I won't go into the reasons, but I will say I resisted. Only she didn't go away and one day I realized she was the only family I had. That without her, I had no biological connection to another person on this planet. That was kind of sobering."

"I know you're trying to help," Evie said grudgingly.

"I would have bet you every penny I had that my mother would never change," Charlie told her. "But I was wrong. And if Dominique can do it, May is more than capable. Your mom cares about you."

"Now," Evie muttered. "But back when it mattered, she was never there for me."

Charlie leaned toward her. "That sucks. She was wrong and she needs to understand that. I just have one question. If she's genuinely sorry and regrets what she did, how is she supposed to make it okay now?"

"I don't understand."

"If she feels remorse and asks for your forgiveness, what will make you grant it? She can't undo the past. So how do you find closure? How do you move on?"

"I don't know," Evie admitted. "I don't think I want to forgive her."

"So you'll both always be in pain? That doesn't sound very pleasant. Are you sure you want to live that way?"

"No, I don't," Evie said before she could stop herself. "But why does she get a free pass?"

"Because in any other alternative, you have to pay, too. Aren't you tired of that?"

Evie nodded slowly. "I want normal," she admitted. "I want to have a family who cares about me and whom I can care about." She wanted so much more than she had.

"You either make it work with the family you have or go find a new one. I hate to break it to you, but you're kind of past the cute kid stage."

Evie managed a smile. "You think? Because I look adorable in a tutu."

She knew Charlie was right. May had acknowledged the past, which was a big step. She was also reaching out. But part of her wanted to stomp her foot and insist it was too little, too late.

Dante had pointed out that she had responsibility for the relationship as it existed today. That if she wanted things to be different, she had to make a little effort.

The past couldn't be fixed, but maybe there was a way for the hole inside of her to be healed. Was being a part of something worth the work it would take?

Just then alarms went off in the station.

"Gotta go," Charlie said as she jumped to her feet and ran toward the engine bay.

Evie stayed where she was until the ambulance and fire engine had left, then she started for home. Dante was picking her up in a few hours. Until then she was going to try on everything in her closet until she found the perfect thing to wear tonight.

As for the question of what to do with her family—that she would release into the universe. Maybe with a little time, the answer would present itself all on its own.

IN THE END, comfort and warmth won over fashion. Evie pulled on long underwear, which meant she wasn't going to fit into her skinniest jeans. She layered a camisole under a sweater, over which she would wear a jacket. As the tree lighting ceremony was going to involve a lot of standing around, cute boots that pinched her toes were out of the question. So much for being dazzling, she thought as she gave in completely and tossed a pair of mittens on the sofa.

She did take the time to use hot rollers, then finger comb her hair into a tangle of curls. She brushed on a second coat of mascara and then applied peppermint-flavored lip gloss in case there was mistletoe. She was ready five minutes before Dante was due to arrive.

Fortunately he was four minutes early. She opened the door and hoped she didn't look as excited as she felt. Maybe being cool was out of the question, but there was no excuse for acting as eager as a puppy.

"Hi," he said as he stepped inside. "You look great."

"Thanks. You, too."

He had on jeans and boots, a leather jacket and a scarf that made his dark blue eyes even sexier. He smelled of wood smoke and pine, and when he leaned in to kiss her, she felt herself melting.

His mouth claimed hers with a combination of hunger and tenderness. After the first brush of skin-on-skin, he drew back and raised his eyebrows.

“Peppermint?”

She shrugged. “It’s seasonal.”

“I like it.”

He closed the front door, then cupped her cheeks in his large hands and lowered his mouth to hers. This time, instead of kissing her, he lightly licked her bottom lip. Tasting maybe, she thought, as wanting made her weak. She pressed her fingers against the cold leather of his jacket, wishing she could get a lot closer.

He waited until she parted for him, then swept his tongue inside. They strained toward each other, kissing more deeply, passion growing until she felt herself start to tremble.

This time she was the one to draw back, her breathing uneven, her head spinning. Spending time with Dante was great. She enjoyed his company, and she felt oddly safe around him. But taking things to the next level? She would have to make sure she kept a firm hold on her heart before she could let that happen. She deserved a little fun but didn't want to let that morph into anything more than that.

"I want to say it's the dance clothes," he murmured, staring into her eyes. "Only you're fully dressed. So it must be you."

She managed a smile. "You're saying I'm a temptation?"

"I'm saying you're on my mind a lot these days."

Words to make her quiver.

For a second she thought about suggesting they pass on the tree lighting ceremony. That her bedroom was only a short staircase away. Except, she needed to be sure she knew what she was doing.

"Don't worry," Dante said, lightly kissing the tip of her nose. "We have a date with a tree and you know how they get if we're late. All sad and then the pine needles fall off. We can't disappoint the children of Fool's Gold just because I find you the sexiest woman in three counties."

That made her laugh. She stepped back and grabbed her coat. "Only three? Who's the competition?"

"A former Miss Apple Valley, four counties away."

"I hate her already."

She zipped her coat. Dante tucked in her scarf, then handed her the mittens. He opened the front door and they stepped into the night.

"You're saying if Miss Apple Valley came calling, you'd dump me in a heartbeat?" she asked, tucking her hand around the crook of his elbow.

"It's a serious possibility."

"And here I was holding out for Matt Damon."

"A married man? I'm shocked and more than a little disappointed."

They were still laughing as they walked toward town.

The evening was clear and cold. Their breath came in white puffs of steam.

"I have a feeling I didn't layer enough," she said as they turned toward the center of town.

"I'll keep you warm," Dante promised.

They weren't the only ones out. The lighting of the town Christmas tree was a big deal, and the sidewalks were crowded. Most of the stores were open. Signs in the windows promised everything from hot chocolate to hot apple cider. There were stands selling homemade cookies and funnel cakes. Christmas music played from speakers.

"Evie, Dante! Good to see you!"

Evie heard someone calling their names but couldn't see who it was. She waved in the general direction of the voice.

"Any clue?" she asked Dante.

"Not even one."

"It's kind of scary that people know who we are."

"As long as they don't chase us with pitchforks."

There were more booths set up by the town square where the crowd was the thickest. Evie hung on to Dante, knowing if they weren't careful, they would get separated.

"Hey, you two." Evie turned and saw Charlie walking toward them. She was with a blonde woman carrying a toddler.

At first Evie wanted to say the woman was Nevada Janack, only the hair wasn't the same and there was something different about her smile. Plus she didn't look pregnant. Clay trailed along behind Charlie, his gaze locked firmly on his fiancée.

"Evie, this is Dakota Andersson. You met her sister Nevada this morning." Charlie leaned close. "You're not going crazy. They're triplets."

"Oh, right. I remember that from the brunch. It's good to see you again."

Dakota laughed. "You, too. My sister Montana is the one who's missing tonight. She's crushed not to be here, but her baby and mine both got a cold and are recovering. My mom is home with Jordan Taylor because we didn't want Hannah to miss tonight." She kissed her daughter's cheek. "Daddy is off getting us hot chocolate."

"It's nice to meet you," Evie said. "This is Dante Jefferson, my brother's business partner."

"Hi." Dakota nodded at him, then turned back to Evie. "I was wondering if there's a toddler class at the dance school. Hannah saw *The Nutcracker* on TV and can't stop talking about it. I know kids can start dance classes pretty young. I went online, but there isn't a website for the studio."

Evie considered the question. "The youngest students I have are six," she said slowly. "But you're right. A lot of girls start much younger than that."

A class for three- and four-year-olds could be during the day, which would be easier on her schedule. Maybe early afternoon. She could even consider a Mommy and Me type class. As for the performance, if the toddlers went first...

There was no point in thinking about that, she told herself. Her plan was to leave town long before next year's show. So the toddlers weren't her problem. But for a second, she thought about how adorable they would be as they danced.

"Let me get through the holiday show," she told Dakota. "If you want to give me a call after the first of the year, we can talk about starting a class for the younger kids. I would enjoy teaching them."

"Thank you. Have a great holiday. I'll be calling."

She walked off with Charlie. Clay paused to give Evie a brief hug before joining his fiancée.

"Can three-year-olds dance?" Dante asked, sounding doubtful.

"Sure. It's good for them to study dance as they're still developing. If done correctly, the practice will improve their motor skills, balance and posture. As long as the training isn't too rigorous or boring. At that age, dance should be fun."

"And when they're older?"

"If they're serious, then it's a lot of hard work." Talent was also required, she thought, remembering what it had been like when she'd been told she didn't have what it took to make it at Juilliard. It didn't matter that she'd trained the longest, had given the most. Without the raw ability, she would never be good enough.

They walked toward the square at the center of town. Light from the streetlamps reflected off the decorations, but until it was lit, the huge tree was little more than a hulking shadow in the darkness.

Evie recognized a few families in the crowd and waved at the people who had taken the time to help with her sets. She leaned into Dante.

"Thanks for talking to my brothers," she said. "For getting them to help."

"I didn't do much."

"You made sure they showed up. That was nice. Thank you."

He groaned. "Not nice. Don't say nice. I would rather be the hot, sexy lawyer you can't resist."

She grinned at him but thought privately that he was all that and more.

He looked at her. "They want to be there for you, Evie. You just have to give them a chance."

Before she could decide if she agreed or not, Shane and Annabelle wandered up and stood next to them. Annabelle was flushed from the cold and munching on a funnel cake.

"I'm eating for twenty," Annabelle announced. "That can't be good, right?"

"You're beautiful," Shane told her.

"I'm going to need my own zip code." Annabelle took another bite and chewed. When she'd swallowed, she looked at Evie. "I need you to be an elf."

Evie stared at her. "Excuse me?"

"Okay, technically it's not me. It's Heidi. Even not pregnant I wouldn't be a good elf. I'm too short."

Evie knew for a fact that Annabelle wasn't drinking, so she had no explanation for the confusing topic of conversation.

Shane put his arm around his fiancée. "You have to start at the beginning."

"What? Oh. The ranch offers holiday sleigh rides. We decorate the sleighs and the horses. Of course if there's no snow, then they're wagon rides. We have hot cocoa and cookies and…"

"Elves?" Dante offered helpfully.

Annabelle nodded.

"I have to get everyone ready for *The Dance of the Winter King,*" Evie said quickly, thinking she didn't have time to be an elf.

"It's only for a couple of evenings. Heidi will know for sure." Annabelle finished the last of the funnel cake, then looked hopefully at Shane. "Do you think I could have a cookie now?"

"Sure."

Dante watched them walk off. "You have a weird family."

"Tell me about it."

"You'd be a cute elf. Do you think the costume has pointy ears?" He sounded hopeful as he asked the question.

"You have a thing for pointy ears?"

"No, but I'm picturing an elf costume. It's very sexy."

"You're as strange as my family."

"I can live with that."

He leaned in as if he was going to kiss her, but just then a voice came over the speaker system.

"Hello, everyone. I'm Mayor Marsha. Welcome to the annual Fool's Gold tree lighting ceremony."

Dante straightened. "Later," he promised.

She nodded.

The crowd moved in around them. Dante shifted her so she was in front of him, his arms around her waist. She leaned into him, enjoying the contact and the warmth.

After a few minutes of announcements, a song from the high school glee club, a cheer from the high school cheerleaders and a drum roll, the lights of the thirty-foot tree came on.

They shone brightly against the dark night sky, and the crowd clapped. There was a bright star at the top, and about half the lights blinked on and off. A few feet away, a little boy asked, "Daddy, do you think it's gonna snow?"

Everyone laughed.

Unfortunately, the skies were clear. Evie found herself agreeing with the little boy—wanting snow on a magical night.

"I have so got to get me one of those," Dante whispered in her ear.

She laughed. "Where would you put it?"

"I'm not sure, but I'd figure something out."

AN HOUR LATER they were back at her place. With the gas fireplace going and the heat up, they'd finally stopped shivering. Without jackets and scarves getting in the way, they could do some very interesting things with each other, as Evie discovered, stretched out on the sofa with Dante.

He had his arms around her and his body pressed to hers. He was all lean muscle—masculine and strong. When he kissed her, she found herself more than willing to surrender. The idea of being sensible was highly overrated.

He kissed her cheek, her jaw and then down her neck. Shivers accompanied the brush of his mouth. Very specific parts of her body were paying attention, and she found herself willing him to touch her breasts.

She wrapped her arms around him and squirmed to get closer, hoping he would get the message. He shifted so he was kissing her mouth again, his tongue tangling with hers. Passion coiled around them, drawing them together.

One of his legs slipped between hers. His thigh pressed against her center. She pushed against the unyielding surface, wanting the contact, the sweetness of his fingers or even his mouth. The image of them naked together filled her mind and made her catch her breath.

He was hard already. She could feel that part of him pressing against her hip. They were both adults. Single. There was no reason not to—

He sat up and stared at her. "I should, ah, go."

It sounded like more of a question than a statement. She could see the battle raging in his eyes. No doubt the fact that his business partner was her brother had something to do with it. And that he'd met her mother. He was being sensible. She should respect that. Which she did. Sort of.

"Okay," she murmured.

"Unless you want me to stay."

She raised her eyebrows. "Did you want me to order takeout? Are you hungry?"

One corner of his mouth turned up. "Now you're messing with me again."

"Uh-huh."

"I expected better."

"No, you didn't."

He grinned. "Was that a yes on me staying?"

She reached for the hem of her sweater and pulled it slowly over her head. As she moved, she felt him stiffen. What she knew and he didn't was that underneath she wore a camisole. She was still completely covered.

Still, as he stared at her, he looked like a man who had just discovered a miracle.

"That was a yes," she whispered as he reached for her.

Ten

EVIE CARRIED A pot of coffee and a plate of toast upstairs. She was tired in the best possible way. Lack of sleep due to a charming, handsome man in her bed was an excuse she could fully embrace. She walked into the bedroom and set the plates and coffee on the dresser. She pulled two mugs out of her robe pockets. Before she could pour, Dante stepped out of the bathroom…naked.

He smiled when he saw her. "You're back."

"Are you surprised? I said I would return with coffee."

"I would have been just as happy to see you if you'd come back without any."

He crossed the space between them, took the mugs from her and put them on the dresser, then pulled her into his arms. As she stepped into his embrace, he pushed off her robe and she let it fall to the floor.

Then his hands were touching her, and she

was leaning in to have a little personal contact of her own.

They'd made love twice in the night, then slept in a tangle of arms and legs. She would have thought he was the type to disappear after the deed, but he'd settled in and she'd been happy to have him stay. Now as he slid his hands over her hips and then up to her breasts, she felt herself starting to melt again. But just as they started to kiss, her stomach growled.

Dante drew back. "You didn't get any dinner last night, did you?"

Food hadn't seemed very important. "I'm fine."

"No way. You're not starving on my watch."

He picked up the robe and draped it around her shoulders, then pushed her toward the bed. She pulled her long hair out of the way, shrugged into the robe and slipped between the sheets. After pouring them each a mug of coffee, he carried one to her and handed her the plate of toast.

"Eat."

"Yes, sir."

He returned with his own mug and settled next to her on the bed. He sipped coffee and watched her finish a piece of toast.

"Better?" he asked when she'd finished.

She nodded. "Like I said, I'm fine."

"You're thin and you spend your day dancing. You need more food."

"I weigh nearly ten pounds more than I did when I was dancing professionally."

He leaned back in mock surprise. "And yet the earth manages to stay in its rotational orbit. Stunning."

She grinned. "You think you're funny."

"I am funny." He touched her face. "You're so beautiful."

"That's the sex talking."

"No, it's me." He leaned toward her. "Maybe later you can model some of your ballet costumes."

She laughed.

"See," he told her triumphantly. "I'm funny."

"You're a riot."

"I'm not kidding about the costumes."

She pushed him onto the pillows, then bent over and kissed him. "Do you have a dancer fantasy?"

"No, I have a fantasy about you. It's specific. It's also my favorite."

She knew he was playing, but his words were oddly touching. "I've never been anyone's fantasy before."

"Sure you have," he said before he kissed her. "You just didn't know." His mouth lingered. Then he drew back and pointed to the toast. "Eat more. You'll need to keep your strength up for later."

"That sounds interesting."

He watched her nibble on the toast, then grabbed

a piece for himself. “So why isn’t there a guy?” he asked between bites. “A husband or a boyfriend?”

“I haven’t met anyone I can imagine falling in love with. Not in a forever kind of way.” She shrugged. “I’ve gotten close a couple of times, but somehow my heart never quite flung itself over the cliff.”

“Interesting visual.”

She grinned. “You know what I mean.”

“I do.”

She finished her toast and tied her robe more tightly around her midsection. “What’s your story? Why isn’t there a Mrs. Jefferson waiting in a suburban paradise somewhere?”

“I’m not that guy,” he said with a shrug.

“Don’t believe in love?”

“Love is too dangerous.” Dante put down his mug of coffee on the nightstand and looked at her. “I was in a gang when I was a kid. I got in early. It was a way to be safe on the streets. My mom didn’t like it, but she was working all the time, so she couldn’t stop me. Plus I was a kid and pissing her off didn’t matter.”

He took her hand in his and stared at their linked fingers. “When I was fifteen, I met a girl. She belonged to a rival gang leader, but we didn’t care. We were in love. And stupid. When he found out, he went after my mom.”

Dante raised his head and looked into her eyes.

"She was killed in a drive-by shooting. To teach me a lesson."

If Evie had been standing, she would have fallen. She could feel her legs giving way and her breathing stop.

"I stole a car to go after him," he continued. "I was caught and instead of being put into jail, I went into a trial program that pulled younger teens out of the gang world and put them in a completely different environment. For me, that was a military school in Texas."

"I'm sorry," she whispered and reached for him. She put her hands on his shoulders and lightly kissed him. "I'm so sorry."

"Thanks. I don't talk about her much. It was a long time ago, but I still miss her."

"Of course you do."

She couldn't comprehend what he'd told her. The words all made sense, but the images were painful, and she was picturing them from a distance.

"I would give anything to have her back," he said quietly. "She was so good to me, and I was a typical teenager. She never got to see me grow up."

"She would have been really proud of you."

"I know." He glanced at her. "I'm not prepared to put my heart in someone else's hands again, but she's the main reason I've pushed you about

May. I would give anything for a second chance with my mom."

The situations were different, but she understood how he would think that. "I can see how you'd want to ride to the rescue. You do that a lot."

"Me? Never."

"You, always."

He kissed her. "Don't make me too much of the good guy." He paused. "I meant what I said before. I don't talk about this. Rafe doesn't know." He hesitated.

She squeezed his hand. "I won't say anything to anyone."

"Thanks."

He drew her down next to him and kissed the side of her neck. "Enough with the serious topics. What are your plans for today?"

She snuggled close, thinking she would happily give up all her plans to spend more time with him. But she wasn't going to push or assume.

"I have laundry," she said. "I might go buy a Christmas tree later, and I have nothing to eat in the house but a loaf of bread and coffee."

"Sounds like a full day," he said, leaning over her. His blue eyes sparkled with something she would like to think was passion and maybe a little anticipation. "Any room for me in it?"

"What did you have in mind?" she asked, her voice breathless.

"A lot of things." He brushed his mouth against hers.

She wrapped her arms around his neck and gave herself over to the sensations washing through her. His hand fumbled with the tie on her robe, then the silky fabric fell free. His fingers caressed her belly before moving higher and—

She stiffened, sure she'd heard something from downstairs.

"What was that?" she asked.

Dante raised his head. "It sounded like voices."

"And footsteps."

She wasn't the type to hear bumps in the night. Besides, it was practically midmorning on a weekend. The sun was out and people were around.

"I'll go investigate," Dante said, sitting up. He reached for his jeans, but before he could pull them on, the bedroom door was pushed open and her brothers rushed inside.

"Are you all—"

Rafe had been speaking. Now his mouth fell open as he stared. Three pairs of eyes widened in identical expressions of astonishment. Evie had a feeling she looked just as shocked.

"You're naked," Clay said at last, obviously horrified by the realization.

All Evie had needed to do was hold her robe closed, but Dante had no such luck. He was caught, sitting on the edge of her bed, jeans in one hand, and that was it.

Rafe's gaze narrowed. "You're sleeping with my sister? We talked about that."

Evie scrambled to her feet and stepped in front of Dante. "You so did not. Because there is no way you have the right to get involved in my personal life. And just because you're paying for this townhouse doesn't mean you have the right to enter unannounced."

Rafe ignored her. "I told you to check on her. To look after her."

Evie spun to face Dante, who was pulling on his jeans. "He told you that?"

Dante stood and fastened his pants. "He mentioned something about it." His gaze settled on her. "You know that's not why I'm here."

She paused, then nodded briefly. "I do. It's okay."

"It's not okay," Shane told her. "Nothing about this is okay."

She turned toward her brothers. "No. You don't get to dictate my personal life. You gave up that right a long time ago and you know it."

She expected them to back off. It wasn't as if

they could have much of an argument. But Clay actually stepped forward.

"Evie, don't you get it? You're our sister and we love you."

FIVE MINUTES LATER Dante finished dressing. Evie had sent her brothers to the kitchen to wait. She drew a sweater over her head, then pulled her hair free. Dante pulled her into his arms.

"Freaked out?" he asked.

"A little."

"Sorry that had to happen. Families are a complication."

She nodded, knowing in this case, he didn't have a problem with complications. She knew he would do anything to have his mom back. Because of that, she wasn't about to complain about her brothers showing up the way they did.

"I'll see you later?" he asked.

"I'd like that."

"Why don't I come over around five with takeout and a movie," he told her. "We can have a quiet evening in."

She stepped into his embrace and hung on for a second. Dante was strong and warm and the kind of guy she would find it easy to fall for. Not that it would be a smart move. After all, he'd made it clear he didn't do long-term, and she had spent years loving people who wouldn't love her back.

He kissed her and then stepped back. “Come on. You can walk me to the door so no one feels compelled to attack.”

“Probably for the best,” she said, taking his hand in hers. “Clay knows martial arts. I think he could kill you with a matchbook cover.”

Dante winced. “I really didn’t need to know that.”

She laughed.

Her good humor lasted until they reached the living room. Dante grabbed his jacket and left, while she had to go face her brothers.

She hesitated, confused by Clay’s seemingly earnest words.

They loved her? That was news, as far as she was concerned. They didn’t act as if they loved her. Until she’d been forcibly moved to Fool’s Gold after her injury, she hadn’t seen any of them in over a year. Except for Rafe, who had shown up in the early part of the summer.

She wanted to say it didn’t matter, except she kind of liked the idea of having family who cared. She’d been alone for what felt like forever.

No, she told herself firmly. She wasn’t getting sucked in to home and hearth and all that crap. It was the season and Fool’s Gold. The town was holiday obsessed. How was she supposed to maintain a sensible amount of emotional reserve when she was going to things like tree lighting ceremonies?

She drew in a breath, then walked purposefully into the kitchen. Her brothers sat at the bar stools by the counter. They each had a mug of coffee and plates littered with dark crumbs. Her lone bag of bread was now crumbled and empty.

"You don't have a lot of food around here," Shane said. "You need to go to the store. Toast isn't breakfast."

Clay nodded at the refrigerator. "You don't even have milk."

"I drink my coffee black."

"Why?"

She sighed. "You can't do this. You can't show up with no warning."

"Because we might find you in bed with a guy?" Rafe asked flatly. "I don't like you sleeping with Dante."

Evie faced him. "You don't get a vote. I'm over eighteen."

"That's not the point."

"It's exactly the point. He's a good guy. I like him. It's not your business."

"I work with him."

"Then don't ask how his weekend was because, believe me, you don't want details."

Clay stood and leaned toward her. "Is it a money thing?"

Evie stared at him, unable to grasp what he was asking. Then she realized he was still talking about the lack of food in her refrigerator and not her reasons for sleeping with Dante.

"It's not money. I don't keep food in the house because if it's here, I'll eat it."

Shane picked up his mug. "What else would you do with food?"

Clay punched him in the arm. "It's about weight, moron." He turned back to her. "You need to eat. You're too thin."

"Is that possible?" she asked, trying to go for humor and suspecting she failed.

"You're not dancing anymore, Evie," Clay told her. "It's okay to be like everyone else."

"Is that what you're doing?"

He patted his stomach. "Charlie's making sure of it."

She waved her hand. "Okay, whatever." She looked at all of them. "While I appreciate the effort, you can't barge in here without calling first. Understood?"

They nodded.

"We wanted to surprise you," Rafe said.

"Then you achieved your goal."

He studied her. "Evie, I know it was bad before. When we were kids."

It had been, she thought. She could be mad at them forever, but to what end? They were her brothers. They'd had their own growing up to do. She'd been a lot younger and the only girl.

"We all did the best we could," she told him.

For a second she thought one of them might ask the inevitable "Even Mom?" But none of them did. Shane walked around the counter and pulled her close. Clay and Rafe joined in for the group hug. For the first time in as long as she could remember, her brothers held her.

When they'd released her, she smiled at Rafe. "Just so you know, I wasn't a virgin."

He groaned and covered his ears with his hands. "Stop! You have to stop."

Clay chuckled. "Feeling pretty good about yourself, aren't you?"

"I am."

Eleven

LATE MONDAY MORNING, Evie parked in front of the Fool's Gold animal shelter. There was a large sign stating that over nine hundred and forty-seven animals had been adopted by the community and that donations were always welcome. When she got out of the car, she heard a couple dozen dogs barking and figured the meeting would be loud, if nothing else.

She walked toward the front door. Another car drove in and she recognized her mother's Mercedes. As May got out of her car, Evie braced herself for whatever was to come. She was relatively sure her brothers would have shared the details of their visit to her place the previous morning. She wasn't exactly thrilled about discussing her sex life with her mother, but she wasn't sure she could actually get out of the conversation.

She waited for her mother to join her. May smiled broadly as she approached.

"This is going to be so exciting," she said happily. "I can't wait to meet all the animals. Rina was telling me that last year there was an iguana up for adoption. Though she said she decided not to give it any special beauty treatment for the holidays."

"Aren't iguanas huge?" Evie asked. "What was she going to do? Paint its toenails?"

"As long as she doesn't expect us to do that."

They walked inside and were met by a pretty young woman in her mid-twenties.

"Hi. I'm Tammy Blalock. I work here at the shelter." Tammy smiled. "I also have a shift at Starbucks. So if you think you've seen me around town, you have."

"You keep busy," May said.

"I know. Life's more fun that way."

"Nice to meet you," Evie said, suddenly feeling like a slacker.

"Rina's already here," Tammy said, leading them through the small office and into the back of the building. "She's putting together a list of who we have to put up for adoption. We already have pictures up on our website and we've done some holiday graphics."

Tammy's long blond ponytail swung as she walked. Evie and May followed her into an open area with a thick outdoor rug and several low chairs. There were also toys and a feline climbing post.

"This is our biggest greeting area," Tammy told them. "Where potential pet parents can spend time with some of our residents. Cats are this way and dogs are over there."

As she spoke, she pointed at two different doors. One had a big cat painted on it, the other had a grinning cartoon beagle.

"Rina's in with the cats," Tammy continued and held open the appropriate door.

Evie and May walked inside. There were dozens of large, airy cages and nearly as many cats. Calicos and marmalades, tabbies and cats in solid colors. Some were sleeping, a few kittens were playing together in one of the larger cages. Evie was immediately drawn to a black-and-white longhaired tuxedo cat with green eyes and a disdainful expression.

Evie crossed to him and offered her fingers for him to sniff. He leaned forward slightly and touched his nose to the edge of her finger, then turned a little, as if offering his cheek. She rubbed his soft fur.

"Hi, handsome," she murmured.

"That's Alexander," Tammy told her. "He's about two or three years old. We're not sure. He was found abandoned and starving a couple of months ago. He's friendly enough around people, but understandably wary. He won't purr for anyone. People want to adopt a cat who purrs."

Alexander looked at her, as if asking if she would be willing to purr, under the circumstances.

"No, I wouldn't," she told him.

Carina McKenzie, otherwise known as Rina, walked into the cat room, clipboard in hand. "Hi, May. Nice to see you again. You must be Evie."

"Hi," Evie said. "Nice to meet you."

"You, too. I really appreciate the help with the adoption. I didn't want to give it up this year, but Dr. Galloway keeps telling me to stay off my feet as much as possible." Rina wrinkled her nose. "She's gotten more stern and is threatening to put me on bed rest if I don't start listening."

Tammy pointed to the door leading back to the getting-to-know-you room just outside the entrance. "Then maybe we should have this conversation out there, where you can sit, young lady."

"Oh, yes. You're right." Rina put her hand on her large belly.

May followed them out. Evie paused, then glanced back at Alexander. The cat stared at her with an expression that said he wasn't the least bit surprised by her leaving. After all, humans hadn't treated him that well. There was no reason for him to trust her, either.

Evie hesitated, then followed the other women out of the cat room.

When they were seated, Rina handed them each several sheets of paper. "This is the layout we used last year at the convention center," she said. "It worked well. The shelter already has the adoptable pets' pictures up on the website. I've got the advertising started. There will be several mentions on the local radio stations and an ad in the local paper. The posters for the storefronts are going to be ready tomorrow."

May had her iPad open. "I already have a note to pick them up and deliver them to the various stores." She smiled. "Glen, Shane and Clay are going to help me. I'm also going to get the flyers."

"Good," Rina said. "We want to hand them out to as many people as possible."

"I would like about a hundred for the dance studio," Evie said. "My students can take them home."

Rina smiled. "Great. Kids are my target audience. Now for the adoption itself. The dogs need to be groomed." She pulled out another list. "Last year I handled most of that, but there's no way I can be on my feet. However, I have a list of volunteers."

Tammy nodded. "I'm heading that group. Rina's been giving me lessons on basic grooming. For the cats, we think a good brushing is enough, and I'm not touching anything that slithers or crawls." She shuddered.

"Cute matters when it comes to adoptions," Rina told them. "Sad but true. So we want fluffy, great-smelling pets. Now here's what we did last year on the actual day."

They went over how many tables they would need and the layout at the convention center. Rina had another list of volunteers who would be delivering pets that morning. Evie was more than stunned when she realized how many moving parts there were to the event and found herself offering to drive cats and dogs to the venue. She was also surprised at how her mother seemed to have a complete understanding of the logistics involved.

"With luck, everything will be done by one or two in the afternoon," Rina said. "I'll be there, and so will Cameron." She smiled as she mentioned her husband. "He's working very hard to keep me off my feet, so I'm not sure how much help I'll be."

"You need to take care of yourself and your baby," May told her firmly. "We can handle this. Having Tammy to contact will be a big help."

She confirmed a few more details, all the while typing on her iPad.

They wrapped up the last of the details, then May and Evie walked out.

"I enjoyed that," May said. "While I appreciate having plenty of free time these days, I've missed the responsibility of having a job."

"The adoption is a lot more work than I realized," Evie admitted as they stood by their cars. "But I'm glad to be helping. Thanks for asking me."

May smiled at her. "I'm the one who needs to thank you. I couldn't possibly do it all alone. Glen is terrified I'm going to bring home all the animals that don't get adopted, but I've promised I won't. Right now we have travel plans. Getting a new house pet wouldn't be fair to the animal. But Rafe and Heidi are thinking of looking at dogs."

Evie thought about Alexander. She wasn't sure how a cat would fit in her life. She'd never had a pet before and hadn't grown up with them, either. For all her love of animals, May hadn't wanted pets around. Probably because she'd had enough to do with four children and little money, Evie thought. Maybe she should look up cats on the internet and find out what was involved with owning one. The guest room of her townhouse faced south, and there was a small window seat. Didn't cats like to lie in the sun?

They worked out when they would next meet to discuss the event, then Evie started to say goodbye. But before she managed to get out the words, her mother touched her arm.

"I heard about what happened with your brothers and Dante."

Evie had managed to forget the incident while they were helping with the animals, so she was unprepared to have her mother bring it up now. She felt herself flush, which was followed by reminding herself she was an adult and what she did in her private life was no one's business but her own. As good as the words sounded, however, she didn't exactly remain convinced.

"My brothers need to knock before walking into my house, and I need to make sure the front door is locked," she said.

"Dante seems very nice," her mother said. "I hope you're being smart about things."

Smart? As in not falling for a man who had made it clear he wasn't interested in a relationship? Smart as in…

"You're talking birth control," Evie said slowly, her stomach clenching as an emotional blow hit directly home.

Of course that was something her mother would worry about. She'd had to deal with the consequences of an unplanned pregnancy. The fact that Evie was the result made things a little awkward.

May touched her arm again, this time hanging on. "No," she said quickly. "I'm talking protecting your health. I hear so many scary things on the news about sexually transmitted diseases. Dante has a bit of a reputation and I was worried."

"Oh. You mean condoms. Don't worry. We used them."

May's expression turned sad. "Is that what you think? That I regret having you?"

"Yes."

"Oh, Evie, I don't. I wouldn't change anything."

May sighed. "All right. That's not true. If I could go back in time, I would do so many things differently, when it came to you. I would be there for you and make sure you felt as if you were a part of the family. But I would never, ever not have you. You're my baby girl."

When Clay had mournfully informed her that her brothers loved her, she'd almost been able to believe his words. But with her mother, she was less sure.

"I want to think that's true," she said slowly.

"I know." May squeezed her arm again, then released her. "You're cautious with me, and I understand that. You've been through so much. I just hope you'll give me a chance and the time it's going to take to win you over. I'm not giving up on us, and I'd like you to get to the place where you feel the same way."

Evie nodded slowly, not sure what she felt. May hugged her briefly, then got into her car and drove away.

Evie continued to stand in the parking lot and thought about all the reasons she could still be angry with her mother. Unbidden, a disconcerting thought popped into her head. She was twenty-six. Her mother had only been a few years older when her husband had died, leaving her a widow with three boys and no money. No doubt she'd been terrified and desperately lonely. One night a handsome stranger had come calling, and May had made a mistake.

The man had disappeared the next morning, and a few weeks later, May had discovered she was pregnant.

For the first time ever, Evie tried to understand what that must have been like. No doubt May had been humiliated and ashamed. She would have also been worried about how she was supposed to pay for the birth, not to mention all the things an infant needed.

What her mother had done to her wasn't right, but maybe, just maybe, it was a little understandable. As Dante and Charlie and even her brothers had pointed out, she had to be willing to accept what was offered. To make peace. Being a part of her family wasn't a given—it required work on everyone's part. May had shown she was willing to go more than halfway. Now Evie had to decide how far she was willing to go herself.

DANTE FINISHED GOING OVER the contract. Most people found the idea of a novel-length legal document daunting, but he enjoyed the challenge. Most of the company's business transactions were straightforward. Still, every now and then, someone tried to screw with them. His job was to make sure that person wasn't successful.

He saved the document on his computer, then

printed out a final copy for signature. As the paper spewed out into the tray, Rafe walked around the corner and paused by his desk.

"Have a minute?"

Dante took one look at his friend's face and knew he wasn't going to like whatever Rafe had on his mind. He also had a good idea what the subject was going to be. But Evie was Rafe's sister, so the man deserved to be heard.

"Sure."

Rafe pulled up a chair and sat down.

"Do I need to kill you?" he asked, his voice deceptively calm.

Dante studied his friend. He could challenge the question—Rafe wasn't the murderous type. But Rafe was more than a business partner and he deserved answers.

"Evie and I like each other."

"And that's supposed to make it okay?"

"It's supposed to tell you that I understand why you might be concerned," Dante told him. "Look, we're spending some time together. I didn't mean for it to happen. You're the one who asked me to look out for her."

"Not by sleeping with her. What were you thinking?"

"That she's a beautiful woman with a great sense of humor who shares my ambivalence about the holidays."

Rafe's gaze was steady. "She's my sister and I don't want her hurt."

"We're clear on what we're doing."

"You're clear," Rafe told him. "But I'm worried about her. Evie isn't like you."

Dante looked at his friend. "You sure about that? From what she's told me, no one in her family knows her very well."

Rafe shifted. "That's true, but I know what you're like in a relationship. I don't want that for her."

Dante understood the complaint. Rafe didn't object to Dante's style so much as the inevitable outcome. There was no happy ending. Ever.

"We've discussed ground rules," Dante told him. "But the next time I see her, I'll bring them up again and make sure she and I are on the same page."

"If you're not and she's upset, I'll have to kill you."

Dante slapped him on the back. "There's that holiday spirit."

Rafe glowered at him. "Dammit, Dante. My sister?"

"I'm sorry, Rafe. I tried to remember that she was your sister, but this attraction was mutual."

Rafe grumbled something under his breath and stalked away. Dante sat at his desk, suddenly less sure he'd made himself clear to Evie. He checked his watch. She would be arriving for work in less than an hour. He would talk to her before her classes began and make sure they had the same expectations. He'd meant what he said—he liked her. The last thing he wanted to do was hurt her.

EVIE ARRIVED AT THE dance studio forty-five minutes before her classes started. The first thing she did was crank up the heat. The old building was drafty and cold in winter. If it were up to her, she would relocate the dance studio to a newer place, with a bigger dance floor and maybe a second practice room. As it was, she waited until she heard the telltale whoosh of the furnace starting, then hung her coat on the rack and went over the classes for that day.

They were getting close to the panic period for the production. In less than two weeks, they would start practicing on stage so everyone could perform in the actual location. The stage was considerably wider than their studio, so that would take some getting used to. There was also the seemingly endless rows of chairs. The thought of an audience could be daunting to even a seasoned professional.

She crossed to the stereo system and connected her phone to speakers, then scrolled through her list of music and found a favorite song. She'd just walked over to the barre when Dante walked in.

She smiled as she glanced from the living, breathing, tempting man to his many reflections in the mirror. Both were appealing although she had to admit she preferred the one she could put her hands on.

"Hi," she said, crossing to him.

"Hi, yourself." He rested his hands on her waist and lightly kissed her. "You going to do some fancy dance moves?"

"I haven't warmed up."

"Can I help with that?"

She laughed. "No. I have students arriving in about thirty minutes."

"Bummer." He drew in a breath. "I had a talk with your brother earlier today."

As the two men worked together, that was hardly news. Except he wasn't sharing a part of a day—instead he was passing on information.

She pressed her fingertips against his chest and winced. "I'm sorry. For what it's worth, I had a talk with my mother."

Dante grimaced. "About the pet adoption?"

"Not exactly. She told me to make sure we were using condoms so I wouldn't catch a disease."

"She didn't."

Evie stared into his eyes. "Do I look like I'm lying?"

"Sorry."

"Me, too. About my brother. Not about the other night."

"Me, either." But he didn't sound completely sure.

She carefully lowered her arms to her sides and took a small step back, pulling away from his light touch. "Dante, this isn't the 1800s. One great night doesn't mean we're engaged."

"I know, I just want to make sure we're on the same page."

She could translate easily enough. He wanted to make sure she remembered their time together was meant to be fun. Not a relationship.

She'd been very clear on what they were doing when they'd started hanging out together. So she couldn't complain about being misled. If she'd started to look forward to seeing Dante more than she should, it was her own business, right? If she was hoping for more than a good time, that was her problem.

She continued to watch Dante's face. "You and I are friends. We like each other and are enjoying spending time together. We're both a little freaked out about the town's obsession with being cheerful and embracing every nuance of all things Christmas. Holidays are stressful and we're getting each other through. The other night we discovered that you earned your reputation with women the hard way and I appreciate that. There are no expectations between us. Does that sum it up?"

She spoke lightly, doing her best to sound as blasé and experienced as any other woman he'd been with. The slight jab of pain in the vicinity of her heart didn't have anything to do with him.

"Perfectly." His blue eyes crinkled with amusement. "I'm glad you enjoyed the other night. I did, too."

"See? We're good. Now you ignore my brother and I'll ignore my mother and all will be well."

"Promise," he told her. He gave her a quick kiss. "We'll both be working late tonight. How about lunch tomorrow?"

"I have to help Annabelle with the book drive."

"There's a book drive? Why? Because the town needed one more philanthropic event?"

"I know. But Annabelle called and asked and I couldn't figure out how to say no. Apparently every child in Fool's Gold gets a book for Christmas. They have to be wrapped, so I'm going up to Ronan's Lodge. We're meeting in the Mountain ballroom." She held up both hands. "I didn't have the heart to tell her I'm not very good at wrapping presents."

"We could practice tonight," he suggested. "Wrapping and unwrapping."

A tempting offer, she thought. But one she wasn't sure her heart could risk her accepting. Before she could decide, she heard footsteps on the stairs. Light footsteps from one of her beginning classes. Dante took a step back.

"Later," he mouthed and walked out of the studio.

As Evie greeted her students, she glanced toward the door. Being sensible about Dante was the smartest move. She had to protect herself and her heart. But deep inside, she knew there was a part of her that wanted more. Wanted to believe in someone. To have a little faith and maybe find love.

Twelve

EVIE PARKED IN front of the Fool's Gold Animal Shelter and got out of her car. She'd called ahead to make sure this was a convenient time for the staff, but now she hesitated. Was she really ready to take on the responsibility of caring for a cat?

"I guess that's what I'm here to find out."

Tammy was waiting for her as she walked into the building. Alexander was sitting on a tall, carpeted platform, his long tail swishing as he looked around the room.

"This is the one, isn't it?" Tammy asked. "You said Alexander, but sometimes people get names mixed up."

"This is him."

Evie walked over to the cat and held out her fingers for him to sniff. "Hi, big guy. How are you doing?"

His green eyes narrowed slightly. He took an obligatory sniff, then turned away.

"Does he hate me?" Evie asked, not sure what his actions meant in the cat world. If she were on a blind date, she would know exactly what he was thinking and it wouldn't be flattering.

"He's making you work for it," Tammy told her. "Keep talking to him and then pet him. He's going to make you earn his trust."

"I can respect that," she said, keeping her voice quiet. "If I were you, I wouldn't be very trusting, either."

She lightly touched his back. While he didn't flinch, he wasn't relaxed, either. His shoulders got a little hunchy. She continued to stroke him, moving slowly and gently, not making sudden moves.

The phone rang.

"I need to get that," Tammy told her. "I'll be right back."

Evie nodded and kept her attention on the cat. She lengthened the strokes so she was petting him from shoulder to tail. After a couple of minutes, he relaxed. By the time Tammy returned, he was actually glancing at her with something slightly warmer than disdain.

"I like him," Evie said. "I need to make sure I'm ready for a cat, but I'm leaning in that direction for sure. Has anyone else said they're interested in him?"

"No. He's not a kitten, which makes his adoption more challenging. But I can let you know if we get any calls before the event."

"That would be great." Evie glanced at her watch. "I have to run. Thanks for this, Tammy."

"No problem. I hope you take him. He's a great guy."

"Bye, Alexander."

The cat looked at her. His eyes narrowed slightly as if he realized she was leaving. Then he turned away. Evie wanted to tell him that she might be giving him a forever home, but stopped herself. Until she was sure, it wouldn't be right to allow him to hope. Unfortunately, explaining to herself that Alexander didn't speak English didn't make her feel any less awful about leaving without him.

EVIE WAS ALREADY LATE. She hurried through town on her way to Ronan's Lodge, glancing at her watch as she went. Thoughts of Dante and her family and the production had kept her tossing and turning much of the night. Now she had to face a morning of book wrapping. She hoped there was an instructional session first.

She glanced longingly at the Starbucks as she passed, but there was no time. As she waited to cross at the light, three teenaged girls came out of the coffee place and spotted her.

"OMG! That's her!" A tall blonde in skinny

jeans and a heavy down coat raced toward her. "Ms. Stryker? Could you wait a second?"

The other two girls with her were both brunettes with big eyes and wide smiles. All three of them were clutching to-go drink containers.

The blonde spoke first. "You're Evie Stryker, right?"

Evie nodded slowly.

"This is so cool. I'm Viv and these are my friends Tai and Wendy. We're cheerleaders." Viv's grin broadened. "I'm actually team captain this year."

"Congratulations," Evie said, hoping the uneasy feeling she had in her stomach was uncalled for and that the girls were just being extra Fool's Gold friendly.

Viv held her drink in both hands. "Every year we do a fund-raiser for the squad. We save money to go to cheerleading camp in the summer."

"Okay," Evie said slowly, the unease turning to sinking. "What kind of fund-raiser?"

"We do a Pom-Pom-A-Thon," Tai, or maybe Wendy, said. "People hire us to go to someone's house and do cheers, only they're Christmas related."

The three of them glanced at each other, then shouted together, "Hey, hey, ho, ho. Merry Christmas and away we go."

Viv laughed. "They're not all that lame, I promise. We were thinking that we're not as good as we could be. So we've got some friends in the creative writing club helping us with new cheers. We were wondering if you could help us with some moves. After all, you were a professional cheerleader, right?"

Evie winced. Her short-lived career as an L.A. Stallions cheerleader had ended badly and wasn't anything she wanted to talk about.

"The Stallions' squad was more about dance than cheering," she said.

The three teens looked at each other, then back at her. "That's what we want," Viv said. "Some ideas to add a little fun to our routines. It would only take a couple of hours. Please."

Evie thought about the book wrapping and the performance, the students she had to work with privately, her volunteering for the pet adoption and how she couldn't seem to take a step without running into someone from her family. This was not the time to take on one more project.

But as she looked at the girls, she couldn't seem to summon the word *no.* She sighed. "Sure. I can help. I have to help wrap books right now and then maybe after that?"

"You're working with Annabelle?" Viv asked. "With the book drive? We're going there, too." She turned to her friends. "We need to work really hard so Evie can have more time with us."

Which would be great for Annabelle and less thrilling for herself, Evie thought, knowing she might as well simply give in to the inevitable.

The four of them made their way to the hotel. Signs directed them to the ballroom. As Evie stepped through the open double doors, she realized she hadn't known what to expect. A few boxes of books and some tables, maybe. It was that times a thousand.

There were at least forty tables set up. On each one was a box, a roll of gift wrap, tape and a sheet of colored stickers. A small crowd was clustered together near the front of the room. Evie and the cheerleaders joined them.

Heidi was there, along with Patience and Charlie. Jo, from the bar where they'd all had brunch on Thanksgiving. She recognized a few other people from town, along with a few of her students' moms. Annabelle checked her watch, then waved to get everyone's attention.

"Thank you for coming," she said. "I'm hoping this won't take very long. I know the season is busy and I appreciate the time and effort you're offering."

Evie felt a warm hand settle on the small of her back. She turned and saw Dante standing next to her.

"What are you doing here?" she asked in a whisper.

"Rafe was supposed to come, but he's on a conference call that's gone long. I offered to represent the company."

He smiled as he spoke. Evie found herself easing toward him, wanting to press her body against his. Remembering the cheerleaders who were no doubt keeping an eye on her, she forced herself to stand straight and pretend she wasn't tingling from the light touch on her back.

"Every table has a box of books," Annabelle was saying. "They are grouped together by age and gender. So please don't trade books with anyone else. When you've wrapped the book, put one of the stickers on the upper right corner. The sticker tells the age range and whether the book is for a boy or a girl. Again, please don't trade stickers."

"There are a lot of rules," Dante whispered into her ear.

Evie fought off a shiver as her body pointed out that every single part of her really liked what this man could do to her and that it had been a while since they'd seen each other naked.

"Behave," she said.

"I am."

She winced, realizing she'd actually been talking to herself rather than him.

Annabelle sent them off to find tables. The cheerleaders took one together and Dante joined Evie.

"Who are your friends?" he asked, motioning

to the teens who were taking books out of the box and unrolling the paper.

"They're on the high school cheerleading squad. I'm going to help them with a fund-raiser they're doing."

He raised his eyebrows.

"I know, I know." She kept her voice low. "It shouldn't take too much of my time."

"You're in demand," he said. "Impressive."

"Overwhelming."

"How can I help?"

She laughed. "Unless you have a secret background as a cheerleader, I'm not sure you can."

"Hmm, there is that year I spent working undercover. Let me see what I can remember."

She laughed and handed him the first book. "Wrap."

"How about I cut the paper and put on the stickers, and you wrap."

"Chicken."

"These are presents for kids. They should look nice."

"Fine. I'll wrap."

They had picked a table with large picture books. For boys, Evie thought, looking at covers with trucks and bugs and camping raccoons.

"I know most women think about having a little girl," she said, taking the piece of wrapping paper Dante handed her, along with the book he'd cut it for, "but I've always pictured myself with sons. I'm guessing that comes from growing up with three brothers."

"Boys are less complicated," Dante agreed. "They want to do things. Girls have feelings."

She laughed. "Are you saying boys don't?"

"I'm saying I understand what a boy feels. Can you see me sitting at a little table having pretend tea with a four-year-old and her toy bears?"

Evie studied him, taking in the deep blue eyes, handsome face and, as always, well-cut, killer suit. She could totally see Dante falling for a little girl. He would be a protective father, one who kissed a boo-boo to make it better and slayed dragons, be they real or imagined. And, yes, she could imagine him sitting at a too-small table and having pretend tea.

They'd both grown up without a father figure in their lives, so she would guess they both knew how important a dad could be. While children weren't on her immediate radar, should that happen, she would prefer to have a man around. She doubted he was the kind of man who would ever consider walking away from his kids.

Under other circumstances he might be someone she wanted to consider hanging on to. Only Dante wasn't into forever, and she was planning on moving on. Although right now her reasons for wanting to leave Fool's Gold seemed a little fuzzy.

"You'd be great," Evie told him and centered the book on the wrapping paper.

In less time than Dante would have thought, the books were wrapped. Evie went off with her cheerleader fans and he stayed after to help load the wrapped books into boxes for delivery.

Gideon joined him, loading the boxes onto a cart.

"Do you know if Evie's gone over my suggestions for the production?" he asked.

Dante straightened slowly and stared at the other man. "What are you talking about?"

"I'm doing the narration for *The Dance of the Winter King.* Didn't she tell you?"

"No. She didn't mention it."

Gideon was tall and moved like someone who knew his way around a fight. Dante recognized the subtle signs from his own early years. The scar by Gideon's eyebrow and the tattoo visible under his rolled-up shirtsleeves were also a clue.

"I had some suggestions to make the transitions smoother," Gideon said. "The premise of the story is interesting. I like the message."

"There's a message?"

"Sure. Every child is special. Unique." He gave a quick smile. "Like a snowflake."

A snowflake? Dante did his best to reconcile the dark, dangerous man in front of him with a guy who talked about children being special snowflakes.

"Okay," he said slowly. "I'll, ah, tell her you're looking for her."

Just then they were joined by a well-dressed, white-haired woman in a suit. It took Dante a moment to put the name with the face.

"Mayor Marsha," he said. "Nice to see you again."

"You, too." The older woman smiled at both of them. "I'm happy to see you're settling in. And you've met Gideon." She turned to the other man. "I'm delighted by the Christmas music. Very eclectic choices. Some traditional songs, of course, but I'm very much enjoying the international selections."

"I like to mix it up," Gideon told her, winking as he spoke. "Keep folks guessing."

The mayor glanced at Dante. "Gideon has recently purchased the two radio stations in town. One AM, one FM. The FM station is playing all Christmas music."

"I'll have to tune in," Dante said politely.

"I'm getting lots of good feedback," Gideon said. "A few local rockers have been by, requesting something else."

"There are local rockers in Fool's Gold?" Dante tried to imagine them being happy in the quiet, family friendly town and couldn't.

"Young rockers," Gideon said, then nodded at the cart. "I need to get these out to the truck. Good to see you, Mayor Marsha."

"You, too."

Dante expected the old lady to move on, but she waited until Gideon had left, then turned to him.

"You're settling in well."

He stared at her, not sure if she was asking a question or making a statement.

"This town is very special," she continued. "A lot is expected of our citizens, but then people get so much in return. Do you know very much about Gideon?"

"No. We've only met a couple of times."

"A very interesting man with a violent history. Then he met a couple of men who changed his life forever. Ford and an angel." She smiled. "Sorry. I couldn't resist."

"I don't get the joke."

"Ford and Angel are men's names. Two men who—" She shook her head. "It's not important. Suffice it to say Ford is the son of one of our founding families. He's coming back, as soon as he figures out how to embrace his past. As for Angel, he'll be home soon, too."

She motioned to the rapidly emptying room. "This is exactly what you need, Mr. Jefferson. You've been on your own for too long. I understand why you've been reluctant to truly settle and admit you're ready to make a home. But here in Fool's Gold we take care of our own. You will always be safe, always welcome."

He stared at the old woman, telling himself there was no way she could know about his past. That no one but Evie knew about his mother and he was convinced she wouldn't have said a word. The mayor was talking in generalities. He was reading too much into her words. Or maybe she was really fishing for information.

He ignored the compassion and certainty in her blue eyes and gave her a practiced smile. "I like Fool's Gold well enough, but I still have my place in San Francisco."

"You'll sell it soon. You belong here, Mr. Jefferson. Fool's Gold has everything you've been looking for. We can't undo the past, but we can heal from it. Oh, and would you please tell May that Priscilla would be more than welcome at the Live Nativity."

The change of subject had him scrambling to catch up. "Excuse me?"

"The Live Nativity. May will worry about Priscilla being left home alone on Christmas Eve Day. She's welcome. Along with her pony."

"You do realize Priscilla is an elephant?"

"Of course."

"In a nativity?"

"God loves all His creatures."

"Won't that look strange?"

"It will look welcoming. No one should be alone for Christmas, Mr. Jefferson. Not even an elephant."

"How is May supposed to get her here?"

"She can walk. It's not that far. Just make sure Heidi doesn't offer to ride her. I don't think that would be a good idea."

He honestly didn't know what to say. He'd seen the stage where the Live Nativity would be on Christmas Eve Day. There was room for Priscilla on either side, along with her pet pony. But still.

Dante drew in a breath. He might never have lost in court, but he recognized a moment when he should simply accept defeat.

"I'll pass along the message."

"Thank you." She touched his arm. "I'm so glad you're here, and we're very lucky to have you as a part of our Fool's Gold family."

She smiled, released him and left. Dante was left standing in the center of the empty room, feeling as if he'd been run over by a freight train. What had just happened? And why did he suddenly want to hug everyone?

Grumbling to himself that the old lady was crazy, he stalked out of the ballroom and headed back to the office. He needed some quality time with a legal brief. That would set his world to rights. Then he could forget all this Christmas crap and get back to being himself.

Thirteen

Evie wrote down another idea for a cheer, then pushed away the paper. She had to focus on her production, and time was ticking. There were less than three weeks until *The Dance of the Winter King,* and she was starting to panic. While helping the cheerleaders was fun, she had to remember her responsibility to her students and the town. Of course, when she thought of it in those terms, she got a little sick to her stomach.

A distraction appeared in the form of footsteps on the stairs. It was several hours until her first lesson, but she'd received an email from Dominique Guérin, her boss. Dominique was flying in for the holidays and had said she would like to stop by the studio that morning.

Another thing to be nervous about, Evie thought, automatically standing, her back straight, her feet in first position. Miss Monica, who had sold the dance studio to Dominique over the summer, had been running the school for years. Evie had only been teaching for a couple of months and had never run anything. For all she knew, Dominique was going to fire her.

"Cheerful, upbeat attitude," she murmured, telling herself not to go looking for trouble. After all, it seemed to have no problem finding her. Besides, she'd met Dominique before, and the woman had been very friendly. Of course, back then, Evie hadn't been in charge.

The door opened and Dominique swept inside. Evie resisted the urge to curtsy in the presence of greatness, instead offering a smile and a handshake.

"Dominique," she said. "It's lovely to see you."

Dominique Guérin had to be close to sixty, but she looked as if she were in her forties. Petite, beautiful, with short gold-blond hair and large eyes, she moved with a dancer's sureness and elegance. She'd been more than a great artist, she'd been a star. She'd graced every famous stage in every country, had danced for presidents and kings and been awarded nearly every honor possible. There were rumors of a title, bestowed by Queen Elizabeth, but Evie couldn't get confirmation on that.

"Evie!" Dominique moved close and hugged her. "You look wonderful. So young. I'm jealous. How are you doing? I read all your emails about

Monica. Running off with a man, at her age. I don't know if I should be impressed or worried about her hip."

Dominique smiled. "But if he's her great love, she shouldn't ever look back. Everyone deserves a great love. Of course, she's left us in a bit of a pickle."

"That's one way to describe it," Evie murmured, offering Dominique a chair.

She'd already made tea and now poured them each a mug, then settled across from her boss and sent out a quick request to the universe that the meeting go well.

Dominique shrugged out of her faux-fur coat and draped it over the back of her chair. Evie eyed the other woman's fitted turtleneck and slim jeans. She doubted Dominique had put on a pound since her dancing days.

Dominique picked up her mug of tea. "Fool's Gold is so pretty. I've been in New York, and while it's beautiful there during the holidays, I do love the small town feel here. And there's plenty going on."

Evie gave a strangled laugh. "Sure. The pet adoption, the book drive, hayrides out at the ranch, the day of giving and, hey, *The Dance of the Winter King.* It's busy."

Dominique smiled at her. "You sound overwhelmed."

"Just some days. I'm supposed to help out with the hayrides. I've been told I'm elf material. And I'm also working on the pet adoption. That's on the fifteenth. It's a lot to get through."

"It is. I wonder if Charlie and Clay would like a pet." Dominique leaned toward her. "Clay and I have been talking. He wants a big wedding. Something the town can be involved in. Charlie wants to elope. She says she's not bride material."

"She would be a beautiful bride," Evie said, thinking her future sister-in-law wasn't traditionally feminine but was still her favorite of the three. Although Heidi and Annabelle had certainly been nice enough.

"We'll see who wins the argument," Dominique said. "I'm betting Clay surprises us all, and Charlie gives in. Either way, a dog might be nice for them. Practice before they give me a grandchild."

Dominique sighed. "I can't believe I'm happy about that, but I am. Charlie has told me to stop asking if she's pregnant. She says they're going to wait at least a year. I've tried to remind her that my wants are more important than hers, but she's not listening. It's very wonderful to have family. You must be pleased to be so close to yours."

"You have no idea," Evie murmured, hoping Dominique didn't press for details. "Are you staying in town through the holidays?"

"Yes. I'm very much looking forward to the production."

Evie pressed her hand against the sudden knot in her stomach. "Great. I've made a few changes from what's been done in the past."

She detailed her thoughts on the transitions and how she wanted to make the story tighter. "The voice-over is being modified, as well. A local businessman is helping with that. He owns the radio stations in town."

"Excellent. I adore community involvement. Charlie mentioned the sets had been refurbished."

"They were. We had a work day." Evie told her about that.

"You do have a challenge on your hands," her boss told her. "I would imagine not every student is gifted."

"Some have to work harder than others," Evie admitted. "I'm working with a few girls privately so they can be in the show. It's not that they aren't willing to work hard," she said, not sure how to delicately share the truth.

"But they have no ability or rhythm," Dominique said drily. "I can imagine. Dance is a gift and given to so few. Normally I would be against lowering the standards. After all, this studio has my name on it. But in this case, the production is for the town. Accommodations must be made—in the spirit of the season."

"Exactly," Evie said.

"You're doing an excellent job. I'm very pleased. You stepped in and took control when you could have simply thrown up your hands and said it wasn't your responsibility."

"I didn't want the students to be disappointed." Evie drew in a breath. "I'm very much enjoying teaching."

"Then you're right where you need to be, aren't you?" Dominique glanced around. "This is a grim little studio, isn't it? Old and drafty. After the holidays, I want you and I to talk, Evie. I'm considering buying a building and putting the studio in it. We would have it redone to our exact specifications. Expand, even. Hire a few more teachers. I'd like you to be thinking about any suggestions you have and if you'd like to be in charge."

Evie stared at her. "But I've only been working for you a couple of months."

"I know, but I like what I see. Believe me, I'm used to sizing people up quickly. I had to know if I could trust my partner not to step all over me, figuratively or literally. I would like us to work together. As partners." Dominique sipped her tea, then nodded. "Interesting. Yes, I think we could be partners. After all, we're practically family, and we will be when Charlie marries Clay."

Evie honestly didn't know what to say. The offer thrilled her. She had dozens of ideas for a new studio and just as many suggestions for different classes.

"Thank you," she stammered. "That's so nice of you."

"Nice?" Dominique raised her eyebrows. "How delicious. I've become a nice person. It's strange, but oddly satisfying."

She rose. "I must go and find Charlie. I wouldn't tell her when I was arriving, so it would be a surprise. She'll be both pleased to see me and slightly annoyed that I kept her guessing." Dominique laughed. "A perfect combination."

She reached for her coat, then paused. "Oh, Evie, please get this sad little studio some Christmas decorations. Use the company credit card. Go wild. I want my girls to be excited when they walk in here."

Dominique smiled again, tossed her coat over her shoulder and swept out of the room. Evie was left in the chair, slightly breathless, as if she'd just survived a small tornado.

Her mind hopped from topic to topic, unable to settle. There was too much to consider.

The Christmas decorations were easy enough. She would ask Dante to help her get a tree. Buying ornaments would be fun. As for the rest of what Dominique had said, Evie wasn't sure. The new studio would be wonderful. As for being a partner, the offer was tempting. Despite her slightly odd ways, Dominique was brilliant and easy to work for. But accepting meant staying, and Evie had always planned to leave Fool's Gold.

Staying would mean being around her family, which was both good and bad. Staying meant being a part of the town, of craziness every Christmas. Staying meant complications with Dante. She'd gone into their relationship with the idea she was leaving. If she didn't, how would things end?

Staying meant belonging.

Evie stood and carried both mugs into the small bathroom. She washed them in the sink and dried them before putting them back into the cupboard. Staying meant reconciling with her mother and accepting that, while May had made mistakes, she was genuinely sorry and wanted to make amends. It meant letting go of the anger she'd carried with her like a talisman.

Perhaps the healthiest decision, Evie realized. But without the hurt and anger, she wasn't sure who she would be.

"I GUESS I DIDN'T think this part through," Evie admitted, trying not to laugh.

Dante obviously didn't find anything about the situation amusing. Probably because he was tired and hungry and wasn't the kind of guy to enjoy shopping for a Christmas tree.

Or maybe it wasn't the shopping itself, but the

fact that she'd asked him to carry a seven-foot-tall tree three blocks in the cold and then drag it up a flight of stairs to the studio.

Narrow stairs, where the too-large tree was now stuck.

"I'm sorry," Evie said, staring up through the branches at the scowling man. "Seriously."

"Uh-huh. You're not sorry. You're having fun."

She bit the inside of her lip in an attempt to keep from smiling. "No, I'm not."

"Right." He grabbed the thick trunk with both hands. "I'm going to give this thing one more try. If I can't get it to move, I'll resign myself to slowly starving to death up here."

He kind of had a point, she thought, realizing the tree blocked the only way up or down.

"On three," she said, taking hold of the top of the tree and planning to push.

"Don't help," Dante told her.

"I'm helping."

"You'll get hurt. I can do this."

As he spoke, he began to pull. Despite his instructions, she pushed from the top. Nothing happened. She pushed harder and felt a little bit of give.

"One more time," she yelled.

"Stop help—"

But it was too late. She shoved, he pulled and the tree suddenly moved free, zipping up the stairs, hitting Dante in the center of his chest. They both went sprawling.

Evie found herself flying forward. She braced herself on her hands and landed somewhat gently on the stairs, facedown.

"You okay?" she asked, almost afraid to stand up and look.

"Fine." Dante's voice was slightly strangled.

"I'm going to order a pizza. Pepperoni all right with you?"

"Sure."

She rolled onto her back and pulled her cell phone out of her pocket, then called the local pizza place and put in their order. After she'd hung up, she stood and brushed off the needles decorating the front of her coat. Finally, she risked looking upstairs.

Dante still lay on his back, the tree on top of him, the base of its trunk maybe three inches from his chin.

"Want to talk about it?" she asked.

"Not really."

She went upstairs and helped roll the tree off of him. He rose and glanced down at the tree on the floor and the layer of needles everywhere.

"Whose idea was this?" he asked.

"My boss's."

"I admire her willingness to delegate."

An hour later the tree was in the stand and the

lights were strung. When the pizza guy arrived, Dante disappeared downstairs to pay him and returned with a pizza box, a bottle of wine and two wineglasses.

"I didn't order wine," she said. "Do they deliver wine?"

"They do not. We have a small wine cellar in the office."

"Because you never know when you're going to need a bottle of merlot to get through the day?"

"Something like that."

While she served their pizza, he opened the wine and then poured. They settled across from each other and each grabbed a slice. The scent of pine mingled with the fragrance of cheese and pepperoni.

"Wine, pizza and a Christmas tree," she said. "What's not to like?"

"Can I get back to you on that?"

"Don't be a Grinch. You know this is fun."

His blue eyes brightened with amusement. "You're fun. Is that enough?"

"It works for me."

He glanced at the tree, then back at her. "You've been talking about getting one of those for your place. Still thinking it's a good idea?"

"I am. I'm also thinking of getting a cat."

"As a decoration?"

"I'm not sure he would like that idea."

"He? You've got a cat in mind?"

She thought about the black-and-white one she'd seen at the shelter. Despite how busy she'd been, he kept popping into her mind.

"Sort of. He was very sweet and needs a forever home." She was still getting used to the idea.

"Cats are okay," Dante said, surprising her.

"I would have thought you were the dog type. You know, slavish devotion and someone to play fetch with."

"I don't have any burning desire to play fetch, and I respect how cats make you earn their interest. Cats are like lawyers. Discreet, quiet and watchful."

She managed to keep from choking as she laughed. "You're a weird guy. You know that, right?"

"It's been hinted at before." He looked at the tree. "Your students are going to be excited."

"I'm sure it will help with the holiday spirit." She thought about what he'd told her about his upbringing. "What were Christmases like when you were a kid?"

He shrugged and reached for his glass of wine. "Quiet. Good. We didn't have a lot of money and it was just my mom and me, but we had fun. We went to midnight services on Christmas Eve. I understood we were poor and didn't expect a lot, but

Mom always made the day special." He hesitated. "I miss her at the holidays."

Evie nodded. "Sure. She was your family."

"She would have liked you."

Evie told herself not to read too much into the statement. "Thank you. I would have loved to have met her."

He sipped his wine. "What about you and your family?"

"Christmases were loud," she said, remembering her brothers getting the family up early to see all the presents. There were other memories—times when she'd felt left out, but she wasn't in the mood to explore them.

"After my mom died and I was sent to the military school, Christmas was different," Dante said. "They kept us on campus. My senior year, one of the sponsors invited a couple of us to his house for Christmas." He reached for another slice of pizza and grinned. "Let's just say it's the first time I figured out the rich really are different."

"Nice house?"

"Nice mansion. It was three stories, I don't know how many bedrooms. I'd never seen a tree that big, even at the mall. The family had presents for us and a stocking. I'd never had a stocking before."

"We always had stockings," Evie said, remembering her twelfth Christmas, when her mother had given her lip gloss and mascara. An acknowledgement that the teen years weren't that far away.

There were good memories, she reminded herself. Maybe instead of focusing on the ones that were bad, she should start looking for the more pleasant ones.

"Have you talked to Gideon?" Dante asked, his voice casual.

"About the narration? Not yet. He left me a message. I need to call him back. He said he has some ideas about the story. Why?"

"He mentioned it at the book wrapping."

She glanced at Dante, wondering if she was imagining things or if he genuinely wasn't pleased about her working with Gideon. In your dreams, she thought, taking a sip of her wine. While the idea of Dante jealous was kind of exciting, reality was very different. He'd made it clear what he was and wasn't looking for in their relationship. Them being together was all about getting through the holidays, about having fun together. Neither of them was committed to anything else, and if she allowed herself to think anything different, she was opening herself up to a world of hurt.

Fourteen

"Extend," Evie said, holding out her arm to demonstrate. "Reach and lift." She turned slowly, then sank down into the final move.

Lillie smiled. "You're so good," she said with an easy smile. "When you do it, it looks right."

"It looks right when you do it, too." Evie stepped behind the girl so they were both facing the mirror. "Now lift and reach and lift."

She moved with Lillie, lightly pressing her palm against the girl's back to keep her straight.

"Lean, turn, stretch."

Lillie did as instructed. She made one last turn and sank down, her fingertips curled delicately, her wrists perfectly bent.

"See," Evie said approvingly. "That was perfect."

Lillie jumped to her feet and spun in a circle. "I got it! I got it!"

"Look at you," Patience said, walking in to the studio.

"Mom!" Lillie ran to her mother, her arms outstretched. "Did you see me?"

"I did. Lillie, that was beautiful."

Lille dashed off to collect her coat. Patience turned to Evie.

"Thanks for working with her. I know she doesn't get the steps as quickly as the other girls."

"She works hard and has fun. As long as she's enjoying the classes, I'm thrilled to have her. She's a great kid."

"Thank you."

Evie knew that Dominique would say Lillie was one of the "unfortunates." Those not blessed with the dancing gene. But Evie found a special kind of pleasure teaching the Lillies of the world. As far as Evie was concerned, if Lillie enjoyed herself and ended up with good memories about her part in the performance, then the experience was a total success for both of them.

"Are you staying sane?" Patience asked. "I heard the cheerleaders wanted your help with their Pom-Pom-A-Thon."

"I'm running ragged," Evie admitted. "But only a couple more weeks and everything will be done. Then I can collapse through New Year's."

"Tell me about it."

Lillie returned, her boots on her feet and her ballet shoes in her hand. "I'm ready, Mom."

"Okay. Off we go. We have to stop at the grocery store and get more supplies. Your grandmother is still on a cookie tear." Patience waved. "Hang in there and I'll do the same."

"Will do."

She and Lillie left. Evie glanced at the clock. She had about an hour until her next class. Time enough to grab something to eat and maybe stop by Morgan's Books for something to read. As soon as Christmas was over, she was going to put her feet up and not move for a week. There were no classes between the twenty-sixth and the first of the year. While she couldn't afford a real vacation, she could hide out and rest.

"You're starting a cult."

She looked up and saw Dante standing in the doorway to the studio. As always, the sight of him set her heart beating a little faster.

"What are you talking about?" she asked.

"Those girls. You're training them to take over the world."

She laughed. "You're not making any sense."

He walked toward her and took her hand, then led her to the window in the reception area.

"Look down there," he said, pointing. "What do you see?"

"Lillie and Patience."

"And how is Lillie wearing her hair?"

Evie saw the braids tightly wrapped around her head, then reached up and touched her own.

"A coincidence."

"I don't think so. All your students are copying you. It's charming." He put his arm around her and pulled her close. "You're their role model."

"I think I'm more of a cautionary tale."

He kissed the top of her head. "You're being too hard on yourself."

He turned her toward him and kissed her again, this time on her mouth.

"What time's your last class?" he asked.

"I finish at six and then I head over to the ranch for the hayrides."

"Me, too." He groaned. "I'd rather be home, having takeout with you."

"Me, too." She put her hands on his shoulders and stared into his blue eyes. "But instead, you're helping my family. You're a really good guy. I don't usually fall for the good ones. I tend to be attracted to the losers of the world."

He leaned close to whisper in her ear. "It's the sex. You can't help yourself."

Evie was still laughing as he strolled down the stairs.

"I DON'T THINK SO," Evie said, staring at herself in the mirror.

"Come on," Annabelle said, handing over a set of pointed ears. "You look adorable. I can't do it." She patted her belly. "I'm pregnant. How would that look? And Heidi has to handle the petting zoo. You know how the goats get when they have company. They're all so happy, they could accidentally knock over a four-year-old."

Evie stared down at herself. She was wearing a green flared skirt, a long-sleeved red-and-green sweater, along with red-and-white-striped tights. Finishing up the outfit was a green hat and elf ears and pointy green elf shoes.

"I don't want to be an elf," she muttered. "What was I thinking?"

Annabelle beamed at her. "That's the spirit."

"I'm crabby."

"Crabby works, as long as you smile for the pictures. Come on. I just heard a car pull up."

Somehow, when she hadn't been looking, Evie had been roped into helping with the annual hayrides at the ranch—a tradition Heidi and her grandfather had started when they'd first moved to the ranch a couple of years ago. Families drove out for an old-fashioned hayride. The various animals were available for petting, families could take pictures, and if they were very lucky, it might snow.

Evie sort of remembered agreeing to help, but

that was before she'd figured out how busy she was going to be with the production and the other activities someone always seemed to be volunteering her for.

"I wrapped books," she told Annabelle. "Isn't that enough?"

Annabelle raised her chin. "Excuse me, but I'm not in charge of the hayrides. That's Heidi's thing."

"Right," Evie muttered, following her pregnant sister-in-law to-be out of the guest bedroom and toward the rear of the house.

She wanted to complain that she'd had to help everyone. Heidi tonight, Annabelle with the books, her mother with the pet adoption. Only all three of her brothers had shown up to refurbish her production sets, so it wasn't as though she could really complain. And in truth it was kind of fun to be with everyone, in a low-key setting. Still, these were the most intense holidays she could remember.

She stepped out the back door and walked down to the lit pathway. The night was freezing, but clear. So far there wasn't any snow in the forecast. Stars twinkled in the dark sky.

The wagon, decorated with swinging battery-operated lanterns and wreaths, stood by the barn. Shane had already hooked up the horses. Christmas music played from a stereo somewhere, and the scent of hot chocolate drifted on the air. Two cars had already pulled up, and children and adults were spilling out into the hay-riding loading area.

Evie watched them, seeing a familiar blonde woman. She was about to wave to Nevada when she realized the hair was all wrong, as was the man with her. Another of the triplets, she thought. Montana, she remembered.

She walked over. "You came for a hayride."

"How could we resist? I can't believe you have time to be here. Everyone is talking about what you're doing with the dance," Montana said. "We can't wait to see it. This is Simon, my husband, and our daughter, Skye."

Evie glanced down at the baby, prepared to give the obligatory coo. New parents expected that. But as she parted her lips to say something, Skye opened her eyes and stared at her. The baby's mouth was a perfect rosebud shape. The corners turned up as tiny hands clapped together in excitement. Skye giggled and reached for her.

"She likes you," Montana said with a laugh. "She's such a flirt. Would you like to hold her?"

Evie nodded and held out her arms. Montana handed over the happy baby.

Skye was lighter than Evie expected, but warm and smelled sweet. The child held her gaze, still smiling and waving her tiny fingers.

Beyond promising herself that she would never want her child to feel about her the way she felt about May, Evie hadn't thought much about having children. She'd seen marriage and kids as some vague future thing. Someday. Just not now.

But holding Skye made her ache in a way she never had before. She saw possibilities and happiness in the baby's face. Parts of her long dormant stirred to life. She wanted to belong, she realized. She wanted what others considered normal or even traditional. A husband. A family. She no longer wanted to live her life on the outside—watching everyone else be a part of something larger than themselves.

She briefly wondered what Annabelle and Shane's baby would look like and suffered a pang when she realized if she kept to her plan of leaving, she wouldn't be here to see him or her born.

"She's so beautiful," Evie murmured, then passed back the baby.

"I wish I could take credit," Montana said with a laugh. "But she gets her looks from her dad."

"Have fun," Evie told her, then reluctantly walked toward the wagon.

More cars pulled up, and the wagon was loaded. Evie was kept busy posing for pictures with the children and helping people up and down the stairs. When Athena, the most wayward of the goats, made a break for freedom, Evie caught her by her red-and-green collar.

"Not so fast, my pretty," she told the goat. Athena dipped her head and nibbled on Evie's shoe.

They did a steady business. Sometime around eight, she took a break.

"You look great," Dante murmured as he passed her with a tray of clean mugs for the cocoa. "Love the ears. Seriously. Do you get to keep them?"

She grinned. "Having an elf fantasy, are we?"

"The outfit is really working for me."

They were by the back door. Music and laughter surrounded them, but they seemed cut off from the rest of the world. She stared into his eyes and wondered what it would be like to get lost in a guy like Dante. What it would be like to not be afraid to love.

"How are you doing with your family?" he asked. "Too much togetherness?"

"I'm doing okay," she said, pleased she was able to say the words and know they were the truth. "They're growing on me." She grinned. "In a good way." She touched his arm. "Brace yourself."

"I'm braced."

"You were right. About me and my mom."

"Can I get that on a statue of some kind?"

She laughed. "No, but I'm going to say thank you. I'm spending more time with her, and it's not too bad. I'm trying to see things from her perspective. She was young when her husband died. There was a lot on her plate. She could have done better, but no one is perfect."

"Forgiveness?"

"I'm getting there."

"I'm glad." He kissed her lightly. "And later, you, me and the ears?"

She was still laughing when she walked back toward the petting zoo.

"There she is!"

Evie turned toward the familiar voice and spotted her mother walking toward her with an older woman. It took her a second to recognize the mayor.

"This is my daughter, Evie," May was saying. "She's a wonderful dancer. She's taken on *The Dance of the Winter King* by herself, and we're all so proud of her."

Evie felt herself flushing, unaccustomed to the praise. "I'm stepping in to help," she murmured. "I didn't want my students to be disappointed."

"I'm sure they won't be," the mayor told her. "Dominique is thrilled with the work you're doing." The older woman took her hand. "I know you're going to be very happy here in Fool's Gold. You need this town and we need you."

The statement was meant kindly, Evie told herself. Even if it was a little spooky.

"Thank you."

She returned to her elf duties. Heidi gave in to

several pleas from children and brought Priscilla down to the barn for pictures. Evie found herself organizing the line and then taking several of the pictures so the families could all be together by the goats and the elephant and the decorated wagon.

"I want you next to me," a little girl said, then turned to her father. "Daddy, can the girl elf be in the picture?"

Dante moved up next to her and took the camera. "I've got this one," he told her. "Go on. Be a star."

"It's the ears," she told him in a whisper. "Apparently they're irresistible."

He chuckled and waved her into position. She crouched next to the little girl and smiled. After that, Evie found herself posing in several pictures. The evening sped by as more families arrived for their hayride.

A little before nine, the last of the cars drove away. Dante and Shane walked Priscilla back to her custom elephant house while Heidi and Evie carried in trays of mugs to be washed.

"That was fun," Evie admitted as she put a tray on the kitchen counter. "Exhausting but good. How many nights do you have the hayrides?"

She glanced at Heidi and saw her sister-in-law standing with her hand pressed against her stomach, her expression joyful and intense.

"Heidi?" Evie took a step toward her. "Are you all right?"

"I'm fine."

"You look… I don't know. *Strange* isn't the right word. You're not sick, are you?"

"No." Heidi glanced around, as if checking if they were alone, then she turned to Evie. "I shouldn't say anything, but I'm just bursting with the news. Can you keep a secret?"

Normally a statement like that would have had Evie backing out of the room. But Heidi didn't look like the information was going to be scary or upsetting. Instead she was practically glowing with excitement.

"Okay. Sure."

Heidi touched her arm and leaned close. "I'm pregnant," she whispered. "I just got confirmation this morning." Her fingers tightened slightly.

Pregnant? Evie stared at her for a second, then hugged her. "Heidi, that's so wonderful. Congratulations. Rafe doesn't know, does he? He was way too calm for a guy finding out he's going to be a father for the first time."

Heidi grinned. "No and you can't tell him. I'm waiting until Christmas Eve, after the performance. I thought telling him then would be the perfect Christmas present."

"He'll be thrilled," she said. And scared. A

baby. She thought of adorable Skye, whom she'd held earlier, and felt a small ache in her heart.

"I'm just so happy," Heidi told her. "We've talked about starting a family, but it wasn't real to me before. Our child is going to grow up here, on the ranch. In Fool's Gold. I feel so blessed."

Evie knew that Heidi had gone through a lot to end up where she was today. The blessings had been earned the hard way. But in the end, she'd had her happy ending. Evie wondered if anyone could find one or if they were reserved for a special few.

Shane strolled into the kitchen, ending any chance to continue the conversation. Evie went outside. She saw Dante leading a very reluctant Athena toward the goat barn.

"You have to go inside," he told the animal. "It's cold outside. You need to be warm."

Athena made a grumbling noise in her throat.

"Fine," Dante told her with a sigh. "Here."

He handed over a piece of carrot. The goat took it and then followed dutifully as he went inside.

She thought about how Dante had been so patient with the children and how he'd teased her about her elf ears. As she'd known for a while, he was one of the good ones.

He stepped out of the goat barn and carefully closed the door, then spotted her and waved. Moonlight touched his face, illuminated the handsome lines, while his broad shoulders cast a shadow on the frozen ground. She thought of the baby she'd held and the longing in her heart, and then she knew.

She'd fallen in love with Dante.

She wasn't supposed to have given her heart. In fact, she would have sworn she was immune to that kind of thing. He'd made it clear he wasn't interested in any kind of long-term relationship, that he didn't do love or forever. He wouldn't risk those kinds of feelings. She knew she'd never been in love before. Not really.

So how had this happened? Was it because of everything else going on? Had she been so caught up in the performance and the town and fitting in that she'd forgotten to protect her heart? Or was it simply that Dante was the one? The one man in the world who was everything she'd ever wanted, and once she met him, falling had been inevitable?

Either way, she was in love with him. A reality that both excited and terrified her. Because she had no idea what she was supposed to do now.

Fifteen

"I'M REALLY MORE a dog person," May said with a sigh. "I hope the cats couldn't tell."

Evie put the last of the brushes and combs on the towel to dry. "You were very affectionate with the cats," she told her mother. "I don't think they had their feelings hurt."

May raised her eyebrows. "Are you mocking me?"

"A little."

"I see." She smiled. "Fine. I suppose it's a silly thing to say. Worrying that the cats will know they're not my favorite."

"Imagine how the fish feel."

They'd just spent an afternoon grooming pets for the upcoming adoption. The adoption was in two days. After that, it was a fast ten days until the performance. Then she could rest. But between then and now was enough work to keep fifteen elves busy.

They collected their coats and walked outside. It was nearly five and already dark.

May looked at her. "Don't you have dance classes today? Did I make you cancel them?"

"No. The school holiday programs are all today, so there weren't any lessons scheduled. That's why I asked if we could do the grooming today instead of tomorrow. Starting on Monday, we get access to the high school's auditorium, and we all get to practice on the actual stage. That will be fun."

And cause for panic, she thought, wondering if she really could pull the show together in time. A problem for tomorrow, she told herself.

"Want to get some dinner?" May asked, her voice suddenly tentative.

Evie was tired and ready for a few hours of quiet, but somehow she found herself wanting to spend more time with her mother. After taking Dante's advice and accepting her share of the responsibility for their continued estrangement, she found herself a little more open to the thought of family.

"Sure," she said.

They discussed options and ended up deciding on Angelo's for Italian food.

They drove into town and found parking behind the restaurant. The whitewashed building had been draped in colored lights that glowed against the pale background. In the spring and summer, a big patio provided outdoor seating, but in the middle of winter, the tables and chairs had been put away. A Christmas tree took their place.

They walked inside and were shown to a quiet booth by the front windows. After glancing over the menu, May looked at Evie.

"Thanks for helping with the hayrides," she said. "I think everyone had a good time."

"They did," Evie agreed. "The kids loved having a chance to pet Priscilla."

"She's very good with children. I think she's happy, all settled with her new herd."

Evie wasn't sure Priscilla would consider a pony and a pig much of a herd, but they were company.

Their server appeared, and they each ordered a glass of wine and the house lasagna. For once Evie wasn't going to sweat the calories. She'd been dancing a lot, and if she had to deal with an extra few pounds after Christmas, then just like much of America, she would make a resolution to lose weight.

"Are you happy with your townhouse?" May asked.

"It works for me," Evie said. "The location is good. I can walk to work, which is kind of fun. I'm sure saving on gas."

May offered her a piece of bread from the basket, which Evie refused, then took one for herself. "You're renting, aren't you? I was wondering if you'd thought of maybe buying something." Her mother picked up the small ceramic container of butter, then put it back down. She glanced at the table, then the bread, then back at Evie. "I would like to help with the down payment. If you plan to stay. In town, I mean."

Evie stared at her mother, confused about the entire conversation until she realized that May was nervous. About the offer and maybe the question of whether or not Evie was planning on staying in Fool's Gold.

As little as two weeks ago, Evie would have announced she was leaving as soon as she had a year's worth of experience. That would have given her enough time to save enough money to relocate. But since talking to Dominique, she was less sure about her plans. Her boss's suggestions for the business were exciting, and the idea of being a partner thrilled her. There was also the unexpected tug of family.

The server appeared with their wine and their salads. Evie waited until she was gone, then drew in a breath.

"I'm not sure what I'm going to do," she admitted. "Whether I want to buy or not. But I appreciate your offer. It's very generous."

Her mother studied her anxiously. "So you might be staying?"

Evie smiled. "Yes. I think I might."

May relaxed against the back of the booth. “That’s good to hear. I had hoped you would like it here. Everyone is so welcoming. The town has an interesting history. You should get Annabelle to tell you about the women who first came here. They’re from the Máa-zib tribe. Very matriarchal. It’s fascinating.” May frowned. “Hmm, didn’t the Mayans predict the world is going to end soon? Sometime this year?”

“If it is, it had better hurry,” Evie said, stabbing a piece of lettuce with her fork. “The year is nearly over. And if anyone is listening, I would really appreciate being able to get through *The Dance of the Winter King* before the world ends. My girls have worked hard and deserve their chance to shine.”

May raised her wineglass. “We’ll toast the girls.”

They sipped their wine. Evie gave in to temptation and took a piece of bread, then put a little butter on her plate. She’d just taken her first, amazingly delicious bite when her mother asked, “How are things going with Dante?”

Fortunately Evie hadn’t started swallowing yet, so she was able to compose herself and not choke. But chewing and swallowing only took so long, and then she was still left with a question she didn’t know how to answer. Despite her tentative peace with her mother, she wasn’t ready to announce she'd fallen in love with a man who didn't want to love her back.

"We're doing well," she said instead. "He's a good guy."

"So Rafe tells me. Although he does have a bit of a reputation with women."

"Dante made it clear from the start that he doesn't do long-term relationships." She couldn't fault him for leading her on.

"You're all right with that?"

"I wasn't looking for a relationship at all," she admitted. "This whole thing started with us getting each other through the holidays. Now it's more than that. We like each other." Which was the truth. After all, she did like him. She also loved him, but she wasn't ready to talk about that yet.

"Tell me about the other men in your life."

Evie wrinkled her nose. "There's not much to tell. I've dated some good guys and some not-so-good guys, but I haven't ever fallen in love. I guess I haven't met the one." Until now, she thought with a sigh. But why go there?

Her mother nodded slowly, as if not surprised. "I'm responsible for that."

"Mom, I'm willing to put a lot on you, but I don't think you get the blame for my sucky love life."

"You were afraid to find someone you could love because you didn't want to be hurt again. Rejected. I would guess you're afraid to love someone because you're convinced he won't love you back."

Evie opened her mouth, then closed it. May's words had a ring of truth. "I have been afraid to give my heart," she admitted slowly.

May blinked several times, as if fighting tears. "I'm so sorry."

"Don't apologize. I picked the guys. Not you."

"But if I'd been there for you…" May held up her hand. "I'll stop now. I want us to have a nice dinner. I've said what I wanted to say and apologized. You can think about it, and we'll deal with it again another time. How's that?"

"I can live with that."

"Good."

They talked about the costumes for the performance. Evie had seen a few of them, although not all. They were scattered around town, being altered and redone by an assortment of volunteers.

"I'm looking forward to comparing this year's dances with what was done in previous years," she said. "I asked Clay to record the whole thing for me."

"You know we're all coming," May said. "I've already bought my tickets."

"I hope you enjoy it."

"I will. When you were little, I loved to watch you dance."

Their server appeared with their entrées. When she'd left, May leaned toward Evie.

"Why did you leave Juilliard? Do you mind telling me? I never understood your decision."

Evie shrugged. "I wasn't good enough. After six months, I was called into the office and told I didn't have the talent. I worked hard, but without the raw ability, I couldn't achieve their standards. Rather than wait until they forced me to leave, I quit."

May's eyes widened. "I can't believe that. You're a wonderful dancer."

"You're not a professional. Trust me, I'm no Dominique Guérin." She thought about being only a few weeks from her eighteenth birthday and knowing she was all alone in the world. She'd had nothing but a shattered dream and the blistered and callused feet of a dancer.

"I wish you'd come home," her mother whispered. "I wish I'd told you I wanted you to come home."

"Neither of us were ready then, Mom," Evie said. "We needed time. I needed to grow up."

"I think I did, too. I missed so much. I'm such a fool."

"You're a good person. You just got a little sideways."

"You're being generous with me. I don't deserve it."

"I think I get to decide that. Not you."

Evie waited for the anger to reemerge, but there was only lingering sadness and a growing sense of peace. Yes, May had made mistakes. She'd been thoughtless. But she'd also had stresses and responsibilities. Evie realized she could spend the rest of her life hating her mother. But to what end? She would only end up bitter and alone. May had acknowledged what she'd done wrong and tried to make amends. Wasn't it better to forgive and take what was offered?

"Is that lasagna?"

Evie looked up and saw Clay standing by the table, his gaze on her plate. She sighed.

"Is Charlie working?"

"Uh-huh. Move over, kid."

She did as he asked, and he slid in next to her.

"Hi, Mom," he said as he reached for the bread with one hand and her fork with another. "You weren't going to eat this, were you?"

"Apparently not."

"Good. I'm starving. So what are you two talking about?"

Evie flagged the server, knowing she would have to order another entrée if she expected to eat. Then she smiled at her mother and said, "Girl stuff. Just girl stuff."

"HE DID NOT," Charlie said as she dumped chocolate chips into a bowl.

"I swear." Evie made an X on her chest. She'd just told Charlie about Clay showing up at the restaurant and eating her dinner.

"I'm going to have a serious talk with him," Charlie promised. "He can't do that."

"He misses you when you're working," Heidi said, stirring butter in a second bowl. Evie wasn't sure, but thought she might be making peanut-butter cookies.

Annabelle handed two eggs to Heidi. "She's right. I mean, I would have attacked him if he'd tried to take food from me, but he got lonely. Like a little puppy."

"A puppy who needs some training," Charlie grumbled.

Evie grinned.

The four of them were in Shane and Annabelle's new house, making Christmas cookies. Evie had gotten the call the previous evening for a Sunday afternoon bake-fest. Just the four "sisters," Annabelle had said. While she had a million things she needed to be doing, she'd found herself saying she would be there.

Now cooling racks overflowed with cookies. By the time these last batches were done, the sugar cookies would be room temperature and ready for frosting.

"When I was a kid," Heidi said, breaking the eggs over the bowl, "Christmas was a big deal. We had our extended, carnival family and planned out who would cook what. Someone took the turkey, someone else the potatoes and so on."

"My holidays were quiet," Annabelle said. "When my parents were together, they were fighting, and after they were divorced, they traveled." She smiled. "Don't feel bad. I liked when they were gone. I spent the holidays with my friends, and their parents felt sorry for me, so they went out of their way to make me feel welcome. It was like being a visiting princess."

"I liked the holidays," Charlie told them. "Especially when my mom was away performing. Then it was my dad and me."

"So we're all dysfunctional," Evie said, keeping her tone light. "Except for Heidi."

"Yes, but not to worry." Charlie grinned. "No one likes her."

"Cheap talk." Heidi stirred the peanut butter into her cookie batter. "I know you all love me."

As far as Evie could tell, no one else knew about Heidi's pregnancy. She really was keeping it a secret until Christmas Eve when she told Rafe. Evie wasn't sure why she'd been Heidi's confidant, but she had to admit she liked knowing about the tiny life growing inside of her sister-in-law.

"What was Shane like when he was a kid?" Annabelle asked. "Any embarrassing stories you want to share? Something I can torture him with later?"

"He was in a band," Evie told her. "When we moved to L.A. For about six months."

"A band?" Annabelle leaned against the counter and sighed. "You've just given me the best gift ever. Did he sing?"

"I think he played bass and maybe sang backup."

Charlie and Heidi both stared at her, their expressions expectant.

"And?" Charlie prodded.

Evie tried to remember what her brothers had done when they'd been younger. "Clay dressed up like Dorothy from *The Wizard of Oz* one Halloween and Rafe crashed his best friend's car the same day his friend got it as a gift."

Heidi's eyes widened in horror.

"It wasn't a bad accident," Evie added quickly. "Just a fender bender. Actually I think it was the fender that had to be replaced."

"Thank goodness," Heidi said. "If it was serious, I couldn't tease him about it."

"He was humiliated, not hurt," Evie assured her.

While they'd been talking, Charlie had finished mixing the chocolate chip cookies and was putting spoonfuls onto a cookie sheet. When she turned to put the trays into the oven, Annabelle picked up the spoon.

"I'm not supposed to eat raw cookie dough, right?" she asked. "It's the eggs."

Charlie pushed the cookie sheet onto the oven rack, closed the door and straightened, then grabbed the spoon from Annabelle's hand.

"No, you're not supposed to eat that." She held up the bag of chocolate chips and shook it. A few rattled inside. "I saved you some."

Annabelle smiled, then sniffed. "You're so good to me."

"I swear, if you cry, I'll…"

"Yes? You'll what? Hit me? Hit a pregnant woman? I don't think so."

"You're so smug."

"I know. It's not as good as being tall like you, but I'll take it."

"They're always like this," Heidi told Evie. "They squabble and then they make up. I think it's because they're total opposites and yet completely alike."

"That's not possible," Charlie said.

Evie studied the two of them. "I see what you mean."

Heidi handed her a fork to start making the cross marks on the peanut butter cookies.

This time last year, Evie had been in Los Angeles, in her tiny apartment, working as a waitress and spending her Sundays as an L.A. Stallions cheerleader. She'd been pretty much on her own, with only a few friends she could depend on. This year everything was different. She was with her family, had new friends and was crazy in love.

Sure there were complications, but she had to admit, when comparing the two scenarios, her life had taken a turn for the better. The much better.

Sixteen

Evie stood on the stage in the high school auditorium and looked out at the rows of empty seats. With the upper-level seating, there were nearly eight hundred seats. That was a huge intimidation factor for her students, which was one of the reasons all their practices were now going to be here. They had to get used to the bigger stage and the—

Her cell phone rang.

"Hello?"

"It's Gideon. Where are you?"

Evie frowned and glanced around at the empty auditorium. She and Gideon had a noon meeting to discuss the changes he wanted to make in the voice-over for the show. He was late. "I'm at the high school. Where are you?"

"At the convention center. The sound system sucks, by the way. I've already put a call into Mayor Marsha. She said I can bring in any equipment I like." He chuckled. "She has no idea what she's agreed to."

"Why are you at the convention center?"

"Because that's where the performance is."

Evie's stomach contracted. "No. It's at the high school."

"It *was* at the high school. But there isn't enough seating. This was all decided months ago. Didn't anyone tell you?"

"No." She had a feeling Miss Monica knew, but that was just one more detail the dance instructor hadn't shared when she'd run off with her gentleman friend. "Wait. The adoption is there. How will there be room?"

"It's a big convention center," Gideon told her. "There's room."

She promised to hurry and raced to her car. It only took a few minutes to drive to the convention center. As she waited at one of the few stoplights in town, she tried to recall the conversations she'd had with her students. Now that she thought about it, she'd always talked about the stage. She'd meant the one at the high school but hadn't been specific. No wonder no one had corrected her. They hadn't known she was wrong.

She pulled into the convention center parking lot and stopped at the entrance that had a large pickup truck in front of it. It looked like the sort of vehicle Gideon would drive. She grabbed her bag and paperwork and raced inside.

Sure enough, a big stage had been set up, and there were rows and rows of chairs.

"Oh, no," she said, coming to a stop and staring at the empty seats. "There has to be room for at least a couple of thousand people."

"Three thousand, two hundred," Gideon said, strolling up to greet her. "Mayor Marsha is convinced the program is going to be a success."

"That's too many people. My girls will freak. I would freak if it were me."

"They'll be fine."

"Easy for you to say. You're not the one doing the dances."

She was still trying to process the change in venue. All this time she'd had the high school auditorium in her head. Why had no one mentioned the convention center?

"Look at it this way," Gideon said with a wink. "At least you won't have far to go after the pet adoption."

"I'm going to throw up."

Gideon held up both hands and took a step back. "No reason for that to happen. Take a deep breath. In for the count of four, hold for the count of four, exhale for the count of four."

She stared at him. "Excuse me?"

"It's a breathing exercise. You work up to a count of ten or twelve, but that takes practice."

"Seriously?"

Gideon surprised her by winking. "I have mysterious depths."

"Apparently."

He was casually dressed in jeans and a long-sleeved plaid shirt, the sleeves rolled up to his elbows. She studied the part of the tattoo visible on his forearm and then looked into his dark, unreadable eyes. She could imagine Gideon doing a lot of things. Holding a gun, giving orders, riding a motorcycle, but she couldn't picture him on a yoga mat practicing his breathing.

"Ex-military?" she asked.

"Maybe."

Despite the three thousand, two hundred empty seats and the incredible list of things she had to get through between this moment and the performance, she laughed. "Because if you told me, you'd have to kill me?"

"Something like that." He shrugged. "I've been places and done things. One day I decided I was done. When my tour ended I went looking for a way to make peace. With myself, at least, and maybe the world. I ended up in a shack in Bali."

"Bali? Not Tibet?"

"I'm more a beach guy."

"Nice work if you can get it."

"There was a teacher there. He taught me—"

For a second something flashed through Gideon's eyes. Evie couldn't say what it was, but she would swear there was pain involved. Something cold and ugly that made her shiver. Then he blinked and it was gone.

"He taught me how to keep on moving forward," Gideon continued. "When I left, I remembered a buddy of mine talking about this place. He grew up here, and when he talked about home, he made it sound like the only place worth living."

"Who was the guy?"

"Ford Hendrix."

"Oh. I know who he is. Well, not him, but his sisters." She laughed. "Did he also tell you that living in this town is like trying to put a puzzle together? I wonder if I'll ever get all the names straight. But I think my mom knows his mom. But he's not here."

"He's still serving. He'll be back soon."

She thought about asking "back from where," but reality returned in the form of all those empty chairs and a ball of panic bouncing off the walls of her stomach.

"Did I already mention I think I'm going to throw up?"

"Yes, but now I don't believe you."

"Fine. Risk your shoes. See if I care." She shook her head. "Okay. I'm focusing. The changes in the script for the narration are great. I love them." She pulled several sheets of paper out of her handbag and shuffled through them. "I want to make sure we're on target with the transitions of the dancers. I've marked this copy with where I think the girls will be moving on and off the stage."

He moved close and studied the pages. "Sure. I see what you're doing. So you want me to pause until everyone is off stage before starting?"

"Right." She glanced up at him. "You're coming to the dress rehearsal, aren't you?"

He nodded. "Give me your schedule. I'll get to at least one other before then, so we can do a run-through from the top."

"That would be great."

DANTE WALKED INTO THE convention center, still not sure why he'd been summoned. Mayor Marsha had called and gone on about a large space and the sound system. Just when he'd started wondering how he was going to politely get her off the phone, she'd asked him to meet Evie right away. He'd agreed, grateful to be able to hang up.

Now he watched her up on stage, standing close to Gideon, their heads bent over sheets of paper. Evie pointed to something and Gideon nodded. His arm brushed hers as he took another paper and held it close to the first.

His head knew there was nothing between

them. That Evie spent most nights in his bed, or he in hers. While neither of them was looking for a serious kind of relationship, they were, in the confines of what they had, monogamous. He'd considered himself civilized for many years now. Law-abiding. He was a lawyer, which made him, by definition, boring.

But deep inside, something stirred. Something heavy and ugly that wanted to propel him to the stage. He didn't just want to step between them, he wanted to push Gideon away. He wanted to hurt the other man and then stand over his broken body and pound his chest as a sign of victory.

The flush of intense emotion faded as quickly as it had risen, but the remnants left him shaken. What the hell was he thinking? Beat up some guy and then do a victory dance? What was he, seventeen again? Mature, sensible people didn't act like that. *He* didn't act like that.

Evie said something he couldn't hear, and Gideon walked away. A couple of seconds later, music filled the open space.

"That's it," Evie called and put down the papers. She shrugged out of her coat, revealing body-hugging dance clothes. As always, the sight of her body in all its perfection moved blood from his head to points farther south.

Then she began to dance.

She moved across the stage. She was strong and

elegant at the same time. Lithe, graceful. He could watch her forever.

Behind him, he heard quiet conversation. He turned and saw several of her students had walked in. They were dressed exactly like her—in black tights and black leotards. Their hair was in braids wrapped around their heads, just like her.

The girls, ranging in age from maybe seven to twelve, didn't notice him. They only saw Evie. A couple of them held out their arms, as if dancing with her. He heard whispers of "Beautiful" and "Oh, look at that turn."

They wanted to be just like her.

He knew Evie had been brought to Fool's Gold under difficult circumstances. The last thing she'd been looking for was a connection with her family. But she'd found that, along with a place to belong. He would guess her plans to leave in a few months were also unraveling. Fool's Gold was now home.

He was a man who had gone out of his way never to form serious connections. Oh, sure, he was friends with Rafe, but that was different. Caring about a woman meant risking more than he was willing to put on the line.

But what if Evie needed him to care now? Everything in her life was coming together. It would only be natural for her to start looking at the future. If her needs had changed, then he needed to back off. To make sure she wasn't expecting more than he could give. Only he wasn't ready to stop seeing her. He *liked* seeing her.

The music ended, and the girls clapped. Evie turned toward the sound and smiled when she saw her students. Then her gaze met his, and the smile became a little wicked.

He grinned in return.

Maybe he was reading too much into the situation, he told himself. Just because she was finding her way with her family and enjoying the town didn't mean she wanted more from him. He would wait and watch. If things seemed different between them, then he would act. Until then, he would hang on and enjoy the ride.

"DO YOU HAVE any idea how many seats that is?" Evie asked, sitting up and reaching for her glass of wine.

"Three thousand, two hundred?" Dante asked.

She turned to him. "I'm seriously on the edge. Don't mess with me."

He leaned in and kissed her. "You don't scare me. I used to be bad."

They were at his place, curled up together in the living room. The gas fireplace flickered away. After an afternoon of practicing with her students on the huge stage at the convention center, Evie was both exhausted and wired.

His mouth lingered, causing her to relax. This

was nice, she thought. Spending time with him, touching him, being touched. Except for her being in love and him not in love with her, it was about as close to perfect as she'd ever gotten.

He drew back and she sighed.

"I feel so stupid."

"It's an honest mistake. Everyone thought you already knew and you didn't."

"I know." She scooted back into the arm of the sofa and rested her sock-covered feet on his lap. "But I'm still playing catch-up. That place is huge."

"Your girls will be fine. You've done a great job with them."

"They're the ones who worked hard." She drew in a breath. "But it's done. We're there and we're practicing, and I'll be fine. I hope."

He rested his hand on her legs. "You'll be fine." He leaned to the side and pulled a flat package out of the drawer of the end table, then handed it to her. "This will distract you."

She stared at the simply wrapped package. "You bought me a gift."

"It's not a Christmas present. Don't freak out."

"I'm not freaking, and it is wrapped in Christmas paper."

"They offered, I said yes. Like I told you, it's no big deal."

Except it was a big deal to her. Dante had bought her something.

She took the package and realized it was a book. After carefully opening it, she stared at the cover.

Cats for Dummies.

She looked at him.

"You're thinking of getting that cat," he told her. "I saw this and thought it would help you decide."

Love flooded her and it was all she could do to hold in the words. She settled on throwing herself at him and hugging him.

"Thank you," she murmured.

"You're welcome." He wrapped his arms around her. "This is nice. I didn't know you responded so well to presents. I'll have to remember that."

"KNOCK, KNOCK."

Dante looked up from his computer and saw May walking toward his desk. It was lunchtime and nearly everyone was gone. Something about a holiday get-together, he thought. Or maybe not. He'd been busy with a new construction contract and not paying attention.

Now he resurfaced long enough to stand and greet his partner's mother.

"Am I interrupting?" May asked. "Silly question. You're focused on something."

"I could use a break." He motioned to the chair by his desk. "Can I get you a cup of coffee?"

"I'm fine." May waved him back to his seat.

"Sit. I'll only be here for a second. I want to ask you something."

She probably wanted gift suggestions for Rafe, Dante thought as he settled back in his chair. He was a guy. He didn't know what Rafe wanted.

"I wanted to thank you," May said. "For helping me with Evie." She smiled at him. "I know you encouraged her to give me a chance, and I'm very grateful."

He wasn't comfortable with praise. "I pointed out that it takes two to fight and asked if that's what she wanted for her relationship with her family."

"You're being modest, which I happen to know isn't like you." She stared into his eyes. "You encouraged her to have an open mind. That allowed her to consider I might be telling the truth when I apologized for all I'd done."

She dropped her gaze to her hands and twisted her fingers together. "I was so wrong and so horrible. I'm still wrestling with how I acted. Evie is being so generous in letting me be a part of her life again. I'm getting a second chance and I'm grateful."

"Ah, good." Dante shifted on his seat and hoped they were done talking about emotions. The only way this could get worse was for May to start crying.

Rafe's mother glanced back at him. "That's why I'm worried about your relationship with her."

Dante realized he'd been wrong. Tears weren't the only way this could get worse.

"You're a good man," she continued. "Rafe speaks highly of you, and I respect his opinion. But he's also said you're not someone interested in a long-term relationship." She stared at him, her eyes pleading. "I just got my daughter back. I don't want her hurt."

He swore silently, wishing he were anywhere but here. "I appreciate your concern, and I share it. I don't want Evie hurt, either. We're both clear on what's going on. We've talked about it."

May's expression softened, and the tension left her shoulders. "You have? Oh, that's a relief. Rafe didn't tell me that. I was afraid…" She shrugged. "It doesn't matter. As long as the two of you are clear on the ground rules. Evie has a good head on her shoulders."

"I agree. We both know this is just for fun." He was careful not to mention the sex. That would only send the conversation back to disaster.

"At the risk of sounding eighty years old," May said with a smile, "I don't understand you young people today. I could never get as involved with a man as Evie is with you and not fall in love. I'm not built that way. Of course, I never expected to ever fall in love again, and look what happened to me. I'm a newlywed. And at my age."

Still smiling, she rose. "Thanks so much for taking the time to speak with me. I know you're busy. We'll be seeing you for Christmas dinner, won't we?"

Dante stood and nodded automatically, but his attention was elsewhere. May's words repeated themselves over and over in his brain, getting louder with each iteration.

"I could never get as involved with a man as Evie is with you and not fall in love."

He was aware of walking May to the door and saying he would see her tomorrow, at the pet adoption. Somehow he made his way back to his desk and settled in his chair. But he didn't bother looking at his computer. After all, he wouldn't really see it.

There were rules, he reminded himself. They'd both been clear. Neither of them would get emotionally involved. But he'd been jealous of Evie when he'd seen her with Gideon. Jealousy meant he cared about her more than he should. What was the next step? Buying spontaneous presents? Looking forward to seeing her and spending time with her? Imagining a future with her?

No. No way in hell. He didn't fall for anyone. He wasn't that guy. He didn't do love.

He'd learned that lesson a long time ago and he

was never going back. Not for anyone. Now the only question was what to do to fix the situation without anyone getting hurt.

Seventeen

"IT'S COMPLICATED," PATIENCE said.

"But they're sisters." Evie glanced at the two fortysomething salon owners, standing on opposite sides of the stage at the convention center. "And they both do hair."

"Yes, but they have competing salons and they rarely speak. It's all very mysterious. No one knows exactly why they're estranged. A few times a year, they show up at the same event. And they've always helped out with *The Dance of the Winter King*. Don't worry. They'll be fine."

"They'd better be, because I can't take on one more thing." Evie eyed the two women, then figured it wasn't her rock to carry. Besides, when it came to family, she was hardly in a position to be critical.

Today was reserved for costume fittings and hair and makeup consults. In front of the stage about ten women sat with pins and tape measures and stacks of costumes. The girls were to show up at a specific time, in groups, so they could try on their costumes all at once. Then they would have their time with the stylists. Evie was already on her second latte and assumed there would be a third.

There was a planned break between twelve and one. Charlie had called the previous night to inform her that the Fox and Hound and Jo's Bar had joined together to donate lunch for the volunteers. But before they got to resting, they had to work.

Fortunately for her, everyone else participating had done this before. The girls were quickly ushered into a makeshift dressing area and sorted by size. The first costumes were handed out. Evie waited anxiously for the parade of seven- and eight-year-old girls in pink leotards and tights with silver tutus and angel wings.

"Bring them over here first," Denise Hendrix told her. "Every year those wings need to be anchored. We don't want any of the angels to have a costume malfunction."

Evie ushered each of the girls to a seamstress who made sure the costume fit perfectly and that the wings were secure. After the girls changed back into their regular clothes, Evie led them to the "hair and makeup" station, on the big stage.

"We want to look like Evie," Lillie told her mom. "With our hair in braids."

Patience smiled. "I think that's a great idea.

With the wings, you'll want your hair out of the way."

She turned to Bella and Julia. "How about silver and pink ribbons woven through their hair?"

Bella, or maybe Julia, nodded. "That would be pretty. Now for the fun stuff."

The girls crowded around the trays of eye shadow and lip glosses. Evie glanced over their heads and realized the colors were bright and glittery. No subtle nudes for her girls. The two sisters tried different glosses on the girls' lips and took the time to discuss options with each of them.

"This is really fun," Evie told Patience.

Her friend laughed. "I know. For me it's nearly as great as the performance itself." She lowered her voice. "On the younger girls, we keep it simple. The eye shadow and lip gloss. We don't put mascara on them until they're older. Still, for most of them, this is really special. The costumes and stage makeup add to the thrill."

Evie noticed that each of the girls was given a few minutes to make her selections, that no one was rushed and that both sisters made a point of encouraging the girls to enjoy being the center of attention.

Her next group arrived right on time. They were her tap girls and would wear red sequined outfits with a tuxedo influence. They also had hats and canes they'd been using as props. But the ones in the studio were old and battered while the canes they would use in the performance nearly blinded with shiny glitter.

And so it went, with group after group moving through hair and makeup. Just before lunch Annabelle and Heidi showed up with the food and drinks. Mayor Marsha made an appearance, along with several of the city council members. By three everyone had been fitted and prepped.

Evie was the last to leave. She walked to the stage and turned to stare at the waiting chairs. Yes, there would be a large audience, but she knew her dancers would be fine. They had practiced and were excited, and this was going to be the best *Dance of the Winter King* ever.

She already had ideas for next year's performance and was excited about starting a toddler dance class. Dominique had said a second time that she wanted to take Evie on as a partner. Everything she'd ever been looking for was right here.

Evie walked to her car. Tomorrow was the pet adoption, which meant a morning of setting up and then the actual event. Three days later she'd help stage the first full-on rehearsal. So far each of the groups had danced at the event center but none of them had gone through the entire show together. In a week, they would have the dress rehearsal and then the performance itself on Christmas Eve.

A busy but satisfying schedule, she thought.

So she really needed to get home and get to bed early. But instead of driving to her townhouse, Evie found herself pulling into the parking lot of the local pet store. Today had shown her where she belonged. That meant it was time for her to take the next step in building a home—adopting Alexander.

She went inside and grabbed a cart, then headed for the cat section. She found litter, a cat box and scooper, food and water dishes, a bed and a few toys. She also picked up a soft cat brush and a blue picture frame with a paw-print and the word Meow in the corner.

As she waited to pay, she made a quick call to the shelter and asked Tammy to put a hold on the cat. She would fill out the adoption paperwork in the morning and make it official. It might take some doing, but she was determined to show Alexander that he could trust her to always be there for him.

"If the pet adoption is here," Dante said, straightening the table. "Why are there booths in the center of town?"

"It's the annual Day of Giving," Evie told him. "I'm not sure exactly what that means. What I heard is various charities are here to talk about what they do so people can make donations and get involved. That finishes at one, and then the pet adoption starts."

They were nearly done setting up for the adoption. The open area they were using was at the far end of the convention center, away from the stage. There was a section for cats, another for dogs and a third area for all other pets. There was a large cage for the kittens to play in and a puppy pen. Tables would hold the cages for the cats, while most of the dogs would be on leashes. Local teens helped with the event, each taking a dog and making sure he or she stayed calm and friendly. The teens also took the dogs outside regularly to mitigate any accidents.

May and Tammy, along with several shelter volunteers, had left to start caravanning the animals from the shelter to the convention center.

"My mom said last year all the animals were adopted. Even an iguana. That's a lot of pressure."

"You'll be fine," Dante told her with a quick smile.

She watched him carefully. She hadn't seen him in a couple of days. With everything going on, she'd been running from place to place. Last night she'd thought they would get together, but he'd still been at the office when she'd gotten home from the pet store. He'd said he would be working late and not to wait up for him.

She told herself not to read too much into his actions, but she couldn't shake the feeling that something was wrong. Although if she was asked to say what, she wasn't sure she could.

They stacked the pet care brochures and made sure there were supplies for the animals, along with snacks and items for cleanup. Then Dante pulled out a chair and patted it.

"Have a seat," he told her. "You're going to be on your feet all afternoon."

She sank down and smiled at him. "You sure I can't talk you into staying for the adoption?"

"No, thanks. I'm going back to work. Contracts don't know a holiday season." He grabbed another chair and sat across from her. "When's the first big rehearsal?"

"In three days. I'm excited and nervous. We'll go through the show several times, then have our big dress rehearsal in a week. Then the performance. Ack!"

"You'll get through it."

"I know. I'm telling myself to stay calm. Oh, if you get a chance, you should come to the dress rehearsal. It won't be as crowded as the actual performance."

A muscle in Dante's cheek twitched. "Evie, you remember what we talked about before?"

The question was simple enough, and on the face of it, not very threatening. Even so, her stomach clenched and her throat went dry.

"You'll have to be a little more specific," she said, forcing herself to smile.

"When this started." He motioned to the space between them.

The "this" being their relationship, she thought. "Of course."

"We agreed it would be easy and there wouldn't be any pressure. No expectations."

He was leading up to something, and she just wanted him to get to the point. Because whatever he had to say, it couldn't be good. This was not a lead-in to "I love you and want to spend the rest of my life with you."

She tilted her head and stared at him. "You're stalling, which isn't your style. Get to the point."

"I'm heading out of town in a couple of days. Flying to Aspen. I won't be here for Christmas."

He was leaving? As in leaving? "Oh," she said slowly, thinking maybe the news wasn't all bad. The holidays could be intense. Fool's Gold required a lot of participation, and Dante was still resisting belonging. "I'm sorry you'll miss the show."

"Me, too." He glanced away, then back at her. "An old girlfriend called. She's meeting me there. I'll be back after New Year's."

Evie was pretty sure Dante kept talking, but she couldn't hear any words. There was only a rushing sound and the sensation of her heart being torn apart. She hoped she didn't go pale or pass out.

Instincts for self-preservation kicked in, and in that moment, all she wanted was Dante gone before he could begin to guess how much this was hurting her.

She managed to stand and felt her thighs start to tremble. She moved behind the chair and placed her hand on the back to keep herself upright.

"That's exciting," she said, hoping her voice sounded normal. "Aspen. I've never been. Of course I don't ski or snowboard, so I don't think I've missed that much. You have a good time, though."

Dante studied her. "Evie," he began.

She waved her hand to cut him off. "Don't," she told him. "This is what we agreed to. Just fun, right? Getting each other through the holidays. Mission accomplished. You're going to miss some delicious cookies, but maybe my mom will freeze some for you."

She glanced at her wrist—not that she was wearing a watch. "Oh, look at the time. I need to grab some lunch before the pets arrive. I'll see you after the first of the year."

She released the chair and willed her body to stay strong. All she had to do was grab her bag, and then she could escape. If she could just have a few minutes by herself, she could get her feelings under control and survive the day.

"Evie, wait."

She kept on walking. She could see her purse on a table. She reached for the handle and continued toward the exit. Once outside, she broke into a run. Her previously injured leg protested a little, but not enough to slow her down. She turned at the first corner she came to, and then another, ending up on the edge of the big park in town. It was cold and gray, but there still wasn't any snow.

She put her hand on the bark of a bare tree and tried to catch her breath. Only instead of inhaling, she began to sob. Deep, soul-ripping sobs that welled up from deep inside of her.

He was leaving. Dante was leaving. Worse, he was going to be with someone else. There was another woman he would laugh with and talk to and make love with. Someone else would hear his silly jokes and know the warmth of his body first thing in the morning. Someone else would be with him for Christmas.

After not being willing to trust herself enough to love anyone, she'd finally given her heart, only to have it tossed back at her. Dante didn't love her, and he certainly didn't want her to love him. He'd told her that from the beginning. She just hadn't been listening. She hadn't believed.

And now he was gone, and somehow, she had to get through days and days of activities, including the performance on Christmas Eve.

She gulped in air, then straightened. She could

do it, she told herself. She was strong. She'd handled worse and survived, she would get through this. The trick was to not let anyone know. Sympathy, while well meant, would only make it harder to go on. When Christmas was over, she would figure out how she was supposed to stop loving him, but for now, she would simply put one foot in front of the other. After all, she was used to dancing through the pain.

Eighteen

"I LOVE HIM!"

The girl speaking was maybe six or seven. She hung on to the large black Labrador mix with both arms. The dog, probably four or five and still skinny from being abandoned and trying to survive in the mountains, wagged his tail back and forth, obviously pleased by the turn of events.

Evie did her best to get lost in the moment, to feel happy for the family and their new pet. The young couple took the offered food and the information on care.

"We went to the shelter several times," the wife said happily. "He's perfect for us. We're calling him Wally."

The little girl beamed up at her parents. "I'm so happy, I almost don't need presents this year."

"That's pretty happy," her dad said.

She nodded. "We could ask Santa to take them to children who don't have a new puppy."

The parents exchanged a look of pride and love.

"That's very nice," her mother said. "Let's talk about that when we get home."

Evie handed over their dog license and the rest of the paperwork. "Have a great holiday," she said and watched them walk away, Wally trotting at their side.

"Another happy ending," May said as she walked over with more completed forms in her hand. "We've found homes for all the puppies and kittens, which isn't a surprise but is still nice. Most of the cats are claimed. Someone took all the fish earlier. Did you see that? I don't understand fish as pets. They can't even interact."

"I think you're just supposed to watch them."

"I'd rather watch a movie." Her mother gave her a quick hug. "I see you're adopting that cat."

"Alexander. I'm taking him home with me this afternoon."

"I hope you'll be very happy together." Her mother studied her for a second. "Are you all right? You've been quiet today."

"I'm fine," Evie said quickly. "Just tired from everything I have to get done. The performance isn't that many days away and we start full rehearsals on the actual stage next week. I need to make sure my dancers are comfortable with the entire show. All those seats are intimidating."

She hoped talking about the upcoming performance was enough of a distraction to get her mother to stop asking questions. Eventually she would have to come clean about what had happened with Dante, but right now she couldn't talk about it. Not only was her heart breaking, but she was also left feeling stupid. It was as if she'd had a party and no one came. There were decorations and food and music, but no guests. While she'd been busy falling in love, Dante had been looking for a way out. He'd found a good one, too.

All she had to do was get through the rest of the afternoon. Then she could go home and have a private meltdown.

May stared at her. Her gaze was so intent that Evie was sure she'd figured out the truth.

"I know what it is," her mother said at last, then startled Evie by suddenly starting to cry. "It's all my fault."

"That's not possible," Evie said, as tears filled May's eyes and spilled down her cheeks.

"Of course it is. You're my daughter and I love you so much. But I lost you because I was stupid, and what if you never forgive me? What if I've done too much damage? What if you can't forgive me?"

She covered her face with her hands and continued to cry.

Evie stood immobilized by shock. She recognized she was at a crossroads, and whatever she decided at this moment would influence the rest of her life.

Yes, her mother had made mistakes. There were reasons, some better than others, for what had happened, but in the end it came down to a choice. Hang on to the past and stay stuck or forgive and move on.

Which meant no choice at all. There was only what was right. While she was still battered and bruised from what Dante had done, she felt a deeper wound finally heal. It wasn't much right now, but later that healing would give her strength. She wanted and needed to be a part of her family.

She reached for her mother and pulled her close. "You didn't lose me, Mom. I'm right here, and I love you, too."

May looked at her. "You do? You swear?"

"I swear. We still have a long way to go. But I've decided to stay in Fool's Gold. We'll hang out together. You can help me find a place to buy. How's that?"

May hugged her so tight, Evie couldn't breathe. But that was okay. Because right now, this was exactly what she needed.

"I do love you," May told her.

"I know. Now you have to promise to stop apologizing. The past is done. From now on, we're just going to deal with the present. Together."

May squeezed again. "Thank you. Thank you so much."

Evie shook her head. "I have to thank you, too, Mom. For making the effort. I'm not sure I would have been able to put pride aside and risk reaching out."

"You mean it about staying here?"

"Yes. Dominique wants to expand the dance school, and I have some ideas for that."

"You could do a dance exercise class for women my age. To help us get in shape. Everyone I know wants to move like you do. You're always so graceful."

"I'd like that."

"I'm not sure what we'd call it. Exercise and dance for old women probably isn't a good name."

Evie started to laugh, and her mom joined in.

May sniffed, then glanced around. While no one was overtly watching, Evie was pretty sure they were the center of attention.

"All right then," her mother said, wiping her cheeks. "Is my mascara running?"

"You look beautiful."

May smiled. "I think that's an exaggeration. I'm going to duck into the bathroom and spruce myself up. Then I'll be back and we can see what we can do about getting the rest of these pets adopted."

"HERE IT IS," Evie said, carefully lifting the cat carrier out of the backseat of her car. "I'm sorry to make you ride back here, but I didn't want to have to worry about the air bag deploying. Not that I'm a bad driver and we're at risk for being in an accident."

She pressed her lips together. "I'm babbling, I know. I'm a little nervous. I've already been rejected by one guy in my life. I guess I'm afraid you'll be critical."

She closed the car door and walked into her place.

The previous night she'd set up the cat supplies. She'd put the litter box upstairs in the guest bathroom. She'd folded an old, soft blanket on the window seat in the guest room. On sunny days Alexander could sun himself there.

The food and water bowls were full and on a placemat in a quiet part of her kitchen. She wasn't sure where to put his cat bed. From what she'd read, he would find where he was most comfortable, so for now, it was in a corner, tucked next to a chair. He could see out, but still feel a little protected.

She took the carrier upstairs to the guest room. She figured they would start near the bathroom and let him find his way from there. She set it on the floor and opened the wire door.

"You're home," she said in a quiet voice. "Alexander, come on, big guy. This is it. Where you belong."

He slowly, cautiously, stepped out of the carrier. After glancing at her, he walked into the bathroom and sniffed. He paused at the litter box, but didn't use it.

"I hope I got the right kind," she said. "It has baking soda in it."

He walked past her and went under the guest bed. Before she could wonder if he was going to hide there for a while, he came out the other side and headed for the hallway.

She'd closed the door to the master, thinking she didn't want to confuse him. He headed downstairs, and she followed.

He made a circuit of the rest of the place, pausing to delicately lap at the water and sniff the dry food. Then he walked to the sofa, jumped up and stared at her.

She paused at the bottom of the stairs.

"I should probably tell you about myself," she murmured, thinking she was being an idiot, but not sure how else to start a conversation with a cat. "I've never had a pet before, so it's possible I won't get everything right. If you could just be a little patient with me, I would appreciate it. I'm, um, a dance teacher, which I like a lot. Do you like children? Because there might be some around, from time to time. I just broke up with the guy I was seeing."

Evie paused, feeling the pain of the words. "I thought he was pretty great. I thought..." She swallowed against the tightness in her throat. "I was in love with him," she whispered, fighting tears. "Stupid, huh?"

She crossed to the sofa, sitting at the opposite end from Alexander, so as not to frighten him. "I've never had a successful romantic relationship, so it's really just going to be the two of us. But I'm hoping you and I can get along. I want to take good care of you."

Steady green eyes regarded her.

"It would really help if you could tell me what you're thinking," she said.

Alexander stood and walked across the back of the sofa. He jumped down on the cushion next to her and then sat, looking at her. Slowly, carefully, she reached out to pet him. She stroked the length of his back, then rubbed the side of his face. When she scratched under his chin, he raised his head up and forward.

"Do you like that?" she asked. "Is that nice?"

Without warning, he jumped onto her lap and stood facing her. She rubbed his soft fur. He turned once and then curled up on her lap and began to purr.

She continued to pet him, feeling the quiet rumble as she rubbed his chin. More tears fell. She didn't try to stop them. She knew that acknowledging the pain was a part of the process. Eventually she would heal, and one day she would be able to look back, saying she'd learned something. Until then she had to figure out a way to survive with a Dante-size hole in her heart.

EVIE FOUGHT AGAINST a pounding headache. She'd spent most of Sunday holed up in her townhouse, getting to know her new cat and sobbing uncontrollably. She'd been forced to duck out for food in the afternoon, then had retreated to her ongoing pity party.

For a second night, she'd mostly been awake, staring at the ceiling, wondering what she could have done differently and asking impossible questions. Like was she ever going to meet "the one" and fall in love?

Alexander had settled the issue of his sleeping arrangements by joining her. He was a thoughtful roommate, curling up at the foot of the bed and sleeping silently. When she'd started crying again at four in the morning, he'd draped himself across her chest and had purred until she'd managed to calm herself.

This morning she'd heard Dante leave around five. As it was way too early for work, she'd assumed he'd been leaving for the airport. Sure enough, she'd checked the parking lot by his office and his car wasn't there. He was well and truly gone, flying off to be with another woman.

All of which made her heart break more but wasn't anything she could deal with right now. After spending the past two hours working with the lighting guy, she had to pull herself together for the dance rehearsal. This would be the first full run-through, with music and lights. Based on her professional experience, it could go very badly and it was up to her to stay calm and positive.

Every part of her hurt. Her eyes were puffy, and she was pale. Falling in love was a bitch, she told herself, but no one else's problem. She had to pull it together for her girls and for the town. In less than a week, she would be done with all this and able to freak out as much as she wanted. She planned to spend the day after Christmas having an emotional meltdown. That would be the end of it. On the twenty-seventh, she would get her act together and move on with her life. What was that saying? She would fake it until she made it.

The rehearsal was due to start at two. By one forty-five all her dancers were there. Grace, the lithe, talented star of the school, had gathered the girls who had the most trouble with their steps and taken them through their section. The tap team was going through their routine, their stocking feet silent on the stage. The rest of the groups were practicing, as well.

Short and tall, skinny and round. All working hard. Happy and determined, she thought.

Gideon walked up to the stage. “Hey,” he said. “I’m here to be the voice from beyond.”

She turned to him. “Aren’t they amazing?” she asked.

He glanced at the girls and nodded. “Beautiful and unique.”

“So speaks the Zen master.”

“Have you been practicing your breathing?”

“Sure. In my free time. I’m also working on a plan for peace in the Middle East.”

“Let me know how that goes.”

She waited until he’d climbed the steps up to the stage, then followed him back behind the side curtains. He would watch the show and do the narration from there. For the dress rehearsal and the actual show, he would be farther away from the action, so there wasn’t background noise. At that point, they would depend on musical cues to stay in sync.

“Thanks for doing this,” she said as she handed him the microphone. “I know it’s been a lot of time.”

He shrugged. “I got the music together and learned a script. No big deal.”

Her voice got a little tight. "It is to me. And the girls. Plus, you're here. We can depend on you."

Gideon's dark eyes narrowed. "Uh-oh. What does that mean?"

"Nothing. Sorry. Personal stuff."

He took a step back. "Are you okay?"

"No, but let's not talk about it."

"What happened?"

She drew in a breath. She was going to have to start telling people at some point. She could practice now. Get the first telling over with. After all, Gideon wasn't a close friend or part of her family.

"Dante and I broke up. I guess it's more accurate to say we're not seeing each other anymore. Breaking up implies a relationship. We never had that." She felt her eyes starting to burn and blinked away the tears. "It's fine. Or it will be. I just wish I hadn't fallen in love with him, you know."

Gideon's face took on the expression of a trapped animal. Despite the ache in her heart, she started to laugh.

"I'll stop talking now," she said. "You look like you're going to faint."

"I don't like the emotional stuff."

"But you're all one with the universe."

"That's different. I can be in the moment."

"As long as it's not an emotional moment?"

"So the system is flawed." He seemed to gather strength. "Are you all right? Can I, ah, help?"

"You're sweet, but, no. I'm fine." She grinned. "So the big tough guy thing is just an act?"

"Some people are afraid of spiders."

"You're afraid of emotions."

He shuddered. "I avoid them. But I could storm a South American country and overthrow a dictator if that would help."

"Not this week, but I do appreciate the offer." She stared at him. "You're really strange."

"I get that a lot." He picked up one of the two microphones and handed it to her. "I'm ready whenever you are."

"I'll get the girls."

She walked to the center of the stage. Gideon was dangerous, she thought. The kind of man who knew things, had seen things, the rest of the world could only guess at. But in the end, Dante was more lethal. Gideon might be capable of overthrowing a government, but Dante had shattered her heart.

The really sad part was if he walked in the door this second and begged her to take him back, she would. In a second. Which meant a trip to the self-help section of the local bookstore was in order. She needed some serious healing.

But that, too, was for later.

She turned on the microphone and faced her dancers.

"Thank you all for coming," she said. "I'm so

excited about this show. Each of you has worked so hard. You should be proud of yourselves." She paused and smiled. "All right. Let's start from the top, shall we?"

Nineteen

"Hey, big guy," Evie said as she walked into her townhouse. She'd just taken her dancers through a second day of rehearsing the entire show. "It went really well. I'm so proud of them."

She paused in the living room, not sure where to find Alexander. The cat had only been living with her for a few days, and they didn't have much of a routine yet. But as she shrugged out of her coat, she heard a soft "meow" from the stairs.

Alexander stood about halfway down, his green eyes wide, his expression expectant.

"Hi, you," she said, walking toward him. "How was your afternoon? Did you sleep in the sun?"

She moved up a few steps, and he moved down. They met somewhere near the bottom. She sank onto the carpeted stairs and began to stroke him. He stepped close and rubbed his head against her hand. His kitty eyes closed, and he purred.

"Wow, that's some greeting," she said. She

slowly picked him up, careful to support his rear, and held him in her arms. He relaxed against her, his whole body vibrating with a contented rumble.

"I'm going to assume you're happy to see me and not anticipating that dinner is in a few minutes."

She set him on her lap. He planted his back feet on her thighs and put his front paw on her chest, by her collarbones, then pressed his nose to hers.

She laughed and scratched his chin. "Okay, so that act in the shelter was you playing hard to get, right? You were making sure I was committed before you gave your kitty heart. I can respect that." Her smile faded. "I should have done the same with Dante. Then I wouldn't feel so sucky about the whole falling in love thing."

She scooped him up in her arms and carried him down the stairs. "I stopped at the pet store and got you some canned food to try." She set him down and reached for the small paper bag she'd carried in with her. "It's organic and supposed to be very supportive of your urinary health. Apparently we're going to have to watch that."

Alexander followed her into the kitchen. She served him a couple of teaspoons of the canned food on a dish and watched him polish off the snack. When he'd finished, he glanced up at her.

"Nice?" she asked. "That was the chicken flavor. I also got tuna."

She put a lid on the can and stuck it in the refrigerator, then paused to survey the complete lack of people food. While she'd gone to the store, her efforts had been halfhearted at best. She had eggs and milk, along with a couple of apples. In the freezer were a few frozen entrées.

She could order a pizza, she thought. Or go get takeout. But that would be so much effort. It had been different with Dante. Easier. She missed that, and his energy. She missed how he made her laugh and the way she felt in his arms. Mostly she missed him.

Before she could make a decision, or simply collapse on the floor and give in to tears, she heard a knock on the door. For a second, her heart froze.

"It's not Dante," she whispered. "He's gone. Off having sex with an old girlfriend."

She walked to the living room and pulled open the door. Instead of a lost tourist or a kid selling who-knows-what, she found herself staring at Patience, Heidi, Annabelle, Charlie and several other women it took her a second to place. She saw her mother waving from the back of the group.

"Hi," she said, not sure what was going on. All the women were holding grocery bags. Was this a shopping intervention?

"We heard," Heidi said. "About what happened."

"This is not the time to be delicate," Charlie said. "We know Dante is a complete jackass and we're sorry." She held up a bottle of vodka in one hand and Baileys mint chocolate liqueur in the other. "We're here to help."

Evie stepped back, mostly because her porch was small and she couldn't figure out how to tell them all to go away.

"I'm Pia," a pretty brunette said. "We've met, but you probably don't remember."

"I brought my own blender," Jo, from Jo's Bar, told her, holding up a very professional-looking machine. "And ice. I didn't know if you had an icemaker."

"Oh, honey," her mother said and pulled her close. "I'm so sorry about Dante."

The women trooped into her living room which, fortunately, was clean. One of the triplets came out holding Alexander.

"I'm Dakota and he's adorable."

"Thanks. I just adopted him last Saturday."

Dakota nodded. "Thanks for the heads-up. I'll warn everyone."

Still confused, Evie followed her into the living room.

"We have a new-to-the-family cat here, ladies," Dakota said, patting Alexander. "Let's try to keep it down."

Evie still wasn't sure what "it" was, although it obviously involved total strangers taking over her house. Jo had already set up her blender and was pouring generous amounts of liquor in with ice. Someone had set out martini glasses and little candy canes.

Charlie was putting out bowls of what looked like dip and guacamole. There were regular chips, tortilla chips, crackers and spreads, plates of cookies, brownies and the largest box of fudge she'd ever seen.

"I'm doing a nonalcoholic cranberry sparkler as soon as I get these peppermint martinis done," Jo called. "For Annabelle and Nevada."

"For me, too," Heidi said. "I ate way too much last night and my tummy's been unhappy all day."

Evie met her sister-in-law's gaze but didn't say a word. Heidi's problem had nothing to do with the volume of food she'd eaten and everything to do with being pregnant. But Evie was going to keep her secret.

Charlie walked up to her and put her arm around her shoulders. "Gideon came to me this morning," she said. "I made a few calls and here we are. We would have come sooner, but you had your rehearsal and we didn't want to get in the way."

"I don't understand," Evie told her.

"It's a Fool's Gold thing. We come, we show support, we get drunk and eat crap. You cry."

"In front of everyone?"

"Trust me, you'll feel better."

"Did you go through this?"

"No. I ran because I wasn't brave enough to face my friends. But you're tougher than me."

"How can you say that?" Charlie was the most impressive person Evie knew.

Charlie stared at her. "Evie, look at yourself. You've been on your own since you were seventeen, with no support. You practically raised yourself and you turned out great. Two months into a new job, you get the whole *Dance of the Winter King* dumped on you and you manage to pull it all together. Who else could do that?"

It was a question she didn't know how to answer. Honestly, she'd never thought of herself as special. In her mind, she'd actually screwed up a lot. She wasn't talented enough to stay in Juilliard and she'd never been able to settle on a job she loved. Until now.

"I'm sorry about Dante," Charlie told her. "For what it's worth, I think he's going to regret losing you for the rest of his life."

"I really hope so."

Charlie grinned. "That's my girl."

Evie was led into the living room and settled in the middle of the sofa. All the other women gathered around. Her mom sat next to her. Jo handed out the peppermint martinis, which turned out to be delicious and went down far too easily.

Evie sipped, aware that everyone was watching her.

"I'll start," a redhead said. She was sitting cross-legged on the floor, Alexander draped over one thigh. "I'm Liz, by the way. Married to Ethan." She pointed at the triplets. "He's their brother."

Nevada groaned. "I suppose that makes what he did our fault?"

Liz laughed. "Technically, it does."

"We're sorry," Montana told her.

"I accept your apology." Liz turned back to Evie. "Ethan and I had a past, which made things complicated."

"And a kid," Charlie said.

"Yes. A son that Ethan didn't know about. When things got ugly, I didn't know what to do. I was trapped here, alone. But everyone came through for me."

"Me, too," Heidi said. "When Rafe was being stupid, my friends had buttons printed up. Team Heidi and Team Rafe." She smiled smugly. "There were a lot more Team Heidi buttons around town."

Charlie shrugged. "I can't bond. I ran."

While Evie appreciated the stories, they all had something in common. Each of the men in question might have acted stupid, but in the end, one by one, they'd come around. There was a shiny wedding band on every left-hand ring finger. Well, except for Annabelle and Charlie, who had engagement rings. No one in this room had lost the man of her dreams. Only Evie.

She swallowed against the familiar tightness in her throat. The last thing she wanted was to start crying. The problem was, she knew the truth. There wouldn't be a happy ending for her. Not really. Dante had the best reason of all to avoid love. He believed the emotion was dangerous. His mother had died because he'd fallen in love.

Tears filled her eyes. She fought them, but one trickled onto her cheek, followed by another. Her mother pulled her close.

"Remind yourself he's a jerk, and one day you won't be in love with him anymore," May murmured.

"Does saying that help?"

"No, but eventually it turns out to be true. You go ahead and cry. When you're done, we'll have ice cream, and I happen to know that really does help."

EVIE'S BREAKUP PARTY HANGOVER lasted for nearly two days. The first day she'd had to excuse herself twice from rehearsal to go throw up, and if she never, ever tasted peppermint again in her life, it would be too soon. The second day the only lingering effects of the alcohol and cookies was a gently pounding headache. On the morning of the third day, she woke feeling like her regular self.

She rolled over and found Alexander was already up and busy with his morning ablutions. She watched him carefully wash his face, first licking the side of his paw, then wiping it across his face and over his ear. He was thorough and patient, but in the end, clean.

"'Morning," she said when he looked up at her.

He started to purr and walked toward her for his cuddle. She pulled him next to her and rubbed him all over before finishing with a good chin scratch.

"You've been very good to me," she told him. "I was really stupid with the martinis. That won't happen again. I've learned my lesson. About liquor if not love."

She rolled onto her back and stared at the ceiling. She'd never been in love before, so had no idea how long it took to feel better. One thing she knew for sure. As soon as she got through the holidays, she was going to start looking for a new place. There was no way she could live next door to Dante. She would be around him too much to forget him.

Her friends would help with finding a place, she thought, that knowledge easing some of the pain. Plus her mom had offered to loan her the money for a down payment. Knowing May, she would probably want to make it a gift, but Evie would prefer to pay her back. It seemed the grown-up thing to do.

"Would you like a yard?" she asked. "Do you like going outside? I can see you lying in the grass, sunning."

Alexander draped across her, his eyes half-closed, his purr comforting her.

She would keep busy, she told herself. Maybe take some classes at the college. There were also her ideas for the expanded teaching schedule. And that exercise class her mom had mentioned sounded fun.

"I'm going to get over him," she told her cat. "I swear I will."

But the ache in her heart seemed bigger every day, and sometimes she wondered how anyone survived losing a great love. How did you learn to forget? To be happy again? She wondered if maybe that was simply a matter of finding small joys in life and stringing them together. Maybe after a while they became bigger than the pain.

She could only hope.

"OKAY," GIDEON SAID from his place backstage. "They win."

Evie looked at the nearly sixty excited, squealing, running, jumping and dancing girls careening around the stage and nodded. "Right there with you. I feel like if we back away slowly and don't show fear, they won't attack."

It was the long-anticipated afternoon of the dress rehearsal. Everyone was in costume for a run-through of the show. Wings quivered, sequins glittered and tap shoes rang out on the wooden stage. Evie had been worried about getting the girls dressed and having them work with their costumes. What she hadn't anticipated was the excitement that would send them into a giggling, bouncing frenzy.

She told herself to simply pick up the microphone and speak with authority. That the girls would instantly quiet and listen. What she didn't know was what she was going to do if she was wrong.

"Breathing isn't helping," Gideon said quietly. "I don't like that."

"They're my responsibility," Evie told him. "I'm going in."

But before she could gather her courage, the door to the convention center opened and Dominique swept inside, followed by Morgan, who played the Winter King.

The petite former dancer moved with a grace that captivated the girls. As one, they turned to watch the elegantly dressed woman. Dominique's hair was perfectly coiffed. She had on a trim, tailored suit, the color of her green eyes, and four-inch heels. She stopped in front of the stage and faced the students.

"Good afternoon, ladies."

"Good afternoon, Ms. Guérin," they answered in unison.

Dominique offered a smile. "I see you're all

ready for your dress rehearsal. What I want you to remember as you prepare for your moment in the spotlight is that each of you is a star. A beautiful shining light that will transform those privileged enough to see you."

She paused. "When I danced professionally there were times when I was tired or hurt or ill. Times when I didn't want to gather myself enough to give my all, but I always did. I remembered that, while this was just one performance for me, this was a memory for everyone watching. They had taken time out of their lives to come see me. They wanted to experience the joy and beauty that only comes from dance. They wanted the experience."

Evie glanced around. Every single girl was staring, riveted by the famous woman's words.

"You will give them that experience. Each of you will offer a memory that can be carried a lifetime. When you feel nervous, breathe deeply. If you start to shake, focus on the music. Evie has taught you well. We are both so proud of you, and I am very much looking forward to watching each of you perform."

Talk about a memory, Evie thought, clapping for her boss, as the girls joined in. For the rest of their lives her students would remember being encouraged by Dominique Guérin.

Evie stepped toward the stage. "Thank you,

Dominique. Now, let's all move offstage. Gideon will start the music and we'll take it from the top."

Nervous energy now channeled productively, the dancers did as she asked. Evie turned off the microphone and walked over to her boss.

"Thank you for this. You're exactly what they needed."

"I'm very excited about the show." Dominique put her hand on Evie's arm. "I heard about your young man. I'm so sorry. After Christmas I'm visiting with friends in Fiji for a few weeks. If you feel the need to get away, I'm happy to loan you my apartment in New York. Charlie has the key."

The unexpected generosity had Evie's eyes feeling a little moist. "Thank you. That's very sweet."

"Some men are idiots."

"I keep telling myself that. So far it's not working, but soon, I hope."

The opening bars of the first song filled the convention center. Morgan settled into his throne as Gideon's smooth chocolate-and-velvet voice spoke over the music.

"Once upon a time there was a magical kingdom ruled by a kind and generous king. He was blessed with many daughters. Each beautiful and wise. The king loved his daughters so much, he decided he would keep them with him forever."

The first group danced onto the stage, their wings quivering and catching the light.

Evie turned her attention to them. Whatever happened or didn't happen with Dante was out of her control. Good ending or bad, she would get through it. Not because she was especially tough or determined, but because she wasn't alone. She had her friends and her family. People who loved her. She belonged, and right now that was more than enough.

On the day before the performance, Evie knew the show was going to be brilliant. Beyond brilliant. Her dancers were amazing, taking to the stage with grace and style. Their costumes fit perfectly, the music was fabulous and Gideon's changes to the narration added a heartwarming element that would have everyone in tears.

She walked into the convention center a half hour before rehearsal, knowing that between them, she and her girls had reason to be proud of themselves. There were—

Her cell phone rang.

Evie grabbed it and glanced at the unfamiliar but local number. "Hello?"

"Evie? Is that you?"

"Yes. Who is this?" She didn't recognize the woman's voice, but she sounded very upset.

"It's Shelley, Grace's mom. I'm so sorry, but there's been an accident." Shelley took a breath. "Grace and her friends went up the mountain this morning to find snow. Unfortunately, they also went snowboarding. I'd warned her not to, what with the show tomorrow and everything, but she snuck off. She slipped and fell and broke her leg."

Evie sank onto the nearest chair. "Is she all right?"

"Yes. It's a clean break. They barely had to do anything to set it, but she won't be dancing anytime soon. She's hysterical, of course. I was terrified, but now that I know she's okay, I'm hoping this teaches her to be more responsible. Teenagers. Which doesn't help you at all. Like I said, I'm so sorry."

"Don't worry about the dance," Evie said automatically, relieved Grace was going to be fine. "We'll figure something out."

"We'll all be there tomorrow night, to watch. Grace will be in tears, just so you're braced."

"Of course she's disappointed."

"And then some. Okay, I need to run. I have to get Grace home. See you tomorrow."

"Bye."

Evie disconnected the call, then stared at the phone, not sure what she was supposed to do. Grace had a full minute solo in the most critical part of the story. It was her dance that finally convinced her father to let the girls go into the world. Her dance began the transformation.

Evie dug through her bag and stared at the

notes she'd made. There was no way to change the music, so there had to be a one-minute transition. Something simple, she thought, wondering who could learn a new dance in a day. She was still working on options when her students began to arrive.

She waited until they were all there to tell them what had happened.

Abby Sutton rolled her eyes when she heard. "It's because she likes this boy who loves to snowboard."

Melissa nudged her sister. "Shh. Don't say that."

"Why not? It's true. Girls do stupid things for boys."

Talk about telling the truth, Evie thought. She'd been an idiot over a guy herself.

"While I'm sure we all feel badly for Grace," Evie said instead, "we have to come up with a way to fill the beats in the music. Grace had a solo at a pivotal moment in the story."

Lillie shrugged. "Why don't you do it?"

Evie blinked at her. "Me? I can't."

"Why not? You know all the steps. You know everyone's steps." Lillie giggled. "You could do the whole show yourself."

"That would look pretty silly," Evie told her.

Melissa and Abby glanced at each other, then back at her.

"You should do it," Abby told her.

"Yeah," Melissa said. "You're better than all of us. Even Grace."

Several girls nodded at that. Then they were all telling Evie to dance the solo.

"You can be one of the daughters, just like us," Lillie said. "Please say you will."

"I'd have to check with Ms. Guérin," Evie said, not wanting to take the spotlight from her students.

"She'll think it's fun," Abby said confidently. "Besides, if you dance in the show, you get to wear makeup and have your hair done. And that's the best part."

Twenty

DANTE STOOD AT the window of his suite, looking out at the mountains. The room was large and well furnished, the view amazing. Logs crackled in the fireplace. New snow beckoned, and room service had just delivered breakfast. Everything was perfect, and he should be one happy guy. Only he wasn't. He'd been through some crappy holidays since his mother's death, but he had to admit this was the worst.

He wasn't anywhere he wanted to be, and he sure as hell wasn't with anyone who interested him. He was alone, on a mountain, on Christmas Eve, and for the life of him he couldn't figure out why he'd thought this was a good idea.

When he'd realized he'd gone too far with Evie, leaving had seemed like the only option. It would make the break quick and clean. He'd thought that would be easiest for her. He'd made up a story about a former girlfriend so Evie wouldn't think they'd get back together when he returned. Then he'd taken off. He'd assumed that by the time the plane landed in Colorado, he would have forgotten all about her.

Only he hadn't. He thought about her constantly. There were plenty of single women at the resort, and more than one of them had made it clear she was interested. He couldn't have been less so. He didn't want just some woman—he wanted Evie. He missed her. He missed talking to her at the end of the day and thinking about her when he should be working. He missed their dinners, their nights, their mornings. He missed everything about her.

Worse, he missed Fool's Gold. He missed the stupid decorations and the idiotic people greeting him every other second when he walked down the street. He missed his friends, and he missed Evie more than he'd thought possible.

Right now she was getting ready for the Live Nativity, which this year would feature an elephant. Where else but Fool's Gold? And was he there, secretly having the time of his life? No. He was stuck in some damn suite in Aspen.

He stalked across the room and told himself he had to get over this. Over her. He had to figure out a way to stop caring about her. Because if he didn't, he would be in real danger. He would start imagining being with her for a long time. Months even. He would start to imagine that it was okay for him to have feelings and then he would… He would…

Dante stopped in the middle of the room. He turned in a slow circle, as if not sure where he was or what to do next. He needed to get home, he realized. Not just to Fool's Gold, but to Evie. Because… Well, hell, he was just going to say it.

"I love her."

That's what his heart had been trying to tell him. He needed her and wanted to be with her. He wanted to give her everything he had and know that she felt the same. He wanted to hold her and protect her and maybe even, someday, have children with her.

He'd only risked his heart once before, and that had cost him everything. So he'd vowed never to take that chance again. But this time he couldn't help himself. Sometime when he hadn't been paying attention, Evie had stolen his heart. The killer was, he didn't want it back. She could have it. If she wanted it.

He ran to the phone and punched in the number for the concierge.

"This is Dante Jefferson, in suite 587. I need to book a flight out of here today."

There was a moment of silence. "Um, sir, you do realize it's Christmas Eve? There aren't going to be any flights. It's going to take a miracle for you to find a seat."

"I'm thinking that maybe miracles do happen, so let's give it a try." He grinned. "Actually don't bother looking for a commercial flight. Find me a private plane. Money is no object."

"All right. Where are you flying to?"

"Fool's Gold, California."

"MOMMY, WHY DOES Baby Jesus have an elephant?"

Evie smiled at the question. The little boy stared up at Priscilla, his expression one of awe.

"Baby Jesus loves all the animals," the boy's mom said.

"Can I have an elephant?"

"Not this year."

"Can I have a puppy?"

"We'll talk about it with your dad."

May linked her arm with Evie's and sighed. "I do love a good nativity."

"This one is very special."

It was midday on Christmas Eve, and the Live Nativity had drawn a huge crowd. Most of the animals had come from the Castle Ranch. The sheep, a couple of goats, Reno the pony and Wilbur the pig. Along with Priscilla, of course.

There were people playing the main roles, although a doll stood in for Baby Jesus. There had been talk of a live infant, but when the temperatures had dropped below freezing, the substitution had been made.

"Are you nervous?" May asked in a whisper.

Evie touched her stomach where butterflies had taken up residence.

"More than I would have thought possible," she admitted. "I haven't danced on a stage in a long time."

"You'll be wonderful. I can't wait to see you. We're getting there early so we can sit up front."

"I'm not sure if that's news that's going to make me feel better," Evie admitted.

Dominique had been thrilled with the idea of her taking over Grace's solo. Evie had spent much of the previous evening practicing. Gideon had come by to cue the music and had stayed through her session.

He was a good guy. Unfortunately she couldn't summon the least little tingle when he was around. And based on how he'd treated her pretty much as a sister, she would say the same was true for him. She was going to have to get over Dante the old-fashioned way. With time and ice cream.

But that was for after Christmas. She'd decided that for the holiday itself, she was going to simply go with her feelings. She was going to love him and not fight it. On the twenty-sixth, she would give herself a stern talking-to and load her freezer with Ben & Jerry's.

"I need to get home," Evie said, kissing her mother's cheek. "I have a thousand details to worry about. Nothing to actually do, but plenty to sweat over."

"We'll see you tonight." May smiled at her. "Should I say break a leg?"

"After what happened to Grace, probably not."

Evie left. She walked back to her house. She saw Alexander sitting in the upstairs window seat. When he saw her, he stood and stretched, then jumped down. She knew he would be waiting on the stairs when she unlocked the door.

She cut across the lawn, then came to a stop as the first snowflakes of the season silently drifted down from the sky.

Evie glanced up at the gray sky, then back at the snow dotting the shoulders and sleeves of her jacket. Then she spun in a circle and started to laugh.

"It's still snowing," Lillie said, plopping down next to Evie.

Evie glanced at the girl and smiled. "You look adorable."

Lillie grinned. "I love my wings."

"You look good in wings."

"Maybe I should have asked Santa for wings instead of a dad."

Evie blinked. "You asked for a dad?"

Lillie wrinkled her nose and leaned close. "I'm old enough to know there's really no Santa, but it doesn't hurt to ask, right? Only Mom says it doesn't work that way."

She leaned close as Evie finished sewing on her shoes' ribbons.

"You have to do that with every pair of pointe shoes?" Lillie asked.

"Uh-huh." Evie showed her where she'd already softened the toe box.

"You can't just buy them finished?"

"It doesn't work that way. Every dancer wants her shoes the way she likes them."

Evie slipped on the shoes, then tied the ribbons and went up on pointe. She walked a couple of steps, came back down, then sank onto the stage floor.

"It's a lot to do," Lillie said.

"It is." Evie flexed her foot and tied the ribbon in place. After cutting the ends, she used clear nail polish to seal them. "I need to put this stuff away."

"Okay."

They both stood. Evie dropped the nail polish and scissors into her bag. By then the ends were dry. She tucked them under the ribbon around her ankle so it was out of sight. A quick check of the large clock on the wall told her they had ten minutes.

"Okay, everyone," she called. "Let's get in place."

Gideon walked by, his headphones and microphone in place. "We're good," he told her.

Morgan, their king for the evening, settled into his throne and gave her a thumbs-up. The dancers separated into their sections and waited for the musical cue. Dominique stepped onto the stage and began with an explanation of the dance. Seconds later, the music began and the curtain went up.

Evie stood with the other girls and watched the younger girls in wings twirl to the center of the stage. Gideon told the story of the Winter King and his beautiful daughters, and the girls danced.

They had energy and enthusiasm. If there was a bent arm here and a misstep there, Evie didn't notice. She waved girls in place and offered an encouraging whisper when she saw a case of nerves. The music flowed and shifted with each section, and at last it was her turn.

She rose on pointe and made her way across the stage. The dance came easily to her, allowing her to feel the music and get lost in the movements. For a second she allowed herself to miss Dante, to wish things could be different, but then she got out of her head and let her body take over.

Gideon's velvety voice told how the king, so moved by his daughter's beauty and joy, realized he must allow his children to go out into the world. They all returned to the stage and danced together, spinning until the girls became snowflakes that fell from the ceiling, and the stage went dark.

There was a moment of silence before the audience exploded into delighted applause. Evie stayed where she was, on the floor of the stage, her arms stretched forward. She rose slowly, the signal for the rest of the girls to do the same. As they'd practiced several times, they formed lines and walked forward, then bowed as one. The first group circled around to the back, and the process was repeated several times until all the girls had had a chance to bow and be applauded.

By the end, the audience was on its feet. The girls gathered around Evie for a group hug as they laughed and jumped up and down. Then a dozen or so young boys climbed the stairs and starting handing out small bouquets of flowers to each of the girls. Parents were clapping and trying to capture everything on their camcorders. Mayor Marsha walked out, a massive bouquet of dark red roses in her arms.

She crossed to Evie and handed her the flowers. "I wish I could say these are from the town," she said, speaking into a handheld microphone. "Although we did buy you flowers, they aren't nearly as lovely as these. Perhaps you would like to thank the person responsible personally."

She motioned to the other side of the stage. Evie

turned and nearly collapsed when she saw Dante walking toward her.

He looked tired, she thought, unable to grasp that he was here. Tired and worried, but, oh, so appealing in a cream-colored sweater and jeans. His blue gaze settled on her face as he moved across the stage.

Hope battled with pain and fear. She was thrilled to see him and terrified she would start crying. She wanted to believe his being here was a good thing, but what if there was some busty blonde waiting in the wings?

Dante walked up to her and took both her hands in his. "You were beautiful," he murmured. "You're so talented, and I can't get over what you did with these kids."

"Who's he calling kids?" Evie heard Melissa grumble.

"You're supposed to be in Aspen."

"I was. By myself," he added. "There's no ex-girlfriend."

Relief threatened her ability to stand a second time. "Then why did you say there was?"

"Because I'm an idiot. I thought…" He squeezed her hands. "Evie, I was scared. Scared of what you'd come to mean to me. Scared of my feelings. You know about my mom and what happened. I promised myself I would never let myself care again. I was doing a good job, too. Until I met you. And then I couldn't help myself."

She was aware of three thousand, two hundred people in the audience, watching. Based on the silence, she would guess that overhead microphones were picking up every word. Not that she was willing to ask Dante to hold that thought so they could go somewhere more private.

"I figured it out this morning. It was Christmas Eve and I wasn't with the people I love. In the place I love. I wasn't with you, Evie. So I chartered a plane to get here in time to see you dance. I knew how much this night meant to you and I wanted to share it with you. I also wanted to tell you that I love you."

Her breath caught. The girls on the stage sighed, as did most of the women watching. Somebody in the audience said something about this "being just like when Shane proposed to Annabelle."

"You do?" she asked.

"Very much. I never believed there could be 'the one' until I met you." He smiled. "I love you and I hope you can forgive me for leaving like that. It will never happen again."

"I believe you."

"About which part?"

"About all of it." The last pain faded away, and her heart began to heal. "I love you, too. I have for a while."

She had more to say, but Dante was pulling her close and kissing her. She wrapped her arms around him and held on. She heard cheers and applause, but they weren't as interesting as the man who held her as if he would never let her go.

SOMETIME LATER, WHEN EVIE had changed her clothes and everyone else had left, she and Dante walked back to their townhouses. It was still snowing, quieting the world and making her feel as if they were all alone…in the best way possible.

"I really am sorry about being such an idiot," Dante told her. "I hurt you. There's no excuse for that."

"I'll let you make it up to me."

"I'd appreciate that."

She glanced at him. "But I do have to tell you that there's a new man in my life."

Dante stared at her. "You went out with Gideon. I knew it."

"No. I got a cat."

He let out a relieved laugh. "Okay. I can handle a cat."

"I don't know. He's pretty handsome and affectionate. And he's a great cuddler."

"You're saying I have my work cut out for me."

"I'm saying we'll have to see who I like better."

He leaned down and wrapped his arms around her waist, then spun them both in a circle. Evie laughed and held her arms out. Being in love really was like flying.

When her head was spinning, he lowered her to the ground and kissed her. "Merry Christmas, my love," he whispered.

"Merry Christmas."

Still wrapped in each other's arms, they made their way home. Tomorrow was for family and friends, but tonight…tonight was theirs alone.

* * * * *

ONLY US: A FOOL'S GOLD HOLIDAY

CHAPTER ONE

"POLISH OR NO polish?" Carina Fiore held up two bottles of pet-friendly OPI nail polish. "I think the traditional choices would be best. Fire-Hydrant Red or Bow-Wow Green."

Eight-year-old Kaitlyn McKenzie laughed. "Rina, she's a cat."

"You're saying cats aren't into fashion? I'm not sure I agree. Just last week I caught this one flipping through *In Style* magazine." Rina studied the petite calico sitting on her grooming table. The calico stared back, her expression slightly defiant, as if daring Rina to try polish.

Rina held in a grin. Her plan was to put festive collars on the cats but she loved making Kaitlyn laugh.

The girl chuckled. "Cats can't read."

"You don't actually know that."

"Dad says they can't."

"Oh, well. Sure. Take the word of a veterinarian over me." Rina gave a heavy sigh.

Kaitlyn stepped around the grooming table and

hugged Carina tightly. "We'll do all the dogs' nails. I promise. I'll even help. We want them to look their best."

"Me too."

As much as Rina hated to admit it, cute pets got adopted faster. And as the person in charge of the Fool's Gold Holiday Pet Adoption, she intended to make sure every single animal looking for a home put his or her best foot forward. Or paw or claw or fin. Not that she would be doing anything to groom the fish. Although she was putting little fish-friendly Christmas trees in the tanks.

Her normally tidy grooming space was currently overflowing with cat collars and doggie bandanas in holiday prints. Over the next two weeks, she would be bathing, brushing and clipping until all the pets up for adoption gleamed.

She glanced at the clock on the wall. "We'd better get you home, munchkin."

Kaitlyn looked up at her, her green eyes as dark and beautiful as her father's. "It's Friday."

"I heard that this morning on the news."

The girl's mouth turned up at the corner. "You know what that means."

"That tomorrow's Saturday?"

"Spaghetti."

"Oh, right. I was thinking of something different for dinner."

"Rina!"

"Maybe liver."

Kaitlyn made a gagging sound.

"Brains?"

Kaitlyn clutched her stomach. "I'm going to throw up."

"Swamp soup?"

Giggling, Kaitlyn ran out of the room.

Rina picked up the cat and stroked her. "What do you think about swamp soup?"

The cat purred.

Fifteen minutes later Rina had finished cleaning off her table and washing her brushes. She collected her backpack and walked toward the break room. One of the veterinary assistants stopped her.

"You have to say something," Jesse told her.

"No."

"Soon."

"Did I just say no? I'm sure I heard myself say no."

Jesse, a pretty blonde whom Rina had known since they were both zygotes, raised her eyebrows.

Rina glanced around to make sure they were alone. Even so, she lowered her voice. "I can't."

"You have to. It's been a year, Rina. This is insane. It's the holidays."

"I'm not sure what the time of year has to do with anything."

Jesse sighed. "It's when you want to be with the people you love. You love Cameron. Tell him."

Rina winced. "Don't say that," she whispered as forcefully as she could. "Not here. Someone might hear you."

"It's Friday afternoon. Everyone is gone but us. Cameron's out at the Castle Ranch, checking on one of the goats there." Her friend moved closer and, Carina noticed thankfully, lowered her voice. "You're my best friend and I totally support whatever you decide, but I also know it's time to tell you that you're acting like an idiot."

"You've told me that every day for six months. It's hardly a news flash."

"Then *do* something. If not now, when? Are you going to waste another year being in love with a man who has no idea how you feel?"

Rina opened her mouth, then closed it. She wanted nothing more than to confess her feelings to the man she loved.

She could still remember the first time she'd seen Cameron McKenzie, DVM. He'd bought the practice from the retiring veterinarian with a promise that all the staff would stay. That included her, the practice's resident groomer. He'd requested everyone meet with him on a Saturday afternoon. She'd walked into the building, not sure what to expect. He'd turned, smiled, and she'd been lost.

Seriously, there'd practically been a swell of music and cartoon animals putting ribbons and flowers in her hair.

She wasn't sure what it was about Cameron that got to her. The wavy dark hair and deep green eyes were only the beginnings of his good looks. Still, her feelings weren't all about how handsome he was. It was the way he cared about his work and how he treated his staff. But if she had to guess, she would say her fate had truly been sealed the moment she'd met Kaitlyn.

She adored the little girl and they had become instant friends. Kaitlyn was smart and funny and just as caring as her dad. The only part of their family that didn't make sense was the absence of a mother. Cameron didn't say much about his ex, so all of Rina's information had come from his daughter. Kaitlyn was fairly matter-of-fact about her past, stating her mommy had left shortly after Kaitlyn had been born. Rina could still remember her steady gaze as she'd said, "Babies are a lot of work and my mommy wasn't ready."

Cameron had shared few details, but those he mentioned were in line with what Kaitlyn had said; his wife had walked away from her newborn and husband and had never returned.

Since then, from what she could tell, he'd devoted himself to being a single father and working hard at his practice. He never dated, hadn't once been caught flirting and showed no interest in one woman over another. In a town with a man shortage, he was practically an irresistible force.

Rina had told herself she would get over her crush, that it was just that Cameron was new and shiny. But as time had passed, her feelings had only grown. Now everything was more complicated because of the fact that she took care of Kaitlyn.

Every school day, Rina arrived at the McKenzie household early, made sure Kaitlyn was up and dressed, then fixed her breakfast and walked her to the bus. After school the girl rode the bus to the veterinary practice where she hung out with Rina until it was time to go home.

Back at the McKenzie house, Rina helped her with her homework and started dinner. In the past few months, she'd begun staying to eat with them. Unfortunately, she couldn't remember exactly how that had started. She wanted to say that Cameron had asked, but she suspected the invitation had come from his daughter.

Cameron paid her as a groomer and as the person taking care of his daughter. And, even though he was friendly and considerate, she couldn't be completely sure he'd ever thought of her as more than a friend. Which meant admitting her feelings put a lot on the line. What if he wasn't interested?

What if telling the truth meant losing her friendship with Kaitlyn *and* her job?

"I'd rather have what I have now than not have anything at all," Rina admitted to her friend.

Jesse shook her head. "You're living half a life, Rina, and that's not you. Your parents were crazy about each other until the day they died. Your grandparents are still in love. Don't you want what they have?"

"I'm scared."

"Love is supposed to be scary. If it was easy, everyone would do it."

Rina knew she was right. The thought of having it all, of being able to admit her feelings to Cameron and having him feel the same way, made her ache with longing. She'd known he was the one from the first second they'd met and her feelings had never wavered. But…

"What if he doesn't love me back?"

"Then you hurt and heal and find someone else."

"I don't want anyone else."

"So you'd rather have half of nothing than take the chance? That's not like you."

"I wouldn't just be losing him. I'd lose Kaitlyn, too."

"You wouldn't have to. You could still be friends with her."

Rina was less sure that was possible. Losing

one would be hard enough, but losing them both would be more than she could handle.

CHAPTER TWO

"TINSEL AND GOATS don't mix," Cameron said, looping his stethoscope around his neck. "Not that she'll listen."

Heidi Simpson nodded as she knelt next to her goat. "I swear, Athena has supernatural powers. She's forever getting out of her pen and doing things she shouldn't. I've been so careful with the holiday decorations."

Cameron believed her. Unfortunately a single box of tinsel had fallen out of her shopping bag and Athena had found it. Like most goats, she was willing to eat nearly everything. The tinsel had tangled in her digestive system, but had finally worked its way through.

"She'll be fine now," he said. "Give her a couple of days for her stomach to calm down." He patted the goat resting in the small goat barn, then rose to his feet.

"You've been great," Heidi told him as she stood as well. "You've been here every day. I really appreciate it."

"Part of the job."

"Still. I know Athena is grateful, too, even if she's having trouble articulating her feelings."

Heidi smiled as she spoke.

Cameron collected his medical bag then followed Heidi to his truck. It was late afternoon on the first Friday in December. The skies were dark and threatening, but the temperature wasn't cold enough for snow in town. Further up the mountain, they could get a good dump in the next couple of days.

Holiday decorations brightened the old house that stood on the ranch. The exterior was a little shabby, but the twinkling lights added a welcoming glow. Heidi was friendly enough. Pretty, he thought absently. Single. He should have been interested, maybe ask her to coffee or out for a drink. Only he wasn't the least bit interested.

He'd dated plenty when he'd been younger and had learned he was the kind of man who wanted to settle down. The problem was with whom.

After his daughter had been born, his ex-wife had announced she was leaving. From his point of view, her desire to leave had come out of nowhere, leaving him blindsided and the single father of a newborn. It had taken him a while to realize that whatever made his wife leave was out of his control.

Over the past few years, he'd become aware of a

nagging sense of having missed something. Fool's Gold had plenty of single women and he'd been set up with more than his share. But he hadn't felt the need for further dates with any of them. Maybe the problem was his—he wasn't willing to trust his daughter or his heart with just anyone.

Heidi paused by his truck. "Thanks again."

"You're welcome. You have my cell number. Call me if there are any problems."

"Don't you ever go off duty?"

"No."

"This town is lucky to have you."

He chuckled. "Remind people of that the next time I raise my rates."

"I will, I promise." She smiled. "Don't take this wrong, but I'm hoping not to see you before the holidays. Unless you plan to bring your daughter by for a horse-drawn carriage ride. We're keeping the tradition in place for the holidays."

"We might have to come by for that." He grinned. "But not for anything else. How's that?"

"Perfect. Merry Christmas."

"The same to you, Heidi."

He got in his truck and started the engine. Heidi walked up the porch steps. He watched her go, hoping for a spark or even vague interest in the sway of her hips.

Nothing.

Twenty minutes later Cameron was pulling into

his own driveway. The Christmas lights he'd spent much of the long Thanksgiving weekend putting up glowed in the darkness. Lit wreaths hung in all the front-facing windows, along with flickering candles. Not real candles. Kaitlyn had informed him those weren't really safe around fabric or children. So she and Rina had bought battery-powered ones from the hardware store in town.

Like most homeowners in Fool's Gold, he had an account at the hardware store. Based on all the packages his daughter and Rina had dragged home from various trips, he wasn't looking forward to that bill. But it was worth it to see his baby girl so excited about the holidays.

He parked in the driveway and turned off the engine. Before he could step out, the front door banged open and Kaitlyn flew across the porch.

As always the sight of her made him want to get down on his knees in gratitude for having her in his world. Sure, the first couple of years had been tough as he and his daughter had figured out how to make a single-parent family work. But every second of fear and worry had been worth it. She was the best part of his life.

He left his bag on the passenger seat and stepped into the night. Kaitlyn flung herself at him, wrapping both her arms around his waist and hanging on tight.

"Hey, baby girl," he said softly, touching her cheek.

She looked up at him, grinning. There was a smudge of flour on her cheeks and a mischievous sparkle in her eyes. "We're making cookies. Rina said we could and it's Friday!" As if the cookies were all the more magical because of the day.

"Christmas cookies?" he asked, already knowing the answer.

"Uh-huh. We rolled them out and then used cookie cutters and now they're cooling and after dinner we're decorating and Rina said you could help." She paused to draw breath. "I can't stand waiting, can you?"

"I'll manage."

His daughter released him, then ran around the truck to get his medical bag, something she'd been doing since she was big enough to drag it into the house. Now she carried it more easily. The time might even come when she couldn't be bothered, preferring to spend her time with her friends. But that was for later. Right now, he was a blessed man.

Kaitlyn led the way into the house. The smell of freshly baked cookies mingled with the spice of marinara sauce. Noah, their sheltie, raced to greet him. A female—despite her name—Noah circled around his legs in an attempt to get closer and express her joy about yet another pack member returning.

"Hey, you," he said, scooping up the dog.

Noah bathed his face in ecstatic kisses. When he lowered her to the ground, she ran off to get her ball.

Rina stepped out of the kitchen.

"Hi," she said, her long brown hair pulled back in a ponytail. "Is Athena all right?"

He nodded. "She feels better than Heidi, who's still feeling guilty about what happened. They should both be back to normal by the morning."

Big blue eyes crinkled slightly as she smiled. Cooking had added color to her cheeks, making her look flushed. Her mouth was full and inviting and the way she moved…

Out of long habit, Cameron pushed away "those" kind of thoughts. Sure, Rina was beautiful and funny and great with his daughter. But while he liked her company and liked having her around, he wasn't ready for a long-term relationship. He wasn't going to let something as fleeting and confusing as romantic involvement with Rina get in the way of his daughter's happiness.

He'd thought he loved his ex. She'd stunned him by leaving with no warning. But in the panicked few weeks that had followed her departure, in the reality of caring for a newborn while trying to keep his practice alive, he hadn't had time to miss his wife. Or maybe he hadn't loved her at all. Either way, by the time he'd resurfaced, his life slightly under control, he no longer regretted her leaving.

Lesson learned, he reminded himself. Friendship he could understand and trust. Rina was his friend. One of his best friends. He was going to do everything in his power to make sure that didn't change.

"I told Daddy he could help with the cookies," Kaitlyn said, walking to the sink to wash her hands without being asked.

Rina grinned. "Did you? Do you think he'll do a good job?"

"I have some creative skills," Cameron told her, shrugging out of his jacket.

"Maybe you could audition," Rina told him. "Do one and if we think it's all right, you can do a second."

His daughter burst out laughing. "She's kidding, Daddy. You can decorate as many cookies as you want."

"Thank you, baby girl." He walked by Rina. "I'll deal with you later," he growled in a low voice.

She glanced at him, then looked away. But in the split second when her gaze locked with his, he would have sworn he saw something. A spark. No, bigger than a spark, because whatever it was hit him hard in the gut. It made him think about being alone with her in a dark, quiet room. Just the two of them and all the time in the world. It made him want to hold her in his arms and kiss her. And more.

He shook off the moment, telling himself it was just the season. Holidays were a time for belonging. While Kaitlyn was amazing, she was his kid, not his partner. Maybe it was time for him to start dating.

He went to the sink to wash his hands, then he and Kaitlyn set the table. When the oven timer went off, he removed the garlic bread and put it on a plate. The dance of preparing dinner was a familiar one, formed over the past year. Rina stirred the sauce, while he dumped the cooked spaghetti into a colander. She combined pasta and sauce, then brought the serving bowl to the table while he poured Kaitlyn's milk and a glass of wine for Rina and for himself. Noah settled into her bed in the corner of the kitchen, a dog biscuit held delicately in her teeth.

"Maybe we could get our tree this weekend," Kaitlyn said, her voice faintly pleading.

"It's a little early," Rina told her, passing the garlic bread. "There's a new delivery coming in next Thursday. They'll be fresh. I love that smell."

"Me, too," his daughter said. "You're right. We should wait. If it's fresh, we can keep it up through New Year's."

Conversation flowed around him. A discussion about whether or not there should be more decorations on the lawn. His daughter talking about practicing for the holiday pageant and how she would start taking dance classes in January. That meant next year she would appear in the Dance of the Winter King. There were also not-so-subtle hints about what she would like for Christmas and a recounted conversation in which Rina had threatened to paint a cat's nails.

"How's the adoption program coming?" he asked.

"Good. I've been putting pictures of the pets up online, so people get an idea of what's available. The shelter has been getting lots of calls." She wrinkled her nose. "There's a family interested in the iguana, if you can believe it. Why anyone would want a four-foot-long lizard that can live twenty years is beyond me. But they have a special room prepared for it and everything."

"Having the iguana adopted out will be a big savings," he said.

"I know. Based on the calls we're getting, we have a lot of good prospective owners interested in other animals, too. I'm hoping for a big turnout."

"You've put a lot of work into the project."

Rina smiled. "The animals shouldn't be stuck in a shelter—not even the iguana. Everyone should have a home to be part of, especially over the holidays."

When he'd bought the veterinary practice in

Fool's Gold, he'd wanted to find a welcoming community to raise his daughter. What he'd found was a place to call home. No one simply lived in the town. They became a part of whatever was going on.

"You're not really going to try to paint the cats' nails are you?" he asked.

"You're going to have to wait and see what I do."

They finished dinner and then sat around the table talking. It was close to seven-thirty when they got up to clear the dishes. While Kaitlyn helped Rina load the dishwasher, Cameron walked Noah. When he returned there were boxes of decorations scattered across the coffee table in the living room.

"Just a few more things," Rina said, with a shrug. "We couldn't resist."

"Where am I supposed to store all this?" he asked. "I'll have to add on a second house."

That made Kaitlyn laugh. She spun in a circle, her long hair flowing out behind her, Noah chasing her. Dog and child collapsed onto the floor in a heap. Kaitlyn opened her eyes.

"Daddy, look!"

He followed the direction of her pointed finger and found a small sprig of artificial mistletoe pinned to the door frame.

Turning to Rina he explained, "She read about

mistletoe when she was six. Now she wants me to put it up every year. It's kind of a family joke."

Only Rina wasn't laughing and suddenly he wasn't either. She was standing right under the tacky little plant—she probably hadn't noticed it until his daughter had mentioned it just now. Emotions flashed through her eyes, emotions he couldn't read. They were friends, he reminded himself. Good friends. Kissing would make things awkward between them and that was the last thing he wanted.

"Daddy, kiss her."

It seemed easier to give in than to explain—at least that was what he told himself. He bent forward and lightly brushed Rina's mouth with his own. There was a quick explosion of heat, then she drew back and sidestepped away.

"Now where are we putting those dancing snowmen?" she asked.

Rina had never been much of a believer in signs, but she was starting to rethink her position. Within a few hours of having a conversation with her friend Jesse about telling Cameron how she felt about him, he'd kissed her. Sure, it had been because of mistletoe and in front of his daughter and his dog. Hardly the hot, I've-been-desperately-in-love-with-you-for-months kiss she'd been hoping for, but still. It was a start.

After quietly leaving a sleepy Kaitlyn in her

bed, Cameron and Carina returned to the living room. Before Cameron could offer her a drink or suggest a movie, Rina decided she had to make her move. Telling him how she felt wasn't anything she could imagine doing, but showing him… He'd broken the physical barrier tonight, and she wasn't going to stop the momentum now.

So when he looked at her and started to ask, "Do you want to—" she was ready.

She put her hands on his broad shoulders, raised herself on tiptoe and put her mouth on his.

For a second he didn't react. There was only the ticking of the grandfather clock in the hall and Noah's sigh as she settled back in her bed. Then slowly, his lips moved against hers.

Rina released the breath she'd been holding and allowed herself to relax. She tilted her head and leaned into him. His hands settled on her waist. But the best part was the sparks.

They were everywhere: floating around, dancing against her skin, swirling through her belly and heating the most interesting parts of her body. Loving Cameron meant wanting him. She'd been aware of the desire lurking inside her, but it was a need without substance. She hadn't known if they had that magical chemistry that would add passion to friendship. Until now.

Now she longed for him even more than before. Her breasts ached to be stroked by him. Her thighs trembled and hunger burned. When he brushed his tongue against her lower lip, she parted for him immediately. When he swept inside, she felt herself getting lost in the moment, in the burning need and the taste of him.

Strong hands pulled her closer. She melted against him, curves to his hard planes, female to his male. At last, she thought. They were both in exactly the right place.

CHAPTER THREE

CAMERON FELT DESIRE rising up inside him, threatening to overwhelm him. Reminding himself that his friendship with Rina was more important than any single night didn't seem to be working. While some might say taking things to the next level made sense, he knew better. If he and Rina were friends, he would never lose her. To do more was to risk what they had and he couldn't imagine his life, or his daughter's, without her.

Carefully, he drew back. His resolve nearly crumbled when he saw the passion in her blue eyes and realized her mouth was swollen with his kisses. She was all lush curves and temptation. He could see her breasts rising and falling with every breath and, for a second, he didn't think he was strong enough to hold back. Then he reminded himself what was at stake and he managed to contain himself.

"Sorry about that," he said lightly. "I guess I got carried away."

He hoped that was enough. That she would accept the words and everything could go back to the way it was before. Wishful thinking, he realized when she spoke.

"I kissed you," she told him.

He nodded.

"You kissed me back."

Another nod.

"Cameron, I want more than what we have."

She laid him bare with her words. But what would happen later, to him and his daughter, if she tired of them and walked away? That had been difficult enough for him to go through once. He couldn't risk Kaitlyn, as well.

He drew in a breath. "I like what we have, Rina. We're friends. Good friends. I don't want that to change."

The passion in her eyes bled away, replaced by despair. "Thanks but no thanks?" she asked, her voice low. Tears glistened before she looked down. "Let me guess. I'm not your type."

"You are. It's not that I don't want you, I do. I just want our friendship more. If we started dating then everything would get complicated."

"Dating?" Her voice rose. "Dating? Is that what you think this is about? I'm in love with you, you idiot. I'm here nearly every night, sharing dinner with you, laughing with you, talking about our days. I'm crazy about Kaitlyn. I'm doing everything I can to show you that I'm exactly who you need, who you should love and want and you think I'm interested in a date?"

He couldn't have been more surprised if she'd taken out a baseball bat and hit him on the head. Love? He couldn't begin to figure out what that meant.

Rina stepped back. In a matter of seconds, she was shrugging into her coat and had her purse in hand. And then she was gone. He was left standing in the middle of his living room, not sure what had happened, but knowing it was bad.

Noah raised her head and looked at him questioningly.

"I haven't got a clue," he told the dog. "Not a clue."

Rina spent most of the weekend working with the holiday adoption committee. She was grateful to be running from meeting to meeting, helping write up descriptions and speaking with prospective owners. Being busy kept her from thinking and not thinking was much easier than feeling the burning emptiness. But come Monday morning, life would get much more complicated.

Her weekday started as they always did, with her going over to Cameron's house to get Kaitlyn ready for school. She almost cancelled, but didn't want to disappoint Kaitlyn. Shortly after Cameron and Kaitlyn had moved to town, Kaitlyn had put in an appearance in Rina's grooming salon. She'd thought the girl was charming and Kaitlyn had asked to spend time there…which had led to the official sitting job from Cameron. But Rina rarely thought of it as a job. Kaitlyn had become so much more to her than her boss's daughter.

Still, Rina wasn't looking forward to seeing the man who had rejected her and trampled her dreams with one carefully worded statement.

She let herself into the house, as usual. The smell of coffee filled the warm and welcoming home. After hanging her jacket on the coat hanger by the door and dropping her backpack on the table in the foyer, she squared her shoulders, drew in a breath and walked into the kitchen.

Cameron was already there. He was freshly showered, wearing jeans and a long-sleeved shirt. His gaze was steady, if a little wary, his eyes the perfect color of green.

She wanted to run. Facing him after what she'd said would take more than she had in her. Only she refused to be rejected *and* be a coward.

"I wasn't sure you'd come this morning," he said.

"We have an agreement."

"I know, it's just…"

She poured herself a cup of coffee. At least her hands weren't shaking. "It's what you said," she told him. "We're friends."

Somehow she would figure out a way to make that okay.

"You're not going to disappear?"

"No."

His body relaxed. "Okay. Good. We can get back to where we were, Rina. I know we can."

Then he was more sure than she was. But she would try. Because of his daughter. Because she wasn't the kind of person to run from trouble. And because friendship was better than nothing.

"I have a spelling test on Friday," Kaitlyn said with a sigh later that afternoon. "My computer checks my spelling for me. Why do I have to learn words myself?"

Rina wiped down the grooming table. She'd already finished her last client and was ready to leave. She'd spent most of Monday trying to act normally, all the while avoiding Cameron. A challenging prospect considering her salon was in the middle of his veterinary practice.

"It's important to be able to spell," Rina said, unable to think of a good reason and hoping Kaitlyn didn't ask for one.

The eight-year-old studied her. "Are you sad?"

"No. I'm fine. A little tired. I was busy with adoption-event planning all weekend."

"Maybe you need a boyfriend."

Rina did her best not to wince. "Maybe."

"You can find one on the computer. Daddy's

looking for a girlfriend there. He told me. He was in a chat room yesterday. I told him I wanted you to be his girlfriend, but he said that was out of the question. I never understand when he says that. I didn't ask a question." She continued talking but Rina couldn't hear her over the fury creating a buzz in her ears. Of all the low-life, rat-fink, weasel things to do. Cameron had said they should stay friends and then he'd gone off to some chat room?

She'd been calm. She'd been rational. She'd told herself that if he didn't want her romantically, that was his right and she would have to get over it. She'd taped her shattered heart back together and had shown up that morning because it was the right thing to do and he'd been in some damn chat room?

"Kaitlyn, will you excuse me for a minute?"

The girl nodded.

"I'll be right back and then I'll take you home."

Rina marched out of her salon. A quick glance at the clock told her that unless there was an emergency, Cameron would be in his office, updating patient records. She walked down the short hall, turned left, then stepped into his office and closed the door behind her.

He glanced up and gave her a smile. She knew that smile, knew everything about his face, the way he walked and how vulnerable he looked when he was tired. She understood his moods, had cared for him when he'd had the flu, had even groomed his dog. She'd loved him and his daughter, offering all she had, including her heart. He'd rejected her and then had gone online looking for love?

"I don't think so," she snapped.

The smile faded and wariness invaded his gaze. "What are we talking about?"

They both spoke in low voices. The practice was in an old house and the walls were thin. While Rina wanted to scream, she didn't want everyone hearing every detail of what could be a very humiliating conversation.

"You went online, looking for a girlfriend?"

He tensed. "Kaitlyn told you."

"Of course she told me. She tells me everything. She loves me."

The reality of what she'd just said slammed into her and she had to clutch the bookcase to stay standing. The affection she felt for Kaitlyn went both ways. They needed each other. How was she supposed to fight against that?

"I'm aware of her feelings," Cameron admitted. "What happened Friday got me thinking about a lot of things. I realized that I haven't been fair to either of you. I've let things go along as they were, without making sure everyone understood the rules."

By *everyone* he meant her. Her strength returned and she straightened. And glared.

"So you thought you'd help both of us by looking for a relationship on the computer?" she demanded.

"I thought if I started seeing someone—" He cleared his throat. "—in that way, Kaitlyn would become less attached to you."

She got the truth then. It cut through her cleanly, a sharp blade against her soft heart.

She'd told herself he wasn't ready. That he had suffered through a horrible divorce, after his wife had simply walked away from him and their newborn child. She'd convinced herself that he was wary of relationships and love and that given time he would see they were perfect together. She'd thought that *Let's stay friends* had meant *not now, maybe later*. Instead he'd been telling her no.

It wasn't that Cameron didn't want to be with anyone, it was that he didn't want to be with her.

Rina's eyes burned, but she refused to cry. Not here, not in front of her coworkers and Cameron and most especially not in front of Kaitlyn. Hope and love and dreams battled with cold, hard reality. As much as she wanted to ignore the truth, she couldn't. Not anymore.

"You're wrong," she said slowly. "About finding someone else. I have been there for you all this time. I know you like me and the way you kissed me proves…" She drew in a breath. "But you don't want to go there. Fine. We won't. I told you that

I loved you and the first thing you did was try to go out with someone else."

She linked her hands together in front of her waist and thought about what it would be like once he stopped looking and started dating. Of being at his house in the evening, taking care of his child, knowing he was out with someone else. She couldn't do it.

"I'm leaving."

He stood. "Leaving? Where are you going? What do you mean?"

She wasn't sure, but as she stood there, the answer came to her. "After the first of the year, I'll be moving my business out of here. You'll need to find someone else to take care of Kaitlyn. I want there to be a gradual transition so she's not upset, but you need someone else for daycare."

"You're cutting us out of your life? You said you wouldn't do that. I thought you cared about us."

"You're wrong. I didn't care. I don't care. I love you both." She stared into his eyes. "That's a whole lot more than caring."

"Then stay."

"No. You don't get to have it both ways. I've spent a year waiting for you to realize I was the one. That's enough time wasted."

With that she turned and left. Her heart pounded hard in her chest and she wasn't sure how long she could keep from crying. The sense of emptiness and loss nearly brought her to her knees. But behind the pain and fear and need to turn back and say, "Yes, fine, half a life is good enough for me," was the belief that she'd made the right decision.

It hurt now. It more than hurt. But with time and a little determination, she would recover. And, she thought, a little help from Fool's Gold wouldn't hurt either.

CHAPTER FOUR

Jo's Bar was a gathering place for the women of Fool's Gold. While the men had a room in back with a pool table and sports playing on TVs, the main portion of the bar was dedicated to women. The walls were painted a skin-flattering mauve, the large-screen TVs featured shopping channels and female-friendly reality shows and the menu included plenty of calorie-light options. During the day, one corner was turned into a play area for toddlers. While Friday and Saturday night brought in the couples crowd, the rest of the time, Jo's Bar was a place for women to feel comfortable. Or have a good cry.

"You did the right thing," Jesse said soothingly. "I know you did."

Rina clutched the tissue in her hand and did her best to stop the steady stream of tears. At the rate she was going, she'd be dehydrated and require emergency medical care within the hour.

"It doesn't f-feel right," she said, her voice

cracking on a sob. "It feels horrible. Everything hurts. I can't do this. I can't go on without him."

Jesse raised her eyebrows, which made Rina laugh. Well, it was more like a hiccup, but still it was an improvement over the crying.

"That made me sound like a stalker," she admitted. "Of course I can live without Cameron." Her humor faded. "I wish I didn't love him. Or that he loved me back. This sucks."

"Yes, it does. It hurts and you feel awful."

Rina looked at her friend and sniffed. "Are you trying to make me feel better? Because it's not really working."

Jesse touched her arm. "Dealing with this will get easier. Once the holidays are over, you can find a place to move your business to and start to cut ties."

Rina nodded and wiped away tears. "You're right. I'm not going to give up seeing Kaitlyn, though. I want to talk to Cameron about working out a schedule. Maybe I can take her a couple of afternoons a week."

"See, you have a plan."

Or at least part of one, Rina thought glumly.

The sound of several women laughing caused her to look to the bar side of the room. At least thirty women were setting up for what looked to be a bridal shower. Rina remembered all three of the Hendrix triplets were getting married over the holidays. Not that she begrudged them their happiness, but ouch.

"This hurts," she admitted. "What a stupid time of year to put it all on the line. I love Christmas. It was always a big thing in my house and I know my grandparents are looking forward to it."

"So you'll be with them and that will be nice."

"I know, it's just..." She swallowed and fought more tears. "We're supposed to go Friday to pick out the tree. That will be hard."

Jesse leaned toward her. "I know it will."

"You're not going to try and talk me out of it?"

"No. If you think you can stand it, you should stick with what's planned. For Kaitlyn. She adores you and getting a Christmas tree is a big deal for an eight-year-old." Jesse studied her. "You've seen him?"

"Since I made my pronouncement yesterday? Briefly. When he came home from work and again this morning when I went to get her ready for school. He hasn't said anything."

This morning he'd simply handed her a cup of coffee and said he would see her at the office. Kaitlyn had been the one to remind her about their date to pick out a tree.

"I'm avoiding him at work," Kaitlyn said. "It's a month, right? I can stand this for a month."

Jesse shifted in her seat. "He came to talk to me this morning."

Rina stared at her. “And? What did he say?”

“That he wasn’t online anymore. Looking.”

Looking, as in… “Oh. You mean he’s not trying to find someone.”

“Right.”

Rina picked up her glass of wine, then put it down. She was sure it was wonderful, but she’d yet to take a sip. The thought of it made her stomach flip, and not in a good way.

“I wasn’t sure if I should tell you,” Jesse admitted.

“Don’t worry. I’m not going to get my hopes up. Cameron isn’t a bad guy. He’s stupid, but not evil. I made it pretty clear that rejecting me and going in search of an online girlfriend in the same day was awful and I’m guessing he believed me.”

“He did.”

“So we’ll fake our way through this. After the first of the year, I won’t have to deal with him anymore.”

The thought should have relieved her but instead she felt sad and empty. Because dealing with Cameron and his daughter had become the best part of her world.

“It’s snowing!” Kaitlyn stared up at the sky, her eyes wide, her lips curving into a huge grin.

Tiny, wispy flakes drifted to the ground. Rina knew they wouldn’t stick and that in a matter of minutes the snow would stop, but for as long as it lasted, it was beautiful. An unexpected gift designed to remind her life did indeed keep moving on.

She and Kaitlyn walked through the Christmas-tree lot. Holiday music blasted out of battered speakers and plastic reindeer and Santas blinked on and off. The two college-age guys helping customers wore sweatshirts with snowmen on the front.

Kaitlyn clapped her mitten-covered hands together. "They're all so beautiful. How will we decide? Daddy said the ceilings are twelve feet tall, so we can't get anything taller than that."

"We could if we put the tree at an angle."

Kaitlyn laughed. "It would look funny and all the decorations would fall off."

"If you're going to be picky."

The girl wrapped her arms around Rina's waist and squeezed. Rina hugged her back, holding on to the moment, knowing that even if she saw Cameron's daughter a couple of days a week, their relationship would never be the same.

"Daddy!"

Kaitlyn released her and raced to her father. Rina gave herself a second to brace herself, then turned to look at Cameron.

Tiny snowflakes dotted his hair and landed on his leather jacket. His green eyes were more guarded than usual, as if he was unsure of how things were going to be between them. Determined to take the emotional high road, Rina gave him a smile.

"We were discussing tree size," she said cheerfully. "Apparently twelve feet is the limit."

"I'd say ten," he told her. "There's an angel to put on top."

Kaitlyn nodded. "She's beautiful and has wings. I'd forgotten about that."

"Ten feet is still a pretty big tree." Rina held out her hand to Kaitlyn. "Let's walk around and we'll figure out which ones we like."

The girl grabbed her father's hand, then Rina's, walking between them. They'd done this dozens of times before. Rina had always enjoyed the connection, but this time there was also a whisper of pain curling the edges of the moment, a reminder that in a few weeks, she would be moving on, no longer a part of the McKenzie family. Not that she'd ever been a member, but she'd foolishly allowed herself to pretend.

The college guys loaded the chosen tree into the back of Cameron's truck. Rina hovered awkwardly, not sure exactly when she was supposed to leave. Cameron was paying for the tree and Kaitlyn had run into a couple of her friends from school. The three girls were huddled together, laughing about something.

Part of her wanted simply to disappear into the

happy crowds on the street, but ducking out without saying good-bye seemed rude. Cameron was doing his best to act normal. She should do the same. Technically, she'd been the one to change the rules by telling him how she felt. Not that she regretted being honest, but it seemed the least she could do was play along.

He pocketed the receipt, then joined her. "She's going to be a while," he said, nodding at his daughter.

"She has a lot of friends."

"I'm glad. When we first moved here, I worried that she wouldn't fit in."

"Fool's Gold is very welcoming. My maternal grandparents lived here all their lives. My mom grew up here. With my dad in the army, we moved around a lot, but we settled here just before I started high school." Now she couldn't imagine living anywhere else.

Cameron studied her. "You must miss your folks."

She nodded. "It's been six years since they died, but yeah, I do. Especially now. Christmas was always a big deal in my house." She smiled, remembering. "We always got holiday pajamas on Christmas Eve. My mom tried to find ones that were exactly alike. Then we wore them on Christmas morning and made breakfast together. It was wonderful."

"That's what I want Kaitlyn to have. Memories. You've really helped with that. Thanks for being here today."

"You know I care about her. Of course I'm here. And I'm still helping with the holiday pageant." She smiled again, but this time it took a little effort. "You're not getting rid of me completely."

"I don't want to." He stared into her eyes. "Rina, I..."

She was pretty sure he was going to tell her he was sorry or suggest they could go back to what they'd been doing before. Neither of which she wanted to hear.

"What are you favorite Christmas memories?" she asked.

He hesitated as if not sure he was willing to go with the obvious change in subject, then he shrugged. "Things were good when I was younger, but after my mom remarried, they went downhill. My stepdad wasn't a bad man, but he was strict and we didn't get along. I spent one Christmas in juvenile detention."

"No way."

He held up a hand, as if offering an oath. "I did. I'd been messing around with some guys and we set a shed on fire. It was stupid. The whole neighborhood could have gone up in flames. Instead of sending me away, the judge sentenced me to a hundred hours of community service. I was fifteen and it seemed like a lifetime of punishment."

Rina had never heard about his early past. "I can't believe you were that kind of kid."

He smiled. "I turned out okay in the end. That community service changed my life. I got assigned to the local animal shelter. I worked ten hours a week, for ten weeks and by the time I was done, I knew I wanted to be a veterinarian. My stepfather had convinced my mother to send me to boarding school. Rather than fight it, I asked them to pick one specializing in science and math so I could get into a good college. I graduated with honors, got a scholarship and the rest, as they say, is history."

"I'm impressed."

"Don't be. There are a lot of kids who suffered a whole lot more than I did. I acted like an idiot and I was punished. What I'm pleased with is that I learned from my mistake and turned things around."

"Your mom must be proud."

"She is and so's my stepdad. We get along now."

"They live in Florida, right?"

He nodded. "We're going to visit them over spring break. You should come with us." He stiffened. "Sorry. I wasn't thinking."

She ignored the sudden ache in her chest. "No problem. I'm sure you two will have a great time. You can go to Disney World."

"Kaitlyn has already started planning what rides we'll go on first." He shoved his hands into his jeans pockets and looked at her. "Rina, I can't go there."

She knew he didn't mean Florida. "You've explained that."

"No, I haven't. I want you to understand. My wife left. There was no warning. Kaitlyn was two weeks old when she packed her bags and said she was leaving. Said she didn't want to be a mother or married to me. I didn't see it coming." He drew in a breath. "I won't go through that again."

"Someone leaving?"

"Yes. I don't want the uncertainty. Friends are different. You can depend on a friend."

"Meaning you won't trust another woman? If you care about someone, she could leave?"

He shifted uncomfortably. "It's more complicated than that."

She wondered if that was true. Was Cameron's entire problem that he was unwilling to take a chance on being hurt again? She was torn between knocking some sense into him and reacting with compassion. She decided that the latter would speak more highly of her character.

"You need to take a chance. If not on me, then on someone. You can't let one selfish, uncaring person scar you for the rest of your life." She stepped closer. "There's more on the line than your heart. Kaitlyn is going to learn about romantic love from what she sees you doing. If you're afraid to trust, that's what you're teaching her."

"She has other role models. Movies. Books. You."

Rina wasn't sure falling for a guy who was unwilling to trust again was something she wanted to pass on to an eight-year-old girl she cared about.

"You're her father. You are the most important person in her world. She'll do what you do."

CHAPTER FIVE

CAMERON WAS STARTING to feel like the antihero in a bad TV show. He would swear his entire staff was glaring at him behind his back. As he'd yet to catch anyone actually glaring, he knew he was in danger of becoming paranoid. Which would not be his best trait.

It was Rina's fault, he grumbled to himself as he carefully checked the sleeping dog on the operating table. The six-month-old Lab-border collie mix belonged to Max Thurman, the guy who owned K9Rx Therapy Dogs. The dog had been spayed right on time and would later continue her training to be a therapy dog. As he touched her shoulder, she stirred slightly, coming out of the anesthesia.

Jesse noted her vital signs. "She seems to be doing well," she said. "I'll stay with her until she's ready to be moved."

Cameron glanced at the woman, checking for hidden meaning behind her words. He knew Jesse and Rina were friends. Rina was friends with everyone around her, and that made him the bad guy in what was happening, which brought him right back to the paranoia that everyone was glaring at him.

The downside to small-town life, he thought as he gave the dog one last pat.

"Let me know if there are any problems," he said. "I'll be in my office." Where he would update the dog's file and scan the list of appointments he had for the afternoon.

As he walked down the hallway, he instinctively paused outside the grooming area. Rina was wielding clippers with the skill of an artist, trimming a small poodle's feet. She carried on a conversation with the animal as she worked, her voice low and soothing. He was familiar with that voice. He'd heard it when he'd had the flu and Rina had practically moved in to take care of both him and Kaitlyn.

He shook off the memory and continued toward his office. On the main hallway wall were hundreds of pictures of pets, donated by their happy owners. Rina had been the one to suggest the picture wall and it had grown. More than one family brought in a new picture every visit to add to the collection.

The bulletin board in the waiting area had a flyer for the adoption event coming up next weekend. Something else Rina was involved with. In his office, he skirted around a planter full of "kitty grass" Rina insisted they keep for their overnight feline guests.

She was everywhere, and he'd never noticed that before. When he'd first arrived in Fool's Gold, she'd been the one who had given him the list of where to shop and how to avoid trouble with the Gionni sisters by making sure he and Kaitlyn alternated between their hair salons. Rina had chided him into joining the Chamber of Commerce and signed him up to speak on taking care of pets at the local elementary schools. She'd taught his daughter to skate, had baked her a birthday cake and carefully curled her hair for the first day of school.

When Rina disappeared from his life, he would lose far more than simply a babysitter or even a friend. A part of him wanted to be angry at her for changing the rules, but another part of him understood why she wanted more than she had.

Which made him wonder, when she walked away, what would *she* lose?

She said she loved him and he believed her. But, thinking about all she'd done for him and how little he'd done for her, he couldn't help but wonder why. He'd never consciously gone out of his way to be kind. She was someone he liked and enjoyed spending time with. When she'd needed a new-to-her car, he'd helped her pick out the one that suited her needs best and then had given her advice on negotiating. He'd fixed a few things in her apartment. She had a crazy phobia about the dentist, so he literally held her hand during her twice-yearly cleaning. But that's what friends did for each other. It wasn't love.

He crossed to the window. While he paid her to take care of his daughter, he didn't pay her to care. That she had given freely.

The holiday pageant was a celebration of cultures and traditions. The translation of that statement was that it challenged the parents of grade-school-aged children with costume design and construction worthy of Broadway.

Rina had spent nearly a month on Kaitlyn's Christmas princess costume, wanting the girl to be thrilled with the results. The hours of sewing had produced a fairy-tale confection in deep red with ruffles and lace and a few beads thrown in for good measure.

Now Rina carefully removed the hot rollers from Kaitlyn's dark hair and finger-combed the ringlets. The girl stayed completely still, as if willing the transformation.

"This would be better if we had some cartoon forest animals," Rina joked, separating a few curls, then reaching for her can of hairspray. "Okay, deep breath."

Kaitlyn obligingly took a breath and held it. At the same time, she put her hands over her face. Rina carefully sprayed the curls into place, made a few last-minute adjustments, sprayed again, and then announced, "Got it."

Kaitlyn lowered her hands to her side. "How do I look?" she asked.

Rina studied the girl, taking in the green eyes so like her father's and the flush on her cheeks. She was lovely, the structure of her face already hinting at the beauty she would be as she grew up.

An ache began in Rina's chest, the knowledge that she would miss so much about Kaitlyn's daily life.

"Almost perfect," Rina told her. "There's just one thing missing." She reached up for the small diamond heart pendant she always wore. The one her mother had given her for her sixteenth birthday.

After unfastening the pendant, she placed the chain around Kaitlyn's neck. "I think you should wear this tonight. Because every princess needs to sparkle."

Kaitlyn touched the heart, then threw her arms around Rina's neck. "I love you so much."

"I love you, too. Always. Remember that. Whatever happens, I'll be there for you."

Kaitlyn straightened and looked her in the eyes. "I know."

Rina made her way to the front of the auditorium and searched for Cameron. He stood up and waved her over. On cue, her heartbeat increased and her whole body longed for him. She'd heard that falling in love was the best thing that could happen to anyone. She was sure that was true for some, but from her perspective, being in love sucked big-time.

She went around the back of the room and came down the center aisle. She knew most of the people in the auditorium and found her progress slowed by greetings and conversation.

"I've got my eye on that calico cat," Edie Carberry told her. "You make sure you let me know if anyone else seems interested."

"I will," Rina said, pausing to admire the older woman's holiday-themed jogging suit. Both the pants and jacket were green velour and there was a sequined poinsettia on the front by the zipper.

A mom with two kids in the pageant stopped her to ask about a border collie mix and Alice Barns, the police chief, spoke wistfully about a small gray kitten.

"With my boys so busy with their own lives, I could use a little furry something," Alice said. "My husband shocked me the other day when he said he wouldn't mind a cat. Coming from him, that's practically an advertising campaign."

Rina finally made her way to the row where Cameron waited and settled into her seat.

"I think the holiday adoption is going to be a success," she said. "I was worried it was a dumb idea, but I'm getting plenty of people interested. Now if only they show up and take the pets they say they're interested in."

"They will."

She braced herself, then glanced at him. His steady gaze locked with hers, making her feel warm inside. He'd always had the ability to make her believe she was safe around him. Too bad that had turned out not to be the truth.

"You can't know that for sure," she told him.

"Yes, I can. This is Fool's Gold and the people here take care of their own."

"Do you mean me or the pets?"

"Both."

The lights dimmed before she could respond.

The production had the usual mishaps. A couple of the kindergarteners were frightened by the bright lights and began to cry. A boy in Kaitlyn's class knocked over a tree and about half the kids forgot their lines. But Cameron didn't care about that. As he watched the skits and listened to the songs, he was once again grateful that he'd decided to move to Fool's Gold.

Kaitlyn looked like the fairy princesses she adored and he knew Rina was the reason. He'd seen the dress in pieces, but not since it had been assembled and it was everything a little girl could want.

"You didn't have to do that," he whispered,

leaning toward Rina. "I never meant for you to spend so much time on her costume."

"I wanted to."

In the dark, it was difficult to read her expression, but he could inhale the sweet scent of her body and feel the heat that tempted him.

For a second, he allowed himself to wonder what it would be like if he permitted himself to give in. To share her feelings and to take what she offered. To touch her and taste her, to let her the rest of the way into his life.

He couldn't risk that, but maybe he could keep the part of her that mattered to him most.

She turned to him. "What?" she asked in a whisper.

"Later," he promised.

After the program had ended, everyone stood up and collected their coats.

"They're serving the kids cupcakes and punch before releasing them back to their families," Rina said with a grin. "Because they're not already wound up from their performances, right? The teachers want to seal the deal with a little sugar rush?"

Cameron knew he should laugh or at least smile, but he couldn't. He grabbed her hand and pulled her to the middle of the rapidly emptying row.

"We need you," he said urgently. "Kaitlyn and

I. We're friends. You said it yourself. Don't go. We can keep things the way they were."

The light slowly faded from her blue eyes. Her mouth straightened.

"You mean give up what I want because having me around is convenient? What do I get out of it, Cameron? Aside from a check every week? A family? Someone to love who loves me back? You want the best of what I have without risk. Without having to share yourself. That's not going to happen. You can buy childcare, but you can't buy me. Not anymore."

"I didn't mean it like that. You can still have a life. Date."

She flinched. "Right. Because seeing me with another man wouldn't bother you at all. Don't you understand that's the best reason for me to leave?"

They were supposed to get Kaitlyn together, to go home and celebrate with popcorn. Put up the last of the decorations. But Rina drew back.

"I'm going to tell Kaitlyn I have to go."

Cameron reached for her, but she was too far away. "Wait."

"No. I'm done waiting. I'm moving on."

CHAPTER SIX

"WHY CAN'T RINA get me ready for school?" Kaitlyn asked, the following Thursday morning.

Cameron carefully brushed his daughter's hair. "She's busy with the pet adoption this coming Saturday and she has a lot to do."

He knew Rina was avoiding him, but he wasn't going to say that. Whatever was going on between him and Rina had nothing to do with Kaitlyn.

"We haven't talked about what we're getting her for Christmas," his daughter informed him. "I don't want to get her a sweater. Rina loves us. We need to give her a present that says we love her, too."

There was a conversation he didn't want to have, he thought grimly. "Love is complicated," he began, but his daughter shook her head.

"It's not. It's simple. Love is when we care more about somebody else than we do ourselves. It's like with Mommy. She didn't love us and that's why she left. Because if she'd loved us, she would have wanted to stay. People who love you want to be with you. And we want the people we love to always be around."

He put down the brush and turned his daughter so she faced him.

"I'm sorry about your mother."

"I know, but it's not your fault." She wrinkled her nose. "Sometimes I get sad about her leaving, but mostly I don't think about it." She beamed at him. "You shouldn't either because we have Rina." Her eyes widened. "I know! Make Rina your girlfriend. Then she would be real instead of an internet girlfriend."

He stared at his daughter, not sure where to start. "I'm not looking for an internet girlfriend."

"You were."

"It was a bad idea."

"What about Rina? We already love each other."

"It's different."

"Why?"

"It just is."

She sighed and mumbled something that sounded a lot like "No, it's not," but he let the comment go. This wasn't a fight he could win.

Kaitlyn turned her back so he could start on her braid. "Rina's pretty."

"Yes, she is."

"She makes our favorite dinners a lot and we laugh together."

"I know."

"You liked kissing her."

That truth kicked him in the gut. He had liked kissing her. A lot, as his daughter would say. But he couldn't get involved with Rina that way.

"Kaitlyn..." he began.

She sighed. "I'll be quiet now."

"Thank you."

Cameron went through a busy morning of appointments. Simon Bradley, a local surgeon, brought in CeCe for her quarterly checkup. These days the small toy poodle was no longer a full-time therapy dog, having been adopted by Simon and his fiancée.

Cameron always enjoyed watching a big, powerful man reduced to cooing over a tiny dog. Not that he would say that to Simon. As CeCe still did some work at the hospital, working with children who had burns, she had to be checked more often to make sure she wasn't carrying any parasites or had the beginnings of an infection.

"You know Rina's not in today," Cameron said as he finished checking CeCe's heart. Usually the poodle was left in the salon for a grooming on her check-up days.

"I know. She told me when she called."

"Rina called you?"

Simon nodded. "To switch appointment days. She mentioned she's relocating her business. That she needs more room to expand."

Cameron nodded. That was the story she'd come up with. He knew she'd decided on the almost-truth to protect Kaitlyn as much as him. Announcing to the world she was forced to move because the man she loved was too stupid or selfish to love her back wouldn't play well. At least not for him. Which she wouldn't want.

He swore under his breath. Why did she have to be so damned good?

"What?" Simon asked anxiously. "Is everything okay with CeCe?"

"Yes. Sorry." Cameron straightened. "She's fine. It's something else. Woman trouble."

"I know what that feels like," Simon admitted with a grin. "Although in my case, it was all my fault."

The grin faded. "Montana put her heart on the line and I walked away. Or tried to. I told myself not being in a relationship was easier than risking losing it. Because then I was in control." He shook his head. "What a crock. There's no control when it comes to the heart. I hate to think about how pathetic I sounded, trying to be brave when I was really terrified. I could have lost everything. For what it's worth, if she's half as amazing as Montana, you should suck it up, apologize for what you did wrong and beg her to take you back."

"Interesting advice."

"Good advice," Simon corrected.

Later that afternoon, when Cameron returned to his office to catch up on paperwork, he found himself unable to stop thinking about what Simon had said about losing what mattered most. The problem was, to risk everything not to do that would mean he couldn't protect himself or Kaitlyn. They could both…

He leaned back in his chair and closed his eyes. Who was he kidding? Protect himself from what? Having Rina in his life? Having her integrated into every moment of his day? Missing her? It was too late for that. Too late for him to protect Kaitlyn from another maternal loss. She might not remember her mother but she would remember Rina. She loved Rina. And as his eight-year-old had wisely pointed out, he loved Rina, too.

He stood, not sure what to think or what to do next. The truth flooded through him. He loved Rina. That's why he'd been so freaked by her confession, why he hadn't wanted to change their relationship. If he loved her, she could hurt him. His ex-wife leaving had been a shock, but he'd gone on. Looking back, he hadn't missed her nearly as much as he should have. But if Rina left, he would be destroyed and so would his daughter.

That's what he'd been afraid of. Losing her. So rather than risk it, he'd pushed her away. As Simon had done with Montana. He had felt that if he decided the course of the relationship, he had the illusion of control.

He shrugged out of his white coat and grabbed his jacket, then stopped. He couldn't just track Rina down and blurt out that he'd changed his mind. That now he wanted her. He'd hurt her and made her feel small. He'd tossed aside what she had offered and then made things worse by trying to keep her around as some kind of on-call child-care staff.

She was the woman he loved, he woman he wanted to be with for the rest of his life. He needed to prove himself to her, to win her. Which meant he needed a plan. A way to apologize and prove to her that she was all he'd ever dreamed about. A tough road, considering how he'd acted.

He started toward the door. He was lucky, he reminded himself. With the pet adoption, Rina wouldn't have had time to go looking for someone else or even to start falling out of love with him. What he had to do was convince her he was worthy. Someone she could trust to be there, no matter what. And he knew exactly how to do it.

The noise in the Fool's Gold Convention Center was nearly deafening. The cement-and-block-wall construction had originally been meant for a big-box store that had never come to town. About eleven years ago, the city had taken over the property and turned it into a convention center, which meant the acoustics weren't perfect. Especially when nearly thirty dogs were barking, kids were running around yelling and a spate of angry hisses came from the kitty corner.

Through it all, Rina smiled, answered questions and confirmed that the paperwork for the adoptions had been filled out correctly.

Holiday decorations brightened their small section of the huge structure, the paper and plastic carefully hung out of dog-reach. She and her volunteers wore cheerful, red, long-sleeved T-shirts with bright letters proclaiming Adopt a Pet, with a cartoon cat and dog under the words. The real dogs wore painted nails and bandanas, the cats, festive collars. She'd left the iguana unadorned.

A crowd had been waiting when the event had begun and adoptions were steady. What confused her were the snippets of conversation she overheard.

"Dr. McKenzie came by yesterday afternoon," Edie Carberry was telling a friend, while holding a carrier containing her new cat. "He made sure I understood the best way to take care of Marilyn." The seventy-something grinned. "I named her after Marilyn Monroe. They have the same eyes."

A family with a beagle mix on a leash stopped by to thank Rina. "We love him," the oldest boy, who was all of ten or eleven, said earnestly. "Dr.

McKenzie talked to us about responsibility. We'll take good care of him. We promise."

Their mother sighed. "He was impressive. Oh, and that certificate for a free exam in six months was great."

"I don't understand," Rina said. "He came to see you?"

The woman nodded. "From what I understand, he went to see everyone who had already expressed interest in a specific pet. He wanted us to be prepared for the first few days of settling in and talked about food and exercise. That was more than enough, but then he offered a free exam. What a great guy."

"I heard that," her husband told her.

The woman laughed.

Rina chatted with the family a few more minutes, then went to find Jesse.

"What do you know about Cameron visiting prospective adoptive families?"

Jesse handed Rina a cloth bag that she started filling with cat food. Each pet was being sent home with a month's worth of food.

"You didn't know?" she asked, sounding surprised. "He spent part of Thursday afternoon and most of yesterday out talking to people who'd said they were interested in adopting. He didn't tell you?"

Rina shook her head. "No. He's offering a certificate for a free exam, too."

Jesse smiled. "He wants your holiday pet adoption to be a success. You should be happy."

"I am, of course. It's just strange."

He hadn't said a word. Not that she'd seen him in the past few days. She'd had the excuse of being busy. Now she just had to get through the holidays, and then she could start forgetting she'd ever fallen in love with him.

Jesse took the full bag of food. "It's a good thing. Maybe you should just accept that."

Rina nodded and got back to work.

By three in the afternoon, all the pets had been adopted, the pet food was distributed and more than a couple of the decorations had started to droop. Rina had accepted help for cleanup and then had sent everyone home. There were only a few chairs left to stack and she could handle that on her own.

She'd just collected her backpack to head to her car when the side door opened.

She opened her mouth to tell the people that the event was over, only to realize they weren't prospective pet owners. Instead, Cameron and Kaitlyn walked toward her.

She hadn't seen either of them in three days and it felt like years. She wanted to rush forward and hug Kaitlyn, be hugged by Cameron and taken home. She wanted to revel in the affection and laughter she always found in their house. But that wasn't to be.

"I heard all the pets got adopted," Cameron said as he approached. "Congratulations."

"You had a big part in that," she said, hoping she was looking friendly rather than desperately in love. "Thank you for your help."

"It's the least I could do." He raised his chin slightly. "I like your shirt."

She glanced down at the Adopt a Pet graphic. "I thought they were festive. It made the volunteers feel special and—"

As she'd been speaking, Cameron and Kaitlyn had started removing their coats. Now she saw they wore similar shirts, only the phrase was a little different. Cameron's T-shirt said Adopt a Vet and Kaitlyn's read Adopt a Vet's Daughter. Instead of a drawing of a cat and dog, there was a picture of the three of them, taken at the end of the summer festival earlier that year.

Hope blossomed. Fragile, brave hope that grew inside her. "I don't understand," she whispered.

Cameron stepped toward her. "Rina, I'm sorry. I was blind and stupid and afraid. I wasn't looking to fall in love, so I didn't recognize it when it happened. I couldn't see the beautiful, special, wonderful woman standing right in front of me."

She drew in a breath. "It happens," she managed.

He took another step and reached for her hands, taking them in his. His steady gaze was full of promise.

"When I kissed you that night, I felt all the possibilities and they terrified me. I was afraid loving meant losing and I couldn't bear to lose you. You are strong and kind and the most giving person I know. I trust you with my heart. More important, I trust you with my daughter."

Rina glanced at the girl, who was practically dancing in place. She'd obviously promised to be quiet, but was having trouble keeping her promise. As Rina smiled at her, Kaitlyn slapped a hand over her mouth and spun in a circle.

"I'm sorry I didn't accept what you offered," he continued, drawing her attention back to him. "I'm sorry I couldn't see what you did for us. But I do know, and I hope you'll give me a chance to prove myself. Kaitlyn and I love you." He smiled at his daughter. "We want to marry you and be a family together."

"Like we are now!" The words burst from Kaitlyn, who rushed toward them.

Then the three of them were holding on as if they would never let go. Rina felt the pain draining away, replaced by the knowledge that dreams really do come true. Loving Cameron and his daughter had been the best part of her. It would continue to be so…forever.

CHAPTER SEVEN

CHRISTMAS MORNING CAME early. Rina found herself being gently shaken a little before six. She opened her eyes and saw Kaitlyn staring down at her.

"You were awake, right?" the girl asked anxiously. "Daddy said I wasn't to wake you."

Rina laughed. "I was awake enough."

"Good. There are presents and it's snowing! I know it won't stick, but there's snow on Christmas! Come on. Get up!"

Rina sat up and stretched. She was wearing red and white candy-cane pajamas, just like the ones Kaitlyn had on. Somewhere in the house, Cameron had on a pair, too. An early Christmas present from her fiancé.

As she got out of bed, her diamond engagement ring caught the light and sparkled. Another early Christmas present that Cameron had given her last night. And after Kaitlyn had gone to bed, things had gotten even better.

Usually she went home after dinner. They had agreed it would be better for her not to spend the night until after they were married in a couple of weeks. Then Kaitlyn had begged for Rina to sleep over on Christmas Eve and sometime around two in the morning, Rina had reluctantly left Cameron's bed to spend the rest of the night in the guest room.

Noah trotted into the room, her nails clicking on the hardwood floor. Cameron followed, looking both handsome and silly in his Christmas pajamas.

"Merry Christmas," he told her. "I have coffee brewing."

"And hot chocolate for me," Kaitlyn said. "And she was already awake. Sort of."

"Give me five minutes," Rina said, smiling at them both. "Then I'll be right out."

She used the bathroom and brushed her teeth, then stepped into slippers and joined Cameron and Kaitlyn in the kitchen. Outside, snow fell. A light dusting covered the deck and backyard. Only Noah's pawprints disturbed the pristine beauty.

Before handing Rina her coffee, Cameron pulled her close and kissed her. Then he held out his arm so Kaitlyn was included.

"Group hug," the girl said with a contented sigh. "Daddy, I'm really glad there are presents, but this is the best one."

"For me, too," Rina said.

"For all of us," Cameron agreed.

Kaitlyn looked up at them and smiled. "See. I told you. We had to give Rina something so she knows we love her. And we gave her us."

* * * * *

Heidi Swain

A Christmas Celebration

SIMON &
SCHUSTER

London · New York · Sydney · Toronto · New Delhi

First published in Great Britain by Simon & Schuster UK Ltd, 2022

3 5 7 9 10 8 6 4 2

Simon & Schuster UK Ltd
1st Floor
222 Gray's Inn Road
London WC1X 8HB

Simon & Schuster Australia, Sydney
Simon & Schuster India, New Delhi

www.simonandschuster.co.uk
www.simonandschuster.com.au
www.simonandschuster.co.in

A CIP catalogue record for this book is available from the British Library

Paperback ISBN: 978-1-4711-9588-4
eBook ISBN: 978-1-4711-9589-1
Audio ISBN: 978-1-3985-1290-0

Typeset in Bembo by M Rules
Printed and bound by CPI Group (UK) Ltd, Croydon, CR0 4YY

Also by Heidi Swain

The Cherry Tree Café
Summer at Skylark Farm
Mince Pies and Mistletoe at the Christmas Market
Coming Home to Cuckoo Cottage
Sleigh Rides and Silver Bells at the Christmas Fair
Sunshine and Sweet Peas in Nightingale Square
Snowflakes and Cinnamon Swirls
at the Winter Wonderland
Poppy's Recipe for Life
The Christmas Wish List
The Secret Seaside Escape
The Winter Garden
A Taste of Home
Underneath the Christmas Tree
The Summer Fair

Praise f

Heidi Swain

'Sweet and lovely. I guarantee you will fall in love with Heidi's wonderful world' **Milly Johnson**

'More Christmassy than a week in Lapland – we loved it!' ***Heat***

'Sparkling and romantic' ***My Weekly***

'The queen of feel-good' ***Woman & Home***

'The most delicious slice of festive fiction: a true comfort read and the perfect treat to alleviate all the stress!' **Veronica Henry**

'Sprinkled with Christmas sparkle' **Trisha Ashley**

'A story that captures your heart' **Chrissie Barlow**

'Grab a glass of mulled wine and enjoy this sparkling, snow-filled romance' ***Culturefly***

'Fans of Carole Matthews will enjoy this heartfelt novel' **Katie Oliver**

'Is Dad there?' I asked before she had a chance to start firing questions. 'Where exactly are you?'

'He is,' she said, her voice drifting away a little. 'We're in the Cayman Islands and it's as hot as hell. We're going to swim with stingrays later . . .'

'Never mind about our schedule,' I heard Dad bluster in the background. 'Ask her if she's all right.'

'You said not to,' Mum tutted.

The line went quiet and I laughed as I imagined the pair of them tussling with the phone.

'Paige,' came Dad's voice. He had obviously won the scrimmage. 'How are you?'

With a lengthy army career behind him, Dad knew that my work in war ravaged countries had never been easy and he had been of the same opinion as my manager, that I was pushing my luck and needed a break.

'Good.' I swallowed

'Because,' he then said, his voice louder again, 'I was going to suggest you headed to somewhere other than the house. Somewhere that you'd find a bit of company, but if you'd really rather be alone . . .'

'Where?' I butted in.

'Wynthorpe.'

'Wynthorpe Hall?' I frowned. 'Why would you suggest I should go there?'

Wynthorpe Hall was nestled in the heart of the Fens and was the family home of my godparents, Catherine and Angus Connelly. It was a wonderful place, but I knew it was far from the silent sanctuary I had been craving in which to hide out and lick my metaphorical wounds in private. As well as two of the three Connelly sons, Jamie and Archie, their partners lived at the hall too, along with a whole host of staff who were so close to the family they were also con-

Catherine. 'Surely there's enough people around and about at the hall to keep him on the straight and narrow?'

'Well, that's the thing,' said Dad. 'Most of them aren't there at the moment. The charity Jamie and Anna run has closed for a couple of months, so they've taken the opportunity to fly out to Africa to visit the project Jamie worked on before he took over management of the hall.'

'But why does that matter if the charity is closed?' I asked, unable to fathom why their absence would be a problem.

'It matters because Anna does a lot of volunteering locally,' Dad explained. 'She's in charge of delivering groceries, library books and prescriptions to people who live out of town and she does a fair bit of ferrying to appointments and things too.'

'In that case, why did she and Jamie leave without having sorted some cover first?' I asked, feeling further confused.

'Because Angus insisted he would be able to sort it.' Dad filled me in. 'He was worried they wouldn't go at all if they were stressing about finding cover so he said he'd arrange it all and sent them on their way.'

'I see,' I said. 'And there really is no one else who can help?'

'Apparently not,' said Dad, 'and Hayley the housekeeper and her partner, Gabe, who maintains the grounds, are also away now too. There wasn't supposed to be much of an overlap with Jamie and Anna's trip but Gabe's sister had a change to her schedule and the run up to Christmas suddenly became the only time they'd be able to get together.'

'Crikey,' I said. 'So who have they got cleaning the hall?'

I knew that there was more to that particular role than flinging a vacuum cleaner about once a week.

'No one at the moment,' Dad explained. 'And you know what a big deal Christmas at Wynthorpe is now, so there's all of that to contend with too.'

I'd momentarily forgotten about the more recent festive changes, but the Wynthorpe Hall Winter Wonderland really was a big deal and, according to the plethora of photos I'd seen posted online, a huge seasonal spectacle. It doubtless took endless organizing and, with fewer people to help set it up, would soon become more of a pain than a pleasure.

'I do know, yes,' I said. 'So, this really is rotten timing for the four of them to be off, isn't it? Whatever was Angus thinking?'

'Since when does Angus think?' Dad laughed. 'You know what he's like. He just wants everyone to be happy.'

That did sound very much like my godfather. Generous to a fault, but often without a thought for the consequences and repercussions. As this current situation proved.

'So, what do you think?' Dad asked.

'About what?'

'About going to the hall. Why don't you go and save the day? You could do the deliveries and flick a duster about the place, couldn't you? You could have a proper Christmas there too. It's been years since you've been in the country at the right time to celebrate that.'

'I suppose . . .' I said, biting my lip.

'I know they'd be thrilled to see you.' I heard Mum chip

in. 'Poor Archie has been pulling his hair out. He's at his wits' end with it all.'

I daresay, as the only Connelly brother in residence it was down to him to pick up the pieces and try to find a way to tidy up the mess his well-meaning father had made.

'It might be just the distraction you find you need,' Dad then craftily added.

And that was how, just an hour after arriving in the UK on November the fourteenth, I found myself boarding a bus for Peterborough and then another for the Fenland town of Wynbridge.

Chapter 2

Exhausted by the emotion of leaving my old life and colleagues behind in Jordan and further tired out by the endless hours of travelling, I had slept through the larger part of both bus journeys from Heathrow to the Fenland market town of Wynbridge, but there was no rest to be found on the actual drive down to the hall.

'You can drop me here if you like,' I soon piped up, taking pity on the taxi's suspension.

The driver had markedly winced when I'd hopped off the bus in Wynbridge, into the back of his car and told him where I wanted to go. I had wondered why at the time, but bouncing along the Wynthorpe Hall drive, in and out of the potholes, his reluctance was explained without a word being said.

'You'll walk?' he asked, twisting around to look at me.

'I'll walk,' I confirmed. 'I know where I'm going.'

As soon as I had climbed out, he made a near perfect three-point turn and slowly headed back to the road and I set off along the winding drive, with my rucksack on my back, excited to catch my first glimpse of the hall and its chimneys which towered above the trees.

The moment I rounded the last corner and spotted it my face broke into a smile. I fixed my gaze on the manor house which had been my idyllic childhood playground and knew Dad had been right; it was a good idea to come and I couldn't wait to see everyone. I only hoped they liked the idea of me turning up unannounced to help out and hadn't managed to make alternative arrangements since Dad had last been in touch.

With the cold really starting to bite, I rushed the final few steps through the courtyard and then rapped on the back door, which was ajar. When no one answered, I pulled off my shabby woolly hat, shook out my hair, which was far longer than I usually grew it and stepped inside, expecting Floss, the family spaniel, to come bowling through from the kitchen to greet me, but she didn't.

'We'll manage,' I heard someone insistently say. 'You know we always do, somehow.'

That had to be Angus.

'That's as maybe,' said someone else, most likely Archie. 'But we haven't so far, Dad, and I can't imagine the situation's going to change anytime soon, can you?'

He sounded thoroughly fed up, but I was relieved. It sounded as though my arrival couldn't have been better timed and alternative arrangements hadn't been made, assuming they were talking about the gaps Anna and Hayley had left.

'We're going to have to get that bog-standard cleaning firm in at the very least,' Archie's voice came again, confirming that I was right.

'But Hayley said . . .' countered Angus.

'Hayley said she'd have our guts for garters if we did,' Archie shot back. 'I know, but we really have no other choice, do we? She drilled me about what to do in minute detail before she left, so I can relay all of that to whoever comes to take over and we'll just have to hope for the best. It's our only option. I can't do it all myself and there's no one else.'

'Not necessarily,' a third voice then piped up. This one didn't sound at all perturbed by the stressful situation and I knew instantly who the soft, dreamy tone belonged to. 'I think the universe has just sent us a solution.' They then happily continued, 'And it's going to manifest any second now.'

A spontaneous cacophony of barking suddenly broke out and rather than find myself welcomed by just one hound skipping around my ankles, I was surrounded by three. Floss was one of them, though she looked much older than I remembered, and there was also a tiny Chihuahua and a colossal wolfhound. What a distinctive doggy pack!

'What's all this?' Angus boomed as he rushed in after the dogs. 'My goodness, Paige!' he cried, pushing through them and pulling me into a swift and all-encompassing hug. 'Is it really you?'

'It is,' I croaked, swallowing over the second lump to form in my throat since arriving back in the country. 'My contract finally came to an end, so I thought I'd come home for a bit.'

It wasn't the moment to worry about the mortifying specifics or go into the details of my earlier than planned departure. Angus squeezed me tighter and then took a step away to take me in properly.

'Paige!' Archie laughed, as he swiftly joined us. 'I can't believe it! What are you doing here?'

'She's come to stay for Christmas,' said Angus, relieving me of my rucksack and struggling under its weight. 'Isn't that wonderful?'

Not one word had been uttered about Christmas, which was still weeks away, but my godfather was clearly convinced I would be in situ for it. There was little point in suggesting that might not be the case. I was fully aware of how 'festive-focused' he could be and like the complications behind my return, I knew it could all wait.

'I'm actually the cavalry,' I told the smiling pair. 'I spoke to Dad almost as soon as my plane landed and he suggested that you might need an extra pair of hands here at the moment.'

Angus positively beamed when I said that.

'I have no idea if I'll be any good at any of it,' I hastily added, before I got his hopes up too high, 'but I'm willing to try – if you're willing to show me the ropes.'

Archie was already untying the apron he was wearing. The capacious front pocket had not one, but three different types of dusters, or cleaning cloths, stuffed inside.

'You'll pick it all up in no time.' He grinned. 'It's so good to see you. Come on through.'

I followed father and son further inside, just as Catherine came into the kitchen from the other end of the room.

'Paige!' she cried, also rushing to pull me into a hug. 'How wonderful to see you after all this time. What on earth are you doing here?'

I took a moment to catch my breath as Angus filled her in, adding to and embellishing the little I had already told him so I really did sound like the all-conquering hero. I took a moment to look around and further gather my thoughts. Having not visited for so many years, I had forgotten how full-on the kind hearted Connellys could be.

I hoped I was going to be able to cope with their exuberance and enthusiasm. The hall was the complete opposite of the silent, empty space I would have found at my parents' house. But then, perhaps that was no bad thing. Time to dwell could be as much of a curse as a blessing and at least throwing myself into helping do whatever was needed at Wynthorpe Hall would ensure I didn't have too much of it.

'Well, this is wonderful news,' said Catherine, when Angus eventually drew breath. 'And so kind of your dear father to suggest that you should come here or even be thinking of us and our dilemma while he and your mother are away on their holiday. We're honoured to welcome you back into the country.'

'It is you!' came another voice, before I could respond. 'Well, I never.'

It was Dorothy, the Wynthorpe cook. She bustled in,

dabbing her eyes with a cotton handkerchief before gathering her wits.

'Right,' she said briskly, looking me up and down. 'Let the dog see the rabbit. Let me see what needs doing. Um,' she then pronounced, 'you look like you need a decent meal to me.'

We all laughed because that had always been Dorothy's stock response whenever anyone arrived at the hall and she knew there was an opportunity to feed them.

'She's all right,' Archie laughed. 'Nothing like the pale and pudgy Paige I remember.'

I shook my head as I realized, he had already resorted to his teasing pre-teen self and childishly stuck my tongue out to match him, which made Mick, the hall handyman who had wandered in from outside, laugh.

'Here, my love,' he said, pulling out a chair for me to sit on. 'Sit yourself down before everyone feels entitled to express an opinion on how you look.'

'My dear Paige,' said the bearer of the dreamy voice, which had so far remained silent, as I made myself comfortable.

'Molly.' I smiled. 'How are you?'

'That's exactly what I was going to ask you,' she responded, pinning me with her pale blue gaze as she tucked an unruly auburn curl behind her ear with one hand and held out the other for me to take.

Out of everyone's scrutiny, I knew Molly's would penetrate the deepest. A self-confessed white witch, she lived in a cottage in the Wynthorpe woods and knew the workings of my heart and head better than any of the others.

When I used to visit as a child and teenager, we had enjoyed a firm friendship. Our sisterly solidarity had run deep as a result of having to deal with all three mischievous Connelly brothers, but we had drifted apart in the years since. Not that that seemed to matter now. I had the feeling we were going to pick up exactly where we had left off.

Momentarily unable to meet her eyes, I realized that she would soon suss out that there was more behind my impromptu arrival than I had let on. In fact, a fleeting glance at her face gave me the distinct impression that she already had.

'Let me get you some tea, Paige,' said Dorothy, rushing about just as she always had and thankfully distracting Molly in the process.

'And I'll tell you more about what's been going on here,' added Archie.

'Or not going on,' I corrected.

'Exactly,' he tutted, throwing his father a look which, true to form, went straight over his head.

Archie told me more about the charity Jamie and Anna had set up, which supported bereaved youngsters and had closed earlier in the year than usual to afford them a break and how Gabe the woodsman, Hayley the housekeeper's other half, was the newest hall recruit.

'And what about introducing me to the dogs?' I asked, as Dorothy poured me another cup of tea. 'I know Floss, of course, but not the other two.'

'Bran, the wolfhound, is Gabe's shadow,' said Mick, patting the gargantuan serene grey dog sitting by his side. 'But he's with us while his master's away as he's not a fan of travelling far.'

'And Suki here,' said Molly, reaching down to scoop the tiny scrap up, 'is mine and Archie's. Dumped here by his ex a few Christmases ago.'

Suki wriggled in Molly's arms and fondly licked her chin.

'I'd forgotten you and Archie are a couple now, Molly,' I said, shaking my head.

This time, it was Archie who stuck out his tongue.

'It's quite the surprise, isn't it?' said Molly with a wry smile, making her better half pout.

'Given the relentless teasing that went on between you when we were growing up,' I laughed, 'it's more than that!'

Archie leant across and kissed Molly's cheek, blushing in the process.

'But clearly a good one,' I relented, pleased to see them both so happy.

I was barely capable of stifling the yawns which had descended by the time I'd drunk my third mug of tea and eaten a huge slice of Dorothy's delicious fruitcake.

'So, exactly how long have you been back in the country?' Catherine asked when she spotted my eyelids starting to droop.

'Just a few hours,' I told her as yet another yawn developed and I forced myself to sit up straighter. 'This time yesterday I was still in Jordan.'

'My goodness,' Catherine gasped. 'No wonder you look all in. You must be exhausted.'

'I am beginning to feel it a bit,' I confessed. 'Even though I did sleep on the bus.'

'In that case,' she insisted, 'you must go and rest.'

'Yes,' said Molly, making me feel wide awake again, 'you really must look after yourself, Paige. You need time to recover.'

Did she mean from the travelling or was she winkling out my secret already? I didn't dare speculate.

'What's it like, working in those camps?' Archie asked.

Catherine and Molly exchanged a look.

'Utterly exhausting, I would imagine,' said Catherine. 'Let's get you upstairs, Paige.'

'The Rose Room is made up,' said Dorothy, making my day.

The Rose Room had always been my favourite. With its own fire and comfy sofa and the deepest tub in the en suite, it was the height of luxury and after so long sleeping on a canvas camp bed, I was going to make the most of it.

'The Rose Room it is then,' said Archie, picking up my rucksack.

Just like his father, he was thrown off balance by the weight of it and groaned.

'What did you expect?' I laughed. 'Practically all my worldly possessions are in there.'

'I would say you travel light,' he smiled back, 'but it weighs a tonne. How on earth have you managed it?'

'She's stronger than she looks,' said Molly with a wink.

I didn't respond to that.

Dinner that evening was the usual jolly Wynthorpe Hall affair and eaten around the scrubbed kitchen table. Dorothy, as always, had cooked enough to feed a thousand and piled my plate high with toad in the hole, mashed root vegetables and thick gravy.

'This looks delicious, Dorothy,' I was quick to say, 'but I probably won't be able to get through half of it. I've been living on rations for so long, I need to be careful.'

I knew from past experience that switching from one diet to another with no settling in period was not a good idea.

'That's all right,' she said, 'you just eat what you can.'

She sounded sincere but I knew she'd be disappointed if I left even the tiniest morsel.

'So,' Angus then keenly said. 'Shall we pick up where we left off earlier?'

'Yes,' said Archie. 'That's a good idea, Dad, and with the arrival of Paige it doesn't feel half as daunting to go through it all again now, does it?'

'Goodness,' I said, letting out a breath. 'I'm not sure my presence warrants that amount of relief, Archie. I am but one person after all.'

'But one person can make a *huge* difference,' Molly prophetically said.

'No pressure then,' I tutted and everyone laughed.

'And you need us every bit as much as we need you, Paige,' she further added. 'It's all meant to be.'

Archie looked poised to ask what she meant, but I cut him off.

'So,' I said, laying my cutlery down and making Dorothy's eyebrows shoot up as a result. 'I know a bit about Anna's volunteering, making the deliveries and ferrying people to medical appointments and so on, but what about cleaning the hall? Is it really not possible to employ a specialist firm to come in?'

'We would have done that with more notice,' explained Catherine, 'but with Hayley and Gabe's plans changing at the last minute we haven't been able to book anyone.'

'I'm up to speed with what needs doing,' said Archie, 'but all the time I'm doing it I'm not getting on with my own work.'

'In that case,' I said, picking my cutlery up again and scooping up a forkful of buttery carrot and parsnip mash, 'you'll have to pass your knowledge on to me, Archie. I should be able to pick it up, shouldn't I?'

I cared very much about the fabric of the beautiful hall and wouldn't be doing a slapdash job like a regular and time-short Mr or Mrs Mop might have settled for.

'It would be wonderful if you could,' Archie gratefully said. 'And if I can manage it, I don't see why you shouldn't be able to.'

'And what about the Winter Wonderland?' I asked next. 'Are you going to need help with that? I'm guessing from what I've been told, it's quite an undertaking.'

I knew there was a trail around the woods for visitors to walk, a variety of seasonal activities to get stuck into, sleigh rides, a Santa's grotto, visiting reindeers and owls, carol singers and a huge variety of festive food and drink as well as some spectacularly decorated trees to admire. The entire weekend was full of fabulous festive delights and even though it was still a few weeks away, doubtless took a lot of planning and implementing.

'Mick and I sort the logistics and do some of the setting up,' Angus told me. 'But Jamie and Gabe generally provide a bit of muscle, along with Archie.'

'Just as well I keep myself fit then.' I grinned. 'Muscle I can definitely manage.'

'If you finish your dinner, you'll have even more heft to offer,' Dorothy put in, capitalizing on the moment.

'I've got mates in town who will help out too,' said Archie. 'To be honest, I think the Wonderland will be fine. It was Anna and Hayley's roles we were really struggling to fill.'

'But not anymore,' smiled Molly.

'No,' I smiled back, already grateful for the timely distractions. 'Not anymore.'

Chapter 3

It wasn't long after dinner before I made my excuses and went to bed. With a fuller tummy than usual and thoughts of a soak in the Rose Room tub swirling around my head, I was feeling drowsy again in no time and hopeful that my sleep would be dreamless rather than filled with the gruesomely blown-up replay of my mistake that it usually succumbed to. The reality had been dreadful enough to endure but my dream state seemed to relish making it all so much worse and restful sleep had been nigh on impossible to come by of late.

'Why don't you come over to the cottage in the morning?' Molly had suggested before I headed up the wooden hill. 'We can have a proper chat.'

I accepted her invitation but reluctantly. I was delighted to reform our friendship, but knew that spending time alone with her, especially so soon after my arrival and before I'd had a chance to put some distance between me and leaving the camp, could well lead to me revealing more than I yet wanted anyone to know.

'And take this,' Molly had further said, pressing a small cork-topped phial filled with pink liquid into my hands. 'It'll help.'

'I'm not drinking this, Molly,' I firmly said, assuming it was one of her potions.

'Good,' she laughed. 'It's for your bath.'

'Oh,' I said, feeling my face flush. 'In that case, thank you.'

I ran myself the deepest bath, pouring the contents of the flowery scented liquid into the steamy stream of water. It mixed seamlessly and created a pleasing amount of bubbles, the soothing scents of lavender, chamomile and something sweet I couldn't identify filling the room and helping me to further relax. I had no idea of the exact ingredients, but whatever had been in that little bottle gifted me a night of deep, mercifully dreamless sleep and I woke feeling refreshed, revived and surprisingly raring to go.

'Just a sec,' I called, pushing back the covers as someone knocked on the door a few minutes after I was awake. 'Hold on.'

I realized, as I turned the ancient metal key in the lock, that the sound hadn't actually been a knock, more of a scratch, which was explained when I opened the door and found Bran, the ginormous wolfhound, standing in the corridor. He loped into the room, hopped on to the sofa and stared at me from under his big shaggy brows. He really was too huge to be believed and would have been impossible to usher out.

'Well,' I therefore said as I closed the door again. 'Good morning to you, too. Make yourself at home, why don't you?'

He patiently waited while I got dressed, pulling on as many layers as I could manage because I was still feeling the cold, and tied up my hair and, together, we went down to breakfast.

'Here you are,' said Dorothy, rubbing the top of Bran's head.

'I didn't dognap him,' I told her. 'He just turned up at the bedroom door, nosed his way in and then refused to budge.'

'Well,' she said, offering me the teapot, 'that's interesting, isn't it?'

Mick shook his head.

'Is it?' I frowned, pouring myself a mug.

Dorothy didn't elaborate, but Bran rested a heavy paw on my lap as if to say, 'don't mind her' and gave me a sympathetic look.

'I'm going to go and see Molly,' I said as soon as I'd finished my tea.

'Aren't you having any breakfast?' Dorothy asked, sounding astounded.

'No,' I said, wrinkling my nose. 'I'm not hungry. I'll have something later.'

I tried to stand up but it was difficult with Bran still welded to my side.

'You can take him with you if you like,' smiled Mick.

'I don't think I'm going to have any other choice,' I pointed out, as Bran's cold nose found its way into my hand. 'Wouldn't he be better off with you though, Mick?'

'Apparently not,' said Mick, clearly unperturbed by his

charge's change of allegiance. 'He's a hound who goes where he's most needed and right now he seems to feel compelled to cling to you, Paige.'

I didn't hang around long enough for that particular topic of conversation to develop.

'Here,' said Dorothy, thrusting a bacon roll into my hands as I shrugged on one of the many waxed coats which hung for everyone's use by the back door. 'You can eat this on the way and you'd better wear wellies. It'll be wet in the woods.'

It was biting cold too. I daresay it was no chillier than it should have been for the time of year, but it was still a long way off the temperatures I'd been used to. Without thinking, I'd started to eat Dorothy's roll as I walked along, but memories of the intense heat and then inevitably, thoughts of the near disaster, filled my head and the mouthful I was chewing became almost impossible to swallow.

'Here, Bran,' I said, holding out what was left for him to take. 'You have it.'

He took it with the softest mouth and swallowed it down in one gulp.

'It'll be our little secret,' I smiled, stroking his back as he paced alongside me.

Molly had opened the cottage door even before I'd reached the path which led up to it and I realized I hadn't given a thought to finding my way. I'd simply followed my feet, marvelling at how everything looked the same, although I knew some of the trees were taller and I could see there was more mistletoe too. Beyond that, however, it was all as familiar as if I'd visited just the week before.

'You found your way then?' Molly smiled, bare-footed in the doorway.

'Of course,' I smiled back.

'I wasn't sure if you'd come,' she added, stepping aside to let me and my shaggy companion in. 'I couldn't help thinking there was a hint of reluctance about your acceptance when you said you would last night.'

'Not at all,' I bluffed, even though her deduction was spot-on.

With a roaring fire in the grate, I didn't mind taking the coat off again and as Molly busied herself in the kitchen, I pulled off the wellies, looked around the room and made myself comfortable among the many embroidered patchwork cushions on the sofa. The place was definitely altered in some respects, but still had the same incense scented and other-worldly vibe. Much like Molly herself.

'Help yourself,' she said, when she came back in through the beaded curtain bearing a tray laden with tempting French toast, fresh fruit and a filled teapot. 'It's breakfast tea, not one of my herbal infusions.'

'Is that Archie's influence?' I asked, grateful that she wasn't going to more forcefully press anything on me like Dorothy had.

'It is,' she confirmed and I was amused to see her cheeks turn pink.

It was a most un-Molly type of reaction.

'He'll be back later,' she carried on, blushing further. 'He can't wait to catch up with you properly. We're all thrilled you're going to take on Anna and Hayley's jobs, but Archie is especially pleased. As you know, Angus means well, but his actions aren't always thought through and this whole debacle was turning into quite a drama.'

'No pressure then,' I said for the second time, making her laugh again.

'And you'll get your reward for your kind and generous gesture because everyone will be arriving in time for Christmas and you'll be able to hand back the reins and properly relax and celebrate then.'

'I honestly can't remember the last time I wholeheartedly celebrated the season.' I sighed, staring into the hypnotic flames of the fire.

'Well, you're certainly in the right place to do it this year,' Molly told me. 'There's nowhere lovelier than Wynthorpe Hall in mid-winter.'

We were quiet for a moment and then I remembered the rinsed-out phial.

'I have no idea what exactly you put in this, Molly,' I said, handing it over, 'but I had the best night's sleep I've had in weeks after taking a long bath filled with it. Thank you.'

Molly took the little bottle from me, her eyes trained on my face.

'You aren't sleeping then?' she probed.

'Oh, Molly,' I said, shaking my head. 'You know very

well that I'm not. Otherwise, you wouldn't have given me the phial in the first place, would you?'

'No,' she lightly said, then paused before adding, 'I wouldn't, but I still can't fathom the details as to why you're not getting the rest you deserve . . .'

Since I had made the colossal error of judgment, I had accepted the fact that I didn't deserve any rest. It had been such a stupid mistake, which carried such dreadful potential consequences, I felt it was more than justified that I should still be experiencing its sting, even though the worst hadn't thankfully happened.

'Paige?'

'Sorry,' I said, tearing my eyes away from the flames. 'What was that?'

'Have you heard any of what I just said?'

I shook my head.

'I was telling you,' Molly tenderly said, 'that I want to help you.'

'You can't,' I blurted out, my eyes prickling with traitorous tears. 'You're right in that there is something troubling me and I know you mean well, but it's something I've got to work through on my own.'

'Is it something to do with Chadia?'

She asked the question so kindly but the shock of hearing my friend and mentor's name on her lips felt like a knife piercing my heart. It was a long time since I'd talked to anyone about the friend whose life had been cut tragically short and even though what had occurred in Jordan wasn't a direct result of what had happened to Chadia, there was a connection. Not that I was willing to acknowledge it.

My fingers strayed towards the precious locket I wore which contained the only photograph I had of my friend, but I soon stopped them, knowing Molly would notice.

'No.' I swallowed. 'Besides, that was years ago.'

'Just because something happened a long time ago . . .'

'It's not Chadia,' I tightly responded.

'Heartbreak then?' Molly suggested, changing course. 'Relationship trouble?'

'Goodness me, no,' I said, with an elaborate eye roll. 'I haven't had a relationship in a *very* long time.'

'Perhaps that's what you need,' she suggested, raising her eyebrows. 'Someone to love and someone to love you back.'

I shook my head.

'Why do loved up couples always want to get everyone else loved up?' I pretended to pout, reaching for a cushion and hugging it to my chest like an armoured breastplate. 'There's no man required in this instance, so don't even think about blending up a love potion or even a quick fling potion. You know that's not my style either.'

'All right.' She grinned. 'I'm not sure anything I could concoct would work its way through that amount of resistance anyway.'

'Well, thank goodness for that.'

'But whatever has got you vexed,' she said, turning serious again, 'feels pretty full on. I can't make sense of your aura at all.'

I resisted the temptation to look about me to see if I could see what she was looking at. Past experience suggested I wouldn't so I kept my gaze locked front and centre.

'I'm sure it will settle down into a more familiar colour now I'm here at the hall,' I said instead.

'I'm sure it will too,' she agreed. 'Throwing yourself into Anna and Hayley's roles is bound to help. Immersing yourself in doing something completely different will keep your mind occupied and you'll heal without even knowing it's happening.'

I hoped she was right. I might have currently felt that I deserved to suffer, but I didn't think it was an emotional state I'd want to carry with me forever.

'Are you going to eat all of this toast?' I asked, reaching for a slice of the cinnamon and vanilla infused brioche and resolutely changing the subject.

Once we had eaten more of the breakfast than I would ever have thought I could manage, Molly picked up the wrapped deck of tarot cards which were never far from her person. She let out a long breath as she began to shuffle them in a well-practiced way and I smiled as she closed her eyes and drifted off because the situation and her expression felt so familiar. The cards had been in her family for generations, passed down from mother to daughter, and were treated with immense respect.

'I'll read yours if you like,' she offered, opening her eyes and clearly making an effort to make it sound as if the idea had only just occurred to her.

'No, thanks,' I quickly said. 'I'd rather you didn't.'

'It might help,' she said innocently.

'Help *you*,' I shot back with a smile. 'You'd get far more out of interpreting the cards than I would and I really don't feel up to sharing yet.'

'Fair enough,' she sighed. 'It was worth a try.'

'You sneaky minx,' I tutted as she put the deck down again.

'Will you carry a crystal instead?' she then asked.

She picked up a bowl from the mantelpiece and began to lift a few pieces out.

'Here,' she said, holding out her palm. 'Take one of these.'

I gave her a hard stare.

'Choose one and I'll stop fussing,' she promised, not at all perturbed by my less than impressed expression.

'They all look the same,' I said, when I peered down at what she was holding.

In her palm were half a dozen pieces of pink crystal. The only real difference between them was their size and a slight variation in their colour. There was one I could see which was shaped a bit like a heart. It was the prettiest of the few she had picked out.

'Just take the one you're drawn to,' Molly insisted, watching me like a hawk.

I bypassed the heart which had caught my attention and went for a smaller piece with rough edges. It was paler than the rest and nowhere near as smooth and tactile as the others looked.

'Happy now?' I asked, showing her the piece I'd picked up.

I couldn't help but wonder if she knew I'd forsaken my favourite.

'I'm almost always happy,' she contentedly sighed, carefully settling the other crystals back into the bowl and returning it to the mantelpiece.

'So, what is this?' I asked, holding my second choice up to the light.

'Rose quartz,' she said. 'It's good for self-healing and self-love.'

'I see.' I sighed, guessing that my clever Wiccan chum had worked out that I didn't even like myself at the moment and was therefore miles off feeling anything like self-love. 'I suppose I'd better get back to the hall,' I said, standing up and slipping the crystal into my jeans pocket.

'Just give yourself time, Paige,' Molly said astutely. 'By Christmas you'll be feeling like a whole new person.'

I couldn't in all honesty believe that, even though it was Molly who had said it.

'You do know that Christmas is just a few short weeks away, don't you?' I said with a wry smile but, on that occasion, Molly didn't smile back.

Chapter 4

I happily whiled away the rest of the day at the hall, with Bran still welded to my side, and was amused to discover that Archie really was still the same teasing terror he had been when we were growing up. In fact, it was more than that and I would have gone as far as to say that he was turning into quite the chip off the old block.

'As you're going to be here while the Winter Wonderland is happening,' he had grinned as we took our seats for dinner and tugged at my ponytail as if we were in infant school rather than two grown-ups, 'I'm hoping you'll be willing to play Santa's Elf for us in the grotto.'

I rolled my eyes and picked a different chair which was out of his reach.

'I think she's too tall for the outfit,' Dorothy said seriously, eyeing me with interest. 'But the tights might stretch a bit.'

'Don't encourage him, Dorothy,' I groaned, knowing he'd soon be looking online for a larger sized festive get up if he sensed even the merest hint that I might be willing to take the role on.

'How do you fancy a trip into town tomorrow?' he then asked me, dropping the subject of stripy tights and hats with bells on once he'd got a plate of food in front of him. 'I thought it would be good to introduce you to a few people and get you up and running as soon as possible.'

I can't deny, I felt a bit nervous, but he was right: the sooner I could make a start the better. Both for myself and the recipients of Anna's generous volunteering.

'Sounds good to me.' I nodded, doing my best to sound more confident than I felt. 'There's no time like the present, is there?'

'Exactly,' he agreed, with another impish grin.

After a reasonably restful night, I discovered it was a fabulously frosty start the next day and even though I was still feeling the cold, the blue sky and crisp rime enhanced the hall and garden making it look even more picture perfect, and the town was a sight to behold too.

'My goodness,' I gasped, as Archie somehow squeezed Anna's tiny Fiat 500, which was going to be one of the vehicles at my disposal while I carried out her role, into an even tinier parking space beside the market square. 'I had no idea it would be this busy.'

When I'd arrived on the bus, I'd been too tired to take much of the town in, but a quick glance showed me it was vastly different to the place I remembered from my last proper visit.

'I know.' Archie beamed. 'Isn't it wonderful? The town has gone through quite a transformation in recent years and it's always busier on a Thursday because the market has a few extra stalls.'

As well as the busy market, I also spotted a smart looking gallery, café and delicatessen within just a few metres of each other and they all looked idyllic. There were a few festive flourishes too, which I assumed were only to be expected as it was already mid-November and I wondered how the rest of the square would look once it was all properly dressed for Christmas. In fact, given the date, I couldn't help thinking that it was a little behind where it should have been for the time of year.

'And the area is fast becoming a magnet for all sorts of artists,' Archie added, when he saw me admiring the gallery and before I had a chance to ask about the lack of decorations. 'Which conveniently justifies our first stop.' He grinned and rubbed his hands together.

He guided me around the market and then through the door of a place called The Cherry Tree Café. The smell of coffee mingled temptingly with the scent of sugar as we crossed the threshold and my stomach growled in response. It was warm too, which made it an even more attractive stop as far as I was concerned.

'Just who I was hoping to see!' called a woman with curly red hair who was standing next to the counter. 'Grab a table and I'll tell Jemma you're here.'

'Brace yourself,' Archie said to me as we found a seat. 'I'm not sure how this is going to go down.'

'What are you talking about?' I asked, my eyes scanning around and taking in the pretty décor. 'It isn't going to be a problem with me taking on Anna's volunteering, is it? You just gave me the impression that you were happy to be coming in here.'

I sincerely hoped his change of heart about our first stop wasn't connected to my decision to step into Anna's shoes. My plan had been to solve problems, not create more.

'Archie!' said a different woman, before he could reply. 'I was beginning to think I would have to come out to the hall myself. Hello,' she then added, her eyes flicking to me. 'Sorry, I don't think we've met.'

'This is Paige,' said Archie, pulling off his scarf and gloves. 'Mum and Dad's goddaughter. She's staying at the hall for a while *and* taking on Anna's volunteering while she and Jamie are away.'

The woman's eyes widened and she gave me the warmest smile. Clearly, Archie's concerns weren't about my stepping into Anna's shoes after all.

'Well,' she said, 'that's wonderful news and what a relief. I know Kathleen was beginning to feel quite frantic about it all.'

I wondered who Kathleen was.

'Your father has a lot to answer for,' she added, pointing a finger at Archie.

'Don't I know it,' he sighed.

'But he means well,' the woman went on, her bright eyes twinkling. 'And I'm delighted to meet you, Paige. I'm Jemma, the currently frazzled owner of The Cherry Tree Café.'

'Oh, crikey,' said Archie, before I could respond. 'You can't be frazzled already, Jemma. You've still got weeks until it's Christmas.'

'I know,' she groaned, fanning herself with an old-fashioned paper order pad. 'I'm close to exhausted already and Lizzie's run off her feet next door. Now, please tell me you've got Hayley's designs, Archie Connelly,' she added, her tone changing to something far sterner. 'It's the deadline soon and I hate cutting it this close.'

Archie looked at Jemma and shook his head.

'You're kidding?' Jemma protested.

'Sorry,' Archie apologized, his shoulders visibly tensing up. 'We still can't find them and her phone is turned off.'

'Well, if they don't turn up soon,' said Jemma, sounding miffed, 'we'll just have to cancel, won't we? It won't go down well with her regulars, but there'll be no other option.'

Once she'd taken our order and gone back to the kitchen Archie told me about the café and its associated businesses. Lizzie, the woman with the glorious red hair, was Jemma's business partner and a well-known sewing and crafting goddess.

'She used to run classes in here along with some sort of knit and natter group,' Archie told me. 'But when her side of things really took off, she moved into the premises next door. It's a popular craft centre now, as well as a gallery, and the pair also have a vintage caravan which they take to events all over the county to serve food and drinks from. They'll be at the Winter Wonderland next month.'

I was amazed Dorothy tolerated that. I had assumed she was in sole charge of the catering, but if she was willing to welcome someone else on site, it went some way to giving me an idea as to just how big an event the Winter Wonderland must be.

'Oh, and they have a themed market stall too, which sells more of their seasonal makes and bakes than they can stock in here and next door,' Archie added for good measure.

'Crikey,' I said, letting out a breath and feeling rather in awe of the resourceful duo. 'That's surely the work of an entire team rather than just two women.'

'There are more people working with them now,' Archie conceded, 'but Jemma and Lizzie are the brains behind the business. They put the rest of us to shame, managing to do the work of ten rather than two.'

He sounded almost disbelieving of what they were capable of and I could hardly blame him. It was an immense empire.

'And what about Hayley?' I asked. 'What did Jemma mean about her designs?'

Archie reached behind him to a display shelf and picked up a mug which had a quirky and bolshy looking little robin painted on it.

'This is one of Hayley's,' he said proudly. 'She created the robin.'

'Oh, wow,' I gasped, taking the mug from him to look at it in more detail.

'She's an amazing artist,' Archie further said. 'And she specializes in painting species of birds and highlighting their different personalities. She's created all sorts over the last couple of years and Jemma has them printed on mugs, cushions and stationery to sell on her behalf.'

'What an incredible talent to have,' I said, turning the mug around.

'I know,' said Archie, also looking at the design. 'I can't even manage a decent stick man.'

'Me neither,' I laughed.

'Unfortunately, though,' he sighed, 'Hayley is as scatty as she is talented and she's left the hall without submitting the designs for this Christmas or telling anyone where she's put them. We've looked high and low, but we can't find them and I know Jemma was hoping she'd have them finished and passed on weeks ago.'

What with it being mid-November, I imagined it was cutting it close to being able to benefit from Christmas present buying too.

'What a thing to forget,' I said, understanding Jemma's frustration.

'That's Hayley for you.' Archie shrugged. 'Although to be fair, she and Gabe did leave in a bit of a rush after his sister's change of plan so I can kind of see why it might have slipped her mind.'

'And why is her phone switched off?' I asked.

'Goodness knows,' said Archie, pulling out his own phone and trying her number for what I guessed was the umpteenth time. 'Still no joy,' he sighed, once the call connected and went straight to voicemail.

'Let's have another hunt for the designs when we get back,' I suggested as a waitress came and filled our table with steaming mugs of coffee and two plates of huge swirled buns. 'Perhaps I might be able to find them. Fresh eyes could be just what you need.'

Archie looked doubtful, but I thought it was worth a shot.

Once we'd eaten every last crumb of the delicious iced and spiced buns which, I had been informed while perusing the tempting menu, were something of a Cherry Tree festive tradition from November onwards, we made our way across the busy square to the library.

We were barely through the door before Archie was accosted.

'Any joy?' asked a woman with perfect grey curls and a neat, trim figure. 'I'm still having more misses than hits, but I haven't given up hope yet.'

The smart and efficient looking woman was probably in her early seventies, but exuded the energy of someone decades younger.

'I am delighted to say I have the answer to your prayers, Kathleen,' said Archie, puffing out his chest and looking peacock proud.

'You have?' she hopefully gasped, her eyes widening in surprise.

'I have,' he confirmed. 'Paige, I'd like to introduce you to Kathleen. Kathleen, this is Paige, Mum and Dad's goddaughter *and*, as of today, your replacement Anna.'

'Oh, my goodness,' said Kathleen, rushing forward,

reaching for my hand and vigorously pumping it between hers. 'It's fantastic to meet you, my dear.'

'Likewise,' I said, feeling rather shell-shocked.

'How wonderful that you're going to save our bacon!' she gushed. 'You really couldn't have stepped up at a better time.'

'Well.' I swallowed. 'I'm going to *try* to save your bacon.'

Clearly, there was a lot resting on my shoulders, certainly more than I'd bargained for and I wasn't sure how I felt about that.

'Come on,' said Kathleen, dashing back to the library counter, whipping out a folder from behind the desk with a flourish and scattering leaflets in her wake which Archie gathered up. 'Let's go and have a look at the list, shall we?'

My stomach twisted a little. The folder looked extremely full. Practically bulging, in fact, and the way she emphasized the list, as if it should have upper case letters, made my heart rate pick up the pace a bit too.

'Excellent idea, Kathleen,' said Archie, returning the leaflets to the counter and nudging me along.

The three of us sat in a corner far away from where the majority of borrowers were browsing. Just like the shops and market square, the library seemed to be thriving too. It was a sight which lifted my spirits, in spite of the fact that my tummy was still having a bit of a moment and my heart was beating a tattoo.

'So,' said Kathleen, spreading papers across the low table. 'Here we are. It couldn't be simpler really.'

It didn't look all that simple to me.

'This sheet covers hospital and clinic appointments,' she explained, pointing at one filled page. 'The majority of which we've got lifts for now.' That was something, I supposed. 'And this one,' she carried on, scooping up another, 'is the fruit and veg delivery itinerary.'

'The Dempster family, who supply the produce and have had a market stall for years, used to do the deliveries,' Archie told me, 'but with Mrs Dempster, Marie, getting ready to branch further out with her floristry business in the new year, they simply haven't got the time now.'

'We did think the delivery of fresh produce was going to have to be cancelled all together until Anna added it to the library books and prescriptions she had already taken responsibility for dropping off.'

'Not forgetting the regular groceries,' Archie helpfully reminded Kathleen. 'And the orders from the butcher's and the baker's.'

'Of course,' said Kathleen, 'not forgetting those. The people registered on the round call me once a week and I order, pick up and pack what they need, often with a discount for a bulk order and Anna, now you Paige, then drops it all off. How does that sound?'

'So, I'm literally just the gopher?' I asked, wanting to make sure I had no further responsibilities to worry about.

'Pretty much.' Kathleen nodded, not quite confirming what I had asked her. 'There might be times when I call on you to assist with the collecting too. Say for example, if picking something up for someone clashes with my dance classes.'

'Kathleen *runs* the dance classes, rather than attends them,' Archie told me.

No wonder she looked so trim.

'Would that be all right, do you think?' she asked me. 'It doesn't happen all that often.'

With nothing else to occupy my time, and having already agreed, I couldn't very well say no to this seemingly minor addition, but I was a little concerned that the parameters of the job were shifting even before I'd started it. I had been hoping for a complete rest from being in charge of anything other than ferrying, especially as my most recent experience of being in charge hadn't ended well.

'It'll be fine,' said Archie, answering on my behalf.

Kathleen was still looking at me.

'Of course,' I said, swallowing hard. 'No problem at all.'

With my new, and already slightly expanded role decided upon and after a hug from a clearly relieved Kathleen, Archie then took me to the butcher's, baker's and the chemist's. He thought that if I did end up doing some of the picking up it would be helpful for the shop owners to have had eyes on me first. Which I supposed was fair enough.

'I would have thought at least the chemist's would have had their own delivery service,' I said as we made our way back to the car. 'That's pretty standard now, isn't it?'

'It is,' Archie agreed, 'but we do things differently here. Anna always spends a few minutes with the people she's dropping things off to because they're the most isolated in the community. Business owners don't have any time to socialize, so this way the recipients get some social interaction and occasionally some help around the house, as well as their books, shopping and so on delivered. It's a very worthwhile community project.'

The description of the job was growing by the minute.

'It certainly sounds like it,' I said, wondering what sort of help around the house I was going to get roped into.

With the housekeeping at the hall to keep on top of too, I was certainly going to have my hands full and there would be little time to dwell on what had happened in Jordan. In fact, during the trip into town I had barely given it a moment's thought. How surprising was that? Was it possible that the plan was working already?

As I lowered myself into the passenger seat of the car, I felt Molly's crystal dig into my hip. I was still a long way off feeling inclined to love myself, but having heard more about the benefits of the scheme I was going to help carry on, and in spite of my nerves, I did like myself a tiny bit more. Wonders would never cease!

'Right then,' I said as Archie started the car, and I shrugged off my apprehension about being able to pull it all off, 'let's get back to the hall and see if we can dig out Hayley's designs, shall we? And then you can show me how to get to grips with where and where not to waft the feather duster about.'

Archie gave me a sideways look as he carefully reversed out of the tight space.

'There's rather more to it than that,' he told me, 'but I have no doubt that you'll rise to the occasion.'

Surely the cleaning had to be more straightforward than the ever-evolving volunteering?

Chapter 5

Back at the hall, and with Bran close by my side again, everyone listened intently as Archie and I relayed the details of what had occurred in town. Molly looked particularly pleased about the situation.

'This is all perfect,' she said, in her dreamiest tone. 'And just in the nick of time.'

I shook my head at her and, picking up that I didn't want anyone else to get wind of the fact that I'd arrived at the hall with more baggage than just my rucksack, she thankfully lowered her voice so only I could hear.

'It's all going to help that crystal I gave you work its magic,' she whispered. 'You'll be feeling much fonder of yourself in no time.'

'That really would be quite a trick,' I whispered back, ignoring the fact that I had already experienced the tiniest shift.

'There's no trick to it,' she told me seriously. 'But by Yule, you'll be a different person. You'll see. The time you spend helping everyone will be the perfect distraction from whatever it is that's got you so vexed. Some distance will give you some perspective.'

Given that I was still spending a lot of my alone time catastrophizing over an outcome which hadn't even happened I didn't think some perspective would be a bad idea. I needed to assimilate and draw a line under what *had* actually happened rather than waste time worrying over what *could* have occurred.

'What do you mean by just in the nick of time, Molly?' Archie asked loudly, making me jump.

'For the people who rely on Anna,' she said back, without missing a beat. 'As Paige is so willing to start the work straight up again, there'll barely be a hiccup in the operation now, will there? And that can only be a good thing, can't it?'

I could tell from Archie's expression that he wasn't entirely convinced that was what she had implied.

'That's true,' he responded nonetheless. 'Kathleen was over the moon, wasn't she, Paige?'

'Yes,' I confirmed, thinking of her reaction. 'She did seem pretty pleased.'

Dorothy sniffed and when I turned to look at her, I found her lips were set in a thin and uncompromising straight line.

'Are you all right?' I asked, wondering what on earth could be the matter.

She had a face like thunder.

'That woman,' Dorothy grumbled.

'You don't like Kathleen?' I was aghast.

Archie let out a long breath and raised his eyes skywards and I realized I'd said the wrong thing. Although, how anyone couldn't like Kathleen with her soft grey curls and can-do attitude was beyond me. I would have thought she and Dorothy would get along like a house on fire. However, it turned out their relationship was more fireworks than comforting glowing embers.

'I wouldn't go as far as to say that I dislike her,' Dorothy tersely said, 'but she's put a lot of people's backs up since she waltzed into town and shook everything up.'

I didn't know what to say to that.

'The only shaking up she's done,' Archie patiently said, 'is on the dance floor during the tea dances and classes she runs at the town hall.'

'Don't you like the dancing?' I asked Dorothy.

Kathleen certainly looked to be thriving on it, but obviously I didn't say that.

'There's nothing wrong with the dancing,' Dorothy conceded. 'What I object to is her going around implying that certain members of the more mature community need to get themselves moving. She's guilt tripping and goading everyone into thinking they need to be more active if they want to live long enough to make the most of their pensions.'

This comment resulted in the biggest eye roll from Archie and Catherine looked unusually uncomfortable. Personally, I thought it was a justified tactic on Kathleen's behalf if it helped keep people healthy, and on their toes, whatever their age. However, I got the impression that there was more to Dorothy's dislike than some clever propaganda on Kathleen's part.

'And a few of us offered to supply an afternoon tea to go with the dances, in line with tradition,' Dorothy then said, turning red, as she got to the true heart of the matter, 'but she wouldn't have it. Apparently, all that stodge, as she put it,' she snapped, sounding increasingly outraged as she banged down the wooden spoon she was holding, 'isn't good for the pipes and she turned us down. What's the good of raising pulses, I heard her snippily say to someone, to then suppress them with all those calories. What a cheek!'

'And Dorothy hasn't spoken to her since,' Archie neatly finished up, drawing a line under the topic. 'Now, where are we at with the vehicle insurance, Mick?'

'All done,' he nodded. 'Paige is now a named driver on the policy for Anna's Fiat and the hall Land Rover, too. You can drive them both now, my love.'

'Do you think you'll be all right in the Land Rover?' Archie asked, as Dorothy continued to mutter.

'Well, I was all right driving through tricky terrain in armour plated vehicles in Jordan,' I told him. 'So, I should be able to handle it.'

'I don't know,' said Mick, my sarcasm going completely over his head. 'She can be a bugger on the gear change from second to third.'

'I'm sure I'll get the hang of it,' I told him as Angus guffawed in the background.

'And *you know who* has sorted the hospital and clinic runs

so you won't have to worry about getting folk in and out of either the tiny Fiat or the high Land Rover,' Archie reminded me in a hushed tone.

'Voldemort?' I innocently asked and he looked daggers.

'I daresay he means that Kathleen,' said Dorothy and Archie groaned.

'How about we go and have a look for Hayley's designs?' I suggested quickly, so as not to set her off again.

'No need,' Angus piped up, with self-satisfied smugness. 'Hayley called while you two were in town and said they're in the secret drawer in the studio.'

He sounded well-pleased to have the answer but Archie was biting his lip and looked more stressed with his father than annoyed with me.

'And did she tell you where the secret drawer in the studio is, Dad?' he asked, pressing his fingers to his temples and moving them in tight circles.

Angus's eyebrows shot up and he cleared his throat.

'Ah,' he said, turning red. 'Well, no, now you come to mention it, she didn't give me the exact whereabouts.'

'Oh, for pity's sake.' Archie sighed.

'But at least we've narrowed it down to one room,' Angus brightly pointed out.

'That's true,' said Molly, jumping up. 'Come on, let's go and look.'

Archie tried to call Hayley again but had no joy and so we all began searching for the drawer which held her designs. The studio turned out to be in the former conservatory and it was a beautiful light and airy space with a view of part of the gardens. I could appreciate why Hayley had set up in there and was very much looking forward to meeting the talented woman in person when she and Gabe arrived back in time for Christmas.

'I would have thought you'd know all the secret hidey holes in the hall by now,' I said to Angus as we ran our fingers along ledges and squinted into dark spaces. 'Surely you've lived here long enough to become acquainted with every nook and cranny.'

My godfather didn't agree.

'This place is still full of secrets,' he happily said. 'There are further surprises around every corner.'

I was about to answer when I received . . . well, a nasty shock rather than a pleasant surprise.

'Sorry,' Archie said, holding up his hands. 'That was my fault.'

I didn't realize what had caused the calamitous crash but my immediate reaction to it had been to throw myself face down on to the cold, tiled floor. I lay on my front with my heart pounding, my ears buzzing and my body trembling.

'What the hell are you doing down there?' Archie laughed as he righted the easel he'd sent clattering and came to pull me up. 'Paige?'

I closed my eyes and tried to swallow.

'Paige?' His voice came again, this time full of concern.

'I'm all right,' I said shakily as I tried to lever myself into a sitting position, even though I wasn't.

'Stay where you are,' said Molly, sitting herself down next to me. 'Just give yourself a minute.'

I felt like such a fool and I knew everyone's eyes were on me.

'Honestly, I'm all right,' I said, shifting again so I was kneeling next to her.

She took my hands in hers.

'It's a standard reflex reaction to loud noises,' I told the assembled group with what I hoped was a nonchalant shrug. 'Old habits and all that.' I smiled, trying to make light of what I'd done.

'I'm not sure I believe that,' said Angus, his brows knitted together and his kind face peering down at mine.

'Me neither,' said Archie.

Molly squeezed my hands.

'It's true,' I told them.

'I daresay it's part of your training, isn't it?' she asked.

'Exactly,' I said, gratefully squeezing back. 'Absolutely standard practice.'

'If you're in the military, I would imagine it is . . .' Archie started but a look from Molly quieted him.

'Your phone's ringing, Archie,' I said, nodding at his shirt pocket.

He pulled it out, still watching me as Molly tenderly helped me to my feet. My legs felt like jelly and I was grateful she didn't let go of my hand while I took a minute to regain my balance.

'Thank you,' I said to my friend, as Archie strode purposefully across the room.

'You know I'm always here if you want to talk,' she softly said.

'I do,' I whispered back.

'That was Hayley,' Archie announced. 'She realized she'd forgotten to tell Dad where the drawer is. It's here somewhere, apparently.'

He fiddled about under the desk for a few seconds and then there was a click and he pulled out a packed A4 envelope with a flourish.

'Thank goodness for that,' he said, letting out a breath.

We all applauded and I sent up a silent prayer of thanks for Hayley and her timely intervention.

Chapter 6

'I can take them to town, if you like,' I offered, once we'd established that even though delivering the designs was a priority, everyone else was pushed for time. 'I can practise driving on the tricky Fenland terrain.'

'Ha, ha,' said Archie, handing the envelope over. 'You'll have to take the Land Rover then,' he added, with a nod at Bran who was once again welded to my side. 'You'll never get the hound in the Fiat.'

'What is that dog's obsession with you, I wonder, Paige?' asked Angus.

'He goes where he's most needed . . .' Molly dreamily said.

Her words came to an abrupt end as she realized she'd put her dainty foot in it and I took the opportunity to quickly head outside, with said dog hot on my heels.

'You won't be able to take him into the café,' Archie said, having handed over a water bottle and Bran-sized bowl as I unwound the windows because the dog's panting had started to steam them up. 'But if you open the door and shout, I'm sure Jemma will come running.'

'Especially when she realizes what I've got,' I said, patting the envelope with the precious contents on the passenger seat.

'Exactly,' Archie agreed.

He handed me Bran's lead and waved us off. However, I had barely reached the start of the drive before Mick flagged me down again.

'Jump cables.' I frowned as he bundled the tangle through the window and into the passenger footwell.

'Just in case,' he said. 'She has been fine, but you can never tell at this time of year. Do you know how to use them?'

I gave him a look and he chuckled.

'I know how to use them,' I told him. 'But I'll need to find something with enough heft to give her a jump.'

'Wynbridge is a rural market town,' he said. 'You won't be short on heft, should you need it. There are always at least three farm trucks milling around the market square.'

The town was short on parking though and I had to leave the Land Rover a few streets away from where we needed to be, not that Bran or I objected to having a bit of a walk. As much as I loved the hall, it was good to get away for a while, especially after the interest I'd raised by throwing myself on to the studio floor commando style.

'I'm not sure this is necessary, Bran,' I said, clipping his lead to his collar as we got into our stride, 'but we'll use it just in case you turn out to be a flight risk.'

He wasn't bothered either way and loped along beside me,

kindly matching his lengthy strides to mine so I wasn't too out of puff when we reached our destination. The café bell tinkled as I pushed open the door and waited patiently on the threshold in the hope of catching someone's eye.

'Are you coming in or not?' asked the customer closest to the draught my lingering was letting in.

'Not, I'm afraid,' I apologized. 'But I'll only be a minute.'

'Can I help?' asked a waitress, who then fortuitously spotted me.

'I have a delivery for Jemma,' I told her. 'But I can't come in to drop it off because I've got a dog with me.'

The woman quickly stepped outside and closed the door behind her.

'Hello, Bran,' she said, giving him a fuss, which he willingly soaked up. 'You must be Paige,' she then said to me.

'I am,' I confirmed. Familiar with how quickly word spread in a small town, I didn't bother asking how she knew. 'And I have this envelope from Hayley to pass on.'

'Her designs at last!' said the woman, sounding delighted. 'Jemma's not here, but you'll find Lizzie in the gallery next door. You can leave them with her.'

I looked down at Bran.

'No one will mind if you take him in there,' she smiled. 'We all know who he is and what wonderful manners he's got.'

I thanked her and headed to the gallery. I peered through the window before going in and hoped she was right about Bran because it looked as though a class of some sort was set up at the back. I wondered if it was one of Lizzie's crafting sessions.

'Come on then,' I said to Bran, who had chosen that moment to flop down on the pavement.

He hauled himself up, looking slightly damp underneath, and we ventured inside. The front half of the gallery was full of shelves packed with beautiful wooden turned bowls, hand knitted scarves and more than a sprinkling of products showcasing Hayley's cheeky feathered flock. The walls were covered in different size canvases, many of them featuring the striking local landscape and wildlife.

I slowly turned my attention from the gallery walls to the class and realized it wasn't a crafting session after all. Some easels had been set up and standing beside them were a group of women, and one man, all wearing the most rapt expressions.

Heads tilted to one side, they were nodding and looking serious and I got the impression that eyelashes were actually being batted in the direction of the person addressing them. There was even a yearning lower lip bite going on and I was consequently intrigued to see the face of the person who was the cause of so much intent interest.

I was just about to clear my throat in the hope that the person facing the group would turn around, when Bran chose that moment to give an almighty shake.

'Oh, Bran,' I loudly admonished.

He had made me jump and I realized I had been as spellbound by the rear view of the man as everyone else was with the front.

'You are a daft dog,' I tutted.

Fortunately, he hadn't got properly wet from his brief encounter with the damp pavement, so there was no harm done, but that didn't seem to be the opinion of the man who had finally turned and was now scowling in my direction.

His stubbled jaw was set hard, and when he pushed his dark hair away from his forehead, his eyes appeared almost black and carried an unsettling hint of menace. Mr Darcy sprang to mind and I felt myself shrink under his disapproving gaze.

'Sorry,' I stammered, frustrated by the shake in my voice. 'I didn't mean to interrupt. I'm looking for Jemma.'

He didn't say anything.

'I mean Lizzie.' I blushed, holding out Hayley's envelope as if that would explain everything. 'I was told she was here.'

The man took a step towards me and my reaction was to take one back. Bran, sensing my discomfiture, shifted so he was standing almost in front of me.

'You can't bring a wet dog in here,' were the man's first furious sounding words.

'He's not wet.' I recovered, standing a little straighter and channelling my inner Elizabeth Bennet in Bran's defence. 'He's barely damp.'

'Well, whatever,' the man gruffly responded. 'You can leave that with me,' he then haughtily said, reaching out for the envelope.

'No,' I said, holding it close again. 'I'd rather not.'

I had no idea who he was so I was hardly going to hand over Hayley's designs to him, was I? He looked rather taken aback by my refusal and I dared him to challenge it, but then Lizzie appeared and the disconcerting stand-off was quickly defused.

'Paige,' she said, striding up. 'It is Paige, isn't it?'

'Yes.' I nodded.

'Archie called a few minutes ago and left a message to say you'd be dropping by.' She beamed.

Without a word, the man turned and walked back to the group who had been interestedly watching on. What a disagreeable person.

'I'm sorry to have interrupted,' I said, loud enough for him to hear.

'Don't mind Brodie,' Lizzie whispered.

'Oh, I won't,' I replied and had the pleasure of seeing his back stiffen. 'These are for you, Lizzie,' I said, holding out the envelope again. 'And Jemma.'

'Do you know what Hayley has come up with?' Lizzie asked, running her fingers along the sealed edge of the envelope.

'Sadly not,' I told her. 'Although I was tempted to take a peek when I drove in, but then thought I should wait along with everyone else until the official unveiling.'

'I admire your ability to resist!' Lizzie laughed. 'But I'm sure your resolve will be richly rewarded.'

'Given what I've seen from previous years,' I smiled, looking at the shelves again, 'I'm sure you're right. Now,' I added, 'I suppose I'd better go in case Bran has another shake and gets in trouble again.'

'Bran's always welcome,' Lizzie said brightly, patting his head, 'and he's not even wet, so no harm done.'

'He's not even damp,' I couldn't resist adding, wallowing in the momentary halt in Brodie's speech to the group.

I left the gallery with a spring in my step and when I looked back was surprisingly gratified to discover the grumpy sod was watching me walk away.

'Right then, Bran,' I said, resisting the urge to wave. 'Let's find something tasty to eat, shall we?'

The market stalls were full of edible treats, so Bran and I wove our way between them tasting samples and picking up a little makeshift picnic as we went, which I thought we could park up and enjoy before we returned to the hall. I'd spotted a concrete pad in the gateway of a field on the drive into town which would be the perfect spot.

'Come on then, Bran,' I coaxingly said in the hope that he'd jump back in the Land Rover unaided after I'd given him a drink.

He willingly hopped in and hunkered down and I turned the engine over which thankfully started on the first try. I drove slowly out of town back the way we'd come, easily shifting the gears from second to third as I had on the drive in and within a few minutes I'd parked up again and was dipping into the bag of treats.

'This sausage roll,' I told Bran as I fed him titbits over the back of the seat, 'is from Skylark Farm which, according to the lady on the stall, isn't all that far from here. What do you think?'

Bran eagerly poked his head further through the gap, keen for another morsel.

'My thoughts exactly,' I agreed. 'Absolutely delicious.'

He wasn't so keen on the apple chutney, also from the same farm, which I had selected to accompany the sausage rolls, but as I dipped the pastry into the pot, I thought it tasted like manna from heaven. Rounded off with a couple of iced biscuits from The Cherry Tree Café makes and bakes stall and washed down with hot chocolate which also served to warm my hands, it was a most delicious feast. My transition from meagre rations to more familiar sized meals was coming along quickly and surprisingly comfortably.

'Shall we have a few more minutes before we head back?' I suggested, twisting round to find Bran fast asleep. 'I guess so.' I smiled.

I had thought about getting out and stretching my legs again with a stride around the headland, but rather than disturb Bran, I opened the windows and pulled my phone out of my jacket pocket instead.

Two messages had landed since I'd left the hall. Most likely because Wynbridge had a better mobile signal than Wynthorpe. The first was from Mum, saying how pleased she and Dad were knowing that I was at the hall with Catherine and Angus and that they would call to see how I was settling in soon.

The second was from Chadia's mum hoping that now I was back in the country, I would be able to visit her. Just like with my parents, I had cited the withdrawal of corporate sponsorship and the consequential staff cuts as being responsible for my early departure from Jordan and, although I felt guilty about the deception, I knew it would be better for me in the long run to keep my explanation simple.

It was Chadia who had set me on the path to overseas volunteering and then working for the charity I had now left. She had been manning the stand at the university recruitment fair I attended in my third year and encouraged me to consider signing up for the same programme she was then involved with. We soon became firm friends as well as colleagues working on the same projects.

I had joined her in Tanzania teaching women's empowerment and working with disadvantaged children, and then we had moved on together, continuing with the same programme in Nepal and Morocco. The skills we taught, which enabled the women to earn their own money, along with raising their awareness, felt basic to me in the beginning, but I soon saw for myself the transformative impact the projects had.

I adored working with Chadia. She was one of those people who always went above and beyond and squeezed every last productive second out of each and every day. She was only a couple of years older than me, but she taught me so much and it was her idea that we should apply to join the charity working in war-torn countries and the resultant camps with a focus on looking after the women and children who found themselves there.

Our applications were successful and we continued to be

the perfect pairing. The work was different to what we'd started out doing, with more emphasis on basic needs, but it was essential, often gruelling and I believe that Chadia came to rely on me as much as I relied on her. However, our partnership came to an abrupt and heart-breaking end.

A brief visit to her family one summer had snatched her from the world, courtesy of a driver who ploughed into her on a pedestrian crossing. I had been devastated by her loss. Chadia's mum had given me the locket with the precious photograph inside and it was the only thing that had been close to my heart since I had become the lone wolf working alongside, as opposed to with, the rest of the charity team.

I had believed that working alone was safest after my friend's untimely death, but given my recent mistake, I had been wrong about that. I blinked away the rush of tears and reminded myself of the perspective I had told myself I needed to gain. My error in Jordan hadn't ended as badly as it might and I needed to take comfort in that rather than constantly imagining the worst-case scenario.

I replied to the message and then a sudden movement on the other side of the field caught my attention. Three Chinese water deer leapt effortlessly across the dyke which separated the field from its neighbour and then disappeared into a distant copse. There had been a painting of a group of deer standing in a frost covered landscape back in the gallery. I wondered who was responsible for creating it. I doubted art teacher Mr Darcy would have such lightness of touch when he filled a canvas.

I tried to fix on something else, but the image of his face, and arresting jean-clad rear view, filled my head. It was a long time since I'd noticed a man in any detail and I hoped my libido wasn't about to leap into life. I had told Molly the last thing I needed was a distraction in the form of the opposite sex and a challenging and grumpy one would be even more unwelcome.

My body gave an involuntary shiver and I realized how cold I'd got sitting in one position, thinking over the details of mine and Brodie's unsatisfactory encounter.

'I suppose we'd better be getting back,' I said to Bran who was still soundly snoring.

I turned the key in the ignition but instead of the comforting roar of the engine there was a clicking sound. I turned the key back, counted to three and tried again, but the engine was as dead as a dodo.

'Damn,' I groaned, resting my head on the steering wheel, after checking that I hadn't left the lights on. 'Damn, damn, damn, damn, damn.'

I located the bonnet lever and hopped out, taking the jump leads with me. Not that they'd do any good when there was no other vehicle to connect them to. I'd have to ring the hall and ask if the vehicle had some sort of roadside assistance cover.

'You need to stay in there,' I said to Bran, who had woken and was whining to join me. 'I'll be with you again in a minute.'

I had just keyed in the code to unlock my phone when I

spotted a large vehicle further along the road heading in my direction and wondered whether I dare flag it down. It was almost level with me when I decided I didn't, but it pulled off the road and on to the concrete pad anyway.

'Are you having a bit of bother?' asked the driver, who was a jovial looking guy about my own age and with a head full of dark curls.

'What makes you think that?' I smiled, relieved to see such a friendly face.

'The open bonnet and the fact that you're holding a set of jump leads was a bit of a giveaway.' He grinned, his eyes crinkling attractively at the corners.

I felt my face flush as I realized my attempt at wit had whooshed right over his head.

'Is that Bran?' he then asked, jumping out and pulling on a waxed jacket which was more battered than any I'd seen back at Wynthorpe. 'You must be from the hall.'

'I daresay you parked up and left your lights on, didn't you?' came another voice.

I looked across the seat the driver had just vacated and felt my shoulders tense up as I came face to face with Brodie, who was glaring at me from the dimly lit interior.

Glowering seemed to be his go-to look, where Bran and I were concerned at least. I couldn't imagine the group admiring him in the gallery had been on the receiving end of such hostility. Their esteem must have sprung from a very different expression and yet my pulse was still racing at the sight of this one, which was most unsettling.

'No,' I primly said. 'I didn't actually.'

'Ignore my brother,' said the other guy, taking the jump leads from me. 'He's been in a foul mood all day.'

'Oh, I'm well aware of that,' I replied sardonically, slamming his truck door shut and turning my back on it. 'Our paths had the misfortune of crossing earlier, back in town.'

The guy chuckled and re-opened the door so he could pop his bonnet.

'I'm Jack by the way.' He beamed.

He couldn't seem to stop smiling and I wondered if Brodie was so glum because his sibling had nabbed all the happy genes in the family.

'I run the Brambles distillery on the outskirts of town.'

'I didn't know Wynbridge had a distillery,' I told him. 'But then I haven't visited for a while. How wonderful.'

'I didn't think we'd met,' he said, as he pulled a slightly dog-eared leaflet out of the pocket of his jacket. 'The distillery is a relatively new addition to the area. You should come along,' he added, handing me the crumpled paper. 'I could give you a tour if you like.'

'That would be great,' I said, finding it impossible not to smile back.

I didn't think he was flirting with me. He was just genuinely happy. Unlike his brother.

'Hurry up, Jack!' Brodie, who was still warmly cocooned in the cosy confines of the cab, shouted. 'I was already late when you picked me up in town.'

Jack let out a long breath and raised his eyes skywards.

'Something tells me you'll be sampling your own drinks tonight,' I laughed.

'You're not wrong.' He joined in. 'Now, let's get you up and running, shall we?'

His powerful truck engine had almost instantly breathed life into the old Land Rover but Jack insisted we exchanged numbers and then followed me as far as the hall drive to make sure I got back safe and sound.

I kept looking at him and Brodie in the rear-view mirror and wondered what they were saying to each other. By the time I waved Jack off, Brodie was looking even more thunderous and staring moodily out of the passenger side window and, from what I could make out, Jack's smile was somewhat strained.

'Well,' I said to Bran, who had forgiven me for abandoning him and plonked his head heavily on my shoulder as we bounced back up the drive. 'That was more of an adventure than we were expecting to have, wasn't it?'

I wasn't even out of my jacket before Molly sought me out.

'I hear you've met the new guy in town,' she said, with a wicked grin as she plucked playfully at my jumper sleeve.

Yet again, the small-town grapevine had been hard at work.

'Who?' I frowned, feigning ignorance.

I knew she could only be talking about one person, but had every intention of playing it cool.

'Brodie, of course.'

'Oh, him,' I said lightly, stepping neatly out of her reach. 'Yes, I have.'

'And what did you think?' she quizzed.

'Miserable,' I announced, turning my attention to the leaflet. 'But his brother Jack, who owns Brambles Distillery, is an absolute sweetheart.'

The look of surprise on her face was priceless.

Chapter 7

My dreams that night were of a different sort, but nonetheless disconcerting. Given that Jack had such a pleasing expression and a whole host of kind words – and deeds – in his arsenal, I felt cheated that it was his gloomy brother who filled my head throughout the longest watches of the night.

Unable to stifle yawns from breakfast to bedtime the following day, Archie said he wouldn't burden me with the instructions on how to carry out the housework until I'd properly got the measure of the volunteering.

'Sundays should be a time to rest,' he said, showing unexpected understanding. 'And we could all do with one day a week to laze about, couldn't we?'

I wondered if his words had been prompted by something Molly had said, but her out-of-this-world expression gave nothing away. However it came about, I was happy to while away the day napping in front of the fire and indulging in Dorothy's legendary Sunday roast.

*

I was feeling a bit jittery on Monday morning and headed back to Wynbridge bright and early to run through that week's schedule with Kathleen. It wasn't strictly necessary but with my confidence having taken such a recent knock, I wasn't leaving anything to chance. I might have only been the gopher, but I would run through the role until I knew it inside out and back to front because the last thing I needed was another mishap.

I knew deliveries were made on a Tuesday, Thursday and even a Saturday if required, and that would leave Monday, Wednesday and Friday to keep on top of the chores at the hall once Archie handed them over. At a push I could do more cleaning on Sunday, but Catherine had already said that wouldn't be necessary. She had assured me that everyone could strip and change their own beds and that Molly would be cleaning her and Angus's room along with Dorothy's and Mick's.

'Did she start first time?'

I had just parked up in the market square when Jack's truck pulled into the space next to me and he and Brodie, the brother Grim, jumped out. I had tried, and failed, on the drive in, to stop myself from wondering if I might bump into them.

'She did,' I said, giving Jack a warm smile. 'But Mick has insisted I keep the jump leads with me, just in case.'

'Sounds like a plan.' Jack nodded. 'And my knowing you've got them means I won't need to follow you around on the off chance that you might get stuck.'

'That sounds a bit stalkerish, Jack,' said Brodie, making his brother blush.

'I didn't mean it to.' He grimaced.

'Ignore him, Jack,' I tutted, dismissing Brodie. 'You were simply being chivalrous. Who knows when I might need rescuing again?'

Brodie fixed me with a level stare and I was rooted to the spot when his face was suddenly transformed by a smile which set my cheeks blazing as brightly as he'd turned his brother's. So that must have been what seduced the group in the gallery on Saturday. It wasn't the glower, but a smile which had held them entranced.

I stared, dumbstruck, feeling both heady and hypnotized as he cocked his head to one side. It was witchcraft and powerful enough to rival even Molly's skills.

'You really don't strike me as the sort of woman who needs rescuing,' he said, which had the immediate effect of turning my cheeks even redder.

'Well,' I swallowed, 'that's as maybe . . .'

My words tailed off and I just stood there, like an idiot.

'You haven't forgotten about my offer to show you around the distillery, have you?' Jack asked, thankfully breaking the spell Brodie had somehow cast over me.

'No,' I said, turning to look at him and instantly feeling more human again. 'Not at all, but it might take me a couple of weeks to take you up on your offer if that's all right? I'm currently settling into a routine of volunteering here in town and helping out at the hall so I haven't much spare time at the moment.'

'That's all right,' Jack said cheerfully. 'But if you want to get the measure of the place, you can always look it up online. My Instagram account will give you an idea of what it's like.'

'Thanks for the suggestion,' I said. 'But I don't have Instagram or any other social media accounts.'

Brodie laughed loudly and clapped his hands together, making me jump.

'There, Jack,' he said, moving to stand next to me and punching his brother on the arm as he did. 'I'm not the only eejit in the world who doesn't have an online presence. Paige is as much of an eejit as I am. No offence,' he quickly added, frowning down at me.

'None taken.' I frowned back.

He was quite transformed and I felt drawn to him like a moth to a flame. I reminded myself of the potentially unhappy outcome of that particular idiom but I couldn't seem to flutter away.

'I wasn't implying that you're an eejit,' he then said, still holding my gaze. 'But that's what Jack called me. He reckons I'm the last person alive who doesn't have an online presence, but he was wrong. There's two of us.'

'So it would seem,' I agreed, hastily forcing myself to look over at Jack before I was further bewitched by his brother.

I hadn't considered that Brodie and I might have anything in common, but surprisingly we had. Jack rolled his eyes and I guessed this was a topic of conversation which had been covered by the sparring siblings many times before.

'I just think,' Jack said, 'it wouldn't hurt for you to have something up and running.'

I risked another glance at Brodie and wondered why, but finding him back in full thundercloud mode, didn't dare ask. He was the master of the speedy mood swing.

'I have to get on,' he snapped, striding off like Darcy on a bad day. 'I'll see you later, Jack. Good luck with your volunteering, Paige.'

'Bye,' I called after him. 'Thanks.'

Jack's expression was almost despairing as he watched Brodie walk away and I was intrigued to know more about the pair of them.

'Are you in town to see me by any chance, Paige?' Kathleen called from across the street, snatching away my opportunity to ask.

'I am,' I called back.

'I'll meet you in the library then,' she said, pointing in the building's direction. 'It's not officially open this early, but just knock on the door and I'll let you in.'

'I'd better get on,' I said to Jack. 'Thanks for keeping an eye out for me.'

'No worries.' He smiled, but I could tell he was still thinking about Brodie. 'I'll see you again soon.'

There wasn't a great deal for me to do on my first stint as delivery driver the next day, but I had soon discovered just how vital a service it was. Some of the long, straight drove roads around and through the Fens only had three or four houses dotted along them with literally miles of empty road in between. There was no bus route so if you lived alone and had no car or other means of transport to take you anywhere, not a lot of company either.

'Well, aren't you a sight for sore eyes,' said the first elderly woman I visited, as she held her front door ajar when it had been my intention to just hand her bag of tablets over and exchange a few words on the doorstep. 'And perfectly timed. The kettle has just this second come to the boil. I know Anna prefers tea, but I have coffee if you'd rather?'

'Tea would be wonderful,' I said, crossing the threshold.

'And I've biscuits too.' She smiled. 'And cake.'

As well as Joan's kind offer, I accepted everyone else's too and my bladder was fit to burst by the time I made it back to the hall. And my throat was a bit scratchy as well. I hadn't talked so much in a long time. It had taken far longer than I had expected to offload everything, but I did get the satisfactory feeling that it was a job well done.

'So,' asked Archie, once I had dashed to the loo, 'how did you get on?'

I looked at the clipboard I had dropped on the table and which had a neat row of ticks running down it and which I had meticulously checked after every stop. I'd also called Kathleen, just to confirm a couple of things. I didn't think I'd got on her nerves. I hoped I hadn't. I had just wanted to be sure that I was getting it all right.

'Good,' I said, showing him the completed checklist and allowing myself to enjoy the feeling of achievement which came with it. 'Mission accomplished. Fruit, veg, meds and tins of soup all delivered and safely stowed away.'

'You must be feeling pretty happy with yourself,' Molly said meaningfully.

'Let's just say,' I answered as I gave Bran, who I hadn't been able to take with me, a fuss, 'I'll sleep easier knowing Harry Hodges can have the baked potato he's been fancying all day for his supper.'

Archie laughed, hopefully unaware that Molly's words were wrapped up with the pink crystal I was carrying around in my pocket.

'And so it begins,' she smiled, beginning to clear the table.

'And tomorrow morning,' I said to Archie, keen to forge ahead as Angus wandered in, 'we can get stuck into everything here and this evening, Angus, I thought we could go through the plans for the Winter Wonderland. I know it's still a few weeks away yet, but there's no harm in being prepared, is there?'

'Five weeks today and we'll be up and running,' said Angus, sounding excited. 'And there's no need to worry about any of it, Paige, but if it will set your mind at rest, we'll check the details. As you haven't experienced it before, it probably would be a good idea to fill you in a bit more on what goes on.'

He sounded sincere, but I'd heard enough tall tales about the mischief and mayhem my godfather had got up to in the name of Christmas in the past, so wanted to be as sure as I possibly could that all was on track and he had no tricks up his sleeve.

I knew that one year he'd had to be rescued by the fire brigade after trying to adorn the hall with lights and got stuck tens of feet in the air in a defunct cherry picker with a concussion as a result and I certainly didn't want a repeat of any such disaster while I was helping out.

'And you mustn't use furniture polish on any of this,' Archie told me, referring yet again to the lengthy list of instructions Hayley had left for him and which I was holding.

I let out a long breath in lieu of a yawn. Angus, Mick and I had stayed up late going through the Winter Wonderland plans and I was feeling tired as a result, but doing my best to keep up with Archie's lesson in how to keep the hall in tiptop condition.

'Or this,' he added. 'Has she written that down? I'm sure she said no polish on this chair.'

'She has,' I said, referring back to the list, which was even lengthier than the one from Kathleen. 'Here, look. No polish.'

Satisfied that he was right, Archie moved on.

'Now this thing,' he said, holding up a little sort of funnel which was an attachment for the vacuum cleaner and looked like it had the foot of a pair of tights taped to the end of it, 'can be used on the upholstery in the sitting room, but only on the lowest setting.'

'Got it,' I nodded. 'And she's written that down and underlined it, so I'm not likely to forget.'

Archie looked at me and raised his eyebrows.

'I'm not being sarcastic,' I told him. 'There's a lot to do, isn't there?'

'Yes,' he sighed, 'there is rather and this is the really pared down version of what usually goes on, on a day-to-day basis.'

'However does Hayley find the time for her art on top of all this?' I asked. 'This is more than a full-time job in its own right.'

'Beats me.' Archie shrugged. 'Are you sure you want to take it on? Molly's going to help out when she can between her readings and Reiki appointments, but it's still a lot for one person.'

'I am.' I nodded. 'Come on, what's next?'

'You won't have to use any of these specialist cleaners,' he said as we ran through the contents of the cleaning supplies cupboard. 'She just wants us to focus on the main rooms and said she'll give everything else a thorough going over when she gets back.'

I hoped she wasn't going to mind that I had taken over from Archie.

'And Mick's going to do the fires,' I said, forcing myself not to worry about it.

'Yes,' Archie confirmed. 'He's dealing with those as usual.'

'Right,' I said, puffing out my cheeks as I scanned down the list to make sure we'd covered everything. 'I think that's it, and don't worry, I won't let you down.'

'Oh,' he laughed, 'I know you won't.'

'No pressure then,' I said and not for the first time since I'd arrived.

'None at all,' he beamed. 'Right, let's go and see if Dorothy needs winding up, shall we? That's a very important part of Hayley's role here too, you know.'

And one I most definitely wouldn't be taking on.

Chapter 8

After my lengthy briefing from Archie about how to best keep on top of cleaning the hall, I began to get an idea of exactly how much work I'd agreed to take on. Combined with what I had already started to do on Anna's behalf, I calculated I was never going to have a spare minute in the run up to Christmas and therefore I'd better stop thinking about the mysterious and contradictory Brodie, who had somehow managed to take up permanent residence in my head, and was too distracting by far.

Having only encountered him all but briefly, he should have been easy to dismiss yet his brooding manner and unexpectedly seductive smile coupled with the discovery that we had something in common had been a game changer. Married to the creative fantasy I'd started to weave around him, the one where he was painting in an idyllic studio and half covered in paint, he was proving impossible to shake off. Admittedly it made a welcome change from fretting over the real reason behind my arrival at the hall, but even so . . .

The Thursday delivery round did go some way to helping me forget about him because there was far more to do. Practically everyone on Kathleen's list had requested something and a longer than usual hold up at the house of Gladys Burdock meant I didn't leave while it was light, which was a little unnerving as I still didn't know my way around and didn't feel particularly comfortable about driving in the dark. Just a few months ago I wouldn't have cared a jot, but now I felt vulnerable and wished I had Bran by my side.

'I'm so sorry to have kept you hanging about,' Gladys apologized as she saw me off and we commented on how quickly the light had faded.

'It really doesn't matter, Gladys,' I reassured her, not wanting her to catch my nerves and feel even worse. 'We got there in the end, didn't we?'

'We did,' she smiled. 'And I'll rest easier as a result.'

'That's more than worth being a bit behind my time for then,' I told her with a smile.

She had been having trouble working out how to use the telephone service to book a long-awaited hospital appointment, but between us we had sussed it in the end and the look of relief on her face when it was confirmed told me that the extra time had been well spent.

I knew it could have been arranged far more quickly had I not worked through the instructions at a snail's pace, checking and re-checking every stage as we went along, but that was all on me. Despite that, we'd eventually got the desired result and I felt an inner glow of satisfaction that I'd been able to help someone who had been struggling.

At that precise moment, Molly's piece of rose quartz rubbed against the car keys in my pocket and I felt relieved that my friend hadn't been in the vicinity to witness my sense of achievement. She would have let no time pass before pointing it out and then been full of herself as a result.

'Now,' I said to Gladys, pushing thoughts of clever Molly away. 'You get back in the warm and I'll see you next week.'

It was already cold, and I could tell it was most likely going to be a frosty night too. I shivered while I waited for Anna's car to warm up and for the windows to clear and then reset the satnav to guide me to my last port of call. With it telling me in a bossy Australian accent, which I had no idea how to change, to do a U-turn, I carefully did as I was instructed, mindful of the deep dykes which ran either side of the verge, and set off.

'Shit!' I swore, after I had taken myriad turns and the device fell off the window, narrowly missing my boot which I then stamped down on the brake pedal.

I swore again when I picked the satnav up and it refused to turn back on, even after I'd given it a shake. Abandoning it, I reached for my phone, thinking I could either fire up Google maps or call the hall and ask someone for help, but there wasn't a single bar of signal showing and, to make matters worse, it was almost out of charge.

'Bugger,' I muttered, feeling frustrated but I refused to be defeated or let my nerves get the better of me. 'Well, there's fuel in the tank,' I commented, checking the gauge, 'so I'll just have to drive about and see where I end up. Not that I can see much . . .'

Eventually the headlights picked out the silhouette of a cottage, set back from the road. The exterior looked to be half covered in ivy which melded it to the landscape and surrounding trees so I almost missed it, but when I stopped with more enthusiasm than grace, I spotted a dim light in a downstairs window. There was no smoke curling out of the chimney, but if there was a light on, then surely someone was at home.

'Civilization at last,' I sighed in relief, steeling myself to step out into the inky darkness. 'Well, almost,' I added, as I pushed open the rickety wooden gate and tripped up the overgrown path to the door.

There was no bell, as far as I could see and I didn't want to use the torch on my phone to check for fear of zapping the last bit of charge, so I knocked.

'Come on,' I said, stamping my feet and rubbing my arms when no one answered and the bitter cold began to bite.

I knocked again, more loudly, and took a step back. The curtains in the window where the light was on shifted slightly, but there was no sound and the door remained closed. I was certain someone was there, but they clearly weren't in the mood to welcome me in.

Then an image of Gladys popped into my head. What if there was someone like her living in the cottage? My hammering had probably scared them witless. I dithered for a second and then, with one last look at the window, went back to the car. If the worst came to the worst, I would just have to stay lost until sunrise the next day.

Fortunately, it didn't come to that, as a while later, I spotted the concrete pad in the field I'd stopped at a few days before (cue the return of those thoughts about Brodie) and managed to navigate my way back to the hall from there. Once I arrived and explained what had happened, Catherine then helpfully took me out to make the last call of the day and Mick turned his hand to fixing the faulty satnav.

By suppertime everything was sorted, but as I lay in bed that night, I couldn't stop thinking about the rundown cottage and the person inside who had moved the curtain. I hoped I hadn't scared them and as I drifted off to sleep, I wondered if I should try to find my way back in the daylight at the weekend to apologize. At least I wasn't thinking about the crack of rifle fire or the arousing artist.

Almost the whole of Friday, throughout which Angus took great delight in reminding everyone that it was now exactly one month until Christmas day, was taken up with cleaning the hall following Archie's instructions and to Hayley's exacting standards, but the weekend was mine to do with as I pleased.

I went down to breakfast a little earlier than usual on Saturday morning with the sole intention of finding the rundown cottage again and apologizing for my previous interruption fixed firmly at the front of my mind. However, I didn't actually make it into the kitchen as Angus was talking to someone and, as I hovered on the threshold and took note of his clandestine tone, I got the impression he didn't want to be overhead.

'I have every faith in you,' I heard him say as I lingered guiltily outside. 'I know you can do it, because I've previously enjoyed the benefit of what you're capable of, remember?'

I was about to do the honourable thing and walk away, but the voice which responded made my ears prick up and my heart pound. No longer on the periphery of my thoughts, Brodie was now in the Wynthorpe Hall kitchen.

'I know you mean well, Mr Connelly . . .' he said, sounding frustrated.

'Angus, please,' my godfather insisted.

'I know you mean well, Angus,' Brodie repeated, though with the more familiar ending, 'but you having faith in me, if anything, makes me feel . . .'

'Encouraged,' Angus hopefully interrupted.

I didn't think that was what Brodie had been going to say.

'And reassured to know that I know you can hit the jackpot again,' Angus keenly said. 'You just need to get on with it. Stop dithering and power through. I'm still expecting to see a return in my faith in you by Christmas, so there really is no time to lose.'

My ears tuned further in.

'But that's less than a month away now,' said Brodie, sounding exasperated. 'And these things take time.'

'That's as maybe,' said Angus, as I heard a step on the stairs behind me, 'but it will be such a disappointment if you don't pull through and I really need it to make this Christmas the best one the hall has ever seen.'

Brodie's sigh was loud enough for me to hear from a few feet away and I couldn't help but wonder what it was that Angus was so desperately in need of. Christmas had always been a highlight at the hall and now, with the addition of the Winter Wonderland, it was, I'd been told, even better. What on earth could Brodie supply my godfather with to make the season even more of a success?

'And this is strictly between us,' Angus urgently added, making me feel more suspicious than intrigued.

I twisted around to find Mick standing right behind me and put my hand over my mouth to deaden the sound of the gasp which had rushed into my mouth. I pointed back along the corridor and we made a stealthy retreat into Hayley's studio.

'What's going on?' Mick whispered, as I quietly closed the door and let out a breath.

'Angus is up to something,' I whispered back.

Mick gave me a look.

'Oh, I know,' I said, shaking my head. 'I know he's always up to something, but this sounds serious. He's talking to Brodie about something and I got the impression he didn't want to be overheard.'

'Who is Brodie?' Mick frowned.

'The brother of the guy who owns Brambles.'

'Oh him,' said Mick. 'I think he's quite new in town, isn't he? I didn't know Angus even knew him.'

'Oh, for goodness' sake,' I huffed, sounding exasperated myself. 'You live here, Mick, so I thought you might be able to tell me something about him.'

Mick ran a hand around the back of his neck.

'I don't know anything about him.' He shrugged.

'What about his job?' I asked. After the way Angus had worded what I'd overheard, I was questioning my artistic fantasy and thought perhaps Brodie wasn't an artist after all. 'What does he do for a living?'

'No idea.' Mick frowned, abandoning his neck and rubbing his hand along his jaw.

I was about to relay exactly what I'd heard, but the door flew open and I screeched in shock.

'What are you doing in here?' Archie laughed.

He was clearly amused by my reaction. I supposed I should have felt grateful that he'd forgotten I wasn't completely my former self and a bit jumpy as a result.

'Nothing,' I shot back before Mick had a chance to open his mouth.

Archie narrowed his eyes, but didn't probe further and I kept schtum. He might still be capable of winding me up, but I didn't want him worrying unnecessarily about his father's potential mischief.

'Molly and I are heading into town now,' he said. 'Do either of you want anything picking up?'

I breakfasted alone, my head abuzz with what I'd overheard and then set off. I did manage to find the cottage again, but more by luck than judgement. I had keyed the postcode of where I had been heading on Thursday into the repaired satnav and then, when I reached roughly the point where I thought it had fallen off the windscreen, I drove about until I struck gold. The cottage was easier to spot in the daylight and as I had taken the Land Rover, I had a more elevated position and could see further ahead.

The little detached house looked even worse in the cold light of day and had I not seen a light on and the curtain move, I would have assumed it was abandoned. It was far from falling down, but the garden was grotesquely overgrown, the windows were filthy and an air of neglect hung about it. I ventured down the path just as it started to rain, which made it all look even worse.

I knocked three times, each increasing in volume, before I got a response and only then was the door opened a couple of inches.

'What do you want?' came the gruff voice of the occupant.

It sounded like an elderly gent but as the person wasn't willing to show their face, I didn't want to assume.

'I'm not buying anything,' they shouted when I didn't immediately answer. 'What are you after?'

In spite of the hostile words, I sensed a hint of fear in the tone and wondered if I had done the right thing in coming back.

'I'm not after anything,' I said, taking a step back and receiving more of a soaking from the rain as a result. 'And I'm not selling anything either. I just wanted to apologize.'

The rain then started to fall harder and I wished I hadn't left my coat in the car.

'What for?'

'I knocked on your door Thursday evening' – I shivered – 'to ask for directions and left when you didn't answer. Then when I got home, I was worried that I might have scared you, so I've come back to say sorry.'

'That was you, was it?' the voice snapped back.

'Yes,' I said, my teeth chattering.

The door opened a little wider and I got my first glimpse of the person who lived inside the cottage. It was a man, most likely in his eighties. He had white hair which had grown out of whatever style it had previously been cut in, deep stubble graced his chin and he was wrapped in a woollen overcoat. The air which wafted out of the door felt even chillier than that outside.

'Thanks for letting me know,' he sniffed, looking me up and down. 'I did wonder.'

Having achieved my goal, at that point, I could have escaped the weather and headed back to the Land Rover, but my intuition kept me rooted to the rain-soaked spot. It had been a while since I had acted on it and, given the temperature, my timing couldn't really have been worse.

'I don't suppose I could trouble you for those directions now, could I?' I asked.

'You don't mean to say you've been lost all this time?' the man asked suspiciously, his bushy eyebrows shooting up as he narrowed the gap in the door again.

'Not exactly,' I said, as my soaked hair began to plaster itself to my head, 'but I never did find my way to where I needed to go under my own steam and I've got to try and go back there next week.'

It suddenly felt imperative that I made it over the threshold. This man was clearly ailing and, even though I had told Kathleen and Archie I didn't want any sort of responsibility, and in spite of the fact that I didn't have a spare second in my schedule to do another thing for anyone else, I felt an overwhelming desire to properly check that this man was all right.

'I suppose you'd better come in,' he eventually muttered. 'But I can only give you five minutes. I've got something very important I need to be getting on with.'

'Thank you,' I said, shivering my way into the cottage and closing the creaking door behind me.

If anything, the action served to keep the cold in and the marginally warmer air out. The door led straight into a sitting room and it was absolutely glacial, bone chillingly cold. I could see the open fire was laid and that there were radiators on the walls too, but neither source of heat was being used and clearly hadn't been for quite some time.

'Stay where you are,' said the man, pointing at the doormat. 'And try not to drip.'

I nodded and folded my arms across my chest.

'I'm Paige, by the way,' I told him.

'Albert,' he said in response, pulling his coat tighter around him, like a protective layer. 'Albert Price.'

'Pleased to meet you, Albert.' I smiled widely, but he didn't return the gesture.

'So where was it you were trying to find?' he frowned.

I reeled off the address and he gave me concise directions which thankfully I didn't really now need to remember, because I was struggling to think of anything beyond how cold I was. While he talked, my eyes scanned quickly around the room. I took in the piles of unwashed dishes, abandoned clothes and stacks of old newspapers. Beneath the general mess there was the evidence of what had once been a comfortable and, had the heating been on or the fire lit, cosy room.

'So, what will you be going there for?' he asked, once he'd told me how to get to the destination I had used as an excuse to gain entry into his glacier cave. 'What would old Franklin Duckett who lives there want with you?'

I told him about the delivery round and the sort of things I dropped off. If anyone should have been on Kathleen's list, it was Albert Price.

'I'm going to be passing your place a lot in the run up to Christmas,' I said, 'so you must let me know if there's anything you need bringing from town or even taking in.'

'Christmas,' he tutted dismissively, ignoring my offer.

I half-expected him to say 'humbug' next, but he didn't.

'I can drop off prescription requests and collect all sorts of groceries,' I reiterated but he impatiently waved my words away.

'Not for me,' he frostily said. 'I can manage well enough on my own.'

Managing was the last thing he looked like he was doing.

'And who is this?' I asked, deciding not to push the issue as I nodded at a scrappy looking little cat which had curled itself into the tiniest ball on one of the armchairs.

Albert squinted in the general direction.

'That must be Bella,' he said huskily. 'She was my sister's cat.'

From the change in his tone, I guessed his sister had either left or died. I couldn't bring myself to ask.

'Shall I write my phone number down for you?' I suggested brightly. 'Just in case you decide you do need something from town, or even a lift in. I'm happy to chauffeur too.'

'There's no need,' he said, trundling off towards the bureau in the corner of the room and scrabbling about for a piece of paper. 'But do it, if it'll get you back out the door quicker.'

I had clearly outstayed my welcome, but I would leave my number.

'I can't find a pen,' he tutted. 'I was sure there was one here somewhere.'

I had wondered why he had felt his way across the room and the fact that he couldn't see the pen which was right in front of him confirmed that, even though he was wearing glasses, he couldn't see particularly well.

'Not to worry,' I said, to save his blushes. 'I'll write it down and pop it through your letterbox next time I'm passing.'

'There's really no need,' he huffed. 'I won't need it.'

'Well, in that case,' I said, 'I won't keep you any longer. Would you like me to put a match to your fire before I go?'

'Of course not,' he snapped. 'I can light my own fire and I can see to my own shopping too. I don't need a do-gooder coming round here poking their nose in.'

That was me well and truly told.

'Has someone sent you?' he then demanded, sounding distraught rather than gruff.

'No, Mr Price,' I said, quickly opening the door. 'No one has sent me. I really did just want to say sorry for disturbing you the other night.'

'Well, you've done that,' he said, 'so you can go now and you won't need to come back.'

He hadn't noticed I'd dropped the scarf I had been wearing on the armchair closest to the door, so I would have to come back, at least one more time.

Chapter 9

That night, and in spite of the fact that further thoughts about Brodie could now be justified as I tried to puzzle out the connection between him and Angus, it was Albert Price and the upsetting state of his cottage which filled my head. Whether it was concern for the elderly gent or a pure coincidence, I had no idea, but my sleep was once again filled with the nightmares I had naively started to think were finally tailing off.

I saw myself, back in Jordan and making the same mistake. I was purposefully striding out of the camp alone and unaided, which was strictly not allowed, feeling determined to liberate the much-needed medical supplies from the broken-down truck just beyond the gate.

At the time I'd done it, I had still been assimilating the outcome of a recent meeting which had broken the news that aid worker numbers were going to be drastically cut as a result of the loss of corporate funding and sponsorship and therefore I clearly wasn't thinking straight. Not that that in any way justified my flouting of the rules.

Rules which were in place for everyone's protection, whether they were a team player or, like me since losing Chadia, the lone wolf type. No matter what your working preference, there were certain protocols everyone had to follow without question, for the safety of all.

Next came the piercing crack of rifle fire, my screams for help and the eventual rescue which had unnecessarily put so many other lives at risk.

When I broke free of the terror, I found myself safely cocooned in the Rose Room and as I lay, damp with sweat and my breath tight in my chest, I felt relieved that I had come to before the nightmare had taken the darker turn it usually favoured. The one which played out the very worst that could have happened as opposed to what actually had. That had to be progress, didn't it?

I lay and pondered the fact that I had walked out of that camp on the misguided assumption that I was following my intuition and I wondered if the fact that the emotion had stirred within me again when I met Albert Price was the reason behind my dramatically interrupted sleep. I did still feel duty bound to help him, but I wouldn't do anything more than mention him to Kathleen. I would pass his name and address on and that would be that.

It was another chilly start on Sunday and Dorothy had decided we all needed hearty breakfasts to prepare us for the hard work to come in the run up to Christmas.

'It's not something I usually do on a Sunday,' she told me. 'But it will stand us all in good stead for what's to come.'

While Mick set the table, I passed around the plates she was filling with eggs, bacon and everything else associated with a full English. I bet Albert wasn't starting his day with anything like the amount of food we were about to tuck into, but then I wasn't supposed to be thinking about him, was I?

'Paige,' came Dorothy's voice. 'I said this one is for Molly.'

'Right,' I said, setting it down in the place where she usually sat.

'She reckons these new veggie sausages don't taste too bad,' Dorothy told me, but she didn't sound convinced.

'They look all right,' said Mick.

'Where are she and Archie?' Dorothy tutted, just as the back door banged.

'Sorry we're late,' said Archie, bounding in. 'We overslept.'

Molly was a few paces behind him, looking as calm and serene as always. Nothing ever seemed to ruffle her. I envied her that. Her eyes sought me out and, knowing the last thing I needed was her all-seeing scrutiny, I turned away and bumped straight into Catherine.

'Are you all right, Paige?' she immediately asked. 'You look a little tired.'

Molly took her seat and I realized that in avoiding her attention, I'd walked right into my godmother's. She might not have been in tune in the same way as Molly, but she had eyes in her head and the bags under my own were a dead giveaway.

'I'm fine,' I said. 'I just didn't sleep very well. I'm not ill or anything.'

'Good,' said Archie, taking his seat and snatching up a slice of toast, 'because you'll need all your strength over the next few weeks to do the work of two people!'

'And not just any two people,' said Angus, who bustled in with the paper tucked under his arm and gave Catherine a kiss on the cheek. 'Eat up, Paige. You're going to need your strength.'

Given that I'd already made a bit of a start on what needed to be done, I knew he was right.

'I've given you an extra sausage,' winked Dorothy, handing me a loaded plate and making Archie huff.

During breakfast, Catherine relayed to us the details of an email she had received from Jamie the evening before. It sounded as though he and Anna were having a wonderful time, now they had got over the tiredness of travelling.

'I better go and check on Jareth,' said Mick, once he'd emptied his plate.

Jareth, I had been told, was a rescue barn owl belonging to Gabe who lived in a large enclosure in the woods. Mick was looking after him while Gabe was away. He was also responsible for Bran, although the daft dog still seemed to prefer my company to anyone else's. Not that I was complaining. I was already used to having him follow me about like an extra-large shaggy shadow.

'We'll walk with you as far as the cottage,' said Archie, taking Molly's hand. 'See you all later.'

That left just Dorothy, Angus, Catherine and me in the kitchen. I loaded the dishwasher and washed the glasses while Dorothy read the magazine which came with Angus's Sunday paper. She had decided to take it easy and had put together a slow cooker stew for dinner rather than the usual big roast.

'Barely four weeks until Christmas now,' I heard Angus say wistfully as I finished putting the glasses away.

'Where has the year gone?' Catherine added, with a sigh. 'I don't know about you, my dear, but the older I get, the faster the time seems to fly.'

'Yes,' Angus agreed. 'I feel the same, which is why we need to make the most of every day and I want Christmas to be extra special this year.'

His clandestine conversation with Brodie flitted into my head again.

'With everyone arriving back in time for it, it's bound to be that,' Catherine pointed out. 'And don't forget Christopher, Cass and the boys will be here, too.'

She was right, of course, and as wonderful as it was going to be to see the eldest Connelly brother and his family again, I had the feeling that Angus's idea of extra special involved something more than kith and kin returning to the fold. I was certain his words had something to do with what I'd heard him and Brodie talking about but still had no idea what that could possibly be.

'And you'll be extra busy the two weeks before Christmas,' Dorothy said to me, further justifying her desire to feed me up. 'What with all those big festive shops to deliver and parcels to run to the post office.'

'Yes,' I said, wondering if I could get away with anonymously dropping a hamper at Albert's door, 'I suppose I will.'

'Are you all ready for the switch-on?' she then asked Angus. 'Have you got your Santa suit out of mothballs yet?'

'All out of its box and ready to go,' he cheerfully said.

'The switch-on?' I frowned, thinking back to how the town had looked the day I went in with Archie. 'That's happening late, isn't it? Though now you come to mention it, I did notice there weren't many decorations on display when Archie introduced me to Kathleen . . .' My words trailed off as Dorothy flashed me a look, but then I couldn't resist adding, 'And why would Angus need a Santa suit for it anyway?'

'Because he now plays Father Christmas on the night the lights go on in town,' Catherine enlightened me. 'And you're right, Paige. It's happening very late this year.'

'I'm amazed it's happening at all,' Dorothy tutted.

'Why?' I asked. 'What was stopping it?'

'Money,' Dorothy said bluntly. 'The council have had so many budget cuts recently, that they simply couldn't spare the cash to fund it.'

My unfortunate first-hand experience meant I could sympathize with the impact the loss of funds could have. Even if I hadn't left Jordan early because of my error of judgment, it was unlikely that I would have secured a new contract now the corporate sponsorship had been lost, even with all of my years of experience.

'So, the Dempsters cleverly set up a crowdfunding page

to make sure it went ahead,' Catherine added, naming the family who I knew supplied the fruit and veg I now delivered. 'We had a similar situation a few years ago, with no tree for the square which they also rescued, but this year there was literally going to be nothing at all.'

'But the event is definitely going ahead now?' I asked, imagining how disappointed everyone must have been when the cancellation announcement was made.

The town was so idyllic it was impossible to imagine it without Christmas lights and further bedecked to celebrate the season.

'Yes,' said Dorothy, with a smile. 'And just in the nick of time. The financial target was finally reached last week after a very generous anonymous donation.'

I noticed Angus shift in his seat.

'So, now it's all set for next Saturday, December third,' Catherine finished up.

'So late.' I frowned, then more cheerfully added, 'But at least it's happening.'

'You must be looking forward to the festivities, my dear?' Angus asked me. 'It's been a long time since you were in the country to celebrate them.'

'I am,' I said. 'There's nothing quite like a traditional Christmas, is there?'

'There's certainly nothing like a traditional Wynthorpe Christmas,' he chuckled. 'And we must make sure you aren't kept too busy to enjoy it. You haven't got an extra PWC on the go, have you? That really would be too much.'

'Of course not,' I tutted, feeling my face flush.

Catherine smiled and shook her head.

'What's a PWC when it's at home?' Dorothy asked.

'Paige's Worthy Cause,' laughed Catherine. 'Don't you remember, Dorothy?'

'Oh, yes,' she said, also laughing. 'Of course. You were always fighting for something or someone, weren't you, my love? There was always a cause to take up, even when you were here on your holidays.'

She was right, but given my recent introduction to Albert and subsequent thoughts about him, I didn't much want to be reminded about that.

'That's because she's always had a hatred of injustice and a desire to help those in less fortunate positions in life,' Angus said proudly, as if he was giving an electoral speech, with me as the hopeful candidate. 'It's her finest quality, in my opinion.'

I didn't say anything, but he was right about my desire to help. It was that which had made me so keen to sign up to the volunteering life Chadia had described the day we met at the university recruitment fair. That, and her own passion for it, of course.

'Do you remember the row over the hens?' Angus beamed.

'I remember the placard,' Catherine reminisced. 'And the chant that went with it.'

Dorothy rolled her eyes.

'Well,' I said, relieved it was just the four of us in the kitchen and Archie wasn't around to start teasing, 'I did eventually understand why you couldn't let them roam completely free.'

'And their run was huge.' Angus winked.

'And fox proof,' Catherine reminded me.

My desire to let the hall's hens run free was a timely reminder that I didn't always get it right, even back then, and that felt like further justification for passing my concerns about Albert over to the real expert, Kathleen. I wasn't passing the buck; I was taking the most responsible course of action.

'You know,' said Angus, with hugely inconvenient timing, 'we're not so different, you and I, Paige.'

'Are we not?'

'No,' he carried on. 'We're not. We both want what's best for people and we always go the extra mile to make sure we help them get it, don't we?'

It was my godfather's words which prompted me to telephone Kathleen that afternoon. However, rather than passing on Albert's name and address, I heard myself asking if there was an optician in Wynbridge who made home visits.

'Yes, my love,' she told me. 'There is. Do you know someone who needs a test?'

'No,' I said, as she reeled off the details. 'I just thought it might be something useful to know if I was ever asked.'

'You're as thoughtful as Anna,' Kathleen praised kindly. 'She always has the measure of what's needed too. It's the little things that make the world of difference, isn't it?'

'Yes,' I had to agree. 'I suppose it is.'

A sight test was a little thing in the grand scheme, but getting Albert to agree to having one, or even to admitting that he couldn't see properly, was a huge hurdle. However, it seemed to me that his lack of vision was the most pressing of his current problems and therefore that's what needed addressing. Perhaps if I could achieve that, my intuition and desire to help might stop nagging and I would then be able to hand him over to Kathleen.

I typed what I hoped was a tactful letter, in a large font, which I intended to post through his cottage door, along with my phone number. The letter, after Angus's reminder that I'd always had a desire to assist, felt like the right compromise.

'You again,' was the welcome I received as I snuck up the path and the cottage door was wrenched open.

'I'm not stopping,' I insisted, shocked at being caught in my clandestine act. 'I was just going to leave this.'

'What is it?' Albert frowned, taking the envelope I held out.

'Just a little note,' I shrugged, as if it was nothing at all.

'You'd best come in,' he sniffed. 'I was actually hoping I might see you again.'

That was a surprise and I followed him inside, grateful that I was wearing my coat and gloves this time. The room was still extremely cold, but I could see he'd had a bit of a tidy up and the few changes pushed a lump into my throat. Here was a man who obviously cared but found himself in a situation that had run away from him and from which he currently had no way of finding his way back from.

'You left this last time you were here,' he said, picking up my scarf.

'Oh,' I smiled, taking it, 'thanks.'

Had he not spotted me, I would have willingly sacrificed it, but then it felt a little damp after its time at the cottage, so it wouldn't have been of much benefit to him.

'So, what's in this here letter then?' Albert asked, squinting at the envelope.

I felt a bit awkward.

'Why don't you read it when I've gone?' I suggested. 'I don't want to hold you up. It's just another apology really and a few words about an idea I had . . .'

My words trailed off.

'As I mentioned before,' Albert said, with a sniff, 'I was hoping to see you. I want to apologize to you too.'

'Whatever for?'

'For being a bad-mannered old beggar,' he said, after a beat had passed. 'I don't get many visitors, certainly none I let in and I was rude to you, which was wrong.'

'No, you weren't,' I insisted.

Albert raised his eyebrows.

'Not really.'

'But it was your own fault,' he then said, taking the edge off his apology. 'You mentioned lighting the fire, which made me realize that you'd noticed . . . things. I don't usually live like this, you know.'

'I can tell that,' I was quick to say, then risked offending him again by adding, 'and you're right, I do notice things. Your glasses, for a start. They're not doing you much good, are they?'

Albert sat heavily in the chair, narrowly avoiding Bella who leapt out of the way in a well-practiced manner which proved my point.

'No,' he admitted. 'Not much.'

'I can help you with that,' I said, emboldened by the fact that he hadn't bitten my head off.

'I'm not going to town,' he snapped.

'You wouldn't need to,' I countered. 'That's what I'd written about in my note.'

I told him how I could arrange to have an optician come out to test his eyes at home and was amazed when he agreed for me to book an appointment. I hadn't expected him to give in so easily, but I was pleased he had, even if his acquiescence made me tear up because it was proof that he really was struggling to see.

'But only if I don't have to go and pick the new specs up,' he gruffly added.

'You won't,' I said. 'I can deliver them for you.'

'And would you be here while I had the test?'

'Certainly,' I said. 'But only if you'd like me to be.'

He mulled that over.

'And then I could get this place sorted out, couldn't I?' he said. 'My sister would turn in her grave if she knew how bad I'd let it get. It's been months since I visited her.'

He was quiet again and I realized that his reluctance to leave the house might be about more than a pair of mislaid glasses.

'I hope you don't mind me mentioning it, Albert,' I said, rubbing my hands together, 'but it really is freezing in here. Shall we go and see if your tank has any oil in it?'

'You go and look by all means,' he said. 'There's a gauge on the side, you'll be able to see it better than I can.'

From the little interaction we'd had, I couldn't be sure if his desire to stay indoors was to do with his limited sight or a fear of stepping outside, but I would hopefully work that out once he'd got his new glasses. So much for not getting involved.

'It's three quarters full,' I told him, once I'd been out to look. 'You should be as warm as toast.'

'I wasn't sure,' he said, sounding heartbreakingly vulnerable. 'And there was a storm which knocked the power out a while ago and I couldn't remember how to reset the boiler. Not that I could've seen to do it.'

I couldn't believe there was no one in his life to offer to do that for him.

'Where is the boiler?' I asked.

'In a cupboard in the kitchen and there's a manual for it in a drawer in there somewhere too.'

I ignored the state of the kitchen and read the manual from cover to cover. According to the paperwork which was with it, the boiler had been serviced the winter before last.

'Won't it go?' Albert shouted.

'I'm just about to try it,' I said, but only when I was completely satisfied that I knew how to do it.

When I had finally reset the keypad, the boiler fired up without missing a beat.

'I can hear the pipes gurgling,' Albert called, sounding almost cheerful.

'I'll check the radiators in a minute,' I called back, while quickly heating a tin of stew I'd found in a cupboard.

It looked to me like Albert had been living out of a hotchpotch of packets and tins for quite a while. There was nothing fresh anywhere and most of what was left was out of date or sailing close to it. I wondered how long it had been since he'd had proper contact with anyone.

'What's that smell?' he asked, sniffing the air.

'Sunday dinner,' I said, carrying through the steaming bowl and a spoon and handing it to him without a fuss.

I didn't give him time to object or become ruffled, but walked immediately away to check the pipes.

'I'll see if any of the radiators need bleeding,' I said briskly, although I didn't really know what that entailed.

'Just do the ones down here,' he said. 'I don't want you going upstairs.'

It was frustrating, but I knew I had to pick my battles.

'All right,' I agreed, 'and then I'd better be off. I'll take your phone number this time too, so I can let you know when the optician can come.'

My business-like manner seemed to do the trick. By the time I'd set the thermostats on the downstairs radiators,

Albert had polished off the stew and his face had taken on a more relaxed expression. I quickly washed the dishes, leaving them to drain dry so as not to push my luck by staying too long. I then took a longer look at him as he fussed Bella who had moved to sit on his lap.

'I'll be off then,' I said. 'I'm going to book that eye test for you as soon as I can.'

'I reckon it's warmer in here already,' he said, sounding drowsy as he went to get up.

'You stay where you are,' I said, lightly laying a hand on his shoulder. 'I can see myself out.'

Having made such a positive impact, I don't know why I sobbed all the way back to the hall, but I did.

Chapter 10

I was up with the lark on Monday morning and, having had a super quick catch up with Mum and Dad on the phone and reassured them that I was happily settled at the hall, I then worked my way methodically through the household chores. I probably could have got through them faster but, as I was flying completely solo, I took my time and it was lunchtime before everything was eventually ticked off to my satisfaction.

'How have you got on?' Dorothy asked as we all congregated around the kitchen table after she'd banged the gong.

'Great,' I said, eagerly accepting a bowl of creamy lentil soup because I had worked up quite an appetite. 'I daresay Hayley works much faster, but I'm all done now.'

'I popped over earlier to ask if I could help,' said Molly as she messily broke a bread roll into pieces on her plate, 'but you looked so engrossed in the vacuuming, I didn't like to disturb you.'

'I'm sorry,' I said, wondering if she had been worried about making me jump. 'I didn't realize.'

'That's all right,' she said, nibbling on a tiny part of the deconstructed roll. 'You were clearly focused and looked like you had something on your mind.'

'Have you got something on your mind?' Catherine asked, sounding concerned.

'You aren't worried about anything, are you?' Angus added.

I wondered if either Mum or Dad had mentioned anything before the phone had earlier been passed on to me. I hoped not. I considered saying something about Albert, if only to distract my godparents from what might have been said, but then decided it wasn't worth the risk.

The Paige's Worthy Cause conversation was still very much at the forefront of my mind and my fragile ego wasn't up to teasing, even of the mildest kind and I obviously couldn't allude to the puzzling Angus and Brodie conversation, which I had been thinking about, either, because I wasn't supposed to know anything about that.

'Well, of course I have something on my mind,' I therefore said jovially instead, latching on to humour rather than my real current preoccupations. 'Hayley will have mine and Archie's guts for garters if she comes back and finds we haven't kept the hall in perfect order. That's enough for anyone to worry about, isn't it?'

Catherine and the others were mollified, but Molly wasn't and I could tell she was still trying to work out why I was back in the country and not sleeping as well as she thought I should.

'Please don't,' I whispered.

'I can't help it,' she whispered back. 'I'm sure it would be better all round if you talked about it.'

'It really wouldn't,' I insisted, 'but being here is helping. Being useful, even though it's only in a small way, is making a difference, so can we please just leave it at that?'

There was no lie in that. Immersing myself in the cleaning had filled my head for hours and stopped me scrolling over the details of my mistake and then blowing it up out of all proportion. Even though I hadn't yet regained faith in my decision making, I was thinking about what had stolen it away less and less.

'All right,' she said. 'And actually, you do look a bit better today. Let's leave it for now.'

I knew I could have told her that my role had simply come to an end because of the loss of corporate sponsorship, but Molly wasn't stupid. She knew there was more to it than that. She had spotted the signs the moment she had first laid eyes on me, and therefore rather than start any sort of explanation, I still felt the best course of action was to carry on avoiding the entire topic.

'Yes, let's,' I agreed. 'I'm heading into town in a bit,' I said, addressing everyone. 'Do we need anything picking up?'

Bran was on his feet almost before I was.

'I won't be able to take you with me this time,' I told him, kissing his shaggy head.

'Can't you go in tomorrow as you'll be heading to Wynbridge to sort the deliveries then anyway?' Mick asked. 'You've hardly stopped since you got here.'

'Afraid not,' I said. 'I won't have time to get done tomorrow what I need to do today.'

'Well, you're going to have to take Bran,' Dorothy said firmly. 'He's been under my feet whining for you all morning. I can't stand an afternoon of it as well.'

'I would have had him with me this morning if he wasn't so scared of the vacuum cleaner,' I said, stroking his wiry back. I hadn't seen him for dust once I'd put the plug in the socket.

'But I need to pop into a couple of shops in town,' I went on, 'so I can't take him with me, can I?'

'It's chilly enough to leave him in the truck,' said Angus. 'He'll be happy enough waiting in the Land Rover with a window open, won't he, Mick?'

'I don't see why not,' Mick agreed. 'It's not as if he's going to overheat.'

There was no way out of it, but Bran was going to be cooped up for ages. As well as booking Albert's eye test, I also wanted to pick up some essentials for him too, so the poor dog would have to stay in the Land Rover while I dropped those off. I had told Albert that I would telephone and let him know when the optician and I would be going, but I didn't think it would hurt to quickly pop in on the pretence of checking that the boiler was still running.

'Right, Bran,' I said, pushing him back as he made to jump out once I'd parked in town. 'I won't be long. You need to stay here.'

He gave me his most forlorn look, then huffed and slumped back down.

'I won't be long,' I reassured him, then raced off to seek out some food which would be easy for Albert to prepare and cook.

Once I'd got a decent selection, along with essentials like bread, milk and biscuits, I headed over to the opticians. I had considered putting the shopping in the Land Rover and checking on Bran first, but I didn't want to test his good manners that far. He looked like a hound who might be partial to a custard cream or three.

'Hello, Paige.'

'Brodie,' I gasped, as I clattered through the optician's door, knocking the bags of groceries on the frame in my surprise. 'Hi.'

He rushed forward to help and having got our hands and the bag handles thoroughly tangled, I felt my cheeks turn even pinker than the chilly Wynbridge wind had already made them.

'Sorry,' he said, once we'd set everything down and I'd taken the seat next to his. 'I wasn't much help there, was I?'

'You meant well,' I laughed, noticing he was as red as I was.

'I don't seem to be much help anywhere at the moment,' he sighed gloomily, sounding fed up.

'Oh,' I said, taken aback. 'I'm sure you are.'

He sat upright and ran his hands through his hair.

'Ignore me,' he said, then asked, sounding brighter, 'How's the volunteering going?'

'Good,' I nodded. 'Really good.'

'Jack's still going on about the fact that you haven't got social media,' he said, leaning his head back against the wall and looking at me out of the corner of his eye.

'Is he?' I asked, surprised that his brother had given it, or me, a second thought.

I tried to look ahead rather than at Brodie because him staring at me from under his long dark lashes and giving me his full attention had caused my heart to flutter again. The way my body continued to react to him was especially disconcerting because he wasn't the type of guy I was usually attracted to at all.

Not that I'd been attracted to anyone or had a relationship in a long time, but my dating history was made up of athletic, blond easy-going, light-hearted guys and Brodie seemed to be the polar opposite in every conceivable way.

'He is.' He then smiled, which was no help in reining the fluttery feelings in either. 'He honestly believes we're the last two humans of our age without it.'

I had to laugh at that.

'He's probably right.' I swallowed, quickly looking away again. 'Funny that we should end up in the same place at the same time, isn't it?'

I could tell he was staring at me even more intently then.

'I suppose it is,' he said thoughtfully. 'We must have been meant to meet, Paige.'

I didn't know what to say in response to that but found my eyes drawn back to his face. Neither of us seemed able to look away. I thought I heard someone clear their throat, but it didn't really register, unlike Brodie's widening pupils.

'Brodie?'

As one, we turned to look back at the shopfloor and standing in front of us, holding a pair of dark framed glasses, was a middle-aged man. He looked amused.

'Would you like to come this way?' he asked my companion.

I sat up straighter and gathered Albert's shopping around me. So mesmerized by our conversation, I'd completely forgotten I was sitting in the Wynbridge opticians and I'd also wasted the opportunity to try and find out what Angus and Brodie had been talking about in the Wynthorpe kitchen. Damn him and his impossibly long and seductive lashes and devastating smile.

'I won't keep you a moment,' the optician said to me as Brodie walked away.

'It's fine,' I said. 'No rush.'

'See you later.' Brodie smiled back at me.

'Uh huh.' I nodded, like a lovestruck fool.

I scolded myself for both the missed opportunity and for falling further under his spell. Developing romantic feelings had been no part of my *take a break at Wynthorpe Hall* plan, but then neither had stumbling across an OAP in need. My R&R trip was taking on a life of its own and pulling me along for the ride.

'What do you think?' Brodie then called over to me, leaning back in the chair and around the screen which had momentarily hidden him from view.

He'd got the glasses on and he looked stunning. All he needed was a book, or a paintbrush in his hands, and I'd be completely undone.

'Great,' I said, giving him a goofy thumbs up. 'They really suit you.'

He disappeared again and I dropped my head into my hands.

'I'm done for,' I muttered. 'I'm completely done for.'

I couldn't take my eyes off him while he was paying and he kept looking across at me too. The heavily framed glasses, which he was still wearing, were the perfect foil for his strong features.

'Will you be at the switch-on, on Saturday?' he asked, coming back over once he'd paid.

'Yes.' I swallowed. 'I'll be there. Will you?'

'I'm aiming to be,' he said. 'I should be back before then.'

He didn't say where from.

'Maybe I'll see you Saturday then.' I nodded.

'I'd like it if you did,' he said, treating me to another of his knee-weakening smiles. 'Perhaps we could go for a drink or something?' he tentatively added.

Was he asking me out on a date or making a casual arrangement? He'd said he *should* be back in town, not that he definitely *would* be.

'Perhaps we could.' I smiled back, my mind racing.

A drink sounded great but to be honest, I was more interested in wondering what the *something* might entail.

'Great.' He nodded, then turned and left without another word.

'I'm so sorry to have kept you waiting,' said the optician, who had also taken a moment to watch Brodie walk out, and before I'd worked out whether our arrangement was set in stone or something that would possibly come off if we happened to run into each other, he went on, 'I'm Mr Wilson. How can I help you?'

Gathering my wits, I explained that I wanted to book a home sight test for a friend and Mr Wilson and I crossed over to the desk. I was sure there was a lingering trace of Brodie's aftershave hanging in the air. I dragged my thoughts back to Albert and forced myself to concentrate on what I'd come to town specifically to do.

'The only at home appointment I have before at least mid-December is for tomorrow,' Mr Wilson said. 'And that's only available because I've had a last-minute cancellation.'

'Tomorrow?'

That regained my attention.

'Yes,' he said. 'Is that too short notice? It wouldn't be until late on in the afternoon.'

'That will be fine,' I said, praying that Albert would agree.

I hoped he wasn't the type who needed time to get used to an idea because waiting even just a couple more weeks was really not an option and I knew I had no hope of talking him into coming to town.

Mr Wilson typed Albert's name into the system and said that both Albert, and his sister, had been customers before. Apparently, numerous reminders had been sent out when they were last due for tests, but none had been responded to.

'Well,' I said, 'Albert can't carry on as he is. The glasses he's currently wearing are no longer fit for purpose. In fact,' I added, 'I wouldn't be at all surprised to discover that they aren't even his.'

'Oh, dear,' said Mr Wilson, sounding concerned. 'That's not good. Is his sister in the same boat?'

'No,' I said, 'it's just Albert now. I've only recently met him, but I do know that his sister has died.'

'Oh, that's terribly sad,' Mr Wilson said. 'Is he struggling on his own?'

'Yes,' I said, 'he is a bit.'

I didn't say anything further. It wasn't my place to talk about Albert's current predicament even if Mr Wilson's question was kindly expressed.

'You should mention him to Kathleen who organizes the dances,' he said, perking up. 'She'd have him sorted in a jiffy. She's got everyone on their toes and she'd get him organized in a heartbeat.'

I knew he was right about what Kathleen could do, and even though getting her onboard had been the sole focus of my original plan, I realized I had changed my mind now. I might not have known Albert long, but I'd established that he was a proud man and one who certainly wouldn't want a fuss. Kathleen bustling in and fixing everything at breakneck speed would be too much for him to cope with.

'Do you know Kathleen?' Mr Wilson asked. 'I can give you her number, if you like.'

'I do know her,' I quickly said. 'I'm working with her, in

fact. I've taken on the volunteering that Anna, who lives at Wynthorpe Hall, usually does, for the next few weeks.'

'Problem solved then.' He beamed.

'Hopefully,' I said, 'but I'm going to keep Albert off Kathleen's radar for the time being. I think he would be . . .' I faltered to find the right word.

'Overwhelmed,' Mr Wilson supplied, with a cheeky smile.

'Yes,' I agreed, thinking of her exuberance. 'She's a wonderful woman, but I think Albert needs to work his way up to a visit from Kathleen.'

'I quite understand,' said Mr Wilson, handing over an appointment card. 'I'll see Mr Price tomorrow and I won't breathe a word about him to Kathleen.'

Once I'd stowed the bags in the Land Rover footwell, I let Bran out for a stetch and a drink and we took a quick walk around the market square, before driving out of town to Albert's. I was amused to note that the drove roads, which had been an unfathomable maze just a few days before, were already becoming more familiar. Whereas previously I hadn't been able to spot any differentiating features, I could now pick out wind tortured trees, different dykes and ditches and I even recognized a few of the farm names.

'I thought you were going to call,' said Albert, when he eventually opened the door after peeping around the curtain to see who it was.

I was delighted to see he wasn't wearing his overcoat.

'I was,' I said, shifting the bags from one hand to another, 'but then I thought I might as well see how the boiler was faring. I can feel from the warm air wafting out that it's still running and I picked up a few bits to tide you over too.'

Albert looked at the bags and scowled.

'I don't want charity,' he bristled. 'I don't need charity.'

'It's not charity,' I said firmly. 'The receipts are in the bags and besides, I'm sure Bella wouldn't object to trying out the box of pouches I've picked up for her, would she?'

I knew Albert had a soft spot where the little cat was concerned.

'Well,' he sniffed, 'you can leave the cat food, but I don't want the rest.'

'Albert,' I said, putting the bags down because they were heavy, 'I haven't got time to sort through it all. Take the lot for now and I'll have back what you don't want tomorrow.'

'Tomorrow?' he snapped. 'Why will you be back again tomorrow?'

'Because,' I told him, 'in the afternoon the optician is going to come and give your eyes a once over.'

'So soon?' he tutted. 'You don't hang about once you've got your feet under the table, do you?'

His tone and manner suggested my feet were far from there.

'It's the only appointment they had,' I said, making to leave before he could turn it down. 'I'll see you at half three.'

'Aren't you going to come in and put this lot away then?' he called after me. 'There's far too much for me to manage.'

I turned to face him.

'I can bring it in,' I said, 'but I can't stop. I've got a dog with me and he shouldn't be shut up for much longer.'

'You can bring him in with the bags, can't you?' Albert said gruffly, disappearing back inside again.

Bran didn't need asking twice. He was off the back seat and up the path before I'd had a chance to close the gate.

'I don't know what Bella will make of him,' I said, as I lugged the bags inside and closed the door with my foot.

'Not much.' Albert pointed, squinting to watch as the tiny cat purred rapturously and wove her way around Bran's skyscraper legs. 'He's a size, isn't he? Even I can see that!'

'Well, I never.' I laughed at the tableau and Albert very nearly chuckled too.

'Life's full of surprises, isn't it, my woman?'

'You can say that again,' I agreed, thinking how quickly mine was being transformed. 'Albert,' I then said, 'it isn't as warm in here as I thought it was.'

'There's nothing wrong with the boiler,' he said quickly. 'I've just been opening the windows to give the place an airing and let the damp out as it warms up.'

'What, even upstairs?'

'I can't get upstairs,' he let slip.

'Oh, Albert,' I sighed.

'I haven't wanted to risk going up,' he said mulishly. 'Not with my sight as it is, but I slept better for being warm.'

'Well, that's good,' I said. 'But where?'

'In the chair,' he said. 'It's a recliner. I'm comfortable enough on there but I'll be back in my own bed if these new specs do the trick and I can get up the stairs again.'

He sounded almost excited at the prospect and as I bent

to carry the bags through to the kitchen, I felt Molly's rose quartz dig into my hip. I still wasn't loving myself, but I did like the feeling I got as a result of helping Albert start to re-embrace life.

'Come and tell me where to put this lot then,' I said, 'and then I'll have to be off.'

I left Bella tucking into chicken in gravy and Albert with a strong brew and an assortment of biscuits on a plate. When Bran and I snuck a look back through the window, Albert looked every bit as blissed out as the cat.

Chapter 11

There was a dramatic drop in the temperature that night and I woke to find Wynthorpe Hall shrouded in heavy fog and a sharp frost and it wasn't only the meteorological atmosphere which had been transformed in the space of a few hours.

In the kitchen, Angus was humming carols, Dorothy had retuned the radio to a channel which favoured festive pop and when I eventually got to town after defrosting Anna's Fiat and driving in cautiously, I found the square a pulsing hive of activity.

Lights were being strung up, trees lifted into place and a sort of stage was being built at one end. Clearly, the countdown to the belated Christmas switch-on was on and the sense of excitement stretched from country to town and back again, inextricably joined by an invisible stand of sparkly tinsel which stretched right across the frosty Fenland landscape.

'Everything looks like it's shaping up nicely,' I said to Kathleen as we ran through the delivery list and loaded a library box packed full of all sorts of books, along with everything else, into the diminutive car.

It was like a game of shopping Jenga and we arranged it all in drop-off order. One misplaced item would send the whole lot crashing down, so the system had to be in sync with the list. There was no point in packing in first what was being delivered first as that would mean me having to empty everything to get it out again.

'Yes,' she agreed, looking around. 'Better late than never and of course it wouldn't be happening at all if it wasn't for that generous last-minute donation. I'd love to know who contributed that.'

Remembering how Angus had gone quiet when it had been mentioned, I thought I had a pretty good idea but didn't say as much. If it was him, then perhaps that would be the extent of his festive mischief for this year and his, according to Archie, reserved mood, was more about him not wanting to croon about his kind gesture than having something else tucked up his sleeve. That was what I hoped, anyway.

'Perhaps all will be revealed on the night?' I suggested to Kathleen with a shrug which hopefully implied that I had no idea about the town's potential benefactor.

'Maybe,' she responded pensively, 'but either way it's going to be a great event.'

'I'm sure it will be.' I nodded, my attention focused back on scrutinizing the packed car, before I fell into the trap of fantasizing about whether I was going to the pub with Brodie during it or not. 'Right, I think that's everything.'

'It had better be,' she laughed, standing with her hands on her hips and also admiring how we'd managed to utilize every available space, 'because you won't get anything else in there now. Thank goodness you haven't got Bran with you today.'

'Oh, don't,' I said, shaking my head. 'I had to sneak out this morning while Dorothy distracted him. Looking at how much there is here today, I think I might need to just use the Land Rover from now on and leave Anna's Fiat at the hall. That said,' I added, puffing out my cheeks, 'I still don't think I'd get Bran in there with the same amount as this to drop off.'

'You're right,' Kathleen laughed, as she pulled a notebook out of her coat pocket. 'Now,' she said, completely changing the subject, 'can I put you down for a ticket to the dance on Friday night?'

'Me?' I laughed.

'Yes,' she said seriously, giving me the once over but unfortunately not noticing my two left feet. 'We could do with some fresh faces and I'm trying to get more of you youngsters involved.'

'But I can't dance,' I told her, feeling myself go hot in spite of the weather. 'I'm useless.'

'Everyone can dance with the right partner,' she said briskly.

'You might think that . . .' I began, but she cut me off.

'Town hall, seven o'clock. Leave the lessons and the dance partner to me,' she twinkled.

have made me promises before and
ve'll see. Whatever happens, I'm still
rage to leave.' She stopped abruptly
he rim of her mug. 'Sorry,' she said,
e no idea why I'm telling you any of
ne to oversharing.'
l,' I told her, imagining at least some
ng away from something, no matter
er easy and with three little ones to
ave been nigh on impossible. You're
med by a sudden smile.
nething behind too,' I was surprised
er. 'Nothing like what I'm guessing
ut it's going to result in a total life
v I'm going to cope in the long-term,
t nothing like your responsibilities.'
ding wise beyond her years. 'It's all
t because your baggage is nothing
embles nothing like yours, it doesn't
of thing I had heard myself say many
king on projects across the world,
empowerment ones.
eterminedly said. 'We both will.'
anged mobile phone numbers and I
r too.
ll the council and make sure they're

'Lessons?' I choked. 'Dance partner?'

'And don't forget to ask Mr Smythe if he needs a lift to the ulcer clinic, next week,' she said, backing away. 'And make sure Gladys has got that appointment date on her calendar. After all the trouble you went to, to book it, we don't want her forgetting, do we?'

I knew Gladys did have the appointment on her kitchen calendar, because I'd written it on there myself, but I added Kathleen's reminders to the bottom of the delivery list anyway. I was still being meticulous about even the tiniest of details and double checking everything.

By the time I looked up again, Kathleen was back in the library, so I made another note to telephone and tell her I wouldn't be attending the dance. She might be easier to say no to on the phone.

'How are the roads?' asked Mr Smythe, welcoming me into his home and eagerly looking through the stack of festive romance novels he'd requested from the library.

'Still a bit icy,' I told him. 'Certainly not what I'm used to driving on, anyway.'

'You should have come in that Land Rover,' he said wisely. 'That thing can handle anything.'

'You're probably right,' I agreed. 'Now, about the ulcer clinic. Are you going to need a lift?'

'Not this time,' he said. 'My daughter's got the afternoon off work, so she's taking me. I'm hoping this will be practically the last time I have to go. It's almost better. Do you want to see?'

I respectfully declined his offer, made a note of the arrangement he had made with his daughter and headed off again. Replacing a light bulb was required of me at my next port of call.

'How's that, Mabel?' I asked as she flicked on the switch and we squinted in the bright light bathing her sitting room.

'Oh, that's better,' said the tiny woman who wouldn't have been able to reach to do it even if she had been able to climb up on to the chair I was balanced on. 'I kept losing count of my stitches last night,' she informed me. 'That table lamp is nowhere near bright enough for close work. Fancy a cuppa, my dear?'

I still had another call to make and was mindful of making it to Albert's in time for his eye test, but accepted anyway.

'Yes, please,' I said keenly. 'That would be great.'

'Are you going to the dance on Friday?' she asked as she offered me the sugar bowl.

'According to Kathleen, I am,' I said, biting my lip.

Mabel chuckled.

'I'm getting a lift in, so I'll see you there then.' She nodded, then surprised me by adding, 'I love a good tango.'

Even though I was sailing close to the wind timewise, I also took my time over my final stop, when I eventually found it. An emergency food parcel and sanitary products and a bundle of picture books for a young mum with three pre-schoolers took me to an out of the way cottage and into the orbit of the woman who hadn't seen another adult for days.

'I'm sorry I'm a bit later than expected,' I apologized,

giving your situation their full attention,' I promised after Alice had said that sometimes she got jittery at night, especially if she heard a car going slowly by.

'Thank you,' she said. 'I'd certainly sleep better with a few other people living nearby and it would be great to be able to walk to the library and get these three to a playgroup.'

'Fingers crossed for a move soon then,' I told her. 'And you can call me at any time,' I insisted. 'If the call doesn't connect because I haven't got enough signal, then ring the hall. No one will mind.'

She promised she would and waved me off. I pulled off the road a little further along and gratefully snacked on the sandwiches Dorothy had packed and Mr Wilson and I arrived at Albert's cottage at exactly the same time. If he was at all surprised by the state of the cottage, he kept his reaction well-hidden and greeted Albert in a professional manner. I was delighted to find he was set up to perform the test in no time.

Albert looked nervous as he handed over the glasses he was currently wearing and I went off to the kitchen, ostensibly to make tea, but really to give him some privacy while they got the test underway.

'But these are a decade out of date, Mr Price,' I heard Mr Wilson say in surprise.

'I'm sure they're not as old as all that,' came Albert's defensive response.

'I'm afraid they are,' said Mr Wilson. 'According to my records, we fitted you with these frames in twenty twelve and it's now . . .'

'I can do the maths,' sniffed Albert.

'You have had new ones since then,' Mr Wilson pointed out. 'Two new prescriptions, in fact.'

'I know,' Albert shot bluntly back. 'But I can't find them, can I?' And that was the end of that.

'Tea,' I said, carrying in the tray and pouring everyone a cup.

The test progressed swiftly, but Albert didn't look happy after his out-of-date frames had been flagged up. He'd whizzed through the glaucoma test, had no double vision or refractive errors and was soon reading from a chart to help Mr Wilson fine-tune his results.

'There's some slight deterioration,' he said, sitting back, once Albert had recited what he could, 'but nothing worse than I'd expect to see in a man of your years, Mr Price.'

He sounded very happy with the result, but Albert was still fed up.

'That's wonderful news,' I said, in an attempt to fill the silence.

'Try these,' said Mr Wilson, handing over a pair of frames which didn't look all that dissimilar to the ones Albert had been wearing before.

Albert put them on. I noticed his hands were shaking a little as he looked about him.

'These are the updated frames which have replaced your last ones,' Mr Wilson explained, 'and the lenses in those match your previous prescription. Your new ones will be a little stronger, but not by all that much.'

Albert didn't say anything.

'How are they?' Mr Wilson asked. 'Can you see better with those?'

'Oh, yes,' said Albert, his voice shaking as much as his hands. 'I can see all right.'

'That's wonderful, Albert,' I said, trying to coax some excitement out of him.

I had thought he would have been on cloud nine when he put them on and saw what a difference they made, but for some reason he wasn't happy at all. Mr Wilson looked at me and I shrugged. Clearly, we were both as confused as each other.

'You can keep those while I make up your new ones, if you like,' he offered, but Albert whipped them off and handed them back.

'No, no,' he said, 'I'll manage and if that's everything, if you don't mind, I really need to get on.'

Mr Wilson took the hint, but then he didn't have much choice.

'Of course,' he said. 'I'll get packed up and if you're happy with these frames I can have the glasses ready to send out on Thursday. I don't want to leave you without them for longer than I have to.'

I was sure that was exceptionally speedy service.

'Thank you,' said Albert. 'I appreciate that and those frames will do.'

'No need to send them,' I said. 'I'll be out delivering again on Thursday so I can collect them and drop them off. That will be better than waiting on the post, won't it, Albert?'

'If you say so,' he said gruffly.

I helped Mr Wilson carry out his equipment and thanked him profusely for coming out to perform the test.

'I'm sure he's happier than he's letting on,' I said, with a nod back to the cottage.

'I certainly hope so,' Mr Wilson chuckled. 'I'll see you Thursday.'

'Well, now,' I said, when I went back inside. 'How brilliant was that? I had no idea it would all be so easy.'

Albert was sitting in his armchair, staring into space. He looked older somehow but that could have been because he wasn't wearing any glasses at all.

'Oh, it was easy all right,' he said grumpily.

'We were lucky Mr Wilson had that cancellation and could fit you in.'

'He's left those behind,' he said, ignoring my acknowledgement of his good fortune and pointing at the frames on the coffee table which were fitted with the lenses that matched his last prescription.

'Oh,' I said, gathering the tea things together and wondering if Mr Wilson had forgotten them on purpose in much the same way as I'd previously left my scarf. 'You might as well wear them then.'

Albert gave me a withering look as I handed them to him.

'Did you ask him to leave them?' he gruffly demanded.

'Of course not,' I frowned, 'you know I didn't.'

Albert looked disbelieving.

'You were in here with us the whole time,' I pointed out,

feeling a bit put out by both the suggestion and his tone. 'Did you hear me ask him to leave them?'

'No, but then you could have said something when you went out just now, couldn't you?'

'But he would have already left them by then, wouldn't he?'

Albert shrugged.

'I don't know why you're being like this,' I said, picking up the tray.

'You can leave that,' he barked and I put it back down. 'In fact, you can leave, too.'

'What?'

'I can manage now. And you won't need to come back.'

'But your glasses . . .' I stammered, my frustration giving way to upset.

'You've just said yourself that I can wear these,' he said, roughly shoving on the pair Mr Wilson had either genuinely forgotten or discreetly left, 'and I can see well enough with them to ring and ask him to send the new ones.'

'Oh,' I said, feeling my cheeks start to flame. 'Okay. In that case . . .'

'I'm not ungrateful for what you've done.'

He could have fooled me.

'But you can go off and busybody on someone else's behalf now. I'll be able to manage on my own again from now on.'

His words hit their mark and tears sprang to my eyes.

'Bye then,' I said, as I walked to the door and opened it.

There was no answer and when I looked back, Albert had carried the tea tray to the kitchen and closed the door behind him. The bubble of excitement I had felt when I got up that morning had disappeared with a pop and for the second time since I'd arrived at Wynthorpe Hall, I left Albert's cottage with tears streaming down my face. Only this time, for a very different reason.

Chapter 12

I felt absolutely wretched after Albert's gruff dismissal and my emotions swung like a badly balanced pendulum. One minute I was feeling frustrated with him and the next I was feeling furious with myself. My inability to stick to the original tasks I'd been assigned since arriving at the hall had caused tumult, both for me and the person I had misguidedly tried to help.

I had foolishly thought I was making progress, but that wasn't the case at all. Within weeks of making the mistake overseas, I had now made another closer to home. I'd told Archie and Kathleen that I wanted zero responsibility and they'd reassured me that I wouldn't have any. I was the one who hadn't been able to resist taking more on and it had come back to bite me, but that was it. From now on, I would be sticking to what was written on the lists and not doing a single thing more.

After a day spent cleaning the hall, I was due back in town early on Thursday but first there was Angus's excitement about the date to contend with.

'Come along! Come along!' he excitedly called on the morning of December the first. 'Come and see what Santa has left us!'

In spite of my upset, I couldn't help but be swept along by his exhilaration and I couldn't suppress the gasp which escaped my mouth when I entered the kitchen either.

'What on earth is that?' I gaped.

'The Wynthorpe Hall advent calendar,' Angus proudly said. 'Every November thirtieth, Santa has his elves hang it back up, ready for us to enjoy the run-up to the big day.'

'Assuming we're all on the nice list,' Archie, who had come over from the woods with Molly, jokingly added. 'If we were in trouble, it wouldn't be here at all, would it, Dad?'

'Quite right, my boy,' Angus merrily boomed.

Well, that was something, I supposed. At least my recent mistakes hadn't been heinous enough to get me booted off Santa's nice list.

'Come along, Paige,' Angus encouraged. 'You're up first this year.'

'Really?' I laughed.

'Of course,' said Angus. 'Come and see what's in drawer number one.'

The calendar was a vast wooden creation, beautifully decorated and filled with different sized drawers and cubby holes. Santa must have had a team of body building elves to do his bidding because it looked like it weighed a tonne. I'd never seen anything like it.

'Go on,' Archie said. 'Hurry up. Some of us have got beds to get back to.'

'Not today,' said Angus. 'I've got a job for you to help me with, Archie.'

I gently pulled open the drawer with number one on it before Archie objected to his father's announcement and found a soft, neatly wrapped parcel inside.

'Oh, Angus,' I smiled as I tore into the paper. 'It's lovely. Thank you!'

'I think you mean, thank you, Santa,' he grinned.

I quickly pulled the reindeer patterned bobble hat on to my head and everyone applauded.

'Santa obviously remembers your fondness for *Home Alone*,' Molly laughed.

'He certainly does,' I enthusiastically agreed.

The hat was almost identical to the one worn by Kevin McCallister and I loved it.

'And he'd probably noticed you had a lovely scarf and gloves, but your hat has seen better days,' Angus added and I rushed to give him a hug.

'I'll be extra toasty on my delivery round now,' I told him. 'Thank you, Santa.'

The excitement of opening the calendar had lifted my spirits, but I still wasn't planning on being out in the Fens for any longer than necessary even if I was going to be warmer. The second my last delivery was made I'd be heading back to the hall, hunkering down and keeping out of further trouble.

'Why don't you come over to the cottage tonight, Paige?'

suggested Molly. I knew she had been watching me closely as I admired my new hat. 'Archie's going out, so it'll be just us girls.'

'And Bran,' added Dorothy. 'You won't be able to leave him today *and* this evening.'

I wasn't sure I wanted to spend an evening alone with Molly. A lot had happened in the last twenty-four hours and she was bound to winkle at least a little of it out of me.

'I'll see you around seven,' she said, before I could come up with an excuse.

'And I'll send you over with some supper,' joined in Dorothy, the pair of them neatly putting the finishing touches on my evening.

When I arrived in town, Kathleen was full of festive bonhomie and the market square, almost ready for the switch-on, was looking even lovelier than before. Lots of the shops now had planted containers flanking their doorways and the lush red and green colour combination looked both seasonal and stylish.

'Good news!' Kathleen announced from her station behind the desk in the library as I walked in.

One of the other members of staff gave her a long-suffering look.

'Good news,' she said again, though more quietly. 'Come with me into the staffroom. We won't disturb anyone in there.'

Had she lowered her voice a little we wouldn't have disturbed anyone anywhere.

'It's about Alice,' she said, closing the door behind her. 'Great hat by the way.'

'Thanks,' I said. 'So, what's going on?'

'Well,' she said, smiling, 'the council have been in touch with her this morning, after my visit to their offices yesterday.' I loved that she'd turned up in person. I'll bet whoever's office she ended up in, didn't know what had hit them. 'And they're going to move her to town before Christmas.'

The sudden elation I felt almost lifted my sleigh of emotions into the air again.

'That's wonderful news,' I said, thinking how excited and relieved Alice would no doubt be feeling. 'It will be far better for her and the children.'

'I know.' Kathleen nodded. 'They're putting her in a flat, but it's a ground floor one with a bit of private outdoor space. The garden is the size of a postage stamp but the children will still be able to get outside for some fresh air and it's only a short walk into town so Alice will easily be able to come here with them, as well as do her shopping and socialize.'

'I'm so pleased.' I smiled, knowing that was exactly what Alice had been hoping for.

When she'd spoken to me about her desire to move, she'd prioritized things for her children, such as going to the playgroup and coming to the library, but I knew it was essential that she should have some benefit from the relocation too.

'The housing officer has arranged for her to look at the flat tomorrow,' Kathleen said. 'I don't suppose there's any chance you could give her a lift . . .'

'Sorry,' I quickly said. 'I can't. I work at the hall on Fridays.'

As excited as I was for Alice and her children, and as much as I liked her, I was determined not to get further involved. I'd made a hash of things with Albert and didn't want a repeat performance with the young mum. There was too much at stake for me to risk somehow ballsing it up.

'And I haven't got access to car seats for the kids,' I further pointed out.

'Not to worry,' said Kathleen. 'I'll sort something. I should be able to get them here and back before I start setting up for the dance. You are still coming, aren't you?'

I was saved from answering, by a knock on the door.

'Chris Dempster is here with the fruit and veg boxes,' said a disembodied voice from the other side. 'Are you ready to start loading them?'

Switching to the Land Rover was definitely a smart move as along with the fruit and veg, there was some dry cleaning to drop off and more general groceries too. I was relieved the delivery route didn't take me anywhere near where Albert lived that day, so there was no temptation to linger outside his cottage trying to decipher how he was getting on.

'I have supper, from Dorothy,' I told Molly when she opened the cottage door to me and Bran that evening, 'and wine, from Angus.'

'You look like Little Red Riding Hood,' Molly laughed, taking the packed wicker basket from me.

'Only the wolf is much friendlier,' I said, giving Bran's back a rub.

He soaked up the fuss and then joined Suki the Chihuahua, already curled up in front of the well-stoked fire. Floss had opted to stay with Dorothy in the hall kitchen.

'Do you want this now?' Molly asked, peering into the basket. 'Or shall I just open the wine?'

The tub of plump green olives from the Wynbridge deli was too moreish to resist and the grissini from the same place paired with Dorothy's delicious homemade houmous didn't last long either.

'So,' said Molly as she picked up her glass, the contents of which looked a little different to mine, and sat back with her feet curled under her, 'how are you enjoying being back at the hall? We've hardly spent any time together since you arrived.'

'It's wonderful,' I told her with a smile as I tucked myself into the corner of the sofa and took a sip of wine. 'Exactly what I needed,' I carried on. 'Especially as I'm in the Rose Room.'

'You do look better than when you arrived,' she said frankly, 'but still not quite your former self.'

'But don't forget you hadn't seen me for a long time,' I reasonably pointed out. 'Time takes its toll on all of us.'

'That's not what I meant,' she batted back. 'And you know it.'

'I do,' I had to agree, 'but given where I've been working and the things I've seen as a result, I was bound to have changed a bit, wasn't I?'

'Yes,' she said with a frown. 'I suppose so. I daresay your work is far more stressful and gruelling than anything I can imagine.'

I didn't refute her, or correct her tense but thought back to the person I had been when, buoyed up by Chadia's exuberant enthusiasm, I had signed up for my first assignment. I'd had this wholly idealistic vision then of what I, undertaking the work, would look like.

What could be more noble, I had thought, than working to help people enhance and rebuild their lives? Even though I had still felt passionate about the roles we eventually took on in the refugee camps, the harsh reality had turned out to be nothing like my romanticized imaginings.

'You should be grateful you can't imagine it,' I said to Molly, as I swallowed more of the wine. 'It was constant pressure and often quite dangerous,' I carried on, the sudden willingness to talk taking me by surprise. 'And there were always at least a hundred more things I felt I could be doing.'

'It can't have been easy,' Molly said softly. 'Especially after what happened to Chadia. It must have been impossible to stay on top of your game under those challenging and grief-ridden circumstances all of the time.'

My former wealth of words suddenly dried up.

'Yes,' I simply said, thinking how in the end I hadn't kept on top of it. 'It was.'

'Will you be ready to go back after Christmas?' Molly then asked.

I let out a long breath.

'It's not relevant whether I'll be ready or not,' I told her, the wine finding its mark and again relaxing my tongue, 'because my position no longer exists. The corporate sponsorship the charity relied on has been withdrawn and roles have had to be dramatically reduced as a result.'

'Oh,' said Molly, looking shocked. 'I see.'

'Mine was one of them,' I added, to make sure she did.

'But you have so much experience . . .' she began to say, then stopped.

'I'd rather no one else found out,' I quickly said. 'I'm not up to explaining it all just yet, especially as I haven't decided what I'm going to do next.'

'Of course,' she said, leaning forward to fill my glass again. 'I won't say anything.'

'Thank you.'

'Other than . . .'

'Oh, Molly.'

'Hear me out,' she insisted. 'I was just going to say that even though what you're doing here isn't on the same scale as what you were doing in Jordan . . .'

'You can say that again.'

'It's still vital work. The food you deliver fills empty bellies and the hospital appointments you help to make potentially save lives. It might not be the same as working in a war-torn country, but it's valid and vital nonetheless.'

Her words reminded me of what Alice had said about our own personal baggage being relevant to each of us. I felt bad that I still hadn't shared with Molly the entire contents of mine, but I just couldn't bring myself to do it.

'I know.' I swallowed.

'You're a good person, Paige,' she said, making me tear up. 'And right now, for some reason, you're being very hard on yourself.'

I had no idea what justified her saying that because, having immediately realized that she would know there was more to my arrival than I was willing to let on, I had gone out of my way to adapt my behaviour and words whenever I was around her. Perhaps my aura was still a muddy colour or something.

'I notice more than you might think,' she then wryly said, confirming that my ruse hadn't worked. 'Now,' she added, thankfully letting the topic drop, 'how about you sample a glass of last year's sloe gin? That's bound to soften you up a bit.'

'Oh, go on then.' I smiled, abandoning the wine. 'I'll give it a go.'

Two generous glasses later and I was beginning to feel more than a little softened up when Bran started barking. Molly and I jumped almost out of our skins and then started giggling as Archie fell through the door with Jack lingering behind.

'Well, well, well,' slurred Archie, falling about as he pulled off his boots, 'what have we here?'

'Hello, Archie,' I said, budging up as he landed heavily on the sofa next to me.

'Have I interrupted a coven meeting?' he loudly whispered.

'I think what you mean is, have *we* interrupted a coven meeting,' said Molly, sounding far more awake than I felt. 'And the answer is, no.'

'We?' frowned Archie.

'Come in and sit down, Jack.' Molly smiled.

'Oh, yes,' said Archie, twisting around. 'Sorry, Jack, where are my manners?'

'Back at the distillery, I would imagine,' Molly tutted.

'Paige, Jack. Jack, Paige,' yawned Archie, pointing at one of us and then the other.

Jack gave me a wide smile and sat in the chair opposite Molly's.

'It's all right,' I said, to Archie. 'You don't need to play the host. Jack and I have already met.'

'Have you?' Archie asked, sounding surprised.

'I jump started her engine,' said Jack. 'The Land Rover engine, I mean,' he quickly corrected.

I couldn't suppress a giggle which seemed to embarrass him further.

'Sorry,' I said. 'It's Molly's sloe gin. It seems to bring out the worst in me.'

'Or the best.' Molly grinned.

'Oh, yum,' said Archie, spotting the ruby coloured gin. 'Is that what we're drinking?'

'No, we're not,' said Molly, her smile vanishing as she firmly put the stopper back in the bottle. 'It's coffee for you, I think. I take it you had a good time at the Brambles tasting evening?'

'I did.' He nodded. 'I tasted everything.'

'Twice,' Jack grinned.

'It was kind of you to bring him home,' Molly said.

'It's the least I could do, given that he'd gone overboard on my watch,' Jack replied.

'Come on, Archie,' she said loudly, because he was starting to nod off. 'You can help me in the kitchen.'

She pulled him to his feet and he staggered behind her out of the room. Suki got up, stretched and trotted after them, but Bran didn't budge. He was pretending to be asleep again, but I knew he was shamming because of the way his bushy brows were twitching.

'So, was it a public event at the distillery tonight?' I asked Jack.

'No,' he said, with a smile. 'It was just me and the lads. That is, Archie, Eli and Beamish. Have you met them?'

'Not Eli and Beamish,' I said.

'Beamish is a mate from town and Eli lives further out but also helps his partner, Fliss, run a supper club in a barn on her family farm,' he explained.

'That sounds swish.'

'It's great,' he said. 'They host events showcasing seasonal and local produce. It's not been going all that long, but it's hugely popular. The tickets sell out in minutes.'

'Do you supply the drinks to accompany the food?'

'Sometimes.' He nodded. 'And I'm currently developing a new range which I wanted Fliss and Eli to try. Fliss couldn't make it though, and neither could Beamish's partner, Hattie, so it ended up being just me and the lads.'

I wondered if Eli and Beamish had sampled as much of Jack's new range as Archie.

'And what about Brodie?' I asked, realizing that he hadn't been included in the party.

'He's gone to London to meet up with some of his city mates,' Jack carried on. 'He told me he should be back in time for the weekend, though.'

'Oh, yes,' I said, thinking back over our previous conversation along with the casual arrangement we'd made to have a drink in the pub. 'He did tell me he was going away.'

I was surprised about where he'd gone though. Brodie didn't strike me as the type to have city friends, but then I supposed that was because I always associated London with suits. I daresay Brodie's mates were part of an artier set. Perhaps I could ask him during our date slash non-date. Assuming it happened.

'I hope you don't mind me mentioning it,' Jack then surprised me by saying, 'but I get the feeling you rather like my brother. Am I right?'

'What?' I blushed. 'Why on earth would you think that?'

'Coffee!' Archie then loudly announced, preceding Molly who was carrying the tray and before Jack could answer.

I drank mine in silence, feeling rather awkward. Jack was right in that I did like his brother but he clearly had something further to say on the matter and I was intrigued to know, even though it was most likely none of his business, what it was.

'So, Paige, what do you think?' I heard someone say and I realized I'd completely tuned out of the conversation.

'Sorry,' I said, clearing my throat. 'I missed that.'

Archie rolled his eyes and leant over from where he was sitting at Molly's feet and slapped my knee.

'Ow,' I protested.

'Wake up, Paige,' he tutted. 'Jack just asked you if you wanted to visit the distillery tomorrow.'

'Oh,' I said, looking from him back to Jack.

'I can show you around, if you like,' Jack offered.

'That would work out great for me,' Archie keenly said. 'Because I could go with you and pick up my car.'

'All right,' I agreed, thinking it would be the ideal opportunity to find out what was on Jack's mind. 'Thanks. I'll come over as soon as I've finished getting the hall ready for the weekend.'

Chapter 13

Jack having sussed I had feelings for his brother, along with difficult to dismiss thoughts of Albert's upset and Molly's sloe gin made for both a heavy cocktail and a sleepless night and consequently I was rather behind my time when Archie came to find me the next day.

'Are you ready?' he asked, right when I was least expecting it.

I let out a screech and leapt into the air, banging my head on the doorframe of the cupboard where I was packing away some of the cleaning supplies.

'Oh, Paige,' he apologized. 'I'm so sorry. I thought you'd heard me come in.'

Ordinarily he would have laughed so I knew he knew that I'd hurt myself.

'Well, I hadn't,' I said, rubbing the tender bump on the top of my head. 'I'm almost done. You can give me a hand with the last of it, if you like.'

With Archie taking on the final bout of vacuuming and

miraculously, with no trace of a hangover, we were soon on our way to the distillery in Anna's Fiat. On the journey I asked a question which I quickly regretted.

'Do you know much about Jack's brother?' I enquired in a light-hearted tone, as I pulled over to let a tractor pass on one of the narrow roads.

'Brodie?' Archie frowned.

'Assuming he's the only brother,' I said, feeling immediately rattled, 'then yes, Brodie.'

Archie grinned and gave me a look.

'What?' I snapped as he caught my eye.

'Oh, Paige,' he teased. 'Has someone got a little crush?'

Had it not been for the bump on the head, I would have realized I was opening the floodgates by asking and kept my mouth shut. Now, not only was Jack privy to my feelings, Archie was going to be convinced of them too.

'Don't be absurd,' I ineffectively bit back. 'I was just wondering . . .'

There was so much I was wondering, and a lot of it was related to working out the connection between Brodie and Angus, but as I had found out about the possibility of that as a result of eavesdropping, I could hardly gossip about it, could I?

'He's a looker, all right,' Archie carried on, still grinning. 'A total head turner, I'll give you that. He's only been here five minutes though, so I can't tell you much. Although,' he added, 'I would have thought he's a bit mean and moody for you. Don't you usually go for fun-loving blonds?'

'Oh, shut up,' I snapped and he laughed. 'Just forget it,' I said, opening the window in the hope that the crisp air would stop me overheating. 'You're still an arse, Archie Connelly. Do you know that?'

Archie nodded and turned up the radio.

'I've never once said I wasn't.'

What was it about our relationship, I wondered, that had us reverting to our teenage selves within seconds of striking up a conversation? Perhaps I should learn the lesson and stop supplying him with such irresistible ammunition.

'Oh.' He beamed, turning the music up even louder. 'I love this one.'

By the time we arrived at Brambles, courtesy of Archie's directions, I'd regained my good humour and we'd sung a tuneless but rousing duet of Mr Bublé's 'It's Beginning To Look A Lot Like Christmas'. With the Brambles' converted barn entrance decked out with warm white twinkling lights and two potted trees standing sentinel outside the main door, my festive spirit received another welcome boost. In fact, in spite of my concerns about Jack's observations, I was still humming as we climbed out of the car.

'Welcome to Brambles,' the man himself expansively said as he strode across the yard. 'Did you hear we're forecast snow?'

'Are we?' I gasped, clapping my hands together and further forgetting the real reason for my visit. 'Oh, how wonderful!'

It had been years since I'd seen snow so I hoped the prediction was right. I might have felt about fifteen after my banter with Archie and singing along in the car, but the thought of actual snow reduced me to no more than five. Coupled with the fun of opening the advent calendar, the sight of Brambles beautifully bedecked, and now the prospect of the white stuff, almost sent me into festive overload.

'You're more excited about that than I am,' Jack laughed at my response.

'I am excited,' I confirmed, feeling very happy indeed.

Archie rolled his eyes.

'What?' I demanded. 'Don't tell me you're against it too. Your father will be thrilled . . .' My words, and some of my enthusiasm, trailed off. 'Ah.'

'Exactly,' Archie agreed. 'He's already in a spin now the advent calendar is up, so throw some snow into the mix and he'll be peaking way too soon and as I recall, Paige, you're every bit as much on Dad duty in Jamie and Anna's absence, as I am.'

'Well,' I said, lifting my chin in defiance, 'I don't care. I'll enjoy it with him.'

'You won't be saying that when you're up in the cherry picker throwing strands of lights over the hall roof.' He grinned.

'When I'm what?' I gasped.

'Thanks for last night,' he then said to Jack. 'I had a blast and I still think the coconut vodka was my favourite.'

Coconut vodka and cherry pickers . . . *My* head was beginning to spin, never mind Angus's.

'About the hall lights,' I began but Archie was walking away.

'Don't worry,' he said, as he pressed the fob to unlock his car, 'we'll talk about it later. I have to get back. Molly's expecting me.'

Jack and I watched him go and I stamped my feet to stave off the cold. I had almost got used to the change in temperature, but that day it certainly did feel cold enough to snow.

'Come inside,' said Jack. 'I want to talk to you before I show you around.'

That had the immediate effect of refreshing my memory and I forgot all about the white stuff again.

'Thanks,' I said, 'it's freezing out here.'

The inside of Brambles was every bit as smart as the outside and Jack quickly showed me into an office just beyond the warm and welcoming reception area where a young woman was talking on the phone.

'Would you like something to drink?' Jack offered, pulling out a chair for me to sit on. 'Great hat by the way.' He grinned as I pulled it off and unwound my scarf.

'Thanks,' I said. 'It was an advent gift from Santa himself.'

'Very cool.' He nodded. 'Tea, coffee, coconut vodka?'

'As curious as I am about that coconut vodka,' I said as I smiled, 'I'd love a tea.'

'I'll sort it if you like,' said the woman, who was now off the phone and eyeing me curiously from the doorway.

'Thanks, Tilly,' said Jack, taking the seat behind his desk and blushing in response to the beautiful smile she gave him.

'She seems nice,' I commented, when she'd gone.

'Tilly?' said Jack, his voice a few octaves higher than

before. 'Yes, she's great. I'd be lost without her.'

I'd wager he thought she was a lot more than great, given his reaction.

'So,' I said, thinking I might as well keep the ball rolling, 'you said you wanted to talk.'

'I did,' he said. 'I do.'

He then stopped again as Tilly came in with our drinks.

'That was quick.' I smiled as she set down the tray.

'I'd literally just boiled the kettle,' she said, her gaze focused back on Jack's face.

'Thanks, Tilly,' he said.

'Shall I close the door?' she asked.

'Yes, please.' He nodded.

'You were saying,' I prompted when he didn't pick the conversation up again.

'Yeah,' he eventually said, sounding uncomfortable. 'I know you're probably thinking it's a bit weird for me to comment on your relationship with my brother . . .'

'I haven't got a relationship with your brother,' I cut in. 'I barely know him.'

'But the thing is,' he carried on as if I hadn't spoken, 'I'm a bit protective of him at the moment.'

Out of everything I had considered he might say, that hadn't featured. I wondered what had happened to make him feel protective, but as he didn't elaborate, I carried on.

'Well,' I said, 'Brodie doesn't need protecting from me.'

Jack nodded.

'I do like him,' I confirmed, 'but I can promise you,

I'm not a danger to him. Our introduction was hardly a classic meet cute,' I joked, 'but I'm not holding that against him.'

'The dog in the gallery day.' Jack frowned. 'Yes, he told me all about that.'

'Did he?'

'Um,' he confirmed, chewing his lip. 'He said he was very rude to you, but he was having a hell of a day. Not that that's any excuse,' he hastily added.

'Well, our conversations have improved a bit since then,' I conceded, thinking of the few we'd had. 'But there haven't been enough to warrant us having the relationship you earlier suggested.'

'That's all right then,' Jack said, sounding relieved as he poured the tea. 'And probably for the best because he's not in a good place at the moment. He's really been through it with his work and I just don't think that getting involved with someone would be a good idea. Not that there's anything wrong with you, Paige . . .'

I was rapidly being nudged towards feeling offended and quickly butted in. There was no way I'd be having that drink with Brodie now. Casual or otherwise.

'Jack,' I cut in. 'Not that it's any of your business, but we're not involved and I'm really not sure you should be telling me any of this, even if we were.'

'Oh, god,' he sighed, putting his head in his hands. 'I'm so sorry, Paige. I honestly didn't mean to make such a hash of things.'

'It's fine,' I said, forcing myself to remember that this was simply one kind, but misinformed brother looking out for another. 'Let's just forget it. I'll pour the tea and then you can give me the grand tour.'

We finished our drinks and I was just about to ask, based on what I'd witnessed in the gallery the day we met, if Brodie was an artist, when Tilly knocked on the door. I was frustrated by the interruption because the question would have further proved to Jack how little I knew about his brother and hopefully set his mind at rest.

'I'm sorry to disturb you,' Tilly apologized, 'but I've got a query about the order from The Mermaid.'

Jack followed her out and I thought what a lucky escape I'd had. I might have had the hots for Brodie and considered his contradictory mood swings captivating, but I wasn't about to spend time with someone who, according to his well-meaning brother, had more baggage than I did.

'Sorry about that,' Jack said, when he came back in just as I had finished relocating my thoughts about his brother. 'Now, how about we take this tour? It feels like I've been promising to show you around forever.'

We only made it as far as the reception again when my mobile started to ring.

'Sorry.' It was then my turn to apologize as I looked at the screen. 'It's the hall number. I'd better see who it is.'

'Of course,' said Jack, taking a step away.

It was Mick.

'I'm sorry to disturb you, love,' he said.

'That's all right. What's up?'

'You've had a call here from a Mr Wilson. He's asked if you could give him a ring at the opticians.'

'OK,' I said cautiously, wondering what he could possibly want.

I had been trying not to think about Albert, but suddenly my heart was racing and my concern had cranked up several notches. I might have been determined to back off, right off, as Albert had asked, but that didn't mean I didn't still care.

'I'll do it now,' I said, checking I had the right number.

'Wilson's Opticians, how can I help?' Mr Wilson answered on the first ring.

'It's Paige, from Wynthorpe Hall.'

'Oh, hello, Paige. It's about Mr Price's glasses. You didn't collect them yesterday.'

'No,' I cautiously said, 'I didn't. Albert told me he was going to ring you and ask if you could send them out rather than,' I hesitated, not wanting to imply that we'd had a falling out, 'have me pick them up.'

'Well,' said Mr Wilson, as he tapped away on a keyboard, 'there's no message logged here, so he can't have called. But not to worry, I'll get them in the post later today.'

'No,' I said, after a moment's hesitation, 'there's no need. I'm close to town so I'll collect them.'

'If you're sure?'

'Absolutely,' I insisted.

That was the right thing to do, wasn't it? Even if I just posted them through the cottage letterbox. That way, Albert would have them sooner than if Mr Wilson put them in the post. I let out a long breath, frustrated that I was still questioning every decision I made. Even those which I knew in my heart were the right ones. Was this lack of confidence going to be a permanent personality trait now? I sincerely hoped not.

'I'll see you soon,' I told Mr Wilson and looked over at Jack.

'Tour postponed?' he correctly guessed.

'Afraid so,' I said, slipping my phone back into my pocket.

'Never mind.' He shrugged. 'There'll be other days. Will you be at the dance tonight?'

I'd forgotten all about that.

'Perhaps,' I said as a few soft snowflakes began to fall. 'Assuming I'm not snowed in at Wynthorpe by then.'

Jack looked at the sky and laughed.

'Not much chance of that,' he said. 'And even if you were, I'm not sure Kathleen would accept that as a valid excuse for missing out on tripping the light fantastic.'

'Perish the thought.' I shuddered.

The snow was coming down heavier by the time I'd parked in town, collected Albert's glasses and driven out again. It was starting to settle too, but Jack was right. I was a long way off being snowed in and exposing my two left feet to the world, well, everyone at the dance anyway, began to feel inevitable.

I eventually arrived at the cottage, braced myself to be called a busybody again and slipped down the snowy path. My initial plan to push the glasses through the letterbox was a non-starter because Mr Wilson had made up a 'comprehensive spectacles care package' and they wouldn't fit, so I had no choice but to knock.

'Who is it?' came Albert's voice, causing a rush of relief to course through me.

At least he hadn't attempted the stairs and taken a tumble, which I had been feeling increasingly worried about.

'It's Paige,' I said shakily. 'Your friendly neighbourhood busybody.'

There was a second's silence and then the door was unlocked and opened.

'I've got your glasses,' I said, holding out the package for him to take. I was pleased to see he was wearing the pair the canny, or forgetful, optician had left behind. 'Mr Wilson called and asked why I hadn't picked them up for you yesterday.'

A flash of something I couldn't fathom crossed Albert's face and he stepped back into the cottage, leaving me still holding the package.

'And did you tell him that I was a stubborn and belligerent old bugger who'd seen you off the second I'd put the glasses on, looked around and realized just how low I'd sunk.'

'Oh, Albert,' I gasped, as the penny dropped.

'Did you let on that my shame about the state of things here had cost me the care and kindness of the only person I'd let over the threshold since I'd lost my sister?'

A sob caught in my throat as I stepped inside and closed the door.

'So,' he said, 'did you tell him that?'

'No,' I said, shaking my head. 'I didn't. I didn't say anything like that, because I stupidly hadn't worked it out.'

I looked around and could see he'd made more of a start on tidying up. There was a roaring fire in the grate too and Bella was asleep in a basket in front of it.

'Huh,' Albert huffed, 'and there was me thinking you'd got a bit about you.'

I had to smile at that.

'I credited you with some sort of intelligence,' he further said, smiling himself.

'My radar's off at the moment,' I admitted. 'It's taken a bit of a battering recently.'

'Sounds to me like we've both been in the wars,' Albert suggested.

'We sure have,' I confirmed. 'It's heavy going on the frontline, isn't it?'

'You can say that again.' He nodded, with a certainty that made my heart ache.

'I think Mr Wilson has sent half the shop along with your new glasses,' I said, setting the padded envelope down. 'How come you didn't ring him to send them out like you'd planned?'

I wondered if it had been a ploy to get me to come back, but it wasn't.

'Bella's been a bit poorly and with these other glasses to wear, thoughts of the new ones went completely out of my head.'

My gaze darted back to Bella.

'She seems better today,' Albert added. 'But I'm still a bit worried about her.'

'Shall I give the vet a call?' I offered, without overthinking. 'Just to be on the safe side. There might be someone available to check her over today and that would set your mind at rest ahead of the weekend, wouldn't it?'

'If it's not too much trouble,' he said huskily. 'That would be grand.'

'It's no trouble,' I responded firmly, unlocking my phone and finding a smidgin of signal. 'Where does she usually go?'

'My sister used to take her to a chap called Will. His firm are the best around here. He was in the wars once too. He's ex-army. A bona fide war hero.'

Albert sounded impressed by the man's reputation.

'Right,' I said, 'I'll take her there. Do you have a carrier for her?'

There was a wicker one, complete with padded cushion, in the cupboard under the stairs.

'And when I come back,' I said to Albert, having secured an appointment, 'we'll talk about arranging for some proper help to get everything straight again. I can get you on Anna and Kathleen's rota for regular food deliveries. How does that sound?'

Albert didn't look too sure, but I wasn't going to back down. He would definitely be more capable with the benefit of his new glasses, but still a long way off being completely independent.

'I know it's hard accepting help,' I empathized. 'Especially when you've been flying solo for so long, but sometimes what we want compared to what we need are two different things. Sometimes, it's better to go with the flow and embrace what's being offered.'

'You sound like you're speaking from experience,' he said insightfully.

'Bitter experience more like,' I admitted. 'I didn't heed my own advice and my life got pretty messed up as a result.'

Had I not been so determined to do everything on my own then my time working in Jordan would have ended very differently. Alone was okay, I realized, but my new and unexpected role was helping me to see that together was better.

'Would you like to talk about it, love?' Albert offered kindly.

'Thank you,' I smiled. 'One day perhaps, but now I need to get Bella to the vets.'

It was still snowing when I set off but Bella was swaddled in a blanket and Albert had made up a hot water bottle for her too. She'd hardly moved when I transferred her from one warm spot to another and I hoped there wasn't anything really wrong with her.

'So,' said Will, Wynbridge's handsome hero vet when he welcomed the pair of us into his treatment room. 'What are we doing for Bella today? I haven't seen her for a while.'

I explained a little about the situation with Albert but only shared the details which I felt were relevant to Bella's current condition, along with who I was in relation to them.

'Let's have a look at her then,' Will said.

He carefully lifted the little cat out of the basket and treated her with such tenderness that I was quite touched. For such a big guy he had a very gentle approach.

'I can't find anything really amiss,' he said, after giving her a thorough examination. 'I'm pretty certain the upset tummy was down to her change in diet.'

'Oh, crikey,' I said, relieved that Bella was all right but feeling guilty because I was the one who had supplied her food. 'That's my fault. I picked up some pouches and I daresay they weren't the variety she was used to.'

'Well,' said Will, 'there's no lasting harm done but ideally a gradual change in diet is best. If she had been fending for herself before she had the pouches the processed stuff would have been quite different. She's got it out of her system now, but is tired as a result.'

'I see.' I cringed. 'I should have thought of that.'

'Honestly,' Will said as he smiled, 'she's fine and the lethargy will soon pass.'

'Okay.' I swallowed, still feeling rotten.

After further reassurance, Will administered a jab and recommended reinstating Bella's worming and deflea regime.

'I haven't met Albert,' he said, 'but his sister was a lovely lady.'

'Albert speaks very highly of you,' I told him as I settled Bella back into her basket.

'He does?'

'Yes.' I nodded. 'He told me you're a war hero.'

Will ran a hand around the back of his neck and turned slightly pink.

'I served my time,' he said lightly. 'And, so I understand it, have you.'

'Sorry?'

'You're an overseas aid worker, aren't you?'

I shook my head in disbelief.

'Life in a small town.' He shrugged. 'There are no secrets.'

'Oh, I know that,' I said. 'Say no more.'

'Where were you last?' he asked, holding the door open.

'Jordan,' I told him. 'In one of the camps.'

'Are you finding it hard to readjust?'

'A little.'

'I was the same,' he said, closing the door again. 'Can I offer you a bit of advice?'

'I suppose,' I said, briefly lifting my gaze to his face.

'Don't be hard on yourself,' he said seriously. 'And don't expect regular life to fall immediately and neatly into place.'

'That's easier said than done.'

'I know.' He smiled.

'But I made this stupid mistake before I came back,' I unexpectedly blurted out. 'Sometimes I can't stop thinking about it.'

'Paige,' Will said patiently. 'Under pressure and in tough circumstances, we've all made mistakes. They're inevitable. We're only human and sometimes things go wrong. No one's infallible. Remember that.'

'Okay.' I nodded.

'And it's almost Christmas,' he added, with a smile. 'Enjoy it. You are allowed.'

Listening to someone who had genuine experience, indeed frontline experience, triggered something in me and knowing that I was getting better at keeping a lid on the catastrophizing which had previously *always* arrived after running through the reel of what I'd done wrong, I could finally acknowledge that I was making progress.

My thoughts after my earlier conversation with Albert were proof that I was readjusting my lone wolf mindset so perhaps, if I carried on in the same vein, the questioning and need for reassurance might fade away too.

'I will,' I therefore told Will, returning his smile.

'Good,' he said, opening the door again.

'Thank you for checking Bella over at such short notice.'

'It's been a pleasure to catch up with her,' he told me. 'You take care, Paige, and remember what I've said.'

Back at the cottage, I gave Albert the good news and his shoulders relaxed.

'I feel bad that it was the food I gave you that put her out of sorts though,' I said, looking at Bella who was in front of the fire, only now having a wash, rather than sleeping.

'Like the vet said,' Albert reminded me, 'no harm done. How much do I owe you?'

'Will said he'd give you a ring about it next week,' I told him. 'Hey, you've changed your glasses. They look great.'

'And they fit well, too,' he said. 'Which is a relief, because

I didn't much fancy having to go to town to get them sorted.'

I wondered again how long it had been since he'd left the cottage but didn't ask. I didn't want to do or say anything which might spoil our re-acquaintance.

'And while you were gone,' he further said, 'I had a think about what you said about getting me some help.'

I held my breath.

'I think it's a good idea.' He nodded. 'I want to get back to sleeping upstairs and the cottage needs a good bottoming out, as my sister used to say.'

'That's great, Albert.' I grinned.

The day was getting better the longer it went on.

'And I want it to be you who helps me,' he then added, which completely took the wind out of my sails.

'Oh, Albert,' I said, 'there are lots of people . . .'

'That's as maybe,' he interrupted, 'but I'm too embarrassed to let anyone else in to see the state of things as they are right now.'

'I'm sure no one would care . . .'

'I would,' he cut in again. 'You've seen me at my worst, so it's you or no one.'

I knew it had taken a lot for him to let me into the cottage in the first place and to let me back in a second time couldn't have been easy either, so I could hardly turn him down.

'All right.' I smiled. 'Where do you want me to start?'

Chapter 14

After a productive few hours spent bottoming out the cottage, I had grasped that agreeing to help Albert get the place back up to his sister's house-proud standards was going to fill all of the few spare hours I had. I also realized, as I carefully negotiated my way back to the hall through the snowy Fenland landscape, that my former resolution to leave Albert alone had now completely taken flight.

After my frank chat with my new friend and the subsequent words of wisdom, born of experience, from Will, my head felt far straighter and I was in high spirits. I was even considering forfeiting the reassurances I'd given Jack about my feelings towards his brother and wondering whether to meet Brodie for that drink after all.

There was no one in the kitchen when I arrived back and I went straight up to the Rose Room where I found Bran waiting for me wearing a martyred expression.

'Sorry,' I said, giving him a fuss. 'I know I'm late, but,' I added, thinking of Albert's new glasses and sunnier disposition, 'I have the most wonderful excuse.'

I didn't have many minutes to revel in the feeling of a job well done, however, as my phone unexpectedly pinged with a reminder that it was high time I started getting ready for the dreaded dance.

'You made it!' Kathleen beamed when she spotted me lingering on the threshold of the town hall. 'I'm so pleased. Now, let me take your coat and we'll find you a dance partner. I have a couple in mind . . .'

I don't know what I had been expecting, but the sight which met my eyes was a surprise, to say the least. Dorothy had mentioned Kathleen's commitment to getting the older generation out of their easy chairs and back on their feet and what I was looking at was confirmation that she was well on her way to achieving that.

The hall was packed with dancing couples of all ages, wearing their glamorous finest, the walls sparkled with the light from the rotating glitterball overhead and there was a palpable air of a good time being had. By everyone except me, that was. I felt completely out of place and was wearing the wrong clothes to boot.

'Ah, Rodger!' called Kathleen, keeping a tight hold of my hand to stop me walking straight back out. 'Might I cut in and ask you to give lovely Paige here a quick lesson in how to waltz?'

Rodger looked thrilled at the prospect, but his partner was a bit miffed.

'Well, don't mind me,' she said sulkily, letting Rodger go.

'Have no fear, Miss Sanderson.' Kathleen beamed. 'I have plans for you, too. Over here, Jack!'

I turned to find Jack lingering on the edge of the throng and looking every bit as awkward as I felt. When he earlier asked if I was going to be in attendance, I had assumed he had a ticket to the event because he was capable of dancing at least one step, but the apprehension on his face suggested not. What was his motivation for coming then?

'You made it,' he said to me as Miss Sanderson, her expression transformed, immediately set about positioning his arms and adjusting his posture.

'Afraid so,' I told him, trying not to laugh as he was manhandled into shape. 'Sadly, there wasn't enough snow to play the stranded at the hall card.'

'I heard that,' said Kathleen, but with no rancour. 'Now come on, the pair of you, otherwise the waltzes will be over.'

Jack and I grimaced at one another and I took some comfort in the fact that I wasn't the only person present who had no idea what they were doing.

'Best foot for… muttered.

'T… Sanderson, mishearing, 'you need … I'm right foot back.'

… giggle and honed in on what … ead I imagined I looked like … ut me through my paces and … all, but in reality, I knew I … impossible not to laugh at

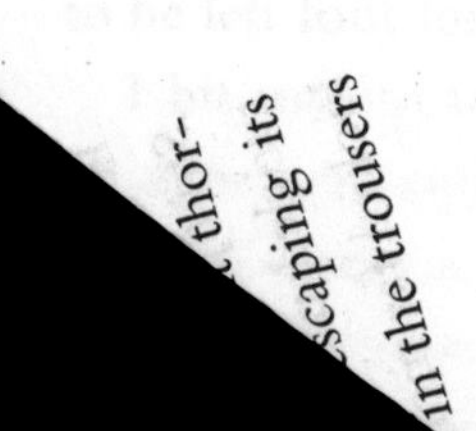

his mortification as Miss Sanderson pushed and pulled and more than once came down heavily on his toes, causing him to turn bright red and insist that it didn't hurt at all.

'Having fun?' I asked when there was an eventual break and we found ourselves next to each other in the queue for glasses of thirst quenching, non-alcoholic punch.

The look he gave me was withering.

'Why did you come?' I asked him as a result. 'I had no choice, what with working with Kathleen. I would never have heard the last of it if I didn't turn up, but you could have got away with staying away.'

He handed me a drink and we moved to the side of the hall.

'Because,' he said, taking a long and clearly much-needed swig, 'I was hoping to spend the evening with someone in particular.'

When I looked at him again, I found he was staring down at me and for the briefest moment wondered if I was the person in question. I hoped not. Jack was a lovely guy, but it was his brother I felt drawn to. Then I remembered how he had acted around Tilly . . .

'So, how are you getting on?' asked Kathleen as she bounded over, cutting through my thoughts and looking the picture of health and without a curl out of place. 'Having fun?'

I, in complete contrast to the way she looked, fel[illegible] oughly dishevelled. I could feel my hair was [illegible] formerly tight ponytail and I was far too ho[illegible] and blouse I had picked out of my limited wardrobe. At least my feet were holding up in flats. I didn't own a single pair of heels so the temptation to wear them hadn't come up. Painful feet on top of everything else would have been too much to bear.

'I'm exhausted,' I told her, 'but yes, I'm having a good time.' I supposed it could have been worse. 'And Rodger is the perfect partner.'

Jack remained stubbornly silent. I daresay the state of his poor toes were stopping him from feeling anywhere near enthusiastic about the evening's entertainment.

'Samba next.' Kathleen beamed. 'You two can buddy up for that. It's ever so easy to pick up, but be prepared to get sweaty!'

She sashayed off again and Jack groaned.

'Bugger this,' he said, draining his glass. 'I've sweated enough for one evening. I'm off.'

'Oh, no you don't,' I said, catching his arm as he went to walk away. 'You're not leaving me, Jack. Kathleen will partner me up with some expert if you go and my muscles will never forgive you. And neither will I.'

Before he could object, the pulsing music started up and our host ushered everyone back on to the dance floor.

'Come on,' I said encouragingly. 'How bad can we be?'

It turned out, we were *really* bad. We spent far more time knocking into each other having not grasped in which order we should be stepping back then forward and were in a constant muddle as a result. The other couples made it look quite sexy and sultry, but Jack and I could only lump about and laugh. A lot.

'I hope no one's recording this,' I giggled breathlessly when there was a break between the beats. 'We'll never live it down.'

Jack shook his head, then fanned me with his shirt which he'd pulled off and tucked into his jeans pocket. The T-shirt he was wearing underneath it looked decidedly damp around the edges and I laughed all the more when I realized it was just the two of us in such a sorry state.

'Having fun?' asked a deep voice behind me and I spun around to find myself face to face with Brodie.

'What are you doing here?' was my immediate response, which I realized wasn't the nicest of greetings. 'I mean, I thought you were out of town.'

'I was,' he said, frowning at Jack, 'but now I'm back.'

'I wasn't expecting you until tomorrow,' said Jack, pulling his shirt back on.

'Clearly.' Brodie scowled, sounding miffed.

'Jack was hoping to see someone here,' I heard myself say, 'but the poor chap has got lumbered with me.'

I don't know why I felt obliged to explain.

'How come you're here?' Jack asked his brother, his bluntness matching how I had started out.

Poor Brodie wasn't receiving the warmest of welcomes back to Wynbridge.

'There was a message for you from Tilly, on the answer phone,' Brodie told him. 'Here,' he added, handing over what looked like a scribbled note. 'I knew you were coming here tonight and when I couldn't get you on your mobile, I thought I'd better bring it.'

Jack read the note, his brow furrowed and I guessed my former thoughts had been right.

'Oh, well,' he sighed, crumpling the paper up and stuffing it in the pocket which had formerly held his shirt. 'Thanks.' He didn't sound particularly grateful. 'You didn't cycle in, did you?'

I was going to laugh, but then realized he was being serious.

'No,' Brodie told him. 'I called an Uber.'

'Well,' said Jack in a slightly more conciliatory tone, 'I really do appreciate it.'

'No problem.' Brodie shrugged. 'I think I'll head off.'

'Oh, no,' said Kathleen who had spotted him and caught him by the elbow just as he was about to turn around. 'You can partner up with Paige for this next dance.'

Brodie looked stricken.

'Let us see if you've got a bit more rhythm than your brother,' she wheedled.

'I'll pass,' he said, making me feel like a withering wallflower. 'Sorry, Paige,' he added. 'Nothing personal.'

'It's fine,' I said, with a shrug to show I didn't care then added, 'I'm all danced out anyway. Jack has really put me through my paces tonight.'

That made his jaw tense up, but I didn't actually want to dance with him anyway. Why would I want to demonstrate to someone I liked, in spite of the fact that he'd just shunned me, that I couldn't even manage the Macarena? I was still feeling hot and sweaty from my samba effort and just wanted to go home.

'Come on then, bro,' said Jack, clearly keen that I shouldn't partner up with Brodie either which, given how he'd warned me off him earlier, was no surprise. 'Let's see if we can catch the Uber that drove you in.'

'What's with some of you men?' tutted Kathleen, standing her ground and refusing to give in. 'One dance won't kill you, Brodie. And to be honest,' she said, in a teasing aside, 'you can't be any worse than this pair were.'

'Hey,' said Jack. 'What we lacked in finesse we made up for in enthusiasm.'

I had to laugh at that, but Brodie was set to full thundercloud mode again.

'Come on then,' he said to me gruffly, taking my hand and causing an unexpected ripple of pleasure to pulse through me as the music started. 'Let's get this over with and then Kathleen might let me go home.'

Had I not been so shocked by the sensations his touch had set off, I would have yanked my hand out of his grasp and told him to stick his dance where the sun doesn't shine, but as it was . . .

'Do you know how to waltz?' he asked, his tone softer as he looked down at me and I felt his fingers graze my shoulder blade through the thin fabric of my blouse.

I closed my eyes for the briefest moment and swallowed.

'Sort of,' I said huskily. 'It's basically step, side, close . . . I go backwards and you come forwards.'

'Oh, I know what it is,' he said, with the smallest of smiles. 'I just wanted to check that you did.'

I don't really know what happened after that. Our eyes locked, our feet moved in perfect synchronicity and, as far as I was concerned at least, there was no one else in the Wynbridge town hall. There was just me, Brodie, the old-fashioned music and the increasingly overwhelming emotions I could feel building to a crescendo inside me. I felt as light as air, fluid, flowing and free. Some seismic shift seemed to have occurred between us as we moved effortlessly around the room.

There was none of my former clumsiness, no desire to giggle and no urge to run away. If I had had my way, the waltz would have lasted a lifetime and the look on Brodie's face inferred he felt the same. Unless I was reading into his expression the emotion I wanted to see . . .

'That was extraordinary!' I heard Kathleen call out in surprise, once the music came to an end. 'Extraordinary!'

Brodie and I sprang apart, both shocked by the rapturous applause and attention our foot-perfect waltz had prompted.

'Goodness me,' said Kathleen, fanning herself as she rushed forward. 'Where on earth did that come from?' Thankfully she didn't wait for either of us to try and answer. 'I'd love to see the pair of you tango!'

'Hear! Hear!' chorused lots of the other attendees.

'You didn't dance like that with me,' Rodger called out, giving me a cheeky wink.

'Or me,' added Jack, with a look of surprise.

He was right. I hadn't danced like that with him or felt like that with him either. Jack and I might have had lots of laughs, but dancing with Brodie had been a wholly different experience. It was expressive, inspired, intimate and a complete shock to the system.

'I'm sorry,' Brodie said, stepping further away. 'I really have to go.'

And just like that, Prince Charming left the ball.

I didn't even try to sleep that night. My head was far too full of music and song, Brodie's face close to mine and the sensations his touch had aroused. Suddenly we'd somehow bypassed going for a drink together in the pub phase and landed on something far more intimate. At least, that was how I felt. I wasn't sure I wanted to delve too deeply to find out if he harboured the same thoughts too, in case he didn't.

If I had my way, Jack was going to be very disappointed with me and I hoped Brodie's connection to Angus wasn't going to turn out to be anything that had the potential to halt our relationship's progress either. I had told Molly I wasn't looking for love, or even a quick fling, and even though I had no idea what it was that I had found with Brodie, I knew I liked it. I liked it a lot.

The third of December dawned bright, clear and cold, which meant the weather was going to be perfect for the long-anticipated switch-on. I knew it was going to be a busy day too, as Angus and his festively decorated sleigh played perhaps the biggest part in the evening's proceedings, but I hadn't expected to find the hall a hive of activity quite so early in the day.

'Morning.' I yawned as I walked into the kitchen.

'Morning,' said Dorothy, pointing at the tea tray. 'I've just refreshed the pot, so pour yourself a cup.'

Catherine was already up too and so, surprisingly, was Molly. I didn't have a chance to ask why she was out of the cottage so early because Dorothy asked a question which shoved all other thoughts clean out of my head.

'So,' she asked, as I plonked myself down, 'how was the dance?'

'Oh,' I said, trying to play it cool. 'You know, much as you'd expect.'

'I suppose Kathleen was putting everyone through their paces?' Dorothy sniffed.

'A bit.' I shrugged. 'Did I miss anything here?'

'Angus on fine form,' Molly laughed. 'And completely over-excited about tonight.'

'Which reminds me,' said Dorothy, thankfully distracted, 'I must finish sewing those bells more securely on his hat. He kept letting the little ones ring them last year and they almost came off.'

There was a knock on the back door which set the dogs barking.

'Come in!' shouted Dorothy. 'It's open.'

Will, the vet I'd met the day before, came shuffling in with a rush of cold air and all three dogs in a tangle around his legs. Clearly, he was as popular with his canine patients as the feline ones.

'Good morning,' he smiled.

'Good morning,' we all chimed back.

'Paige,' said Catherine, 'this is Will, our local vet.'

'We've already met.' He nodded at me. 'Haven't we, Paige? How was Bella after her trip to the practice yesterday?'

'She was fine,' I told him. 'Still a bit sleepy, but happy enough.'

'Who's Bella?' Dorothy frowned.

I hadn't had anywhere near enough caffeine to feel up to explaining that I'd embraced a PWC which had nothing to do with my recently assigned roles and therefore picked my next words with care.

'A cat who belongs to one of the people I see on my rounds,' I simply said.

'I thought you just did Tuesdays and Thursdays,' Molly piped up. 'It was Friday yesterday.'

Thank you, Sherlock.

'I do as a rule,' I confirmed, 'but the cat was poorly so I offered to take her to see Will to set the owner's mind at rest ahead of the weekend. Anyway,' I rushed on, 'how come you've been called out, Will? I'm guessing it's not to see any of the dogs.'

They were all still nudging around him at various heights, trying to get his attention. Just at that moment the back door opened again and, along with another blast of bitterly cold air, Angus, Archie and Mick came in. They were all bundled up and their cheeks were glowing. I made a mental note to wrap up extra warm before I headed anywhere.

'We're ready for you now, Will,' said Mick, sounding rather grave.

'Morning, Paige,' said Archie, looking only marginally happier than Mick. 'How was the tour of the distillery?'

'I still haven't had it,' I told him succinctly. 'Something came up and I had to leave before we got started.'

'Right,' said Angus, clapping his hands together before Archie had a chance to ask what, 'that's enough chat. We'd better get on.'

The men ventured back out into the near dark and Catherine explained what had prompted them to call Will out.

The evening before, Mick had gone to shut the ponies up and found one of them a little lame. Usually, he would have treated her himself. Given that he had years of equine experience, he had the measure of what to do and it wouldn't have been an issue.

However, with the ponies poised to pull Angus around the market square in Wynbridge as part of the illumination celebrations, he had called Will in for a second opinion. The ponies also gave sleigh rides at the Winter Wonderland and he and Angus didn't want anything to jeopardize that. Unless, of course, the pony was still lame and then she would be rested and receiving further treatment.

By the time Catherine explained what was going on, Will and Angus were back.

'Well,' I heard Angus say as they stamped their boots on the mat, 'it's disappointing, but she comes first and it can't be helped.'

'I'm sure she'll be fine in time for the Winter Wonderland,' Will reassured him, 'but today's trip to town is out of the question.'

They came back into the kitchen and Angus shook his head. I knew he must have been feeling upset that his trot around town was cancelled, but true to form, he was more concerned about his pony's welfare and her recovery than missing out on shouting a few extra 'Ho, Ho, Ho's!'

'So, no lap of honour tonight then?' asked Dorothy.

'Nope,' said Will.

'Can't you phone around to see if anyone could lend you another pony?' I suggested.

'Sadly not,' said Angus. 'Pulling that sleigh is an art form and the ponies have been trained and regularly schooled with it here throughout the year.'

'So, what will you do now?' Dorothy asked. 'You can't cancel.'

'I wouldn't dream of it!' Angus shuddered. 'Perish the thought. It was bad enough when we thought there was going to be no switch-on! We can't have it happen now without Santa and his sleigh.'

He sounded as though he'd forgotten that he was the man in the red suit and believed that it was the real Father Christmas who was set to descend and hand out the presents Dorothy had told me the Women's Institute members had spent the best part of the week wrapping.

'Mick and Archie are now loading up the sleigh on the trailer,' he explained, 'and I've already phoned Chris Dempster. We're going to drop the sleigh in the market square now, before it gets busy, rather than hide it at the council office car park as we usually would and there's a team on standby to set up a sort of tableau to make more of a feature of it.'

Personally, having had a peek at it in the stable, I thought it was enough of a spectacle in itself, but Angus sounded keen on the extra festive dressing and I was impressed by how quickly the people in town had swung into action.

'And I better get on,' said Will. 'I'm on call this weekend and have a few things to do at the practice between calls.'

'Thanks for coming out,' said Angus, slapping him on the back.

'It was no problem,' he said. 'Mick was right to trust his gut. And Paige,' he added, 'let me know if Bella doesn't bounce back during the next couple of days, won't you?'

'Will do,' I said, wishing he hadn't mentioned her again.

'Bella?' Angus frowned.

'Never mind,' said Catherine. 'Go and see Will off and then we'll check your suit one last time.'

'Yes,' said Dorothy, looking pointedly at his rotund figure. 'There's only a little allowance left on the seams now.'

With the wheels of Operation Switch-On running smoothly again, I wasn't needed and so I headed to town to pick up the few groceries and some extra cleaning supplies that Albert had asked me to collect – and to check that Kathleen hadn't been spreading the news about mine and Brodie's unexpected coming together on the dance floor. I might have been feeling like a *Strictly* professional as a result, but I'd rather keep the details of what had occurred under wraps.

The square was a hive of activity and the sleigh, already arranged next to the Wynbridge Christmas tree and bedecked with holly, ivy and mistletoe, looked even more spectacular than it had back in the Wynthorpe Hall stables.

The further drop in temperature meant the snow which had fallen the previous day, along with a little more overnight, had frozen solid and I hoped it wouldn't turn to slush too soon. I might not have experienced a Christmas in England for a very long time, but the rush of memories and thrill of excitement induced by the sight of the snow felt both comforting and familiar and I couldn't wait to see the town all lit up.

'Yoo-hoo!' I turned around to find Kathleen heading in my direction. 'How are you feeling after last night?' she called, from along the street. 'Aching in all the right places, I hope.'

'I'm fine,' I said quietly, when she reached me. 'Kathleen, you haven't mentioned to anyone about me and Brodie waltzing, have you?'

'Not specifically.' She smiled.

'Good,' I said, letting out a breath. 'Great.'

'But then,' she nudged, 'I wasn't the only person there last night, was I?'

'No,' I had no choice but to agree as I imagined everyone else talking about it. 'You weren't, were you?'

She eyed me for a moment and I could tell she had something further to say.

'You know,' she said confidingly, 'You and Brodie looked absolutely perfect together on that dance floor. Made for each other, in fact. I don't know why you'd want to keep that waltz a secret.'

'Oh, Kathleen.' I blushed.

'Don't *oh Kathleen* me,' she laughed. 'And I'm not just talking about seeing the two of you as dance partners. Is there a little romance in the offing?' she then brazenly asked. 'I certainly hope so.'

'I don't think so,' I told her. 'I barely know him.'

'Well,' she said, 'it's Christmas, isn't it?'

'So?'

'Magical things happen at Christmas and the pair of you . . .' she said dreamily, then gasped. 'And talking of Christmas.' She frowned, looking at her watch. 'I'd better get on. I'm supposed to be at the town hall, wrapping a few last-minute presents for Santa to hand out. Is he all set to enchant the children?'

'You know Angus,' I told her. 'He's always all set to enchant everyone.'

I couldn't get what Kathleen had said out of my head that day.

'Are you all right?' Albert frowned, as I finished putting the shopping away and handed him the empty bag.

'Hm,' I said, zoning back in.

'Are you sure all this isn't going to be too much for you?' he asked worriedly. 'I felt a bit bad after you'd gone last night. You're obviously busy already and I felt as though I'd goaded you into helping.'

'Oh, Albert,' I said, giving his hand a squeeze. 'You didn't goad me at all. If you remember, I was the one pushing myself in here and insisting on running your heating and getting your eyes tested. I want to do this for you. And much more besides.'

In spite of the recent distraction, I was still determined to find a way to get him further than the front door.

'Well.' He frowned. 'As long as you're really sure.'

'I am,' I told him. 'And believe it or not, you're actually helping me as much as I'm helping you.'

'What do you mean by that?' He looked confused.

'Oh, it doesn't matter,' I said. 'I'll explain another day, but please be reassured that I really am happy to do these things for you.'

'In that case,' he chuckled, 'you'd better do them properly. You've just put the tinned goods in the fridge and the milk in the cupboard.'

I rolled my eyes, sorted the muddle and then got ready to go.

'Are you sure you don't want to come with me tonight?' I again offered as I zipped up my coat. 'It's going to be a wonderful night and I'd love you to come and see it all.'

I knew that if Albert accepted my offer, I would have to

tell everyone who he was and run the risk of the Wynthorpe clan crooning that I had found a PWC after all, but it would be worth it if it got my new friend out of his cottage. Unfortunately, however, he wouldn't change his mind.

'I'm sure,' he said, looking towards Bella, who was sitting up in her basket. 'I know she's looking brighter today, but I don't think I should leave her, just yet.'

'All right,' I said, not wanting to push him. 'As you wish.'

Chapter 15

Back at the hall, after settling the dogs, we drove to town in convoy. Mick had taken the lead in the Land Rover with a carefully hidden Santa hunkered down on the back seat, and the not-so-incognito Archie, and I followed on with Catherine next to me and Dorothy and Molly squeezed in the back.

The Fiat wasn't a vehicle which easily accommodated four fully grown women and Molly said she'd make the return journey in the Land Rover. However, the cramped conditions and steamed up windows were quickly forgotten after we left the confines of the car and walked to the market square.

My senses were lit up – even though the town wasn't yet – by the spectacle which met us. The market had even more festive stalls and there were carols being sung by a choir dressed in Victorian style outfits. I could smell mulled wine and cider and, thanks to the tantalizing scents wafting from the food carts, I could practically taste The

Cherry Tree Café warm mince pies and iced gingerbread tree biscuits along with the spicy sausages on the Skylark Farm stand.

It was biting cold, but that didn't matter. If anything, it added to the ambience and, as I stood and gazed at the seasonal spectacle in front of me, I knew with one hundred per cent certainty that, in spite of the current turmoil I was feeling about Brodie, my decision to come to Wynthorpe Hall had been the right one.

'Come on,' said Molly, her eyes shining with excitement, 'what shall we do first?'

Catherine and Dorothy had already headed over to the Women's Institute stall. I had spotted Kathleen there already and I could tell from her and Dorothy's body language that a potential stand off was in the offing. I hoped they wouldn't forget it was actually the season of goodwill and that there were multiple family groups present.

'Would you look at those two?' Molly tutted, following my line of sight.

'Do you think we should go over just in case they kick off?' I asked as Dorothy picked up something from the plate Kathleen was holding out and sniffed it.

'No,' Molly said firmly, pulling me away. 'They're grown women. They can sort themselves out.'

'In that case,' I said, looking around again and wondering if I was going to catch sight of Brodie among the crowd, 'you lead the way. I want to see everything. What do you suggest we look at first?'

'Well,' Molly asked, having given it a moment's thought, 'have you got any Christmas shopping to do?'

'Yes,' I said, pulling out a list. 'I have presents to buy for everyone at the hall.'

'In that case,' she said, steering me towards The Cherry Tree Makes and Bakes stall, 'I think we should sort that first because some of the stalls sell out really fast and it's busy already.'

By the time we'd crammed the car boot with bags of carefully chosen presents, we were both ready for something to eat and drink. I'd been thrilled by the array of gifts on offer and loved that I could talk directly to the business owners and talented crafters who had created them. It gave the gifts I'd selected even more meaning and I vowed to make an effort to add a more personal touch to every present I gave from then on.

'Right,' said Molly, linking her arm through mine, 'let's see if you're any quicker deciding what you want to eat and drink than you are at buying presents.'

'I wouldn't bank on it,' I giggled as we joined the crowds again and I spotted a familiar face.

'Hello, Alice,' I said, as we slowly inched up the queue to buy food and drink from the Skylark Farm contingent.

'Paige.' She smiled, spinning around and almost taking both me and Molly out with the pushchair. 'How lovely to see you.'

'Likewise,' I said, thinking she was a braver woman than me, bringing three children to such a busy event. 'Are you having a good time?'

'I am,' she said. 'Kathleen kindly picked us up and we're very excited to see Santa, aren't we, guys?'

Three little voices chorused their agreement and the eldest girl, who wasn't in the pushchair but holding tightly on to the handle, looked shyly up at Molly.

'I like your coat,' she said, admiring the velvet sapphire-coloured folds of fabric.

'It's a cloak,' said Alice.

'Like the magic one in my book?' the girl gasped, wide-eyed.

'Knowing the lady wearing it,' I confided, 'it might well be.'

Molly winked at the little girl and received a diffident smile in response.

'Shall we find somewhere quiet and all eat together?' I suggested to Alice. 'Many hands and all that.'

'Oh yes, please.' Alice smiled and Molly held out her hand for the little girl to take. 'But only as long as you're sure? I wouldn't want to interrupt your evening.'

'Of course I'm sure,' I told her. 'Come on.'

'I'm Molly,' Molly said softly, making the introduction I hadn't got around to.

'And I'm Saffron.' The girl smiled back and their friendship was sealed.

The three of us opted to drink the seasonally spiced apple juice on offer. It was just as warming as the cider, but without the alcoholic hit. We also picked up regular apple juice for the children, sausages in crusty rolls embellished with apple and plum chutney, and pumpkin pasties from a stall selling vegetarian and vegan bakes.

'That was so good,' I said, wiping my mouth on a serviette once we'd eventually finished. 'Those pasties were amazing.'

'I really liked mine,' said Saffron, who had a whole host of crumbs around her feet.

Her siblings had crumbled their fair share too, but everyone appeared happy enough, or they were until Alice unleashed the wet wipes and tidied them all up.

'Shall we stick together?' I asked her, once the objections had died down. 'Molly and I still have loads to see.'

'Thank you,' she said, 'but I'm going to go and find Kathleen. I said I'd check in and let her know I was okay before Santa put in an appearance.'

'All right then,' I said, pleased that she and the children were having a good time but aware that Alice, as a result of what she'd been through, might not find it all that easy to slip into new friendships. 'I'm sure we'll bump into you again later.'

I made a mental note not to be full-on where getting to know Alice was concerned and to tell Dorothy about Kathleen's further acts of kindness. I couldn't see how she could object to someone who was so community spirited, even if she did favour low-calorie and low-fat options in the kitchen.

'Bye, Saffron,' said Molly, giving a little curtsey and making her young admirer laugh. 'See you later.'

The four of them were barely out of sight when I heard someone calling my name.

'Paige!'

I spun around to see Jack waving from behind a stall bearing a Brambles banner. He and Tilly looked to be doing a roaring trade, but there was no sign of Brodie. Once Molly and I had walked over, I bit back the urge to ask if he was around.

'Coconut vodka?' Jack offered, holding out a shot in a tiny plastic cup. 'You missed out on the tour, so it's the least I can offer you in its place.'

'Thank you,' I said, feeling relieved that he hadn't started the conversation off by mentioning the dance, 'that's very tempting, but I'm driving tonight, so I'd better not.'

He looked crestfallen.

'I wouldn't mind trying it though,' said Molly and he handed it to her instead.

She took a surprisingly small sip and licked her lips, a wide smile readily forming.

'Wow.' She grinned. 'That's amazing.'

'And moreish, right?' added Tilly.

'Ever so.' Molly nodded, but I noticed that she didn't drink the rest. 'I know now why Archie came home the worse for wear the other night. I'll have this, please,' she said, picking up a bottle and handing it to Tilly who expertly wrapped it. 'It will be a nice surprise for Archie. I'll give it to him on the solstice. The coconut can be an extra reminder that the sun and light are poised to take over from the dark, short days again.'

I looked at her and raised my eyebrows.

'I know that's a tenuous link,' she laughed, 'but you'll understand once you've tasted it, Paige.'

'It fills me with an urge to dance the samba,' grinned Jack, clicking his fingers.

'Each to their own,' Molly laughed.

'How about you, Paige?' he asked me. 'Are you still in the mood for a dance?'

His teasing and cheeky tone suggested that now he'd seen me and Brodie dancing, he was no longer concerned about us getting together, or at least by the sight of us being together. It was such a turnaround, given how resistant he'd been at Brambles just the day before, it almost gave me whiplash. Had it been just the two of us talking, I would have asked what had prompted the change of heart but as it wasn't, I didn't.

'We'd better go and see what Dorothy wants, Molly,' I said instead as I spotted her windmilling from the other side of the square. 'She's going to do herself a mischief if we don't go over.'

We said goodbye to Tilly and Jack and sped over to the gallery.

'You're just in time,' said Dorothy, pulling us inside and closing the door.

'Hayley's designs,' Molly and I said together.

We joined the crowd, which included Alice and her three little ones, around the table at the back of the gallery. It was covered in a pretty holly and ivy patterned cloth, the mounds and hillocks under it an indication that there was treasure hidden beneath.

'Thank you for joining us,' said Jemma, stepping forward.

'I know lots of you have been looking forward to finding out what Hayley has been working on for this collection and, even though she can't be with us in person tonight, she is here . . .'

She stepped back and Lizzie handed her an iPad which she set up on a plinth.

'Well, I never,' laughed Catherine as a young woman's face filled the screen.

'Evening, everyone,' she beamed.

'Evening,' we all laughed back.

She then told us about the inspiration behind the collection and that the bird she had focused on represented rebirth, boldness and protection.

'It's wrens,' Molly whispered in my ear. 'I bet there are dozens of wrens waiting to take flight under that cloth.'

After a few more words from Hayley, Jemma lifted the fabric and Molly's guess was proved right. The exquisite collection was met with rousing applause and lots of 'oohing' and 'aahing'. Set out on the table were mugs, cushions, notebooks, all sorts of things featuring a tiny but intricately detailed wren motif.

My favourite design featured the little bird nose to tail with the one in front of it. One had its beak in the air, the next its tail upright. Somehow Hayley had captured the staccato bobbing action wrens are known for perfectly. Noticing how fast the table was emptying, I quickly picked up a mug which had the design printed around the top.

'Great choice,' grinned Hayley, when I joined Catherine

at the iPad and had been introduced as her goddaughter and current home help. 'Is everything all right at the hall?'

'Everything's fine,' I reassured her. 'Although I have no idea how you manage to fit in all that upkeep *and* your art.'

Her face flushed with pride.

'I'm the ultimate multi-tasker,' she laughed.

'You must be,' I told her. 'I'm looking forward to meeting you when you get back.'

I left her talking to Catherine then went to pay for my purchase so I could go and find Molly, Alice and the children who had walked back to the square ready for the switch-on.

'It's a shame about the ponies,' Molly said, when I found them, 'but the North Pole aesthetic works well, doesn't it?'

The team drafted in that morning to create the tableau around the sleigh had done a wonderful job and it all looked as if it could have been lifted straight out of Lapland.

'It really does,' I agreed, then switched my attention to the stage where Chris Dempster was waxing lyrical about the community coming together and thanking everyone who had contributed via the crowdfunding page and also by giving their time to set everything up. 'This really is a Christmas miracle, isn't it?' I whispered.

'You old romantic,' said Molly, pulling me into her side.

'It's the ultimate Hallmark movie moment,' said Alice, sounding a little choked herself.

'It really is,' I agreed. 'This is going to keep my festive feeling topped up.'

'You're staying at Wynthorpe Hall,' Molly reminded me

with a nudge. 'You won't need to worry about losing the festive feeling again now!'

'Three, two, one!' everyone joined in with the countdown and then a button was pressed.

A collective cheer rang out as the market square was flooded with light and a display of fireworks soared into the air. They looked spectacular and I didn't realize it until they'd finished, but I had watched them all without flinching once. I blinked back my tears and swallowed hard, focusing my gaze on the brightly lit tree, lampposts and sparkling strands which seemed to be strung everywhere. I felt proud that I was finally moving on and could now endure a bang or two without succumbing to drastic action and bad memories.

'Santa!' I then heard Saffron shout. 'Come on, Mum!'

'Father Christmas!' yelled someone else.

While we had all been admiring the town lights and fireworks, Santa himself had climbed into his sleigh and was now waving at the crowd who rushed to form an orderly queue to meet him. I felt quite emotional as the sleigh bells rang out and for a moment, I almost forgot that it was my godfather inside the suit and not the man himself.

'I'll see you again soon,' said Alice as she rushed to join the queue.

'He really looks the part, doesn't he?' said Archie, coming over to me and Molly. 'You could almost believe it was him.'

'For a moment there,' I admitted, shaking my head as my eyes swept again over the glossy red sleigh which looked even better under the lights. 'I did.'

Flanked by two elves, Santa called the adoring crowd to order and a steady stream of children took their turn to meet him and receive a small gift. It was a truly joyous sight and I was so happy to have had the opportunity to see it.

'Come on,' said Archie, after we'd been watching for a few minutes, 'let's go over to the pub. There's been a change of plan regarding getting home. Mick is going to run Mum and Dorothy back and then come and pick Dad up later, so we can be as long as we like now. That is, if you still don't mind driving and not drinking, Paige.'

'Not at all,' I happily agreed, wondering if I'd find Brodie in The Mermaid.

As much as I was enjoying watching Santa make wishes come true, especially those of a very happy looking Alice and her brood, the cold was beginning to get to me and I willingly followed Archie and Molly over to the pub. It was standing room only and I was introduced to so many people my head was soon spinning even though I'd drunk nothing more potent than a glass of Coke.

Brodie wasn't among them, but there was Beamish and Hattie, then Lottie and Will, who I did know of course and was happy to tell that Bella was doing fine. Then came Amber from Skylark Farm and Fliss and Eli from Fenview Farm, along with Ruby and Steve from the market.

'I hope no one's planning to test me on names later,' I shouted to Molly, who raised her glass in response, having clearly not heard what I'd said above the cacophony of laughter and chat.

It was like that for about an hour and then folk began to drift away. I gratefully flopped down on a chair the second one became available and only then noticed that Brodie was sitting all alone at a table next to the fire. He had receded so far into the shadows he reminded me of Aragorn from *The Lord of The Rings* who could make himself disappear in just a few well-placed strides.

I was just wondering how long he'd been there, when he looked up and our eyes locked. I felt my face flush and turned away. I twisted around to talk to Molly to hide my discomfiture at being caught staring but she was still standing with Archie and they were engrossed in conversation with another couple. Feeling further exposed, my gaze flicked back to Brodie and found his was still trained on me.

There was nothing else for it and so, while trying to suppress the memory of his body moving close to mine lest my legs give out, I picked up my glass and walked over.

'Hey, Brodie,' I said, ignoring the speedy thump of my heart. 'I was wondering if I might see you tonight.'

'You were?' He frowned.

'Yes,' I said, feeling awkward. 'We said about having a drink tonight the day we met in the opticians, remember?'

'Oh, yeah,' he said. 'We did, didn't we? But of course, that was before the dance.'

'Yes,' I said, 'I'm sorry you got roped into that. You obviously didn't want to be there and you took off before I could apologize that Kathleen . . .'

'It's fine,' he cut in. 'Although I'm sorry I wasn't as much fun as Jack to dance with. Everyone has been telling me all day what a laugh you had with my brother.'

'I think we were laughing more to cover up our ineptitude than anything else.' I smiled. 'I . . . I much preferred my waltz with you.'

Brodie's frown was replaced with a look of surprise.

'Well, that's a first,' he said.

'What is?'

'Someone preferring me over him.'

I got the feeling we weren't talking about being dance partners anymore and guessed that Jack hadn't mentioned anything about having worked out that I had the hots for his brother. I was grateful about that.

'Oh, I can't believe that,' I said, the words catching.

'It's true,' he said, pushing out the seat opposite him with his foot. 'Do you still fancy that drink?'

I sat down, my jelly legs grateful for the intervention.

'So,' I said, letting out a breath.

'So,' Brodie responded, pushing his glasses further up his nose.

I could still see his long, thick lashes behind the lenses and they were as sexy as hell. I tried not to keep honing in on them but they seemed to have some sort of magnetic pull. If I'd had my wits about me, I would have immediately started making inroads into working out what the connection between him and my godfather was and whether it was going to impact on us possibly getting to know each other better, but all avenues of conversation seemed to have dried up the moment my backside touched the seat and my eyes were level with his.

'I'll just go and get us another drink,' he said, bumping the table in his haste to get up.

I was talking to Will when he came back.

'I don't think I'll ever get used to them,' the wonderful vet had just confided. 'The booms are too much. I'm going to suggest the silent type, next year, but I'm pleased you can still enjoy the noisy ones, Paige.'

'Fireworks,' I said to Brodie, who was looking confused.

'I haven't been able to stand the noise since I came out of the army,' Will further explained. 'It's triggering. Sets off my PTSD.'

'I'm sorry to hear that,' said Brodie, eyeing me curiously.

'Will wanted to know if I felt the same,' I said, 'but I was fine tonight.'

'Which is great,' said Will, raising his glass. 'Okay, I better go. Enjoy the rest of your evening, guys.'

'Thanks.' I nodded. 'You, too.'

'What was that all about?' Brodie frowned the second Will was out of earshot. 'You're an aid worker, aren't you?'

'Yes,' I said. 'I've recently been working in refugee camps.'

'Is gunfire an issue in refugee camps?' He frowned.

'It can be.' I swallowed.

Especially if the aid worker in question has put their colleagues at risk.

'Can we talk about something else?' I asked, regrouping. 'Why don't you tell me about your work?'

The artistic fantasy I'd woven around Brodie didn't marry up with my godfather's request to 'see a return' from him and before I fell further for the man with a tendency to turn all Mr Darcy at the drop of a hat, I thought I should try to get my act together and get to the bottom of it.

'Or just more about you,' I added, making my enquiry more general. 'Because beyond knowing that you've only recently moved here and that you're living with your brother, I don't know anything. Are you planning to stay or just passing through?'

Brodie pushed his hands through his hair.

'Well,' he sighed, 'the jury's still out on that one at the moment.'

'You're older than Jack, aren't you?'

'Yes.' Brodie nodded. 'I am the eldest. Unfortunately.'

'That was a loaded answer.' I laughed. 'Why is being the eldest an issue?'

'Because it meant that I was the brother who was pressured into following our father and grandfather into the family career.'

'That sounds rather old-fashioned,' I unnecessarily pointed out.

'It's a ridiculously out-of-date attitude,' he agreed. 'But I was given my grandfather's name and as a result, I was raised with the mindset of following in his footsteps and sticking to the business our family have always excelled in.'

Neither Brodie's words or expression suggested that he was enthusiastic about the family career path or that it had anything to do with wielding a paintbrush. My assumption the day we met in the gallery, that he was about to instruct an art class, must have been wrong. Perhaps he had just been holding the fort until Lizzie came back in. I still hoped not though because my artistic fantasy suited him so well.

'So,' I tentatively asked, 'what is the business that your family excels in?'

'Making money,' Brodie said on an out-breath. 'Making lots and lots of money.'

'Oh.' I swallowed. 'Right.'

I felt a torrid mix of emotions when he said that. The thought of him spending his working life making money was so far removed from what I had imagined him doing, it was a real jolt to my system. As was the realization that our careers couldn't have been more different. I had spent a decade with my bank balance sailing close to zero, but Brodie's most likely had a whole host of zeros embellishing it and all in a far more lucrative order.

'When I became a hedge fund manager for D and C,' he carried on, unknowingly delivering yet another blow, 'I thought Dad was going to die of pride. He came down to London to celebrate the weekend before I started and I'd never seen him so happy.'

I took a moment to catch my breath as the puzzle that was Brodie broke apart and reformed into an entirely different pattern. The return Angus was hoping to see, I realized, was of a financial variety and the London mates Brodie had left

Wynbridge to catch up with were in fact suits and not some arty group in a creative up and coming part of the city.

But it was even worse than that. Jack had said that his brother had been really going through it with his work and hearing the company name fall from Brodie's lips, I realized that the man sitting opposite me could well be responsible for so much more than trying to swell the Wynthorpe coffers.

I swallowed down the bitter tang of disappointment and upset as I kissed goodbye to the image of Brodie wearing over-sized knitted sweaters to paint in and replaced it with one of him in a designer suit behind the wheel of an ostentatious and overpriced car and not giving two hoots for the consequences of his misplaced investments.

'I'm sorry,' I said, putting my glass on the table, with a less than steady hand. 'But I'm not feeling very well. I think I'd better go.'

Brodie looked at me and frowned.

'Crikey,' he said. 'You do look a bit pale. Here, let me help you.'

He pushed back his chair as I stood up.

'No,' I said, shrugging him and his concern off. 'It's okay. You stay where you are.'

'Can we meet again soon?' he asked, as I walked away.

'Sure,' I said, making for Molly and Archie who were fortuitously signalling that they were ready to go. 'I'll call you.'

Chapter 16

I drove back to the hall with rather less caution than I'd exercised on the way in to town and in a mood that in no way reflected the earlier part of the evening which I had enjoyed very much. Thankfully neither Molly or Archie noticed my change of temper and I was left to try and get my head around what I had discovered in peace.

Nothing could lull me to sleep and long before anyone else was up, I crept into the family sitting room, the only place where I'd found a remotely decent signal for my phone, and fired it up. It didn't take many seconds of searching to confirm that my reaction to Brodie mentioning the name of the company he worked for was justified.

'Davey and Clarkson,' I whispered. 'Shit.'

Not only had the lavish lifestyles and reckless insider trading, along with dodgy investments and even dodgier pay outs led to the downfall of one of the biggest city funds the UK had ever known, it had also ensured the charity I had worked for had lost a huge chunk of its benevolent funding and had to cut essential jobs as a result. Mine included, in a roundabout sort of way.

No wonder Jack had told me his brother was going through a rough time with his work. With Davey and Clarkson as a former employer, it was hardly surprising that Brodie was keeping his head down and hiding out in the Fens. Keeping a low profile would have been high on his agenda and might possibly even account for the duplicitous artistic impression he had adopted. I can't have been the only person in Wynbridge to have been taken in by that?

I wondered if anyone else in our circle knew about his questionable credentials and more to the point, why had he mentioned them in front of me? Had he assumed that because I was only recently back in the country I wouldn't know about the scandal or had mentioning the company by name been a genuine slip of the tongue after he'd downed a couple of drinks?

With more questions than answers now filling my head, I shut my phone down again, feeling nonetheless grateful that I now knew more about the man I had been formerly falling for. It appalled me to think that Angus had been drawn into something risky, but there could be no other explanation. Going forward, I would watch him and Brodie like a hawk and take whatever action was required to stop my godfather suffering a financial loss.

'So,' I briskly said to Albert, when he opened the cottage door to me a little later, 'I thought we'd see about sorting out a few things upstairs today.'

'Is it day?' he asked, peering out. 'It still looks like the middle of the night to me.'

'I know it's early,' I said, 'but there's no time like the present and as you'll only let me help you, we have to capitalize on the limited time I have available, don't we?'

He stepped aside to let me and Bran in.

'I'm sorry,' he said, closing the door. 'I know it's not ideal . . .'

I reached for his hand feeling wretched. I couldn't let my upset over Brodie and my concerns about Angus spill into my time supporting Albert.

'Please don't apologize,' I said quickly. 'I didn't sleep well and I'm in a bit of a grump. I didn't mean to bite your head off and I really am happy to be here.'

At least I could be certain of who I was dealing with at the cottage. There were no secrets or skeletons waiting to be unearthed at Albert's. The situation with him couldn't have been more straightforward and that's what I needed. Something simple to keep me occupied while I decided how best to tackle the Brodie conundrum.

'Why didn't you sleep?' Albert asked.

'Too much excitement in town last night,' I blagged. 'It was quite an evening. Now, what shall we do first?'

'Have some breakfast,' Albert said decisively. 'You've got a determined look about you this morning, so I'm going to need some sustenance to keep up.'

After we'd eaten, Albert tidied away and I went to see what the bedrooms and upstairs bathroom were like. It was fortunate that his sister had had a downstairs shower room installed, otherwise Albert would have been really stuck during the last few months.

'So, how is it?' he asked, when I went back down.

'Not bad at all,' I told him. 'I've turned on the radiator in your room, stripped the bed and opened the windows to let the space air and I've given the bathroom a bit of a scrub. Not that it needed much.'

There were three bedrooms upstairs but I'd only gone into the one which had the door open and Albert had described as his. He'd insisted he would deal with the other two.

'I've missed having a soak in the bath,' he sighed, looking wistfully at the stairs.

'I had a feeling you'd say that,' I smiled. 'Which is why I've run you a bath and filled it with some of the pine scented bubble bath which was on the shelf.'

'A bath at this time of day,' he tutted. 'Whatever next? That's far too decadent.'

'Well, it's run now,' I said enticingly, 'and it would be terrible to waste all that water, wouldn't it?'

His eyes twinkled.

'Well, as you've already gone ahead,' he said, 'I suppose I could hop in, couldn't I?'

'I don't know,' I laughed. 'Are you up to hopping?'

'Let's see, shall we?'

With his new glasses, Albert was more than capable of negotiating the stairs which, thankfully, weren't of the old-fashioned Norfolk variety, and already had double handrails fitted. Getting used to them again was just going to be a matter of confidence and practice.

'If we come up and down a few times before I go,' I told him as he neared the top with me behind, 'you'll be fine to come up to bed on your own tonight.'

'If you make me do this a few times before you go,' he chuckled, 'I'll be too tired out to do anything other than go straight to bed this morning.'

'And where would be the harm in that?' I scandalized him by asking.

Once he was safely on the landing he turned and looked back down.

'I wasn't too keen when we had the extra handrail fitted,' he told me, 'but I can appreciate now that it made all the difference to Stella.'

'Stella?'

'My sister.' He swallowed. 'Haven't I ever mentioned her name?'

I shook my head.

'Well.' He nodded. 'There you are, now you know and thinking about it, you'll need to go into her room for sheets to make up my bed again. That's the room.' He pointed. 'The airing cupboard is in there. And as you're going in, you might as well turn the radiator on, but I'll still do the other room.'

'How about I remake your bed while you swim in the tub?' I suggested. That way I knew I would be able to keep an ear out for him without making it obvious that I was hanging about. 'Do you think you'll be able to get in and out on your own?'

'Oh,' he said, 'I hadn't thought about that.'

In the end we reached a compromise. He undressed and pulled on a bathrobe and I then went in and helped him step over the side into the bath. I then left again so he could disrobe and lower himself in.

'Are you down?' I shouted through the closed bathroom door when I heard a splash.

'I am,' came the slightly muffled reply. 'But what if I can't get out?'

'We'll worry about that when you've turned into a prune,' I said, hoping it wasn't going to be an issue. 'How is it?'

'Bloody lovely!'

'Albert Price!' I gasped. 'Language, please.' He chuckled. 'I'll leave you to it.'

Who would have thought that something so simple as running someone a bath could give so much pleasure and satisfaction? And not just to Albert. I was feeling pretty pleased about it myself. Had Molly known, she would have been thrilled.

'I hope you don't mind, Stella,' I said, as I tentatively opened her bedroom door. 'I won't be a moment.'

Almost before I had taken the room in, Bella shot between my legs and jumped up on the bed, purring loudly. The sight of her circling and settling on the pillow where her mistress's head would have once rested brought a lump to my throat.

'Don't get too comfy,' I told her, looking at the crocheted doilies which adorned every surface and the bottles of flowery Yardley scent lined up along the dressing table, 'I'll be closing the door again in a minute.'

The airing cupboard was a paragon of tidiness and I easily found a neatly ironed bed set with lavender scented sachets tucked in between the shelves.

'How are you doing in there?' I called to Albert once I'd re-made his bed, flicked the feather duster about and closed the window again.

There was still snow on the ground so it was chilly in the room, but it would soon warm up again and it felt all the better for being aired. The whole cottage did. It was finally getting back to being what I imagined it once was.

'Grand,' Albert said dreamily. 'I've topped the hot water up, so I might as well have a few more minutes, if that's all right?'

'You take as long as you like,' I told him. 'I'm going to make another brew.'

I had a feeling he would be exhausted by the time he was dry and dressed so topping up his blood sugar would help combat the toll the exertion would take. Having refreshed the pot, I nudged Bran aside to clean out the fire, laid it again and then immediately lit it, all still with one ear on what was happening upstairs.

'The tea's made,' I then told Albert through the bathroom door. 'Do you want it in there or downstairs?'

'I'll have it downstairs please,' he said, sounding a little less buoyed up than before. 'That's assuming I can get down there again.'

'Are you stuck?'

'I think I might be,' he said shakily. 'I can't work out how to get out.'

'Can I come in?'

'I think you're going to have to, but you have to promise you won't look.'

I opened the door a couple of inches.

'I'll have to look a bit,' I told him. 'Otherwise, I won't be able to pass you the towel.'

It took some working out and some discreet towel manoeuvring, but we got the bath emptied and Albert out in the end. I made him sit on the toilet seat to get his breath back while I put his socks on and helped him into a clean shirt and pullover. I tried not to look at him or say anything beyond what I needed to while I was doing it.

'Well,' he eventually said, 'that was far from dignified, wasn't it?'

I looked at him and bit my lip.

'I'm so sorry, Albert,' I apologized. 'I didn't think it through, did I? I was so keen to get you in there, I didn't spare a thought about how we'd get you out.'

'I can't believe,' he said, his shoulders starting to shake, 'that within days of letting you into the cottage, you've seen me naked! I've had romantic relationships that have moved slower.'

'Oh, Albert!' I said, with a smile. 'Are you laughing?'

'How can I not?' he chuckled.

It was a relief that he could see the funny side. If I'd been in his position, I'm not sure I would have been able to.

'But we'll have to do something about this situation,' he

said, pointing at the bath as he got to his feet. 'I wonder how hard it would be to have one of those bath chairs fitted?'

'I've no idea,' I told him. 'But I can find out if you like.'

'See if there's a way we can do it without letting anymore busy bods in, can you?' He winked. 'And let's have that tea, before it stews in the pot.'

Once he'd had a moment, rather than being worn out from the exertion of having a bath, Albert was full of energy. Within the last few days, he'd been transformed from a man who was so cold he wore his coat in the house, to a sprightly gent with a wicked sense of humour and the fluffiest white hair I'd ever seen.

The transformation was psychological as well as physical and I thanked my lucky stars, and his, that I'd got lost and stopped to ask for directions. Things with Brodie might have turned bad but the Albert situation was very much on the up.

'Right,' I said, as the morning of hard work came to an end and I realized I had hardly thought about Brodie's revelation at all. 'I'd better head back to the hall. Dorothy is cooking a roast today. A lovely joint of beef and huge Yorkshire puddings.'

'Very nice.' Albert smiled, smacking his lips.

'You're more than welcome to join us,' I told him, thinking again that my PWC would be justifiably exposed if it got Albert out of the house. 'We're four down, what with Jamie and Anna and Hayley and Gabe being away, but Dorothy won't have factored that into her portion control. There'll be more than enough to go around.'

'Thank you for the offer,' Albert graciously declined, 'but I'm happy to stay put. I'm planning to try one of those pies you've put in the freezer today.'

'As you wish,' I said, feeling a little disappointed that I couldn't capitalize on the morning's momentum and tempt him beyond the front door. 'I'll just go up and find Bella.'

She'd completely abandoned Bran but he didn't seem to mind. As long as I was in sight for most of the time, he was happy enough.

'She's on Stella's bed,' Albert told me. 'I spotted her before I came down.'

'Would you like the room closed again?'

'No,' he said softly. 'It'll be nice to go to bed and see the door open.'

'And you'll take the phone up with you and let me know when you're all tucked in.'

'Yes, Mum,' he said, rolling his eyes.

'Because if I don't hear from you . . .'

'I'll call,' he promised. 'Scout's honour.'

Bran and I left him to it and headed back to the hall. It was marginally warmer and the snow was making a rapid disappearance. I could make out the colour of the fields again and the roads were wet rather than slippery.

As I wove my way back along the drove roads and then up the bumpy drive, thoughts of Brodie and Angus filled my head. I had been grateful for the distraction at Albert's but I knew I mustn't let the pair slide off my radar for long.

I wondered if I should keep my concerns to myself or if I

should perhaps involve Archie. Angus was his father, after all. Remembering what Angus had said to Brodie about wanting to see a return by Christmas, I knew I had just three weeks to intervene and with everything else going on, the time was going to fly by.

'Just in time,' said Dorothy as I walked in and she opened the Aga door, releasing a delicious waft of Sunday dinner. 'I was just about to ring you.'

'And talking of phone calls,' said Mick, holding up the notepad which sat next to the muddle of papers and magazines beside the phone, 'you've had at least half a dozen.'

'Have I?' I frowned. 'No one's rung my mobile.'

I pulled it out of my pocket and only then realized that I hadn't turned it back on after my pre-dawn Googling.

'Oh,' I said, 'it's not been on.'

'And you two are sailing close to late too,' Dorothy tutted, banging the oven door closed again as Molly and Archie drifted in.

'Almost, but not quite.' Archie grinned, giving her a kiss on the cheek and getting swatted with the tea towel as a result.

'All of you, wash your hands and sit down,' she said. 'Before this lunch spoils.'

'Four calls from the same number with no message,' Mick carried on, as Catherine and Angus also joined us. 'And a further two, with a request for you to ring them back.'

'What's the number?' Angus asked, assuming Mick was talking to him.

'Brambles distillery,' Mick told him, 'but the calls were for Paige, Angus, not you.'

'Oh,' said Angus, throwing me a smile. 'That'll doubtless be Jack, trying to re-schedule your tour, Paige.'

'It wasn't Jack,' said Mick. 'It was the other one, Brodie.'

'Brodie,' said Angus, sounding slightly less sure of himself. 'I didn't realize you knew him, Paige. Are you sure he didn't want me, Mick? Because I am expecting him to call.'

'No,' insisted Mick. 'It was definitely Paige he was after.'

'You were with him in the pub last night, weren't you, Paige?' Molly then piped up. 'Perhaps you left something behind. You were in a bit of a rush to leave, weren't you?'

I could sense Angus looking at me.

'You know,' I said, 'you might be right. I couldn't find my scarf this morning.'

'That'll be it then,' Molly said.

'Must be,' I agreed. 'It can't be anything else.'

'Right, come on,' Dorothy said impatiently. 'Come and carve this joint, Angus, otherwise we'll be eating at teatime.'

I made a point of filling Dorothy in about what Kathleen had done for Alice and her children the evening before and I was just beginning to sense that she was starting to soften when the phone rang again. It was a wrong number, but it reminded Angus that I had a call to return.

'When you speak to Brodie,' he said to me, 'could you please remind him he needs to give me an update?'

'About what?' I brazenly asked, hoping Mick might overhear, but he took no notice.

He'd apparently forgotten all about the conversation we'd had in the conservatory the morning I'd heard Angus and Brodie whispering in the kitchen.

Angus tapped the side of his nose.

'I hope you aren't up to anything, Angus,' I said loudly. 'With the Winter Wonderland on the horizon, the last thing we need is any sort of disruption, isn't it, Catherine?'

'Paige is right, Angus,' she said sternly. 'You mustn't get up to any tricks before the Wonderland.'

'What about after it?' He grinned and everyone groaned.

We set the kitchen to rights and then all of us, including the dogs, went up to the family sitting room, where the fire was already lit.

'You can use the phone in the kitchen if you can't get a signal here,' Catherine kindly offered. 'If Brodie has called that many times, then I daresay you should ring him back.'

'Actually,' I said, only partly to stop further mention of him, but mostly because I felt it was time, 'as we're all together, there's something I'd like to talk to you about.'

'It's not to do with your workload, is it?' Mick asked. 'I've been worried that we've put too much on you.'

'No,' I said, 'it's not that. I'm managing everything well enough. So well, in fact, that there's turned out to be a bit of space for something else.'

'Is it a new relationship?' suggested Archie, waggling his eyebrows.

'Be quiet, Archie,' Dorothy tutted. 'Ignore him, Paige.

What is it that you've found time for? I'm amazed you've been able to find a spare minute for anything.'

'Well,' I said, taking a deep breath, 'I suppose you could define it as a PWC.'

'No way,' Archie laughed, earning himself a stern look from his mother.

'Go on,' said Angus, sitting up straighter and looking intrigued.

'It's all come about by accident really . . .' I began.

'There are no accidents,' Molly cut in.

'I was out doing the delivery round one day,' I carried on, not mentioning that it was right at the beginning of me taking it on, 'and happened upon this rather neglected looking cottage.'

'There are a few of those around here,' said Mick.

I was pleased about that because it hopefully meant no one would be able to pinpoint exactly the one I was talking about. I might have wanted to pick their brains for suggestions about how to further help Albert, but not at the expense of exposing his identity until, or unless, it became absolutely necessary.

'Yes,' I said. 'You're right, Mick, and this one belongs to someone elderly, who now lives alone and has been struggling to keep on top of things.'

'They sound like an ideal candidate for Kathleen,' I was then surprised to hear Dorothy say. 'What?' She frowned at my look of surprise. 'I know she's not all bad, really. And those healthy mincemeat flapjacks she was handing out last night were almost edible.'

Praise indeed.

'Well,' I smiled, 'I'm delighted to hear that and you're right about this person being right for her and Anna to help. However, they're also fiercely private and quite stubborn to boot and as a result, and probably because they're feeling a bit vulnerable, the only person they'll let help them at the moment, is me.'

'So, that's where you've been disappearing off to when you haven't been officially working.' Dorothy smiled.

'I have already helped them with a few things,' I confirmed, 'and they're managing better . . .'

'A PWC already sorted by the sounds of it then,' interjected Angus.

'Not quite,' I further explained. 'There are a few practical adjustments I'd still like to help them make and officially adding them to Anna's round is also a priority, but it's not the main one right now.'

'So, what is?' Mick asked.

'My main concern is that they haven't left their home in a very long time and, if for any reason they had to, then I think they'd struggle. I asked them to lunch here today, because it's a safe and reasonably quiet place, but they turned me down and that's not the first time I've offered to take them out.'

'Maybe they didn't like the sound of Dorothy's cooking,' said Archie.

Dorothy threw a cushion at him, narrowly missing the top of Bran's head.

'I'm being serious, Archie.' I frowned. 'There may come a

time in the future that they have to leave, say if they become ill or something and if they haven't done it in a very long time then it will make the situation even more stressful.'

'Sorry,' Archie said, sounding repentant. 'I didn't think. So, how have they been managing with food and things?'

'They've been living off frozen stuff and processed packets and tins for a while.'

Dorothy's sharp intake of breath said it all.

'And lots of it was out of date when I arrived on the scene and stocks were running dangerously low.' I shook my head. 'I dread to think what would have happened had I not turned up when I did.'

'Like I said,' Molly kindly whispered, 'there are no accidents.'

Perhaps she was right.

'And it's not just their diet which is suffering,' Angus said thoughtfully. 'Although that's dreadful enough, but they're missing out on so much more, too. Life must be very limited when it's restricted to four walls.'

'Not to mention lonely,' Catherine added.

'Exactly,' I agreed. 'I don't want to force them out. To be honest, I don't think I could, but I do think they need to broaden their horizons a bit.'

'What did you say their name was?' Dorothy frowned.

'I didn't,' I said, 'and I'm not going to tell you. Not yet anyway. Even talking about them feels like a betrayal of trust.'

'It's not that,' Angus said kindly.

'But I understand where you're coming from,' said

Dorothy. 'And I wasn't trying to trick it out of you. I just couldn't remember if you'd said.'

'Well,' said Mick. 'I don't know about the rest of you, but I'm not sure what the answer to this one is.'

'Leave it with us though,' said Catherine, 'and we'll see what we can come up with.'

'Yes, we will,' said Archie, then abandoning his previous good behaviour added, 'and in the meantime, Paige, you'd better ring Brodie back.'

I picked up Dorothy's cushion and threw it at him far harder than she'd managed and with vastly improved accuracy.

Chapter 17

As I was still assimilating what Brodie had told me, I made no attempt to call him back and he didn't ring me again either, but I was nonetheless pleased to turn my phone back on and find that Albert had remembered the promise he'd earlier made.

'I'm in bed,' he proudly announced, a little after nine. 'I took my time and it was a doddle.'

'Well done you,' I said admiringly, keeping still so as not to lose the signal. 'I knew you could do it and to be honest, I'm pleased you've called and I don't have to turn out to check up on you, because it's a filthy night, isn't it?'

As the afternoon had turned to evening, the last of the snow had been replaced by driving rain and a roaring wind.

'It's certainly rattling the rafters,' Albert agreed. 'I've got Bella up here with me and before you say it, I have been watching out for her under my feet and I did remember to put the guard up in front of the fire.'

'I'm pleased to hear it,' I said. 'And tomorrow, I'm going to see what I can find out about getting you a bath chair that doesn't need electrically installing. If I can source one, then I'm sure we'll be able to work out how to set it up and use it between us.'

'You're a good lass.' Albert sniffed, sounding a little teary. 'I don't know what I did to deserve you turning up on my doorstep.'

'Well,' I told him, blinking hard myself. 'For a start, I was lost so it was a fluke that I turned up at all and secondly, you've seen what I'm like. I'll push myself in anywhere if I can, won't I?'

I ignored Molly's voice in my head telling me there were no such things as flukes and said goodnight to Albert, happy in the knowledge that, for the first time in a long time, he was tucked cosily up in his bed. Given the horrible turn in the weather, it couldn't have happened at a better time.

There was no improvement in the weather the next morning, if anything it was worse. I could hear the wind pummelling the hall even above the noise of the vacuum cleaner and poor Bran had no idea where to be at. If such a thing as doggy earplugs existed, I would have fitted him with a pair there and then.

As I tried to soothe him, I wondered if there was something unpleasant in his past, like mine, which could be triggered by loud and unpredictable noises. If that was the case, was it our shared trauma that he had sensed when I first arrived and which had drawn him to me? I was taming my memories and my reaction to them, aided by the balm of

Wynthorpe Hall and the passing of time, and I hoped that Bran would one day be able to do the same.

'I never had you down as a lover of musicals,' said Dorothy as I waved my phone about in the kitchen trying to find a bar of signal so I could look online for a bath chair for Albert.

'Me neither,' agreed Molly, who was knitting the sleeve of a very big sweater in rainbow coloured wool. 'What's that tune from?'

'*South Pacific*,' said Dorothy, without missing a beat and then she and Molly began to sing in unison.

'What are you two on about?' I asked, from my perch on the counter top under the window which was proving to be if not a signal hotspot, then a lukewarm one.

'You've been humming about hair washes all morning,' Molly laughed.

'Yes,' said Dorothy. 'Is there any man in particular that you're trying to forget by washing him right out of your hair?'

'I have no idea what you're talking about.' I blushed, heading off to the printer which was hopefully spitting out the info I'd found for Albert.

Molly and Dorothy carried on singing and when I went back after collecting the pages, Angus had added his baritone to the din. I rolled my eyes, folded the sheets and put them in my jacket pocket. I'd barely swallowed the last mouthful of Dorothy's delicious lunch before Angus starting singing 'Hello Dolly' and I made my excuses to leave.

'I have an errand to run,' I said, looking at Bran who had finally settled. 'I think I'll leave him here,' I quietly added.

'How about you take me instead?' Archie pleaded, as Catherine began crooning too. 'Save me, Paige.'

'No way,' I said as I ducked out quickly. 'You're on your own.'

As Mick had given Anna's car a wash and polish and the roads were filthy, I took the Land Rover instead, which a layer of mud somehow seemed to enhance. It was just as well I did too as en route I came across a traveller squatted at the side of the road examining a very flat bicycle tyre. I pulled alongside, as close as I could without giving them a further soaking, and unwound the window.

'Are you all right?' I shouted above the noise of the wind, which was whipping across the flat fields without a buffer to halt its blast. 'Can I give you a lift somewhere?'

The rain, with the sharp gusts behind it, felt like a slap in the face, and when the cyclist stood and met my gaze, I felt like I'd received another.

'Oh.' I swallowed. 'It's you.'

'Hey,' said Brodie, his face screwed up against the onslaught. 'Yep, it's me.'

'Hi,' I said, taking in that he was wet through. 'What are you doing out in this?'

'Nothing.' He sniffed, shaking off the worst of the rain. 'At least not now. I've got a flat tyre.'

'I can see that,' I said sardonically.

'I've been trying to call you,' he told me, pushing his soaked hair out of his face.

'Oh, have you?' I said lightly, as if it was completely fresh news.

He gave me a look. It was one of his brooding best and I was instantly transported back to the day we met. My heart skittered and I reminded it of the other version of the man in front of me. Not the charming one in a chunky knit, but the slick city one with the designer suit and six-figure salary who worked for the company which had played fast and loose with my charity's much-needed cash as if it was Monopoly money.

He was the reality, not the man I was watching getting buffeted by the wind with a crappy bike that looked like it had been lifted straight from the scene in *Butch Cassidy and the Sundance Kid* at his feet.

'Do you want a lift then?' I begrudgingly offered again, because I could hardly leave him there. 'I can take you back to Brambles, but I have an errand to run first.'

'If it's not too much bother,' he said, 'that would be great.'

'No.' I shrugged. 'No bother.'

He manhandled the bike into the back and then squelched on to the passenger seat.

'So,' he asked, 'where are you headed?'

I pulled back on to the road, the vast puddles spraying muddy water into the deep dykes which ran along either side.

'To see a friend,' I told him, as the wipers struggled to dislodge the deluge. 'I just need to drop something off, so I won't be long.'

'Take as long as you like,' he said. 'I'm just grateful to be out of the storm.'

I didn't say anything. I didn't know what to say. Had I not been so focused on the road, I might have asked some leading questions, but the conditions were pretty treacherous and I needed to concentrate.

'I should have asked before,' he said, when I didn't comment. 'Are you feeling better?'

'Better?'

'Yes,' he said. 'When you left the pub Saturday night you weren't feeling well.'

'Oh, yes,' I said, remembering that he didn't have a clue about where my head was at as a result of his upsetting revelation. 'I'm fine now.'

'That's good then,' he said, shivering. 'And I know now's hardly the time, but I'd really like to carry on with our conversation. That's why I was calling you, to ask if I could take you on a date.'

'A date?' I squeaked, swerving a little. 'What, as in a *date* date?'

'Yes,' he said, ducking his head. 'A *date* date.'

Just a couple of days ago, his words would have been music to my ears and I would have eagerly accepted, even though I would have been going against everything I'd told Jack. But a lot had happened since then and even though I did want, need even, to talk to Brodie, the last thing I wanted was to have that conversation labelled as part of a date.

'I really like you, Paige,' Brodie carried on before I had the chance to say that I didn't want to date him, 'and, having thought more about our dance and got my head around what you said about preferring me over Jack, I was beginning to think that you might like me too.'

'Here we are,' I blurted out as Albert's cottage came into view. 'I'll be five minutes. Ten at the most.'

I turned off the engine and jumped out. I'd got jelly legs again. My thighs often seemed to be in a state of collapse when Brodie was in the vicinity and they were at their worst having heard what he'd just said. I pulled up the hood on my coat and wobbled up the path to the cottage door.

'Albert!' I shouted, when there was no response to my knocking and I was in danger of becoming as soaked as Brodie.

The strength of the wind carried my voice away and I knocked again, only harder. With no sight or sound of either Albert or Bella, I stepped across the border which ran under the front window and peered through the glass I still hadn't got around to polishing. I could see Bella curled up on the sofa, but there was no sign of Albert. I stepped back and tried the handle, but the door was locked.

'What's wrong?' asked Brodie as I retreated to the Land Rover and pulled out my phone.

'I don't know that anything is,' I said, trying not to imagine Albert stuck upstairs having had a fall in the night. 'I'm sure it's nothing.'

I rang the house phone, but there was no answer.

'Damn,' I muttered as I cut the call off.

'Shall we try the back?' Brodie suggested. 'There must be another way into the house besides the front door.'

As loathe as I was for him to come with me, I was too worried to insist he stayed put.

'Yes,' I confirmed. 'There's a door in the kitchen which leads into the garden.'

'Come on then,' he said, jumping out and letting a roar of wind in.

The strength of it pulled the driver's door right out of my grasp.

'This is locked too,' I said once we'd shuffled around to the back and tugged at the door handle. 'I think I'm going to have to break in.'

'Are you sure?' Brodie asked. 'What if they've just popped out?'

It was a perfectly reasonable question, but I knew that Albert wouldn't have just popped anywhere. I hadn't been able to tempt him over the threshold, even with his new specs on, so he certainly wouldn't have gone off on a jaunt in the middle of a raging storm.

'They won't have gone out,' I told Brodie, but he wasn't listening.

I turned to find him walking down a path I hadn't noticed before.

'Hey!' I called after him. 'Where do you think you're going?'

'What about down here?' he shouted over his shoulder. 'Could they be in this shed, do you think?'

Chapter 18

I'd never noticed that there was another building on the site, but Brodie was right. Tucked at the furthest end of the garden, and almost completely camouflaged by mature shrubs and trees, there was an ancient looking Nissen hut. Had the storm not torn a branch from the bottom of the tree planted closest to it, I'm sure it would have remained unexposed and unnoticed.

Once a common site across East Anglia, you were now more likely to find a converted hut trendily decked out and listed on Airbnb than housing aircraft on a military base, and I blinked hard, just to make sure my eyes weren't deceiving me.

'How cool is this?' Brodie gawped when I reached him, the branch having thankfully not fallen across the path. 'What's it used for?'

'I've no idea,' I said, looking back towards the cottage. 'I didn't even know it was here. I think we should go back . . .'

Brodie put a hand on my arm and cocked his head.

'I can hear music.' He grinned. 'I think we might have found whoever it is you're looking for.'

'That's not possible,' I began, but then stopped as I also caught a few notes carried on the wind.

'What is that?' Brodie asked, frowning in concentration. 'Oh, hang on. I think I recognize it. It's Glenn Miller, isn't it?'

Before I could answer, he'd stepped up to the door, narrowly avoiding the long stems of the shrubs being whipped about in the wind.

'Wait!' I called after him but he didn't stop.

His hand was almost on the door handle by the time I was beside him.

'Wait,' I said again, batting him away. 'You can't just go barging in.'

'I wasn't planning to,' he said, sounding hurt.

'Albert!' I shouted, knocking on the door. 'It's me, Paige. Are you in there? Albert!' I yelled again when there was no answer.

During a brief lull in the wind, I went to call again, but Albert's reedy response meant I didn't have to.

'Who is it?' he shouted warily. 'Who's there?'

'Oh, thank God,' I muttered, my shoulders sagging. 'It's me, Paige!' I yelled as the wind immediately gained in strength again. 'Are you all right?'

'Yes,' he called back. His voice sounded close to the other side of the door and the music had been turned down. 'Yes, I'm fine. You go back to the cottage and I'll be with you in a minute.'

'Are you sure you want to walk back to the house on your own?' I asked. 'It's very windy out here.'

'Yes,' he said again. 'You go. I'll be just a few paces behind you.'

His words were followed by an almighty crash and a cacophony of swearing I wouldn't have thought my octogenarian friend capable of.

'I'm coming in,' I said, shoving Brodie, who was still standing in front of the door, aside. 'You wait here,' I said forcefully.

I turned the handle, pushed the door open and my jaw dropped. The wind rushed in, threatening to cause another rumpus and I quickly stepped inside properly and, unable to keep Brodie out, closed the door behind both of us.

'I told you to go back,' Albert said gruffly as he bent to right a metal bucket and I rushed to reposition an easel which had tumbled over as a result of me opening the door.

'I'm so sorry,' I began.

'And who is this?' he scowled, pointing at Brodie. 'I don't want either of you in here.'

I shot a glance at Brodie, expecting to hear him apologize and hoping to see him leave, but he was rooted to the spot. His eyes were scanning around and his mouth had formed a perfect O. He appeared every bit as shocked as I felt, only perhaps I had more reason. So much for thinking that Albert's life held no secrets.

'I'm sorry, Albert,' I apologized again, trying to look only at him and not, like Brodie, gawk at the array of easels and canvases filling the hut. 'I tried to find you at the cottage and when you didn't answer, my . . . friend spotted the hut and suggested we tried the door.'

Brodie finally came to his senses and stepped forward, his hand outstretched for Albert to shake.

'This is not a hut, Paige,' he said, his tone full of admiration. 'It's an artist's studio and it's an honour to meet you, sir. I'm Brodie. I'm so sorry we interrupted you.'

Albert, justifiably smarting over our unwanted intrusion, wasn't in a forgiving mood and ignored Brodie's hand.

'Shall we go back to the cottage?' I suggested. 'And get the fire going? You're going to need it today.'

On any other day, I would have been delighted that Albert had left the confines of the cottage and, in spite of the intrigue I felt towards what I was surrounded by, I would have apologized again and left him to it, but with the storm still raging, I couldn't possibly leave him to negotiate the path to the cottage alone, especially as the tree outside had already lost one limb, even though he did want Brodie and I to go.

'There's a fire in here,' said Brodie, pointing out the area further inside the studio which housed a large and lit log burner. There were a couple of old-fashioned and well-worn armchairs arranged either side of it on a huge rug too.

It did feel cosy and my eyes quickly scanned around. I could see a kitchen area as well as glass doors and additional windows which flooded the place with light, even on such a stormy day. There were no further home comforts, however, and the rest of the space, as Brodie had already pointed out, was a clearly defined studio. There were filled canvases of every size stacked along the walls and a few were hung, but most were arranged in piles.

I looked back at Albert and found him watching Brodie who was far less discreet in his appraisal than me. I felt like my head was about to implode. I had thought I had Albert fathomed, but the discovery of the studio made me realize there was far more to him and his life than I had assumed. There was that wretched A word again.

I opened my mouth to ask the question I couldn't resist a second longer, but Brodie beat me to it.

'I have to ask, sir,' he said deferentially. 'Is this your work?'

Albert moved to turn the CD, which had continued to play Glenn Miller, completely off. I could hear the wind had dropped again, but inside the studio the tension and awkwardness made me feel every bit as buffeted as I had been outside.

'It's extraordinary,' Brodie continued, walking over to more closely examine one of the canvases which was filled with rich, vibrant colour and had an energy, which even I, a complete novice when it came to art, could appreciate. 'Isn't it, Paige?'

Even though I was in complete agreement, I didn't answer. I had only just got my relationship with Albert on an even keel, and wasn't going to risk saying or doing anything which might tempt him to permanently banish me from his recently improved sight again. That said, taking in his thunderous expression, it might have already been too late.

'Come on, Brodie,' I said loudly, trying to draw his

attention and get him moving towards the door rather than further inside. 'Let's go.'

'And this one,' he said, apparently not hearing and moving along. 'I love the marks you've made here.'

He reached forward and for a second, I thought he was going to actually touch the canvas, but he pulled back at the last moment. As frustrated as I was that he was ignoring me, I was curious too. Not about the marks on the canvas, but about him.

For a man more used to handling bank notes than a sketch book, he was utterly absorbed by the image in front of him. I might have still been smarting over my disappointment that we weren't compatible, that I had complicated baggage he still wasn't aware of and that I'd read him all wrong, but I was beginning to wish I'd stayed in The Mermaid long enough to hear more of Brodie's life story.

'And this . . .' he said, darting off to examine another painting.

There was clearly more for me to discover about both him and Albert, but that didn't alter the fact that he was currently oblivious of, and therefore ignoring, Albert's wishes.

'Brodie,' I said warningly.

'They're my sister's,' Albert said at exactly the same time. 'She was the artist and I'd appreciate it if you'd leave her work alone now, young man.'

'Stella painted these,' I breathlessly said.

I didn't know what Stella had looked like, but with her penchant for flowery scent and fussy doilies, I couldn't marry her up to the image of creating such bold paintings at all.

'I think you've got quite close enough,' Albert added.

There was something in his tone which finally broke through Brodie's enchantment and he turned bright red and took a step away.

'I'm so sorry,' he apologized. 'I didn't mean to—'

'I'm sure you didn't,' Albert cut in, 'but it's time you went.'

'I'm sorry too, Albert,' I said, moving to stand next to him. 'We really didn't mean to intrude. I was just so worried about you.'

He nodded, but didn't say anything.

'Shall we go back to the cottage?' I tried again.

'I'll go back when I'm ready,' he said, neatly dismissing me.

'I've got that information I said I'd look out for you,' I told him, desperate to make amends and not have things spoiled between us again.

'You can leave it on the side,' he said, with a nod to a table. 'Thank you.'

I did as he asked, still wishing I could convince him to head back to the safety of the cottage but knowing he wasn't going to budge.

'Brodie,' I then snapped, because he was edging his way towards another painting.

'Sorry,' he said. 'I just want to . . .'

'Come on,' I growled, making for the door.

'It was a pleasure to meet you, sir,' he said to Albert, once he'd torn his eyes away.

His tone was full of regret and it was obvious he didn't want to leave. Given the chance I knew he would have stayed and asked a million more questions, but Albert looked no way inclined to give him that chance and I couldn't blame him. Oh, how I wished I'd left Brodie stranded and soaked on the side of the road.

'Your sister had an incredible talent, Albert,' I softly said as I opened the door to go back out into the wind.

Albert nodded.

'Would you consider . . .' Brodie started again and with a groan, I quickly reached out and pulled him by his sleeve through the door.

'I'll call you later, Albert,' I said, as he ambled off towards the chairs next to the fire.

'No need,' he said, but not unkindly. 'And there's no need to mention any of this to anyone either. I hope you can make that clear to your friend out there?'

'I will,' I said vehemently. 'I absolutely will.'

I didn't say anything until we were well out of earshot of the studio and Brodie didn't either. He seemed to be in a daze. Walking just ahead of me, his legs looked to be as wobbly as mine usually were in his presence. Not that I had an issue with mine then though. I was so angry, every part of me was rigid.

'What the hell was that?' I started as the cottage came into view.

He turned to look at me.

'What?' He frowned.

'You barging in and asking twenty questions is what!' I scowled.

'Did you not see those paintings?' he asked incredulously. 'They were extraordinary. That work is exceptional.'

'Never mind "the work",' I snapped, making air quotes with my fingers. 'What about Albert?' I raged. 'He's extraordinary too and he's an extremely private person. I've been working so hard to gain his trust and try to help repair his life and you just barge straight in and undo it all in a matter of minutes!'

Brodie looked shellshocked.

'I didn't do that,' he said, glancing back in the direction of the studio. 'Did I?'

'Put yourself in Albert's shoes,' I told him. 'Just for two seconds.'

Brodie swallowed and looked at his own shoes.

'You're a total stranger and you waltz in and start poking about and asking a hundred questions,' I stormed on, recreating the scene. 'How would you have felt if someone had done that to you?'

He didn't answer.

'Given that no one around here knows a lot about you, I get the impression that you're a private person too, Brodie,' I fumed. 'Like Albert, you're hiding away from the world right now, aren't you?'

'Why would you think that?' he asked, his head snapping back up.

'Never mind,' I said, refusing to spell it out for him. He was clearly still unaware that I knew any of the unsavoury details about the company he had formerly worked for or had sussed out that he was lying low as a result. 'Let's not make this about you. Think of Albert.'

Brodie bit his lip and shook his head.

'Shit,' he eventually said. 'I'll go back. I'll go and say I'm sorry.'

'You will not,' I said, blocking his path. 'You'll do no such thing.'

'Paige?' came another voice, from closer to the road.

'Who the hell is this now?' I demanded.

I ushered Brodie back along the path and found Jack's truck parked next to the Land Rover on the road.

'Oh, and Brodie,' he added when he spotted the pair of us emerging from the hidden path. 'You haven't got a flat battery again, have you, Paige?'

'No,' I said, making sure Brodie was still in front of me where I could keep an eye on him. 'I've just been visiting a friend.'

I hoped Albert was still my friend.

'I didn't even realize there was a cottage here,' Jack said, scratching his head. 'I haven't noticed it before.'

I hoped both he and his brother would soon forget it existed.

'So, what are you doing here?' he asked Brodie. 'I thought you were out on the bike.'

'He was,' I said, unlocking the Land Rover and answering on Brodie's behalf.

'I got a flat tyre and Paige kindly picked me up.'

Was that a note of sarcasm I detected?

'I was going to drive him back to Brambles,' I said, ignoring him and opening the door to drag the bike out, 'but as you're here, Jack, you can take him.'

'No, I can't,' he said, as I thrust the bike at Brodie. 'I haven't got time. I was on my way to meet Tilly.'

'I'm sure she won't mind if you're a bit late,' I said, thinking that given the longing looks I'd noticed her lavish on him, she would probably forgive him if he didn't turn up at all. I then turned my attention to Brodie. 'And regarding what you've seen in that hut this afternoon,' I said in a low voice which I hoped held enough force to carry weight, 'you need to forget about it.'

'I'm not sure I can—' he started.

'Well, you better,' I interrupted, 'for Albert's sake. If I find out you've told anyone what we've seen today, I can promise you, you'll regret it.'

It felt absurd that I was threatening him but, in that moment, I was prepared to do or say anything to protect Albert. I walked away before Brodie argued back and quickly climbed into the driving seat. Thankfully, the engine turned straight over.

'Bye then,' said Jack, looking confused as he also got ready to drive off.

I didn't pull away until he was out of sight and on the journey back to Wynthorpe my bad mood expanded tenfold. Given that I had been in Brodie's company for no more than an hour, there was an awful lot to unpack and none of it was good.

For a start he'd said he liked me and that he wanted us to go on a date. A week ago, I would have been ecstatic about that, but knowing now a little of his history and how it impacted on mine as well as those I had worked for and respected, it wasn't an option. I would, however, have gone along with it for the sake of finding out what he and Angus were cooking up, but then came his reaction to what he saw in the studio in Albert's garden and yet again what I thought I knew about him was blown out of the water.

When faced with a plethora of painted canvases you didn't look the way Brodie had looked and you didn't say the things he'd said, unless you were speaking from a place of education and understanding. So, who really was this man? Some rogue banker by day and an artist by night? And where did that potential twist in his story leave my feelings for him?

As I parked up at the hall, I had no idea where I ranked on the liking or not liking Brodie-meter but I did know that had he been more sensitive and more aware of Albert's reaction to us discovering his sister's studio and left when he had first been asked, I might have been feeling more inclined to go to the trouble of finding out.

'You must be joking,' I heard Archie say as I hung my coat by the back door and pulled off my still sodden boots. 'There's no way I'm letting you do that, Dad. You haven't got the skills for a start.'

Angus mumbled something inaudible and Archie groaned in response. What the hell had I walked in on now?

'No, she wouldn't,' Archie then said. 'She'd be furious.'

'What's going on?' I frowned, my thoughts about Brodie, Albert and Stella momentarily set aside.

'Paige,' said Archie, running a hand through his hair. 'Good. You've got a head for common sense.'

Angus shook his, but whether he was disputing Archie's words or inferring that the situation didn't require common sense, I couldn't be sure. Given it was my godfather I was dealing with, he was most likely disputing the latter.

'You don't need to bother Paige with this,' he said dismissively.

'We've just been up in the cherry picker,' Archie carried on as though his father hadn't spoken.

This was the second time the cherry picker had been mentioned since my arrival, and I felt no more inclined to be thrilled by it being dropped into the conversation now than I had the first time I'd heard it.

'We were just checking the fittings for the lights which will be going up this week,' Angus elaborated.

It was the second time the lights had been mentioned too. I had thought Archie had been joking about the hall being covered in them, but clearly not.

'And we found that some of the ornate stonework around a couple of the uppermost windows at the back is looking a little worse for wear,' Archie continued.

'So, get an expert in to quote to repair it then,' I said, frighteningly aware of what was afoot in Angus's head and wanting to express an immediate counter opinion.

'There!' Archie exclaimed, pointing at me. 'Did you hear that, Dad? Get an expert in.'

'What else would you do?' I frowned, although I already knew the answer.

'According to Dad there are no experts around here, so he's going to have a go at repairing it himself,' Archie said, confirming my fears.

'Oh, Angus,' I groaned.

'It will cost a fortune to get someone in from further afield,' he insisted, 'and it really is only minor repairs that need doing. I'm sure I can do it.'

Archie shook his head and I hoped his father wasn't penny pinching because he wasn't expecting his return from Brodie to pay off.

'You need to get a professional in,' I said to Angus. 'This is the very fabric of the building we're talking about. It's all well and good tinkering with the odd thing inside and in the garden, but you could do irreparable damage to the stone decoration. Or worse, damage that will end up costing more to repair in the long run. You should leave well alone.'

Angus looked hurt.

'You don't think I can do it,' he said sulkily.

'I *know* you can't do it,' I said back firmly. 'Stonemasons take years to train. Sticking up a bit of mortar and crossing your fingers in the hope that it won't drop off won't cut it, will it?'

'Though as you're so keen, Dad,' Archie soothingly said,

'we could ask if the stonemason, or stone carver would be willing to let you watch them work.'

'Well, I suppose you might be right,' Angus reluctantly agreed after a few seconds of deliberation.

'We'll have a look online later,' Archie further said, discreetly pocketing the key for the cherry picker. 'There's bound to be someone reasonably local who can help.'

'Help with what?' asked Catherine, as she came into the other end of the kitchen with Dorothy and the dogs close behind.

'Oh, nothing important,' said Archie, winking at me.

I took the hint and helped Dorothy set the table. As I did so, my annoyance with Brodie sprang back up again. I thought I had been even more forthright with him when I wanted him to back off at Albert's than I had just been with Angus, and yet he'd completely ignored me.

'As grateful as I am for your help, Paige,' said Dorothy, prising the cruet from my grasp, 'I can't cope with the noise.'

'What noise?' I frowned.

'The noise you're making,' said Mick who had joined us and brought Molly in with him. 'You're slamming things down as if you've got a grudge against them.'

'I'm sorry,' I said, my shoulders slumping as I fussed Bran who I realized I had so far ignored. 'I'm in a bit of a grump, I'm afraid.'

'Why are you so rattled?' Molly asked, setting out the plates with the lightest touch. 'Or should I say *who* has got you so rattled?'

'It's not your PWC, is it?' Angus asked. 'I'm still thinking about how you might be able to tempt them out. I haven't forgotten about that.'

'No,' I said, boycotting further thoughts of Albert still sitting inside Stella's studio. 'It's not them. It's your mate, Brodie, actually.'

'My mate?' Angus repeated, turning slightly pink.

'Oh, of course,' said Molly, as if she had known all along, which was impossible.

'Yes,' I huffed. 'He was very rude to Albert earlier. In fact, I'd go so far as to say Brodie has probably irrevocably damaged all the progress I've made with him so far.'

'What on earth did he do?' asked Dorothy. 'And who's Albert?'

'So, you're off Brodie now, are you?' Archie grinned.

'I was never on him,' I shot back, refusing to acknowledge the innuendo.

'Albert who?' cut in Angus. 'Not Albert Price?'

'Damn,' I swore.

In venting my annoyance over Brodie, I'd given Albert's name away. I'd bet he wasn't thinking he was lucky to have me in his life today. First, I'd interrupted him in Stella's studio and now I'd blurted out his name to everyone I currently lived with.

'Is that who you've been visiting, Paige?' Angus asked again.

'Yes,' I said, knowing there was no point denying it.

'Well, I never.' Angus laughed, slapping his hand down on the table and making the cutlery bounce.

'I take it that name means something to you, Dad?' asked Archie.

'I should say,' he said. 'If this isn't serendipity in action, then I don't know what is.'

'I don't understand,' I frowned.

'Me neither,' Archie laughed.

No one else had a clue either, so Angus sat down to explain.

'Albert Price is,' he beamed, 'or was until he retired, a renowned master stone carver. His work on both the Peterborough and Norwich cathedrals is much admired. I had no idea he still lived in the vicinity, let alone practically on our doorstep.'

'Well, I never,' Archie laughed again, the sound almost identical to his father's familiar chuckle. 'What are the odds of that?'

'I don't believe it,' I frowned, trying to team up the image of the elderly man I knew with someone capable of carving huge stones and carrying out intricate repairs.

I couldn't quite make it fit, but then I hadn't matched fussy doily lover Stella to those flamboyantly coloured canvases either, had I?

'This is wonderful.' Angus smiled at me. 'We've killed two birds with one stone, haven't we? No pun intended.'

'What are you talking about, Angus?' Catherine asked.

Angus briefly explained about the repairs which needed doing.

'And if Paige,' Archie added, cottoning on, 'suggests that

Dad's going to do the repairs himself to Albert, then he's bound to want to take a look. This might be how you can get your friend further than his front door, Paige!'

'Oh, Angus, you're not really going to try and do the work yourself, are you?' Catherine cried.

'No,' he said sheepishly. 'Of course not, but Paige can say that as a ruse, my dear.'

'You know, you might be right,' I said, thinking it over and ignoring the fact that Albert had now already ventured further than his front door because it had only been a few steps down the garden path. 'It's worth a try, but I'll have to be discreet. I don't want to let on that I've been talking to you about him . . .'

'You'll find a way,' said Molly.

I was flattered that she had such faith in me.

'If only we could find a way to smooth the way for you and Brodie so easily, too,' she then cheekily added. 'To begin with I thought it might be Jack who stole your heart, but even though I don't know much about him, I'm guessing that Brodie—'

'Don't worry about Brodie,' I snapped, ignoring Archie's guffaw. 'I've recently discovered something about him which makes us entirely incompatible, so no one's heart is going to be stolen this Christmas.'

'You have?' Molly frowned.

'Yes,' I said, wondering if Angus was feeling worried about the turn the conversation had taken. 'In fact, that combined with something he did this afternoon has made me seriously question whether we can even be friends.'

'Oh, no,' said Molly, sounding more upset than I would have expected. 'That's terrible.'

Given that I had hardly talked to her about him, I had no idea why she should be so put out. I wondered if she'd somehow read my tarot cards without my permission and deciphered more than she should.

'It's no big deal.' I shrugged.

'So, what have you found out about him then?' Archie asked curiously. 'Jack has never really said much about him other than that he's going through a rough time and has come to Wynbridge for a bit of time out.'

'Jack said pretty much the same to me,' I said, thinking of our conversation at the distillery ahead of my aborted tour. 'I know now that Brodie has a very particular reason for wanting to take some time out . . .'

'So,' Angus loudly interrupted, 'what are you going to say to Albert to tempt him to come and look at our deteriorating stonework then?'

I looked at him and shook my head. Obviously, he *was* concerned I'd been going to spill the beans.

'If he's half the craftsman you say he is,' I told him, 'then telling him that you're going to bodge it should get him moving, shouldn't it?'

'Yes,' Angus agreed, sounding put out that his determination to change the subject had prompted such a rude remark. 'I suppose it should.'

Chapter 19

The storm had pretty much blown itself out by the time I went to bed, but my head was every bit as tempest tossed as the garden and grounds around Wynthorpe Hall had been. I was certain, given his reaction when the subject came up, that Angus hadn't wanted me to tell everyone what I'd discovered about Brodie and that didn't bode well. It more than implied that he was up to mischief and I would have bet my last few pounds in the bank that whatever the pair of them were scheming had nothing to do with the Winter Wonderland.

And then there were my thoughts about Albert to realign, not to mention my concerns that he'd been knocked off his feet on the walk back to the cottage. I was tempted to call and check up on him, but forced myself to stop catastrophizing (something I was becoming better at, in spite of the current hiatus) and considered it might be more beneficial to give him some space, even though my head was full of questions.

I was amazed to think that Albert had once been a master

stone carver and that he had an incredibly artistic sister with a fondness for crocheted doilies. Neither were professions or pastimes I would have imagined either of them having. And, if I had been so wrong about the Price siblings, had I made further mistakes about Brodie too?

There were multiple deliveries to make on Tuesday, including a stack of flat-packed boxes which Kathleen was lending to Alice, who was getting ready for her move to town.

'I knew this lot would come in handy for someone else one day,' Kathleen told me as she helped me load them. 'That's why I hung on to them.'

'And you never know,' I said, wedging the last of them into place behind the front seats, 'you might want to use them again yourself, mightn't you?'

Kathleen looked at me and laughed.

'What?' I frowned.

'Sorry,' she said. 'I thought you were joking. Why on earth would I want to leave Wynbridge? Why would anyone ever want to leave Wynbridge? You can't tell me you don't feel the connection, Paige. You've been coming here all your life, haven't you? And it's pulled you back again now and my guess is, right when you need it.'

'That's true,' I conceded, wondering if she was actually as perceptive as Molly, although in a less obvious way, 'and even though the majority of my visits when I was growing up were centred around the hall, I always loved coming into the town and now, of course, it's even better.'

'It is?' Kathleen asked, sounding surprised.

'Oh, yes,' I said. 'It was lovely before, but with all the changes to the shops and businesses and the stronger sense of community bringing everyone together it's an even lovelier place to visit now.'

'So, you could say,' Kathleen smiled, 'that you're even happier to be here now than you were before?'

Had it not been for Brodie then inconveniently striding out of The Cherry Tree Café and popping into my line of sight, I would have told Kathleen I was indeed far happier but then, I could hardly take out his shortcomings on the wonderfully improved town, could I?

'I am,' I therefore agreed, as I jumped back into the Land Rover. 'It's a really fantastic place.'

Appeased by my response, she waved me off and I headed out of town by the fastest route possible. I had an idea forming about when I would talk to Brodie and what I would say and it certainly didn't involve a bungled conversation in the packed market square.

I had lots of calls to make that day, all of them equally important and involving endless cups of tea, but one was more memorable than the others.

'I'm sure I could hear something rattling in the pipe when I used it this morning,' an elderly lady called Daisy worriedly told me as she showed me her washing machine. 'I've tried ringing all the plumbers listed in the local trade magazine but no one's got back to me.'

'I'm not sure I'll be able to do anything,' I said cautiously, because washing machine repairs were way beyond my capabilities, 'but I'll take a look.'

'It's the drain thingy,' she said, pointing at the pipe in question. 'I'm worried there's something stuck in there and if it gets wedged and blocks it, the machine will flood.'

I pulled the outlet pipe out and squinted into it.

'I can't see anything,' I said, giving the pipe a squeeze, 'but there is something in there. I can feel it. It's a few inches down.'

Daisy squeezed it too.

'Oh,' she said, turning pink. 'I think I might know what that is.'

She bustled off and came back with a wire coat hanger which she was hellbent on bending out of shape.

'See if you can hook this around it?' she said, handing me the wire and taking hold of the pipe.

It took some manoeuvring, but little by little the bump in the pipe shifted until it was high enough for me to flick it out with a flourish. Without thinking, I raised my hand and caught whatever it was that had been causing the trouble.

'There,' said Daisy. 'I've been looking for these for months. I even had a new set fitted when I resigned myself to the fact that they were lost for good.'

I opened my hand and found a set of dentures in my palm. A top set, not that it mattered.

'I must have left them in my cardigan pocket,' Daisy tutted, scooping them up and rinsing them at the sink. 'These new ones have never fitted the same.'

She deftly swapped the new for the old and having refitted the pipe and washed my hands, I beat a hasty retreat, just about managing to stave off my laughter until I had driven off. Thankfully, the rest of the drop-offs were without the same level of drama. Last call of the day was to Alice who was looking forward to her imminent move to town.

'I don't think I'll need half of these,' she said, as she shifted her youngest a little higher on her hip and I carried the boxes in. 'I haven't got much because I left my last place in such a rush; I could only take what I could carry and with the kids, that wasn't a lot.'

'But you've been given things since then, haven't you?' I reminded her as I looked around. 'You might have more than you think.'

'That's true,' she said. 'Everyone has been so kind.' It upset me that she sounded so surprised and gave me a further insight into her previous life. 'I can't wait to get into town now.'

'Kathleen said the flat is perfect.' I smiled. 'And I'm looking forward to seeing it. Although you probably won't need me to deliver there, will you?'

'It is perfect,' she confirmed happily, then added with a blush, 'And no, I most likely won't, but I'm hoping we'll keep in touch.'

'Me too,' I said, thinking how nice it was that the suggestion had come from her. 'I'd really like that.'

'And Saffron hasn't stopped going on about Molly and

her magic cloak,' Alice laughed, 'so I'm hoping we'll see her again too.'

'Oh, I'm sure you will,' I told her. 'Molly is always popping up where you least expect her.'

'I'm not used to having friends,' she then blurted out, confirming what I'd pretty much guessed. 'I'm probably going be crap at it.'

'You won't be,' I insisted. 'But I'm someone prone to keeping myself to myself, so I'm out of practice too. I've only really got Molly and now you.' I nudged her and she smiled. 'So, are you all sorted for the day of the move?' I asked, not wanting to make too much of the heart to heart.

'Yes,' she said. 'Chris and Marie Dempster and their son have offered to help me because they've got a van.'

'That's great,' I said, thinking how much stress that would eliminate and how kind it was given how busy the family were with their own businesses. 'And you know you can ring me if you get stuck with anything, don't you?'

'Thank you,' she said. 'Everyone's been so helpful.'

'It's that sort of place.' I nodded, pulling out my phone. 'Now, you have got my number, haven't you?'

When I glanced at the screen, I noticed I had a missed call from Albert.

'Yes,' she said. 'You gave it to me when I said I sometimes get a bit jittery at night.'

'I'm sure that will change when you're living in town.'

'I think you're right,' she said. 'In fact,' she added, 'I'm feeling less worried and a little more confident every day.'

'Oh, Alice,' I said, as the little one she was holding called Tansy, wriggled to be put down. 'You're an inspiration. Do you know that?'

'Me?' Alice laughed, turning red.

'Yes, you,' I insisted. 'Wynbridge is full of strong women and your moving to town will mean the place has gained another one. I think you're amazing.'

I left her looking pensive and I hoped she could see the value of the choices she'd made and the brave action she'd taken which was already benefitting her children's lives as well as her own.

I sat in the Land Rover outside her gate and took a deep breath before listening to the message Albert had left for me. It was a huge relief to hear that I wasn't banished and that he wanted to see me.

'Perfect timing,' he said, as he opened the door when I arrived. 'The kettle has just boiled so you can make us a brew. No Bran?' he added, looking around me.

'No,' I said, feeling relieved that we seemed to have slipped back into our former way of talking with no awkwardness or ill feeling. 'Not today. I couldn't fit him in with all the deliveries and to be honest, he doesn't seem quite so desperate to stick to my side these days.'

I hadn't really noticed it before, but he was definitely shadowing me less. If he thought I was making progress, then I must have been moving on.

'You had a lot to drop off then?' Albert asked.

'Crikey, yes,' I puffed. 'I can't believe how quickly

everyone gets through so much fresh stuff, which reminds me,' I added, dashing back out again.

'What have you got there?' Albert frowned.

'Three carrots, two parsnips and a swede,' I told him. 'I found them rolling about under the seat so they must have fallen out of one of the boxes. Chris had overfilled a few.'

'I can't abide swede,' Albert said sniffily, screwing his face up which made me laugh.

'You won't even know it's there when I've finished with it,' I told him, flicking the kettle on again. 'How do you fancy soup for your dinner?'

I enjoyed having something productive to do and with the soup simmering and the tea things washed up and put away, Albert called me through to the sitting room where he'd set a match to the fire.

Bella was curled up on his lap and the scene was one of blissful domestic harmony. It was as if the time in the Nissen hut had never happened and the studio didn't exist. I had been tempted to look to see if I could spot it when I arrived, but Albert had been so quick in opening the door, I hadn't dared.

'So,' he said, reaching down the side of the chair and pulling out the printed papers I'd previously left, 'let me tell you why I've asked you to come.'

'Have you decided on a bath chair?'

'Almost.' He nodded. 'Or at least, I reckon I have. What do you think of these inflatable contraptions?'

We spent a while looking at the two he was most keen

on and, once he'd made up his mind, I said I'd order it and promised to be on hand when it was delivered. With it all settled, I blitzed the soup and warmed a couple of the part-baked crusty baguettes I'd picked up in my original shop.

'Don't do that bread for too long,' Albert called through to me. 'My teeth can't cope with it when it's rock hard.'

That set me laughing again about what had occurred at Daisy's, but I didn't share the anecdote. We enjoyed our meal and Albert didn't once mention the swede and when everything was cleared away again, we sat listening to the crackle of the fire.

'Are you all right?' he asked after a few minutes had passed. 'If you keep frowning like that, the lines will stick. That's what Stella always used to say.'

I hadn't realized I had been frowning and when I looked at him, I noticed his cheeks had flushed a little at the mention of his sister. I wondered if he'd been going as far out of his way not to mention her as I had.

'Have you got something on your mind?' he asked. 'If you're working your way up to asking about the studio, I'd rather you didn't.'

'No,' I told him. 'It's not that.'

'Good,' he said. 'I appreciate that, because I'd hate for us to fall out, but I can tell there's something. What is it?' he further probed. 'Trouble in paradise?'

'Trouble where?' I laughed.

'Paradise,' he repeated. 'Have you and your young man had a falling out?'

'I haven't got a young man.' I further frowned.

'That chap who came here with you the other day. Are you not stepping out together, as we used to say in my day?'

'Goodness me, no,' I hastily corrected him. 'Absolutely not.'

Perhaps I wasn't the only one guilty of making assumptions.

'Shame,' Albert said, eyeing me speculatively. 'Because for all his pushy ways, you made a handsome couple.'

I rolled my eyes at that.

'What is it that's on your mind, then?'

I had actually been thinking about Brodie, but thought I'd try to use Albert's gift of an opportunity to my advantage.

'It's Wynthorpe Hall,' I said, shaking my head, 'and Angus, my godfather.'

'Is he up to mischief again?' Albert smiled.

'You know about his impish antics, do you?'

'I can't imagine there's a soul for miles who doesn't. What's he up to that's got you so vexed? More Christmas tomfoolery? Mr Connelly's Christmas reputation is legendary in these parts.'

I couldn't help but laugh at that. Mr Connelly's Christmas Reputation would be a great film title. Or even a stage play. A farce, of course.

'Surprisingly,' I smiled, 'it's not his idea of festive fun that's got me worried.'

'Oh?'

'It's the hall,' I sighed. 'There's some stonework around the top windows on one side that needs some attention and Angus has got it into his head that he can fix it himself.'

Albert's horrified expression was exactly the reaction I'd been hoping for.

'Why isn't he looking to get an expert in?' he demanded.

'He reckons there aren't any around here and it will be too expensive to have someone come from further afield.'

'It might cost a bit,' Albert said wisely, 'but if the daft beggar makes a hash of it, which he undoubtedly will, it will end up costing more than double to fix it.'

'You sound like an expert, Albert,' I said, but he didn't take the bait.

'It's just common sense.'

'That's what Archie, his son, said.' I sighed again. 'But you've heard what Angus is like and once he's got a bee in his bonnet about something, he always sees it through. Shall I make another pot of tea?' I said, standing up. 'Then I'd better get off. It's getting late.'

I left him to mull over what I'd said and busied myself in the kitchen, checking there was still plenty of food in the fridge freezer and cupboards. As well as trying to get Albert to spread his wings a little I was going to have to get him officially added to Anna's rota.

'How's that tea coming on?' he called to me.

'All done,' I said, carrying it through. 'And there are biscuits too. That should keep you going for a while.'

I sat back down, ostensibly to retie the laces on my boots, but really to see if he was going to say anything further. I was on tenterhooks waiting to find out if my subterfuge had worked.

'You know,' he said, 'I used to do that job.'

'What job?'

'Stonemason.'

'You were a stonemason?' I asked, sounding suitably surprised.

'A stone carver actually,' he said, his chest swelling with pride.

'Oh, Albert,' I said. I was already genuinely in awe having made an online search of the work stone carvers carried out. 'That's amazing. Stone carving requires so much skill. It must have taken years to learn how to do it.'

'I worked in the trade for nigh on five decades.'

'My goodness,' I gasped. 'That's a lifetime. You must have loved the work to do it for that long.'

'Well,' he said, his chest deflating and his tone losing its former lightness, 'I don't know about that, but my father told me at fifteen that he knew where there was an apprenticeship going and that it would be a solid career for life. And he was right.'

That was the second time since my arrival in Wynbridge that a man had told me their father had played a part in influencing their careers. I wondered if Albert's father had been as demanding as Brodie's?

'So given that you gave almost fifty years of your life to the craft,' I said with emphasis, 'you must have a pretty good idea of what's what.'

'I suppose,' he said, sounding suspicious.

'Look,' I wheedled, 'I know it's a lot to ask, but would

you consider taking a look at the bit of hall Angus has set his sights on . . . defacing?'

Albert winced at the word, which had been my intention.

'Can't you get photos?' he asked.

'I don't think so,' I said. 'Certainly not of the quality you'd need to make a detailed assessment.'

'In that case, I'm sorry.' He shrugged. 'There's nothing I can do.'

'It's such a shame.' I sighed. 'I hate the thought of any part of the hall being compromised. It's such a beautiful building and having recently seen some of Angus's handiwork for myself . . .'

'I know it's a beautiful place,' Albert said. 'I've visited in the past. And it's historically important too. He really shouldn't be touching any of it given its listed status.'

'I'm sorry you can't help, Albert,' I further said, 'because you really do sound like someone who could convince him of that.'

'I'm not up to climbing ladders.'

I daresay ladders hadn't been climbed to do the work he used to carry out in a very long time.

'Angus has a cherry picker which he uses to reach the top of the hall,' I countered. 'I wouldn't dare go up in it, but I imagine you must have worked at some heights in your time.'

'Almost as high as the sky sometimes,' Albert reminisced.

'So, the top of Wynthorpe Hall would be a doddle for you, wouldn't it? And I would have thought there'd be a generous consultancy fee involved.'

'I wouldn't want paying,' Albert sniffed and I knew he was warming to the idea.

'I could drive you there and back,' I added temptingly, 'and it really wouldn't take any time at all.'

'And you wouldn't try to trick me into making a detour to go somewhere else?'

'Oh, Albert.' I swallowed, upset to hear the vulnerability in his tone. 'Of course not.'

'Because if I do agree to do it, it'll be straight there and back with no funny business in between.'

'I wouldn't dream of trying any funny business,' I sincerely told him. 'I just want to save the hall from a great dollop of mortar being applied in the wrong place.'

Albert shook his head at the prospect.

'All right,' he eventually said, 'I'll come.'

I resisted the urge to jump up and punch the air and settled for giving him a kiss on the cheek instead.

'There's no need to go overboard about it,' he said, but with a smile, 'and I can't be away for too long because Bella's not used to me going out.'

'We'll be there and back in a flash,' I promised, thrilled that I was finally helping him break free from the confines of the cottage.

Chapter 20

Everyone was thrilled when I told them that I'd managed to convince Albert to visit the hall the very next day. I had craftily told him that Angus was in a rush to make the repairs before the Christmas lights went up and the sooner the assessment could be made the better. The reality was that I didn't want to give him time to stew over the excursion and change his mind and therefore felt the diminutive deception was justified.

During dinner that evening, I reminded everyone that Albert was never to know that I had been talking about him or that it had been my intention to get him away from the cottage to broaden his horizons again.

'He's coming in a purely professional capacity,' I said for about the hundredth time. 'And it will only be a flying visit. I doubt we'll even get him inside the hall.'

'I'm going to prepare a high tea,' Dorothy said as if she hadn't heard a word.

'There's no need,' I insisted. 'Because Albert won't be coming in.'

'No harm in being prepared just in case though,' she smiled. 'And if he doesn't, I'm sure it won't go to waste.'

'You know you can rely on me to put it out of sight.' Archie winked.

'And me,' Angus added.

'Now,' Dorothy mused, 'shall I make savoury scones or sweet?'

'Both,' chorused the Connelly men, in perfect synchronicity.

'I suppose I could,' she agreed. 'Kathleen has given me her recipe which cuts some of the calories so I don't suppose the seams on your Santa suit would be in too much jeopardy if you had one of each, Angus.'

We all exchanged stunned looks, but no one said a word. Clearly, a ceasefire in hostilities had occurred but no one spoke for fear of ending it.

The kitchen had more cakes than Jemma's display counter in The Cherry Tree Café by the next afternoon and Dorothy was wearing the Christmas motif patterned apron Santa had gifted her from the advent calendar that morning, to add the finishing touches to them. The big man really was in tune with the Wynthorpe Hall goings on.

'I'll see you in a bit,' I said as I nervously got ready to go and collect Albert.

Bran had sensed something had got me jittery again and was insistent that he should come along.

'The cherry picker is all right, isn't it?' I asked Archie, as I turned the key in the Land Rover ignition.

'It's just been serviced,' he reassured me, sounding serious for once. 'Albert will be completely safe.'

'Good,' I said, letting out a breath. 'Right, here we go,' I added and set off with my heart hammering in my chest.

'I'm almost ready,' said Albert when I arrived at the cottage. 'I wasn't sure I'd still get into these, but I must have lost a bit of weight during the last few months.'

He was just stepping into a smart pair of navy overalls and they looked more than roomy. Given that he'd been eating hardly enough to keep a sparrow alive when I first met him, I thought he'd probably lost more than a bit of weight.

'You look very smart, Albert,' I told him. 'Is that a tie I can see under your pullover?'

'Of course,' he said. 'Now, where did I put my keys?'

With Bella settled and after stepping up into the cab with the help of an old apple crate, Albert fussed Bran and then settled in his seat. I had expected him to be a bit edgy given how long it was since he'd been properly out, along with what I'd experienced of his former reluctance to leave, but he didn't seem fazed at all. His hands were a little shaky, but that appeared to be the extent of his nerves and I realized I was more stressed than he was.

'This is a bit of all right, isn't it?' he said, looking around as I negotiated the Fenland roads back to the hall. 'I like being this high up. You can get a good look at everything.'

I made sure I took my time so he could take in the wintry landscape.

'Do you drive, Albert?' I asked.

'I used to,' he told me. 'Would you look at that?' he then gasped, as he spotted a hare pelting across a fallow field at full speed. 'I wish I could shift as fast as that.'

'Me too,' I agreed. 'I'd get loads more done every day.'

'You do more than enough, gal,' he said, giving me a rosy-cheeked smile.

'I do try.' I swallowed. 'I like to keep busy.'

'But you shouldn't be busy all the time,' he said sagely. 'Thinking time is every bit as important as doing time, you know.'

'When did you get to be so wise?' I smiled.

'It's taken over eighty years to hone my intelligence,' he chuckled.

'What are you like?' I laughed along with him. 'Now, here we are. Hold on to your hat, Albert, because the drive has seen better days.'

His teeth were positively rattling by the time I parked, but his first glimpse of the hall again had elicited the same response as mine had been just a few weeks before.

'What a place,' he said, his eyes roving over the fabulous façade, elaborate chimneys and mullioned windows. 'We mustn't let Angus gets his mitts on this exterior, Paige.'

'That's why we need you, Albert,' I said, reminding him of his importance. 'If anyone can make him see sense, you can. I've had a look into your former line of work. There's more to it than wielding a chisel, isn't there?'

'I should say so,' he said. 'Now, help me out and we'll see what's what.'

My fears that Albert might succumb to anxiety began to evaporate as he shook hands with Angus, Archie and Mick. Once they'd made their way over to the cherry picker, he donned the hard hat Archie offered and then turned to discreetly wave me off and they disintegrated completely.

'You could go and help Molly and Dorothy set out the tea,' Archie called over to me. 'I'm sure we'll all be in need of a bite to eat by the time we're done out here, won't we? What do you reckon, Albert?'

'I think you might be right, my lad,' he amazed me by responding and, letting Archie's tongue-in-cheek chauvinistic divvying up of the jobs pass, I practically skipped across the courtyard.

'So,' I said, when the four men eventually returned to the kitchen, had washed their hands and I'd helped Albert out of his overalls, 'what's the damage? You've been out there for ages. I hope that's not an indication of how bad things are.'

'We've been so long,' beamed Angus, 'because we were giving Albert a tour of the grounds as well as looking at the stone work I was so worried about.'

'Oh,' I said, surprised.

'What a place,' Albert said again, looking even pinker than he had before. 'The gardens are a credit to you, Mick. In my line of work, I came to appreciate structure and form and now pretty much everything's dormant that's exactly what you can see out there in the planting. It's beautiful.'

'Thank you, Albert,' said Mick.

I looked at Albert and something about what he had just

said niggled. It didn't have time to develop, however, because Dorothy thrust a cake stand into my hands, Molly set out the last of the cups and saucers and the ritual of tea began.

'So, all in all your fears were unfounded,' Catherine said to Angus as Albert explained in layman's terms what he had discovered.

'Not entirely,' Angus corrected.

'There's work to be done,' said Albert, 'but nothing that can't be left until the spring and I know just the person who can help.'

Catherine looked relieved.

'It's not you, is it, Mr Price?' Molly smiled at him.

'No, my love,' he said. 'My days as a stone carver are long over.'

'But I can tell you've still got the desire to create within you,' she said and I felt that niggle irritate again.

'Can you now?' he said, his smile faltering for the first time since he'd arrived.

Once tea was over, I expected to take Albert back to the cottage, but he informed me that there had been a change of plan.

'Angus has offered to show me around inside,' he said. 'I won't be able to manage all of the stairs, but there's still plenty to see. Do you think Bella will be all right? I can postpone it if you think she's missing me?'

I was delighted that Albert's original brief foray back out into the world was turning into an entire excursion.

'I think Bella will still be fast asleep,' I reassured him. 'She won't even notice you're not there. This is the perfect time to look around, Albert.'

Reassured, he, Angus and Catherine set off into the main hall.

'What a lovely man,' said Molly as she and Archie pulled on their coats to walk back to their cottage in the woods. 'I can see why you were so drawn to him, Paige.'

'I was lost,' I reminded her. 'And stopped to ask for directions. It was just a fluke that it was Albert's cottage I happened to stop at.'

'There are no such things as flukes, or coincidences,' Molly patiently reminded me.

'The universe guides us to exactly where we need to be,' Archie carried on, quoting word for word what she was going to say next, 'at exactly the time we need to be there.'

'Well,' I said, rolling my eyes at the pair of them, 'that's as maybe. I'm just pleased I've been able to help him get back on his feet.'

'Which proves my point exactly,' Molly sighed happily.

'Do you think Albert's the reason I came to the hall?' I asked her.

'I think there are lots of reasons why you came,' she said dreamily. 'Some still to be revealed. And don't forget you've been helping more people than just that dear man since you arrived.'

'So many more,' Archie agreed, sounding sincere for the second time that day.

'I do hope you appreciate the value of what you're doing here, Paige.' Molly frowned. 'I know it's very different to your former work, but it's no less valid.'

'I know,' I said, but sometimes I did wonder if the little things were enough. 'And it's keeping me out of mischief while I'm here,' I added, trying to lighten the moment.

'Um,' Molly said, 'I'm not so sure about that.'

'She's still getting into mischief, you mean?' Archie grinned.

'No,' said Molly. 'I'm beginning to wonder about how long she'll be here.'

'Not much longer,' I said. 'I'll be off after Christmas and as soon as Anna and Hayley take up their roles again and that's only about three weeks away now, so . . .'

'We'll see,' said Molly, with a twinkle in her eye. 'Come on, Archie.'

It was curious that Molly had suggested I might not be leaving as soon as I had originally planned because the tiniest seed of an idea had been sown since I had met Alice and I had started to wonder if there might be scope for me to utilize, enhance and put into practice again the knowledge I had gained while working with Chadia on the women's empowerment projects. The seed hadn't yet germinated, but it was there, poised and waiting for the ideal conditions to burst out of its coat and put down roots.

Albert's tour of the hall lasted until it was almost dark and with him teetering to accept Catherine's offer of dinner, I volunteered to drive back to the cottage to check on Bella to help him make up his mind. I knew he wouldn't be able to relax with thoughts of her filling his head so it seemed the most practical solution.

'Are you sure?' He frowned, when I suggested it. 'It feels like a huge imposition.'

'I really don't mind,' I told him. 'I'll be no time at all and then you'll be able to properly enjoy the evening.'

'I can't believe I'm doing this,' he said, sounding amazed at his own daring. 'I have you to thank for this, Paige.'

'No, you don't,' I told him. 'This is all down to you, Albert, and your decision to try and help save this old hall from Angus's well-intentioned handiwork.'

'Well,' he said, looking quite transformed, 'when you put it like that.'

Just as I'd known she would be, Bella was fast asleep in her basket under the radiator in lieu of the fire being lit. I refreshed her food, gave her a fuss and resisted the temptation to go and peek through the windows of the studio in the garden.

Had it still been daylight I might have succumbed and I wasn't proud of that admission, but there were a few things I'd heard Albert say, comments of an artistic kind, which had got me wondering if I could find a way to check out the real provenance behind the many canvases tucked away in the unlikely looking studio.

However, I turned my back on the place, forced myself up the path and into Anna's Fiat, returning to the hall, feeling slightly spooked because a large vehicle had followed me all the way. Right up the drive and into the courtyard, in fact.

'Brodie,' I said, breathing a sigh of relief when I realized it was him and in spite of the fact that he wasn't flavour of the month. 'What are you doing here?' I asked, moving to halt his progress towards the hall.

With Albert inside, I had no intention of granting Brodie entry. I might have had the willpower to resist peeking into the studio, but I didn't know if he would be able to resist asking about the paintings again. Given his initial reaction to them, I didn't think it was worth the risk.

'Don't worry,' he said gruffly, clearly still feeling the sting of our previous parting, 'I'm only going to be a minute.'

I didn't budge.

'What are you doing?' he frowned. 'I need to talk to Angus.'

'He's in a meeting,' I said, 'a private, family one. That's why I was out,' I lied. 'To give them a bit of space.'

'Oh,' he said, looking over my shoulder towards the hall. 'I hope everything's okay?'

'I'm sure it is.' I nodded. 'I'll tell him you stopped by.'

He ran a hand through his hair.

'Was there something else?' I asked when he didn't move.

'Your friend,' he said, 'the chap with the studio.'

'I know who you're talking about,' I snapped.

'Have you seen him?'

I looked at my feet.

'I've been thinking about him,' he carried on, 'about how I would have felt if I'd been in his shoes and I feel terrible. I was so rude and I genuinely didn't mean to be. I've been thinking about going back . . .'

'There's no need,' I quickly cut in. 'I have seen him and he's been fine about it.'

'He has?'

'He has.'

'Oh, thank God,' Brodie said, smiling.

'So, there's no reason for you to go back,' I further insisted. 'In fact, I know he'd prefer it if you didn't.'

'All right,' he agreed. 'The last thing I want to do is further jeopardize you being able to help him.'

'I appreciate that,' I said, thinking it would be so much easier to permanently switch off my feelings for him if he was consistently blunt and bad mannered. This thoughtful Brodie was still frustratingly appealing in spite of my knowledge about the questionable work he had once been involved in. 'I'd better get on.'

'I don't suppose there's any chance we could still go out for that drink, is there?' he asked, sounding hopeful.

'There is,' I said, because I did still need to talk to him, although it would have to happen somewhere more private than in The Mermaid in town and certainly not on the Wynthorpe drive with Albert in the vicinity. 'I'll call you at the distillery.'

'All right,' he said, 'but I'll see you tomorrow, anyway.'

'You will?' I frowned.

'Yes,' he said, 'for the greenery gathering.'

I had no idea what that was. I knew there was a Christmas tree auction and bake sale happening on Saturday in Wynbridge and that it was too early for the solstice celebration, but a greenery gathering did sound a bit like a Pagan rite.

'Apparently, we're gathering holly and ivy to sell at the auction on Saturday,' he elaborated, 'and mistletoe, of course. Jack has told me that the greenery is collected in the woods here and then sold in town. I thought you'd know that, what with it being a Wynthorpe tradition?'

'It must be a new one,' I said, feeling embarrassed that he knew more than me. 'Something that has started since I last visited. So how come you're involved?' I then truculently asked.

'Jack helped last year and with fewer people here than usual, Angus has invited me to join in too. I was planning to tell him that I'll definitely be here,' he said, looking over my shoulder at the hall.

'You could have called about that,' I pointed out.

'I needed to see him about something else, too.'

The return from the jackpot my godfather was expecting him to hit, no doubt.

'Well, I'm sorry you can't, but I'll happily pass on a message.'

'No,' he said, 'it's okay. Thanks, though. I'll talk to him about it tomorrow.'

It was cold standing outside, but I didn't go in until I had watched him drive away and was certain he was off the premises.

'Would you like some mulled wine, Paige?' Angus offered during dinner, as he poured more into Albert's glass.

'No, thanks,' I declined. 'I'll be driving later, so I'll pass.'

'I'll take Albert home if you like,' offered Mick, who never drank alcohol. 'That is, if it's all right with you, Albert?'

'Yes,' he said, turning his attention to Mick. 'That's fine with me. This whole afternoon has been an adventure and I'm feeling quite giddy having already changed plans once this afternoon. Another deviation from the schedule won't hurt.'

'I think you'll find the giddiness is down to Angus's wine,' I laughed, noticing Albert's flushed complexion. 'He makes it rather strong.'

'You know,' Albert cheerfully said, looking into his glass, 'I think you might be right.'

It made my heart soar to see him so changed from the man I had first met and I made a mental note to ask Mick to see him safely all the way up the stairs when he took him back to the cottage, just in case he got carried away and tried to take them two at a time.

Chapter 21

After the delicious dinner, Dorothy retired to her room and Mick went to check the ponies which just left Catherine, Angus, Albert and me. Albert had insisted that with his old bones so relaxed he could make it up the stairs to the family sitting room and we were all soon settled around the fire, with the dogs at our feet. Angus handed round generous measures of brandy in elegant balloon glasses, which after the wine, I felt none of us needed, but we all accepted anyway.

'So, Albert,' said Angus, sitting down heavily on the sofa next to Catherine after stoking the fire, 'tell me more about your work. You had a hand in working on both cathedrals and castles during your career, didn't you?'

'I did.' Albert nodded. 'I had the good fortune of working on some of the most beautiful buildings this country has to offer.'

'Including here now.' I smiled. 'In a roundabout sort of way.'

'Indeed.' He smiled back, raising his glass to toast the comment.

'I can't begin to imagine how long it must have taken you to learn the skills to work at such a high standard,' Angus continued.

'Years,' said Albert. 'Decades really.'

'You clearly had a passion for it,' Catherine said.

Albert looked thoughtful, then he set his glass down and laced his fingers together in his lap.

'You'd think so, wouldn't you?' He swallowed. 'But in truth, my passion lay elsewhere. Don't get me wrong, though, I was decent at my job.'

'One of the best,' Angus interjected.

'Perhaps,' Albert graciously said, 'but it was never the thing which set my soul on fire.'

I felt my face grow warm and it wasn't because I was sitting too close to the grate.

'Was there something else that set your soul on fire, Albert?' I whispered.

'You know there was,' he said, looking straight at me. 'There still is. You've seen it.'

'Oh, Albert,' I gasped.

'What is it?' Angus frowned, looking concerned. 'What's wrong?'

'Nothing's wrong exactly,' Albert said softly. 'I've just made a confession that's been decades in the making.'

'Given that you've taken so long to say it,' I urged him, 'please don't hastily say anything else now that you might later regret. You've had more to drink tonight than you've probably had in a very long time and I'd hate for the alcohol to loosen your tongue. Please don't say things you're going to later wish you hadn't, Albert.'

Albert smiled and held out his hand. I reached for it and he squeezed my fingers tightly in his.

'It's all right,' he said simply. 'I want to explain.'

'Are you sure?'

'I am,' he said, sounding certain. 'I've been thinking about sharing this secret all week and that's down to you, Paige, and not just because you caught me out. You've banished my loneliness and given me my spark back. I thought it had been snuffed out completely after Stella died, but it wasn't and I want to embrace life again and enjoy every moment because, let's face it, at my age, I might not have many moments left. If I don't talk about this soon, I might not ever get the chance.'

'Don't say that,' I said, squeezing his hand harder.

'It's true,' he laughed, patting my hand with his free one and then letting mine go. 'Let me seize this moment and tell my story.'

Catherine and Angus had listened to our exchange and Angus's eyes were shining with excitement as he waited to hear what Albert had to say.

'I would very much like to tell you about the thing that sets my soul on fire,' my friend then began, 'but it's quite a long story.'

'Well, we would be honoured to hear it,' Catherine said kindly and Angus nodded in enthusiastic agreement.

'Yes,' he said, 'we're not going anywhere, Albert.'

'All right,' he said, pulling in a breath. 'In that case, I'll start right at the beginning.'

I felt every bit as intrigued as my godparents sounded, but I was nervous for Albert too. This was obviously a massive step he was about to take.

'There are huge parts of my entire life,' he bravely began, 'which have been twisted out of shape by the bullying of my father and his inability to let me be the person I always wanted to be.'

You could have heard a pin drop. Even the dogs had stopped snoring.

'I never wanted to be a stone carver,' Albert carried on. 'My illustrious career came about as a result of the compromise I made the summer I left school in order to keep a roof over my head and my father in good temper.'

His head dropped for a moment and I felt my heart contract.

'Oh, Albert,' I whispered, my breath catching.

'You see,' he carried on, looking up again. 'You see,' he then more loudly said, 'I was born with a paintbrush in my hand, not a chisel.'

'You're the artist,' I whispered, although I already knew and he nodded.

'An artist?' Angus echoed.

'All I ever wanted to do was paint,' Albert added, 'but my father wouldn't hear of it.'

'Whyever not?' Catherine quietly asked, sounding as affected by the emotion in Albert's tone as I was.

'Basically because of his bigoted views,' Albert said distastefully. 'He wouldn't entertain the idea of a son who wanted to be an artist. He said he'd be a laughing stock among his friends and that I would be labelled . . . well . . . I won't use any of his foul words, but I'm sure you get the gist.'

'I see,' Angus sighed.

'His homophobia was shocking,' Albert continued, 'but sadly not unique. There were plenty of people around here with similar views at that time and as a result my father flagged up the apprenticeship, as a sop to my creativity, I suppose, and I took it to keep the peace.'

'Did you ever think about leaving?' I asked. 'Weren't you tempted to move away?'

'I couldn't,' he said, sounding sad. 'I promised my mother before she died that I'd look after Stella, who was younger than me and that I'd help Dad as best I could, too. Not that I could stand him. He was a cruel man and I wouldn't have abandoned Stella to his tyranny for every easel in the world. So, I kept the vow I'd made to Mum and I stayed.'

'And in doing so,' Catherine said, 'sacrificed your paintbrushes.'

'Yes,' Albert confirmed. 'I swapped the few brushes I had managed to keep hidden from him for chisels and I didn't set them down again until the day I retired.'

'My goodness,' Angus sighed, 'half a lifetime spent working at something you didn't enjoy.'

'Oh, I did enjoy it,' Albert said. 'That was why I carried on with it after Dad had gone. The carving became adequate, although it was never enough to replace what I thought I'd lost.'

'So, the studio in your garden,' I said. 'All those paintings . . .'

'What studio is this?' Angus asked, sitting up. 'What paintings?'

'Well, now you know they're not my sister's work.' Albert chuckled. 'She couldn't paint for toffee. Her skill was with a needle and thread. Her embroidery was exquisite.'

'My goodness, Albert,' I said, it finally properly sinking in that he was the one responsible for creating the vibrantly filled canvases. 'This is incredible.'

'Yes,' he proudly acknowledged. 'It is rather, isn't it?'

'I think I need to take a look at these paintings!' Angus joined in.

'I can't believe I've just claimed them as my own,' Albert said, the colour returning to his face.

'Here,' I said, passing him his glass of brandy. 'You'd better have some of this. And I'll have more of mine too.'

We both took a restorative gulp from our respective glasses.

'So, Albert,' I said, as I felt the alcoholic warmth spread through me, 'you obviously found the courage to start painting again. How did that come about? And more to the point, how did you manage to keep an entire studio hidden in the garden?'

'I did,' he mischievously smiled, 'but the studio didn't arrive until after my father's death. You'll probably think us a terribly wicked pair,' he explained, shaking his head, 'but

Stella and I pooled the money our father left us to buy the studio and get it set up and then we filled it with everything I was going to need to catch up on all the years I'd wasted.'

'All the years you'd lost,' Angus corrected. 'They weren't wasted and their loss wasn't down to you, my friend.'

My godfather was right and I rather liked the thought of Albert and his sister creating the studio. I imagined it must have given them a great deal of excitement.

'How ironic to use your inheritance.' Catherine smiled at his daring.

'I'm surprised the old tyrant hasn't come back to haunt me.' Albert grinned. 'It took me a while to get used to not living under his rule and wake my creativity up again, but once it happened . . . Well,' he said to me, 'you've seen how many paintings there are, Paige. You know I made up for the wasted . . . I mean, lost years in the end.'

'I'm feeling jealous, Paige,' said Angus, his tone suggesting he meant it. 'You hadn't uttered a word about this studio or its contents at all.'

'I promised I wouldn't,' I told him. 'Although, Albert,' I then felt duty bound to confess, 'I did mention your name here, and once Angus had made the connection to your work and because he needed advice about the hall repairs, we felt it would be the ideal way to tempt you away from the cottage. I hope you can forgive me.'

Albert looked at me and smiled.

'Of course, I can forgive you!' he laughed. 'I know I've said it already, Paige, but you've changed my life. I can't find enough words to tell you what it means to have a warm house and a full belly again and now to have finally taken ownership of those paintings . . . well . . . it's the cherry on a very special cake.'

'Oh, Albert,' I choked. 'Do you really mean it?'

'Of course, I do,' he said. 'You've given me a whole new love of life. I stopped painting completely after Stella died, but I think I'm ready to start again now.'

'That's wonderful,' I sobbed, through a sudden torrent of tears. 'I'm so happy.'

'You look it.' He beamed and we all laughed.

It was thrilling to think that all of this change had come about as a result of me getting disorientated in the darkening Fens. Molly's words about there being no such things as flukes and coincidences popped into my head again.

'You've truly woken me back up, Paige,' said Albert, looking teary himself, 'and I'll never be able to thank you for that.'

The warm glow in my heart and the realization that I had helped to make this happen was all the thanks I was ever going to need.

'You don't need to thank me, Albert,' I said firmly, making a revelation of my own. 'Because you've helped me every bit as much as I've helped you. I came back to the hall with baggage I haven't wanted to share with anyone, but my friendship with you has lightened the load so much, that I'm ready to cast it aside now.'

'Oh, Paige,' Catherine whispered. 'We could all tell there was something . . .'

'It's fine,' I told her, feeling for the first time that it almost was. 'I made a stupid mistake at the camp which very nearly ended in disaster and then, even though it didn't have the worst possible outcome, I let it get to me and grow out of all proportion.'

'So, you didn't leave Jordan just because of the funding cuts?' Catherine asked.

'I asked Molly not to say anything about that,' I sighed. 'But not even she knows the whole of it because I haven't told her.'

'She hasn't said a word about any of it,' Angus piped up. 'It was your dad who told me the details of the changing financial situation and I was very sorry to hear about it.'

I wondered how he would feel if he knew it was his buddy Brodie's firm which had been responsible.

'I have to ask,' Catherine softly said, 'why haven't you talked to anyone about what happened, Paige? I'm sure Molly would have been able to help you work through everything in no time at all?'

I felt my eyes fill with tears.

'I suppose I was ashamed.' I shrugged. 'My actions put other people's lives at risk and I was mortified. I didn't want anyone to know what I had done. I'd rather not dwell on the details now, but I can promise you I am finally beginning to accept what happened, although I'm not quite ready to completely forgive myself just yet.'

'But no one was hurt?'

'No,' I said, 'thankfully not. The situation was quickly and safely resolved but I decided it was time for me to bow out as a result. There most likely wouldn't have been a renewed contract because of the funding cuts, but I wouldn't have been going back, even if there was. At the time I thought I'd lost my edge, but now I'm beginning to think that it was simply time for me to move on and find something new.'

'Or someone old.' Albert smiled.

'Quite.' I nodded, blinking hard.

'Well, we're delighted you decided to come here,' said Catherine. 'And I hope you'll find your something new to go with the old, in the vicinity.'

'Me too,' I agreed, then, feeling that I had said more than enough for one evening, asked, 'So when exactly are you going to start painting again, Albert?'

'And more to the point,' added Angus, 'when can I come and see what you've already done?'

'In answer to your question, Paige,' Albert announced, 'I'll be picking up a paintbrush tomorrow.'

'That's fantastic!' I smiled, raising my glass again.

'And as for your question, Angus,' Albert then said, looking at my godfather, 'I'm afraid you can't see it. I'm not going to share any of it, but if I ever change my mind, then you'll be the first to know.'

Angus looked exceedingly disappointed and I felt relieved he didn't have Albert's address. I would have to ask Mick to keep it under his hat.

'That's fair enough.' He nodded, but I got the feeling that cogs were beginning to whir.

I hoped they wouldn't whir too fast because I still had to find a way to call a halt on his and Brodie's connection and I didn't need something else to worry about on top of that. It was just ten days until the Winter Wonderland and less than a fortnight until everyone returned to the fold and I was determined to have everything on track, with none of the hall's finances jeopardized, in time for that.

'How are we doing in here?' asked Mick, popping his head around the door.

'Very well,' said Angus and Catherine gave him a look. 'How's it doing out there, Mick? Is it freezing yet?'

'No,' he said. 'I don't think there'll be a frost tonight.'

'Good,' said Catherine. 'It's the greenery gathering tomorrow so the milder the better.'

'That reminds me, Angus,' I said, only just remembering. 'Brodie dropped by earlier and said to tell you that he'll be here tomorrow and that there's something he needs to talk to you about, in person.'

His gaze shifted to Catherine for the briefest moment before he answered.

'That's great news,' he said. 'Many hands and all that. Isn't that right, Mick?'

'Absolutely,' he agreed. 'The more the merrier.'

'Well,' said Albert, putting down his glass and shifting forward in the armchair, 'I would offer to help, but I'm not as sprightly on my pins as I once was.'

'And you'll be busy tomorrow anyway,' I said with a wink as I helped him stand up.

'I certainly will,' he agreed. 'So, don't worry about calling in.'

'Are you sure?'

'Absolutely,' he insisted. 'I'll have plenty to keep me occupied.'

'Perhaps you might consider coming with me to town on Saturday though,' I suggested. 'I'd love to get you a tree for the cottage from the auction.'

'Ooh,' he said, 'I'll think about that. I didn't have any decorations up last year.'

'No decorations,' Angus gasped. 'That's a tragedy.'

'Don't worry,' said Catherine, patting his arm. 'I'm sure Albert will have a very different Christmas this year. Paige will make sure of that.'

'I will,' I confirmed.

'And perhaps you'd like to come here for Christmas day?' Angus asked, standing up. 'You'd be most welcome.'

'Something else to think about,' said Albert. 'Thank you. And thank you so much, for welcoming me to your beautiful home today.'

'You're welcome any time, Albert,' Angus insisted, shaking his hand.

'I'm hoping you'll consider overseeing the work we need doing in the spring.' Catherine smiled, standing to kiss his cheek.

'I'm sure I could help with that,' he said, looking well pleased.

'Are you certain you don't want me to come back to the cottage with you?' I asked.

'No, no,' he said, squeezing my hand. 'I'm sure Mick won't mind seeing me up the stairs.'

'I won't mind at all,' said Mick. 'I'll look after him, Paige.'

'You get off to bed, my dear,' said Albert, 'you've got a busy day tomorrow yourself.'

'That I have,' I agreed, wondering if more than greenery would end up being gathered.

Chapter 22

After thanking Albert again for his help in assessing the hall stonework, Angus saw him and Mick off and I went to bed. I slept right through the night and woke the next morning feeling such a lightness of spirit that I was almost giddy. I had to lay still for some minutes before I felt ready to risk putting my feet on the floor and standing up.

I wouldn't go as far as to say that I was free of the memory of my mistake, but I was finally more accepting of it. Errors of judgement, as regrettable as they are, do happen and I was grateful that I was now able to move on from mine.

The feeling had been growing during the previous couple of weeks and on the morning of the greenery gathering, I was ready to wholeheartedly embrace it. Whether the change was the result of the passing of time, my fledgling friendship with Alice or the joy I felt at playing a part in Albert's rediscovered love for live or even a combination of the lot, I couldn't be sure, but I was very happy to seize the moment and forge ahead.

I still had decisions to make about what I was going to do with my life when the new year dawned. There were fresh ideas forming about that but first, I had Christmas at Wynthorpe Hall to enjoy and I was determined to make the most of that most wonderful time of the year. Even the Brodie-shaped blot on the festive landscape couldn't suppress the upsurge in my spirits. My feelings for him had been well and truly stamped on but, at least I forced myself to believe, I hadn't been involved with him deeply enough to feel his loss too strongly.

'You're sounding very chipper this morning,' said Angus, when I literally waltzed into the kitchen. 'Could it be anything to do with Albert's visit by any chance?'

'It might be,' I said, then hastily added, 'But please don't forget we're not supposed to be talking to anyone about certain parts of that.'

'Have no fear,' he said, 'I'm the soul of discretion.'

I gave him a look.

'I am.' He pouted. 'You'd be surprised at the secrets I'm currently keeping.'

'Would I?' I pounced.

'You would.'

'I'd wager at least one of them has something to do with Brodie, doesn't it?' I then suggested blatantly.

My forthrightness was no doubt the result of my lightness of heart and happier mindset.

'Given that I've just told you how good I am at keeping secrets,' Angus said infuriatingly, 'I can't possibly comment on that, can I?'

'Surely you can tell me,' I said, leaning in. 'I'm discreet too.'

He lips remained tightly zipped.

'Well,' I said, stepping back, 'if it is to do with him, it can't be anything too deep and meaningful, because he's only been here five minutes. I can't imagine that you know him well enough to carry his darkest secrets, do you?'

Did he even know that Brodie had worked for Davey and Clarkson? If their collusion was of a financial variety, and what else could it possibly be, then I sincerely hoped so. I had done a little further digging about the scandalous business and, although not all employees had been named and shamed, the situation had come to a head at roughly the time Brodie had done a city bunk and turned up at Brambles. That had to be too much of a coincidence for him to be completely in the clear, didn't it?

'I know him well enough,' Angus said mildly, turning away.

'But do you know . . .' I began, before Dorothy bustled in and it was impossible to carry on.

I watched his retreating back thinking that I would separately corner him and Brodie at the gathering. I couldn't risk wasting more time trying to puzzle out what they were up to. Really, I should have dealt with it sooner, but as Molly was always so keen to remind me, things happened when they were meant to and not a moment before. I hoped, on this occasion especially, that she was right.

'Who could that be at this time?' I said, as someone rapped on the back door.

'I've drafted in some help,' Dorothy said mysteriously, then rushed off and came back in with Kathleen.

I looked from one woman to the other in surprise.

'We've settled our differences,' Dorothy said, noting my shock as she took Kathleen's coat and gloves.

'We've *almost* settled our differences,' Kathleen corrected her. 'It's early days yet.'

'But we're off to a good start,' Dorothy further stunned me by saying. 'Kathleen's been showing me how to cut some calories out of my baking without compromising on the taste . . .'

'And, to return the favour, Dorothy's offered to assist with the teaching at a couple of the dance classes now there are so many attendees,' Kathleen said in response.

I didn't know which revelation rocked me the most. Cutting calories in the cakes was surprising enough, but in the end, it was the thought of Dorothy dancing that was the real clincher.

'I didn't know you could dance, Dorothy,' I said, still looking from one woman to the other.

'Well,' she said coquettishly, 'every woman should have her secrets. Isn't that right, Kathleen?'

'Absolutely,' her former enemy eagerly agreed. 'And the more mysterious the better.'

They both laughed as if they had been co-conspirators forever and I shook my head.

'Anyway,' Kathleen said to me, 'I forgot to tell you, Paige, I've managed to get the deliveries for today covered.

I thought you might prefer to stay here and help with the gathering all day.'

'Oh, thank you,' I gratefully said. 'I wasn't expecting that.'

Her kindness would give me further time and opportunity to work on Brodie and Angus which was most welcome.

'I did offer to look after Alice's little brood,' she carried on, 'so she could come and help too, but she turned me down. I didn't mind that she said no, of course, but I thought she might appreciate the break.'

'I'm not sure she's ready to leave the children in someone else's care just yet,' I said, trying not to be indiscreet. 'I'm sure she wouldn't have meant any offence in turning you down.'

Kathleen struck her forehead.

'Of course,' she said. 'I should have realized that.'

'Are we all set?' asked Archie, as he then bounded in.

He stopped dead at the sight of Kathleen now seated at the table, drinking the tea Dorothy had just made.

'Just about,' I replied, before he said something foolish and put his foot in it. 'But where's Molly?'

'Already in the woods,' he told me, still regarding the two women suspiciously. 'And she has been for ages.'

'She isn't gathering already, is she?' I frowned.

It was barely light.

'Of course not,' he tutted, as if I should have known and when he turned his attention fully to me.

'What's she doing then?'

'Asking for permission,' he said seriously. 'She always asks before we take. The ritual is an important part of the day and guarantees another good harvest next year.'

'How's Molly getting on?' asked Angus, who miraculously reappeared now all opportunity of a conversation with just me was lost.

He looked every bit as surprised to find Kathleen in the kitchen as both Archie and I had.

'Almost done, I should think,' said Archie. 'Any chance of a bit of breakfast before we get out there, Dorothy?'

'Of course,' she huffed. 'Why do you think I'm standing here with a pan in my hand?'

While Dorothy filled us up, I mulled over the idea of checking in with Albert but then remembered he was supposed to be indulging in a late start. I hoped he didn't harbour any regrets when he woke up and recalled what he had told Catherine, Angus and me.

'So, we've cleared the air,' Dorothy was saying when I tuned back in, 'and discovered we have quite a lot in common. I'm going to help out with some of the classes.'

'And start the catering,' Kathleen, who I noticed had filled up on scrambled eggs, grilled tomatoes and mushrooms, added, 'in the new year.'

'Well, that is good news,' said Catherine, sounding relieved. 'I always thought the two of you would make fine friends if you could get over your little misunderstanding.'

'Ready,' said Molly, as she wafted in. She looked paler than usual, but sounded happy enough. 'Let the gathering begin.'

Archie jumped up.

'You need to eat something and make sure you're grounded before you head back out,' he masterfully said.

I was amazed she did as she was told and keenly tucked into the full English vegetarian option Dorothy had prepared for her. Clearly, asking the woods for permission was quite an undertaking. It had certainly given her an appetite.

'Before we head out,' said Angus, 'let's do the advent calendar. It's your turn again today, Paige.'

'Is it?' I asked, surprised.

He nodded and beckoned me over.

'I hope it's a pair of gauntlets,' I joked. 'I've seen the holly already and some of it looks pretty vicious.'

It wasn't any sort of protection from whatever Mother Nature had to share with us, but a beautiful red Moleskine lined notebook.

'It's lovely, Angus,' I said, turning it over in my hands. 'Thank you.'

'You're going to find it especially useful during the next couple of weeks,' he said, with a twinkle in his eye.

'Am I?' I asked, looking more suspiciously at the book. 'And why would that be?'

'All in good time.' He beamed. 'I can't say anything yet, but watch this space.'

'It isn't anything to do with the Winter Wonderland, is it?' Catherine asked exasperatedly. 'You did, promise, Angus . . .'

'No, my dear,' he said reassuringly. 'I can say, hand on heart, that it's absolutely nothing to do with the Winter Wonderland.'

'That's all right then,' she said, sounding relieved, but I wasn't much soothed.

'Come on,' Mick rallied us as he came in. 'We best get organized. Folk are starting to arrive.'

In the absence of Jamie, Anna, Hayley and Gabe, Angus had asked a few locals who could spare the time to help out. I already knew that Brodie was going to be a part of the group, but when he turned up in Jack's truck, I realized the old adage was wrong. Being forewarned actually offered no insurance of being forearmed at all.

'Damn,' I muttered as I surreptitiously watched him pull on a battered pair of safety boots and the equally worn wax coat.

The chunky navy jumper encasing his broad chest was the perfect foil for his thick dark hair and eyes and the fact that he hadn't shaved, cranked up the seductive man of the woods image even more. He couldn't have looked further from a city suit if he tried and I felt my breath catch as his gaze sought out mine and held it for a brief heart-stopping second, a slow smile spreading across his face.

'You all right?' Molly asked.

'Yes,' I croaked, then cleared my throat. 'Yes.' I swallowed, turning my back on Brodie. 'I'm fine.'

But I wasn't fine. There was a Brodie shaped net closing in around me and I wished I really could turn off my feelings for him, rather than pretend to myself that I already had. In spite of the fear that he may have put the Connelly finances at risk and that his behaviour at Albert's had been dreadful, I still fancied him like crazy and it was most inconvenient.

The fact that he looked like the epitome of a Hallmark hero and had now apologized for his behaviour didn't help either. My heart twanged at the sight of him and my head seemed to have little problem ignoring the red financial warning flag with a big pound sign splashed across it.

'Right,' shouted Mick. 'Let's get started.'

Angus thanked everyone for coming and then Mick and Archie organized the troops. We were assigned specific teams and I was relieved not to be in Brodie's. Even though I still needed to talk to him, I didn't think I would have a hope in hell of contributing to the event or finding out anything if I had to witness the seductive sight of him turning all hunter-gatherer.

'Come on,' said Archie, handing me a hard hat, 'we're on mistletoe duty.'

Armed with a variety of equipment, Archie, Tilly from Brambles, who had arrived with another friend, Molly and I went off in search of the trees which had the most to crop. It wasn't a particularly bright day and in places the woods felt a little foreboding. I was pleased to have woken up with such a sunny disposition. Had I not, I might have felt spooked. Tilly kept close to my side and I wondered if she felt it too.

'Jake and Amber from Skylark Farm are harvesting mistletoe from their orchard to add to ours,' Archie explained as we stopped under a poplar tree and got set up. 'It sells out quicker than the holly and ivy, so we need to gather as much as we possibly can.'

'Or as much as the trees want us to pick,' Molly said meaningfully.

Tilly didn't look as though she knew quite what to make of Molly, which I could understand.

'That's what I meant,' smiled Archie. 'Right, come on. Let's get cracking.'

Just like his father, Archie had a passion for tools and took charge of the telescopic loppers. It wasn't long before we were all warmed up and Tilly, immersed in the work, appeared far more relaxed. I wasn't though.

'Hey,' I shouted at Archie again.

He was allegedly trying his best to steady the descent of the cut bunches to maintain as many of the berries as possible but there were a couple of pieces which fell fast and unchecked, mostly whenever I was directly underneath them.

'You're supposed to shout *below* when you've cut a piece,' I testily reminded him as I readjusted my hard hat.

The bunches he'd caught me with weren't heavy, but they did gather a bit of momentum on their descent and had knocked my hat skew-whiff.

'Sorry.' He grinned.

'Yeah,' I tutted. 'You look it.'

By lunchtime, we'd gathered quite a haul and Mick collected the bags in the trailer attached to the hall quad and ferried them back to the courtyard. The three of us followed on, taking the tools with us as we probably wouldn't find them again.

The Wynthorpe woods felt bigger as we walked back and

although I had easily traced the path to Molly and Archie's cottage before, there were parts which felt unfamiliar that morning. There seemed to be something afoot too. Nothing I could grasp because I wasn't in tune like Molly, but there was definitely something off-kilter.

'How have you got on?' Angus asked, once we'd pulled off our boots and joined everyone in the packed kitchen.

It was standing room only by the time we'd washed our hands and Dorothy and Kathleen were in their element. Dorothy had prepared two batches of soup and baked bread and potatoes which she piled high with a variety of cheese and set next to Kathleen's huge trays of warm brownies and healthy flapjacks.

The level of chat was proof that everyone was enjoying themselves and the dogs skittered around and through our legs making sure no dropped crumb sullied the flagstone floor for many seconds.

'We've got on really well,' said Archie. 'Great, actually. Molly was right, the mistletoe crop is huge this year. We've filled more bags than ever.'

'So, watch out.' Molly smiled at me. 'It's bound to weave its magic and we'll all be kissing beneath it by the end of the day.'

'Anyone here you fancy locking lips with, Paige?' Archie piped up.

I ignored him and turned sharply away, bumping straight into Brodie. I heard Archie guffaw behind me and felt my cheeks turn bright red.

'Oh, no,' I gasped, as one half of the cheese-packed potato I'd just put on my plate, fell to the floor. 'I'm so sorry.'

The other half had splattered into Brodie's chest and there was a huge lump of melting Stilton stuck to the front of his lovely sweater.

'It's fine,' he said, as I reached for a paper napkin and tried to wipe it.

His chest felt solid and I blushed even brighter as I handed him the sticky serviette.

'This sweater has seen worse than a blob of Stilton,' he added, taking it from me and also turning red.

I went to apologize again, but was knocked off balance by Bran who had spotted the potato on the floor and wasn't going to leave it for either Floss or Suki to clear up. It was the classic school playground moment, when some wit comes up behind you and takes your knees out, resulting in you creasing like a pack of cards. Only in this instance, I didn't fold because Brodie caught me.

'And now I need to apologize,' he said, setting me upright again and steadying me while I abandoned the plate to the table.

In his heroic moment, he'd caught me with the Stilton-covered serviette and I had a patch to rival his on the arm of my top.

'I'd say that makes us equal,' I said, smiling up at him and then checking myself.

'And you're both going to stink,' Archie unhelpfully added. 'We're swapping teams this afternoon and I bagsy not being in either of yours.'

'I only stood to free up a chair,' Brodie told me. 'I really am sorry.'

'It's my fault,' I said, easing around him. 'I should have been looking where I was going. It would have been fine if Archie hadn't been playing the fool.'

'You still haven't answered my kissing question,' the man himself loudly said.

'I think I'll go back out,' said Brodie, clearly keen to distance himself and I could hardly blame him. 'I'm sure Mick could do with a hand stacking the bags.'

Mick was still eating but Brodie headed off anyway.

'That was not helpful.' Molly frowned, digging Archie in the ribs.

'I was just trying to give them a nudge in the right direction,' he said innocently.

I ignored them both and reached for another plate and potato wondering what I could do to avoid having to go back out and run the gauntlet of being paired up with Brodie. My sunny disposition had dipped a little as a result of the strange feeling in the woods and Archie acting up had dimmed it further. I no longer even felt inclined to carry out my plan to corner either Angus or Brodie and get to the bottom of their connection.

'Right!' shouted Mick. 'I know we all want to have a snooze now Dorothy and Kathleen have filled us up, but if we make a concerted effort, I reckon we can be done in a couple of hours.'

With work still to do, I couldn't bail and took the inevitable hand fate then dealt me squarely on the chin.

'See you later, stinky Stilton twins,' Archie laughed as he waved me and Brodie off, along with a couple of the others.

I hadn't enjoyed being bopped on the head by falling bunches of mistletoe, but cutting the holly turned out to be worse. I was pricked more than once, in spite of the thick gloves Mick had given me and I kept catching Brodie's eye without meaning to. I tried to position myself far away from him but somehow, we still ended up side by side.

It felt like far longer than a couple of hours before I heard Dorothy bashing the gong to tell us that time was up and there was tea and cake in the kitchen. To avoid further ribbing from Archie, I decided not to head back with everyone else and ducked off the path when no one was looking. I might have felt a little disconcerted by the woods that day, but what I would doubtless face in the kitchen would be far worse than being a bit spooked.

As I strode out, moving quickly to keep warm, I wondered if I might happen upon the Wishing Tree. I hadn't thought about it since I'd been back but knowing how much faith Molly had in the ancient hawthorn's abilities to make wishes come true, I wondered if it might be able to help me properly turn off my feelings for Brodie. I quickened my pace as I heard the trinkets and charms secured to the branches melodiously tinkle ahead of me and stumbled into the clearing which surrounded it.

I took a deep breath and walked over to it, noticing how many more additions there had been since my last visit while rifling through my pockets for something to add to accompany my wish. I didn't have anything, so instead placed my hands lightly against the trunk and closed my eyes.

'Paige?'

I let out a squeal and practically jumped out of my skin, as the one person I didn't want to see stepped into view from the other side of the trunk. The tree was so huge that Brodie had been completely hidden and I felt irrationally cross with the hawthorn for not giving me some sort of warning that I was not alone.

'Brodie,' I gasped, one hand on my chest. 'You frightened me half to death.'

That said, I still recovered far quicker than I would have done even just a couple of weeks ago.

'Sorry,' he said huskily. 'I thought everyone had gone back to the hall.'

'So did I,' I said, a little tightly. How ironic that the one person I wanted to avoid was in precisely the place I'd come to avoid him. 'What are you doing here?'

'Nothing,' he said, wiping his face with his jacket sleeve.

'Are you all right?' I asked, taken aback to see his eyes were full of tears. 'Sorry,' I added. 'Obviously, you're not.'

'I am really,' he said, sniffing hard. 'I don't know what happened. I just stepped into the clearing and some . . . feeling came over me.'

'What sort of feeling?'

'I can't explain it,' he shrugged.

I looked at the tree again.

'What is all this?' he asked, peering up into the branches.

'It's a Wishing Tree,' I said softly. 'People come here to make a wish, or say a prayer, and leave a token as thanks to the tree for granting it.'

'Oh, wow,' he gasped. 'I've never seen anything like it.'

'It's pretty special,' I sighed. 'And people have been coming here for years.'

'I can see that,' he said, stepping back to take more of it in. 'Why this tree, do you think?'

'Well,' I said, recalling Molly's words. 'All trees are special, of course, but in Celtic mythology the hawthorn was considered sacred and it symbolized love and protection, or so Molly once told me.'

'And she'd know,' Brodie laughed, moving to stand a little closer again. 'I guess that makes it the ideal choice for a Wishing Tree, doesn't it?'

'I guess so,' I said, biting my lip. 'She also told me that it's known as the Fairy Tree and that fairies live under it to guard it.'

'Hm,' said Brodie, sounding thoughtful.

'What?'

'Fairies are supposed to be mischievous, aren't they?' he asked.

'I'm no expert, but rumour has it that they are very impish indeed.'

'I wonder if they account for the strange feelings I've had today,' he mused. 'I've been here before and enjoyed walking among the trees, but there's been something strange in the atmosphere today.'

I hadn't known he'd visited the woods before.

'I've felt it too,' I said, looking over my shoulder.

'I wouldn't say it's sinister,' Brodie elaborated, 'but there's just . . . something.'

'I agree.' I swallowed, my gaze shifting back to him.

There was a sudden gust of wind which threw us off balance and pushed us closer together. We reached out to steady one another and in the next moment, our eyes had locked, our pupils dilated and in the second after that, we were wrapped in each other's arms and Brodie was lowering his lips to meet mine. I didn't for a single moment think about pushing him away.

My knees buckled as his mouth met mine and the kiss which started as tender, soft and sweet deepened and Brodie groaned with pleasure. The sound reverberated through his chest and I kissed him even harder.

If there was fairy mischief afoot it kept us connected for a very long time. When we eventually drew apart, we were both breathless and flushed and every bit as surprised as each other. I took a few seconds to process what had happened and Brodie did the same.

'Is this what you were wishing for?' he eventually laughed, smiling down at me.

I shook my head.

'No,' I said, 'in fact . . .'

'In fact, what?' he asked.

I had been about to say that I was going to ask for the polar opposite of what had just happened, but stopped.

'In fact,' I said, collecting myself, 'I hadn't had time to make my wish before you appeared.'

'And I didn't even know what the tree was,' he laughed again. 'So, you can't blame me. Where did that wind even come from?'

'I have no idea,' I said, looking around as if I might be able to spot the source of it.

It was a perfectly calm end to the day. Correction, it was a perfectly calm end to the day in the woods, but inside my head and heart, a storm was brewing. I wondered if Brodie's thoughts and insides were as churned up as mine?

'Molly said everyone would end up kissing today, didn't she?' he self-consciously said. 'But where's the mistletoe?'

I squinted up into the hawthorn's uppermost branches.

'There,' I pointed. 'Right at the top.'

'Ah.' He nodded.

'And in that case,' I said, 'I think we should put what just happened down to . . .'

I didn't get to finish the sentence because Brodie's phone started loudly ringing.

'Sorry,' he said, pulling it out of his pocket. 'This is the last place I'd expect to find a mobile signal.'

'You'd better answer it,' I told him.

He turned away and I wondered which direction I could slope off in.

'Angus,' he then said and I decided to stay put. 'All right,' he finished up after my godfather had concluded relaying whatever he'd called to say. 'I'll be with you in a minute.'

Brodie ended the call and turned back to face me.

'Angus wants to talk to me,' he said, following me out of the clearing. 'He says he's got something of interest to tell me.'

'I'm intrigued,' I said, grasping the nettle. 'I didn't realize the two of you knew each other so well.'

'Between you and me,' he said, perhaps assuming that now we'd kissed he could share a confidence, 'I'm doing something for him, but I'm not allowed to say what.'

'I see.' I swallowed, my emotions all over the place. 'That sounds a bit cloak and dagger.'

'Well, it is a secret,' he admitted and my heart thumped. 'You won't mention it to anyone, will you?'

'Of course not,' I promised.

Surely, if he was so willing to admit that he was doing something secretive for Angus, it couldn't be anything too risky, could it?

'We've known each other a while,' he then further added. 'We first met in London a few months ago.'

But then, on the other hand . . .

Chapter 23

Brodie hadn't elaborated further and I managed to avoid everyone back at the hall, grab some snacks and head upstairs to hunker down and process in the Rose Room. The day had dawned with such promise and excitement but it had ended in a right old muddle.

The truth was, I liked Brodie. I liked him so much, in fact, that even when he had revealed to me what his job was and who he had worked for and I had abandoned the romantic fantasy I'd woven around him, I had still clung to a tiny fraction of hope that I'd somehow got the revised version of him wrong.

That hope, shored up by Brodie's reaction to Albert's studio, had been the reason I hadn't yet made a concerted effort to find out what he and Angus were conspiring about. It was also the reason why I had left my heart dangerously close to the line that our kiss in the woods had sent it leaping across. However, now that Brodie had revealed where and when he and Angus had met, I knew that speck of hope had to be swept aside. Allowing it to exist had been a grave mistake.

It was time to get to the bottom of whatever was going on and I was going to have to orchestrate an opportunity to expose the truth and risk upsetting Angus. If he deemed my interference unforgivable then I would forgo Christmas at the hall and leave.

There was less than a fortnight now until everyone arrived back and there were others who would rally around in the interim. My heart would ache for the Connelly clan, the town and even Alice who I was looking forward to getting to know better and it would doubtless take time to recover from my surprising feelings for Brodie, but so be it.

But what about Albert? Remembering the change that had come over him during his visit to the hall I took comfort in the knowledge that he would now be able to cope with my earlier than planned departure and might even be willing to let Kathleen help him, too. That said, I dreaded the thought of leaving him so soon and hoped it wouldn't come to that.

With a heavy heart and trying not to think of either our foot-perfect dance or the blissful pressure of Brodie's mouth on mine, I slipped into bed, with Bran welded to my side. How was it conceivable that the most wonderful day had dawned, full of excitement for the celebrations to come and within a few hours I was contemplating the possibility of calling premature time on my stay at Wynthorpe Hall?

*

There was plenty to do the next day and after I had exchanged messages with Mum admiring the many photos she had sent via WhatsApp and making all the right noises to reassure her and Dad that all was well, I tidied and cleaned, using the time to try and come up with an idea that would get Angus, Brodie and I together in a location which wouldn't rouse suspicion.

I felt jittery all day, and every time the phone rang, I wondered if it might be Brodie, but he didn't call. Not for me anyway and I tried not to dwell on why I felt more disappointed than relieved about that. I did receive one call, however, from Albert, telling me he was going to be in the studio all day so I didn't need to worry about going to see him again.

'That's wonderful.' I smiled. 'I hope you have a productive day.'

'Thank you,' he responded. 'And I've been thinking over what you said about getting a tree from the auction tomorrow,' he added.

'Oh, yes?' I said, crossing the fingers on my free hand.

'I'd like to do that,' he delighted me by saying. 'It would be good to get the decorations out of the loft again, but only if you can spare the time. I don't think I could manage the ladder like I used to.'

The thought of us decorating a tree and enjoying some mince pies and mulled wine by his fireside caused a lump to form in my throat. Seeing the cottage further transformed would be a wonderful and, if I did end up leaving before Christmas, very precious memory.

'Of course, I can spare the time,' I keenly told him. 'I'll come over early in the morning to get the decs down and then we'll head to Wynbridge. We could even have lunch out.'

'I think I'd like that,' he said, making my eyes prickle.

What an incredible turnaround. It was only a few weeks ago that I was trying to coax him to open his front door and now he was willing to stride out of it.

'See you tomorrow then,' I finished up, blinking back the tears.

'I'll be waiting,' he chuckled, completely unaware of my emotion.

Saturday was one of those unforgettable winter days, gifted with bright blue sky, endless sunshine and a dip in the temperature capable of turning your nose red almost before you'd set out.

'Shall we go to town together this morning?' Molly asked, when she bounded into the kitchen looking and sounding every bit as excited as everyone else.

Angus had already been crashing about for hours. He was planning to buy trees at the auction but was also taking delivery of a couple directly from a supplier called Wynter's Trees, which was situated just inland of the north Norfolk coast.

'Sorry,' I told her. 'I can't. I have a date.'

'Oh,' she said, clapping her hands. 'You and Brodie have got it together at last.'

'About time.' Archie, who was close behind her, grinned.

'Don't be absurd,' I tutted, willing my face not to flame. 'I'm talking about Albert. I'm going to buy him a tree and then help him decorate it.'

'Oh,' Molly said again, only this time with rather less enthusiasm.

'I have no idea what Brodie's doing,' I said, shrugging, 'but his plans have absolutely nothing to do with me.'

After a hurried breakfast, I defrosted the Land Rover and set off.

'I hope you've got a thermal vest on under that sweater,' I said to Albert, the second he let me in. 'How did you get on yesterday? Is it chilly in the studio?'

'Are you all right?' He frowned after my bombardment of questions.

'Of course,' I said, avoiding his eye. It was hard trying to pretend nothing was wrong, when potentially, everything could be. 'I'm just excited about our trip to town.'

'Too much sugar on your Coco Pops, I reckon,' he laughed. 'Yes, I've got my thermals on. Yes, I got on well in the studio yesterday and no, it isn't chilly in there because I keep the wood burner going.'

'Have you got enough wood down there to keep it well stoked?' I further asked.

'Yes, yes,' he said, brushing the question off. 'Stop fussing.'

'Come on then,' I said, unbuttoning my coat, 'let's get the decs down and then we'll go. I want to make sure we bag you a decent tree. This room will take a big one, I reckon.'

After carrying down the Price family decorations, of

which there were quite a lot, I downed a glass of water and we headed into Wynbridge. It was already busy and I wondered how Albert would cope being among so many people.

'All right?' I asked as I helped him out of the cab.

I didn't want to make another fuss, but couldn't not ask.

'It's busy, isn't it?' he said, linking his arm through mine and looking around.

'Busier than I thought it would be,' I told him. 'Is that all right?'

'I am a bit worried,' he said.

'Oh, Albert,' I said, tucking him closer.

'I'm worried that if we don't hurry up, all the best trees will be gone.'

I wasn't sure if that was bravado or the truth, but we quickly made our way to the square where the trees were being auctioned off and bagged ourselves a beauty.

'Thanks, Steve,' I said to the Dempster's son who kindly carried it back to the Land Rover and helped me strap it down securely.

'No worries,' he smiled, looking very much like his dad. 'Don't forget your mistletoe.' He winked at Albert, before rushing off to help someone else.

'Would you like some greenery?' I asked Albert. 'I could get you some straight from the Wynthorpe woods if you don't want to get caught up in the square again.'

'I'm not bothered about mistletoe,' he said, 'but perhaps we could have a look for a wreath for the door on the market.

Let's have a drink somewhere first though, shall we? I could do with defrosting.'

Encouraged that he wasn't in a rush to leave, we managed to squeeze our way into The Cherry Tree Café. There was no sign of Lizzie, but Jemma was rushing about, expertly juggling orders and clearing tables.

'What can I get you?' she asked. 'Hello, Paige. How's it looking out there?'

I introduced her to Albert, filled her in on what was happening in the square and requested two iced and spiced buns and hot chocolate with the works.

'My goodness,' Albert gasped, when it arrived. 'There'll be no stopping me this afternoon.'

'That's my plan.' I nudged him. 'We'll have the cottage transformed in no time after a sugar hit like this.'

While we thawed out and filled up, I told Albert about the gallery next door.

'They showcase all kinds of local artists' work,' I innocently said, 'and I'm sure they'd have room for one more.'

Albert fixed me with a steely stare.

'Don't worry,' I told him, when I realized I'd pushed my luck too far. 'I wouldn't really dream of trying to convince you to exhibit.'

'Good,' he said, wiping cream from his upper lip. 'Because I'd hate for us to fall out again.'

'So would I!' I laughed, feeling proud of how far we'd come. 'You're really not going to share your work though, are you?' I sighed.

'No,' he said gruffly, 'I'm really not.'

Knowing he wouldn't back down, I changed the subject.

'Hello, Paige,' said Kathleen, who came in with Dorothy close behind. 'How are you enjoying the town in full festive flow?'

'Very much,' I told her.

'What about you, Albert?' asked Dorothy. 'Has Paige sorted you out with a tree yet?'

'She has.' He nodded. 'A wonderful one. Although it is a little on the large side. I reckon we'll have to lop the top off to get it in the cottage.'

Dorothy rolled her eyes.

'She's getting as excited as her godfather, this one.' Dorothy nodded at me which made my cheeks flare. 'They're going to be as bad as each other by the time it's the Winter Wonderland weekend.'

I hoped Angus would be sticking to his promise not to do anything untoward that weekend, especially if we'd had words by then.

'Look at her,' Kathleen teased, misinterpreting my reaction. 'You've gone bright red just thinking about it, Paige!'

'Have you dropped your cakes off?' I asked Dorothy to draw attention away from my glowing complexion.

She had been in a bit of a flap when I left the hall, worrying that she wasn't going to get them to the bake sale in time.

'Mick and I have just done it,' she said, 'which is why I've come in here for a restorative cuppa. I honestly didn't think we were going to make it.'

'Dorothy has made the prettiest Christmas cakes for the bake sale which is happening in the town hall,' I explained to Albert.

'And don't worry, Albert,' she said, patting his arm. 'I've got a smaller one back at the hall with your name on it.'

'Now that is kind.' He smiled. 'Thank you. I'm partial to a slice of Christmas cake and I reckon yours will be top notch.'

Dorothy grew a couple of inches taller when he said that, no doubt pleased her new friend was in earshot to hear the praise and I realized I hadn't introduced Albert to Kathleen. With that soon remedied and Kathleen making me promise to add Albert officially to the delivery rota, I paid our bill and vacated the table so she and Dorothy could secure it.

'Is that the gallery you were talking about?' Albert asked, when we were out in the busy square again.

'Yes,' I said, 'that's the one. I've only been in a couple . . .'

The words died in my throat as I spotted Brodie coming out of the door.

'Shall we go and see if we can find you a wreath, Albert?' I brightly suggested, turning us in the opposite direction, but it was too late.

'Paige!'

My heart sank. Obviously, I needed to talk to Brodie, but not with Albert in tow.

'Brodie.' I swallowed, turning back again. 'Hi.'

Looking between me and Albert, he didn't seem to know what to say next and was probably wishing he hadn't called out as much as I was.

'It's lovely to see you again, Albert,' he finally said, in a surprisingly familiar tone.

'Likewise, young man,' said Albert, taking me further aback.

'I was hoping I might see you,' Brodie then said to me.

'You were?' I croaked.

'Yeah,' he said, shoving his hands through his hair. 'I really need to talk to you. Any chance we could go for that drink we haven't managed yet?'

I bit my lip. The pub was far from ideal for what I had to say.

'Brodie!'

'I think Jack wants you,' I said, as he called out again. 'You'd better go. If you ring the hall, we'll sort something out.'

'I'd rather arrange it now,' Brodie said, 'because I can never seem to get you at the hall, but you're right. Jack's going to burst if I don't get over there.'

The Brambles stall was swamped and Jack was struggling on his own. I wondered where Tilly was.

'I can see that,' I said. 'I really think you should go.'

'Okay,' he said, his shoulders dropping. 'Bye, Albert. I'll call you later, Paige.'

Albert and I watched him walk away.

'I don't understand you two,' said Albert, shaking his head. 'You're clearly into each other. That's what you youngsters say these days, isn't it? And yet between you, you can't get your act together.'

'I do believe that is the youthful vernacular,' I confirmed, but didn't acknowledge the implication of what he had said. 'Come on,' I added, 'let's find you a wreath for the cottage door and a stand for the tree, unless you've already got one?'

'That's a point,' said Albert, thankfully distracted. 'I didn't think of that.'

By the time we'd finished in town, having stayed longer than planned because Albert decided to do a little festive shopping, he was too tired to start decorating. I manhandled the tree indoors, set it up after some swearing and cajoling and promised to go back the next afternoon, once I'd helped decorate the hall in the morning.

'Are you really sure you can spare the time?' he asked. 'It's Sunday tomorrow.'

'I know,' I told him, 'and I definitely can. I want you to enjoy getting the cottage ready for Christmas and you'll do that far better after a decent night's rest.'

'I am going to sleep well tonight,' he said, shaking his head. 'What a day!'

'Have you enjoyed it?'

I already knew the answer, but wanted to hear him say it.

'I have.' He nodded. 'I was a bit overwhelmed when we first arrived. We couldn't have picked a busier day to go shopping, could we?'

'We couldn't,' I agreed. 'I'm sorry about that.'

He put up a hand to stop me.

'Don't apologize,' he insisted. 'We needed to go today to get the tree and it was wonderful to be able to soak up the atmosphere. And what's more, with you by my side, Paige, I knew I'd be able to cope.'

'Oh, Albert,' I choked.

'It's true,' he said, looking a little misty eyed himself. 'I know I've already said it, but you really have transformed my life and there'll never be words enough to express my thanks for that.'

We had a warm hug and then I lit the fire and made sure he had everything he needed in time for his favourite Saturday night game show.

'I'll see you tomorrow,' I said, as I slipped out the door.

'Tomorrow,' he cheerfully said, holding his mug of tea aloft. 'And perhaps you might want to think about ringing that young man before he rings you? That's how you young independent women operate these days, isn't it?'

I gave him a look and left him to it.

Chapter 24

By the time everyone at the hall fell into bed that evening, the multiple trees, some of which I was fascinated to see were growing in pots, were set in their final positions and we had spent what felt like endless hours ferrying the decorations down from the loft, ready for adorning everywhere the following day and, given the amount there was to do, even beyond that.

If I'd thought Albert had a lot of boxes, it was nothing compared to what Angus had been squirelling away over the years and he'd got the next week, which was how long he told me it would most likely take to embellish both the interior and exterior of the hall to his satisfaction, organized with military precision.

I was surprised to find everything so orderly as he generally favoured a more chaotic approach, but Christmas, I realized, was the one occasion which was not to be trifled with and I knew it would be picture perfect as a result.

It was Mick's turn to receive a gift from Santa the next

morning and once we'd admired the many packets of seeds he would be sowing in the spring with a view to creating cut flower beds in the walled garden, and filled up on breakfast, we began the pleasurable task of decorating the hall.

I threw myself into Angus's operation with gusto and unboxed many fragile tissue wrapped treasures, some of which I remembered from Christmases past spent visiting the hall with my parents. Along with the beautiful glass baubles, there were worn and faded homemade angels crafted by the three Connelly boys too and more recent papier-mâché additions from the two grandsons.

With carols playing and everyone in such a buoyant mood the morning was a joy and by lunchtime great areas of the hall glistened, shone and sparkled. There was some special adornment or tableau in practically every spot and the glow of the warm white fairy lights softened everything and made it feel cosy, even in the middle of the bright day.

After lunch I excitedly headed to Albert's, taking Bran with me, for a repeat performance and there was a sense of relief coursing through me too. In spite of his many lists and tight schedule Angus had been so bitten by the decorating bug that he wanted to go off track for a while and get the cherry picker and lights ready for decking the outside of the hall earlier than planned. I felt very happy about not being there to be roped into helping with that.

'Aha,' I laughed as I crossed the threshold of Albert's cottage. 'I see you've started without me!'

'I couldn't resist.' He smiled. 'I woke feeling as excited as

I used to on Christmas day when I was a child and thought I'd start unpacking a few things and arranging what I could.'

'You really shouldn't have moved some of these boxes on your own though, Albert,' I scolded mildly.

I knew how cumbersome they were because I had carried them downstairs.

'Well,' he said, looking a little flushed, 'it's done now. Tell me what you make of what I've done so far?'

The fireplace was adorned with silk foliage swags and there was a similar arrangement on the table and more lining the windowsills.

'No wonder you didn't want any greenery,' I said, fingering a trailing strand of ivy, just to make sure it wasn't actually real. 'These are stunning.'

'All Stella's handiwork,' Albert said proudly. 'I told you she was a dab hand with a needle and thread.'

'You did,' I remembered, 'but I had no idea she was as skilled as this. Did she hide her light under a bushel too?'

Albert rolled his eyes.

'She didn't have to,' he said. 'My father reckoned sewing was a far more acceptable pastime than painting.'

I was about to apologize for bringing it up, but Albert laughed.

'Stella used to dare me to take it up,' he said, his eyes further lighting up at the memory, 'just to see Dad's face, but I never did. Probably just as well.' He shrugged. 'Now, how about you make us some tea and then we'll be all set to carry on.'

With tea to hand, along with the tub of mince pies and sausage rolls Dorothy had insisted I bring with me, we set about exploring more of the boxes. There were a few which Albert looked in and said he didn't want to unpack, which saved us some time, but there was still more than enough to decorate the tree and festoon the walls and ceilings.

'I daresay this is nothing like the bespoke and antique collection you've been setting up at the hall,' he said as he handed me another faded carrier bag from Woolworths. 'This is all high street stuff. Apart from the angel.'

The beautiful seraphim was yet another of Stella's incredible creations and wore an elaborate gold dress and had sheer but sparkling wings. They looked dazzling when they caught the light.

'You're right, Albert,' I said, hanging a couple more baubles around the back of the tree. 'This is all very different to the Wynthorpe decs, but it's a treasure trove nonetheless. This collection of yours is pure vintage and the fact you have most of the original packaging makes it quite valuable.'

'Get away with you,' he tutted, assuming I was teasing.

'I'm being serious,' I told him as I opened up a pair of honeycomb bell and holly wall decorations. 'These must have been with you since the fifties and there's another whole box full just like it. They're precious, Albert, and in this condition, pretty rare.'

He stood and looked at them with his head cocked to one side.

'Well, yes,' he conceded. 'I suppose they have been in the

family a good long while. Most of them would have been picked up from Woolies in town.'

'There you are then,' I said. 'You want to keep looking after them. I daresay if you ever sold them you could retire on the proceeds.'

'I'll bear that in mind,' he laughed. 'But now I think it's time for another cuppa, don't you?'

The light was fading when we eventually finished and I was beginning to feel all decked out by the time Albert bestowed upon me the honour of turning on the tree lights. I held my breath as I pressed the switch, even though I'd tested them before carefully draping them around the tree.

'There now.' Albert beamed as the little orange, green, blue, pink and red bell-shape lights sprang into life. 'Doesn't that look a treat?'

The lights were very different to those at the hall too and they didn't twinkle or chase each other up and down the tree in time to music, but they were beautiful and perfectly fitting for Albert's retro vibe.

'No one would doubt the cottage is occupied now,' I sighed wistfully, thinking how lovely the tree would look to anyone driving by.

Albert shook his head.

'Let's not think about unhappy times,' he said, wiping away an unexpected tear. 'But focus on the fun we've got ahead of us and the fresh future on our horizons.'

I was thrilled he had such a sunny outlook, but I couldn't bring myself to think that far ahead, especially now my

Christmas was potentially shaping up to be different to the one I had been planning. Willing myself not to worry about whether there really was trouble ahead, I blinked away my own tears and embraced the moment, enjoying seeing Albert and his home so completely transformed.

'And talking of the future,' he said, 'is there any news about my bath chair?'

'Oh, yes,' I said. 'It should be here sometime next week. There was some hold up in the delivery chain which is why it's taking so long, but it's back on track now. I meant to say yesterday, but forgot.'

'Perhaps there's been a run on them for secret Santa presents,' he joked.

'That's bound to be it,' I giggled, imagining Santa ferrying about a sleigh full of the chairs and other aids geared towards independent living.

'I'm rather looking forward to my next swim in the tub,' Albert smiled.

I would have to make sure a bottle of bubble bath formed part of the pile of Christmas presents I was getting ready for him. I wondered if he had a fondness for Radox.

'Good,' I said, 'it's important to have something to look forward to in life.'

'What are you looking forward to?' he then forthrightly asked me.

'Today it has to be my bed,' I told him, avoiding any potential seriousness or deep dive into my as yet still hazy future. 'It's been a long and very busy day.'

And it wasn't done with me yet.

'So,' I said as I pulled my coat on to leave, 'we've got your lights set on a timer, so you don't have to worry about turning them on and off. You've got your dinner warming in the oven and the fire's lit. So, you're all set, yes?'

'I am,' Albert agreed. 'Thank you. And I've got plans in the studio for the next couple of days, so you needn't worry about calling in. With the Winter Wonderland to set up on top of everything else, you probably won't have the time anyway!'

'You're right,' I said, letting out a long breath.

Along with finding a way to get Brodie and Angus to confess to whatever they were up to in that time too, it really was going to be jam packed.

'It's going to be very busy.' I swallowed. 'I'll give you a ring to check in though,' I further said, giving Albert a kiss on the cheek, 'and you know you can always call me.'

I waited until he had locked the door and pulled the curtain across and then walked up the path with Bran to the Land Rover. It was a chilly night and I was pleased the vehicle started first time. I was looking forward to an early, and hopefully restorative, night ahead of cleaning the dust the decorating would have kicked up throughout the hall.

I turned on the headlights once the cab had warmed up a little but didn't make it as far as first gear.

'What on earth?' I frowned.

Turning on the lights had illuminated a bike which looked as though it had been half buried in the hedge just beyond the gate. I daresay I wouldn't have spotted it had I set off in the daylight, but there was no unseeing it then and I knew exactly who it belonged to.

My heart was racing as I pulled away from the cottage, just far enough for Albert to think, should he happen to be watching, that I had left. Coming to a halt again, from my elevated position I could see a square of light towards the back of the garden. I turned off the engine, let Bran out again, then doubled back and crept through the gate. With my heart thumping loud enough for even Albert with his less than sharp hearing to pick up, I snuck through the garden to the studio.

Just as I had suspected, there was someone inside. I could hear music playing quietly and a voice humming along to it. I stood for a moment like a rabbit caught in the headlights wondering whether to burst in or make a stealthier approach.

With a shaking hand, I reached for the door handle and quietly turned it, settling on stealth rather than surprise. Already knowing who I was going to see, my emotions were a tumultuous and heady mix. On the one hand I was furious that Brodie had ignored my warning and come back to the cottage, but on the other, as long as he was doing what I thought he was doing, I was relieved because it might mean he wasn't the person I had recently assumed him to be.

I dithered on the threshold and then a timely nudge from Bran set the next chain of events in motion.

'Brodie,' I whispered, my breath catching as I peeped

inside and saw him, with his back to the door, painting with passion.

His solid frame kept the canvas he was working on largely hidden from sight, but he was utterly absorbed. I went to close the door again with a view to going back to the cottage to ask Albert for an explanation when Brodie whipped round, most likely having caught the change in temperature the open door had created, and our eyes locked.

'Paige!' he gasped.

I let go of the door and it swung open wider.

'What are you doing here?'

'What am I doing here?' I repeated. 'What are *you* doing here?'

He didn't say anything.

'I asked you not to come back,' I reminded him.

His face, which had drained of all colour when he spotted me, then flushed red.

'You ignored me,' I said, feeling hurt.

He might now turn out to be the man I had always hoped he was, but if it was at the cost of putting Albert in a difficult position then the price of the revelation was too high.

'I didn't ignore you,' Brodie said quietly.

'The evidence in front of me suggests otherwise,' I tersely responded.

'I'm only here,' he said, taking a step closer to me, 'because I was invited.'

'You were invited?' I frowned. 'Or you pushed your way in?'

'I was invited,' he said firmly.

I turned to go back to the cottage and discover what Albert had to say about that, but Brodie darted around me, blocking my path.

'What are you doing?' I demanded. 'Get out of my way, Brodie.'

'Please don't go,' he begged. 'Not yet. Let me explain first.'

I looked up at him and felt my annoyance that he hadn't taken my warning to stay away seriously start to crumble. He wouldn't *really* have forced his way in, would he?

'You walked out on me once before,' he reminded me, 'and everything between us, apart from that unforgettable kiss, has been off centre ever since. I'm not letting that happen again. I can't.'

'Oh, Brodie,' I sighed.

'Come on,' he said. 'Come and sit down and let me tell you everything.'

Chapter 25

I walked further into the studio with Bran as close to my side as it was possible for him to get and headed towards the wood burner which was burning brightly. Albert had been right about it keeping the place warm. I realized then that, feeling dazed, I hadn't capitalized on the opportunity to look at the canvas Brodie had been working on. He had now turned the easel to face the other way, so I had missed my chance. Damn.

'Won't you sit down?' he asked, as he swilled some brushes in a jar. 'Why don't you follow Bran's lead?'

The huge hound had already forsaken me in favour of the heat source and curled up on the rug in front of the fire. I slowly lowered myself into one of the armchairs next to him.

'What was it that gave me away?' Brodie then asked.

'The bike,' I said huskily. 'The Land Rover lights picked it out.'

Brodie shook his head.

'I didn't plan to leave it there,' he tutted. 'But you were

already here when I came back and I was worried that if I tried to wheel it through the gate, you'd hear it squeaking.'

'When you came back?' I frowned. 'Exactly how often have you been here?'

Brodie wiped his hands on a paint-stained towel and looked sheepish.

'Quite a lot over the last few days,' he confessed, 'and this morning, too.'

'In that case,' I said, 'I'm very much looking forward to hearing what you have to say.'

He sat in the chair opposite mine and ran both hands through his hair. I noticed there was now a streak of cobalt blue running through one side.

'I think I'd better start from where we broke off in The Mermaid on the night of the switch-on, when you fell ill,' he began.

I tried not to think of the time I had wasted as a result of my phantom ailment.

'There was so much more I wanted to share with you then . . .' His words trailed off as he stared at the flames dancing behind the door of the fire.

'Go on,' I encouraged because I couldn't wait to hear it now.

'Well,' he said, his gaze returning to mine, 'as you may remember, I had got as far as telling you that I had reluctantly followed the family career path my father had so desperately wanted me to take.'

'The money-making family career path, you mean,' I said disparagingly, confirming that I had far from forgotten.

'Yes,' he sighed, shaking his head, 'that was the one. There was something else I wanted to do, but my father made it very clear that if I pursued that, then I would never gain his approval and at the time, I wanted that more than anything else.'

I couldn't help thinking how what he said mirrored some of the words Albert had spoken during the evening we'd spent together at the hall.

'Therefore,' Brodie continued, 'when I reached the age where I had to make those educational decisions that would shape my future, I took the only option which would gain his support.'

'That can't have been easy,' I swallowed, feeling a relatively surprising pang of sympathy.

'It broke my heart,' Brodie said sadly, 'but,' he then added, 'the fact that I turned out to have an aptitude for investment softened the blow.'

My compassion ebbed away somewhat when he said that.

'My portfolio quickly grew beyond all expectation,' he carried on, 'and my father did indeed respect me. And it was that which made me believe that my sacrifice had been worth it and that the lifestyle I had immersed myself in as a result was the one I wanted.'

I imagined it was one of fast cars, long haul holidays and extortionate city living.

'So, I'm guessing you made a lot of money?' I pointlessly asked.

'During the next few years, I made a fortune,' he confirmed. 'Millions, both for myself and my clients.'

'Then you're a very rich man,' I said sniffily, imagining him and his work buddies living on the proceeds which had previously been assigned to the charity I had worked for. 'Congratulations,' I added scathingly thinking how much better that money could have been spent, even though the charity only ever received a fraction of it.

Brodie laughed and shook his head, apparently not catching my sarcastic tone.

'In some ways I am rich,' he said, 'but not in others and that's mostly down to Jack.'

'What's that supposed to mean?'

'Things began to change for me the day he called to tell me he was starting up his own distillery,' Brodie elaborated. 'He'd been working in the industry for a while with ambitions to go it alone and suddenly, Brambles was happening.'

'Go on.'

'I started to travel up from London to help him at the weekends,' he then surprised me by saying, 'and I soon saw something in Jack's life that was lacking in mine.'

'An empty bank account?' I suggested.

'Passion,' Brodie corrected, looking at me so intently, I felt my cheeks flush. 'Jack had found something which made him so happy and that he believed in so deeply, it had become his life's purpose. I knew I'd felt like that about something once, and before you say it,' he quickly added, 'it wasn't money.'

'What was it then?' I asked, wanting him to spell it out.

'Painting,' he said, looking around the studio. 'That was what I'd given up when I chose a business degree over art school. In my effort to keep my father happy, I'd set aside my heart's desire and replaced it with pounds and pence. For a while, I'd become as obsessed as he was, but the scales fell as I watched my brother create something he truly loved.'

'I see,' I swallowed, now completely absorbed and momentarily forgetting how his lavish lifestyle had impacted on my infinitely more frugal one. 'So, what did you do? After Jack's wake-up call, what came next?'

'Nothing,' he sighed, 'and it drove Jack to distraction.'

'Knowing Jack,' I said, 'I can imagine it would.'

'So, one weekend, he took matters into his own hands,' Brodie continued, smiling at the memory. 'He handed me a sketch book and a box of pastels and told me to get on with it. He drove me out to the countryside and practically forced me to draw.'

'Bravo for Jack and his direct action.' I smiled back.

'Indeed.' Brodie beamed. 'Because that was exactly what I did. And I didn't stop. I couldn't. It was as if a dam had burst and I had no desire to plug it.'

Utterly entranced, the joyous change in his tone made tears spring to my eyes.

'That's amazing,' I choked.

'It was,' he laughed.

'But what did your father say?'

'Nothing to begin with, because I kept it a secret. Painting was something I did at the weekends and I kept my supplies at Brambles to resist Monday to Friday temptation. But it didn't last. Within weeks, I was painting at my flat and every surface was covered in canvases.'

'Is that when he found out?' I asked, leaning further forward in my seat.

'It wasn't quite that soon,' Brodie recalled. 'But it wasn't long after because fate stepped in and gave me the biggest nudge.'

'What happened?'

'Well,' he said, a sense of wonder in his tone. 'One night, I was painting when a friend turned up with a guy I didn't know. I didn't want to let them in, but my mate was a bit drunk and very noisy, so I admitted them both before they woke the neighbours.'

'That was considerate of you.'

'I'm a considerate person.' He smiled.

'Go on,' I urged.

'Well, the guy I didn't know turned out to be a buyer for a gallery and he fell into raptures over my work. I know that sounds big-headed,' he quickly added, 'but that's what happened. He loved it and said that he wanted to sell it.'

'That's amazing,' I gasped.

'It was.' Brodie nodded. 'And it all happened so fast.'

'Did you say yes?'

'No,' he said. 'I was too shocked at the time. I told him I needed a couple of days to think about it but when I told Jack, he reckoned I should just get on with it.'

'And did you?'

'I did.' Brodie grinned. 'I told my father, who I'd tricked

into attending the gallery the evening my work first went on sale, that I would keep working during the day and paint at night and it would all be fine.'

'What did he make of that?'

'He didn't believe it would pan out for a second. And it didn't. Within a month I'd left the firm.'

'You worked for Davey and Clarkson, didn't you?' I asked, knowing it was impossible to ignore the elephant in the room any longer.

I had loved listening to how Brodie had been reacquainted with his paintbrushes but it wasn't the whole of the story and if we were going to move forward then everything needed to come out, whether it was going to tarnish his fairy tale or not.

'Yes,' he nodded, 'and from your tone, I'm guessing you've heard of them?'

'Who hasn't?' I wryly smiled.

Brodie shook his head.

'I was so lucky I got out when I did,' he told me. 'I had absolutely nothing to do with any of what shut the company down and was gone long before it all kicked off. I did know a couple of the people involved, but not well. That said, I was pleased to have left before my name could be associated with the scandal, because mud sticks.'

'It does,' I nodded, wholeheartedly relieved that he hadn't been in any way involved but wondering what this meant for Angus's words about the return he wanted to see.

Brodie looked at me, his eyes widening as understanding dawned.

'You thought I was involved,' he stated, sounding appalled. 'Oh my god, is that why you . . .'

'I did have my suspicions after you'd told me who you worked for,' I cut in to confess. 'Especially as it seemed like you'd just turned up in the area and no one knew much about you.'

'I see,' he said, sounding more upset.

'But my hatred of Davey and Clarkson runs deeper than you having worked for them, Brodie.'

'What are you talking about?'

I pulled in a breath.

'The money they used to donate to the charity I worked for,' I explained, 'funded a wealth of volunteering positions and since those selfish bastards played fast and loose with the millions that didn't belong to them . . .'

'The funding has been lost,' Brodie surmised.

'And so were the jobs.'

'Yours included?' Brodie gasped.

'I was probably going to go anyway,' I said, not wanting to get caught up in explaining the other details surrounding my decision to leave. They weren't relevant to this particular conversation. 'But the loss of the company donation meant there wouldn't have been another contract available to me even if I'd wanted it.'

'Oh, Paige. I'm so sorry.'

'I'm more sorry for all the people we can't now help.'

'I had no idea.'

'There's no reason why you should, but,' I then carried on

because we weren't finished with the revelations surrounding the implications of finding out the name his former employee had had just yet, 'there's more.'

'More?' Brodie frowned.

'Yes. I heard you talking to Angus,' I blurted out, 'in the kitchen at the hall. He said he was expecting to see some sort of return from you before Christmas and after you'd told me about your work, not to mention who you worked for, I assumed . . .'

'That it was of a financial variety?'

I nodded.

'And then after you said you'd met him in London,' I added to try and further justify the assumptions I had made, 'I didn't think I could possibly be wrong.'

'Had I been in your position,' Brodie generously said, shoving his hands into his hair again, 'I would have most likely thought the same, but to be fair we could have met in London for any number of reasons.'

'That's true,' I said, biting my lip and looking around. 'But Angus wasn't talking about money anyway, was he?'

'No,' Brodie said.

It was a huge relief to hear him confirm that.

'So, what does he want then?' I asked, feeling as if a weight had been lifted. 'What exactly is it that my godfather is expecting from you?'

Brodie looked at me for a moment.

'I will tell you,' he eventually said. 'But only because I don't want there to be any more confusion between us.'

'Me neither,' I said vehemently.

'But Angus mustn't find out that you know,' he added seriously.

'If he finds out you've spilled the beans, I'll tell him I forced it out of you.'

Brodie's face broke into a smile and his eyes twinkled.

'And how exactly would you go about forcing this secret out of me?' he asked.

I rolled my eyes.

'This is not the time,' I laughed. 'Just tell me what he wants.'

'All right,' he said, sitting back again and picking up the thread. 'As I'm sure you can imagine, my father was furious when I told him I was giving up my career to paint full-time.'

'Even after what had happened at Davey and Clarkson?'

'Yes,' he said. 'He reckoned none of that mattered because I'd got out before it went belly up and that I would easily secure another position because I hadn't been involved.'

'He sounds like quite a piece of work.'

'Oh, he is, but I told him I wasn't stepping back into that world and he and his former approval disappeared faster than a hare across the Fens.'

'That must have been tough, given that it was his approval you'd wanted all along.'

I was surprised to see Brodie shake his head at that.

'It was easier to get my head around than you might think,' he carried on, sounding upbeat. 'Because I met Angus shortly after that and discovered what genuine approval and respect meant.'

That made sense.

'How did you meet?'

'Well, he's a friend of the owner of the gallery where my paintings were being shown and he came to the exhibition after being told there was work on display which featured the Fens. When he told me where he lived and I explained my connection to Wynbridge, it felt as though the stars had aligned.'

'Oh,' I said, clapping my hands. 'Molly would love this. According to her there are no accidents or flukes. Everything that happens is meant to and it occurs at precisely the moment it's supposed to.'

'I agree with her entirely.' Brodie smiled. 'You should have seen Angus's face when we were looking at one of my landscapes and I told him it was the Wynthorpe estate I'd been trespassing on to create it!'

'Oh my god!' I grinned. 'What were the odds of that?'

'Like I said,' Brodie laughed, 'fate lent a hand.'

'Many hands!' I added, clapping mine again and momentarily forgetting that I still didn't know what Angus was expecting, although it wouldn't take a genius to work it out now. 'So, now you've embraced your life's purpose?'

'More or less,' he said. 'Although I didn't come back to the studio here uninvited as you no doubt suspected when you saw my bike in the hedge.'

My face flushed when he said that.

'It was Angus who put me in touch with Albert and our mutual friend gave me a warm welcome, which has had a huge impact. He's told me a lot about his life and what he went through with his own father and I'm so grateful to know I'm not alone.'

No wonder they'd appeared so pally in town and Brodie hadn't defied my warning at all. It was my wily godfather who had worked out the two men would get along and then put them in touch. It struck me how similar Brodie and Albert's journeys had been. They had both suffered disapproving fathers, but had eventually embraced their art.

'But it's slow going,' Brodie added, with a glance back at the easel and sounding less chipper than he had before.

'How so?' I asked.

The look on his face when he turned back fractured my heart a little. This reaction to his hard fought for artistic freedom was not the one I had expected.

'I've been in the wilderness for months,' he told me, his voice cracking. 'I gave away practically all of my money to charity and to Jack to invest in the business, in the misguided belief that I could live off the money I made from selling my paintings.'

That was a brave move, given how much money I reckoned he would have had to part with.

'It would have been manageable and I felt that it was the right thing to do. There was some integrity in starting over, completely fresh,' he further added. 'And it would have been fine, had something in me not gone wrong.'

'What do you mean?' I asked quietly.

'When I left London and moved in with Jack,' he said, sounding wretched, 'I found I couldn't do it anymore. I couldn't paint. Whether it was the shock of taking the plunge or the pressure, I don't know . . . but I just couldn't do it.'

'Oh, Brodie.'

'It was killing me,' he said. 'I taught a few classes in town to tide me over but they just made the situation worse because I couldn't stop thinking about why I was having to give them.'

No wonder he had been in such a bad mood the day we met. He had been enabling others when he couldn't help himself. Painting had been a pleasure when he had cash in the bank, but by giving it away his creativity had become his bread and butter. He *had* to paint in order to live and the pressure had killed his passion stone dead.

'That must have been tough,' I sympathized.

'It was,' he said, 'and your well-meaning godfather made it tougher too.'

'How so?'

'Because,' Brodie explained, 'having snapped up practically my entire original collection, Angus then announced that he wanted more, much more. Starting with a painting which he can give to Catherine for Christmas.'

'So that's the return he's expecting?' I asked, wondering where Angus had put the rest of Brodie's work at the hall.

'That's it.' Brodie shrugged. 'He's offered me a generous commission and I have to come up with something by the twenty-fifth to earn it. I think he thought that a deadline and something specific to focus on would burst through my creative block and Jack was of the same opinion.'

I felt like finding Angus and Jack and banging their heads

together. Poor Brodie. No wonder he looked like Darcy on a bad day so often!

'So, tell me,' I said in a tone which left him in no doubt that I already knew the answer, 'how has that immense pressure been working out for you?'

'Not well,' he laughed, playing along.

'I can't believe you can laugh about it.'

'Up until a few days ago, I couldn't,' he said. 'But now I've met Albert and everything has changed. Ever since he welcomed me to the studio and shared his life story, it feels like something has actually been unlocked.'

'Oh, Brodie,' I said, feeling relieved on his behalf. 'That's wonderful. Albert's an incredible man, isn't he?'

'He certainly is,' he agreed. 'And we just clicked the moment I came back after Angus said I'd be welcome. I'd painted something by the time I went home that day. And I've barely had a brush out of my hand since.'

He sounded so happy. What a rollercoaster he'd been on. Even the re-telling of this journey had caused a plethora of emotions to pour out of him, so goodness knows how he had felt while he had been living through it.

'We even painted together this morning.' He grinned.

'You didn't?' I gasped.

'We did.' Brodie nodded. 'It was amazing.'

I pictured him and Albert working side by side. In stature and age, they were at opposite ends of the scale, but in terms of personal journey, they were peas in a pod. An externally unlikely pairing, but an internal match made in heaven.

'I suppose it was you who shifted the decoration boxes around in the cottage, wasn't it?' I asked, thinking how Albert hadn't looked at me when I'd told him off.

'It was,' he confessed. 'I told Albert you'd be suspicious about that.'

I shook my head.

'What a pair of conspirators, you are!'

'Are you cross?'

'How can I be?' I laughed, my transformed mood matching his. 'After everything I've been assuming about you but not found the courage to get to the bottom of, I hardly have the right to be even a tiny bit miffed.'

Brodie looked at me and smiled.

'Why do you think you didn't get to the bottom of it?' he asked.

'I don't know.' I swallowed as he stood up and held out his hand.

'Could it possibly have had anything to do with the fact that you didn't want to believe it?' he suggested.

'Maybe,' I said softly, taking his hand and letting him pull me to my feet.

'Could it be that you had developed feelings for me and that you knew deep down there was no way I was some city high flyer who specialized in dodgy investments and who was planning to take off with the Connelly fortune?'

We both laughed at that because hearing him say it out loud, I knew it was absurd.

'Given how long I let the situation run for, there could

be some element of truth in that.' I smiled, as he pulled me close and wrapped me in his arms.

'You really wanted me to be a penniless artist because you thought that would make us more compatible, didn't you?'

'All right, clever clogs,' I sighed. 'I think we've got to the bottom of it all now.'

'So,' he said, lowering his lips tantalizingly close to mine, 'why don't you do something to shut me up?'

Our second kiss tasted even sweeter than the first because there was no mystery, guilt or muddle caught up in it. I only wished it could have lasted a bit longer.

'Well, I never,' I heard Albert chuckle as he opened the studio door. 'And about time too!'

Chapter 26

I was so happy on the journey back to the hall that I didn't feel the bone shaking impact of a single one of the potholes. The evening's relief-inducing revelations, the power of Brodie's second kiss, the sight of him and Albert set up for another painting session and the realization that I would not now have to risk upsetting Angus and would therefore be spending Christmas in Wynbridge had sat me firmly on cloud nine and it was a very comfortable place to be.

Of course, I was still very much aware that I had some big decisions to make about my future, but there was no desperate need to dwell on them in the run up to the celebrations. For the time being, I fully intended to focus on the present and squeeze every last drop of excitement out of it.

As I parked the Land Rover in the courtyard and kissed Bran on top of his grey head, I congratulated myself on just how far I'd come since I'd arrived and how I was going to enjoy an unexpectedly fabulous end to the year.

Accepting that, like every other human on the planet, I

had flaws and made mistakes was the most beneficial thing I had done for my mental health in a long time. By taking on Anna and Hayley's work, I had rediscovered the joy of working in harmony with others and now witnessing Albert and Brodie's blossoming friendship, along with how they flourished better together than alone, was further inspiration, too.

'Right,' I said, just before lunch the next day. 'I'm going out. I'll see you all later.'

'How on earth have you managed to finish so early?' Dorothy asked.

'I started before six,' I told her.

She shook her head.

'You're working too hard,' she scolded.

'I'm fine.' I smiled.

She eyed me astutely.

'I'd like to know what's got you in such a buoyant mood all of a sudden.' She smiled back. 'I thought you'd be fed up with all the extra dust the decorating kicked up.'

'I'm just excited about Christmas,' I told her, although it was so much more than that. 'A bit of extra dusting didn't hurt, especially now the hall looks so beautiful; it's put me right in the mood for it.'

'Oh, yes,' said Archie, who never had sharper hearing than when he thought he could raise a smile by saying something rude.

'Dear, dear,' Dorothy tutted. 'You are naughty sometimes, Archie.'

'What?' he gasped. 'I never said a word, but as you are so in the mood for Christmas, Paige,' he then said to me, 'how about giving us a hand to get more of the hall lights up this afternoon?'

'Sorry,' I said, reaching for my coat. 'I'll never be *that* keen.'

Before heading down to the studio, I let myself into the cottage using the key Albert had given me before I left the previous evening, to make a plateful of sandwiches and see if there were any mince pies left from the last batch Dorothy had sent.

I knew neither of the two new men in my life would think of their stomachs once they were ensconced in front of their easels and it was my plan to keep them filled up so they had the energy to keep painting. They both had a lot of catching up to do and I was going to make it my mission to enable their endeavours at every opportunity.

'Come on,' I said to Bran, who was still looking for Bella, after I'd done. 'She'll be in the studio.'

All was calm and silent as we headed across the garden and we slipped inside as quietly as we could. We must have been sitting next to the wood burner for at least half an hour before our presence was acknowledged and I had been starting to worry that the sandwiches were going to curl.

'Paige.' Albert beamed, when he eventually looked up from his easel. 'Is it that time already?'

Just as I'd guessed, they had completely lost track of the hour.

'Just about,' I said quietly, taking in how different he looked. 'How are you getting on?'

He looked back at the huge canvas he was standing in front of and nodded.

'Not bad,' he said, but he didn't invite me to look.

Infuriatingly, both him and Brodie had set up at the far end of the studio facing the door, so there was no chance of a sneaky peek as I went in. I could see Brodie was working on a smaller canvas than Albert and that there were a further two stacked by his side, both with their images turned the wrong way for me to see them.

'What about Brodie?' I asked, inclining my head in his direction.

The space around his feet was also littered with what looked like pencil sketches. I hoped that wasn't a bad sign. Now Albert had helped unlock his creativity again, I wanted him to be able to forge ahead all guns blazing.

'Don't worry,' Albert reassured me. 'It might look a bit messy, but it's all part of his process. He's not been here long. He went off sketching first. The other two canvases are from last night and they're both finished.'

'Oh, right,' I said, thinking that was super speedy work. 'That's great.'

'It is.' Albert smiled, coming over to where I'd set the tray down on a little table next to the armchairs.

He picked up a sandwich with one hand and Bella with the other, plonked himself down, then settled the cat and started to eat. His movements were so free flowing and natural. He had none of the stooped stiffness which had all but crippled him when we first met.

'What?' he asked, as he chewed.

'Nothing.' I shrugged, my lips twitching into a smile as I leant over to pour the tea which was past its best.

Brodie still hadn't even noticed I'd arrived, but I didn't take it personally. It was a pleasure to watch him work. Even if I could only see his legs.

'I'm so pleased about you two.' Albert smiled, following my line of sight. 'I knew you'd make a decent match, right from the moment I heard you scolding him for coming in here and sticking his nose in where you thought it wasn't wanted.'

I blushed at the memory.

'We didn't get off to the smoothest of starts,' I admitted, 'but hopefully things will be plainer sailing now.'

'Well,' said Albert, 'you know what they say about the course of true love . . .'

At that moment, Brodie's head popped comically up above the top of the canvas he was sitting in front of and he jumped to his feet, pulling out an ear bud.

'Paige!' He beamed. 'When did you get here?'

Without waiting for an answer, he pulled out the other bud, rushed over and kissed me full on the lips.

'I didn't hear you arrive,' he said, kissing me again.

I might have been fascinated by brooding Brodie when we first met, but this new version was a total joy and the impact of his kisses were a revelation.

'Literally ages ago,' I told him between them. 'Sorry, Albert,' I apologized.

'Don't mind me,' he chuckled. 'From what Brodie's told me, he's wanted to kiss you from the moment he set eyes on you, so by all accounts, I reckon he's got some lost time to make up for.'

'Albert!' Brodie cried, sounding embarrassed. 'That was for your ears only.'

Laughing, I waved Brodie's mortification away.

'Go on, Albert,' I encouraged. 'What else did he say about me?'

'Nothing I daresay you don't already know,' Albert chuckled again, reaching for another sandwich.

'That's the last time I trust you with a secret, Albert Price,' Brodie pretended to huff.

'Given how many you've told me over the last few days, my lad,' Albert countered, 'I reckon I know them all now anyway.'

'You're probably right,' Brodie agreed, pulling me to my feet in one smooth movement.

He then sat himself in the armchair and pulled me on to his lap.

'So how are things at the hall?' he asked, as I offered him the rapidly emptying plate. 'You haven't told Angus that I've let you in on our secret, have you?'

'Of course not,' I told him. 'I've hardly seen him this morning because I was cleaning in a frenzy to make sure I got here in time to shove some food down the pair of you.'

'That's all right then,' he said, jiggling me about which prompted a hard stare from Bran who looked less inclined to tolerate our messing about than Albert did.

'And no one knows about us either,' I added, loving that there was now an 'us'.

'If you carry on like this though,' Albert pointed out as Brodie kissed my cheek, 'you won't be able to keep your relationship under wraps for long.'

'Albert's right,' I said, twisting around to look at Brodie, who was quite irresistible close to. 'What are we going to do?'

Brodie stared deep into my eyes and I watched his pupils dilate.

'Nothing.' He shrugged, laying a hand lightly on my thigh. 'We're together now and there's no reason to keep it a secret, is there?'

'None at all,' I agreed, feeling even happier. 'Although we might have to put up with the odd person insisting that it's down to them that we're together.'

'I can handle that,' he laughed. 'As one of Wynbridge's most successful matchmakers perhaps Kathleen might give us discounts on tickets to the next dance. I'm very much looking forward to waltzing with you again, Paige.'

I felt a prickle of tears. I couldn't think of a time when any of my former relationships had made me a part of a bona fide couple. I hadn't had relationships while working overseas, and none of the occasional hook-ups during leave or any of the patchy university dates I'd been on, had warranted the title.

'She might,' I said, clearing my throat. 'I'm looking forward to that too.'

I had told myself I wouldn't keep thinking about what

was going to happen after Christmas, but now Brodie had so comfortably and openly declared our togetherness, I was desperate for my seed of an idea to further sprout, especially if it would keep me in Wynbridge or very close by.

Albert stood up, resettled Bella and walked over to his easel again.

'I don't suppose there's any tea left in that pot, is there?' he asked.

'I'll go and make some more,' I offered, shifting to stand up, but Brodie held me back.

'Are you okay?' he quietly asked.

'Yes.' I nodded. 'Of course.'

'Am I moving too fast?' he asked, his eyes searching my face. 'You'll have to tell me if I am.' He added, 'I've never felt anything like the way I feel for you for anyone else and I'm worried it's making me a bit needy and presumptuous.'

'Oh, Brodie.' I swallowed.

'I mean it,' he said.

'You're not being needy or presumptuous,' I told him. 'This is uncharted territory for me too.'

He nodded at that.

'Well,' he said, 'you're not being either of those things either. In case you were wondering.'

'That's enough chitchat,' said Albert, drawing a line under our heart to heart. 'Come and get back to work, Brodie. You'll be moaning in an hour that the light's gone.'

After another kiss, I took the lunch things back to the cottage, washed them up and made more tea and a flask of coffee. I was just about to carry it down to the studio when there was a knock on the door.

'Delivery for Albert Price,' said a woman in a high-vis waistcoat when I answered it.

'Oh, perfect,' I said, spotting the label. 'Thanks very much.'

I was tempted to open the box, but thought it should be Albert's treat.

'That parcel you've been waiting for has just turned up,' I told him as I reversed into the studio so as not to knock the tray.

'Is that your bath chair, Albert?' Brodie asked.

'It must be,' he said.

'It is,' I confirmed. 'I read the label. I can't wait to see it. I'll come back and set it up for you tomorrow, if you like.'

'Come back by all means,' he said, 'but Brodie has said he'll put it together for me.'

'Oh,' I said. 'Fair enough.'

'Don't pout about it.' Albert smiled. 'I've not turned into a misogynist who thinks reading instructions and putting things together is man's work.'

Brodie's head popped up again and he grinned.

'It's just that we're aware that he's got more time than you at the moment,' Albert further explained. 'What with looking after the hall and doing the deliveries.'

'And,' Brodie said, 'I wanted to do something to thank Albert for letting me use his studio. I feel far more productive here than I ever did set up in Jack's spare room. Not that I'm not grateful to my brother,' he quickly added.

'That's fair enough.' I happily accepted, because the arrangement would save me some time. 'Right, there's tea here and coffee. Please don't let it stew. I'd better get back to the hall,' I added, checking the time on my phone. 'I should be safe now.'

'From what?' Brodie asked, stepping away from his easel.

'Being talked into going up in the cherry picker to help string up the hall lights.' I shuddered.

'You could do that no problem,' Albert said. 'That thing's as safe as houses.'

'Says the man who is used to working hundreds of feet up in the air.'

'Not hundreds,' he corrected.

'Well, whatever,' I said. 'I'd rather keep my feet planted firmly on the ground, thank you very much. How about you, Brodie?'

He didn't answer and when I looked at him, he seemed to be in a daze.

'Are you thinking what I'm thinking, lad?' Albert then asked, turning to look at him.

'I think I might be,' he said. 'It's all a case of perspective, isn't it?'

'It could well be,' Albert said thoughtfully.

I had no idea what either of them were on about.

'Come on, Bran,' I said and he started to slowly haul himself to his feet. 'Let's leave the artists to it.'

'Wait,' said Brodie, coming out of his reverie. 'I'll walk you back to the road.'

'No need,' I said, but he insisted.

And I was pleased he did because he had the most wonderful way of saying goodbye.

The next day played out in pretty much the same way, only with a plethora of deliveries replacing the hours of cleaning. With the incentive of seeing Brodie again, I would have liked to whizz through them, but I was mindful that the interaction for the recipients was every bit as beneficial as what I dropped off.

Alice didn't need anything delivered, but I was excited to see how she was settling into her new flat and I had a card from the gallery for her too, so I made sure I had plenty of time to call in and say hello once the Land Rover was empty of perishables and prescriptions.

'I can't believe you're unpacked already,' I told her as she led me through the freshly painted rooms once I'd handed over the card and she'd made us both coffees.

'I was determined we'd feel settled by Christmas.' She grinned. 'And to be honest it already feels like we've been here far longer than just a few days.'

'I can totally understand that.' I nodded. 'I hadn't visited the hall or Wynbridge for years, but I was barely back anytime at all before it felt like home.'

The thought of leaving made my stomach twist and I knew it would be too much of a wrench to leave, especially now Brodie and I were finally stepping out together, as Albert loved to say.

'There's some magic in Wynbridge,' Alice said wistfully, as she looked around. 'I'm certain of it.'

'I think you might be right,' I agreed.

'And everyone tells me there's even more at Wynthorpe Hall.'

'Oh, definitely,' I laughed. 'The place is awash with it.'

'I can't wait to experience it for myself.' She beamed. 'Kathleen has offered to give us lifts to and from the Winter Wonderland at the weekend. I haven't told the kids anything about it though,' she quietly added as her eldest came in, 'otherwise I'd never get any peace.'

'Mum's the word,' I said, tapping the side of my nose.

'Is it all set up yet?' she asked.

'We're starting tomorrow,' I told her. 'And I haven't visited it before either, so I'm really looking forward to it, too.'

'How exciting,' she said, 'but you must be rushed off your feet.'

'I am a bit,' I responded, 'but I do feel bad that I wasn't about to help you move.'

'You needn't,' Alice insisted. 'I told you the Dempster clan had it all in hand and to be honest, I don't think I could have coped with more people involved.'

That made me feel a bit better.

'Even a new friend,' she then added with another smile.

I smiled back.

'I'm going to start looking for a part-time job in the new year,' she confided as we finished the tour, 'so I might well be drafting you in to help out then.'

'Draft away,' I told her. 'Whatever you need. And I have an idea about an opportunity of my own brewing, but I'm not at the sharing stage yet.'

Alice was intrigued and I promised I'd keep her in the loop, then set off for Albert's.

As I drove along, my thoughts tracked back to the Winter Wonderland. There was an awful lot of work to be done for something which would this year last just forty-eight hours. But then, they were going to be forty-eight magical hours which would hopefully create standout and special festive memories for so many people and that would make the graft worthwhile. If I was lucky, I might even bag a few special moments myself.

I also couldn't help thinking how fast the weeks had flown by since I had arrived at the hall. I'd certainly packed a lot in to that time, and Dad had been right. Keeping busy and helping out had proved to be a great healer, transformative even. My life had changed an extraordinary amount and Albert's and now Brodie's had too.

'Everything all right?' I asked when Brodie opened the cottage door as I let Bran out of the Land Rover. 'I thought you'd be in the studio by now.'

He beckoned me into the house and I rushed to follow him inside.

'I should be down there really,' he said, after closing the door and giving me a tender kiss. 'Your nose is cold,' he added, kissing the end of it.

'I know,' I said, giving it a rub. 'So, why aren't you then?' I asked. 'In the studio, I mean.'

Brodie pointed towards the ceiling.

'It's Albert,' he said. 'I can't get him out of the bath.'

'Oh, no,' I gasped. 'Is he stuck? I thought with that new chair . . .'

'Let me rephrase that,' Brodie said quickly. 'The chair is set up and Albert *can* get himself in and out now, but he *won't*.'

I had to laugh at that.

'He keeps saying he'll just have another quick top up and the water must be almost over the side!'

'So, why haven't you left him to it?' I asked, laughing again.

'I didn't like to,' he said. 'He told me he'd be fine and that I should go, but I just couldn't.'

'I tell you what,' I said, because I could see he was itching to get started. 'You go down there now and I'll wait here and listen out for him.'

'Are you sure?'

'Yes,' I said. 'Go on.'

'You're bloody brilliant, you are. Do you know that?'

'I did hear a rumour,' I said, reaching for the front of his jumper and pulling him close. 'Now go on,' I said, after giving him another lingering kiss. 'Go now, or it won't be worth it.'

I busied myself in the kitchen, keeping an eye on the ceiling to make sure there were no drips or damp patches starting to show, and it was getting on for an hour later before Albert finally came down the stairs looking dapper and smelling of cologne.

'Paige,' he said, sounding blissed out. 'I didn't know you were here.'

I looked up from the paper I had been reading in lieu of anything else to do.

'Hello, Albert,' I smiled, looking him up and down. 'You look taller than I expected you to.'

'Taller?' He frowned.

'Yes,' I said, 'you've been in the bath so long I thought you were bound to have shrunk.'

'Oh, you,' he said, his face splitting into a smile. 'That chair's a godsend. It's so easy to use.'

'You'll be cursing it when your water bill arrives,' I warned him.

'No, I won't,' he said cheekily. 'I'm like you and Brodie. I've got a lot of time to make up for, only on the bath front. I'm only using the water now that I haven't over the last goodness knows how long.'

'It's funny you should mention time, Albert,' I told him. 'Because I've worked out that it's a month tomorrow since I arrived at the hall.'

'A month?' Albert frowned again, sounding disbelieving. 'That can't be right.'

'It is,' I said. 'I've just checked. It was the fourteenth of November.'

'So how long is it since you scared me witless by knocking on my door?' he asked, lowering himself into his armchair.

He was never going to let me forget how we met.

'Um . . .' I said as I worked it out. 'It'll be three weeks on Thursday.' Albert shook his head. 'Three weeks the day after tomorrow.'

'I don't believe it,' he said.

'I know,' I said. 'I can't believe it either to be honest. I've known Brodie just a week longer than I've known you, Albert.'

'It doesn't seem possible, does it?' he said, staring into space. 'How can so much have happened in such a short space of time?'

'I've no idea.' I shrugged.

'My goodness,' he added. 'It makes you wonder what the next three weeks is going to bring, doesn't it?'

'That it does, Albert,' I said, letting out a breath as I wondered what else was in store for us. 'That it does.'

Why was it that ever since I'd told myself I would focus on the present and not think about the future, it had become impossible to do anything else?

Chapter 27

If I thought I had been achieving a lot before, it was nothing compared to what I managed to get through during the next few days. Thankfully, I wasn't asked to step into the cherry picker as Archie and Mick had finished setting up the hall lights in the time I was visiting Albert's cottage.

As well as my cleaning and delivery duties, I had helped set up the Winter Wonderland areas in and around the woods which would house the visiting wildlife. We would be playing host to both local rescue owls and reindeer from further afield and there had also been a discovery trail through the trees to prepare, along with Santa's grotto in the walled garden and summerhouse.

That was the smallest part of the whole event, but it had taken the longest to create because it was the most detailed. There were multiple strands of lights to arrange, life-size emperor penguins and smaller polar bear figurines to position among the shrubbery, a faux fire for the grotto itself and an armchair – and, of course, a huge sack of presents.

On Thursday evening, Jemma and Lizzie arrived to set up the pretty Cherry Tree Café vintage caravan and there were other food and drink suppliers coming too, but they would arrive ahead of opening early on Saturday morning.

Hot chestnuts, along with a hog roast and apple-based drinks from Skylark Farm had proved popular the year before so they were coming back and Jack from Brambles, ably assisted by Tilly, would be providing mulled wine. At Molly's suggestion, the people who supplied the switch-on with a vegetarian and vegan feast had been invited too. Dorothy had been in a baking frenzy for days and, in spite of what she said, was loving every minute.

I barely had time to miss Brodie and Albert, but I had been checking in with them in the evenings. From what I could make out, Brodie was practically living in the studio and they'd both enjoyed a productive few days. I'd also received another call from Mum and even texts from Jamie who was keen to check that his father was behaving. It was a relief that I could honestly reply that he was.

By Friday lunchtime everything for the Wynthorpe Hall annual Winter Wonderland was in place. The beautiful reindeer and their keepers were settled in their quarters, the previously lame pony had been declared fit to pull the shining sleigh and, to further add to my excitement, when I stepped out of the hall to take the dogs for a walk after finishing the cleaning, I found Brodie puffing up the drive on his battered old bike.

'Brodie!' I exclaimed, rushing to meet him. 'I didn't know you were coming.'

'Bit of a last-minute plan,' he said, jumping off the bike and taking a moment to catch his breath.

'You really should have thought about keeping enough money from your former life to buy a car,' I told him as he pulled a rucksack off his back and I steadied the bike. 'This thing has definitely seen better days.'

'I know,' he said, trying to smile. 'I've been thinking the same myself.'

'Have you got your breath back now?' I asked, stepping closer.

'Just about.' He nodded.

We were both more than a little breathless by the time we'd finished kissing.

'Well, well, well,' said a voice behind us and we broke apart. 'What have we here?'

'Nothing more than your better half has probably already predicted, Archie Connelly,' I told him, turning to find both him and a very happy looking Molly walking towards us.

'You took your time about it though,' he further teased.

'Actually,' I said primly, taking Brodie's frozen hand in my gloved one, 'I've only been here a month, so you can hardly tease us about that.'

Molly looked as though she would have still liked to.

'I'm just about to walk the dogs,' I said quickly before she had the chance. 'Shall we all go together?'

'I can't, I'm afraid,' Brodie told me, squeezing my hand. 'I'm actually here on a mission. I've come to take a ride in the cherry picker.'

'You can come with us to do that instead, if you like, Paige,' Archie suggested.

I gave him a withering look and he laughed.

'I'll walk the dogs with you,' Molly said, putting Suki, who she had been carrying, down, 'and we'll meet in the hall after you've done, shall we?' she added to Archie.

'Good idea,' he said. 'And you'll stay for dinner, won't you, Brodie? Dad's turning on the hall lights when it gets dark. You won't want to miss that.'

'Well,' Brodie said, looking at the rickety bike, 'I'll think about it. The roads around here are a bit dicey in the dark.'

'I can take you back to Brambles in the Land Rover if you like,' I offered. 'It would be lovely if you could stay.'

'All right,' he said, pulling me close again. 'That would be great. Although I'm not going back to Jack's, but we'll talk about that later.'

'Yes,' said Archie, 'come on. I've moved the picker to where Dad told me you wanted it, so let's make the most of the light. I don't suppose you're going to tell me why you want to go up in it, are you?'

The pair of them walked off and Brodie threw a parting smile over his shoulder which made my heart flutter as if I was a thirteen-year-old rather than an early thirty something. I blew him a kiss back and guessed his visit was most likely something to do with Angus's commission so Archie had no hope of wheedling any details out of him.

'Come on then,' I said to Molly. 'Let's go before we freeze to the spot.'

We walked the woodland trail, checking everything was properly in place and lingered a long time at the reindeer enclosure. There was a calf among the group which had been born in the spring and was keen to bump noses with Bran through the fence. Floss wasn't interested in the beautiful beasts, but Molly had picked Suki up again as she was prone to yap and dart under the fence.

'Are these all female?' I asked one of the keepers as I ducked to avoid a magnificent velvet covered antler when the largest of the group wandered over to say hello.

'Yes,' said the guy who travelled with them. 'We have a mixed herd but it's the females who keep their antlers until after they've given birth in the spring. The males shed after the breeding season in December.'

I thought about that for a moment, then looked at Molly who smiled.

'So, Santa's reindeer . . .' I began.

'All girls,' said Molly with a gleeful grin.

'Really?' I gasped.

'Extremely likely,' confirmed the keeper.

'Well, I never,' I said. 'I never knew that.'

Having gingerly petted the majestic matriarch, we said goodbye and took a detour to the Wishing Tree. The atmosphere in both the woods and the hawthorn clearing felt completely different to the day of the gathering. There was a light breeze weaving its way through the branches but nothing like the gust which had pushed Brodie and I together.

I watched as Molly walked up to the tree and then around

it, one hand resting on the trunk as she circled. I stood further back, thinking of that unforgettable kiss, along with everything else that had happened since. Sometimes it felt as though I'd been staying at the hall for far longer than a month.

'Molly,' I said, when I noticed she'd stopped walking, 'are you all right?'

She took a few seconds before answering and even though there was nothing unusual in that, I got the feeling there was something amiss. For a start, she hadn't quizzed me once about the shift in mine and Brodie's relationship and she hadn't asked about the impact the rose quartz she'd pressed on me when I first arrived was having either.

They were both topics I would have expected her to broach, especially as it had been a while since we'd been alone. I had been fully prepared for her to capitalize on our solitary walk and gift me with more of her other-worldly wisdom as we took it.

'Yes,' she sighed. 'I think so.'

'You don't sound very convinced,' I said, beginning to feel concerned.

She moved a little away from the tree and turned to face me.

'I'm sensing big changes,' she said, a frown creasing her forehead and making her look nothing like her usual serene self. Molly had never gone in for frowning. 'But I can't see what they are yet. It's unsettling.'

'Big changes for you?' I asked, moving closer to her side.

'For lots of us,' she said. 'I think we're all going to feel their impact.'

'Molly,' I said, 'you're scaring me.'

'It's nothing bad,' she said quickly, the frown disappearing as Bran nudged her hand and she rested her fingers lightly on top of his head, 'but it is big. A huge shift. Time will tell.' She smiled.

'Well,' I said, 'I hope we're not kept waiting too long.'

'I can understand that,' she said. 'Especially as you're going to be impacted by them all. Don't look so worried,' she then laughed, linking her arm through mine. 'You've come so far already. I don't think there's anything now that you can't handle.'

I hoped she was right about that.

'Now,' she said, as we walked back to the path which would lead us to the hall. 'Tell me all about you and Brodie.'

'Thank the goddess for that,' I laughed. 'I thought you were never going to ask!'

I told her that we were now officially a couple, but didn't mention that I had concerns about what would happen after Christmas. I daresay, Molly being Molly, she already had an inkling, so I focused instead on the good stuff and then, during dinner, Brodie and Angus filled in some of the blanks and explained to everyone more about how they knew each other.

By the time we were ready to watch my godfather light up the hall everything, apart from his secret Christmas commission for Catherine and Albert's extraordinary talent, had been openly discussed.

I was relieved that Albert and his studio hadn't been mentioned. He might have picked up his brushes again but I knew that his paintings were still for his, and now, Brodie's eyes only and they most likely always would be.

I completely respected that, but I would have dearly loved for him to develop an urge to step out of the shadows and share his work with the world. He wasn't getting any younger and I worried that he might one day come to regret keeping it all hidden away.

I knew that if I were to suggest that to him, he would wave my words away but it was only three weeks ago that he had been living in freezing cold near-squalor and literally couldn't see further than the end of his nose. Molly's words about change rang around my head, but I didn't have time to pin down further thoughts about them because Archie was calling for quiet and Angus was bouncing up and down in barely contained excitement.

'If he's this geed up now,' Brodie whispered into my ear, making my skin tingle, 'you're really going to have your work cut out tomorrow.'

'I was just thinking that myself,' I whispered back.

We counted down from ten to one and then, with a flourish and a drumroll loud enough to rival Clark Griswold's, Angus flicked a switch and the hall was bathed in the soft glow of warm white lights.

'No way,' Brodie gasped, stepping back to take it all in.

'Oh, Angus,' I beamed, bouncing up and down myself. 'It's beautiful.'

We all took several paces down the drive and Angus stood between us, with his hands on his hips, his eyes tracking from one side of the building to the other.

'This is definitely better, Dad,' said Archie, who sounded every bit as thrilled as his father looked. 'I think we've cracked it.'

Every window had lights around it and so did the door. It was elegant and sophisticated and from what Mick explained, it was a rather different look to the one Angus had originally favoured when he'd started stringing up lights a few years ago. Apparently, there had been an accident then and a far more chaotic approach to the project which Angus had tried to keep a secret.

'I think you're right, son,' Angus said, clapping Archie on the back and shaking Brodie's hand. 'This is just perfect.'

'There you go, Molly,' I quietly said. 'There's one big change for you.'

'What do you mean?'

'Angus has just agreed that the hall has enough lights. Surely, he'd usually be clamouring for more.'

'You're right,' she laughed and I was relieved to see her looking more like herself.

Photos were taken and then Molly and Archie went back to their cottage and Catherine, Angus, Dorothy and Mick headed back into the hall, leaving me and Brodie to further admire the sensational seasonal spectacle.

'If we had Instagram,' he pointed out as we stood close together and scrolled through the pictures I'd taken on my phone, 'we could upload these.'

'You're right,' I said, slipping the phone back into my pocket and giving him a kiss. 'But I can live without it.'

'Me too,' he said, zipping up his coat.

It was the battered old Barbour again and it suited him perfectly.

'Ah,' I said, as the penny dropped. 'I get now why Jack was on at you that day to have an account. He wanted you to upload your work, didn't he?'

'Yep,' he said. 'And he's still on about it.'

'Maybe you should,' I said, biting my lip.

'Don't you start,' he said, lunging to tickle me. 'I get enough nagging from him.'

I let out a squawk as his fingers found my waist.

'No more,' I begged, when he wouldn't stop. 'I hate being tickled.'

'Me too,' he said, dropping his hands. 'So don't get any ideas,' he added as I immediately darted back at him.

'I suppose I'd better drive you home,' I said reluctantly. 'It's getting late and if I don't get some sleep, I won't be any use to anyone tomorrow. You are coming to the Wonderland, aren't you?'

'Not tomorrow,' he told me. 'I need to work on Catherine's painting, but I'll come on Sunday.'

'Do you think we'll be able to get Albert to come then, too?'

'I hope so,' Brodie said. 'I think he'd enjoy it.'

'Me too,' I agreed. 'He loved the auction in town, even though it was busy. The Wonderland is more spread out so it should feel a little quieter. I'll ring and ask him in the morning.'

'Or I could ask him?' Brodie offered. 'That's where I'm staying tonight.'

'At the cottage?'

'Most likely in the studio. I'm planning a long night.'

'Given the amount of time you're spending there now,' I smiled as we loaded his bike into the Land Rover, 'you'd be better off moving in.'

He didn't say anything.

'Brodie?'

He turned to look at me.

'I'm not supposed to say anything,' he said, 'but Albert has offered me his spare room in the cottage.'

'He never has?' I gasped.

'He has,' Brodie confirmed, a frown forming.

'And what have you said?' I asked, noting his expression. 'Don't you want to take it?'

He ran his hands through his hair, so I knew the decision he had to make wasn't an easy one and that he was giving it careful consideration before deciding.

'I really do want to take it,' he confided. 'More than anything. Tilly and Jack are obviously becoming more than colleagues now . . .'

'Are they?' I cut in. 'How wonderful is that? I knew there was something going on between them the day I had my almost-tour of the distillery, even if they didn't.'

'Yes,' said Brodie, 'and I'm really happy for them, although gooseberry has never been my favourite fruit. And it would be wonderful to be so close to the studio,' he added. 'That funny little place has transformed me.'

'So, what's stopping you saying yes to Albert's offer?'

'It's just all so quick,' he said, sounding wary. 'I've barely known Albert any time at all and this would be a huge change, for both of us.'

He was right, of course. It was a huge commitment for anyone to make, especially to someone you'd met just days before.

'You're right,' I had to agree, but couldn't help thinking of what Molly had said and how convinced she had seemed that the changes coming would be good ones. Perhaps this was one of them. 'It is quick,' I further said, 'but Albert knows his own mind and he's extremely keen to embrace life again and live it to the full.'

'Thanks to you,' Brodie said, making me blush.

'Well,' I said, 'I've played a part, but it's been his choice to run with it all and perhaps inviting you to stay is part of that. I think, if I were you . . .'

'Yes?'

'I'd go for it,' I told him. 'It will be a huge change, but an exciting one for both of you, I reckon.'

'I know you're right,' he said, sounding more sure. 'And I do feel in my heart that it's meant to be. It's my head that's a bit cautious, but my heart and my gut are right behind the idea.'

'In that case,' I said, thinking of my own heart as I reached for his hand, 'I'd still take your head into account, but I'd follow your gut and your heart.'

It was very late by the time I got back from dropping Brodie at the studio. Albert's cottage had been in darkness, so I'd left him at the gate. I didn't expect anyone to still be up when I got back to the hall, but Angus was waiting for me in the kitchen.

'I had my key,' I told him. 'You could have gone up.'

'I know,' he said, warming milk on the Aga and snatching the pan up just before it spilled over, 'but I wanted to talk to you.'

With a mug of cocoa each, we sat at the table and I held my breath. I hoped I hadn't let his recent impeccable behaviour lull me into a false sense of security. Was I about to have the rug pulled out from under me?

'Is it about tomorrow?' I tentatively asked.

Angus chuckled.

'Absolutely not,' he promised. 'That's all going ahead exactly as planned. I really did mean it when I said I was satisfied with the set up.'

I felt my shoulders drop.

'Good,' I said, daring to breathe again and blowing into my mug. 'Great. That's all right then, because I really have got enough on my plate right now.'

Angus looked at me for a moment and I felt my shoulders stiffen again.

'I can appreciate that.' He then freaked me out by saying, 'But I hope there's room for a little something else?'

'Oh, Angus . . .' I groaned.

'It's nothing bad,' he insisted. 'I promise.'

'What is it then?' I asked, wanting him to put me out of my misery as quickly as possible.

'Well,' he said, 'I thought it would be nice if we had a party. A sort of Christmas celebration if you like.'

'Oh,' I said, feeling a little less freaked.

That didn't sound too bad, but I was still reserving judgement until I'd heard the whole of it.

'Everyone will be arriving on the twentieth,' he reminded me, 'and I thought it might be nice to have a get together with friends and family to celebrate on, say . . . the twenty-third.'

'That's very close to Christmas day,' I pointed out.

'It is,' he acknowledged, 'but that will give you more time to organize it.'

'Me?' I said, spluttering through my first sip of cocoa.

'Yes,' he said. 'I'd like you to set it up, Paige. You can plan it all out in the notebook Santa gifted you.'

Exactly how long had he had this party idea in mind? He could have given me a heads up before.

'You want me to plan a party, to be held here, on the twenty-third?' I asked, just to be sure I'd heard him correctly.

'That's it,' he confirmed.

I mulled it over and came to the surprising conclusion that it didn't sound like too much of a stretch.

'So, what do you think?' he asked eagerly.

'It should be doable,' I tentatively said. 'As long as you're not expecting too much of an extravaganza.'

'So, you're willing to go ahead?'

'I suppose,' I said. 'Yes, I'll do it.'

'That's wonderful,' he said, as he pushed back his chair and stood up. 'Oh,' he then added, as if the next idea had just occurred to him, 'and it might be nice if we could perhaps have some of Albert and Brodie's paintings on display when it was happening.'

'What?'

'I was thinking that it might be the ideal opportunity to reveal the two newly discovered local artists to the world,' he said, taking a step away from the table.

'Oh, Angus,' I tried to interrupt, but he carried on.

'And as you're the person who knows them the best,' he wheedled, 'I'm thrilled you and Brodie are now a couple by the way, *and* you're the person who'll be organizing the celebration, you're most conveniently placed to convince them that it's a good idea.'

My mouth opened and closed like a trapdoor but no sound came out and Angus took advantage of my stunned silence and rushed out of the room and up to bed, leaving a trail of splashed cocoa in his wake.

Chapter 28

Having helped to set up the Winter Wonderland, admired the hall lights and fallen head over heels in love with the idea of Brodie and Albert living in the cottage together, I had thought the rest of the run up to Christmas was going to be plain sailing, but Angus's late-night chat at the kitchen table had thrown everything into chaos.

Sleep was impossible to come by and when it was time to get up, rather than spring out of bed as I had imagined I would on this special and long anticipated day, I lay there, limp as a used dishrag and with a thousand jumbled thoughts flying around my head.

The Christmas celebration I could willingly get on board with, but creating an exhibition of Albert and Brodie's art to run alongside it was going to be impossible to pull off. Brodie, having already publicly shared his work, might be easier to convince, although given his recent creative block even his acquiescence wasn't a given, and as for Albert ... the words *complete non-starter* sprang to mind.

'Angus,' I said, when I went down and fortuitously found him alone, 'about the Christmas celebration.'

'You've been thinking about that, have you?' he beamed, sounding pleased. 'Well, I suppose you should be, given that this time next week it will be the morning after!'

I didn't want to acknowledge that. Even without the impossible exhibition element, it was still a very short amount of time in which to pull off a party. And being so close to Christmas made it all the more complicated. A truly stylish seasonal soiree should have been months in the making. I might have thought that it would distract me from stressing over post-Christmas plans when I said I'd do it, but at what cost?

'And I did say that I want to keep it a complete secret from Catherine, didn't I?' Angus then added.

'No,' I said, thinking that it would make it even harder to get off the ground. 'I'm pretty certain you didn't mention that.'

'Oh,' he said. 'Well, if you can keep it from her, that would be great. Obviously, you'll have to tell the rest of the family about it and I'll give you a list of who to invite from further afield, but as far as the exhibition goes, that's just for you, me, Albert and Brodie to know about until as close to the time as possible.'

I tried to think calming thoughts, take slow breaths in and out and count to ten but when faced with my self-assured godfather who nothing seemed to faze, it wasn't easy.

'Look,' I said, before the moment was lost, 'I think the

celebration is a fabulous idea, and I know you've got your heart set on the exhibition element of it, but there's no way I'll be able to talk Albert into it.'

Angus looked at me and shook his head.

'I think you're underestimating your capabilities, my dear.' He smiled benignly.

'I'm really not,' I responded.

'Albert has told me that when you turned up on his doorstep he was living in a cold house, surviving on tinned rations and had pretty much given up all thoughts of seeing another spring.'

I felt a lump form in my throat. Not only was I shocked Albert had shared something as intimate as that, I also hadn't realized he'd been feeling that low.

'And look at him now!' Angus said triumphantly. 'He's back on track and living his best life and it's all thanks to you, Paige.'

'That's as maybe . . .'

'And it could be even better,' he hastily added. 'He'll have an even richer life when you get him to share his paintings and further reignite those feelings along with the ambitions he had before his father quashed his dreams.'

'Look,' I said, keen to put a cap on Angus's enthusiastic and fanciful daydreaming. 'He's painting again. Isn't that enough? Who says he wants recognition? Who says the feelings he's already experiencing aren't even better than those he had before?'

I wanted to believe what I was saying, but I had to admit

there was a tiny part of me that agreed with Angus. I had watched Albert tutor and guide Brodie during my recent visits to the studio and had thought then how much he had to offer.

I had even imagined him giving a lesson or two at the gallery in town, but that was pure fantasy and I felt sure Albert wouldn't appreciate me trying to pressure him into making that, or exhibiting his work, a reality. Our friendship was still very new and therefore potentially fragile and I didn't want to do anything which might jeopardize it. I'd been rebuffed once before and it hadn't been a pleasant experience.

'The best thing you can do,' Angus said, as we heard the back door open, 'is forget all about it for today and just enjoy the Winter Wonderland. Just let the whole thing sit and settle and I'm sure inspiration will land right when you least expect it.'

'But you just said yourself that there's less than a week to sort it . . .'

'I know,' he told me, 'but in my experience, fretting over problems never makes them easier to solve. Put your worries about convincing Albert to exhibit on the backburner and a solution as to how to talk him round will soon present itself.'

I had absolutely no faith in Angus's words of wisdom. However, I did manage to forget my worries when Kathleen arrived early on with Alice in the passenger seat of her car and three extremely well-wrapped up children in the back.

In spite of the early hour, visitors had already been arriving in droves and I had been helping to man the ticket office and clear tables for Lizzie and Jemma who were serving hot drinks and tempting snacks by the bag full.

'Hello, Alice!' I called as she and Kathleen set up the buggy and strapped the two youngest in.

Saffron skipped around them, her eyes eagerly taking everything in.

'Hi!' Alice called back.

'Paige!' said Kathleen. 'Just the person.'

I walked over and Saffron beamed up at me. I could almost feel the energy and excitement radiating from her little rosy-cheeked face.

'You're keen,' I said to Alice. 'It's still early yet.'

'We're here at this time because of me actually,' Kathleen explained. 'Although these four were keen to get here too, of course. Originally, we were all set to come a little later, but Dorothy rang to ask if I'd have time to help her in the kitchen, so . . .'

'Oh,' I said. 'She hasn't said anything to me.'

'She was going to ask you,' Kathleen further said, 'but she told me that when she came to find you, it looked like you were needed elsewhere. It's busy, isn't it?'

'Ever so,' I said, 'and we've barely been open an hour yet.'

'I want to see Santa's reindeer,' said Saffron, tugging at Alice's coat as the two in the buggy squirmed to get going too.

'In a minute,' said Alice, kissing the top of Saffron's head.

'Are you still as busy as you were earlier when Dorothy saw you?' Kathleen asked me.

I held out my hand for Saffron to take.

'I'm going to be for the next few hours,' I told her with a grin, 'because I'm going to give Alice and the children the ultimate Winter Wonderland guided tour.'

Kathleen smiled and I guessed that's what she had been hoping I would say.

'Oh, will you?' Alice gasped, looking even more relieved than Kathleen. 'Will you really?'

'It would be an honour,' I told her, thinking how much I was going to enjoy seeing the children react to everything. 'I've seen it all already, of course, so I'm quite the expert,' I pretended to brag, 'but I would love to see it again through the eyes of these three.'

Kathleen gave Alice a hug and quickly bustled off and we then collected tickets and maps which, I noticed, had been designed by Hayley, and set off. There were points of interest marked all around the woodland trail and if visitors stamped all the spots on their maps using the ink pads at the corresponding site, they got an extra gift from Santa in the grotto.

'So,' I said, as Alice and I fell into step after the initial excitement had calmed a little, 'how are things in town? Still good, I hope?'

Alice looked at me with the biggest smile lighting up her pretty face. Her cheeks were flushed and she looked far less tired and worn out than she had the first time we met.

'The flat's still great,' she said, with a twinkle in her eyes, 'and moving there has changed so much more than my address.'

'It must be that Wynbridge magic you mentioned before.' I smiled.

'Without a doubt,' she laughed.

'Are you still planning to look for a job in the new year?'

'Definitely,' she said firmly, 'because I've realized now just how detrimental to my mental health the time spent entirely on my own at the cottage with just these three actually was.'

'I get that.' I nodded, her words sparking another idea.

'I had thought,' she carried on thoughtfully, 'that when I got out of my relationship, if you could call it that, that I'd be done with people. That I would want to keep myself to myself for good, but I was wrong. Time spent in company, even just an hour a day chatting in the market, or visiting the library, has made a huge difference to the way I feel.'

'I love that,' I said, knowing I had experienced something similar myself since arriving at the hall.

After losing Chadia, I had been ruthlessly independent, working alone for years and making no attachments and forming no ties. I had thought it was for the best. The one sure way to prevent my heart from further assault. However, the anguish I experienced after my mistake, which most likely wouldn't have even happened had I been a team player, was proof that my heart hadn't, in fact, been protected at all.

However, since arriving at the hall and working with others, forming bonds, friendships and a romantic relationship, I had come to realize the true value of what made for a happier and fuller life. It was other people and I was feeling a million times better for letting them in.

I wondered how many other people there were, in the Wynbridge area alone, who might need to experience that for themselves? Not everyone might have been looking for romance but we all needed friends. How many of the people I visited in their isolated cottages had regular opportunities to get together in person?

'And keeping busy is helping me find myself,' Alice continued confidently. 'I'm even thinking about taking an adult education class or two and, even though I won't be ready for a new relationship for a very long time,' she stoically added, having clearly thought it all through very carefully, 'I'm already thinking that I should never say never.'

'Oh, Alice.' I sniffed, feeling simultaneously choked and delighted. 'That's amazing.'

'It is,' she laughed. 'If you'd told me this time last year, that I'd be here now, with my kids living a completely different life, with so many new friends and such wonderful support, I never would have believed it.'

'Reindeer!' shouted Saffron as we rounded a bend in the path and the enclosure came in sight. 'Come on, Mum. Look, there's Rudolph!'

'It's Rachel actually,' I whispered to Alice, taking the buggy handles from her so she could enjoy the special moment with her daughter. 'I'm so happy for you, Alice,' I told her.

'So am I.' She beamed in return.

'You're an inspiration,' I told her again.

'Well.' She blushed. 'I don't know about that.'

I stayed with her for the largest part of the day and after Kathleen had driven her and the exhausted children back to town, I walked around the trail again on my own. I wanted to go back and see the owls which were being shown by a lad called Ed and his mum, Mags. I had seen their stand earlier, but one of the owls was having a flap on its perch which had scared Alice's youngest so we hadn't lingered.

'Hello, Paige,' said Will, who happened to be visiting the stand at the same time.

'Hi,' I said. 'How are you?'

'I'm good.' He nodded. 'Thrilled to have been able to give the all clear for the sleigh rides to go ahead. Have you been for a ride in it? I'm guessing you have by now.'

'No,' I told him. 'I haven't yet. I'm saving it for tomorrow.'

I rather liked the thought of Brodie and I, and Albert, if he fancied it, going for a ride with Mick at the helm. I had seen the resplendent red sleigh going up and down throughout the afternoon and it looked even more spectacular in motion than it had set up in Wynbridge market square on the night of the switch-on.

The only thing missing from it was Santa, but that was because he was entertaining visitors in the grotto and two Father Christmases in one place would have taken some explaining. Mick had been cajoled into wearing a Santa hat though and he didn't look impressed about it when it kept slipping down over his eyes as the ponies trotted along. I was just grateful there had been no further suggestion that I should play the elf.

'You'll love it,' Will said. 'It's really exhilarating and brings out the child in all of us.' I could believe that. 'Do you know Ed, by the way?' he asked, turning back to the lad who was in charge of the owls.

'We met briefly when he arrived early this morning,' I explained, 'but the owls weren't set up then which is why I've come back for a look.'

'Hi,' said Ed, as he soothed a barn owl who was looking a little ruffled.

'Hi.' I smiled and he turned bright red.

'That's not an owl, is it?' I then said to Will, having spotted a small hawklike bird at the back.

'No,' he said, 'that's a kestrel.'

'It's beautiful,' I said, taking in the prettily speckled plumage and inquisitive dark eyes.

'You can hold her if you like,' said Ed. 'This is her first time at an event, which is why I've put her at the back. It can be a bit overwhelming, so I introduce them gradually to the display and if they don't settle, Mum takes them away again.'

'What's her story?' I asked, as Will helped me put on a thick glove.

Before I had a chance to get too nervous, Ed carried her over and the little kestrel, who was incredibly light, hopped on to the glove and he then wrapped a strap around it. Thankfully, she seemed relaxed.

'She was liberated,' Will said with emphasis, and I wondered at his choice of word, 'from someone who had bred her and was keeping her in appalling conditions.'

I looked from him to the tiny face and thought of the sad start the diminutive bird had had. I was tempted to stroke her, but wasn't sure how she'd react.

'That's awful,' I said. 'Will she ever be released?'

'No,' said Ed. 'Sadly not. She sustained a couple of injuries when she was young which means she's not a good flyer.'

'Or hoverer,' added Will.

I remembered seeing kestrels hovering over ditches and dykes as they tracked their prey. If she couldn't do that, she'd have no hope of fending for herself in the wild.

'Well,' I said, a minute later as Ed took her back to her perch and prepared to pack up for the day, 'I daresay she's very happy with you.'

'I hope so.' He blushed again.

'I know so.' Will smiled. 'Ed and I have worked together for years and there's not a bird he's encountered which he hasn't been able to soothe, settle and tame.'

'Says the man with the true healing touch.' Ed grinned.

'You sound like a dream ornithological team,' I laughed, thinking that here was another example of teamwork in action and this time, from an unlikely pairing.

'We should have that printed on a T-shirt,' Will laughed back.

Having thanked Ed for the privilege of holding one of his beloved birds and said goodbye to Will, I made another quick trip to the reindeer enclosure and then headed back to the courtyard. The last few cars were leaving and Archie was chatting with the remaining stallholders and catering crews.

'Great news about you and Brodie,' said Jack, once Archie had moved on from the much-depleted Brambles stall and we were alone. 'I've never seen him so happy.'

'It's a while since I've been so happy too,' I unguardedly told him, feeling my cheeks flush almost as brightly as Ed's had when I'd smiled at him. 'But you've changed your tune,' I reminded Jack. 'That day at Brambles . . .'

'Please don't.' He winced. 'I'm still feeling bad about that and after watching the pair of you at the dance, well . . . I realized that some things in life are just meant to be.'

I wondered if Brodie had told his brother how we were connected through his former employer? At least I now knew the rough time Brodie was going through with his work that Jack had referred to was with his creative block and not embezzling money from dodgy financial portfolios. Not that I could ever really have believed he was capable of that.

'You were just looking out for him,' I said generously, hoping to make Jack feel better. 'Protective brother and all that.'

'I really thought I was.' He smiled.

'You had his best interests at heart.'

'I did.' He nodded. 'I still do. And I get the feeling that he's finally painting again which is certainly in his best interests. You wouldn't happen to know anything about that, would you?'

'A little,' I confessed, 'and he is but I'm not going to elaborate. Firstly, because I'm not sure Brodie would want me to and secondly, because I don't know much other than he's picked up his brushes again.'

'That's fair enough.' Jack nodded. 'I'm just happy to see the eejit with a smile on his face. Clearly art and amore suit him.'

'It's a bit early to be talking amore,' I laughed, 'but we're having fun.'

'I know my brother,' Jack said with a smile, 'and I know the look of love when I see it – and it's the first time I've *ever* seen him wearing it.'

I didn't know what to say to that, but if Jack was right, then I did know that I had to think even more carefully before making any decisions about what I was going to do once Christmas was over.

Chapter 29

Sadly, Angus's suggestion that I should put my concerns about how to get Albert to exhibit on the backburner to allow a solution to magically appear didn't work that day and inspiration didn't strike on Sunday either.

However, I did spend the whole of Saturday evening making plans and lists for the celebration in the notebook Santa had gifted me with a view to drafting Dorothy in to help with the eats and drinks, first thing Monday morning.

The party was going to be a simple affair and I hoped that as the rest of the Connelly clan would only have been back at the hall for a couple of days when it took place, their being together would make the gathering feel like more of a celebration.

Angus's desire to host an art exhibition as well as a party was surplus to the seasonal requirements as far as I was concerned, but I had promised I would try to pull it off, and I would do my best but if it failed, then at least the love of family returned to the fold for the festivities would add to the excitement.

Before I immersed myself too deeply in the super speedy

planning though, I was determined to squeeze every last drop of fun out of the Winter Wonderland.

'You'll need a hat, scarf and gloves,' I told Albert who looked every bit as excited as I did when I went to pick him and Brodie up on Sunday morning.

I was delighted Albert was so keen to join in the fun and I was resolute that we'd get him in the sleigh, even if we had to lift him up and in.

'All here,' he said, picking up a mismatched collection of woollen accessories. 'And I've got a pair of those handwarmer things you heat in the microwave, too.'

'You're all set then,' I praised. 'But what about your protégé? Where's he?'

Albert rolled his eyes and shook his head.

'Still in the studio,' he told me. 'And I wouldn't let him hear you call him that.'

'He can't *still* be painting.' I frowned. I hadn't been able to rouse him at all the evening before and when I telephoned the cottage earlier that morning, Albert had said he still hadn't come up for air. 'Shall I go and fetch him?'

'Best not,' Albert said wisely. 'I made him take an alarm clock set to the time you said you'd be here so, assuming he hasn't turned it off, he knows when he's expected.'

'That sounds a bit extreme,' I said, giving Bella a fuss.

'Perhaps,' conceded Albert, 'but better than interrupting him in person.'

'I take it the muse has struck,' I said, as I tuned into heavy footfalls thundering along the path.

'You could say that,' said Albert. 'Look out.'

I was just clear of the door when Brodie came bounding through it. He looked exhausted and his hair was sticking up all over the place. I was rather taken aback by the dazed look in his eyes which suggested he'd been somewhere very far away while he was sweating over the canvas. If only in his head.

'How are you getting on?' Albert asked him.

'Better.' He smiled, planting a quick kiss on my lips and looking more like himself with every second. 'But not brilliant. There's still work to do and I was wondering if I might give the Wonderland a miss. Or maybe,' he quickly added, having taken in my reaction to the suggestion, 'cycle up later this afternoon and catch the end of it.'

'No way,' I sternly said. 'You've been ensconced in that studio long enough. And as thrilled as I am that the paint is flowing again, I think you need a break. Don't you, Albert?'

I hoped he'd agree with me, but being an artist himself, he might think it better that Brodie carried on until his creativity was spent.

'Paige is right,' Albert thankfully sided with me. 'As usual. You do need some time out, Brodie. And a shower.'

'Sorry.' Brodie blushed. 'I suppose I have gone a bit feral.'

'And a little distance from your work will give you some perspective,' Albert wisely added. 'Come back to it again this evening with fresh eyes and a full belly and you'll be far more productive than if you try to carry on with it now.'

Brodie wasn't initially inclined to completely agree, but

eventually relented and headed off to shower while I made tea and buttered toast.

'There's tea here, Brodie,' I called through the shower room door, 'and toast.'

'Bring it in, will you?' he called back. 'I am decent.'

The sight which met my eyes when I opened the door and peered through the steam was very decent indeed. Wrapped in a low-slung towel I was treated to the admirable view of a beautiful broad chest and a deliciously toned torso. I had a desire to run my fingers down it as Brodie roughly rubbed his hair until it was almost dry.

'There you go,' I said, resting the mug and plate on top of the laundry hamper. 'Don't be too long.' I swallowed, struggling to keep my empty hands to myself. 'Otherwise, we'll never get to the front of the queue for a ride in the sleigh.'

Brodie grinned and turned to face the sink which didn't help quell my desire at all as his muscular back and defined waist looked every bit as perfect as his front.

'Happy Christmas to me,' I wistfully sighed and Brodie laughed.

I laughed too and quickly stepped out of the door to find Albert waiting.

'Everything all right in there?' he asked, with his eyebrows raised and sounding like a stern old-school headmaster.

'Yes,' I squeaked. 'Everything very all right. I was just taking Brodie his breakfast.'

'That's all right then,' he said, with a smile. 'Now, come

on, Brodie!' he called. 'There's a bag of hot chestnuts up at the hall with my name on it!'

Sunday was even busier than Saturday and we took our time looking at everything the Winter Wonderland had to offer. Brodie had begun the expedition wearing a bit of a thundercloud expression, and muttering about needing to get back, in spite of the smile he had given me in the shower room, but as the morning progressed, he started to unbend and relax a bit. Finally, after a glass of his brother's excellent mulled wine, served by a very content looking Tilly, brooding Brodie was banished and my much happier beau had popped up in his place.

'A sleigh ride next,' I said, rubbing my gloved hands together in anticipation of the Wonderland highlight. 'And look, the queue's not too long.'

'You young things go and enjoy that,' said Albert, 'and I'm going to take a breather with Catherine in the morning room.'

Right on cue, my godmother appeared, wrapped in a stunning shawl and with her hair in an elegant wispy bun. She looked as if she could have stepped straight out of the pages of a Forster novel.

'Come along then, Albert,' she said, offering him her arm. 'Let's go and warm up inside, shall we?' Then, sensing my disappointment added, 'I've booked a ride in the sleigh for the two of us a little later, Paige, so don't worry. Albert won't miss out.'

Their time together had obviously been pre-arranged

and I loved that the two of them had been in touch since Albert's initial visit to the hall and that he was forging lasting connections with my godparents. I knew there would be no chance of him slipping back into his former frugal ways with the Connellys keeping an eye on him and if Brodie moved into the cottage full-time that would be even better.

I watched the pair walk away and a sigh escaped my lips.

'Penny for them?' Brodie asked, pulling me back to the present.

I looked up into his handsome face and felt my heart-rate quicken.

'I was just thinking what a comfort it is to know that Albert is going to be looked after so well should I have to . . .' My words trailed off.

If my seed of an idea about what I could do with my life next did germinate there was going to be every chance that I wouldn't be leaving Wynbridge in the new year, so why upset the apple cart by mentioning the possibility of it?

'Should you have to what?' Brodie frowned.

'Take on more festive deliveries and have less time to check in with him,' I blagged.

'I think he's more than capable of looking after himself again now.' Brodie smiled down at me. 'And,' he happily added, 'I've decided I'm definitely moving in with him, so you won't have to worry about him no matter how many deliveries you have to make. How do you feel about that?'

'Ecstatic!' I told him, giving him a hug. 'Although

given the amount of time you've been spending in the studio recently, I was beginning to think you already had moved in.'

'I suppose I pretty much have,' Brodie laughed, 'but I've still got the rest of my stuff to shift from Jack's place.'

I said I'd help him move his things as soon as he was ready and we joined the queue for the sleigh rides. The trip turned out to be even more exhilarating than I expected.

'It feels much faster than it looks when you're watching it go around, doesn't it?' I laughed as Mick treated Brodie and I to a second lap and tendrils of hair escaped from under my hat and whipped around my face.

We had a blanket tucked around our knees and our fingers were laced together underneath it. The sound of the sleigh bells rang out and I don't think I'd ever experienced anything so romantic. Not even Archie blowing kisses as we rushed by halted the feeling. Brodie smiled at me, then let go of one of my hands and wrapped an arm around my shoulders, pulling me close to his side.

Clearly, I was forgiven for prising him away from the studio and I hoped he would be as easy to win around when I broached the subject of the exhibition and the Christmas celebration. Perhaps I should ask Angus to keep the sleigh on standby, as a softener, just in case I encountered more resistance than I anticipated.

'That,' I said to Mick, as Brodie offered me a hand to climb out and I found my knees were shaking a little, 'was incredible.'

'You liked it?' he asked, pushing the Santa hat further back on his head.

'I loved it!' I said, patting one of the ponies on the back.

Their breath steamed into the chilly air and they looked every bit as happy as I felt. They obviously loved the part they played in making the weekend so memorable and that made it all the more special.

'It's always popular.' Mick grinned. 'Shame we haven't got snow to make the scene complete though.'

'That really would have been something,' Brodie laughed. 'Maybe next year,' he added, smiling at me.

'You never know.' I smiled back.

We left Mick resting the ponies and, as the light was beginning to fade, strolled over to the walled garden to admire the grotto all lit up.

'Oh, wow,' gasped Brodie. 'How beautiful is this?'

There were still a few families milling about and I didn't think Santa had left his seat all day. He was going to have a numb backside for a few days, but his 'Ho, Ho, Ho's' sounded as genuine and cheery as ever.

'When we were setting it up, I knew it was going to look good,' I told Brodie. 'But it's turned out even better than I imagined.'

'Didn't you come and look at it in the dark yesterday?' he asked.

'No,' I said, 'like the sleigh ride, I wanted to save it for today and share it with you.'

'Well, thank you.' Brodie smiled cheerfully. 'I really

appreciate that you did that. This whole day has made me feel like a kid again and I've loved it.'

'I'm so pleased,' I told him. 'For a while this morning, I didn't think I was going to get you to come.'

'For a while I was going to try to convince you that I couldn't,' he admitted. 'Thank goodness, I didn't. You know . . .' he then started to say, but stopped.

'What?' I softly asked, squeezing his hand in mine.

He took a second before answering.

'I was just going to say,' he then said, 'that my life has been so much better since you landed in it and I really hope you're going to be around for a very long time.'

'How about for ever?' I whispered, hoping with the whole of my heart that I would be able to develop my fledgling plan and turn it into reality to enable my infinite suggestion.

I then gasped as Brodie lifted me off the ground and spun me around.

'I suppose that would be all right.' He grinned, humorously playing the moment down but not making a convincing job of hiding his excitement at all.

'Well, as long as you're sure.' I shrugged, playing along.

'Oh, Paige,' he said, cupping my face in his hands, 'I really got the feeling that you were going to take off after Christmas and as much as I hate to sound like a needy bloke, and knowing that you're completely entitled to do what you like and go wherever you want, I can't deny that I was absolutely dreading it.'

I wasn't sure what I had specifically said or done to make

him think that and wondered if everyone else had assumed the same thing.

'When I first arrived, it was my plan to leave again after Christmas,' I told him honestly. 'But not now. Now, I can't bear the thought of leaving. I don't know how I'm going to make a living or where I'm going to live, but I do have an idea for a possible community project taking shape, so I'll see how that develops and just take things from there.'

'That sounds exciting,' Brodie said interestedly. 'Are you going to tell me about it?'

'Not yet, but I will soon.'

'I can't wait,' he said, punctuating each word with a tender, soft kiss. 'I know that whatever you're planning in that clever and kind-hearted head of yours will be amazing and I hope we'll be able to take it forward together.'

I was beginning to feel certain that if I ever managed to grab five minutes to puzzle it out, I'd get the finer details straight in my head and knowing then that Brodie would be waiting to help me take it further, was wonderful. I'd listened to Alice, Ed and Will all talk about life enhancing collaborations and it was time to participate in a few of my own.

'I haven't mentioned anything to anyone else yet,' I told Brodie as I kissed him back. 'Not even that I'm thinking about staying for good, so let's keep it between ourselves for now, okay?'

'That's fine by me,' he sighed. 'Whatever you want.'

'Great.' I smiled, all the while thinking that if I could

further develop my idea ahead of the Christmas celebration, I might be able to announce it then and that might sweeten Angus's upset should I fail to get Albert to share his paintings at the party. 'That's exactly what I want.'

Chapter 30

Having shared my decision that I would be staying in Wynbridge after Christmas with a very happy Brodie, it felt like there was nothing I couldn't do and in the spirit of embracing togetherness, I was awake with the lark Monday morning and went to find Dorothy in her private sitting room, with a view to bringing her up to speed about the celebration and to ask if she would be happy to help.

'Well, now,' she said, taking both my explanation and request in her stride, 'I've been waiting for this.'

'You have?' I frowned.

'Of course,' she laughed. 'There was no way Angus was going to pass up on the opportunity for a party once everyone was together, was there?'

'No,' I said, scratching my head, 'I suppose not.'

'You didn't see it coming?' she asked.

'No,' I told her. 'With everything else going on, it didn't even enter my head.'

'You've been away from here for too long.' She smiled.

'But I'm keeping my fingers crossed that you won't be in a rush to get off again once Christmas is over. I don't think you're quite topped up with enough Wynthorpe spirit yet.'

'Well,' I said vaguely, cursing the colour which I knew was creeping into my cheeks. 'Nothing's decided. I just want to enjoy Christmas and I'll think more about what I'm going to do next after Boxing Day.'

'If I had a man like Brodie hanging on my every word,' Dorothy confided, with a mischievous wink, 'wild horses wouldn't drag me away.'

'Oh, Dorothy,' I said, blushing brighter.

'Now,' she said, reaching for a notebook which looked similar to my own. 'Let's have a think about what we're going to need for this Christmas celebration.'

It didn't take long to go through the arrangements for the catering as Dorothy was an old hand and more than capable of providing a feast in a trice. It also helped that she had been filling the freezers with festive snacks for weeks and the savoury and sweet treats she'd already prepared merely needed defrosting and reheating. She wasn't at all concerned that I couldn't yet give her guest numbers and was willing to wing it.

As I later whizzed through the cleaning, I realized that were it not for the exhibition element of the event, I wouldn't have had anything to worry about. The hall was already decorated, the food and drink was sorted and the majority of guests would be in situ by Friday so even issuing invitations wasn't that big a deal. However, there was the exhibition element to fret over – and worry about it, I did.

By the time I'd completed my hall duties, which that day included making up extra rooms, the Winter Wonderland was almost dismantled and thoughts were turning to everyone's arrival the next day. Anna and Jamie were already en route back to England and Hayley and Gabe and eldest son Christopher, his wife Cass and their two sons would be setting off for the hall soon, too.

'I can't believe your time doing Anna and Hayley's work is almost up,' Molly said as we shared an early lunch ahead of me going to Albert's to explain what Angus had in mind for him and Brodie. 'It only feels like five minutes since you walked in and saved the day.'

'I know,' I agreed. 'It's gone every bit as fast for me too.'

'And we never did properly discuss what it was that sent you flying here, beyond your contract coming to an end, did we?' She wryly smiled.

'No,' I said tentatively, 'we didn't.'

'Don't worry,' she quickly added. 'I'm not going to try and force it out of you now.'

'You're not?'

'No.'

'Why not?'

'Because I can tell you've worked through it and accepted it,' she stated rather than asked, accompanying her pronouncement with one of her trademark all-seeing stares. 'You haven't forgotten it,' she further said. 'But it hasn't got a hold on you anymore.'

'You're right,' I confirmed. 'But I would like to tell you what happened.'

I had no idea where that announcement came from, and Molly looked as surprised as I felt, but I went with it, safe in the knowledge that the memory of what had occurred could no longer harm me.

'I can appreciate now that I was distracted,' I began, 'but that was no excuse for my resultant irrational actions.'

'Go on,' Molly encouraged, settling in her seat.

'Well, we'd recently had a meeting at the camp and been told that due to a severe cut in corporate funding, volunteer numbers and programmes across the globe were going to be sharply reduced and, in some cases, scrapped completely.'

'I can imagine you must have been devastated.'

'I was,' I said, 'we all were and I was still mulling it over the day we were due to receive urgent medical supplies. They were being driven to the camp by truck and I'd been waiting for it to arrive for hours, when I got word that the vehicle had broken down just outside the gates.'

'That must have been frustrating?' Molly frowned.

'It was,' I said, biting my lip. 'And I was so wound up that I . . .'

'That you . . . ?'

I took a deep breath before carrying on.

'That I decided to take matters into my own hands and, without consulting anyone else, marched out of the camp, found the truck and began offloading the supplies by hand.'

Molly's eyes widened.

'I know,' I said. 'It was a huge error of judgement and the

eruption of rifle fire which rang out during my second trip to the truck, made sure I knew it.'

'Oh, Paige,' Molly gasped. 'You must have been terrified.'

'I was,' I said, 'not only for myself, but more for the rest of the team who had to launch a rescue and put themselves in danger to get me back.'

'Was anyone hurt?'

'Thankfully not,' I said, wiping my eyes, 'but that didn't stop me catastrophizing over what might have happened from then on and losing all confidence in my ability to make even the smallest decision.'

'And it made you jittery too,' Molly said thoughtfully. 'That was why you hit the deck that day in Hayley's studio when we were looking for her designs, wasn't it?'

'Yes.' I swallowed. 'That's exactly why I reacted like I did. That's not happening anymore though,' I told her. 'And the nightmares have stopped too.'

'Nightmares?'

'Yes,' I said, 'they were pretty bad when I first arrived, but being here has helped so much. I'm making decisions for myself again and I've learnt a valuable lesson too.'

'Which is?'

'That working in isolation didn't protect my heart,' I was able to admit. 'I've come to relearn that working in a team and doing things with other people, just like I did when Chadia was alive but had lost sight of since she died, is far more beneficial to my mental health than keeping myself to myself and my emotions locked up tight.'

Molly moved to wrap her arms around me, embracing me in an incense scented hug.

'I'm so sorry I didn't tell you sooner,' I said, letting my tears fall unchecked. 'I know you were willing to listen but . . .' My words trailed off.

'Don't be sorry,' Molly said, kissing my hair and pulling away a little so she could look right at me. 'If you had been meant to tell me before now, you would have done. This was the time it was all meant to come out,' she insisted, sounding more Molly-ish than ever. 'Not before or after, but now. Yes?'

'Okay,' I said, wiping my eyes. 'Okay, yes.'

She let me go but didn't take her eyes off me.

'You've finally moved on.' She smiled. 'And you've found someone to love and who loves you back and as a result made huge decisions about your future.'

'I still think it's a bit early to be talking about love,' I quickly said, not wanting to further discuss the future either. Not until it was at least a little more decided in my head and in spite of the fact she had sussed so much out already.

'I don't,' she firmly responded. 'Anyone can see that you love the very bones of Albert and he feels just the same about you.'

I bit my lip, grateful that I hadn't said Brodie's name as that was who I had assumed she was referring to.

'Actually,' I said as I smiled back, 'you're right. Keeping myself busy, helping Albert and working in a collaborative way again has helped me process and come to terms with what happened and the work and my involvement in it has made my life richer too. It's been the best Christmas present I could have wished for.'

'You're truly blessed,' said Molly, standing up and stifling a yawn. 'We both are and I'm so happy for you, Paige. I feel honoured that you were able to share this part of your journey with me.'

'Thank you,' I said. 'Reaffirming our friendship means so much to me.'

'And to me too,' she responded. 'And do keep in mind that this incident will only now fade with time. By this time next year, you'll barely recall the depth of negative emotion it induced at all.'

I had a feeling she was going to be right about that.

'Now,' she sighed, 'would you mind if I went and had a bit of a rest?'

'Are you all right?' I asked.

I hoped my unburdening hadn't zapped her cosmic energy.

'Yes,' she said, colouring a little, 'but it's the solstice celebration in a couple of days and I need all of my strength in order to make it a truly memorable one.'

I stood up too and gave her another hug. She was comfortingly warm but as ever, felt as light as air.

'I think I'm ready to give you this back,' I said, sliding the rose quartz out of my pocket. 'I'm happy to say that I love myself a whole lot more than I did when I first arrived.'

Molly smiled and closed my fingers around the crystal, the feel, shape and texture of which had become so familiar.

'You keep it,' she said, 'as a reminder of how far you've come and how much you can change in such a short space of time.'

'And there are more changes to come, aren't there?' I said, thinking of our conversation at the Wishing Tree clearing.

'Oh, yes,' she smiled. 'Lots.'

I tried to pack my nerves away as I headed off in Anna's Fiat to talk to Albert and Brodie. I had been going to take the Land Rover so Bran could come with me but he had preferred to stay curled up with Floss in front of the Aga. I wondered if he could sense that Gabe was heading back as I kissed the top of his head and silently thanked him for the strong and silent support he'd given me during the last few weeks.

I shed more tears when I left him because it felt as though some hugely important phase or cycle was coming to an end and once the calendar flipped to the new year, I would be stepping into a new one. My tears didn't spring from a place of upset, but rather from one of excitement and a little trepidation. Life really was full of surprises.

And talking of surprises.

'What's all this?' I asked, as I pulled up in front of the cottage and found Brodie unloading cardboard boxes from the back of a car I didn't recognize. 'I thought I was going to help you move. Although looking at the size of a couple of those boxes, the Fiat wouldn't have been big enough. You said you didn't have more than a few bags to shift!'

'I know,' he said, looking into the cavernous boot of the

decrepit looking Volvo he was standing next to. 'And I didn't until earlier, but then I got a bit carried away at the art supplies place in town.'

'A bit,' I laughed.

'So,' he said, putting the box down and stepping further away from the car so I could see the whole of it. 'What do you think?'

'To what?'

'The car, of course,' he said, rolling his eyes. 'This is my new set of wheels.'

'This is yours?' I laughed again. 'And it's new?'

'Hey,' he said. 'Don't laugh. It's new to me and the best I can afford. The guy I got it from had loads of others in his yard, so if something falls off . . .'

'If?' I interrupted.

'All right,' he said, kicking the tyres as people for some reason were apt to do when discussing cars, '*when* something falls off, he'll have a spare for me.'

'I see,' I said, climbing out and walking around the vehicle which had probably been more than once around the clock. 'Well, she looks sturdy enough.'

'Built to last.' Brodie beamed, fondly patting the roof. 'It's a classic really.'

'You haven't got a clue what you're talking about, have you?' I teased.

'Nope,' he confessed. 'My last car was a brand-new Mercedes and it cost me over a hundred grand. I only had it because it was the most expensive one available at the time.'

'What?' I gasped. 'A hundred thousand pounds!'

'I know,' he said, biting his lip. 'Please don't judge. That was the old blinkered Brodie. You know, the one I told you about who'd got his priorities all wrong when he was trying to live his life to please his father.'

I was relieved I hadn't known that Brodie. He was nothing like the scruffy-jumper wearing clapped-out Volvo driver standing in front of me.

'No judgement,' I said, holding up my hands. 'So, how much has this one set you back? Not quite six figures, I would imagine.'

'Less than two grand,' he said, grinning and rubbing at a patch of scuffed paintwork with his sleeve, 'and I love it a hundred times more than the Merc already.'

'Um,' I said, watching his hands-on approach, 'I'm beginning to feel jealous.'

'Don't be,' he said, abandoning the car and pulling me into his arms. 'There's more than enough room for both of you in my life.'

'That wasn't quite what I was hoping you were going to say,' I tutted.

'How about, there's room in the back for a mattress then,' he tried again, that time suggestively waggling his eyebrows.

'What are you, eighteen?' I teased. 'And in this weather, you've got to be kidding!'

I helped him carry in the last of his boxes, while he told me how he and the new super car had completed his move from Brambles in one swift journey, the trip to buy further art supplies aside. So entranced by the retelling, I had completely forgotten the purpose of my own journey until Albert piped up.

'I'm guessing Brodie has told you about my offer to share the cottage as well as the studio,' he said, looking happier than I'd ever seen him.

'He has,' I confirmed, 'and I'm thrilled for you both. I think you'll get along a treat.'

'So do I,' he agreed, then ruined the moment by adding, 'and before I forget, Angus called to say that you've left your notebook behind, Paige. He said he wasn't sure you could manage without it, whatever that means.'

'What's that godfather of yours on about now?' Brodie chuckled.

I looked from one of them to the other.

'Let's sit down for a minute,' I suggested. 'And I'll tell you.'

'It's not more hall repairs, is it?' Albert frowned. 'I told him they can wait until the spring.'

'No,' I said, 'it's nothing like that.'

'What then?' Brodie asked.

'Well,' I said, easing myself into the explanation, 'as you know, the rest of the Connelly clan are all due to land at the hall tomorrow. Jamie and Anna and Hayley and Gabe will be arriving back from their travels and the eldest brother, Christopher and his family will be arriving to spend Christmas there, too.'

Albert nodded.

'Catherine was telling me on Sunday how much she's

looking forward to having everyone together for the festive period,' he said. 'You're going to have your hands full though, Paige. Will you still be on cleaning duty?'

'Probably,' I said. 'And even if I wasn't officially, I'd still be helping out.'

'You're a good lass,' he praised.

I hoped he was still thinking that when I got to the heart of the matter.

'It's only fair,' I said, 'giving that I'm still living there gratis.'

'So, what's all this about a notebook?' Brodie frowned.

'Well,' I said, licking my lips, 'Angus has tasked me with planning a party. We're having a Christmas celebration on the twenty-third to further enjoy everyone being together and I've been using the notebook to keep track of the planning.'

'That sounds wonderful,' said Albert. 'I can't think of anywhere more suited to a Christmas gathering than the hall.'

'And you're both invited, of course,' I added.

He immediately accepted. 'We'd love to attend, wouldn't we, Brodie?'

Brodie nodded, but didn't say anything. He'd clearly guessed there was more to Angus's party idea than I had so far let on. It was now or never.

'In fact,' I carried on breezily, 'Angus is counting on you both being there, because he'd like to make it a celebration with a twist.'

'What sort of twist?' Brodie frowned.

Thinking on my feet, an idea formed which would make

more work for me, but hopefully soften the request I was about to make.

'He wants me to put together an exhibition. Lots of local art work is going to be included, but he would like to make yours and Albert's the main focus,' I said in a rush, mentally crossing my fingers in the hope that I would be able to get other artists on board at such short notice. 'He wants you to display your work at the hall as a sort of gentle introduction, or reintroduction in your case, Brodie, to sharing it with the wider world.'

My words were met with silence. As the seconds ticked by, I looked from Brodie to Albert and back again but couldn't work out what either man was thinking.

'So,' I said, when I couldn't bear the quiet any longer, 'that's why he thought I might need the notebook, because that's where I've been making notes about how many sausage rolls and mince pies Dorothy has got stashed in the freezers, along with who will be exhibiting alongside you. Hopefully, alongside you . . .'

My light-hearted comment didn't encourage either man to speak and I was just thinking I'd leave them to mull it over when Albert cleared his throat.

'So, who will be in charge of arranging the displays?' he asked. 'And exactly how many paintings would Angus like us to send?'

My mouth fell open in shock.

'You can't be serious?' Brodie gasped. 'Surely, you're not thinking of doing it?'

Albert sat up straighter in his chair.

'Yes,' he said firmly. 'Yes, I am.'

'But just a few days ago you swore us to secrecy . . .' Brodie reminded him.

'I know,' Albert said. 'I know I did, but now an amazing opportunity has come along and I want to grab it. If you remember, I also told you that I was going to live my life to the full again, didn't I?'

Brodie didn't answer that.

'And sharing my paintings with a few people, even if it is just during a Christmas party, will be a chance to fulfil a boyhood dream.'

'But what if it doesn't end there?' Brodie asked, sounding concerned. 'You know what Angus is like, he could get the press involved.'

Albert shook his head.

'We'll cross that bridge when and if we come to it,' he said resolutely. 'Not that I can imagine for one second that anyone would be interested.'

'So, you're absolutely on board, Albert?' I asked, just to be sure I hadn't misinterpreted what I thought was his positive, and surprising reaction to the idea.

'Definitely,' he said, leaving no room for confusion. 'I think it will be a lark. I'm not getting any younger, am I? So, I'll happily embrace any larks which happen to come my way from now on.'

I gave him a double thumbs up thinking it was a huge turnaround for him. I couldn't wait to tell Angus that

Albert was going to take part. I was thrilled he was so keen, but one glance at Brodie's face hastily wiped the smile off mine.

'And you, Brodie?' I asked, even though there was no doubting his reaction.

'Absolutely not,' he said, shoving his hands through his hair.

'Brodie . . .' Albert began.

'No,' he said, cutting him off. 'No way. I've only just started painting again and I've been working my nuts off to try and complete this commission Angus wants in time for Christmas. That's what he said he wanted me to do, what he pressured me to do and that's what I've done. Why he has to keep moving the goalposts, I have no idea.'

'He keeps moving them,' Albert said mildly, 'because he sees real talent in you and he wants you to succeed.'

'And he probably didn't think the idea would be all that much of a leap for you,' I added, 'because you've displayed your work before.'

Brodie raked his hands through his hair again.

'You gave up everything to do this with your life,' I reminded him. 'And you've been through a truly difficult and transformative time as a result . . .'

'Exactly,' he huffed, cutting me off. 'So, why can't I now be left to do it in peace?'

'Because you've come through it,' I reiterated. 'It's done. The time for peace is over and it's time to forge ahead. Make up for the lost months and start the new year with a different sort of exhibition under your belt and with your work sitting side by side with the man who has helped you break through your block and embrace your brushes again.'

I stopped to draw breath and received a nod of approval from Albert. I was rather proud of my speech, but it didn't have any impact on making Brodie change his mind.

'I can't,' he said, standing up.

'You can,' said Albert, 'and you should. Opportunities like this don't come along every day and just because you're young and probably think there'll be others, that doesn't mean you should waste this one. Life's too short to waste moments like these.'

Brodie looked at Albert and then at me.

'I can't do it,' he said again, slamming the door behind him as he strode out.

I made to go after him, but Albert stopped me.

'Leave him,' he softly said. 'He's simmering right now and you won't get anywhere with him while he's coming to the boil.'

I sat back again.

'I daresay you're right,' I said, feeling awful. 'I've ruined moving day, haven't I?'

'You've certainly stirred it up a bit,' Albert chuckled.

'I thought you were going to be the tricky one,' I told him, only then noticing he had splashes of red paint in his hair. 'I expected you to be the one shouting and storming out.'

'If only I could move that fast,' he said wistfully, which made us both smile.

I would like to have waited to see which way the wind

blew when Brodie finally came out of the studio, but with so much happening at the hall the next day, I had to leave.

'You get off and tell Angus to put some display boards up,' Albert said, which reminded me that I now had other artists to invite and boards to source to hang their work on. 'And leave boy wonder to me. I'll bring him round.'

Albert sounded very sure of himself, but having seen and heard Brodie's reaction to the idea, I couldn't in all honesty say that I thought he would succeed.

Chapter 31

Angus was both absolutely thrilled *and* surprised when I told him that I thought we should invite more artists and that Albert had very happily agreed to take part. I winced as I relayed Brodie's reaction to the idea, but it was then my turn to feel surprised, because my godfather wasn't fazed at all.

'That's wonderful news, Paige,' he said, pulling on his coat and indicating that I should do the same. 'I told you you'd have no trouble getting Albert onside, didn't I?'

'You did,' I said, 'but his decision was nothing to do with me. He said yes as soon as I'd finished explaining what you had in mind, whereas Brodie . . .'

'Will come round.' Angus shrugged, literally waving my concern away. 'Now come outside and tell me what you think of these boards. I think they'll be ideal to hang the paintings on.'

The boards turned out to be a variety of white modular display stands which fitted together in endless configurations.

'These are perfect,' I said, examining them. They were both sturdy and unobtrusive. Ideal for our purpose. 'Why have you got them?'

We were in one of the offices in the stable block which had been converted to house the charity Anna and Jamie ran.

'They look expensive,' I added.

'They've been used by the charity and they weren't cheap,' Angus confirmed, 'but as Jamie always says, you buy cheap you buy twice, and these have paid for themselves already and have been used at multiple fundraising and awareness raising events.'

They'd been well looked after too. There wasn't a mark on any of them.

'I thought we could set them up in the main hall,' Angus said, 'in whatever layout you think will work best.'

'I'd like to give each person who is exhibiting their own space,' I said, as I began to picture the party in my head and hoped I would be able to convince more artists to turn out so close to Christmas. 'That way they'll be able to talk to the guests more intimately.'

'That's a great idea,' Angus agreed.

'And talking of guests,' I said, 'if we don't invite some, along with more artists soon, they won't come. Christmas is a busy time, and I daresay most people have already made plans. To be honest, I think it might be too late to expect much of a turn out.'

Angus shifted further around the office.

'It's all in hand,' he squeaked.

'How so?' I asked.

'Well,' he said, peeping around the boards and giving me a mischievous smile, 'I had a similar idea on the extra artist front myself a couple of days ago and got Lizzie, from The Cherry Tree Café on the case.'

'I see,' I said.

'And,' he added, disappearing from view again, 'the other guest invitations were sent out a couple of weeks ago.'

I couldn't believe it.

'So, what was the point of drafting me in then?' I gasped. 'You made out that it was a completely new idea when you talked me into helping with it, but it sounds like you've got it all in hand already and you don't need me at all.'

I wasn't sure whether I felt exasperated or relieved, as was so often the case when dealing with Angus Connelly.

'Of course, I need you!' he said, facing me again. 'First and foremost, I needed you to convince Albert and Brodie to exhibit. That was the main thing. But then there's the nuts and bolts of the thing to get sorted, too. I've only asked guests and artists. Nothing else.'

As ever, he was the ideas man and someone else was left to do the more mundane graft. In this instance, me.

'And what about the artists?' I asked. 'Have you had much of a response?'

'I have,' he said, sounding serious. 'Show stands are so expensive that lots of small creators can't afford them, so Lizzie has asked people who haven't had an opportunity to exhibit like this before.'

'Oh, wow,' I said, thinking what a wonderful opportunity the potential exposure for them was going to be. 'That's fantastic.'

Angus and Lizzie's success took the pressure off me a bit which made it even more fantastic.

'And I specifically asked you to help because I wanted to give you something to focus on once Anna and Hayley got back,' Angus then kindly said. 'I was worried you might feel a bit redundant with less to do when they took over again.'

'Well,' I said, tears prickling as a result of his thoughtfulness, 'I appreciate that.'

'You do know that we don't want you to go, don't you, Paige?' he said, looking a little bright eyed himself, 'so I'm going to be coming up with all sorts of plans to stop you.'

I rushed into his arms and he hugged me tightly. In the current absence of my own father, Angus was doing a wonderful job of stepping into the breach. Even if at times he did still have a tendency to be a bit maddening.

'I take it that's all right?' He smiled.

'It's more than all right,' I told him, feeling excited for the time when I could tell him the plan I'd been cooking up for myself.

'That's the spirit.' He beamed, giving me a tighter squeeze before letting me go. 'Right,' he then said, 'we'd best get back. Tomorrow's going to be a busy day.'

'It is.' I nodded. 'And we still need to work out how we're going to keep this party a secret from Catherine when we've got so much setting up to do.'

'Oh, don't worry.' Angus winked. 'I've thought of a way around that too.'

It seemed to me that the only thing I had to worry about was Brodie, but that was more than enough.

Having thought over what Albert had said about Brodie coming up to a boil, I decided it would be best if I left him to simmer and focused my attention the next day on getting my deliveries finished early so I could be back at the hall in time to welcome and meet everyone.

It turned out to be quite a race against the clock as there had been far more library books than usual to deliver and the vast majority of them were festive fiction titles. Multiple Sarah Morgan and Trisha Ashley paperbacks filled the boxes and there were plenty bearing Milly Johnson's name too.

'Did you get any lunch in town?' Dorothy asked once I'd finally made it back and flopped down into a chair.

'Not a morsel,' I told her as my tummy loudly rumbled, confirming exactly how hungry I was. 'There was no time.'

'I did tell you to take something with you,' she scolded. 'Here,' she added, handing me a bowl. 'There's soup on the Aga and I'll pop one of those part-baked rolls in to warm.'

Dorothy usually made all of the hall bread, but with so many visitors poised to descend she had to cut a few corners and laid in supplies of the part-baked baguettes and rolls amongst other things.

'What time did Mick leave for the airport?' I asked, ladling thick chicken and tarragon soup and hearing my tummy rumble again as the delicious aroma filled the air.

'Getting on for three hours ago, I reckon,' she said, glancing at the clock next to the advent calendar. 'They should be back about three.'

I sat at the table again and tucked into my belated lunch.

'My tummy still feels a bit funny,' I said, once I'd finished.

'There's cake in the tin,' Dorothy automatically responded.

'I don't think it's hunger,' I told her, with a smile. 'It's excitement. Christmas is really going to begin once everyone gets here, isn't it?'

'You're not wrong,' said Angus, rushing through the door wearing a Santa hat at a rakish angle.

It wasn't his *proper* Father Christmas hat as that only came out when the real Santa was in residence.

'Here you go, you two,' he said, pulling another two hats out of a bag. 'Get these on and we'll be all ready to line up outside when everyone arrives.'

I was happy to wear mine, but Dorothy wasn't at all keen.

'I only washed my hair yesterday,' she tutted.

'If I have to wear one,' said Catherine, following Angus in, 'so do you, Dorothy.'

I looked at my godmother and chuckled.

'It suits you,' I told her.

She was definitely one of those women who could pull hats off. Even white faux fur-trimmed ones with bells on the end.

'Whereas I look hideous,' moaned Dorothy, as she resignedly pulled it on and too far down.

I straightened it for her and we posed as a group as Angus insisted on taking a selfie.

'Afternoon clan,' laughed Archie, who then arrived with Molly.

They were both wearing hats too, but Molly's was dark green and matched her newest cloak which had tiny tinkling silver bells sewn on to the ribbon ties. The colour set off her hair beautifully.

'You look stunning, Molly,' Dorothy sighed. 'Far better than us in these red get-ups.'

'Just count yourself lucky I talked Dad out of buying the matching jackets with buckle belts,' Archie told her, which made her laugh.

'Thank you, Dorothy.' Molly smiled. 'I've just finished making it.'

'Is everything all set for tomorrow?' Catherine asked.

'It is,' Molly said, a rush of colour warming her pretty pale cheeks. 'I'm all ready for the solstice ritual and Dorothy has baked the cake to celebrate Anna's birthday.'

Fortunately, I had been reminded that it was Anna's birthday the next day and had wrapped her a present in the spare few minutes I'd found to parcel up the Christmas gifts I'd picked up on the night of the switch-on. As I hadn't yet met her, I hoped she'd like it.

'Come on then,' said Angus, as the clock struck three. 'It's not too cold outside today, so let's go out and assume positions.'

The hall lights were already twinkling and the trees which

stood sentinel either side of the beautiful arched door were lit too. I couldn't imagine there had ever been a homecoming like it and we and the dogs weren't waiting many seconds before we caught sight of the first set of headlights winding their way along the bumpy drive.

'Who is it?' Catherine excitedly asked. 'My money's on Christopher,' she quickly added. 'He said the boys were bursting to get here when I spoke to him and Cass last night.'

Her prediction was right and the four of them were barely out of the car before Bran barked and stood stock still as a truck appeared and pulled up alongside Christopher's car. The daft dog then became almost puppyish as he skittered round to the driver's door, vastly hindering his beloved owner's ability to climb out.

'I told you he was missing you, Gabe,' the woman I recognized as Hayley from the iPad screen on the night of switch-on, laughed. She then hopped out and ran to hug us all in turn. 'Paige,' she said, when she reached me. 'It's lovely to meet you in person at last.'

'Likewise,' I said, as her tree of a partner, Gabe, was finally able to climb out of the truck and joined us with Bran melded to his side in much the same way the dog had previously been stuck to me. 'And you too, Gabe.'

'I understand Bran has been shadowing you since I went away.' He smiled down at me.

'You could say that,' I laughed, 'and a very fine job he's done of it, too.'

Last and by no means least, Mick came along just a

minute later and deposited a tired but buoyant Jamie and Anna. Having travelled the furthest by far, they were the most world-weary, but even they were full of bonhomie and thrilled to be home after their long journey.

'We meet at last.' Anna warmly smiled in greeting once Jamie had introduced us. 'Thank you so much for taking on the deliveries.'

'You're most welcome.' I smiled back. 'I've absolutely loved doing it.'

'That's probably just as well,' she said mysteriously.

It was a very happy rabble who tumbled back into the warm hall, all wearing the hats the patriarch insisted were befitting of the occasion.

Gathered around the kitchen table with endless mugs of tea, huge slices of all sorts of cakes and toast for Anna because she'd mentioned that she'd missed the taste of Marmite, we listened to everyone's adventures and the grandsons, Hugo and Oscar, expanded upon their lengthy Christmas lists.

'So,' Christopher said to me, when there was an eventual lull in the conversation, 'how are you, Paige? It feels like forever since the last time I saw you.'

'I'm good,' I told him. 'I've had such fun being back.'

'She's been doing mine and Anna's work in our absence,' said Hayley, looking around and making the bell on her hat tinkle. 'And from what I've seen so far, she's been making a decent job of it.'

'Well,' I said, 'no one can keep this place in as fine fettle as you, Hayley, but I've given it my best shot.'

'Catherine told us you'd saved the day by stepping in,' Cass said kindly.

'I'm not sure about that,' I said with a smile, 'but keeping busy has been a big help to me. I arrived in a bit of a muddle, but I'm feeling much better about life now.'

'And rumour has it you're in lurve,' Jamie shouted down the table, loud enough for everyone to hear. 'According to Archie you haven't been too busy to squeeze in a bit of *upendo*.'

'A bit of what?' Hugo, the eldest grandson, frowned.

'*Upendo*,' said his uncle. 'It means love in Swahili.'

Hugo turned bright red and pretended he hadn't heard and I wished I could do the same.

'Ooh,' said Hayley, 'what's this?'

'I've just started seeing someone,' I said vaguely, hoping she'd let it drop.

'Details!' she loudly demanded.

'You've a lot to answer for, Jamie Connelly,' I tutted, pointing an accusatory finger down the table to where he sat with his arm around Anna. 'I thought Archie was the champion pot stirrer around here now, but clearly you're still a rival for the title.'

This had the desired distracting effect and the two men started an infantile arm wrestle which almost upset the teapot and had Dorothy demanding that everyone cleared out of her kitchen so she could get on with making the dinner.

'I'll help Gabe with our bags,' Hayley said, 'and then I'll give you a hand, Dorothy, and Paige and I can get to know each other better. You can fill me in on the details of this budding romance.' She winked at me, before sashaying out.

Anna said she'd be up for hearing all about it too, after she and Jamie had sorted their luggage, but whereas Hayley was back in the kitchen in a trice, Anna was nowhere to be seen.

'She's fallen asleep,' Jamie explained with a yawn when he came down again.

'You look as though you could do with a nap yourself,' Dorothy said, scrutinizing the dark circles under his eyes.

'I'm all right,' he said. 'I'd rather catch up on the goss and try to sleep tonight.'

I rolled my eyes.

'You might as well get it over with,' tutted Dorothy, setting the two extra helpers to work peeling and chopping veg. 'You'll get no peace until you do.'

'Well,' I said, thinking I might as well ham it up as they weren't going to leave me alone, 'I actually have two new men in my life.'

'Blimey,' said Hayley, looking at me appraisingly. 'I wouldn't have thought you were the type.'

'One's in his late eighties,' I told her with a grin, 'and now also a firm friend of the family.'

Jamie shook his head and Hayley laughed.

'And the other?' Jamie asked, not waiting to hear about how I'd met Albert or how our friendship had developed as a result.

'Is someone who has only recently moved to the area,' I told the pair.

'Is he an octogenarian too?' Hayley quipped.

I thought of Brodie's wonderful towel clad physique in Albert's steamy bathroom.

'Absolutely not.' I smiled.

'You're blushing,' teased Jamie.

'I don't care.' I shrugged.

'So, who is it then?' Hayley urged.

'A guy called Brodie,' I said, loving the way his name sounded on my lips.

'Is that Jack's brother?' Jamie pounced, his eyes lighting up.

'Who?' Hayley frowned.

'The guy who owns the distillery,' Jamie said impatiently. 'His brother turned up not all that long ago.'

'It is Jack's brother,' I said. 'And that's all I'm going to say, so you can just keep peeling the veg while I go and check the fires.'

I didn't respond to any of the subsequent barrage Jamie bombarded me with as I walked out but I did hope that I was still going out with Brodie once the dust kicked up by the exhibition request had settled.

After a delicious dinner and an evening spent around the fire getting to know each other, catching up with everyone's news and admiring the many photos Anna and Jamie had taken during their African adventure, we all went to bed so we would be rested for the solstice and Anna's birthday the next day.

The Rose Room felt empty without Bran and I was

tempted to search out a signal hotspot so I could call Brodie to try and get the measure of how he was feeling, but I didn't. As a result, I lay in bed feeling restless and didn't sleep particularly well.

'Happy birthday to you!'

Everyone sang to wish Anna the happiest of days late the next morning. She and Jamie had slept in, which added to the anticipation of celebrating with her and when we showered her with presents along with the gift Santa had hidden in the capacious advent calendar, grandson Oscar's excitement had almost reached fever pitch. Goodness knows how exhilarated he would be by Christmas Eve.

'Cake!' demanded Archie, making his youngest nephew further roll about in his seat. 'Cake for lunch! What do you say, boys?'

Both boys sided with him, of course, and we enjoyed the delicious chocolate covered confection Dorothy had created, although I noticed Anna didn't finish her slice. She still looked a bit peaky, but then given how far she and Jamie had travelled in such a short space of time, I wasn't surprised. From my own experience, I knew that sometimes I could shrug the miles off but there were other occasions when they would floor me for days.

'Paige,' said Molly, sidling over. 'I was wondering if you could help me get ready for the ceremony this afternoon? It's going to be a bit different today and I could do with a hand carrying a few extra things into the woods.'

'Of course,' I said, wondering what she had in store.

'Hayley said earlier that the hall looks so good it doesn't need cleaning today, so I'm at your disposal.'

We slipped out into the stunning but chilly sun-filled day and I spotted Brodie's Volvo bouncing up the last stretch of the drive.

'Oh,' said Molly, also watching it, 'I meant to say, I've invited Brodie to join us. I had a feeling that he might need to hear what I have to say more than anyone else.'

I had no idea what she meant by that, because I didn't know what she was going to say, but her words didn't sink in anyway. The beat of my heart and the thoughts flying around my head were suddenly a jumbled mess as I wondered what sort of mood Brodie was going to be in. If he'd agreed to come to the hall, then perhaps it wouldn't be such a bad one.

Molly carried on walking ahead, but I waited for him to climb out of the car. There was no brooding Brodie scowl, but his smile wasn't the sunniest I'd ever seen either.

'Hey you,' I said, walking over and wanting to break the ice straightaway.

'Hey yourself,' he said, immediately reaching for my hand and pulling me into a hug.

'It's good to see you,' I sighed, breathing the scent of him in before leaning back to look up at him.

'Likewise,' he said, brushing my willing lips with a soft kiss. 'And before Angus starts giving me the third degree,' he added, looking over my shoulder towards the hall, 'I just want to say that even though I'm here, I haven't changed my mind about displaying my work at the celebration.'

'That's okay,' I said, trying not to let my disappointment transfer into my tone.

'And also,' he said more urgently, 'I want to tell you that I'm not cross with you about it. I know you were just the messenger, Paige, so it wasn't fair to shoot my annoyance over it in your direction. I'm sorry I did that.'

'It's fine,' I told him. 'If I were in your shoes, I would have reacted in exactly the same way.'

I didn't add that I had hoped with the whole of my heart that if I gave him some space and left Albert to talk to him, he might change his mind, because he clearly hadn't. So much for Angus's insistence that I wasn't to fret and that everything would fall into place.

Brodie kissed me again and I felt relieved that we were back on track, even if the celebration was going to happen without the inclusion of his work. None of which I'd still had the honour of seeing.

'Come on then,' he then said. 'Molly was very keen that I should join in with the solstice celebration, but I have no idea what that involves, do you?'

'Not a clue,' I told him as we set off after my friend, 'but I bet hand holding and chanting's involved.'

Brodie looked rather unnerved by that.

'How's Albert?' I asked quickly, for fear that he'd take off.

'He's good.' Brodie smiled. 'He said I should come today and that it was important that I told Angus face to face that I wasn't going to change my mind.'

I was surprised Albert had said that but then wondered if

he thought Brodie wouldn't be able to go through with it when faced with my generous and kind-hearted godfather.

'Oh,' Brodie then added with a sheepish grin, 'and I've finished the commission . . .'

'Oh, Brodie!' I said, stopping in my tracks. 'That's wonderful. He'll be so pleased! And indeed, so am I and I hope you are too!'

'I am,' he said, his grin growing. 'It's a relief to be honest.'

I could appreciate that.

'I hope Angus likes it,' he said, looking back in the direction of the hall again. 'And Catherine, of course, but more than anything, I hope it will sweeten the blow of letting Angus down.'

I wanted to say that by not taking part he was letting himself down, but thought it sounded a bit harsh, so didn't.

Molly, Brodie and I had just finished setting everything up in the woods when the sound of voices met our ears. The sun was already sinking and Molly was keen to capitalize on every second, so wasted no time in saying a few words and then sending us all out to search for Yule logs. I couldn't help but feel relieved that there had been no immediate opportunity for Angus to corner Brodie and wondered if Molly had engineered it that way.

'Do we really have to ask the woods for permission before selecting a log?' Brodie asked me in a low voice, as we set off to look for something which would fill Albert's grate.

'Yes,' I told him. 'You heard Molly, she said that's really important.'

It wasn't long before we found one and, having self-consciously asked if we could take it, headed back to the clearing. Hayley and Gabe soon came back with a log for their cottage, Archie with another for his and Molly's and last of all came Hugo and Oscar. They had selected a huge specimen for the hall. It took many hands to shift it but they looked thrilled with their choice as it was dragged into pride of place.

Molly then instructed us to make ourselves comfortable on the blanket covered logs around the central blazing fire she had set going.

'What's that smell?' Oscar asked.

'It's frankincense,' Molly told him in a dreamy voice.

'It's lovely.' Oscar beamed at her, clearly smitten, as well he might be because she looked so beautiful standing wrapped in her cloak and with the dancing flames matching her ethereal cloud of hair.

She smiled at him and then, without another instruction or any guidance at all, we all fell silent and spent a few minutes staring into the fire. I don't know what everyone else thought about during that precious time, but I thought back over the last twelve months and all the things that had happened during them.

It had been a year of exciting highs and crushing lows. I was still sad that my time working overseas had ended with a blunder, but also thankful that I had eventually had the sense to see it for what it actually was rather than keep playing over what it could have been.

As I watched the flames lick and curl, I realized that had I not made that error of judgement then I would never have come to the hall. I would never have met Brodie, and Albert would most likely still be holed up in his damp, dank cottage with little hope of surviving the winter. Molly was right after all, there were no such things as mistakes.

I lifted my eyes and found her watching me. I swallowed hard and she nodded, smiling as if she knew what I was thinking and the realization I had just made. I smiled back, but then felt Brodie shudder beside me. I looked at him and saw tears coursing unchecked down his cheeks. I went to reach for his hand, but stopped myself. Whatever each of us was experiencing as we sat around that fire, it was private and for no one else to intrude upon.

'And now,' Molly eventually said, 'would the Oak King and the Holly King please come forward?'

Hugo and Oscar stood up and went to join her. She handed them beautifully crafted papier-mâché masks which they solemnly pulled on and then also picked up toy swords. There was a crown for Hugo too.

'Behold the Holly King,' Molly said loudly and Hugo bowed, almost knocking off the crown. 'And the Oak King,' Molly carried on and Oscar followed his brother's lead only with more success because he was less adorned.

She then lyrically told the story of the battling kings and how the Holly King held power over one half of the year and the Oak King the other. As she talked, the boys mildly tussled around us, suppressing the occasional giggle. As the tale reached its climax, the battle intensified until eventually the Oak King slayed the other and reclaimed the crown with a fantastic flourish and unsuppressed delight.

'And so, on this day,' Molly reverently said, 'in this very moment, we celebrate the rebirth of the sun, we celebrate the return of the light and from this day forward we rejoice in the lengthening of days. Take this timely shift in the wheel of the year to your hearts and let the light fill you up as you move forward to embrace the power it affords you. Be brave, be bold and above all be merry. Happy Yule!'

We all stamped, clapped and cheered, welcoming in the shifting season and even though I knew the worst of the winter was still to come, the days were going to get longer and lighter from that moment on and all would be well. Looking at the sea of smiling happy faces around me, I knew everyone present felt the shift too.

'Thank you, Molly,' I called over to her, trying to make myself heard.

She rushed over to me as Brodie stood up and walked away.

'Look,' she said, plucking at my sleeve, with her cheeks brightly shining in the firelight. 'The magic is working already.'

I followed her gaze and watched as Brodie strode up to Angus, took him to one side and whispered something in his ear. Angus looked ecstatic and slapped Brodie on the back before shaking his hand and then, having looked at Catherine, whispered something in return.

Brodie laughed and catching my eye, gave me a thumbs up.

'I don't know what's just happened,' Molly laughed, 'but something has.'

'I do,' I told her, knowing that Brodie had just found his own way to embrace the returning light. 'I know exactly what's happened and you won't have to wait much longer to find out.'

Chapter 32

'Hurry up, Dad!' Archie exasperatedly called from his position next to the main hall door. 'They'll be here any second!'

'I'm coming.' Angus beamed as he bumbled along, stopping to welcome someone else and turning Archie's face so red as a result, I thought he was going to combust. 'Thank you all so much for coming.' Angus continued to dawdle.

'Dad!' Jamie practically screeched, adding his desperate plea to that of his brother.

'I'm here,' Angus said mildly, stepping between his two sons. 'There's no need to shout,' he added, making everyone laugh.

Brodie looked at me and shook his head.

'That man,' he sighed.

'I know,' I agreed. 'How are you feeling?'

'Sick to my stomach.' He grimaced.

'You'll be fine,' I said, looking deep into his eyes and thinking how wonderfully his navy-coloured shirt set the intensity of them off. 'Everything will be fine.'

'If I can do it, lad,' Albert stoically said, from Brodie's other side as he smoothed down his tie, 'then I'm damn sure you can.'

It had been a rush to get everything ready that morning. Angus's insistence that the Christmas celebration should remain a surprise for his wife had caused untold issues and hold-ups as nothing could be set up until she was off-site.

Thankfully, Anna and Cass had come up with the ingenious idea of taking her on an impromptu trip to Wynter's Trees on the Norfolk coast which gave us a bit of extra time. As well as selling and renting out potted Christmas trees, the place sold all kinds of bespoke and local crafts, the creators of which were set up in a street of little beach huts.

To convince Catherine to go, Anna had come up with the excuse that she hadn't seen the sea for a while and that she hadn't had any opportunity to buy Christmas presents and off the three of them had gone to this wonderful sounding one-stop festive shop. I would have loved to have gone to see the place for myself but obviously that wasn't an option because I was in charge of coordinating the speedy set up at the hall.

There were more decorations and twinkling fairy lights to go up and the display boards were arranged to give each of the six invited artists a booth of their own. Albert and Brodie's work remained covered and wouldn't be revealed until the guest of honour returned which, according to the desperation in Archie's tone, would be very soon. I was glad about that because I still hadn't had so much as a peep at Brodie's work.

Among the exhibitors, along with my two favourite men, there was a young woman called Bec who Angus had rather a soft spot for and when I met her, I immediately understood why. She was a whirlwind of infectious energy and had as many off the wall ideas as he did.

Bec's canvases were huge colourful abstract affairs. She had somehow managed to wedge them into her bright yellow 2CV with the roof down, which itself caused quite a stir when it arrived. It looked even more decrepit than Brodie's Volvo and I wondered if all penniless artists favoured quirky, have certainly seen better days, modes of transport.

She and Albert were getting along like a house on fire and from the few glimpses of his work that I had caught in the studio, I wasn't surprised about that. I hadn't seen all that much though and my memories of what had been prominently on display when I first went into the studio were a little hazy because I had been so angry that Brodie had barged in that day. Most of the canvases had been hidden after that and therefore, I was looking forward to examining Albert's work every bit as minutely as Brodie's.

There was also a watercolour artist, a textile artist and a lino print artist. I had already viewed their work, along with Bec's, and I was fascinated by it all. Each of them favoured different techniques and mediums and yet all managed to capture the essence of the Fenland landscape which is why Angus had been so keen for Lizzie to invite them. I didn't think there could be another family in the whole of East Anglia who were more melded to the landscape than the Connelly's.

'They're here!' Archie yelled, making everyone jump and Brodie groan.

We all fell silent which, given the number of cars parked in front of the hall was a bit of a waste of time, but it added to the atmosphere and Catherine's face was a picture when Angus took her hand as she came in, then gave the signal for the lights to go on.

'Surprise!' everyone shouted.

'My goodness,' she laughed, one hand on her chest. 'What's all this? I guessed something was going on, but I wasn't expecting quite so many people.'

Everyone was thrilled with her response and welcomed her home so warmly you would have thought she'd been gone for months rather than a few hours. I felt deeply touched and recognized practically everyone in the crowd and I felt a fond affection for them too. It was amazing to think that just a few weeks ago, many of them would have been total strangers.

'You know Dad,' said Archie as he led Catherine further in.

'He never does things by halves,' chorused Jamie and Christopher.

'Never a truer word spoken.' Catherine smiled as she looked about her.

Angus then explained the purpose of the party, telling everyone that it was in part to celebrate the arrival of Christmas, but also to champion and appreciate the work of local artists.

'I have recently discovered not one' – here he pointed at

Brodie who was looking greener by the second – 'but two new artists in our midst,' he continued, with a sweeping gesture which took in Albert, who gave a little bow and betrayed no sign of nerves even though I was sure he must have been feeling some. 'And I thought it would be a wonderful end to the year to give them, and everyone else here, the recognition they deserve in creating such beautiful work, which captures the unusual landscape we live in so beautifully.'

'Albert?' Catherine asked, sounding surprised. 'Are you going to share your work?'

'Yes,' Albert confirmed, blushing as far as his boots. 'Yes, I am.'

'Well, I never,' she gasped, looking at the covered boards. 'I think this is a wonderful idea,' she then said to Angus, kissing him on the cheek. 'Where shall we begin?'

Angus beckoned Brodie forward and as he refused to let go of my hand that meant I got pulled to the front of the crowd with him.

'With this fine young fellow, I think,' Angus announced. 'He's the reason why I came up with the idea of the celebration and I've commissioned him to paint something special for you, my dear.'

He stood aside to reveal a large cloth-covered canvas resting on an easel.

'Would you do the honours?' Angus asked Brodie.

His hand slowly released mine and he stepped closer to the work which, in so many respects, had held him captive for so long.

'I hope you like it,' he said, as everyone leant in closer to get the first tantalizing glimpse of whatever it was that he'd painted.

I could see his hands were shaking as he began to pull at the cloth and my heart went out to him. He might have displayed his work in a gallery in London, but that had been with the safety net of a six-figure salary behind him. At that time, it had been a hobby, but now he meant to make his living from his brushes and the pressure must have felt immense.

'Oh, my goodness, Brodie,' Catherine gasped, her hand flying to her chest for the second time. 'That's extraordinary.'

Brodie had painted the hall, but from a good way down the drive and from an elevated position, which explained his trip in the cherry picker. The aspect he'd picked meant that as well as the hall, he was also able to include the wider landscape, including the garden and woods and the far-reaching, Fenland sky. The colours he'd used were vibrant oils which gave the composition a deep warmth, encapsulating the essence of the hall perfectly.

'This is amazing,' said Archie, patting him on the back.

'Look,' said Angus, leaning right in, 'I can even see the dogs on the drive.'

'You can't have Wynthorpe Hall without the dogs,' Brodie laughed, sounding relieved that his work was being so well received. 'And they were all milling about the place the day I came to sketch.'

'How on earth have you painted this in such a short space of time?' Archie asked in wonder.

That was a question I was keen to hear the answer to myself.

'We only went up in the picker just a few days ago,' Archie added.

'Well,' said Brodie, one hand finding its way through his hair. 'I've pulled a few long days since then.'

'And nights!' came Albert's voice from the back which made everyone laugh.

'And nights,' Brodie acknowledged. 'But I'd already got lots of preliminary sketches, which helped. That said,' he further explained, 'I couldn't put my finger on why, but they weren't giving me quite what I wanted. However, when we went up in the cherry picker everything fell into place and this is the result.'

A round of applause started and Brodie turned red in response.

'I'd really like to do four,' I heard him say to Angus. 'One for each season and all from the same angle.'

'Oh yes,' said Catherine, clapping her hands, 'that would be wonderful.'

'I agree,' Angus nodded keenly.

'Obviously it would be a passion project . . .' Brodie tried to say, but Angus wouldn't allow that.

'We'll discuss the details later,' he said, as the guests began to talk among themselves. 'You just enjoy this moment because you've done it, Brodie. You've slayed your demons and conquered your fears and there's nothing that can hold you back now.'

'I couldn't have got to this point without you,' he said to Angus, his voice choked with emotion. 'And you,' he added, reaching for me again. 'And Albert,' he beamed, as the man himself came to offer his congratulations.

All three of us had enjoyed the benefit of working together rather than struggling on alone since fate had pulled us in the same direction. We might not have been your average friendship group, but who cared about that? Somehow, we were a fabulous fit and that was all that mattered.

'It's your turn now, Albert.' Angus smiled kindly. 'Are you ready?'

Albert took a deep breath and I felt for him even more deeply than I had for Brodie. My friend had waited almost a lifetime for this moment.

'As I'll ever be,' he said, taking in the hall, and the many people gathered inside it.

Angus nodded.

'Right,' he then loudly said, drawing everyone's attention again. 'I would now like to introduce you to another unsung artist I've recently discovered living not all that far from here and this fortuitous introduction was all down to my wonderful goddaughter, Paige.'

I hadn't expected a mention and willed him to move quickly on, which thankfully, he did. The unveiling of Albert's paintings caused as big a stir as Brodie's. In fact, the sudden surge forward from the gallery owner Angus had invited, along with a journalist he knew who worked on the arts and culture section of a popular broadsheet, suggested it was even bigger. For a moment, Albert looked quite overwhelmed, but I stepped up to take his hand and he soon recovered.

Everyone wanted a piece of my two wonderful men that afternoon and their work was much admired. The other artists, who were similarly swamped, were fascinated by the paintings, some of the guests were clamouring for commissions, the journalist wanted to set up an interview and take photos and the gallery owner had plans to host a joint exhibition.

'It's going well, I think,' Angus said to me as the afternoon swiftly turned to twilight and no one showed any sign of wanting to leave.

'Extremely well,' I said, giving him a hug. 'This was inspired, Angus.'

He looked delighted.

'Albert has taken to it like a duck to water,' he chuckled. 'He's refusing to be interviewed at home or grant anyone access to the studio which of course is adding to the intrigue and creating even more interest and demand.'

'I love that,' I said, watching my friend hold court from a seat which had been positioned next to his stand.

'The journalist is fascinated by Albert and Brodie's friendship as much as anything, so Catherine has suggested they could be interviewed here when we hang Brodie's paintings, alongside one of Albert's, of course.'

'That's wonderful.' I smiled, thinking how lovely it would be to see the two friends living, working *and* being displayed side by side.

Albert's paintings were nothing like Brodie's. They were abstract in form like Bec's and, even though I knew little about artistic interpretation, I could appreciate their strong sense of place. Seeing his and Brodie's work together would be incredibly striking.

The celebration went on far longer than anyone expected and ended with everyone gathered around the huge hall fire enjoying more of Dorothy's mouth-watering mince pies and savoury snacks and Angus's trademark mulled wine.

'Do you think he'll let me set him up with an Insta account now?' Jack asked me with a nod in Brodie's direction.

It was the first chance we'd had to talk all afternoon but I had noticed he was there, looking extremely proud of his big brother and happily holding hands with Tilly.

'I doubt it,' I laughed.

'You're probably right,' he said, shaking his head. 'What an end to the year you've gifted him, Paige.'

I shook my head at that.

'He's done it himself,' I tried to say, but Jack wouldn't allow it. 'A collab then,' I settled on. 'Brodie, Albert and I have all gifted each other a wonderful end to the year.'

Jack did accept that and as he went off to cheekily negotiate a price for a canvas for the Brambles reception area, Lizzie from The Cherry Tree stepped forward.

'Oh, Paige,' she said, looking delighted, 'that journalist guy is going to come to the gallery. He wants to interview the other artists in the new year as well as Brodie and Albert.'

'That's fantastic,' I told her, wondering if Hayley would be seeing her name in newsprint. 'Angus will be thrilled.'

'And I hope you are too,' she said. 'You've played a part in making this happen. I've even got Albert to promise to teach a few classes alongside Brodie next year, once the dust has settled.'

My face must have been a picture, because she laughed at whatever expression I had pulled.

'I know,' she said. 'I was surprised too.'

'I thought Brodie hated . . .' I began, but my words trailed off as I realized he probably didn't want Lizzie knowing how much he had struggled to teach when she had been kind enough to offer him the work.

'I know he hated it,' she said perceptively anyway, 'but he told me earlier that now he's painting, he wants to give it another go and with Albert by his side, I'm sure the lessons will be a huge hit.'

'Well, that is wonderful,' I was happy to say.

After singing a couple of carols, led by Angus who was wearing his Santa hat again, the guests began to slowly drift away and the artists dismantled their stands.

'Angus has said we're just going to move mine and Albert's booths to the side of the hall,' Brodie told me as he bounded over looking quite transformed. 'That way, he and Catherine can decide at their leisure which work they want. What?' he then asked.

'You,' I laughed. 'I've never seen you so . . . bouncy.'

'Bouncy?' he laughed, picking me up and spinning me around.

'Yes,' I puffed when he eventually put me back down. 'Bouncy.'

'Well, why wouldn't I be?' he grinned. 'Today has been one of the best days of my life and I have you to thank . . .'

'And Albert and Angus and Jack and . . .' I tried to reel off but he silenced me with a kiss.

'Hey!' Archie shouted. 'Don't think you can stand there snogging until Christmas just to get out of the clearing up!'

'I wouldn't dream of it,' said Brodie, rushing off again and leaving me feeling quite breathless.

Chapter 33

After the excitement of the Christmas celebration, Christmas Eve was calm by comparison. Everyone had their list of tasks to complete to make the next day as relaxing for everyone else as possible and we went about our work, giddy with excitement and full of festive cheer.

Brodie and Albert spent the day at the cottage but I didn't mind not seeing them as they were going to be with us at the hall for the whole of Christmas day. I didn't see much of Anna or Molly either, however they joined the rest of us around the fire when it was time to eat a light supper and listen to carols from King's.

There was no containing the anticipation for the next day by then and even though Hugo resolutely said that he was too old to listen to his grandfather read *The Night Before Christmas* or put out a small feast for Santa, he still participated in both.

'Just to keep Oscar happy,' he muttered as he carefully arranged the carrots out of Floss's reach and the adults exchanged secret smiles over his head.

I went to bed wondering if I would find any surprises in my stocking the next day, and there were a few as I tore into it before it was even light, but the biggest two of all were waiting in the kitchen.

'Oh my god!' I squealed, as I rushed into the room having recognized the two voices even before I'd opened the door.

My parents jumped up as Dorothy discreetly stepped back and I ran into their waiting arms with tears pouring down my cheeks and my breath tight in my chest. I realized then just how much I had missed them and exactly how long it had been since I had seen them.

'What are you doing here?' I sobbed, once they'd practically hugged the life out of me. 'I thought you were still on your cruise,' I choked, holding on to Mum's arm as tightly as if my life depended on it.

She was as emotional as I was, so Dad found the words to explain.

'Until just a couple of days ago, we were,' he told me, with an uncharacteristic catch in his voice. 'Then we docked in Barcelona and decided to cut the trip short and fly back to be here in time for Christmas.'

'Angus had been sending us such wonderful reports of what you were getting up to between our phone calls,' Mum then found voice enough to add, 'and I couldn't bear the thought that the year you were finally back in the country for Christmas we weren't, so . . .'

I had no idea my godfather had been doing that.

'We packed our bags and jumped ship,' Dad finished up. 'I take it you're pleased to see us?'

I rushed from Mum's side to his and he held me close, making more tears spring to my eyes. It had been a long time since I'd received a hug from my father and so I cherished it all the more.

'So,' I said, looking up into his tanned face, 'tell me, what exactly has Angus been telling you?'

Breakfast was a very merry affair and, with so many of us all wanting to eat at the same time, quite a squeeze.

'Thank goodness we set the dining room up yesterday, instead of opting to eat Christmas dinner in here,' Dorothy said to me as Archie and Molly arrived, flushed from their walk from the woods. 'At this rate we'll need to add another leaf to the table.'

She looked absolutely thrilled and not at all stressed that she had more mouths to feed and might not be able to make the meals stretch that far. Where Dorothy was concerned, not having enough to eat, or drink, was never a consideration.

As well as Brodie and Albert, Kathleen, Alice and her children and Jack and Tilly had been invited too. Kathleen had accepted the offer on the condition that she could be kitchen porter for Dorothy and Jack and Tilly would be arriving in time for dinner in the afternoon. Alice, however, although immensely grateful to be included, had wanted to spend the day quietly – or as quietly as she could with three little ones – in her new home.

As I knew she wasn't coming to the hall, I had telephoned

and talked her through my community project idea on Christmas Eve and she was every bit as excited about it as I was. She was also keen to be involved in some way and I promised that as soon as I had a few life things sorted I would begin setting it up in the new year.

I wished she was spending Christmas day with us and would be there when I shared the plan with everyone else, but I appreciated that she needed her space and more time to process everything she'd been through. It would take time for her to come to terms with how utterly transformed her life had been since she'd bravely found the courage to change it.

'And we'll definitely need that other hostess trolley,' Dorothy added, counting heads again. 'It's not as big as the others, but I'd rather have it than not.'

I'd already prepared two the day before, marvelling at their retro appearance. Dorothy assured me they were a godsend when catering for the extended clan and I had to agree with her, especially as the dining room and kitchen were quite a distance apart.

'I'll just tell Mum and Dad what I'm doing and then I'll go and sort it,' I told her.

The morning was pushing on and Hugo, Oscar, and Angus of course, were eager to see their presents under the tree, even though they wouldn't be opening them until later.

'I'll be back in a sec,' I said to Archie, as I went to slip out but he lightly caught my hand.

'Can you just hang on?' he asked, sounding so unlike his usual mischievous self that I stopped in my tracks.

'What's wrong?' I frowned, instantly on alert.

'Nothing,' he said quickly, as Jamie came to stand next to him. 'Nothing's wrong.'

'Before we all head off to get dressed and peek at the presents under the tree,' Jamie said, loud enough to draw everyone's attention as I moved to sit down again. 'Can we just have a minute of your time?'

'It'll have to be a brief one,' said Dorothy, brandishing a wooden spoon.

'Oh well, in that case,' said Archie, looking at his brother and sounding more like his old self. 'We'd better go together.'

Jamie nodded and laughed as Anna and Molly went to stand next to their Connelly men.

'One, two, three,' they called out and then there was the briefest pause before they shouted, all four in perfect synchronicity, 'we're pregnant!'

Each and every mouth fell open and then the whooping, cheering and clapping began.

'Both of you?' called Angus above the noise as he pointed first at Anna and then at Molly.

The two women nodded and laughed.

'Yes,' said Anna, looking at her friend, 'both of us. I'm due first in early summer.'

'And I'll be a couple of weeks later,' Molly ecstatically added.

'I don't believe it!' Angus cried, pulling at his hair until it stood on end. 'This is the best Christmas morning I've ever had!'

Catherine was then on her feet and hugging the two women she loved as if they were her very own daughters and Jamie and Archie were clapping each other on the back and looking immensely proud of their manly prowess.

'Isn't this wonderful?' Dorothy gasped, abandoning her spoon. 'Two babies!'

I took a moment to absorb the news. Molly had told me that more changes were coming but I'd had no idea she had foreseen something as dramatic and thrilling as this, but then I wondered, had she realized that herself?

'Two babies,' Hayley sighed, coming to link her arm through mine. 'What the hell are we going to do now?'

'What do you mean?' I asked her.

'Well,' she said, with a sly wink, 'Anna won't be able to keep lugging those deliveries about, will she? You know yourself how weighty those fruit and veg boxes are and the library books aren't exactly light either, are they?'

There was no chance to answer as Angus was popping champagne corks and making toasts and for a few minutes the whole scene fell into wonderful chaos, punctuated with kind kisses and warm congratulations.

The day continued in much the same vein and my face wore a permanent smile which only grew wider when Brodie and Albert arrived in the tinsel-toting Volvo.

'All dressed for the occasion, I see!' I laughed as I rushed out to meet them.

Not only was the Volvo festively adorned, but the two men were wearing matching Christmas jumpers too.

'These were the most garish ones I could find,' Albert told me with a chuckle.

'Albert insisted,' said Brodie, looking as if he'd rather be wearing anything but a gingerbread and snowman patterned sweater. 'He thought Angus would appreciate them.'

'Oh, I know he will,' I laughed. 'I only wish you'd got one for him.'

Brodie threw me a squishy, soft parcel, while he grabbed more bags of presents.

'What do you think that is?' he asked, rolling his eyes.

The second he was handed it, Angus tore into the present and was pulling the jumper over his head.

'I think this calls for a selfie,' he demanded, standing proudly between Albert and Brodie in the kitchen. 'Or should that be Elfie?' he added, laughing at his own joke.

'And we'll have to take another when Jack arrives,' said Brodie, 'because Albert insisted on getting one for him too.'

What a quartet!

'Oh, Albert,' I laughed.

'I'm making the most of today.' He smiled. 'It's been a while since I've enjoyed Christmas.'

'Me too,' I told him, giving him a tight hug. 'Me too.'

With the baby news shared again and introductions to my parents made, I didn't think the day could possibly get any better. Everyone was dreamily milling about the beautifully decorated hall and we all looked as though we had been entranced by the twinkling fairy lights, softly scented candles and brightly shining baubles.

It genuinely felt as though some spell had been cast over every minute that ticked by and every word that was uttered. I'd never experienced an occasion like it and I knew I'd certainly picked a good year to spend Christmas at Wynthorpe Hall. Although, if Molly had been privy to that thought, she probably would have said that it had picked me.

'You look so happy,' said Brodie, taking a moment to pull me into the empty main hall and lingeringly kiss me under a fortuitously placed bunch of mistletoe.

'That's because I am,' I told him. 'I came here just a few weeks ago in such a muddle and feeling sadder and lonelier than I could have ever thought possible and now I'm . . . blissful.' I beamed up at him.

'And so you should be,' he said, softly brushing his lips against mine again. 'Look at all the wonderful things you've done since you got here.'

'It's been a joint effort,' I told him. 'So many people have been pulling together to make so many others so happy, that it's quite taken my breath away.'

'Um,' said Brodie, 'and there was me thinking that I was the person who had done that.'

'Oh, you have,' I told him. 'But in a rather different way.'

'Is that canoodling I can hear going on?' came Albert's amused voice from the other side of the door.

'It is, Albert,' Brodie called back.

'Jolly good,' he laughed. 'Carry on.'

'Happy to oblige,' Brodie responded.

'No,' I said, giggling and pulling away, 'we mustn't. Come

on, otherwise we'll be late for Dorothy's legendary Christmas dinner. And Jack and Tilly will be here any minute.'

There were twenty-two of us seated for dinner that afternoon. Twenty-four if you counted the babies, twenty-seven if you included the dogs and yet, in the spirit of Connelly clan togetherness, the gathering still somehow felt like an intimate one.

Between the three courses Dorothy served, ably assisted by Kathleen, we all switched places to ensure there was every opportunity to chat and by the time the flaming pudding had been served I was delighted to find myself seated between Albert and Brodie with Mum and Dad and Molly opposite.

'So, Paige,' Angus called down the table. 'What's the plan? Have you made any decisions about what you're going to do next?'

I looked first at Albert and then at Brodie.

'I have,' I said, turning my attention back to Angus. 'Obviously I can't leave Wynbridge because there's no telling what this pair will get up to if they're left to their own devices.'

Everyone cheered at that.

'Very true.' Angus beamed, smoothing down his jumper.

'And then of course, there's you to keep an eye on too, my dear godfather.'

My own father laughed at that.

'Me?' Angus gasped. 'I'm as good as gold these days, but perhaps you should keep an eye, just in case I have a relapse.'

'The only problem,' I said, biting my lip, 'is that I've come up with this fabulous idea about what I want to do next, but I'm not sure if it will pay, so I've no money and nowhere permanent to live.'

'That's easily remedied,' said Catherine from her end of the table. 'The Rose Room is yours for as long as you need it, so that's the roof over your head sorted and obviously we won't be charging you rent.'

'Thank you.' I beamed, imagining the excitement of living longer at the hall. 'Thank you so much.'

'Thank *you* for stepping in and helping out,' Angus said back.

'I was hoping you might be able to help carry on with the deliveries now I'm pregnant,' Anna said, echoing what Hayley had earlier hinted at, 'but I'm intrigued to know what your new idea is.'

'I'll be more than happy to carry on with the delivery round,' I hastily reassured her. 'My idea might take a while to get up and running, so I'll easily be able to juggle it.'

'So, what is it?' Angus asked, wriggling in his seat.

'Well,' I said, looking from him to Kathleen, 'it's another project for the local community. During the time I've spent making the deliveries, I've come to realize that lots of the people who receive them often don't see another soul from one drop-off to the next and are lonely as a result.'

'Which is why you've been so brilliant, following Anna's lead and spending a few extra minutes with them as you've gone around,' Kathleen praised.

'It's actually been one of my favourite parts of the role,'

I told her, 'but,' I carried on, taking a deep breath, 'it's not enough. During the last few weeks, I've learnt to appreciate the importance of human contact more than ever and I've met people who have suggested, either through their words or actions, that they feel the same.'

'I know I do,' Albert said encouragingly.

'And therefore,' I continued, buoyed up by his understanding, 'I want to set up opportunities for people to get together, and I don't mean a mother and toddler group or an over seventies luncheon club. I want to mix everyone up and bring all age groups together.'

'What a wonderful idea.' Angus smiled.

'I was thinking it could happen in the town hall, two or three times a week. I've loads more research to do, but ultimately, I want to apply for funding to buy a minibus so I can collect and drop people off, as well as coordinate the whole thing. We could even arrange group trips eventually.'

'Oh, Paige,' said Kathleen, 'this sounds amazing and you're right about mixing everyone up. We already have specific age-defined groups for various things, but something which blends them all together would be wonderful.'

'We can share stories,' Albert joined in.

'And even perhaps skills,' added Brodie, also sounding keen.

Everyone had something to say after that and all of it was positive.

'So,' I said, when we'd eventually exhausted the topic and my parents looked fit to burst with pride, 'that's the plan, Angus.'

'And a blooming good one it is, too,' he pronounced, raising his glass and everyone else following suit. 'To new adventures,' he toasted, 'and new life,' he added, with a smile for Anna and Molly.

'To new adventures and new life,' we chorused.

'You're amazing,' Brodie softly said into my ear, 'do you know that?'

'It's this place,' I told him. 'It's brought out the best in me. I've loved every minute of being here since I've been back.'

'Even the minutes when you got lost in the Fens?' Albert asked, listening in.

'Especially those minutes,' I told him. 'I loved those stressful minutes on the road more than any of the others because they led me to somewhere so wonderful.'

'That's true.' He swallowed, reaching for my hand.

'If you're interested, Paige,' Jack then piped up, stretching the neck on his jumper which he'd gamely pulled on over his shirt, 'I'm looking for part-time staff to help in the distillery. I'd be happy to fit the hours around everything else you're planning. What do you think?'

'Oh yes,' I said, swallowing away the lump in my throat as Brodie reached for my other hand and Molly smiled at me across the table. 'Thank you, Jack. That sounds great.'

Suddenly, a whole new future and a brand-new life was within my grasp and I was eager to reach out and grab it. The thought of bringing everyone together and giving them the opportunity to embrace new friendships in the way that I finally had, was the most thrilling aspect of the plan of all.

'Next year is going to be amazing.' Brodie beamed as Angus asked everyone to stand for another toast. 'And I'm so excited that we're going to be together to experience it.'

'Me too,' I agreed.

'Me three!' piped up Albert.

As everyone again raised their glasses, Brodie slipped his arm around my waist and Albert squeezed my hand, I thought how blessed I was to have so many wonderful people in my life and how much better my existence was for letting them all into it.

Our togetherness had overcome my sadness and banished my loneliness and that was the very best way to celebrate what had turned out to be the most memorable Christmas of all.

Acknowledgements

Every book is special, but a trip to Wynthorpe Hall at Christmas has a little extra something and I feel that *A Christmas Celebration*, the third winter Wynthorpe visit, is no exception. There really is magic there and it spreads further than the woods and the beloved Wishing Tree. Thank you for picking the book up. I hope the Connelly clan, Wynbridge and the new residents have given you an appetite for the seasonal excitement to come!

I started writing this book living in one house and finished it in another and on top of turning fifty in the spring I, like Paige, have been through quite a transformation this year. Consequently, I have lots of people to thank for helping me through it. Whether you've shifted boxes, conjured kind words, poured fizz or been endlessly available to chat, your friendship and support has been much appreciated and if you could stick around for 2023 that would be fab!

Massive thanks to Amanda Preston, Clare Hey and the

entire Book and The City team, Claire Howard, Sue Baker, Fiona Jenkins, Jenni Keer, Clare Marchant, Rosie Hendry, Ian Wilfred, every member of the Heidi Swain and Friends Facebook Book Club, the championing book bloggers and of course you, dear readers. You have all been Team Heidi this year and that has been an endless source of comfort and pride. What a wonderful crew to have in my corner. Thank you all.

Thank you also to wonderful Rob Reed who very generously bid on the Authors For Starlight auction organised by Tamsyn Murray last autumn. The lot was to have a character named in my next Christmas title and, having won, Rob told me that he had bid to have his Mum's name included and that when she was younger, she loved to dance.

Kind-hearted Kathleen swiftly proved herself to be a generous and much-loved addition to Wynbridge and her passion for dancing has provided me with the opportunity to write one of my favourite scenes in the book. Thank you, Rob. I hope I have done dear Kathleen justice.

And last, but by no means least, thanks to Dennis and Roy and their perfect pack for making my daily walks so memorable.

So, my loves, this really is it for another year. I wonder what the next will bring? A whole raft of exciting opportunities would be my guess. However, in the meantime, if you find yourself alone this winter, be like Paige and Albert and reach out because, as I have discovered for myself, together really is better.

Until we meet again, may your bookshelves – be they virtual or real – always be filled with fabulous fiction.

With love,
H x

About the Author

Heidi Swain lives in Norfolk. She is passionate about gardening and the countryside, and collects vintage paraphernalia. *A Christmas Celebration* is her fifteenth novel. You can follow Heidi on Twitter @Heidi_Swain or visit her website: heidiswain.co.uk

Underneath the Christmas Tree

Wynter's Trees is the home of Christmas. For the people of Wynmouth it's where they get their family Christmas tree, and where Christmas truly comes to life.

But for Liza Wynter, it's a millstone around her neck. It was her father's pride and joy but now he's gone, she can't have anything to do with it. Until her father's business partner decides to retire and she must go back to handle the transition to his son Ned.

When Liza arrives, she discovers a much-loved business that's flourishing under Ned's stewardship. And she's happy to stay and help for the Christmas season, but then she has other plans. But will the place where she grew up make her change her mind? And can it weave its Christmas cheer around her heart . . . ?

The Summer Fair

Beth loves her job working in a care home, looking after its elderly residents, but she doesn't love the cramped and dirty houseshare she currently lives in. So, when she gets the opportunity to move to Nightingale Square, sharing a house with the lovely Eli, she jumps at the chance.

The community at Nightingale Square welcomes Beth with open arms, and when she needs help to organise a fundraiser for the care home they rally round. Then she discovers The Arches, a local creative arts centre, has closed and the venture to replace it needs their help too – but this opens old wounds and past secrets for Beth.

Music was always an important part of her life, but now she has closed the door on all that. Will her friends at the care home and the people of Nightingale Square help her find a way to learn to love it once more . . . ?

A Taste of Home

Fliss Brown has grown up living with her mother on the Rossi family's Italian fruit farm. But when her mother dies, Fliss finds out she has a family of her own, and heads back to England with Nonna Rossi's recipe for cherry and almond tart and a piece of advice: connect with your family before it is too late . . .

Fliss discovers that her estranged grandfather owns a fruit farm himself, on the outskirts of Wynbridge, and she arrives to find a farm that has fallen into disrepair. Using her knowledge gleaned from working on the Rossi farm and her desire to find out more about her past, Fliss rolls her sleeves up and gets stuck in. But what will she discover, and can she resurrect the farm's glory days and find a taste of home?

The Winter Garden

Freya Fuller is living her dream, working as a live-in gardener on a beautiful Suffolk estate. But when the owner dies, Freya finds herself forced out of her job and her home with nowhere to go. However, with luck on her side, she's soon moving to Nightingale Square and helping to create a beautiful winter garden that will be open to the public in time for Christmas.

There's a warm welcome from all in Nightingale Square, except from local artist Finn. No matter how hard the pair try, they just can't get along, and working together to bring the winter garden to life quickly becomes a struggle for them both.

Will Freya and Finn be able to put their differences aside in time for Christmas? Or will the arrival of a face from Freya's past send them all spiralling?

Poppy's Recipe for Life

Things haven't always been straightforward in Poppy's life but her dreams are finally within her reach.

She's moving into a cottage in beautiful Nightingale Square, close to the local community garden, where she can indulge her passion for making preserves and pickles. She may not have the best relationship with her family, but she is surrounded by loving friends, and feels sure that even her grumpy new neighbour, Jacob, has more to him than his steely exterior suggests.

But the unexpected arrival of Poppy's troubled younger brother soon threatens her new-found happiness, and as the garden team works together to win community space of the year, Poppy must decide where her priorities lie and what she is prepared to fight for . . .

Snowflakes and Cinnamon Swirls at The Winter Wonderland

Moving into Wynthorpe Hall to escape the town's gossip, Hayley finds herself immersed in the eccentric Connelly family's festive activities as they plan to host their first ever Winter Wonderland. But Hayley isn't the only new resident at the hall. Gabe, a friend of the Connelly's son Jamie, has also taken up residence, moving into Gatekeeper's Cottage, and he quickly makes an impression on Wynbridge's reformed good-girl.

As preparations commence for the biggest event of the season, the pair find themselves drawn ever closer to one another, but unbeknownst to Hayley, Gabe, too, has a reason for turning his back on love, one that seems intent on keeping them apart.

Under the starry winter skies, will Gabe convince Hayley to open her heart again once more? And in doing so, will he convince himself?

Sleigh Rides and Silver Bells at The Christmas Fair

When Anna takes on the role of companion to the owner of Wynthorpe Hall, on the outskirts of Wynbridge, she has no idea that her life is set to change beyond all recognition.

A confirmed 'bah humbug' when it comes to Christmas, Anna is amazed to find herself quickly immersed in the eccentric household, and when youngest son Jamie unexpectedly arrives home it soon becomes obvious that her personal feelings are going all out to compromise her professional persona.

Jamie, struggling to come to terms with life back in the Fens, makes a pact with Anna – she has to teach him to fall back in love with Wynthorpe Hall, while he helps her fall back in love with Christmas. But will it all prove too much for Anna, or can the family of Wynthorpe Hall warm her heart once and for all . . . ?